THE
VICTROLA
BOOK OF
THE OPERA

STORIES OF THE OPERAS

WITH ILLUSTRATIONS & DESCRIPTIONS

OF VICTOR OPERA RECORDS

SEVENTH EDITION

Rewritten and Revised

NOTE — Acknowledgment must be made to Oliver
Ditson Co. and G. Schirmer for kind permission to
quote occasionally from their copyrighted publications. Both these houses have set new standards
with their operatic publications—the Schirmer with
superbly printed opera scores and collections of
opera airs entitled "Operatic Anthology"; and Ditson
with the Musicians' Library, masterpieces of music
typography

Copyright 1924 by

VICTOR TALKING MACHINE COMPANY

Camden, New Jersey, U. S. A.

*Prices shown herein are Victor Company's
current list prices*

"HIS MASTER'S VOICE"

INDEX

INDEX — (*Continued*)

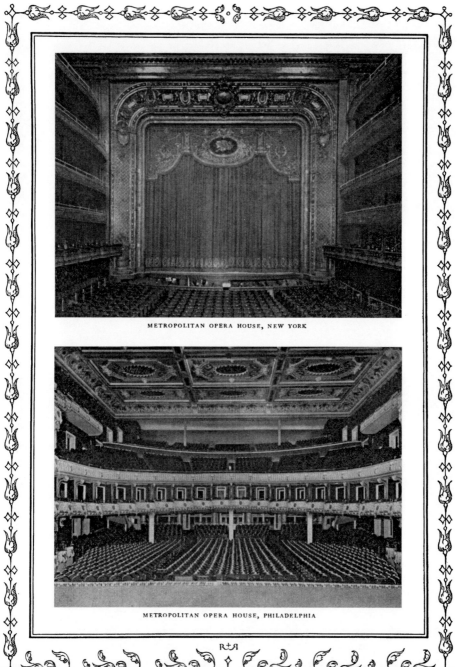

METROPOLITAN OPERA HOUSE, NEW YORK

METROPOLITAN OPERA HOUSE, PHILADELPHIA

THE MARIENSKOI OPERA, PETROGRAD

THE OPÉRA, PARIS

FAMOUS OPERA HOUSES OF EUROPE

THE OPERA, PARIS

FRENCH OPERA, NEW ORLEANS

MUNICIPAL THEATRE, RIO DE JANEIRO

METROPOLITAN, PHILADELPHIA

METROPOLITAN, NEW YORK

NATIONAL THEATRE, SAO PAULO, BRAZIL.

FAMOUS AMERICAN OPERA HOUSES

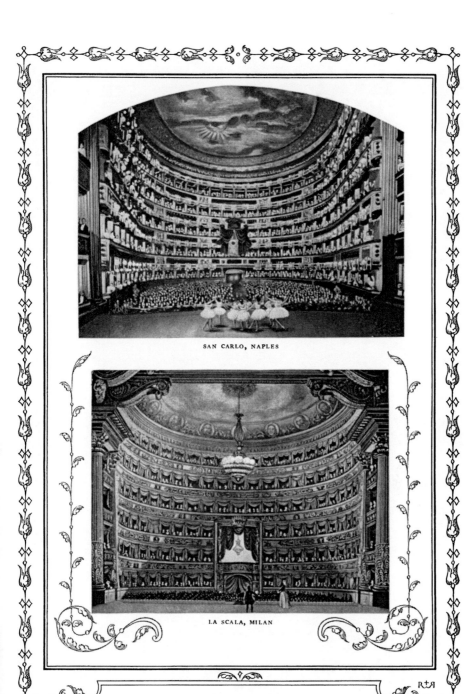

SAN CARLO, NAPLES

LA SCALA, MILAN

FAMOUS OPERA HOUSES OF EUROPE

SOME OF THE GREAT SINGERS
OF THE WORLD

All of whom have made Records for the Victor

PREFACE

THIS seventh edition of the Victrola Book of the Opera, like all previous editions, has been prepared for the purpose of telling the stories of Grand Opera as completely as seems necessary for general understanding and to show the wealth of operatic music which is available on Victor records for study and for entertainment.

For the convenience of the reader and in order that the flow of the narrative may not be interrupted, the Victor records from each opera are listed at the end of each story.

In addition to the operas listed in this book there are many others from which only isolated arias, duets, marches, overtures, and so forth, have become part of the world's musical repertoire. Among them are many veritable gems of which splendid Victor records are listed in the Victor Record Catalogs, but not referred to here because the complete operas are not in current use.

Revised editions of the Victrola Book of the Opera are issued at intervals of about two years. New Victor Records are issued every week so that at any given time the most recent issues of operatic records will be found in supplements to the Victor Catalogs.

There is still another source of supply and one which is of the utmost interest to the connoisseur and to the student.

From time to time over a period of many years records have been withdrawn from the catalogs because, though rendered by famous artists, they were made before the art of recording had reached its present perfection.

These records, showing the individual interpretations of the great artists in the parts on which their fame is based, from the time the first serious work in recording music was undertaken, have all the charm, all the interest, all the historic value which attaches to "limited editions" in any form. A special catalog listing these numbers is available to any music-lover who is interested in records not now in general circulation upon application to dealers or to the Victor Company.

WHAT IS AN OPERA?

COMPARATIVELY few of the hundred and ten million inhabitants of these United States ever have seen an opera. Most of the remainder never will see one. A considerable number of educated people occasionally go to the opera, and have been there perhaps a half dozen times in all. And a still smaller proportion, probably very small, may be classed as "opera fans," going regularly every season. With these we are not so deeply concerned, but with the two former classes we are, and especially with those who go once in a while.

Frequently those who attend the opera but rarely, come away disappointed, for the simple reason that they have gone expecting something that is not there. Consequently they have failed to get the full value of what *is* there—through their not having noticed it. It is not to be expected that one can attend this exotic form of entertainment and at once comprehend its deepest subtleties. We may very well ask ourselves, therefore, what to expect when going to the opera, and to answer some of the criticisms of the opera which sometimes arise through lack of understanding.

Most people, if asked what an opera is, would answer "A play set to music," but this is true only in the most general way. An opera is indeed a drama, but it consists of Action, Speech, Song and Stage-setting. Since an ordinary spoken drama provides these things without the music, it follows that the "song" is really the chief thing in an opera, and the one thing to which the other factors are sacrificed in greater or less degree. All too often, Americans go to the opera expecting plenty of "action," and are correspondingly disappointed when they find that there is really "very little doing." A moment's thought will show them that it is impossible for a human being to have enough breath to negotiate a high C and at the same time give way to violent action of any kind. If there is any "violent action" in an opera, it usually takes place "off-stage," or is reduced to a few stereotyped motions. In a "real" play, for instance, a duel can be fought out with great verisimilitude, as it usually is in "Hamlet"; but in an opera a duel is generally reduced to a few stereotyped motions more or less in time to the music, as in "Faust." And a great deal of the time, the artists are grouped about the stage in picturesque attitudes in which motion is reduced to a minimum for reasons easily apparent; those actually singing need their breath, and any vigorous movement apart from them would distract the attention of the audience.

As a matter of fact, music being the language of the emotions, the emotions in an opera are naturally of paramount importance. We are supposed to be interested not so much in what our hero, heroine or villain may do, as in how he feels before and after the action is performed. Thus, for instance, in "Il Trovatore," when *Manrico* learns that *Azucena*, whom he supposes to be his mother, has been captured, his immediate desire is to rescue her; but instead of dashing off at once, as he might dash in real life, he steps to the front of the stage and sings a song expressing his mad desire for vengeance. To the average American, unaccustomed to the conventions of opera, there is in this, perhaps, naturally something very strange; but the humor strangely lies in his own naïve confusion between Life itself and Art, which mirrors the emotions and reactions of life. In more familiar forms of art, even dramatic art, he is ready enough to accept the conventions without question. If the same scene occurred in a photoplay, for instance, we should undoubtedly have a "close-up" in which *Manrico*, before setting off to rescue his mother, would come to the front of the screen and by facial expression make clear his emotions. We are so used to this that we accept it without question, presumably entertained in watching an actor "register" make-believe horror, hatred and vengeance! In the photoplay, however, action is the chief thing, and we should have to see him attempt the rescue and fail, instead of going right on to the next scene, where we find *Manrico* in a dungeon with *Azucena*, again melodiously expressing his feelings. Unless you go to the opera prepared to accept its conventions, you may be disappointed.

Another thing that may confront the operatic neophyte is the comparative scantiness of the kind of melody that can be readily whistled. Here again, he forgets that in true opera, melody is a lyrical outburst attainable only in moments of climax. It is all very well for *Madame Butterfly*, worked up to an intense pitch of belief in *Pinkerton's* return, to sing "Un bel di vedremo"; but how is the *Pinkerton* in the same opera to invite the American Consul to have a whiskey and soda? He does it in a *parlante*, a sort of recitative in which the voice follows the normal inflections of spoken voice, and the orchestra plays music typifying his particular mood. There is no room for melody, no reason for it. The demand for melody was so great in days gone by, when opera-goers went mainly to hear this or that great artist, that melody was often employed to a degree detrimental to the development of the opera, threatening to degenerate the art into a glorified concert; but such reformers as Gluck, Wagner and the later Verdi perceived the danger and led the art back to its higher levels.

Those who go to a modern opera expecting a "Celeste Aïda" every other minute, are doomed to disappointment. If there is any "melody" at all (and ultra-modern opera composers may seem to avoid giving us any!) it is reserved for the great moments, coming only once or twice in an evening. In its place, however, there is a portrayal (and it can be a wonderfully subtle one!) of the workings of the human emotions, the cross-purposes, the combinations and permutations of feeling, suggested by the interplay of strange harmonies, fragmentary melodies, and the voicing of strings, woodwind and brass.

Another question that sometimes arises is: "Why don't they sing in English?" If every town and village in America had an opera-house attended by Americans to hear American singers sing American operas, no doubt they would. With us, however, opera is a foreign importation. We have very little opera, but what there is is the very best in the world. We hear French, Italian, German opera as it is to be heard only in France, Italy and Germany, usually sung by the pick of the artists from those countries. To force these artists to sing in a hastily learned English would be as unpleasant for them as for us. Moreover, the opera with us is a luxury, supported by the wealthier class, many of whom keep a "working acquaintance" with one or more European languages. They much prefer to hear operas unmarred by translation. Only those who have read the English translations of foreign operas know how terrible these translations can be. The plain fact is that an opera loses much of its flavor when translated even by a master of English when that master is compelled to conform to the needs of the *music*.

It is sometimes urged, also, that English is "unsingable" owing to the fact that most English words end in consonants. If these consonants (many of which are sibilants) are slurred over, the words are unintelligible, yet if the consonants are pronounced they result in a series of little explosions not satisfactory to the ear. Even German, they say, is better because so many words end in vowel sounds. We believe, however, that if Americans really desired it, a way would be found in which to sing the musical language of Shakespeare and Milton, Byron, Keats and Shelley. The Victor Company has met the "English problem," as far as possible, by having records sung in English by acknowledged masters of the art, as well as records sung by foreign artists in their own tongue. Generally speaking, it seems as though most Americans prefer to hear the best artists sing the melodies in the best way, regardless of language, for the great demand for operatic records sung in the original seems to point in that direction.

In this newer edition of the "Victrola Book of the Opera," besides retelling the stories of the opera, we have included much biographical, historical and critical matter relating to the chief works, believing they will be better appreciated if better understood. Only those well read in music know how much confusion exists in the average mind regarding the different "schools" or varieties of opera. We are acutely aware that much has been omitted, but we have done our utmost to keep free of mistakes of any kind, and to maintain the broadest and most inclusive critical spirit in what criticisms may appear. For they are not made to opinionize, but only to make easier the way.

HISTORY OF OPERA

A BRIEF OUTLINE

FORMS of dramatic entertainment in which music plays a prominent part have been known from the earliest times. But to a group of Florentine nobles and art-lovers, Count Bardi, Peri, Caccini and others, who flourished at the end of the sixteenth century and the beginning of the seventeenth, belongs the honor of having founded modern opera. The music of that period was chiefly polyphonic, that is to say, based upon the strict laws of counterpoint and the combination of melodies into canons, fugues, and the like. This was admirable for ecclesiastical uses, but it was quite unsuited to the drama; so these Florentines, turning, as did all art-lovers in that age of the Renaissance, to the ancient glories of Greece and Rome, strove to reproduce what they believed to be the original Greek form of musical declamation. Their efforts, revealed in such works as "Euridice" and "Dafne," were crude enough, yet they opened up new possibilities in composition, of which more able musicians, such as Carissini, Monteverde, and especially Alessandro Scarlatti, soon availed themselves. Opera quickly passed from the narrow circle of the Florentine nobles, and achieved a new function when it was used to glorify the great princes of the Italian cities. Scarlatti took it a step further by popularizing it with the masses; so that opera-houses soon appeared. These were definitely devoted to the new art, the first of its kind being the Teatro di San Cassiano, in Venice, 1637.

Opera quickly spread to other countries, where it developed for the most part along national lines. Space does not permit an elaborate account of its development, but a brief summary of the part each country played in the history of opera may be attempted.

ITALY

Being the original birthplace of the new art, Italy naturally dominated the minds of opera composers for many years. And when other countries established and maintained it, upon lines peculiar to themselves, Italy still kept its musical independence of style. The Italian opera gradually developed into a form in which especial attention was paid to melody and to vocal display, yielding, at its height, such works as the masterpieces of Rossini, Bellini and Donizetti. Despite their beauties and those of less significant works the domination of the voice in these led to a certain degeneracy in style—a true lack of artistic balance. Italian opera became a string of coloratura arias with accompaniments for the orchestra of so slight a kind as to be trivial. The "plots" also were of secondary importance. Dramatic interest failed, and the opera might just as well have been sung off stage. There are notable exceptions to this, as in the case of Rossini's "William Tell," but composers in other countries had shown that a higher standard of art was possible. The first to realize this was Verdi, whose early works followed the Rossini-Bellini models. He was too great an artist to remain unaffected by the general development of opera elsewhere, and soon adopted a virile course of his own in which, while remaining true to Italian ideals of plentiful melody, he gave more attention to the drama, and to the fuller emotional expression made possible by modern harmonies and an improved orchestra. In such works as "Rigoletto," "Traviata," "Aida," and finally in "Otello" and "Falstaff," he brought Italian opera back to its traditionally high standards. His successors such as Giordani, Ponchielli, Puccini, Mascagni and Leoncavallo, have maintained his achievements. They have held to Italian ideals as to melody, but have fully availed themselves of all modern resources. Their plots have tended to be "realistic," often melodramatic, but in this they have but followed the general artistic trend of the age.

FRANCE

Italian opera was introduced into France by Lulli, about fifty years after the Bardi-Peri experiments in Florence. Here it was quickly grafted on to the older French art of the Ballet, and it developed along lines of its own. Lulli's initial efforts were succeeded by those of Rameau, a Belgian (1683-1764) and some very necessary reforms which affected opera in all countries were brought about in Paris by Gluck (1714-1787). France has been peculiarly indebted to foreigners for the development of her opera, but has naturally produced many opera-composers of her own. The French gave special attention to the art of declamation and they have, in this respect, steadily maintained their prestige. The opera-bouffe is a form of opera peculiar to France, for which the world remains in her debt. French ideals were maintained by such composers as Halévy, Auber, Thomas, and later, Gounod and Bizet with "Faust" and "Carmen" respectively. Saint-Saëns and Massenet did much to develop French art in the latter part of the nineteenth and beginning of the twentieth centuries, and still further advances have been made in recent years by Debussy and others. The latter-day French have steadily adhered to the French ideal of faithful declamation rather than melodic inventions, which accounts for the fact that the modern French operas yield few "tunes" for the multitude to whistle.

GERMANY

The first distinctively German operas were given us by Reinhard Keiser, who flourished in Hamburg, where Händel also made his first operatic ventures. The first genuine "Singspiel" publicly performed was Johann Theile's "Adam and Eve," produced in Hamburg, 1678. This form is somewhat akin to the English "ballad-opera," consisting chiefly of a dramatic story interpolated with songs and ballads. Even Mozart, who generally followed Italian models, was attracted by this novel form. A notable advance in German opera was Beethoven's "Leonore," in which the great master followed lines of his own, somewhat resembling those of Gluck. The modern German romantic opera is generally said to have been founded by Weber with "Der Freischütz," in which he falls back for his subject upon German legend. Spohr and Marschner also contributed to this movement, which certainly paved the way for Richard Wagner, without doubt the greatest dramatic composer the world has yet known. Not only did Wagner exert a profound influence upon German art, but he affected the composers of all nations, in instrumental as well as in dramatic music. Since Wagner's epoch the greatest of the German opera composers has been Richard Strauss, with "Salome," "Elektra" and kindred works. Other notable followers of the Wagnerian model, whose works are known in this country, have been Humperdinck, Goldmark and Smetana (whose "Bartered Bride" is a Bohemian work specially characteristic of latter-day nationalistic efforts). A notable contemporary of Wagner was

16

Meyerbeer, who for awhile dominated the French stage. Meyerbeer was a law unto himself, however, producing works along German, French or Italian lines with equal facility, contributing here and there to the general development of opera yet founding no school, and having no disciples. The Germans have excelled both in declamation and in melody, and have greatly enriched and dignified the resources of opera with their great learning in the arts of harmony, counterpoint, instrumentation, stage-setting, as well as by their highly idealistic standards of beauty. In recent times these qualities ran to seed somewhat, and much that was beautiful gave way to that which was merely "kolossal"; but Germany today is, if anything, as deeply affected as ever by the splendid traditions of Beethoven and Wagner.

ENGLAND

In England the operatic ideas of the Italians were grafted onto the Masque as in France they had been grafted onto the Ballet. Purcell, Thomas Arne and others made a splendid beginning. Händel contributed something before turning his attention to oratorio; but on the whole England has not added anything to opera worthy to rank with her splendid contributions to literature and the stage. The most distinctive type of opera England has given the world has been the ballad-opera—such as "The Bohemian Girl" and "Maritana" (both by Irish composers!). The lighter forms of opera have been developed in this country with some success. "The Beggars' Opera" was an early effort in this direction. In more recent times, a more distinctive type of satir-ical comedy-opera had a promising beginning with Gilbert and Sullivan, but so far there has been no successor to "H. M. S. Pinafore," "The Mikado" or "Patience," in which the movements and personalities of the day were held up to salutary ridicule.

RUSSIA

At first Russia followed strictly Italian models, but in "A Life for the Czar" (1836), Glinka showed what might be drawn from Russia's own immense resources in national folk-music, and since his day such composers as Moussorgski, Balakireff, Tschaikowsky, Rimsky-Korsakoff, Borodin and others have produced some highly original works. These are steadily growing in favor.

AMERICA

Receptive to all schools of opera, the United States has as yet produced no distinctive type, the works of Victor Herbert, Cadman, Horatio Parker and others being apparently founded more or less on German or French models. The Metropolitan Opera House in New York (if we except the opera in New Orleans) so far is almost the only organization that has persisted over a number of years in producing the greatest works in the best style. It seems probable that Chicago may succeed in maintaining a permanent organization of its own, but efforts to establish permanent independent opera in such cities as Philadelphia and Boston have so far proved abortive. Our other cities are dependent solely upon local amateur efforts, upon visits of the Metropolitan or Chicago Companies, or the more or less successful itinerant companies which struggle for existence.

17

NOTE ON PRONUNCIATION

LIKE all systems of pronunciation involving foreign languages, the system of pronunciation followed in the "Victrola Book of the Opera" cannot hope to reproduce every sound exactly.

Many European languages contain sounds, especially vowels, which have no exact equivalents in English. Certain French sounds are exceedingly difficult for many English-speaking persons to learn—the vowel sounds of u and eu, for instance, and certain terminal consonants, such as the n in words like *charmant*. The German ch, to many, also is difficult, and the vowels, ä, ö and ü. The best practice is to Anglicize these frankly, where the exact pronunciation cannot be learned by word of mouth. There is no harm in referring to "L'Africaine," for instance, as "Lafricayn"; anybody who knows the French name of this opera will understand you, will accept your pronunciation, and you need be in no fear of ridicule. If you cannot say Alberich, call this character Alberick. It is best, of course, to learn each pronunciation, but where this is not possible, the best thing is to pronounce the name as it is given in the "Book of the Opera". Imperfect knowledge is a thousand times better, in such matters, than blank ignorance.

If Italian pronunciations seem confusing, it is well to remember that c, before e and i, is pronounced like ch in cheese; before other vowels, like k. The Italian ch is "hard," like our own k. G, before e and i, is soft, as in *gem* and *gin;* before other consonants hard, as in *gate, go*. In French there is no syllabic accent, or stress, all syllables being sounded equally. But here and there, in French names, we have placed an accent mark over a syllable, to indicate that it must be pronounced as clearly as the others, and not slurred over.

Many of the standard operas have several names, according to the language into which they may be translated. Wagner's *Fliegende Holländer*, for example, in French first became *Le Vaisseau Fantôme*, which is not a translation at all, and in English it is *The Flying ` Dutchman. Pagliacci*, in French, becomes *Paillasse;* the first English translator rendered it simply *Clowns. Romeo and Juliet* in Italian is *Romeo e Giulietta,* and in French *Romeo et Juliette*. Here and there throughout the volume, for greater intimacy with English-speaking audiences, a character originally English in origin (as Othello), is not translated into Italian except in the title to the opera. Happily most operas bear titles (like Aïda), for example, which are the same in all languages.

The nomenclature of the operas is that by which they are most familiarly known in America. The titles in the index include all the variants, in different languages, likely to be called for by an English-speaking public. Where a name is similar in several languages, the original article is not changed.

It is believed this procedure, while affording liberal cross-references, will save a good deal of vexation. Nothing is more exasperating, to the music-lover unschooled in operatic history, than to hear, or to come across, references to some strange work which proves to be only a familiar one under an unfamiliar name. European countries, despite their knowledge of one another's speech, cling pertinaciously to their own titles for operatic works.

L'AFRICAINE

(THE AFRICAN)

MEYERBEER might be called the Chameleon of Music. In the arts, he was all things to all persons, writing for public demand. He was born in 1791, in Berlin, of Jewish parentage. His father was a rich banker named Beer, and the composer added the "Meyer" in compliment to an uncle bearing that name. He early exhibited musical powers, and wrote much music, in a stiff and formal style. He adapted this first, however, to the needs of Vienna, then to the needs of Italy, where he was hailed as a sort of new Rossini. In France he grew more Gallic, it would seem, than the French.

Meyerbeer was a slow and uncertain workman. He wrote and erased and re-wrote interminably. He received the libretto of "L'Africaine" in 1838, and it occupied him for years, not being actually produced until after his death. The plot was tinkered with and modified times out of number—so much so, that the present hero, *Vasco di Gama*, was added to the characters as an afterthought!

"L'Africaine," says Grove, "is the most purely lyrical of Meyerbeer's operas. None is so melodious or so pathetic, or so free from blemishes of conventionality. . . It approaches the domain of poetry more nearly than any of his other operas." It was one of the longest, requiring six hours to produce, so that it had to be cut down radically. It is one of the best, however, of Meyerbeer's works; it is rich in melody and contains many famous numbers, some of them recorded.

THE OPERA

OPERA in five acts. Text by Scribe; music by Meyerbeer. First produced at the *Opéra*, Paris,

April 28, 1865, with a cast including Sasse, Batteo, Naudin and Faure. First London performance in Italian, under the French title, at Covent Garden, July 22, 1865; and in English at the Royal English Opera, Covent Garden, October 21, 1865. First American production December 1, 1865. Mmes. Hauk, Moran-Olden, Bettaque, Breval, Nordica and Litvinne are some of the famous *prime donne* who have appeared as *Selika* in America. *Vasco di Gama* has been sung by Campanini, Giannini, Perotti, Grienauer, Dippel, de Reszke and Tamagno; and *Nelusko* by Faure, Scotti, Stracciari and Campanari. Produced at the New Orleans Opera December 18, 1869. Important New York revivals occurred in 1901 with Breval, de Reszke, Adams, Plançon and Journet; and in 1906 with Caruso (his first appearance in the rôle), and again in 1923.

CHARACTERS

SELIKA, (*Say-lee'-kah*) a slave, formerly an African princess...................Soprano

INEZ, (*Ee'-nez*) daughter of Don Diego.............Soprano

NELUSKO, (*Nay-loos'-koh*) a slave, formerly an African chief....................Basso

DON PEDRO, (*Don Pay'-droh*) President of the Royal Council.................Basso

GRANDE INQUISITORE.........Basso

DON DIEGO, (*Don Dee-ay'-goh*) Member of the Council...Basso

HIGH PRIEST OF BRAHMA (*Brah'-mah*).............Basso

VASCO DI GAMA, (*Vahs'-koh dee Gah'-mah*) an officer in the Portuguese Navy........Tenor

19

CARUSO
AS VASCO DI GAMA

Chorus of Counsellors, Inquisitors, Sailors, Indians and Attendant Ladies

The Action occurs in Portugal, on Don Pedro's Ship at Sea, and in India

(The Italian name of the opera is "L'Africana," *Laf-ree-kah'-nah*; the French is "L'Africaine", *Laf-ree-kahn*).

ACT I

SCENE—*Council Chamber of the King of Portugal*

VASCO DI GAMA has returned after an expedition with news of a new and strange land; he has brought papers, charts, and two slaves, *Selika*, formerly an African princess, and *Nelusko*, a former chieftain of hers. *Vasco* is a blend of quixotism and practical ability, uniting the sailor's bluffness with the poet's idealism. He is eager to do in the East what Columbus did in the West, and to add a new El Dorado to the Portuguese realms. We find him in Council, and we hear a dignified opening chorus, "Dio che la terra venere" (Thou Whom the Earth Adores). The slaves are presented—Indian in feature though he bought them in Africa. *Vasco*, unknowingly enough, through his love for *Inez*, daughter of *Don Diego*, has awakened the enmity of *Don Pedro*, President of the Council, and when he asks for funds for a new vessel to explore the new territory, his request, to his amazement, is followed by his arrest, and he is led off between guards.

ACT II

SCENE—*Prison of the Inquisition*

VASCO sleeps fitfully, *Selika* watching. As she sings a lullaby of her own land, *Nelusko* enters with a knife to slay him. She reminds *Nelusko* of his debt to *Vasco*, who saved his life, and, awakening the sleeper, saves *Vasco's* in turn. *Selika* tells *Vasco* the route to the land of his heart's desire. He embraces her, and she believes she has won him. *Inez* and *Don Pedro* enter. The girl's father and the courtier have told her that *Vasco* loves *Selika*; it seems true, and *Inez* renounces him, declaring she is now the affianced of *Don Pedro*. *Vasco* is set free, and he removes her jealousy by giving her the two slaves.

Vasco learns that the *King* has given *Don Pedro* the expedition and the governorship of the new country. *Don Pedro* offers to buy the slaves—to learn the route. *Nelusko* is overjoyed, for this will separate *Vasco* and *Selika*. As *Vasco* leaves the prison, he learns that *Inez* has wedded his arch-enemy.

ACT III

SCENE—*Deck of Don Pedro's Ship*

THERE is an orchestral prelude, in placid vein, typifying the lapse of time; a plaintive melody for the cor anglais is prominent. The rising curtain discloses the ship's deck, where *Nelusko*, who has misguided her course, planning escape, sings the weird "All' erta, Mariner!" (What Ho, Mariners!) followed by the weirder ballad of "Adamastor, Re dell'onde profonde" (Adamastor, King of the Seas). This rolling stave, mocked with a trombone, affects all with superstitious fear. A storm arises, a ship is seen in the offing, and *Don Pedro's* ship heaves to. *Vasco*, with true chivalry, comes aboard. He has come off on his own account, and he comes to warn *Don Pedro* of danger. *Don Pedro* orders him slain, when *Selika* rushes at *Inez* with a poised knife, threatening to kill her unless *Vasco* is released. *Don Pedro* complies; but *Vasco* is imprisoned in the hold. *Selika* is led to be flogged, when the storm breaks and all find occupation. Suddenly the ship is boarded by Indians. *Don Pedro* and his host are slain. *Nelusko* is acclaimed leader, and *Selika* queen.

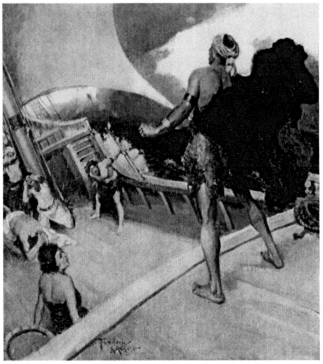

THE BALLAD OF ADAMASTOR

ACT IV

SCENE—*A Temple of Brahma*

TO the semi-barbaric strains of the "Marcia Indiana," or "Indian March", *Selika* is placed upon her throne. The women survivors of the ship are being marched to the deadly grove of mancinilla trees, whose influence is poison. Concealed in the ship's hold, *Vasco* is discovered later, and he is brought before *Selika*, already sentenced to death. Left alone with his guard, he sings the lovely "O Paradiso" (Oh Paradise), a smooth, lovely cantilena with an eloquent climax. Then the crowds return, demanding his death. *Selika* is with them; she can save his life only by claiming him as her husband. She compels *Nelusko's* consent by threatening suicide. The priests consent, but demand a ritual marriage in native style. Thinking *Inez* dead, *Vasco* consents. Alone with his bride, he hears the voice of *Inez*—who has escaped.

ACT V

SCENE I—*The Queen's Garden*

INEZ is recaptured. *Selika*, with swift insight, learns her love is true, pure and worthy of her own sacrifice. She gives *Nelusko* some tablets declared poisonous, and tells him to place *Inez* and *Vasco* on a homeward-bound ship; the tablets, to be administered on the way home, of course are harmless. Then *Inez* prepares for death.

22

SCENE II—*A Promontory by the Sea*

A MANCINILLA tree overlooks the broad ocean. *Selika*, standing beneath it, gazes at a distant sail. She sings a long and sorrowful farewell, "Gia l'odio m'abbandona" (All Thoughts of Hate). She seizes some of the deadly flowers, and inhales the perfume. *Nelusko*, seeking her, finds her swooning. He, too, drinks of the poisoned air of the flowers, and sinks beside her.

THE VICTOR RECORDS

(Sung in Italian unless otherwise noted)

ACT III

ALL' ERTA MARINAR!

(What Ho! Mariners!) TITTA RUFFO, Baritone 817 10-in., $1.50

ADAMASTOR, RE DELL' ONDE PROFONDE

(Adamastor, Ruler of Ocean) TITTA RUFFO, Baritone 6262 12-in., 2.00

NELUSKO:
Adamastor, monarch of the pathless deep,
Swift o'er foaming waves

To sound of fierce winds tramping;
When his dark steeds vex the misty sea,
Beware, mariner! Beware, mariner!
When the gale rolls o'er the deep,
Then beware, then beware!
See, the lightning's flash reveals to thine eye,
How the dark waves seek the storm-laden sky
All hope now is lost,
For the doomed wretch no tomb,
None, none but a watery grave!

ACT IV

O PARADISO!

(Oh Paradise!) ENRICO CARUSO, Tenor 6007 12-in., $2.00

BENIAMINO GIGLI, Tenor 6138 12-in., 2.00

GIOVANNI MARTINELLI, Tenor 6193 12-in., 2.00

EVAN WILLIAMS, Tenor *In English* 6308 12-in., 2.00

VASCO:
Hail! fruitful land of plenty,
An earthly Paradise art thou!
Oh Paradise on earth!
Oh azure sky, oh fragrant air
All enchant my heart;
Thou fair new world art mine!
Thee, a radiant gift,
On my native land I'll bestow!
O beauteous country—mine thou art at last!

VASCO AROUSES THE JEALOUSY OF INEZ

23

HOMER
AS AMNERIS

THE RETURN OF RHADAMES—ACT II

AÏDA

GIUSEPPE VERDI was almost sixty. He had worked long, hard and successfully, and he felt he had earned the right to retire. But the Viceroy of Egypt was to open the new Grand Opera House in Cairo, he wanted a new opera for the dedication, and Verdi seemed the logical composer to write it. A work dealing with the past grandeurs of Egypt was to be the subject—to which Verdi's genius for the grandiose seemed especially fitted. When approached, however, he sought to evade the commission by naming an exorbitant fee—a method by which Grieg, in later years, sought to avoid the rigors of a sea voyage and an American concert tour. Verdi, like Grieg, was embarrassed when his offer was accepted. Unlike Grieg, he could not plead ill health, and he set to work. He soon became interested, as he felt the opera growing beneath his hand. When completed, it was realized to be the greatest work of his career. He little dreamed that sixteen years later he was to bring forth an even greater one!

"Aïda" was successful from the first. It lacked none of the composer's earlier fire, but it was more mature in style and more convincing in dramatic power. Its vivid plot, its golden pageantry, its richness of melody, of harmony, and of orchestral scoring, marked it not simply as one of the best of Verdi's works, but as one of the greatest of all time. And years have rather increased than diminished its reputation.

In "Aïda," Verdi realized he was preparing a pageant—an opera in magnificent setting, with plenty of room for display. He was composing for large masses of people, and he did not fail to provide melody in its simplest and most impressive form, in a setting of

25

harmony and orchestration all might appreciate. Yet there is careful characterization throughout. The music of *Rhadames* is bold and romantic; the vanity, pride, anger, jealousy, terror of *Amneris* find ample expression. The simple, loving *Aïda* is no less carefully drawn; so it is with minor characters,—*Amonasro, Ramfis, The King.* Nor is the proper background wanting—the blazing pageantry of *Rhadames'* return; the soft beauty and mystery of Egyptian night; the awe-inspiring ritual of the priests of Isis, Osiris and Ptah. The more one studies "Aïda" the more one is amazed at the lavish genius of the composer. It is a landmark, not only in his own development, but in that of opera itself.

THE OPERA

OPERA in four acts. Text translated from the French of Locle by Antonio Ghislanzoni. Music by Giuseppe Verdi. First produced in Cairo, December 24, 1871; at La Scala, Milan, under the direction of the composer himself, February 8, 1872; at Naples in March, 1872; at Parma, April, 1872; Berlin, 1874; in Paris, at the *Théâtre Italien*, April 22, 1876; revived at the same theatre in 1878; and given at the Opéra, March 22, 1880, where it has since been one of the most popular of all works. First London production at Covent Garden, June 22, 1876; produced at St. Petersburg, in Russian, 1879. First performance in America at the Academy of Music, New York, November 26, 1873, the cast including Torriani, Cary, Campanini and Maurel. Produced in Philadelphia, December 12, 1873; and at the New Orleans Opera December 6, 1878. The opera has always been a favorite one in America, and holds the Metropolitan Opera record for the largest number of performances. In 1904 Caruso made his first appearance at the Metro-

politan as *Rhadames*. A highly impressive open air production was given in 1912 at the foot of the pyramids of Egypt.

CHARACTERS

AÏDA, an Ethiopian slave (*Ah-ee'-dah*) ....Soprano
THE KING OF EGYPT............Bass
AMNERIS, (*Am-nay'-riss*) his daughter.........Mezzo-Soprano
RHADAMES, (*Rahd'-ah -maze*) Captain of the Guard......Tenor
AMONASRO, (*Am-oh-nahz'-roh*) King of Ethiopia....Baritone
RAMFIS, (*Rahm'-fiss*) High Priest....................Bass
A MESSENGER................Tenor
Priests, Priestesses, Ministers, Captains, Soldiers, Officials, Ethiopian Slaves and Prisoners, Egyptians, etc.

The Scene is laid in Memphis and Thebes, in Pharaoh's time.

ACT I

SCENE I—*A Hall in the Palace. Through the Great Gate at the rear may be seen the Pyramids and the Temples of Memphis*

TO a soldier, the knowledge of his country's danger must act as a trumpet-call; to *Rhadames* it implies even more. *Ramfis*, the high priest, the power behind the throne, has told him the Ethiopians are about to rise against Egypt, and that an expedition is to go forth to prevent them. He intimates that the sacred Isis, the omnipotent goddess of his people, has chosen a certain brave and young warrior to command. He departs, leaving *Rhadames* to ponder his words.

But the young warrior is not dream-

AÏDA SUNG AT THE FOOT OF THE PYRAMIDS IN 1912

ing simply of war. He thinks also of his victorious return to his beloved *Aïda* —the slave, captured from the very people he proposes to attack. In his triumphs he will have full power to atone for her present misfortunes. In the visions of his new power and the intoxication of his love, he sings the beautiful "Celeste Aïda:"

This melody, sung against a shimmering background of string-tone, expresses to the full the devotion of *Rhadames*. Its beauty has made it the most popular number in the opera, and the number most frequently played by itself. Yet as a part of the opera it is even finer—establishing, by sheer musical beauty, the intensity of *Rhadames'* love in such a way as to make his subsequent sacrifice on *Aïda's* behalf both logical and inevitable.

His musings are broken by *Amneris*,

the king's daughter, a woman whose demure aspect conceals a passionate and highly charged nature. She rallies the hero upon the unwonted fire of his glance, declaring the woman who may inspire it is to be envied. A strange and ardent light indeed gleams there, but it gleams, not for *Amneris* but *Aïda*, who is seen approaching. Her woman's wit quickened by jealousy, *Amneris* comprehends. She, a royal princess of Egypt, ignored for a foreign-born slave!

Her anger is delayed by the entrance of the *King*, with his guards. A messenger brings the news that the Ethiopian invasion is an accomplished fact—that the enemy approaches under *Amonasro*. ("My father!" exclaims *Aïda*, aside.) Amid excitement, *Rhadames* is appointed leader, and *Amneris* enjoys a proud moment as she presents him with the banner beneath which he is to go forth.

The *King* enjoins the Egyptians to guard with their lives the sacred Nile, and they depart to make ready for war.

27

LANDE   THE GREAT CONSECRATION SCENE

Aïda, with conflicting feelings, is left alone on the stage. There she sings the remarkable aria, "Ritorna Vincitor," blaming herself for the words of encouragement she had given the hero when about to set forth against her own father, yet confessing to herself again the racking power of her love for *Rhadames*.

The girl is horrified, as much at herself as at the workings of circumstance; but she sincerely loves *Rhadames* and wishes for him to return in glory. The varied melody, the shifting harmonies of the music here, supported by ever-varying orchestral touches as conflicting ideas seize her, make this a memorable instance of Verdi's mature genius. *Aïda* seems ready to collapse. But she recovers, calls wildly upon the gods for aid, and goes out slowly as the curtain falls.

SCENE II—*The Temple of Vulcan. In the center is an Altar illumined by a mysterious Light from above*

RHADAMES has come to seek the blessing of the gods. *Ramfis* and his priests and priestesses intone blessings upon the expedition, while an invisible choir chants the praises of Ptah. *Rhadames* enters and receives the consecrated veil. He is solemnly blessed by *Ramfis*, responding with a fervent prayer to his gods to protect the sacred land of Egypt, of which he is now the sworn champion and leader. *Ramfis* then sings the closing invocation, "Nume custode e vindice" (God, Guardian and Avenger). This is a broad, dignified melody, against a steadily beating orchestral accompaniment in which a majestic contrapuntal bass is heard. Soon the air is taken up by *Rhadames* and the chorus with rich and gorgeous effect. *Rhadames* is invested with the sacred armor, and as the priestesses go through the mystic dance, the curtain falls. Never is *Rhadames* farther, than at this moment, from the thought of treachery to his beloved country. Wait and see!

28

ACT II

Scene I—*A Hall in Amneris' Apartment*

RHADAMES has been away for some time—long enough for him to have justified his command with victory, and more than long enough to set *Amneris* thinking upon his strange behavior with the slave-girl. She lies indolently upon her couch, her own girls chanting songs in his praise. She herself calls upon love to fulfil her soul with rapture and to heal her own jealousy. The girls' chorus, "Chi mai fra" (His Glory Now Praise), is rich and heavy with Oriental coloring. As they sing, *Amneris* takes up the melody. There is a beautiful, long-drawn trumpet note in the accompaniment.

Seeing *Aïda* approach, *Amneris* prepares for a moment of revenge. It is deftly achieved. She treacherously consoles the girl just long enough to gain her confidence; then when the secret is out, she turns upon her like a scorpion. "Time will heal the anguish of thy heart," she declares, "and more than this, a powerful god-love." Sympathy is the last thing the captive looks for, and she is melted. The talk of love disarms her, and the crafty princess, watching with cat-like eyes, has no difficulty in reading the pallor upon her rival's face.

"Among the braves who fought so well,
Has someone a tender sorrow awakened in
   your heart?"

This is enough. "What say'st thou?" cries the unhappy girl, and her secret is out. *Amneris* then confesses her own love for the hero—the love of the king's own daughter.

Then follows a powerful scene. *Aïda* is dazed. She can but implore mercy—from the merciless. She makes no denial, only pleads, helplessly, for pity. *Amneris* first threatens her with death, but refines upon this by demanding that she shall witness *Rhadames'* triumphant return, and his obeisances to herself as she sits beside her father, the *King*.

Scene II—*Without the City Walls*

THE scene changes to a gate of the city of Thebes. The *King* and his court are assembled about a great throne to receive and welcome the conquering army. A majestic chorus is sung by the people and the priests, leading up to the famous "Grand March."

This is introduced by trumpet calls, in an introductory crescendo, broad, suave, melodious, followed by the martial strains so familiar to all. Specially designed trumpets are used here. They are long and straight, like the trumpets used in Renaissance art. Each has a tiny valve concealed beneath the trumpeter's hand.

The pomp and the splendor of this scene are unsurpassed by anything in the range of opera. The Egyptian troops, preceded by the trumpeters, enter, followed by chariots of war, ensigns, statues of the gods, dancing girls carrying treasures, and finally *Rhadames*, riding in triumph under a canopy borne by twelve slaves. An additional brass band, as a rule, is employed on the stage here, in addition to the trumpets. The effect is magnificent beyond description.

The *King* descends from the throne to embrace *Rhadames*, as the saviour of his country. At his own command, *Amneris* crowns the victor, who is asked to name any boon he desires.

At that moment the prisoners enter, including *Amonasro*, dressed as a plain officer. *Aïda* cries out "My father!" but she is signaled not to betray his rank. *Amonasro* then acknowledges his daughter, admits defeat, and de-

29

scribes how the "King of the Ethiopians", (himself!) transfixed by wounds, died at his feet. That this duplicity is not simply a means of salvation but of revenge is shown in his plea to the *King*, whom he asks to be merciful, as Fate may bring him his own misfortunes on the morrow!

Amonasro's bluff, soldierly manner commends itself to the *King*. The populace and prisoners beg his release; the priests demand his death, and that of the other captives. *Rhadames* pleads for mercy, and recalling the *King's* promise of whatever he desires, demands life and liberty for the Ethiopians. The *King* yields, stipulating only that *Aïda* and *Amonasro* remain as hostages. So far, all is well; but he announces that *Rhadames* shall have, for further reward, the hand of *Amneris*.

Then follows a magnificent finale. *Amonasro*, released, swears secret vengeance, already planning, a bad man but a true man of action. *Amneris* is triumphant, her vengeance complete. But as the curtain falls, *Rhadames* and *Aïda* gaze upon one another in blank despair. The hand of Fate has struck them, and struck hard.

ACT III

SCENE—*The Banks of the Nile; Moonlight. The Temple of Isis can be seen behind Palm Trees*

FROM out the temple is heard a sweet, mysterious chant of praise, "O tu che sei d'Osiride" (O Thou who art Osiris). Oboes and wood-winds, against a gently persistent rhythmic accompaniment, yield tranquil but weird suggestions of the Orient night. The calm is portentous, however, as before a storm. A boat approaches with *Ramfis* and with *Amneris*, who has come to give thanksgiving for victory, and to pray that *Rhadames* shall be hers forever. The pair enter the temple, when *Aïda* comes cautiously forward, in hope that *Rhadames* himself may appear. She sings a tender

COPY'T MISHKIN
DALMORES AS RHADAMES

CARUSO AS RHADAMES

COPY'T DUPONT
EAMES AS AÏDA

and despairing song of the lovely land she may never see again. This air, "O Patria Mia" (My Native Land), is one of the loveliest in the work. Blending with its melody is a weird, wandering strain for the oboe, faint, high, sweet and mysterious.

Turning to go, she sees *Amonasro*, who conceives in her love for *Rhadames* a means of escape, and even victory. Skilled plotter, he plays, even as *Amneris* had played, upon the feelings of the innocent girl. He tells her, almost brutally, he knows of her love, and the princess's jealousy. Agonized, she cries out that she is in the power of *Amneris*, when he tells her how she may gain happiness with her lover and return to Ethiopia.

The proposal is an ugly one; the way for it is laid by a harrowing picture of the Ethiopians' treatment by their conquerors. And that is too much for the girl, who recoils. Then follows a terrible scene, in which the woes of her people are laid upon her own head. She cries out for pity—but what are the woes of a girl beside the ambitions of kings and the fates of peoples? At last she yields, and the tragedy moves on.

Rhadames at this moment appears, *Amonasro* concealing himself among trees. The hero seeks to embrace his beloved, but, scientifically prepared, she bids him prove his affection by fleeing with her. The scene, "Fuggiam gli ardori" (Fly With Me), is a remarkable dialog in music, the pleading accents of the girl and the agitation of the hero being in sharp contrast. He resists, but the glamor of her presence, the spell of the night, and the desperate prospects of his marriage to *Amneris*, weaken his resolve. He in turn succumbs; and caught up, by reaction, upon the surge of his own emotions, he gives way, freely, to his vision of an easy future. The music follows and expounds all. In yielding, he lets slip

the information that the Egyptian army must go out by the pass of Napata. And *Amonasro* then leaps forth.

Rhadames, commander of the Egyptians, has let loose his plans. But his fatal devotion to *Aïda* is too strong, and it is too late to repent. *Amonasro*, with subtle casuistry, points out that he is guiltless, that his betrayal is Fate. He paints an attractive picture of what lies, for all of them, in Ethiopia. *Rhadames*, as a man, is done.

The worst is yet to follow. Among the still palms, there has been a double eavesdropping. *Amneris*, coming from the temple, has overheard.

Mad with jealousy she rushes in and denounces the trio, her wrath blazing forth with especial virulence against *Rhadames*, the betrayer of his country, his gods and herself. So blind is her passion, that *Amonasro* escapes, and with him *Aïda*—who sees, in a flash, that her one hope is to help her father in his attack on the Egyptians, if *Rhadames* ever is to be rescued.

ACT IV

SCENE I—*A Room in the Palace. One side, a Door leading to Rhadames' Prison Cell*

AMNERIS is passionate, hot-blooded, vindictive, but she is a woman. If self-love is the guiding star of her life, she nevertheless loves *Rhadames* with the full hunger of a selfish nature. As the curtain rises, she is seen in despair, weighing the cost of her own action in giving up her lover to the priests. Her rival has escaped; *Rhadames*, through her own act, awaits a traitor's punishment—how unjustly only she herself knows; for he was controlled by human impulse, not design. Could he learn to love her, she yet might save him! She resolves to try, and he is brought in. Then begins the first great duet of the act; "Gia i sacerdoti" (The Priests Assemble). Exerting all the power of

31

her beauty and her womanhood, she offers to save *Rhadames* if he will renounce *Aïda*. He refuses, and is told that death is the alternative. What does *Rhadames* care for death? As the scene wheels on, "Aïda, a me togliesti" (Aïda, Thou Hast Taken), he speaks again of his rapt affection for the slave-girl. The duet rises to supreme heights when he declares that his death for *Aïda's* sake can be counted as the highest blessing he can desire. Then the pity of *Amneris* subsides into the darkness of hate, and she calls upon the gods for revenge. The men-at-arms appear, and conduct *Rhadames* into the judgment room.

Amneris must suffer too. *Rhadames* once gone, she cries out against the very fate to which she has sent him. This is a most beautiful moment; "Ohime, Morir mi sento!" (Ah, Me, Death Approaches!) sings the unhappy princess. Then she turns, to see *Ramfis* and the *Priests* filing past her and entering the judgment hall. "Behold," she cries, "the fatal ministers of death— Ah, do not let me behold those white-robed phantoms!" But the law now is stronger than the will of *Amneris*. Her lamentation, the stern voice of *Ramfis* and his priests, from behind the scenes, conducting the trial, combine to produce a doubly tragic sense of foreboding. It is marvellously reflected in the music. The bass tuba in the orchestra sounds with baleful effect, and the hollow voices of the priests, chanting in unison, add to the gloom that prevails. *Amneris*, in torture, covers her face with her hands; but she cannot shut out the terrible voices of *Rhadames'* accusers. Throughout all, he remains silent. Finally the voice of *Ramfis* pronounces the sentence— death by burial alive beneath the altar of the gods whose nobler attributes—of faith and justice—he has offended. The priests re-enter, and again file impassively across the room, before the

AÏDA: "Clasped in thy arms, love, I resolved to perish!"

despairing eyes of *Amneris*. The wretched woman denounces them, but they repeat that their work is done. She departs in wild despair, her last hope gone; for nothing now can save the man she loves from the terrible doom that awaits him beneath the temple-floor.

SCENE II—*Interior of the Temple of Vulcan—below, a Subterranean Apartment, the Tomb of Rhadames*

THE setting of the last scene is one of the most remarkable in opera; Verdi himself is said to have devised it. The work, in the words of Camille Blaigue,"finishes in serenity and peace, and such terminations are the most beautiful. Above, the temple full of light, where the ceremonies continue immutable in the sanctuary of the indifferent gods; below, two human beings dying in each other's arms." The stage, indeed, is divided; the upper half shows the temple, where the chanting priests intone their endless litanies; the lower half, underneath the very statue of Osiris, the deity of the nether world,

is the tomb where *Rhadames* awaits death by starvation.

The hero, dedicated to death, believes himself alone, and his reflections are embodied in the incomparable music of the aria, "La Fatal Pietra" (The Fatal Stone), which is swung into place overhead. He laments, not suffering and death, but separation from his beloved. As the last sounds die out above he sees, among the shadows, the outline of a human figure. He is not mistaken, not delirious, it is she! She has come to partake of death beside him. Her father is slain, his troops scattered; she has crept to earth like a stricken animal, her heart foreseeing the sentence to be passed upon *Rhadames*.

The great duet between the pair is one of the supreme moments in all opera. It is known as "O terra addio" (Farewell, O Earth). Its melody is in broad calm phrases, tranquil as the sea of Eternity. It is sung in unison—even the blending of the voice-parts symbolizing the absorption of their souls into a union free of all earthly dross. Together they bid farewell to earth and its sorrows, and await the Dawn.

THE VICTOR RECORDS

(Sung in Italian unless otherwise noted)

ACT I

CÉLESTE AÏDA!

(Heavenly Aïda!) ENRICO CARUSO, Tenor 6000 12-in., $2.00

GIOVANNI MARTINELLI, Tenor 6192 12-in., 2.00

RHADAMES:

Heavenly Aïda, beauty resplendent,
  Radiant flower, blooming and bright;
Queenly thou reignest o'er me transcendent,
  Bathing my spirit in beauty's light.
Would that thy bright skies once more beholding,
  Breathing the soft airs of thy native land,
Round thy fair brow a diadem folding,
  Thine were a throne next the sun to stand!

RITORNA VINCITOR

(Return Victorious!) ROSA PONSELLE, Soprano 6437 12-in., 2.00

AÏDA:

Return victorious! And from thy lips
Went forth the impious word! Conqueror
Of my father—of him who takes arms
For me—to give me again
A country; a kingdom; and the illustrious name
Which here I am forced to conceal!
The insane words forget, O gods;
Return the daughter
To the bosom of her father;
Destroy the squadrons of our oppressors!
What am I saying? And my love,
Can I ever forget
This fervid love which oppresses and enslaves,
As the sun's ray which now blesses me?
Shall I call death on Rhadames—
On him whom I love so much?
Ah! Never on earth was heart torn by more cruel agonies!

33

ACT III

O PATRIA MIA
(My Native Land) ROSA PONSELLE,
Soprano   6437   12-in., $2.00

AÏDA:

My native land, no more to thee shall I return!
O skies of tender blue, O soft airs blowing,
Where calm and peaceful my dawn of life
  pass'd o'er,
O hills of verdure, O perfum'd waters flowing,
O home beloved, I ne'er shall see thee more!
O fresh and fragrant vales, O quiet dwelling,
Promise of happy days of love that bore.
Now hope is banish'd, love and yonder dream
  dispelling,
O home beloved, I ne'er shall see thee more!

ACT IV

GIÀ I SACERDOTI ADUNANSI
(The Priests Assemble) LOUISE HOMER,
Contralto and ENRICO CARUSO, Tenor
          8012   12-in.,   2.50

AÏDA A ME TOGLIESTI
(Aïda Thou Hast Taken) LOUISE HOMER,
Contralto and ENRICO CARUSO, Tenor
          8012   12-in., $2.50

OHIMÈ! MORIR MI SENTO
(Death Approaches) BIANCA DE CASES,
Mezzo-Soprano and Chorus
          6351   12-in.,   2.00

LA FATAL PIETRA
(The Fatal Stone) Final duet, Part I
JOHANNA GADSKI, Soprano and ENRICO
CARUSO, Tenor   8015   12-in.,   2.50

O TERRA ADDIO
(Farewell, Oh Earth) Final duet, Part II
JOHANNA GADSKI, Soprano and ENRICO
CARUSO, Tenor   8015   12-in.,   2.50
LUCY MARSH, Soprano and JOHN
McCORMACK, Tenor   8034 12-in.,   2.50

BLACK LABEL AND BLUE LABEL RECORDS

Céleste Aïda! (Heavenly Aïda!)......................*Paul Althouse, Tenor*	55045	12-in.,	$1.50
Ständchen (Serenade) (Schubert) (In German).........*Paul Reimers, Tenor*			
Ritorna vincitor (Return Victorious!)..............*Lucy Marsh, Soprano*	55135	12-in.,	1.50
O patria mia (My Native Land)....................*Lucy Marsh, Soprano*			
Aïda—Grand March...........................*Vessella's Italian Band*	35265	12-in.,	1.25
Rondo Capriccioso...........................*Vessella's Italian Band*			
Fuggiam gli ardori (Ah! Fly With Me) *Lucy Marsh, Soprano and Paul Althouse, Tenor*	55058	12-in.,	1.50
Madame Butterfly-O quanti..*Olive Kline, Soprano and Paul Althouse, Tenor*			
Aïda Selection.................................*Arthur Pryor's Band*	35195	12-in.,	1.25
Attila—Grand Trio (Verdi)......................*Kryl's Bohemian Band*			
Aïda Selection.....................*Hurtado Brothers Marimba Band*	35559	12-in.,	1.25
Lucia Sextette.....................*Hurtado Brothers Marimba Band*			
Gems from "Aïda"—Part I...................*Victor Opera Company* Chorus, "Almighty Phtha"—Solo, "Heav'nly Aïda" (Céleste Aïda)— Women's Chorus, "Come Bind Thy Flowing Tresses"—Soprano Solo, "Love, Fatal Power"—Chorus, "On to Victory".			
Gems from "Aïda"—Part II...................*Victor Opera Company* Chorus, "Glory to Isis"—Solo, "My Native Land"—Solo and Chorus, "Oh King in Thy Power, Transcendent"—Solo, "Priests of Isis"—Finale, Duet and Chorus, "Fatal Stone"	35726	12-in.,	1.25

ANDREA CHENIER

OPERA in four acts; libretto by Luigi Illica; music by Umberto Giordano. First produced at La Scala, Milan, March 28, 1896. London, 1903, Carl Rosa Company, in English. First American production Academy of Music, November 13, 1896. Revived in 1908 by Hammerstein. Metropolitan, 1922.

THE Countess de Coigny is giving a ball to church and state dignitaries. Chenier, whose verses have found interest, is to be a guest. Gerard, a footman, soon to be revolutionary leader, sees his aged father, a lackey, at work; he sings the powerful dramatic air, "Son Sessant' Anni" (For Sixty Years) decrying his servitude. The guests arrived, the Countess asks Chenier to improvise; he refuses, consenting when her daughter Madeleine pleads. He outrages all but Madeleine, a sincere, spirited girl, by his idealistic social and human creed. This is sung in the aria, "Un di all 'azzurro spazio," criticizing church and state. A troop of beggars enters, introduced by Gerard as "His Serene Highness, Prince Poverty," and is ejected, with Gerard. Chenier follows.

In Act II, Chenier becomes a Revolutionary. Roucher appears with a passport for him, counselling flight. He refuses without Madeleine, who arrives in disguise, and begs him to save her from Gerard, now a Revolutionary power who is attracted to her. They start, but are caught by Gerard, who seizes the girl. Gerard and Chenier fight, while she is spirited away. Gerard is hurt, but magnanimously counsels Chenier to save the girl. He tells the crowd his assailant is unknown to him.

Later on Gerard presides over a Revolutionary tribunal. A spy announces Chenier's arrest, urging Gerard to denounce him. The papers are signed after the great scene, "Nemico della patrie" (The Enemy of His Country). Madeleine appears and offers to give up her life for Chenier, who, denounced as a traitor, pleads his own cause. Gerard would relent, but the mob thirsts for blood and Chenier is led off for execution.

The last act is in St. Lazare prison, where Chenier is writing his last verses, the beautiful "Come un bel di di Maggio" (As Some Soft Day in May) expressing his belief in truth and beauty. Madeleine bribes her way in. Gerard brings her, then goes for a last vain appeal to Robespierre himself. At dawn the death-tumbril comes for Chenier. Madeleine goes to death with him. Gerard, self-redeemed, has for his reward the consciousness of his own lofty self-sacrifice.

THE VICTOR RECORDS
(Sung in Italian)

ACT I

SON SESSANT' ANNI
(Sixty Years Hast Thou Served Them)
TITTA RUFFO, Baritone
817   10-in., $1.50

UN DI ALL' AZZURRO SPAZIO
(Once O'er the Azure Fields) ENRICO
CARUSO, Tenor   6008 12-in., 2.00
BENIAMINO GIGLI, Tenor
6139 12-in., 2.00

ACT III

NEMICO DELLA PATRIE?
(The Enemy of His Country?) TITTA
RUFFO, Baritone   6262 12-in., 2.00

ACT IV

COME UN BEL DÌ DI MAGGIO
(As Some Soft Day in May) ENRICO
CARUSO, Tenor   516 10-in., 1.50
BENIAMINO GIGLI, Tenor
975 10-in., 1.50

BARBER OF SEVILLE

(IL BARBIERE DI SIVIGLIA)

(Italian)

WHEN told that Rossini had composed "The Barber" in thirteen days, Donizetti replied: "Very possible; *he is so lazy.*" The remark was at once a tribute and a censure; for Giaoachino Antonio Rossini was one of those men upon whom Providence most lavishly scatters gifts.

Superficially, Donizetti's taunt is deserved in "The Barber." It bears all the signs of a work hastily flung together. The original overture was lost and the present one belongs to a totally different opera—"Elizabetta"; the opening of the cavatina "Ecco ridente" is borrowed from "Aureliano"; the air of *Bertha*, "Il vecchietto cerca moglie" was suggested by a Russian tune, and the eight opening measures of "Zitti, Zitti" are taken from Simon's air in Haydn's "Seasons." Yet these numbers are at least well chosen, and the rest of the opera is so rich with original melody, so joyous in its abounding good spirits, so spontaneous and fresh, so subtle in its characterization and so brilliant in its climaxes that "The Barber" is regarded by many as the greatest of Rossini's works. Not even the fact that the incomparable Mozart himself had dealt with the same *Figaro* in another episode from the comedy of Beaumarchais "The Marriage of Figaro" dims altogether its lustre.

"The Barber of Seville" was a violent failure when first produced in Rome. In this it fulfilled an almost fixed tradition with meritorious, or afterwards popular, works.

Aware that his opera was good, Rossini took failure with philosophy; he believed that the opera would ultimately succeed, and the belief was justified. To this day, "The Barber of Seville" has the place of honor among the twenty operas Rossini wrote in the eight years from 1815 to 1823. It is only surpassed—if it *is* surpassed—by "William Tell," written in 1829—the last opera the composer wrote, though he was not yet forty years of age.

Rossini's greatest contribution to music in "The Barber" is his joyous spontaneity. The melodies are so fresh and vigorous, so lavish in their bubbling fertility, that they disarm technical analysis; but one technical gift Rossini *did* possess—a thorough understanding of the human voice; and this gift is displayed to the utmost in "The Barber of Seville." The "Largo al factotum" is possibly the best basso buffo number ever written and among coloratura arias none is more famous than "Una voce poco fa." In these, only the initiated can tell how artfully the composer has contrived to give the singer every chance to make the most of vocal skill without in any way lessening the flow of natural melodic inspiration.

THE OPERA

COMIC opera in two acts; text by Sterbini; founded on the trilogy of Beaumarchais. Music by Rossini. First presented at Rome, February 5, 1816. The opera was at first called "Almaviva," to distinguish it from Paisiello's "Barber." First London production, 1818. At Paris, in Italian, 1819; in French, 1824. First production in Germany at Brunswick, 1820. Produced at Vienna, 1820; Berlin, 1822. First N. Y. production November 29, 1825, by Manuel Garcia and company; sung at the New Orleans Opera, March 9, 1828. Many notable revivals have occurred in America of recent years—in 1892 with Patti, her last appearance in New York as *Rosina;* in 1898, for Melba, who made her first American appearance as *Rosina;* for Sembrich's farewell operatic appearance in 1909; by Hammerstein, for Tetrazzini; the New Theatre production with Lipkowska, and the Metropolitan revival, February 5, 1916, on the 100th anniversary of the first production, with Barrientos, Mattfeld, de Luca, Damacco and de Segurola.

CHARACTERS

COUNT ALMAVIVA (*Ahl-mah-vee'-vah*)
Tenor
BARTOLO (*Bahr'-toh-loh*) physician
Bass
ROSINA (*Ro-zee-nah*) his ward. Soprano
BASILIO (*Bah-seel'-yoh*) music master
Bass
BERTHA, Rosina's governess. . Soprano
FIGARO (*Fee'-gah-roh*). . . . . . Baritone
FIORELLO (*Fyo-rel'-loh*) servant to
the Count. . . . . Tenor

*Scene and Period: Seville, the
Seventeenth Century*

(The original Italian name of the opera is "Il Barbiere di Siviglia", *Eel Bahr-be-ay-reh dee See-veel'-yah*).

ACT I

SCENE I—*A Street in Seville.
Day is Breaking*

THE handsome and distinguished *Count Almaviva* is deeply in love with *Rosina*, the ward of *Doctor Bartolo*, a physician both mean and suspicious. Not wishing to have the glamor of his rank influence the girl, *Count Almaviva* has taken the name of *Lindor*, and as such, we find him serenading the lady of his heart. Not very successfully,

it must be admitted, for she pays no attention though the musicians wake the neighborhood. He sings a lovely serenade, "Dawn With Her Rosy Mantle," but as it fails, he conceals himself to watch a newcomer who is vigorously making known his identity. It is *Figaro*, the factotum, the jack-of-all-trades, the debonaire *Barber of Seville*—the same hero who figures again in Mozart's "The Marriage of Figaro." *Figaro* is thoroughly well satisfied with himself, and gives a list of his accomplishments in the famous "Largo al factotum" (Room for the Factotum). It should be remembered that in the days of perukes, powder and patches, the barber was not only "tonsorial artist," but also a dentist and chirurgeon who bled his customers as readily as he shaved them. Incidentally, he was a privileged person, whose easy access to the homes of the distinguished made him a convenient instrument for the plots and schemes of young lovers and old *roués*.

This brilliant and loquacious "Largo al factotum" (Room for the Factotum) sung at breakneck speed, is a severe test of the singer's art. The music is as merry and forceful as the words.

Figaro is accosted by the *Count*, who asks him to arrange a meeting with the fair *Rosina*. They have no sooner made an alliance than *Rosina* and old *Bartolo* appear at the balcony window. If *Rosina* has seemed unresponsive to the serenading *Lindor*, her very suspicious guardian has been watching her. After the *Count* again serenades her with the "Se il mio nome," (If my name you would know) she contrives to drop him a note.

Shortly after, *Bartolo* leaves the house, ordering that nobody shall be admitted save *Basilio*, a music master, and incidentally a matrimonial agent. Meanwhile, however, *Figaro* has plotted to gain admittance for the *Count*. Troops are coming to the city, and

37

Almaviva, disguised as a dragoon, may easily be billed on the unwilling *Bartolo*. This is a grand idea!

SCENE II—*A Room in Bartolo's House*

ROSINA is discovered reading a note from *Lindor*. She is agitated, as one might expect, and she lets loose her feelings in an ever-delightful coloratura aria, the "Una voce poco fa" (A LittleVoice I Hear). It is one of the gems of the work.

Almost every resource known to the coloratura singer's art is employed in this glittering number. Rapid scales, detached, legato; brilliant arpeggi, now soft, now loud, now high, now low, surprise the ear, and in their bubbling gaiety express the full charm of the equally gay and charming words.

At the end of it *Rosina* runs out of the room when her guardian appears in company with *Basilio*. *Bartolo* is telling the matrimonial agent that he wishes to marry *Rosina* himself, but that her hand is sought by one *Count*

Almaviva, though he little suspects that the serenader of the night before and the *Count* are one and the same. *Basilio*, scenting profit, is sympathetic, and they agree to produce a story that will disgrace him. "A calumny!" cries *Basilio*. "What is that?" asks the *Doctor*. In reply the musical matrimonial agent gives his famous description in song, "La calunnia" (Slander's Whisper), full of bombastic humor.

With the departure of the two plotters, *Rosina* returns accompanied by *Figaro*, who tells her that her guardian plans to marry her himself. She laughs at the idea and asks *Figaro* who the young man is she has seen from the balcony. *Figaro* admits he is an excellent youth, but has one failing. "A failing?" cries the girl. "Yes, a great one," answers the factotum blandly, "he is dying of love." The girl, greatly interested, presses for further details, and learns that the adored maiden is none other than *Rosina* herself. "You are mocking," she cries; and the two make merry in

MELBA AS ROSINA

TETRAZZINI AS ROSINA

SEMBRICH AS ROSINA

a delightful duet, the "Dunque io son" (What! I?). And all seems well.

The comedy so characteristic of the whole work here gallops through the music. *Figaro* leaves after telling her his scheme to billet *Lindor* upon the household, and *Bartolo* returns, to accuse *Rosina* of writing a note and dropping it from the balcony. He misses the very sheet of paper: "Manca un foglio" (Here's a Leaf Missing), declares he.

The old *Doctor's* anger and the girl's impertinent replies are admirably treated in the music. He points out an ink-mark on her finger, to which she answers that she used the ink as a salve for a small cut. He calls attention to a freshly trimmed quill pen and the missing sheet of paper; and she replies that she used the paper to wrap up some sweets for a girl friend and the pen to design a flower for her embroidery; the old man is in a violent and quite just rage.

A loud knocking is heard at the door—the *Count* in his soldier's guise, pretending to be drunk. A comic scene follows, in which *Lindor* manages to get a word with *Rosina* before the police are called in. The *Count* escapes arrest by secretly declaring himself to the commandant, when the astonished official salutes and takes his men away. *Bartolo* is so enraged he can hardly speak; he does, though, and the act ends with the brilliant quartet, "Guarda Don Bartolo" (Look at Don Bartolo).

ACT II

Scene—*A Room in Bartolo's House*

THOUGH the soldier scheme has fallen through, *Figaro* soon invents another by which the *Count* may obtain entry to *Bartolo's* dwelling. As the curtain rises, we find the old *Doctor* wondering if the drunken soldier may not be an emissary of *Count Almaviva*. He is interrupted by a stranger, none less than the *Count* himself, but this time disguised as a music-master. He explains that *Don Basilio* is ill, and that he has come to give *Rosina* her music lesson in his place. He makes himself known in a melodious greeting, the "Pace e gioia" (Heaven Send You Peace and Joy). Neither is at hand.

COPY'T MATZENE

RUFFO AS THE BARBER

In this interesting number the *Count* exhibits himself as a specially humble and obliging music-master, but *Bartolo* suspects he had seen a man of similar build before. To allay these suspicions the *Count* does a bold thing; he produces the note written by *Rosina* to her charming *Lindor*, asserting that he found it at the inn where *Count Almaviva* is staying, and he offers to make *Rosina* believe she is the *Count's* dupe. The idea pleases *Bartolo*, *Rosina* enters, and the famous lesson scene begins. Rossini wrote a special trio for this scene, but unfortunately the manuscript is lost and *Rosina* usually interpolates an air *ad libitum*, sometimes a strange one!

As *Bartolo* insists on remaining it looks as though the *Count* would have to make good his promise to deceive *Rosina*, but the resourceful *Figaro* arrives and declares this is the *Doctor's* day for shaving. He contrives, moreover, to secure the key to the balcony for future use. The game once more approaches a disastrous end when *Don Basilio*, the real music teacher, appears expecting to give *Rosina* her lesson. The *Count* is resourceful, however, and reminding *Bartolo* of their scheme to deceive *Rosina*, he points out that the matrimonial-agent-music-teacher must be gotten rid of. *Doctor Bartolo* immediately detects in *Don Basilio* the symptoms of an imaginary fever. The *Count* and *Figaro* promptly follow his lead. The mystified *Don Basilio* is disposed to insist on the excellence of his health, but with a fat purse the *Count* manages to convince him he is suffering acutely. The shaving is renewed after *Don Basilio's* departure and *Rosina* and the *Count* under cover of the music lesson, talk elopement. The situation cannot last, however, and soon *Bartolo* becomes suspicious. He approaches the preoccupied lovers, to realize that he has again been duped. The three conspirators laugh at him and run out, followed by the *Doctor*, who is purple with rage.

The pertinacity of *Figaro* and the *Count* is such that *Doctor Bartolo* is now determined to play his last card. He shows *Rosina* the note, saying that her supposedly devoted *Lindor* is conspiring to give her up to *Count Almaviva*. The furious *Rosina* offers to marry *Bartolo* at once, tells him of the plan to elope and bids him have *Lindor* and *Figaro* arrested as soon as they arrive. *Bartolo* goes for the police and for the marriage broker. He is barely out of sight when the *Count* and *Figaro* enter by means of the key which *Figaro* procured during the music lesson. *Rosina* greets them with a storm of reproaches, accusing *Lindor* of duplicity. The *Count* promptly makes known his true identity and the lovers are soon embracing amid a shower of blessings from *Figaro*.

They are interrupted by *Don Basilio* who has returned in the office of notary and marriage broker, to unite *Rosina* and *Bartolo*, but with the aid of a pistol he is persuaded to unite *Rosina* and *Count Almaviva*. No sooner is the marriage completed than *Bartolo* arrives with the police. The commandant demands the name of the culprit,

BARTOLO ARRIVES WITH THE SOLDIERS—FINALE, ACT II

but finding he has to do with the distinguished *Count Almaviva*, already married, he declines to interfere, and *Bartolo* submits with the best possible grace, the opera closing with the garrulous good wishes of the irrepressible *Figaro*.

THE VICTOR RECORDS

(Sung in Italian)

ACT I

ECCO RIDENTE IN CIELO

(Dawn With Her Rosy Mantle)
Tito Schipa   965   10-in., $1.50

LARGO AL FACTOTUM

(Room for the Factotum) Pasquale Amato, Baritone   6039   12-in., 2.00

Emilio de Gogorza, Baritone
     6068   12-in., 2.00

Titta Ruffo, Baritone   6263   12-in., 2.00

Giuseppe de Luca, Baritone
     6077   12-in., 2.00

Figaro:
   Room for the city's factotum here,
   La, la, la, la, la, la.
   I must be off to my shop, for dawn is near,
   What a merry life, what pleasure gay,
   Awaits a barber of quality.

SE IL MIO NOME

(If My Name You Would Know) Tito Schipa   965   10-in., 1.50

UNA VOCE POCO FA

(A Little Voice I Hear) Luisa Tetrazzini, Soprano   6337   12-in., $2.00

Amelita Galli-Curci, Soprano
     6130   12-in., 2.00

Rosina:
   A little voice I heard just now:
     Oh, it has thrill'd my very heart!
   I feel that I am wounded sore;
     And Lindor 'twas who hurl'd the dart.
   Yes, Lindor, dearest, shall be mine!
     I've sworn it, and we'll never part.
   My guardian sure will ne'er consent;
     But I must sharpen all my wit:
   Content at last, he will relent,
     And we, oh, joy! be wedded yet.

LA CALUNNIA

(Slander's Whisper) Marcel Journet, Bass   6174   12-in., 2.00

Feodor Chaliapin, Bass
     6059   12-in., 2.00

Basilio:
   Oh! calumny is like the sigh
   Of gentlest zephyrs breathing by;
   How softly sweet along the ground,
   Its first still voice is heard around.
   So soft, that sighing amid the bowers
   It scarcely fans the drooping flowers.
   Thus will the voice of calumny,
   More subtle than the plaintive sigh,
   In many a serpent-wreathing find
   Its secret passage to the mind;
   Thus calumny, a simple breath,
   Engenders ruin, wreck and death;
   And sinks the wretched man forlorn,
   Beneath the lash of slander torn,
   The victim of the public scorn!

AN OPEN-AIR PERFORMANCE OF BARTERED BRIDE AT ZOPPSOT

THE BARTERED BRIDE

FRIEDRICH SMETANA strove to do for his native Bohemia what Liszt had done for Hungary—nationalize its music. One result was "The Bartered Bride." He wrote eight operas and a set of symphonic poems, all in national style. In late life, like Beethoven, he grew deaf, yet produced some of his finest music during this deafness. He was born in 1824, studied with Liszt, and first became known as a conductor. The "Founder of the Bohemian School," it was he who first recognized and aided Dvořák.

THE OPERA

COMIC opera in three acts; libretto by Sabina. Music by Friedrich Smetana. First performance, Prague, May 30, 1866, where the success of the work led to Smetana's appointment as director of the Prague opera. Produced at the Vienna Music Festival 1892. First London production in 1895. First heard in America at the Metropolitan, February 19, 1909, with Destinn, Jörn, Didur and Reiss, under the direction of Gustav Mahler.

HANS, a servant in the household of *Kruschina*, has won the love of that rich peasant's daughter, *Marie*, who is planned, at the instance of a marriage broker, *Kezal*, to be married by her father to the rich but half-witted *Wenzel*, son of *Kruschina's* friend *Micha*. *Kezal* offers *Hans* 300 crowns to renounce her; he agrees if the contract shall contain the words "*Marie* shall be married only to a son of *Micha*." *Marie* refuses to believe *Hans* has sold her; but on meeting him, he seems quite joyous over the affair. *Micha* and his wife arrive in time to recognize in *Hans* their long-lost eldest son. The contract remains valid, and the marriage broker is out 300 crowns.

The opera is lively, brilliant, and is written in finished style. Perhaps the best-known individual number is its Overture, inspired by Bohemian airs and treated with consummate musicianship.

BLACK LABEL RECORD

{ Bartered Bride Overture.....................................*Pryor's Band* }35148 12-in., $1.25
{   *Madame Butterfly—Selection (Puccini)*....................*Pryor's Band* }

RUDOLPH AND MIMI

LA BOHÊME

PUCCINI is one of the few composers of recent times whose operatic successes are both numerous and lasting. Indeed, he is matched only by Massenet as to numbers, and so far as frequency of performance is concerned, the Italian composer far surpasses the Frenchman, in America at least. No doubt this is largely due to the highly melodic character of his works. Puccini's music is modern without being ultra-modern. You will hark in vain for the trills and tremolos, the musical frills and furbelows, of old-time "Italian Opera;" and you will hark just as vainly for the non-melodious murky obscurity characteristic of some more recent operatic developments (of course we exclude Massenet from the latter class). For the rest, his harmonies and orchestration are opulent as to color and his melodies informal in character, breaking in on the thread of musical discourse only when justified by the dramatic situation, and apt to be repressed as rapidly as they have been begun by some sudden turn of dramatic events.

Not only is "La Bohême" rich in melody, but the melody is of the most appealing kind. Puccini, like his heroes, *Rudolph, Marcel, Colline* and *Schaunard*, was in his youth an artist whose riches were measured in terms of genius rather than hard cash. He, too, lived in an attic wherein he found the problems of existence more baffling than those of Harmony and Counterpoint. His life was touched also by the romance, the beauty of living, interspersed with that drudgery and discomfort which only become tolerable when viewed through the mists of memory. Experiences such as these, hallowed by time and made precious by success, could hardly fail to influence him in composing the music of "La Bohême." It is said, indeed, that some of the incidents in the opera came directly from his own experience, and, while the opera is, of course, founded on Mürger's novel, "La Vie Bohême," it varies considerably from the original in detail, though most faithfully preserving the spirit of the work, a spirit in which comedy and tragedy, charming idealism and harsh reality, are richly interwoven.

THE OPERA

OPERA in four acts. Text by Giacosa and Illica; music by Puccini; being an adaptation of part of Mürger's *La vie Bohême*, which depicts life in the *Quartier Latin*, or the Students' Quarter, in 1830. First produced at the Teatro Reggio, Turin, February 1, 1896, under the direction of Toscanini. In English as "The Bohemians," at Manchester (Carl Rosa Company), April 22, 1897, and at Covent Garden with the same company, October 2d of the same year. At the *Opéra Comique*, Paris, June 1898. In Italian at Covent Garden, July 1, 1899. First production in the Americas at Buenos Ayres in 1896. First U. S. production at San Francisco March, 1898, by the Royal Italian Opera Company, following their tour of Mexico. The company later sang the opera in New York, Wallack's Theatre, May 16, 1898. Given in English by the Castle Square Opera Company at the American Theatre, New York, November 20, 1898. The first important production in Italian was that given by Melba's Company in Philadelphia, December 29, 1898. Produced in 1907 at the Metropolitan, with Caruso, Sembrich and Scotti.

CHARACTERS

RUDOLPH, a poet............Tenor
MARCEL, a painter........Baritone
COLLINE, a philosopher.........Bass
SCHAUNARD, a musician.....Baritone
BENOIT, an importunate landlord..Bass
ALCINDORO, a state councilor and
    follower of Musetta...........Bass
MUSETTA, a grisette........Soprano
MIMI, a maker of embroidery..Soprano

Students, Work-girls, Citizens, Shop-keepers, Venders, Soldiers, Waiters, etc.

Scene and Period: Paris, about 1830.

ACT I

SCENE—*In the Attic*

TWO of the four inseparables of art are at home. *Marcel* is busy painting at his never-finished canvas, "The Passage of the Red Sea," blowing on his hands from time to time to warm them. *Rudolph*, the poet, is gazing through the window over the snow-capped roofs of Paris. The attic itself is roomy, but sparsely furnished—a fireplace empty of fire, a table, a small cupboard, a few chairs, a few books, many packs of cards, an easel, and the riff-raff of an artist's studio. *Marcel* is first to break the silence; he complains of the cold, saying he feels as though the Red Sea were flowing down his back. *Rudolph* answers in kind, and finally *Marcel* ceases painting and is about to break up a chair, but *Rudolph* offers instead the manuscript of one of his own plays. They burn it act by act, warming their bodies and feasting their eyes on its meagre flames. The acts burn quickly, and *Rudolph* admits that brevity is the soul of wit, finding his drama quite sparkling. *Colline*, the philosopher, enters, stamping with cold. Suddenly, however, *Schaunard* comes, too, bringing wood for the fire, food for the table, wine and money—and plenty of each. The three others gaze in rapturous

COPY'T MISHKIN   PHOTO BERT   COPY'T DUPONT

GLUCK AS MIMI   FARRAR AND SCOTTI AS MIMI AND MARCEL   SEMBRICH AS MIMI
                              (ACT III)

45

amazement. *Schaunard*, pressed for an explanation, informs them he has been giving a music lesson to a rich English amateur—this was before the days of the American tourist-invasion of Paris. They begin to feast merrily, but are interrupted by the landlord, who wants his rent, having, after the manner of his kind, scented the riches from afar. They show him money and give him wine—more wine—and again wine—till he becomes in turn jovial, melancholy and maudlin, after which they throw him out of the room. "I have paid the last quarter's rent," remarks *Marcel*, shrugging his shoulders as he locks the door.

Though more comfortable, or perhaps because of it, *Rudolph* is still disposed to be pensive; so he refuses to go with the others when they hilariously depart to spend the money they have saved from the landlord's clutches —*Colline* wearing the splendid coat which he has so far contrived to keep in spite of its obvious salability. It covers a multitude of sartorial shortcomings, that coat!

A timid knock is heard at the door. It is *Mimi*, the girl from the room above. She is a slight girl, frail but graceful, with a complexion that has the white velvety bloom of the camelia, though suffused with a warm glow that would have warned anybody but a poet that her health is not of the best. "This frail beauty allured *Rudolph*," says Mürger, "but what wholly served to enchant him were *Mimi's* tiny hands that, despite household duties, she contrived to keep as white as snow." She has come to ask for a light for her candle, and the two fall into conversation. She asks him, artlessly enough, what his occupation is, and he tells her in the familiar "Narrative."

This air is one of the great numbers from the opera, and one of the most popular of recorded numbers. The tender sympathy of the opening— "Your little hand is cold;" the bold avowal, "I am a poet;" the glorious beauty of the love motive at the end, and the final brilliant high note are unforgettably lovely.

She in turn tells him her story—how she makes artificial flowers for a living —the while she yearns for the blossoms and green meadows of the country; that she leads a lonely life in her garret among the housetops. She gives us insight into her tenderness, her youth, her tremulous but infectious gaiety, so that we, with *Rudolph*, feel the magnetism of her charm, and sympathize with her desire for a fuller and richer life.

Soon the two are close friends. They hear the other three artists hilariously shouting as they make their way across the courtyard below, and move to the window to watch *Marcel*, *Colline* and *Schaunard* depart. A flood of moonlight envelops *Mimi*, and *Rudolph*, looking at her, knows that life for him will never be the same again. The act closes with the beautiful duet, "O soave fanciulla," in which *Rudolph* and *Mimi* awake to a realization of each other. The lovely melody with which the duet begins is associated with *Mimi* all through the opera, and is employed with touching effect in the death scene of Act IV.

Mimi shyly begs *Rudolph* to take her with him to the Café Momus, where he is to rejoin his friends, and the curtain slowly falls as they leave. The "little white hands" have fastened themselves on *Rudolph's* heart forevermore.

ACT II

Scene—*A Students' Café in Paris*

THE Café Momus is one of those odd restaurants in Paris much frequented by artists, and by those of the outside world who wish to do as the artists do—vain searchers after the elusive joys of "Bohemia" which can

SCENE FROM ACT II

come only to those who can suffer as well as rejoice; a class whom the artists themselves have dubbed "Philistines," who may suitably be despoiled by the Children of Light. Hither come *Rudolph* and *Mimi* to join their companions, who are already here. So also is *Musetta*, a delightful little lady who is enjoying the hospitality of one *Alcindoro*, a rich Philistine. She makes eyes at her old friend *Marcel*, and is not a whit abashed when his offended jealousy makes him pretend not to see her. She gets rid of her elderly admirer and joins the party, singing the charming "Musetta Waltz."

This number is not only charming in itself, but it typifies the lightness, the joyous abandon, the freedom of the "Quartier Latin." The melody is familiar to every one, and indeed there is no better waltz melody in modern music. It has wings. It floats airily and lightly in one's brain, after the record is silent.

The fun now becomes fast and furious. *Musetta* is finally carried shoulder high by the friends, while the foolish old banker, *Alcindoro*, is left to pay the bills of the entire party.

ACT III
Scene—*A City Gate in Paris*

BUT good times cannot last forever, and one bitter cold morning we find *Mimi* shivering as she asks the officer at the gate in the environs of Paris if she can see *Marcel*. *Marcel* has left the studio, and is staying at an inn on the Orleans road, painting not landscapes but tavern signs for a living. He is surprised to find *Mimi*, who has come to tell him that she can no longer live with *Rudolph*—she cannot endure their continual quarrels. Love in a lofty garret, it seems, is no nearer heavenly bliss than love in a cottage when the cupboard is bare. *Marcel* expresses his astonishment in "Mimi io son."

This duet affords a fine glimpse of *Marcel's* sympathetic nature, and his concern on discovering that *Mimi* is not only unhappy but physically ill.

47

Much disturbed, he goes into the inn, where *Rudolph* has come to visit him—to tell his version of the trouble with *Mimi*. *Mimi*, meanwhile, secretes herself, and is not surprised to overhear *Rudolph* accusing her of fickleness.

Marcel is once more placed in the position of a sympathetic observer as his friend upbraids *Mimi* with flirting, apparently not without cause.

A distressing fit of coughing, however, puts an end to *Mimi's* eavesdropping, and brings *Marcel* and *Rudolph* out to her.

Mimi bids farewell to her lover with exquisite pathos. Her "Farewell" melody is one of the loveliest in the entire work, and is a universal favorite. Most tenderly does the poor girl's "Farewell, may you be happy" come from her simple heart as she turns to go. *Rudolph* protests, something of his old affection having returned at the sight of her wan beauty.

They are interrupted by the entrance of *Musetta*, who is in turn accused by *Marcel* of flirting. A pretty quarrel ensues—a vulgar but human and wholesome "scrap" in sharp contrast with the depth of feeling underlying *Rudolph's* quarrel with *Mimi*. The other two, however, are drawn into the discussion, and a remarkable quartet ensues, the "Addio, dolce svegliare."

In this remarkable modern ensemble the emotions expressed are as diverse as they are in the famous "Rigoletto" quartet, though it in no way resembles that number in style. The sadness of *Mimi's* farewell to *Rudolph*, his last-minute tender efforts to induce her to remain, the fond recollections of happier times—and in contrast the sharp bickerings of *Marcel* and *Musetta;* all these differing moods find plastic expression in Puccini's music.

With this the Act closes, the love affair of *Rudolph* and *Mimi*, which began so prettily in the moonlight, having ended rather dismally in the fogs of misunderstanding and recrimination.

ACT IV

Scene—*Same as Act I*

BEREFT of their sweethearts, the two men are living sad and lonely lives. "At this time," says Mürger, "the friends for many weeks had lived a lonely and melancholy existence. *Musetta* had made no sign, and *Marcel* had never met her, while no word of *Mimi* came to *Rudolph*, though he often repeated her name to himself. *Marcel* treasured a little bunch of ribbons which had been left behind by *Musetta*, and when one day he detected *Rudolph* gazing fondly at the pink bonnet *Mimi* had forgotten, he muttered: 'It seems I am not the only one!' " In the opening scene *Marcel* stands at the easel pretending to paint, while *Rudolph*, apparently writing, is furtively gazing at *Mimi's* little pink bonnet. The true state of affairs is finely revealed in the famous duet, "Ah, Mimi, tu più" (Ah, Mimi, False One). The music is remarkably rich in feeling and melodious in character. This number is so familiar that to describe it would be to gild the lily. Its depth of feeling, however, and the spontaneity of its melody make it one of the rarest and richest numbers in modern music.

The two men pretend to brighten up when *Schaunard* and *Colline* appear with materials for supper. This scene of rather forced gaiety is interrupted by *Musetta*, who has come, wide-eyed, to tell them that *Mimi* has been deserted by her viscount and is coming home to die. The poor girl is brought in and laid on *Rudolph's* bed, while he is distracted with grief. The friends hasten to aid her, *Marcel* going for a doctor, while *Colline*, in order to get money for delicacies for the sick girl, decides to pawn his famous overcoat.

He bids farewell to the coat in a song that is not without its touch of whimsical pathos,—the "Vecchia zimarra" (Farewell, Old Coat), the delight of the operatic basso.

This little flicker of comedy in a scene otherwise overburdened with tragedy affords a charming relief. The coat affords one of the byplays of comedy throughout the opera. No matter how destitute the four insep011arables may be, *Colline* refuses to raise money on this garment. Yet in the hour of *Mimi's* necessity he parts with it like the good fellow he is.

Colline and *Schaunard* go softly away, leaving *Mimi* and *Rudolph* together, and they sing their beautiful farewell song. This is the last thing before the passing of *Mimi*. In dreamy tones the dying girl recalls other days they spent together, and with heartbreaking pathos they plan yet happier days together.

There is something pitifully tragic in this last scene, as they discuss a future which shall be free from jealousies and quarrels, for *Rudolph* at least knows that such a future is only too likely for both of them, *Mimi's* end being now very near.

Just as *Mimi*, in soft accents, recalls their first meeting, she is seized with a sudden faintness that alarms *Rudolph*. The young man's grief is pitiful.

The music of this final moment is touching in its simplicity, suggesting indeed, that "peace which passeth understanding," toward which the unhappy girl is bound.

Rudolph quickly summons his friends who are returning with the delicacies for which, alas, there is now no need; for the young girl, weakened by disease and privation, passes away in the midst of her weeping friends, and the curtain falls to *Rudolph's* despairing cry of "Mimi! Mimi!"

THE VICTOR RECORDS
(Sung in Italian unless noted)

ACT I

RACCONTO DI RODOLFO
(Rudolph's Narrative) ENRICO CARUSO, Tenor   6003   12-in., $2.00
GIOVANNI MARTINELLI, Tenor   6192   12-in.,   2.00
JOHN McCORMACK, Tenor   6200   12-in.,   2.00
ORVILLE HARROLD, Tenor   6151   12-in.,   2.00

MI CHIAMANO MIMI
(My Name is Mimi) NELLIE MELBA, Soprano   6210   12-in.,   2.00
GERALDINE FARRAR, Soprano   6106   12-in.,   2.00
LUCREZIA BORI, Soprano   6048   12-in.,   2.00
FRANCES ALDA, Soprano   6038   12-in.,   2.00

O SOAVE FANCIULLA
(Thou Sweetest Maiden) NELLIE MELBA, Soprano and ENRICO CARUSO, Tenor   95200   12-in.,   2.00
FRANCES ALDA, Soprano and GIOVANNI MARTINELLI, Tenor   8002   12-in.,   2.50
LUCREZIA BORI, Soprano and JOHN McCORMACK, Tenor   3029   10-in.,   2.00

ACT II

MUSETTA WALTZ
ALMA GLUCK, Soprano   649   10-in.,   1.50

ACT III

MIMI, IO SON
(Mimi, Thou Here!) GERALDINE FARRAR, Soprano and ANTONIO SCOTTI, Baritone   8023   12-in.,   2.50
FARRAR-SCOTTI   10007   12-in.,   3.50

ADDIO
(Farewell) GERALDINE FARRAR, Soprano   6106   12-in.,   2.00
NELLIE MELBA, Soprano   6210   12-in.,   2.00
ALMA GLUCK, Soprano   649   10-in.,   1.50

QUARTET, "ADDIO, DOLCE SVEGLIARE"
(Farewell, Sweet Love) GERALDINE FARRAR, Soprano, GINA C. VIAFORA, Soprano, ENRICO CARUSO, Tenor and ANTONIO SCOTTI, Baritone   10007   12-in.,   3.50

ACT IV

AH MIMI, TU PIÙ
(Ah, Mimi, False One) ENRICO CARUSO, Tenor and ANTONIO SCOTTI, Baritone   8000   12-in.,   2.50

VECCHIA ZIMARRA
(Farewell, Old Coat) MARCEL JOURNET, Bass   698   10-in.,   1.50

BLACK LABEL AND BLUE LABEL RECORDS

Mimi è una civetta (Cold-Hearted Mimi!) (*In Italian*)
de Gregorio, Casini and Ferretti 68453 12-in., $1.25
Trovatore—Soldiers' Chorus (*Verdi*) (*In Italian*)......*La Scala Chorus*

Bohême Selection......................................*Pryor's Band* 35077 12-in., 1.25
Jolly Robbers Overture..............................*Pryor's Band*

Bohême Selection ....*Vessella's Italian Band* 35353 12-in., 1.25
Madame Butterfly Fantasia 'Cello...................*Rosario Bourdon*

Musetta Waltz (*Whistling Solo*)......................*Guido Gialdini* 16892 10-in., .75
Carmen Selection Xylophone..........................*Wm. H. Reitz*

Ah, Mimi, tu più (Ah Mimi, False One) (*In Italian*) *Murphy and Werrenrath* 45182 10-in., 1.00
Faust Trio—Prison Scene, Part III....................*Victor Opera Trio*

GILLY AS MARCEL

FARRAR AS MIMI

CARUSO AS RUDOLPH

PHOTO BYRON

THE CARNIVAL AT PRESBURG—ACT II

THE BOHEMIAN GIRL

THE never-failing melodic charm of "The Bohemian Girl" is neither Latin nor Teutonic but Celtic, at least by geography. The composer, Michael William Balfe, was a Dublin boy, born 1808, the son of a dancing master. Early proficiency as a violinist ripened into the greater gifts of musical composition, with a special faculty for writing simple but effective tunes. Of Balfe's many operatic works, "The Bohemian Girl" is by far the most famous; and its popularity is justified by its melodious character. The composer's fame extended all over Europe, and he was particularly admired by the French. "The Bohemian Girl" won him the French decoration of Chevalier of the "Legion of Honor" as well as other honors from other governments. He lived chiefly in England, where he died in 1870.

THE OPERA

OPERA in three acts; text by Bunn; music by Balfe. First produced at Drury Lane, London, November 27, 1843, the cast including Harrison, Rainforth, Betts, Stretton and Borrani. An Italian version was brought out at Drury Lane, February 6, 1858. First American production November 25, 1844, with Frazer, Seguin, Pearson and Andrews. The work, after its English success, was translated into many languages, and produced in Italy as *La Zingara* (at Trieste, 1854); in Hamburg as *La Gitana*; in Vienna as *Die Zigeunerin*, and in Paris as *La Bohémienne*.

CHARACTERS

ARLINE, daughter of Count
    Arnheim...............Soprano
THADDEUS, a Polish exile.......Tenor
GYPSY QUEEN.............Contralto
DEVILSHOOF, Gypsy leader......Bass
COUNT ARNHEIM, Governor of
    Presburg..............Baritone
FLORESTINE, nephew of the
    Count..................Tenor
    Retainers, Hunters, Soldiers,
      Gypsies, etc.

51

Time and Place: Presburg, Hungary;
Nineteenth Century

ACT I

SCENE—*Country Estate of Count Arnheim, near Presburg*

A MERRY hunting party is in progress in the Castle grounds at Arnheim, and the assembly is completed by the arrival of the *Count* himself, who greets his little daughter *Arline* before joining the hunt. As soon as the hunters depart, *Thaddeus*, a young Polish nobleman, appears. He is a fugitive escaping from Austrian political enemies, and in a desperate case. *Devilshoof* and a party of gypsies then arrive, and are about to attack *Thaddeus*, when he explains his condition, and is made a member of the band. No sooner has this occurred than a great noise is heard. Little *Arline*, it appears, is in danger from a wild stag, and all is confusion as the huntsmen come rushing back. *Thaddeus* alone keeps his head, and, seizing a rifle, he manages to shoot the beast. The child is taken to the castle, badly scared, and slightly wounded in the arm, while *Thaddeus* is invited to the feast and freely lionized. His refusal to drink the health of the Austrian Emperor, however, causes trouble. Seeing him in danger, the *Count* flings him a bag of gold and bids him depart. *Thaddeus* indignantly refuses the gold and is attacked by the guests. *Devilshoof* comes to his rescue and he escapes, but the gypsy chief is himself captured and imprisoned in the castle. While the feast is resumed, *Devilshoof* not only gets away, but kidnaps the unfortunate *Arline*. He is seen, and the hunters go in pursuit, but *Devilshoof* kicks away a tree that is the only bridge across a rocky ravine and so gets off. The *Count* falls fainting at the loss of his daughter.

ACT II

SCENE—*Gypsy Camp in the Outskirts of Presburg*

T WELVE years elapse before the gypsies again return to Presburg. They make their presence known by robbing *Florestine*, the self-indulgent and drunken nephew of the *Count*. He parts in good grace from his watch and jewels but laments the loss of a valuable medallion. A pretty romance between *Thaddeus* and *Arline*, follows the girl's recital of her vision, "I Dreamt I Dwelt in Marble Halls." *Thaddeus* tells her of her noble origin and capture by the gypsies, and the two plight their troth. The *Gypsy Queen*, who is in love with *Thaddeus*, attempts to separate them, but only succeeds in hastening a gypsy wedding between the two lovers. Her opportunity for revenge occurs in the next scene—a carnival in the public square. *Florestine* attempts to flirt with *Arline* but is repulsed. Observing this event, the *Gypsy Queen* gives her the medallion stolen from *Florestine* the night before. This is subsequently discovered by *Florestine*, and *Arline* is arrested as a thief and brought before *Count Arnheim*. The *Count* has just been ruminating over his long lost daughter, singing "The Heart Bowed Down." When *Arline* appears he is struck by her beauty and obvious innocence, and later discovers the scar on her arm from the wound made by the stag. By this he knows her for his own child and the Act closes in a happy reunion.

ACT III

SCENE—*Castle of Arnheim*

A RLINE, restored, nevertheless is pining for her gypsy lover and husband, *Thaddeus*, and is overjoyed when *Devilshoof* contrives to bring him to her chamber. The sweethearts are interrupted, however, by *Count*

Arnheim and his friends, and *Arline* barely has time to conceal *Thaddeus* in a closet. A veiled woman enters the room and approaches the *Count.* It is the *Gypsy Queen,* and she bids him look in the closet where *Thaddeus* is concealed. A highly dramatic scene follows this disclosure, and though *Arline* pleads boldly for her lover, the angry *Count* bids him depart. Before leaving, however, *Thaddeus* shows that he is of noble blood, and *Arline* reminds her father that *Thaddeus* saved her live. This softens the *Count* and all appears to be about to end happily. But the vengeful *Gypsy Queen* directs one of her followers to shoot *Arline.* He puts the rifle to his shoulder and is about to fire when

Devilshoof intervenes and turns the rifle in the direction of the *Queen* herself, who falls as the shot is fired. The safety and happiness of *Thaddeus* and *Arline* is thus assured, and the curtain falls on a joyous scene.

THE VICTOR RECORDS

ACT II

I DREAMT I DWELT IN MARBLE HALLS
MABEL GARRISON, Soprano
641 10-in., $1.50

HEART BOW'D DOWN
CLARENCE WHITEHILL, Baritone
6307 12-in., 2.00

THEN YOU'LL REMEMBER ME
JOHN McCORMACK, Tenor
747 10-in., 1.50

BLACK LABEL AND BLUE LABEL RECORDS

{Overture to Bohemian Girl.........................*Arthur Pryor's Band*} 16287 10-in., .75
{ *La Czarine Mazurka (Ganne)*.....................*Arthur Pryor's Band*}

{I Dreamt I Dwelt in Marble Halls...........*Elizabeth Wheeler, Soprano*} 16398 10-in., .75
{Then You'll Remember Me........................*Lewis James, Tenor*}

{Then You'll Remember Me and I Dreamt I Dwelt...........*McKee Trio*} 18190 10-in., .75
{ *Good-Night, Beloved (Nevin)*.........*(Violin-'Cello-Piano) McKee Trio*}

{Selections from Bohemian Girl.....................*Arthur Pryor's Band*} 35081 12-in., 1.25
{ *Yelva Overture (Reissiger)*........................*Arthur Pryor's Band*}

{Gems from Bohemian Girl—Part I..................*Victor Opera Company*}
  Chorus, "Away to Hill and Glen"—Solo, "I Dreamt I Dwelt in
  Marble Halls"—Solo, "Heart Bow'd Down"—Mixed Quartet, "Si-
  lence, the Lady Moon"—Solo, "Fair Land of Poland"—Chorus,
  "Happy and Light"
{Gems from Bohemian Girl—Part II.............*Victor Opera Company*} 35603 12-in., 1.25
  Chorus, "In the Gypsy's Life"—Solo and Chorus, "Come with the
  Gypsy Bride"—Solo, "Bliss Forever Past"—Duet, "What is the
  Spell"—Solo, "Then You'll Remember Me"—Solo and Chorus,
  "Oh, What Full Delight"

BORIS GODOUNOW

MOUSSORGSKY'S life and genius were strangely erratic and disordered. He died in poverty hastened by dissipation. His musical training was irregular; yet he was perhaps the most original composer Russia ever produced. "Boris Godounow" has powerfully influenced the music of our own day, and from it many composers have gathered fresh and vivid material.

THE OPERA

OPERA in three acts. Text arranged by Moussorgsky, based on a historical drama by the famous Russian poet, Pushkin. Music by Modeste Moussorgsky. Portions of the opera were given at St. Petersburg in February, 1873, but the production of the work in its entirety was delayed until January 24, 1874. Produced at Moscow in 1889. In 1896 the orchestration was somewhat revised by the composer's friend, Rimsky-Korsakoff. Given at Paris in 1908 by a Russian opera company, with Chaliapin in the title rôle. First American production at the Metropolitan Opera House, New York, November 19, 1913, with the original Paris costumes and scenery. First Berlin performance, 1924.

CHARACTERS

(With the Cast of the First American Production)

BORIS GODOUNOW, Regent of Russia .... Adamo Didur
XENIA, his daughter . . Leonora Sparkes
THEODORE, his son . . . . Anna Case
THE NURSE . . . . Maria Duchêne
MARINA . . . . Louise Homer
CHOUISKY . . . . Angelo Bada
DIMITRI . . . . Paul Althouse
VARLAAM . . . . Andrea de Segurola
MISSAIL . . . . Pietro Audisio
TCHELKALOFF . . . Vincenzo Reschiglian
PIMENN . . . . Leon Rothier

A SIMPLETON . . . . Albert Reiss
A POLICE OFFICER . . . . . . Giulio Rossi
TWO JESUITS . . { Louis Kreidler / Vincenzo Reschiglian

Time and Place: About 1600; Russia

(The name of the opera is pronounced *Boh'-reess Goh'-doo-noff*).

THE first scene is before the Novo-dievitchi Convent, Moscow. *Boris Godounow* is regent for *Czar Feodor*, son of Ivan the Terrible. In an ambitious moment *Boris* has murdered his nephew *Dimitri*, Ivan's younger brother, to whom the throne would have passed upon the tyrant's death; but seized with remorse, he has fled to the Novo-dievitchi Convent to expiate the sin. He has a wide following among the people, who are unaware of the murder. And they have thronged, with nobility at their head, to beg him to take the throne.

The scene changes to a cell in the Convent of Miracles. *Pimenn*, an old monk, reveals to *Gregory*, a young monk, the story of *Dimitri's* death. *Gregory*, learning that *Dimitri* was of his own age, resolves to spread the report that *Dimitri* was never slain, and to usurp the Russian throne. Again the scene changes; *Boris*, among great pomp, consents to take the throne as regent. This scene affords a magnificent half-barbaric stage setting.

The second act, in the opera as usually given, opens in an inn on the Lithuanian border, whither *Gregory*, with two companions, has escaped from the Convent. He hopes to cross the frontier and raise an army, but is prevented by a Government order issued after escape. He just misses arrest, by making a soldier believe one of his companions the offender, then leaping off through a window. Meanwhile, *Boris*, in the *Czar's* palace in the Kremlin, a prey to fear and remorse, is talking with his young son, *Theodore*, when an old accomplice, *Chouisky*, appears, to bring the news that people are in revolt, under the belief that *Dimitri* still lives. They are actually at the Russian border; and if they once enter the country, the country must fall. *Boris*, a superstitious mystic, actually wonders if the ghost of *Dimitri* has risen to appear against him.

In the third act *Gregory* awaits the lovely *Marina*, a Polish lady who serves the interests of Poland by helping him play *Dimitri*. He lurks in her garden during a great banquet. When this is ended, *Marina* appears, to stir up together his ambition for the throne and his love for herself. This is the remarkable "Garden Scene," with its wonderful slow-swinging, seductive rhythm and melody, like nothing else in music.

The next phase of the work is in the Forest of Krony, where peasants are making sport of a nobleman who has fallen into their hands. The scene, written years ago, is a prophecy of what since has happened in Russia. *Gregory*, as the false *Dimitri*, enters, and the people, dissatisfied with *Boris*, join him in revolt. As they disappear, a village *Fool* sits alone in the snow, singing a heart-rending ditty on the hopeless condition of the empire. The simple irony of this touch is unsurpassed in opera.

Finally, the Duma gathers in the Imperial Palace to meet *Boris*. *Chouisky* plans treachery, and hints to the assembled boyars, or nobles, something of the real truth regarding *Dimitri*. *Boris*, entering, is confronted by *Pimenn*, who tells how a blind man has been restored to vision at the tomb of the murdered youth. *Boris* listens with horror, and finally interrupts with a cry. He is dying, and he asks for *Theodore*. He passes away begging the son to rule wisely and to protect *Xenia*, his sister. The opera ends abruptly, leaving the inference that *Gregory's* rebellion must perish, the true facts of *Dimitri's* death being known.

THE VICTOR RECORDS

BORIS GODOUNOW

PHOTO WHITE

ALTHOUSE AS DIMITRI

(Garden Scene—Finale, Act III) MARGARETE OBER, Contralto and PAUL ALTHOUSE, Tenor *In Italian*
76031 12-in., $1.75

Farewell of Boris (Farewell, My Son, I Am Dying) (Act IV) FEODOR CHALIAPIN, Bass 88661 12-in., 1.50

In the Town of Kazàn (Act II) FEODOR CHALIAPIN, Bass
558 10-in., 1.50

55

THE DEATH OF CARMEN—ACT IV

CARMEN

CARMEN is among the three or four most popular operas of all time; yet recognition came to it but slowly. For one thing, its originality was against it. "Carmen" appeared at a time when Wagnerian theories of opera were bringing consternation among conservative musical critics; and, as Bizet adopted innovations in his scorings he was charged with imitating Wagner. Unquestionably, Bizet was influenced by Wagner's ideas, like any progressive composer; but he was no imitator, and the fact was recognized in due course. It was declared, too, that the work was "immoral,"—for Paris was going through the "crinoline stage" of prudery. Again, internal politics at the Paris Opera were against it. But these things died out after the first overwhelming success of the work in London; today the work has no rival in Paris, unless, perhaps, "Faust" itself. Bizet regarded "Carmen" as his *magnum opus*, and he was distressed at its first failure, which is said to have hastened his death, three months after its first performance. He never knew that he had given the world what is to this day, perhaps, the finest example of French operatic art.

George Bizet was born in Paris, October 25, 1838; he died there June 3, 1875. He studied at the Conservatory, winning the coveted *Prix de Rome* in 1857, with its period of study in Italy. In this year his first opera, "Docteur Miracle," was produced in Paris. He had studied with Halévy, whose daughter he married. The career thus auspiciously begun, however, was not to continue so fortunately. Other works of his were produced, among them "Les Pecheurs des Perles," "La Jolie Fille de Perth," the incidental music to Daudet's play, "L'Arlesienne," but their success was trifling. Bizet's chronic poverty is revealed in a letter in which he complains that he has to waste valuable composing time in making cornet-arrangements of popular tunes—an experience also of Wagner's. But many friends acknowledged Bizet's genius,—among them Liszt, for

FARRAR IN ACT I

CARUSO AS DON JOSE

AMATO AS THE TOREADOR

THE QUINTET—ACT II

FARRAR AS CARMEN—ACT III

THE METROPOLITAN REVIVAL OF 1915

when did Liszt ever fail to recognize genius? Nor did he lack recognition from fellow-craftsmen,—which, no doubt, helped him endure somehow the slings and arrows of an unnecessarily outrageous fortune.

Bizet's was not an obscure genius; considering his gift of melody and his talent for clothing his tunes in warm harmonies, his want of success is hard to understand. Perhaps he was not finally happy in his choice of subjects; not until "Carmen" did he "find himself" and display his magnificent mastery over "local color." This opera, with its gypsy scenes, its Spanish setting, furnished him with every picturesque opportunity he could wish for, and the drama itself, with its clear play of elemental human passions moving logically and inevitably to a tragic end, revealed in Bizet an unexpected dramatic ability, worked out with adequate power of treatment but fine restraint. There is no ranting in "Carmen." The conflict of passions set up in the first act, works out simply and majestically to its certain consummation. Despite his talent for local color, the composer never pauses to paint pretty but unessential tone-pictures. His gift is used as a means to an end; notwithstanding the lively scenes, gay melodies, one feels throughout the sense of foreboding, of impending disaster, maintained with growing intensity until the curtain falls. Only a master of musical dramatics could ensure to us this steady crescendo of emotion.

Carmen, a beautiful, audacious gypsy girl, has been working in a cigarette factory in Seville. To the square, opposite, comes a troop of dragoons, among them *Don Jose*. *Don Jose* is affianced to *Micaela*, who comes from his native village to see him, with money and a message from his mother. *Don Jose* loves the girl, but he is attracted by *Carmen's* deliberate coquetries. *Carmen* is arrested for stabbing one of the factory girls in a quarrel, and is placed in charge of *Don Jose*. She induces him to untie the rope that binds her, and she escapes. For this *Don Jose* is arrested and himself imprisoned. *Carmen* repairs to a tavern near Seville, frequented by smugglers, to await *Don Jose's* release.

Carmen passes her time gaily at the inn, where she meets *Escamillo*, a toreador, whose courage and dash attract her. When *Don Jose* comes to the inn, she says nothing of *Escamillo*, but endeavors to make the dragoon join the smugglers. She fails, but he overstays his leave. His officer, entering, tries to flirt with *Carmen*. He orders *Don Jose* to depart to barracks, and strikes him. A fight follows, and the pair are separated by *Carmen's* friends. But *Don Jose*, now guilty of insubordination, is forced to desert and join the smugglers. He goes off with them and with *Carmen*. whom he now adores passionately.

Don Jose is not happy in his new surroundings; *Carmen* mistakes his feeling for cowardice. Quarrels arise. *Carmen*, perplexed, "reading the cards," is appalled when she turns up spades— "a grave!" The smugglers go off on a mission of their own, leaving *Don Jose* as sentinel; he fires a shot at a stranger in the distance. He proves to be *Escamillo*, who has come after *Carmen*. *Don Jose* is enraged and a fight ensues. The pair are separated by the gypsies and *Carmen*, attracted by the shot. *Don Jose* is for having it out, then and there, when *Micaela* appears with the news that his mother is dying and would see him. He departs, after *Escamillo* has invited all to the bull fight.

The closing scene is at Seville, outside the bull ring. The crowd has gathered to receive *Escamillo*, now in

58

his glory, and *Carmen*, who has followed him. The toreador and his admirers enter the ring, but *Carmen*, despite warnings, awaits *Don Jose* outside. He arrives, and piteously begs her to remain true to him. She refuses. His anger arises; when she remains obdurate, he stabs her to the heart—just as the victorious *Escamillo* emerges from the doors of the bull ring to receive her congratulations. He finds her dead, and *Don Jose*, in agony, throws himself across the body.

THE MUSIC

With such a theme in such a setting, Bizet came into his own. Each number of "Carmen" is a musical masterpiece, brilliant with life and color; yet no number is out of keeping with the rest, and the principal airs stand out like jewels in a perfect mounting. Bizet united French logic, Gallic fitness, to a vivid Jewish imagination. Moreover, in his characterizations he displays a profound psychology; and despite his easy, flowing style, his inexhaustible tunefulness, his dash and brilliancy, which cannot hope but captivate the most superficial audiences, his music withstands the scrupulous analysis of those who really look underneath the surface.

He is especially tuneful in delineating *Carmen*—who is far from being the unconventional, "Bohemian" sort of person early critics considered her. If she does not live according to the conventions of the village-bred *Micaela*, it is because she neither understands nor appreciates. She has been reared among smugglers and bandits and outlaws—with whom wildness and audacity are the true "conventions." They are gamblers who play with life and liberty—who stake a full stomach and a fat purse against a bloody death, who know no greater disgrace than to fail to pay their own strange debts of honor. If these are conventions, then *Carmen* is the most conventional of all. She, too, is a gambler, taking gamblers' chances with what cards are dealt her. Her cards are her own audacious beauty, her wild coquetry, the dangerous fires of human passion; against the prize she plays for, the hearts of men, she can stake only—herself. If we do not accept this as the basic psychology of *Carmen's* nature, the last act of the opera becomes meaningless. Why should she face *Don Jose* alone when she might have gone into the bull ring, or commanded a body-guard of her own friends? She knows that *Don Jose*, a ruined man, is desperate and fearless when aroused. Yet she chooses to stay deliberately. According to gypsy law, she is his until the union is broken by mutual consent. Her "gamble" has been that he will weary of her when she wearied of him; and she has lost. Well, she will pay. None can accuse her of fear or falsehood. She owes that much to her self-respect in conformity with gypsy convention. So she stands alone and "faces her man."

All this is revealed in the music. The "Fate" motive which sounds so ominously at the end of the overture, is echoed again and again through the score, changing its form in a dozen ways. In the card scene it flickers through and through, like an angry tongue of flame in a bank of smoke. At the end, when the tragedy is done, it blazes forth luridly. *Carmen's* own music is saturated throughout with her own seductive charm. No less care is given *Don Jose*, a normal, well-regulated man with a dark streak of passion woven into his being; observe his tenderness toward *Micaela*, his devotion to his mother, his sense of shame at deserting! All this contrasts darkly with *Carmen's* recklessness. Incompatibility is bound to spring up

CARMEN SINGING THE "HABANERA"—ACT I

—and worse, for these are people of strong passion; contempt for each other's way of life is sure to bring tragedy. *Micaela*, the modest exemplar of civilized convention, is all maidenly shyness, all gentle loyalty; these give her the quiet courage necessary to make her way to the smugglers' abode and *Don Jose*. *Escamillo* is brave as he is boastful. To each the music fits, as the flesh fits the spirit.

THE OPERA

OPERA in four acts. Text by Meilhac and Halévy, founded on the novel of Prosper Mérimée. Music by Bizet. First production at the Opéra Comique, Paris, March 3, 1875. First London production June 22, 1878. First American production October 23, 1879, with Minnie Hauk, Campanini and del Puente. First New Orleans production, January 14, 1881, with Mmes. Ambre and Tournie. Some notable revivals in New York were in 1893, being Calvé's first appearance, the cast including Eames, de Reszke and La Salle; in 1905 with Caruso; and the Hammerstein revivals of 1906, with Bressler-Gianoli, Dalmores, Gilibert, Trentini and Ancona; and 1908 with Calvé. After five years' neglect the Metropolitan, in 1915, staged a brilliant revival with an "all-star" cast, including Farrar, Caruso, Alda and Amato. The opera is frequently given today.

60

CHARACTERS

Don Jose (*Don Ho-zay'*) a Brig-
  adier...................Tenor

Escamillo (*Es-ca-meel'-oh*) a
  Toreador..............Baritone

Dancairo (*Dan-ky'-roh*).....Baritone

Remendado (*Rem-en-dah'-doh*)..Tenor
  (Smugglers)

Zuniga (*Tsoo-nee'-gah*) a Captain. Bass

Morales (*Moh-rah'-lez*) a Brig-
  adier.....................Bass

Micaela (*Mih-kah-ay'-lah*) a
  Peasant Girl...........Soprano

Frasquita (*Frass-kee'-tah*) ⎱ Mezzo-
Mercedes (*Mer-chay'-dayz*) ⎰ Soprano

  (Gypsies, friends of Carmen)

Carmen (*Kar'-men*) a Cigarette Girl,
  afterwards a Gypsy.....Soprano

An Innkeeper, Guide, Officers, Dragoons, Lads, Cigar Girls, Gypsies,
  Smugglers

*Scene and Period: Seville, Spain;
  about 1820*

ACT I

Scene—*A Public Square in Seville*

THE prelude to "Carmen" is vivid, inspiriting, intense, bidding the blood to tingle as it calls up visions of the crowds gathering outside the bull ring in Seville. The women are magnificent dark beauties, with sumptuous black hair and flashing black eyes that glitter like half-hidden gems from beneath their lace mantillas. They are garmented in silks that are stiff and heavy with embroideries and tassels, and they are shod with black "zapatos," high-heeled shoes that give to the graceful Spanish gait an added charm and mystery. Their escorts are lean, swarthy men, tanned with the sun and hardened with outdoor life. They, too, are clad in gala attire. The dashing "March of the Tore-

adors," the first theme of the prelude, is probably one of the most invigorating themes in all opera. It gives way to the proud, steady step of the world-famous "Toreador Song," goes back to the march theme, and then dies out with the ominous "Fate" theme which pursues *Carmen*, an audible shadow of disaster, until the very end.

There is an odd story told of this theme, which is said to be of Eastern origin. The legend is that when Satan, according to Mohammedan tradition, was cast from Paradise, he remembered only one strain of the music he had heard there. This was known as "Asbëin," or the "Devil's Strain," and Bizet used it with fine symbolic as well as perfect musical fitness.

The effect in the prelude, after the bright measures of the Toreador's music, is almost appalling; the lugubrious notes of the brasses, heard beneath the flickering tremolo of strings, giving true and poignant expression to the tragedy of *Don Jose* and his gypsy sweetheart, whose fickleness only aggravates her charm. This movement breaks off with a sudden detached chord as the curtain rises. This short but brilliant prelude is a summation of the whole opera, and a key to it. It is complete in itself, and makes an admirable record.

The curtain rises upon the noon-hour of the cigarette girls. They are gathered in little knots, chatting gaily with the men. Most of them surround *Carmen*, who is piqued at *Don Jose's* indifference to her charms, as well as by his handsome figure in his dragoon's uniform. It is less to the others than at *Don Jose* that she sings the "Habanera" (Love is Like a Wood-Bird).

This is the first "air" of the opera, and one of the best known, though, strangely enough, Bizet did not write its music. He selected it, a typical Spanish tune, from Yradier's "Album des Chansons Espagnoles." The rather slow, seductive tempo, the dreamily sensuous melody, are most aptly placed; the refrain is particularly fascinating.

With this *Don José's* fate is sealed. He is not in love with *Carmen*—yet; but he cannot banish her image from his mind, even when, later, *Micaela*, his betrothed sweetheart, appears with the letter from his mother, who also sends him a kiss—most shyly and modestly delivered.

A lovely duet follows, "Parle-moi de ma mere" (Tell Me of My Mother). It shows, as plainly as music may, that *Don José's* affection for the girl is real, and that she, in turn, has given him her whole heart. *Micaela's* air develops into a broad, sustained melody

of real lyric "swing" and power, *Don José* taking it up as the memories of his old home crowd back upon him—the valley, his mother, his first love for *Micaela*.

When the girl departs, *Don José* is left alone with his thoughts. But it is not for long. A commotion breaks out in the factory and the reading of his mother's letter is interrupted by the outpouring of an excited rabble. *Carmen* has quarrelled with another girl and stabbed her. She is brought before the officer of the guard and arrested.

The girl behaves with insolence. Her hands are therefore tied behind her, and she is left in charge of *Don José* while the soldiers drive off the crowd. Alone with him, she proceeds to bring to bear upon the dragoon all of her powers of fascination; she is frankly charmed by the handsome youngster and piqued by his apparent indifference. Does she know it is not real?

PHOTO REUTLINGER
THE CARDS PREDICT CARMEN'S DEATH
(EMMA CALVÉ)

PHOTO WHITE
ALDA AS MICAELA

She proceeds, woman-wise, to bring these powers into play. She sings to him the famous "Seguidilla," another famous dance-song, composed in an insidious yet powerfully rhythmic vein. Its cadences cannot fail, in his present state, to move the heart of *Don Jose*. She tells him of her plans to go to the inn of Lillas Pastia, near the ramparts of Seville. The tormented dragoon knows that she is making the vulgarest love to him, for purposes of her own; yet he cannot resist her beauty and her song—especially when she tells him that she will meet at the inn a soldier whom she loves. Who can this be but *Don Jose* himself? Blind to all but his infatuation, blind to his duty, forgetful of *Micaela*, heedless of what may happen, he unties her hands. When the soldiers come to take her away, she pushes *Don Jose* aside, and in the confusion escapes—to the inn of Lillas Pastia.

Between the first and the second acts, a graceful orchestral interlude serves to typify the lapse of time until *Don Jose*, free of prison, is able to rejoin *Carmen*. This interlude is a gem. It is complete in itself, yet it gives continuity to the opera, where it is placed with the certainty with which a single deft note is placed in a melody and with as much significance. Its dancy, gypsy rhythm and its many-colored orchestral setting, figure forth the new world in which *Don Jose* is to find himself—a light-hearted, reckless, but jealous and high-blooded community of smugglers and thieves and vagabonds.

ACT II

SCENE—*Tavern in Suburbs of Seville*

CARMEN is in her element. Gypsy smugglers have come down from the mountains. They are having a gay time—dancing, feasting on rabbits and olives, and drinking muddy wine. They break into a dashing gypsy song, "Les tringles de sistres," one of the most typical gypsy numbers in the opera. Its eager rhythm, the clash of tambourines, the freshness and origi-

COPY'T DUPONT
DE LUSSAN AS CARMEN

EMMY DESTINN AS CARMEN

COPY'T DUPONT
CALVÉ SINGING THE GYPSY
SONG—ACT II

nality of the harmonies and modulations, which never grow stale repeating, the delicacy of the instrumentation—all are in Bizet's happiest vein.

The dance is repeated, the smugglers are ready to go, and they invite *Carmen* to join them. But mindful of *Don Jose*, she refuses. Meanwhile, before her lover appears, she makes a new friend —*Escamillo*, the Toreador, who introduces himself in what is perhaps the most famous air of the whole opera; and what is certainly one of the most clever pieces of description in all music.

This fiery tale of the bull fight itself is admirably set in the melody and its accompaniment, while the refrain is one that sets the heart beating. The refrain is that previously heard in the "Prelude," and it occurs, in different forms, throughout the opera whenever the Toreador comes to the scene. Its effect on *Carmen* is singular. She is loyal to *Don Jose*, but she is rather upset by the Toreador.

Don Jose is heard singing in the distance. *Carmen* and her friends peer through the shutter. They admire his appearance and agree he would make a fine smuggler. *Carmen* pushes them from the room and prepares to meet him, as he enters singing the last high note of the soldierly air, "Halte la! Qui va la?" (Halt There). He is greeted with joy.

Carmen dances for *Don Jose*—to an odd little air of her own composing, with castanets. She begs him to join the smugglers. Beat for beat, however, the bugles sound against her odd song. Affairs come to a climax, in a splendid piece of dramatic writing. *Carmen* pitches *Don Jose* his cap and sabre, and bids him begone. He is more enslaved than ever; he is mortified by the prospect of losing her, and his passion surges up to the boiling-point. Now is the moment for a really great love song—and we have it, in the "Air de la Fleur," or Flower Song.

Don Jose reminds *Carmen* of the flower she threw to him at their first meeting, and he tells her, in touching accents, how he kept it through the dreary weeks of his prison life.

The young man pours out his heart in this rich and tender romanza. *Carmen's* wild heart is touched, and she grows more determined than ever that he shall go off with her to the joy and the freedom of the gypsies' life— the adventures and the dangers and escapes, the long nights under the free winds and the stars.

He and *Carmen* sing of them together "La bas dans la montagne" (Away to Yonder Mountains); but *Don Jose* is determined, for the time being, to go back to his duties as a soldier. His love affair seems likely to come to an end when his captain, *Zuniga*, enters the inn. He insolently orders *Don Jose* to be off, and he turns upon *Carmen* an eye of proprietorship. *Don Jose* refuses, *Zuniga* strikes him, and the trooper, mad with rage, draws the sabre which *Carmen* had thrown him a little while before.

Carmen screams for help—to prevent bloodshed. Officer and man are separated and overpowered, and for *Don Jose* the life of a law-keeping subject and soldier is done. Guilty of insubordination, of an attempt upon a superior's life, he can only go with the gypsies, desert and become an outcast —however much the lover of *Carmen*.

Before the next act there is another interlude of great beauty—a pastoral melody of exquisite and touching grace. Its melody is given by a flute against plucked strings:

It is taken up in "imitation" by other instruments. Its song-like sweetness and purity are like cooling waters after the heady and intoxicating vintages of the second act. They refresh the emotions for the struggles yet to come.

ACT III

SCENE—*A Wild and Rocky Pass in the Mountains at Night*

THE drama sweeps on. *Don Jose* is lost. He has burned his bridges; he is passionately in love with *Carmen*. He has forgotten *Micaela*, he has forgotten his mother, he has abjured the laws which governed him, he has broken all authority, he is an outcast with a price upon his head. And *Carmen?* He is her slave; woman-like she is tiring of him, because she has discovered his weakness. *Don Jose* is hardly a good smuggler. Loyal unto the band, he despises the life, is resentful against her even while he loves her; then, in the background, is *Escamillo*. Already in spirit *Don Jose* and *Carmen* are separate—separate by the strange forces of heredity and circumstance that by determining society, control life, even as against the very passions that bind them together.

The stage is dark. It is the hour before dawn; the smugglers arrive in groups, set down their bundles and light a fire. Here occurs the famous Sextette. *Carmen* and *Jose* are at open odds. *Carmen* drifts to where *Frasquita* and *Mercedes* are "reading the cards."

Here she sings the "Voyons que j'essaie" (Let Me Know My Fate) trying to read her own fortune. Out of the orchestra steals the terrible "Fate-theme." Spades, spades, spades, the emblems of death and disaster! She throws them aside with fury—but with despair. The camp is ready, the

CARUSO AS DON JOSE—ACT III

CALVÉ AS CARMEN

DALMORES AS DON JOSE

smugglers retire. Then, though *Don José* is on guard, there steals in the pitiful figure of *Micaela*.

Don José's mother is dying, and the girl, for all her terrors, has brought the news into the mountains. In a beautiful air, "Je dis que rien ne me'epouvante" (I am not Faint-Hearted) she calls upon heaven to protect her. The music takes on the softer and tenderer coloring appropriate to her pure devotion to *Don José*. The solo is touching in this tenderness, and in curious contrast to the weird gloom of the card scene.

A shot is fired, and the girl runs into a cave. *Don José* has seen a stranger, and fired at him. It is *Escamillo*, who has come to join *Carmen*. He appears examining his hat, which the bullet has pierced. He introduces himself with fine bravado: "Je suis Escamillo" (I am Escamillo). The two men learn they are rivals. In a moment knives are out, when *Carmen* and the smugglers, attracted by the shot, again appear and intervene. *Don José* again would bring the matter to a finish, but *Micaela* appears with her news, and *Don José* must leave to see his mother before her death. All else is forgotten.

Carmen scornfully echoes *Micaela's* request, the music echoing *Don José's* jealousy. The Toreador song chorus returns, as it to indicate *Escamillo's* ascendency, but it dies out in strangely distorted echoes. *Don José* and *Micaela* disappear in the opposite direction. *Carmen* leans faintly against a boulder and watches them depart. With a shudder she remembers the message of the cards. Well, whatever will be, will be. Such is fate.

ACT IV

SCENE—*A Square in Seville, before the Entrance to the Bull Ring*

A THIRD intermezzo indicates again the changed scenes of the opera. It is lively, delicate yet vigorous, like a swift dance—only the oboe has a few plaintive notes. Then the curtain rises on the crowd outside the great "Plaza de Toros." A brilliantly dressed throng awaits the procession into the ring and the entrance of *Escamillo*. The brilliant opening theme of the prelude rings out again with irresistible verve. Street hawkers with oranges, fans and favors, are vigorously pushing their wares. Soldiers

BYRON   CARD SCENE—ACT III

and civilians, cits and peasants, aristocrats and bull-ring loafers, black-haired, black-eyed women with towering combs and floating mantillas and embroidered silken shawls, throng the open square. *Escamillo* appears with *Carmen*, both magnificently dressed. *Carmen's* own brilliant attire proclaims its own story, and hers. The "Toreador Song" greets *Escamillo*, who takes leave of *Carmen* before he enters the ring, in the song, "Si tu m'amas" (If You Love Me!), he promises to fight all the better for her love; for *Escamillo*, despite his rough life and his gayeties, is a brave and gallant Spanish gentleman. *Carmen*, won to him, yet half-conscious of what Fate is bringing her, avows, in return, her own willingness to die for *Escamillo*. As the Toreador enters the ring, *Carmen* is warned of *Don Jose's* nearness. But she is no coward herself and she replies that she does not fear him. Alone upon the stage she waits his reappearance—which does not take long.

Then the clouds of tragedy lower in truth.

For the first few moments the air is tense; question and reply are swift, the one pleading, the other merciless. *Don Jose* pleads in impassioned accents; *Carmen* for a moment seems even to waver; but from the interior of the ring come the plaudits of the crowd, the first theme of the prelude reappearing, reinforced with magnificent choral harmony. *Carmen* faces it out, but her heart is chill, for she knows that the end is come. *Don Jose's* rage increases when the applause of the multitude again crashes forth. *Carmen*, seeming uplifted, throws at *Don Jose's* feet the ring he has given her. He draws his knife and rushes in. *Carmen* has seen death.

When *Escamillo* appears, a moment later, among the crowd, at the wide-flung doors, *Carmen* is lying there and *Don Jose* has surrendered. But at the sight of his rival, *Don Jose* frees himself a moment, and flings himself, as if to join her in the death he cannot yet hope for, across the body of his beloved. Another magnificent phrase peals out, "My Adored Carmen!" and Fate has had its will.

THE VICTOR RECORDS
(Sung in French unless noted)

ACT I

PRELUDE
Philadelphia Orchestra   796 10-in., $1.50
FANTASIE
ERIKA MORINI, Violinist 6445 12-in., 2.00
(Soldiers Changing the Guard)
STOKOWSKI AND PHILADELPHIA ORCHESTRA
1017 10-in., 1.50
HABANERA
(Love is Like a Wood-bird)
GERALDINE FARRAR, Soprano
621 10-in., 1.50
GABRIELLA BESANZONI, Contralto *In Italian*
6047 12-in., 2.00
SOPHIE BRASLAU, Contralto
550 10-in., 1.50

CARMEN:
Ah! love, thou art a wilful, wild bird,
And none may hope thy wings to tame,

If it please thee to be a rebel,
Say, who can try and thee reclaim?
Threats and prayers alike unheeding;
Oft ardent homage thou'lt refuse,
Whilst he who doth coldly slight thee,
Thou for thy master oft thou'lt choose.
Ah, love!
For love he is the lord of all,
And ne'er law's icy fetters will he wear,
If thou me lovest not, I love thee,
And if I love thee, now beware!
If thou me lovest not, beware!
But if I love you, if I love you, beware!
beware!

PARLE-MOI DE MA MÈRE
(Tell Me of My Mother) LUCY MARSH,
Soprano and JOHN McCORMACK, Tenor
8034 12-in., $2.50
SEGUIDILLA
(Near the Walls of Seville) GERALDINE
FARRAR, Soprano   6108 12-in., 2.00

67

CARMEN (*airily*):

Nigh to the walls of Sevilla,
Soon at my friend Lillas Pastia
I'll trip thro' the light Seguidilla,
And I'll quaff Manzanilla,
I'll go seek out my friend Lillas Pastia.
(*Plaintively, casting glances at Jose*):
Yes, but alone one's joys are few,
Our pleasures double, shared by two!
So just to keep me company,
My beau I'll take along with me!
A handsome lad—deuce take it all!—
Three days ago I sent him off.
But this new love, he loves me well;
And him to choose my mind is bent.

ACT II

LES TRINGLES DE SISTRES

(Gypsy Song) GERALDINE FARRAR,
Soprano   6109 12-in., $2.00

Ah! when of gay guitars the sound
On the air in cadence ringing,
Quickly forth the gypsies springing,
To dance a merry, mazy round.
While tambourines the clang prolong,
In rhythm with the music beating,
And ev'ry voice is heard repeating
The merry burthen of glad song.
Tra la la la, etc.

CANCION DEL TOREADOR

(Toreador Song) PASQUALE
AMATO, Baritone *In Italian*
6040 12-in., 2.00

HALTE LA! QUI VA LA?

(Halt There!) GERALDINE FARRAR,
Soprano and GIOVANNI MARTINELLI,
Tenor   8019 12-in., 2.50

AIR DE LA FLEUR

(Flower Song) ENRICO CARUSO, Tenor
6004 12-in., 2.00
ENRICO CARUSO, Tenor *In Italian*
6007 12-in., 2.00
GIOVANNI MARTINELLI, Tenor
6191 12-in., 2.00
JOHN MCCORMACK, Tenor *In Italian*
6200 12-in., 2.00
FERNAND ANSSEAU, Tenor 6348 12-in., 2.00

DON JOSE:

This flower you gave to me, degraded
'Mid prison walls, I've kept, tho' faded;
Tho' withered quite, the tender bloom
Doth yet retain its sweet perfume.

Night and day in darkness abiding,
I the truth, Carmen, am confiding;
Its loved odor did I inhale,
And wildly called thee without avail.
My love itself I cursed and hated,

*   *   *   *   *

Then alone myself I detested,
And naught else this heart interested,
Naught else it felt but one desire,
One sole desire did it retain,
Carmen, beloved, to see thee once again!
O, Carmen, mine! here as thy slave, love binds
me fast,
Carmen, I love thee!
From Schirmer score. Copy't G. Schirmer

LÀ-BAS DANS LA MONTAGNE

(Away to Yonder Mountain) GERAL-
DINE FARRAR, Soprano 6108 12-in., $2.00

ACT III

VOYONS QUE J'ESSAIE

(Let Me Know My Fate) GERALDINE
FARRAR, Soprano   6109 12-in., 2.00

CARMEN:

Come, let me know my destiny.
Pictures! spades! a grave!
They lie not; first to me, and then to him,
And then to both—a grave!

(March of the Smugglers)
STOKOWSKI AND PHILADELPHIA ORCHESTRA
1017 10-in., 1.50

JE DIS QUE RIEN NE M'ÉPOUVANTE

(I Am Not Faint-Hearted) (Micaela's Air)
FRANCES ALDA, Soprano   6038 12-in., 2.00
ALMA GLUCK, Soprano   6145 12-in., 2.00

MICAELA:

I try not to own that I tremble;
But I know I'm a coward, altho' bold I
appear.
Ah! how can I ever call up my courage,
While horror and dread chill my sad heart
with fear?
Here, in this savage retreat, sad and weary
am I,
Alone and sore afraid.
Ah! heav'n, to thee I humbly pray,
Protect thou me, and guide and aid!
I shall see the guilty creature,
Who by infernal arts doth sever
From his country, from his duty,
Him I loved—and shall love ever!
I may tremble at her beauty,
But her power affrights me not.
Strong, in my just cause confiding,
Heaven! I trust myself to thee.
Ah! to this poor heart give courage,
Protector! guide and aid now me!

ACT IV | C'EST TOI!

ARAGONAISE
(Prelude) Toscanini and La Scala Orchestra   839   10-in., $1.50

C'EST TOI!
(You Here?) Geraldine Farrar, Soprano and Giovanni Martinelli, Tenor   8019   12-in., $2.50

BLACK LABEL AND BLUE LABEL RECORDS

Carmen Selection....................................*Sousa's Band*
  Prelude, Act I—Entr' acte, Act IV—Toreador Song
  Freischütz—Overture...........................*Sousa's Band*   35000   12-in., $1.25

Toreador Song..............................*Werrenrath and Chorus*
  Pagliacci—Prologue (In Italian)........*Reinald Werrenrath, Baritone*   55068   12-in., 1.50

Toreador Song (*In English*).....................*Alan Turner, Baritone*
  Trovatore—Tempest of the Heart (In English).....*Alan Turner, Baritone*   16521   10-in., .75

Carmen Selection (*Xylophone*)............................*Wm. Reitz*
  Bohême—Musetta Waltz (Whistling).................*Guido Gialdini*   16892   10-in., .75

Carmen Selection..............................*Vessella's Italian Band*
  Prelude—Toreador Song—Habanera
  Coronation March (Le Prophète) (Meyerbeer).......*Vessella's Italian Band*   35610   12-in., 1.25

Prelude (2) First Intermezzo...................*Victor Herbert's Orchestra*
  Prelude—Finale and Third Intermezzo...........*Victor Herbert's Orchestra*   55103   12-in., 1.50

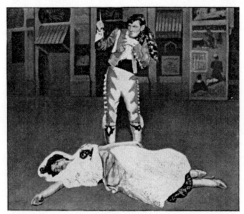

DON JOSE AND CARMEN

PHOTO LANDE CARUSO TOSCANINI DESTINN GATTI-CASAZZA, HOMER MARTIN

A REHEARSAL OF CAVALLERIA AT THE METROPOLITAN OPERA HOUSE, NEW YORK

CAVALLERIA RUSTICANA

UNLIKE many suddenly successful works, "Cavalleria Rusticana" continues to hold its own
as one of the most popular of operas.
Nor is this hard to understand. The
plot moves directly and simply to its
predestined end; the music is forceful
and strong, intensely dramatic in feeling and rich in harmony and orchestration. Best of all, Mascagni manages
to combine a good deal of straightforward melody in a score which otherwise
follows the modern idea in having no
set arias and ensembles.

For Pietro Mascagni, the production
of "Cavalleria Rusticana" proved as
dramatic a turn in fortune's wheel as
any such turn, perhaps, in the history
of opera. The son of a poor baker of
Leghorn, born December 7, 1863, aided
by a friendly uncle, he entered the
Cherubini Conservatory against his
parents' wishes. Some preliminary successes not only reconciled his father,
but brought aid from Count Florestano
de Larderel, a wealthy amateur, who
sent him to the famous Conservatory
at Milan. Here success for a time
deserted him. Resenting the dry studies of harmony and counterpoint, he
soon left his teachers, not unwillingly,
to mould artistic temperaments less
assertive than his own. He found
himself conductor of an obscure touring
opera company visiting the smaller
Italian cities with no very brilliant
prospects for the future, though he
learned many practical details of his
art which he might never have learned
at the Conservatory. Wearying of this
life of constant travelling, he married
and settled down to the humdrum
career of a music teacher at Cerignola,
near Foggia. About this time, how-

70

ever, there was need felt in Milan for short, concise one-act operas, and a prize for such a work was offered by Sozogno, the music publisher. Securing a libretto, Mascagni worked feverishly, and in eight days wrote "Cavalleria Rusticana." Not only did he win Sozogno's prize, but he won the yet greater prize of universal approval, and while still in his twenties this obscure music teacher found himself hailed as a genius, one of the newest and brightest stars in Italy's lustrous host of operatic composers. Medals were struck in his honor. His native city, Leghorn, welcomed him back with torchlight processions and illuminations, and the King of Italy conferred upon him the order of the crown of Italy, an honor not bestowed upon Verdi until middle life. "Cavalleria" was hailed with rapture all over Italy, and soon was equally popular in all music-loving countries. Mascagni's subsequent career has been devoted largely to operatic composition, but has produced no work quite rivalling "Cavalleria" in popular esteem. His "Piccolo Marat," first given, in Italy, in 1921, remains to be more thoroughly known.

The story of "Cavalleria Rusticana" is so simple that it can be told in a sentence. *Turiddu*, a young Sicilian peasant, returns from the wars to find his old sweetheart *Lola* wedded to *Alfio*, and he makes love to *Santuzza;* but in *Alfio's* absence he renews relations with *Lola*. *Santuzza* in despair informs *Alfio* upon his return, and the two men fight it out with knives till *Turiddu* is slain. The raw facts of the plot are so simple as to savor of every-day police court news, but the charm of the Sicilian setting, the interplay of human nature as the various characters thread out their destiny, the passionate intensity of the music, are such as to lift this tragedy of low life into a vivid and heart-searching drama. In contrast with the love of two women for *Turiddu* is the love of a third—his mother. Through all the misfortunes which his escapades bring him, the mother-love is unfailing, and *Turiddu's* mother is no less sympathetic with the wronged and outraged *Santuzza*. This, and the simple religious piety of the peasant-folk at Eastertime, lift the tragedy out of the commonplace.

The music of "Cavalleria Rusticana" is a happy blend of the old and the new. In its melodiousness it adheres to the older tradition. Tunes abound, so simple in character that any person with an average ear for music can readily grasp them. In this respect the work is obviously a descendant of the old Italian school of opera; but the method in which the melodies are used is modern. There are no set arias, no elaborately arranged ensembles halting the movement of the plot while the singers display their vocal charms. The melodies occur naturally and spontaneously, and, moreover, they are arrayed in all the panoply of modern harmony and orchestration. There is none of the stiff recitative of the older day. The recitative, on the contrary, is flexible and natural, giving a just musical presentment of the speaking voice's inflections with an accompaniment for the orchestra which faithfully follows the mood of the moment. Emotional crises develop, reach their climax and pass away; or again, they reach a point where the lyric outburst of melody seems natural, and indeed inevitable. This flowing continuity of style is essentially modern, being one of the innovations in operatic treatment for which we are indebted to the genius of Richard Wagner. Ultra-modern composers have carried the idea forward to such a degree as practically to eliminate melody in the ordinary sense of the word; but the success of their efforts is still in doubt.

71

THE OPERA

OPERA in one act. Libretto adapted from the book of Verga by Targioni-Torzetti and Menasci; music by Mascagni. First performed at Rome, May 17, 1890; in Germany, at Berlin, October 21, 1891; London, 1891; Paris, January 19, 1892. First United States production in Philadelphia, September 9, 1891. Given in New York October 1, 1891.

CHARACTERS
and Original American Cast

SANTUZZA (*San-toot'zah*), a village girl.....Soprano (Kronold)

LOLA (*Low'-lah*), wife of Alfio
Mezzo-Soprano (Campbell)

TURIDDU (*Too-ree'-doo*), a young soldier........Tenor (Guille)

ALFIO (*Al'-fee-oh*), a teamster
Baritone (Del Puente)

LUCIA (*Loo-chee'-ah*), mother of Turiddu...Contralto (Teale)

Chorus of Peasants and Villagers.
Chorus behind the Scenes.

The Scene is laid in a Sicilian Village. Time, the Present.

(The name of the opera is pronounced *Kah-vahl-leh-ree'-ah Roos-tih-kah'-nah*. Its English translation is *Rustic Chivalry*).

SCENE—*A Square in a Sicilian Village. At the right in the Background is a Church. At the left, the Inn and Dwelling of Mamma Lucia. The Time is Easter Morning in the Present Day.*

THE opera really begins with the Orchestral Prelude, which takes the form of a fantasia on the principal airs of the work, welded together with splendid musicianship. During the performance, however, the voice of *Turiddu* is heard from the curtained stage singing the "Siciliana," one of the most popular airs in the whole work:

It is a love-song pure and simple; but in its long-drawn cadences, its darkly colored harmonies, is some hint of the tragedy which is the consummation of *Turiddu's* love for *Lola*. It is a serenade, and the composer has given the melody a guitar-like accompaniment which is unusually charming, but of course the main significance lies in the melody and the ardent wooing of *Turiddu:*

O Lola, fair as flow'rs in beauty smiling,
Love from thy soul-lit eyes
Softly is glowing;
He who would kiss thy lips, red and beguiling,
Blissful and favored were he
Such heaven knowing!

* * * *

It is Easter Day, a festival that means as much to the Sicilians as Christmas to us. Moreover, it is springtime, and the air is fragrant with the odor of orange blossoms, and the lark rises singing from myrtles in full bloom. The warm beauty of the day is eloquently suggested in the opening chorus, "Gli aranci olezzano" (Blossoms of Oranges). This is sung first by women, and then by men, and during its melodious progress the curtain slowly rises, showing the people of the little village crossing the square to enter the church opposite the inn where *Lucia*, mother of *Turiddu*, plies her trade.

No sooner has the happy crowd entered the church than *Santuzza* appears and calls for "*Mamma Lucia.*" "What is it?" asks the old woman, coming from the house. "Where is *Turiddu?*" questions the girl. Something in her manner warns *Lucia*, and she evades

72

the repeated question with "Do not ask me. I don't know. I want no trouble." But *Santuzza* pleads, asking her to be merciful as the Saviour was merciful to the Magdalen. This leads to the "Dite, Mamma Lucia" (Tell Me, Mother Lucia).

Lucia replies that *Turiddu* has gone to Francofonte for wine. "No," declares *Santuzza*, "someone in the village saw him last night." The older woman's suspicions are quickly aroused and she invites the girl to enter; but this the unhappy *Santuzza* cannot do. In this little Sicilian village the moral code is strict, and she is an outcast, excommunicated for her sins! "What of my son?" questions the mother; but before *Santuzza* can reply, the cracking of whips and jingling of bells announces the arrival of *Alfio*, the carrier, who presently enters, followed by the crowd. He sings the "Il cavallo scalpita" (The Sturdy Steed), a vigorous description of a carrier's career. The lively rhythm and swift changes of harmony are particularly exhilarating, and this number is one of the most brilliant in the opera.

Alfio has every reason to be happy, for as a public carrier he possesses much prestige, and he thoroughly enjoys the life. Moreover, is he not the husband of the beautiful *Lola?* All his simple satisfaction bubbles over in this number, the latter part of which is given over to his joy at returning home for Easter, and the welcome that awaits him from his adored one. He has no suspicion that a few hours earlier another man has been likening the lips of the dusky *Lola* to crimson berries. The chorus joins gaily in his lively music, and afterwards disperses, some into the church, and the rest about their business, *Alfio* among them.

The gaiety of *Alfio's* song gives place to the Easter music which now fills the air. Two records present the "Regina Coeli" (Queen of the Heavens) and the "Ineggiamo al Signore" (Let Us Sing Before the Lord).

This Easter music is exceptionally rich in melody and harmony. Its tranquil beauty and sanctity of feeling deeply emphasize the part religion plays in the lives of these simple, pas-

AMATO AS ALFIO

SANTUZZA PLEADING WITH TURIDDU—ACT I
(DESTINN AND CARUSO)

GADSKI AS SANTUZZA

toral people. There is splendid breadth and dignity in its familiar tunes.

With the departure of *Alfio* and his admirers, *Santuzza* and *Mamma Lucia* are left alone again, and *Santuzza* pours her sad story into the kindly ears of the sympathetic *Lucia*. Before *Turiddu* went away to serve his time in the army, it appears, he was in love with *Lola*, who seemed to return his love. But when his time was up, and he returned to the village he found *Lola* married to *Alfio*. To console himself, *Turiddu* made violent love to *Santuzza*, who yielded to his ardor all too completely. Now, it seems, *Turiddu* is again paying court to *Lola*, who receives him with favor, and *Santuzza* finds herself doubly disgraced by his desertion. The story of *Santuzza* is set forth in the "Voi la sapete" (Well Do You Know Good Mother).

This is one of the most powerful, and indeed one of the most beautiful numbers in the opera, the melody being familiar to everybody:

Lucia is not wholly surprised, but deeply grieved. She looks with foreboding upon the future, and she does her best to console the unhappy girl, who pleads for her prayers, in the "Andante, O mamma" (Implore Your God to Save Me).

Lucia tries to comfort her, remaining patient even when the frantic *Santuzza* threatens vengeance against her son; then even *Santuzza's* mood softens as she thinks of the love she has lost.

Lucia leaves *Santuzza* to enter the church, and a moment later *Turiddu* himself appears. Then follows the duet, "Tu qui, Santuzza" (Thou Here, Santuzza?), in which the two quarrel violently.

This number is a melodious semi-recitative which presents the quarrel with growing intensity. "Thou here?" asks *Turiddu*, and *Santuzza* explains that she has come to see his mother. She then confronts him with the fact that he did not go to Francofonte, as he was supposed, but instead to *Lola*. *Turiddu* accuses her of spying upon him, and is soon beside himself with anger. *Santuzza* insists that he has been seen by *Alfio*, *Lola's* husband himself, but *Turiddu* refuses to listen, taunts her with jealousy and ingratitude, bidding her to leave him.

They are interrupted by the sound of a woman's voice, singing from behind the scene as she approaches. It is the unsuspecting *Lola*, on her way to church, carolling out the lovely "Fior di giaggiolo" (My King of Roses).

The music is adapted to suit the words, which express her love for *Turiddu*:

My king of roses,
Radiant angels stand
In Heav'n in thousands;
None like him so bright
That land discloses,
My king of roses!

She enters—and grasps the situation at a glance. The two girls converse with thinly veiled irony; the embarrassed *Turiddu* contributes but little. Finally *Lola* proceeds to church, inviting her lover to follow. *Santuzza* claims him, however, and they continue their former quarrel. This is carried on in one of the loveliest numbers of the entire work, the "Ah, No, Turiddu, rimani" (No, Turiddu, Remain!).

The melody is tender and pathetic, rising to a great climax as the distraught girl begs *Turiddu* to return to her. He refuses, and the scene that follows is passionate and intense. The girl's frenzied agony is no less powerful than *Turiddu's* violent anger, and finally, when *Santuzza* advances threateningly upon him, *Turiddu* seizes her and throws her down, hastening into

SANTUZZA: None should go
But those who have not sinned!

church in pursuit of *Lola*. "Accursed!" cries the wretched girl, "accursed at Easter, thou false one!" and yields herself up to despair.

She is aroused by the arrival of *Alfio*, and another great scene ensues, which is set forth in three records, "Turiddu mi tolse l'onore" (Turiddu Forsakes Me), "Comare Santa, allor" (Santuzza, Grateful Am I), and "Ad essi io non perdono" ('Tis They Who Are Shameful).

In these the duet is presented with extraordinary dramatic force, and interspersed with the semi-recitatives are melodic passages unsurpassed in modern dramatic music. *Santuzza* tells all she knows. At first *Alfio* finds it hard to believe in *Lola's* guilt. His anger is immediate and passionate— "If thou art lying I'll have thy heart's blood"—but in the end he is convinced. *Santuzza* repents having told him, and reproaches herself; but *Alfio*, who is at bottom generous by nature, tries to calm her. He breaks out again in sudden fury against *Turiddu* and *Lola*— " 'Tis they who are shameful! Revenge I'll have upon them, this day and hour."

They go out, leaving the stage empty

while the beautiful "Intermezzo" is played. The calm serenity of this music, and the peaceful scene upon the stage, are in sharp contrast with the highly charged scenes of a moment ago, and that which is to come. It provides a moment of relief for which the audience is grateful, and serves to emphasize the devout religious spirit of the Sicilian peasants despite their hot-blooded conduct in human affairs.

This exquisite interlude, with its heavenly melody at the end, is doubtless the most familiar single number in the entire work, and is complete in itself. Not only is the melody beautiful, but the harmony is rich, and the orchestral scoring, with its fine contrasts of woodwind and strings, is a beautiful piece of musical tone-painting.

PART II

AS the last strains of the Intermezzo die away, the people begin to leave the church, and soon a merry crowd is assembled outside the inn of *Mamma Lucia*. They sing "A casa, a casa" (Now Homeward), a lively chorus which prepares the way for the

75

Brindisi—"Viva il vino spu meggiante" (Drinking Song).

This is a lively number, in striking contrast to the prevailing tragic tone of Mascagni's opera. It has a most fascinating swing, and is full of life and color, beginning:

The "Brindisi" is sung by *Turiddu* as if he had not a care in the world, though perhaps his gaiety is a trifle hysterical, for the end is already at hand. As the "Brindisi" draws to a close, *Alfio* approaches in time to see *Lola* drink in response to *Turiddu's* toast. Watched with tense interest by the assembled crowd, *Turiddu* offers *Alfio* a glass of wine. "A voi tutti salute" (Come Here, Good Friends), sings he.

Alfio scornfully refuses, to the horror of *Lola*. *Turiddu*, still in a mood of bravado, pours the wine carelessly on the ground, and the peasants, realizing the situation, withdraw leaving the two rivals face to face. A challenge is quickly given and accepted, after the Sicilian fashion, *Turiddu* biting *Alfio's* ear, and the men arrange to meet in the garden.

Now follows an affecting scene in which *Turiddu* bids farewell to his mother, in the "Addio alla madre" (Turiddu's Farewell) and the "Mamma quel vino e generoso" (Too Much Wine, My Mother)—Turiddu's Farewell, continued, and finale of the opera.

Without explaining the details, *Turiddu* pretends to have been drinking, and declares the wine-cup to have passed too freely among his comrades. He must go away, he says, and he would bid his mother farewell. *Lucia* is not deceived; his distraught manner, the passionate tenderness of his fare-

well, tell her more than words could say, and she watches him horror-stricken as he tears himself from her arms and rushes away, first bidding her take care of *Santuzza*.

There is but little more to tell. *Santuzza* enters and throws her arms about *Lucia*. People crowd about them, and soon a woman comes running with the cry "Neighbor *Turiddu* is murdered!" Several other women rush in, terrified. *Santuzza* falls swooning, and *Lucia* is supported by other women in a fainting condition. The curtain falls rapidly as the crowd gathers round the unhappy pair, and all is over.

NOTE—*The quotations from Cavalleria Rusticana are given by kind permission of G. Schirmer. (Copyright 1891.)*

THE VICTOR RECORDS
(Sung in Italian unless noted)

ACT I

SICILIANA
(Thy Lips Like Crimson Berries) ENRICO CARUSO, Tenor   516 10-in., $1.50
GIOVANNI MARTINELLI, Tenor
                            734 10-in., 1.50

VOI LO SAPETE
(Well You Know, Good Mother) MARGARETE MATZENAUER, Contralto
                            6327 12-in., 2.00
MARIA JERITZA, Soprano 687 10-in., 1.50

SANTUZZA:
Well do you know, good mother,
Ere to the war he departed;
Turiddu plighted to Lola his troth,
Like a man true-hearted.
And then, finding her wedded
Loved me!—I loved him!—
She, coveting what was my only treasure—
Enticed him from me!
She and Turiddu love again!
I weep and I weep and I weep still!

AVE MARIA
(Adapted to the Intermezzo) JOHN McCORMACK, Tenor and FRITZ KREISLER, Violinist, 3021 10-in., 2.00

ADDIO ALLA MADRE
(Turiddu's Farewell to His Mother)
ENRICO CARUSO, Tenor 6008 12-in., 2.00

THE COMPLETE CAVALLERIA RUSTICANA (IN ITALIAN)

Every part of Mascagni's popular opera has been recorded in this new series. On account of Parts 6, 10, 11, 14, 15 and 16 being in 10-inch size it has not been possible to double the series in regular order, and the records should be played just the way they are numbered. For example, 35686-A should be followed by 18549-A, etc.

No. 1. Prelude and Siciliana (Thy Lips Like Crimson Berries) *Francesco Tuminello, Tenor, and La Scala Orch.* No. 2. Prelude, Part II.........................*La Scala Orch.*	35680	12-in.,	$1.25
No. 3. Introduction and Chorus of Villagers (Gli aranci olezzano) *La Scala Chorus* No. 4. Chorus of Villagers, Part II...........*La Scala Chorus*	35681	12-in.,	1.25
No. 5. Dite, Mamma Lucia...............*G. Ermolli and E. Ravelli* No. 7. Easter Hymn, Part I (Regina Coeli).........*The Opera Chorus*	35686	12-in.,	1.25
No. 8. Easter Hymn, Part II (Inneggiamo al Signore) *Giorgina Ermolli, Soprano and Chorus* No. 9. Voi lo sapete.......................*Giorgina Ermolli, Soprano*	35685	12-in.,	1.25
No. 6. Alfio's Song (Il cavallo scalpita).........*Enrico Perna, Baritone* No. 10. Andate, o mamma..................*Giorgina Ermolli, Soprano*	18549	10-in.,	.75
No. 11. Tu qui, Santuzza?.....................*Ermolli and Tuminello* No. 14. Turiddu mi tolse l'onore...................*Ermolli and Perna*	18558	10-in.,	.75
No. 12. Fior di giaggiolo...............*G. Ermolli, Tuminello and Ravelli* No. 13. Ah, No, Turiddu, rimani.................*Ermolli and Tuminello*	35687	12-in.,	1.25
No. 15. Comare Santa, allor.....................*Ermolli and Perna* No. 16. Intermezzo............................*La Scala Orchestra*	18557	10-in.,	.75
No. 17. A casa, a casa.................*Tuminello, Ravelli and Chorus* No. 18. Brindisi—Viva il vino spumeggiante.......*Tuminello and Chorus*	35688	12-in.,	1.25
No. 19. A voi tutti salute.............*F. Tuminello, Perna and Ravelli* No. 20. Mamma, quel vino é generoso.............*Tuminello and Ravelli*	35689	12-in.,	1.25

MISCELLANEOUS CAVALLERIA RECORDS

Prelude *Vessella's Italian Band* Introduction to Act I *Vessella's Italian Band*	35453	12-in.,	1.25
Gems from "Cavalleria" (*In English*)...................*Victor Opera Co.* Gems from "Pagliacci" (*In English*)..................*Victor Opera Co.*	35343	12-in.,	1.25
Prelude..*La Scala Orchestra* Selection ("Alfio's Song," "Easter Chorale," "Intermezzo"). *Pryor's Band*	35104	12-in.,	1.25
Intermezzo...................................*Victor Concert Orchestra* Tales of Hoffman—Barcarolle..................*Victor Concert Orchestra*	17311	10-in.,	.75
Intermezzo.................................*Victor Herbert's Orchestra* Spring Song (*Mendelssohn*)..................*Victor Herbert's Orchestra*	45186	10-in.,	1.00
Intermezzo.................................*Pietro's Accordion Qt.* Pagliacci—Vesti la guibba (*Accordion*).......................*Pietro*	17941	10-in.,	.75
Intermezzo...................................*Vessella's Italian Band* Minuet (*Boccherini*)...........................*Vessella's Italian Band*	67896	10-in.,	.75

CHIMES OF NORMANDY

(LES CLOCHES DE CORNEVILLE)
(French)

COMIC opera in three acts. Text by Clairville and Gabet; music by Robert Planquette. First produced at the *Folies Dramatiques*, Paris, April 19, 1877, where it ran for 400 continuous performances. First New York production at the Fifth Avenue Theatre, October 27, 1877.

Time and Place : Normandy ; Time of Louis XV

(The French title of the opera is "Les Cloches de Corneville," *Lay Klohsh duh Korn'veel*).

HENRI, *Marquis de Valleroi*, is romantic and adventurous. In his absence from home, singular things have happened. *Gaspard*, the warden of the estate, has turned miser, and has planned that *Germaine*, his supposed niece, shall wed the *Sheriff* and ward off investigation. *Germaine*, however, loves *Grenicheux*, who saved her, she believes, from drowning. *Grenicheux* seeks her hand,—also the supposed wealth she will inherit; and he has jilted *Serpolette*, a girl of unknown parentage, found as a baby in the fields by *Gaspard*. Villagers, at a fair, try to tease *Serpolette*, but fail. She claims she is a nobleman's daughter and cares nothing for *Grenicheux*. *Henri* returns, in Mexican costume, and is not recognized.

Corneville castle is "haunted." Chimes ring there mysteriously. *Henri* will investigate. *Germaine* and *Serpolette*, with *Grenicheux*, enter his service, and he reveals his rank. They discover, after blood-curdling experiences, that *Gaspard* is using the castle as a treasure-house and ringing the chimes to keep away the curious-minded —and the superstitious. *Gaspard* is discovered counting his money-bags, and the shock drives him insane.

Henri further makes himself known, and gives a fête. *Serpolette* arrives in fine raiment, announcing she is the long-lost *Marchioness de Lucenay;* but *Henri* has doubts. *Grenicheux*, who has been masquerading as her factotum, claims the hand of *Germaine* in return for his rescue. But it transpires that *Henri* rescued the girl himself, and *Grenicheux* is joyously kicked out. *Gaspard* becomes suddenly lucid, and reveals that *Germaine* is the true *Marchioness*. *Henri* and *Germaine* marry, and *Grenicheux* and *Serpolette*. The chimes ring out for a double wedding.

THE VICTOR RECORDS

DANS MES VOYAGES
(With Joy My Heart) RENATO ZANELLI, Baritone, *In French*   879 10-in., $1.50

BLACK LABEL RECORDS

{Selection of the Principal Airs.........................*Pryor's Band*}	35738	12-in.,	1.25
{ Poet and Peasant—Overture (*von Suppé*) ....*Pryor's Band*}			
{Selection of the Principal Airs.................*Victor Concert Orchestra*}	35583	12-in.,	1.25
{ Erminie Selection......................................*Victor Orchestra*}			

LE CID

MASSENET, for all of his popularity, was a modern. He was lavish in orchestral effects, subtle in his presentation of character, and his score, though melodious, afforded few "set pieces." He revelled in the picturesque and the heroic—of which "Le Cid," from the life of the great Spanish warrior, is a characteristic example.

THE OPERA

OPERA in four acts. Text by A. D'Ennery, Louis Gallet and Edward Blau, based upon the play of the same name by Corneille, glorifying a famous Spanish hero, *El Cid* (1040-1099). Music by Jules Massenet. First production at the Opéra, Paris, November 30, 1885, with a notable cast including Jean and Edouard de Reszke and Pol Plançon. The first American production occurred at the New Orleans Opera. First New York presentation February 12, 1907, with the de Reszkes, Plançon, Lassalle, de Vere and Litvinne.

CHARACTERS

KING FERDINAND..........Baritone
DON URRAQUE, his son.......Baritone
COUNT GORMAS................Bass
CHIMÈNE, his daughter.......Soprano
DON RODRIGUE, known as The
    Cid.....................Tenor
DON DIEGO, his father..........Bass
LEONORE, maid to Chimène...Soprano
Courtiers, Soldiers, Townspeople

Time and Place: Seville, Spain; Twelfth Century

(The name of the opera is pronounced *Luh Seed*; in Spanish it is *El Theed*, with the *th* as in "thread.")

THE CID, (from the Arabic *el seid*, "The Conqueror,") has returned from victory over the Moors, and the curtain rises to show him receiving knighthood from *King Ferdinand*, at the house of *Count Gormas*, whose daughter, *Chimène*, loves the warrior with a love that is returned in full. The *King* and his family approve, for the *King's* daughter herself loves *The Cid*; a match, however, is impossible between her and one not of royal blood.

But the *King* bestows upon *Don Diego*, father of *The Cid*, a governorship expected by *Count Gormas*. The *Count*, enraged, insults *Don Diego*, who, too old to fight, calls upon his son to uphold his honor—without naming his adversary.

The Cid accepts the task, and is dismayed to find himself set against the father of his beloved. By accident more than design he kills *Count Gormas*. He expires in the arms of his daughter, who sets aside love and swears vengeance. The *King* refuses her entreaties for justice, influenced, of

ORIGINAL POSTER BY CLAIRIG

course, by his daughter, who loves *The Cid*, but also by the fact that the Moors again are advancing. Before he departs to fight them, *The Cid* gains audience with *Chimène*, who finds her love as strong as her wish for retribution. After a dramatic scene they part, both torn with anguish.

The Cid's encounters turn out badly at first, and *Chimène* and the *King* both hear he is dead. The girl's vengeance is fulfilled, but her love is racked with despair. A second report turns the news. He has routed the enemy, and is alive. He returns, to find the girl still implacable. The *King*, shrewdly enough, now promises her he will punish the warrior. He has no intention of complying, but with Solomon-like wisdom he asks her to pronounce, herself, the death-sentence. His judgment is correct; *Chimène* cannot bring herself to this. Finally, when *The Cid* draws his own dagger and threatens to end his own life if she will not wed him, *Chimène* is forced to acknowledge that Love is triumphant, *The Cid* a conqueror in love as in war.

VICTOR RECORD

Ô SOUVERAIN, Ô JUGE, Ô PÈRE!
(Almighty Lord, Oh Judge, Oh Father)
ENRICO CARUSO, Tenor *In French*
6013 12-in., $2.00

SCENE FROM LE CID

THE GALLEY OF CLEOPATRA (MONTE CARLO OPERA)

CLEOPATRA

CLEOPATRA, like the even less-known "Panurge," is a posthumous work of Massenet's. Rumor has it that really the opera was written before "Manon," but that Massenet was not satisfied with it. Whatever the truth, it was not given until after the composer had passed away.

THE OPERA

OPERA in four acts. Text by Louis Payen; music by Jules Massenet. First produced at Monte Carlo, February 23, 1914, with Marie Kousnezoff, Alfred Maguenat and M. Roussiliere. First American performance by the Chicago Opera Company, January, 1916.

CHARACTERS

CLEOPATRA, Egyptian Queen
               Mezzo-Soprano
MARK ANTHONY, Roman Emperor................Baritone
OCTAVIA, betrothed to Mark Anthony..............Soprano
CHARMIAN, Cleopatra's maid..Soprano
SPAKOS, Egyptian Freedman, in love with Cleopatra........Tenor
ENNIUS } Roman Officers.....Baritone
SEVERUS }
AMNHES, tavern keeper of Alexandria................Baritone
ADAMOS...................A dancer
A VOICE...................Baritone
Greek and Egyptian Slaves, Roman Officers, Gift-Bearers, Jugglers, Guards of Mark Anthony and Octavius.

The Scene: Vicinity of Alexandria, Asia Minor; and in Rome

MARK ANTHONY, encamped in Asia Minor, is in the first act receiving pledges of fidelity from defeated enemies. *Spakos*, an Egyptian freedman, arrives to announce *Cleopatra. Mark Anthony* is not pleased, but the *Queen's* beauty impresses him and he falls in love. Despite orders recalling him to Rome, he decides for Egypt with her. They enter the royal barge, to the chagrin of *Spakos*, himself in love with the *Queen*.

Anthony wearies of his prize, and he returns to Rome to wed his former betrothed, *Octavia*. An officer from Egypt arrives at the wedding festivities, in the second act, with the intelligence that *Cleopatra* has lightly consoled herself with *Spakos*. *Anthony* becomes jealous, leaves his bride and hurries back to Egypt.

His action is hastened, no doubt, by his reading over some letter-tablets *Cleopatra* has sent him in the past. These awaken the emotions told of in the "Air de Lettre—Tes Messages d'Amour" (Letter Song—Thy Messages of Love).

The next scene is in the notorious quarter of Alexandria, where *Cleopatra*, disguised, is seeing the dissipations of her people. *Cleopatra* takes one of her sudden fancies for a boy named *Adamos*, head of a company of dancers. *Spakos*, in a rage, endeavors to kill him. The mob is about to close in upon the strangers when *Cleopatra* makes herself known.

In the midst of this, *Charmian* arrives, to tell the *Queen* that *Anthony* awaits her at the palace. *Spakos* tries to detain her, but she has him placed under arrest, hastening back to welcome her old lover.

The third act sees another fête, in *Cleopatra's* gardens. *Octavia* arrives, and pleads with *Anthony* to return, as the Roman army is marching against Egypt. *Anthony*, his infatuation strong as ever, refuses, going out at the head of Egyptian troops, while *Octavia* sadly returns to Rome.

The last act sees *Cleopatra* awaiting the victorious return of *Anthony*. *Spakos* informs her that her hero believes her dead. *Cleopatra*, enraged, stabs the man. *Anthony*, his army vanquished and himself mortally wounded, appears in time to die in the *Queen's* arms. *Cleopatra* then, overcome with grief, applies to her breast a poisonous asp, which bites her, and she dies.

THE VICTOR RECORD

AIR DE LETTRE — TES MESSAGES D'AMOUR
(Thy Messages of Love)
MARCEL JOURNET, Bass *In French*
699   10-in., $1.50

MME. KOUSNEZOFF (CLEOPATRA)

MAGUENAT AS ANTHONY

WHITE　　　　　　　ARRIVAL OF KING AND QUEEN

LE COQ D'OR

(THE GOLDEN COCK)

WITH a story as fantastic as anything out of the Arabian Nights, "Le Coq d'Or" (The Golden Cock) was in the first instance written as an opera. Its first production in Russia was a failure. It then was rewritten as an "opera-pantomime" for the Diaghileff Russian ballet, the text being sung by vocal artists and the chorus; the action being performed, in dumb-show, by the ballet. The fate of the opera was almost exactly that of the composer's "Scheherazade" suite, originally a pure concert work but which developed into one of the "classical" ballets of modern music. Ballet or opera, it is imaginative and original.

THE OPERA

OPERA pantomime in three acts. Text by V. Bielsky, founded on a fairy tale by Pushkin; music by Rimsky-Korsakoff. First performance September 24, 1909, at Zimin's Private Opera House, Moscow; at Petrograd January, 1910. The revised version was produced at the Paris Opera June 9, 1914; London, June 25, 1914. First American performance at the Metropolitan Opera House, March 6, 1918.

CHARACTERS

(With the Original American Cast)

CHARACTERS	SINGERS	PANTOMIMISTS
THE PRINCESS	Maria Barrientos	Rosina Galli
THE KING	Adamo Didur	Adolph Bohm
AMELIA	Sophie Braslau	Queenie Smith
THE ASTROLOGER	Rafaelo Diaz	Giuseppe Bonfiglio

83

Characters	Singers	Panto-mimists
The Prince	Pietro Audisio	Marshall Hall
The General	Basil Ruysdael	Ottokar Bartik
A Knight	Vincenzo Reschiglian	Vincenzo Ioucelli
Voice of the Golden Cock	Marie Sundelius	

Boyars, Court Ladies and Nobles, Soldiers, Oriental Dancers, Giants, and Dwarfs.

(The name of the opera is pronounced *Luh Cokh Dohr'*).

ACT I

Scene—*Palace of King Dodon*

DODON (which is Dodo), an aged king, is conferring with his boyars or princes. He is weary of rule and warfare, but his council is incapable of advice. The Crown Prince *Girdon* suggests that troops be concentrated at the capital, but General *Polkan* objects, and there is a quarrel. The *Astrologer* appears, and offers to *Dodon* a *Golden Cockerel* which will always give warning when danger is near. The bird is put to bed with much ceremony. The *King* is doubtful, though he accepts the gift, saying if the *Cockerel* proves worthy, he will give the *Astrologer* anything he may demand. The bird soon warns the *King* there is an invasion at his borders. The blood-princes go off to repel the attack.

ACT II

Scene—*A Narrow Gorge in a Mountain Pass*

DODON is warned by the *Cock* to go aid his sons. He finds their bodies and sheds a few tears over them, but sorrow is forgotten when a beautiful woman appears from a tent on a hillside, singing, in the opera, the unique "Hymn to the Sun." In a strange wailing canticle, tinselled through with extraordinary chromatic scales and weird modulations, this beautiful but vain creature asks if in her own "dear land" the roses yet grow in splendor and the "lilies burn in fiery sheaves;" if in the evenings, the maidens come with soft songs to the fountains of mystical water.

The white-bearded *Dodon* falls in love with the *Queen*, singing to her in a voice like a bee in a bottle, and dancing in front of her a clumsy and fantastic dance. Rheumy-eyed, thick-ankled, yet the *Queen* returns his love and promises to marry him.

ACT III

Scene—*Outside Dodon's Palace*

THE people await the *King* and his new *Queen*, who arrive in fairy-tale splendor. But the lady is bored with her doddering old lord and master. There is a way out. *Dodon* sees the *Astrologer* passing, and he asks him to name his reward for the gift of the *Golden Cock*. The *Astrologer* demands the *Queen*, and *Dodon* strikes him dead on the spot. A storm threatens, and when the *King* turns to his *Queen*, in helpless terror, she scorns him. Suddenly, among thunder, the *Golden Cock* is heard crowing. He flies at *Dodon*, pecks him on the skull, and the monarch, in his turn, falls dead. It has grown dark during the storm, but when light breaks, a moment later, the bird and the *Queen* have gone, and over the body of *Dodon* the folk sing a weird lament.

THE VICTOR RECORDS

HYMNE AU SOLEIL

(Hymn to the Sun) Mabel Garrison, Soprano *In French*   638   10-in., $1.50

Amelita Galli-Curci, Soprano
   In French   631   10-in.,   1.50
Fritz Kreisler, Violinist   6183   12-in.,   2.00
Mischa Elman, Violinist   6100   12-in.,   2.00

L'ART DU THEATRE   THE RIDE TO HELL—ACT V

LA DAMNATION DE FAUST
(DAMNATION OF FAUST)

HECTOR BERLIOZ'S dramatic legend in four parts; book based on de Nerval's version of Goethe's poem, partly by Gandonniere, but completed by Berlioz himself. First performed December 6, 1846, at the *Opéra Comique*, Paris, in concert form. In New York under Dr. Leopold Damrosch, February 12, 1880. It was given at Monte Carlo as an opera February 18, 1893, with Jean de Reszke as *Faust.* Revived there in 1902, with Melba, de Reszke and Renaud. First American performance of the operatic version in New York, 1908.

CHARACTERS

MARGUERITE (*Mahr-guer-eet'*).Soprano
FAUST (*Fowst*) . . . . Tenor
MEPHISTOPHELES (*Mef-iss-tof'-el-leez*) . . . . Baritone or Bass
BRANDER . . . . Bass

Place: A Hungarian Village

(The name is pronounced, in French, *Lah Dam-nass-see-ohn duh Fowst;* its English equivalent is "The Damnation of Faust.")

FAUST soliloquizes upon the vanity of life; young folk are heard in the distance, then Hungarian soldiers tramping past to the "Rákóczy March." He is about to take poison when he hears the strains of Easter music. *Mephistopheles* joins him, and suggests they see the world together.

The story, in the main, follows the Gounod "Faust." They go to a beer cellar in Leipzig, leaving in fire and smoke; then to a forest, where *Faust* sleeps, to see the vision of *Marguerite.* The next scene corresponds to the Gounod garden scene, *Mephistopheles* distracting the maid's attention with a serenade,

while *Faust* enters the room of the sleeping *Marguerite.* The girl wakes in a kind of trance. Endeavoring to enter the church, she is withheld by the malevolent power of *Mephistopheles.* She returns and falls into the arms of *Faust.*

The last part contains four scenes: a moonlit room where *Marguerite* sings her lament; a rocky pass where *Meph-*

85

istopheles tells *Faust* she is about to be executed for murdering her mother, and where *Faust* barters away his soul to save hers; a "Ride to Hell" on the infernal steeds Vortex and Giaour, shown, as a rule, by a moving panorama, and a vision of the town with angels hovering overhead to rescue the soul of the pardoned girl.

THE VICTOR RECORDS
RÁKÓCZY HUNGARIAN MARCH

Toscanini and La Scala Orchestra

6300   12-in., $2.00

BLACK LABEL RECORDS

Dance of the Sylphs.............................*Victor Concert Orchestra*	19249	10-in., $0.75
Sylvia Ballet—Pizzicato Polka...................*Victor Concert Orchestra*		
Rákóczy March.....................................*Conway's Band*	67965	10-in., .75
Radetzky March ....*Conway's Band*		

PHOTO BERT

DAMNATION OF FAUST—FOURTH SCENE—PARIS OPÉRA

86

THE DAUGHTER OF THE REGIMENT

BY the year 1840, Donizetti had written fifty-three operas; and during that year he added five more to his credit. His insanity and his death, late in the "fatal thirties," are attributed to overwork.

Donizetti's operas set no new standards; they are for the most part typical of what the average music-lover calls "Italian Opera of the old school." Yet his gifts were personal; even when he followed the stereotyped rules of his day, he could not help investing his work with a tender lyric charm vouchsafed to but few.

"The Daughter of the Regiment" is a brilliant little opera, with rollicking songs, drums and military fanfares, a vivacious heroine and a comic character—the old *Sergeant of the Twenty-first.*

THE OPERA

COMIC opera in two acts. Words by Bayard and St. Georges. Music by Donizetti. First produced at the *Opéra Comique*, Paris, Febuary 11, 1840; Milan, October 30, 1840; Berlin, 1842, at the Royal Opera, and during the next sixty years it had two hundred and fifty performances on that stage. Produced in London, in English, at the Surrey Theatre, December 21, 1847, and during the same year, in Italian, with Jenny Lind. The first American performance of which the author has knowledge was that at the New Orleans Opera, March 7, 1843. Jenny Lind, Sontag, Lucca, Patti, Richings, Piccolomini, Albani and Parepa Rosa have all appeared here as *Marie.* Given by the Strakosch Opera Co. in 1871 with Cary, Capoul and Brignoli. Maretzek produced the opera just after the Civil War broke out, emphasizing the military features, with Clara Louise Kellogg as *Marie.* Sung in English by the Boston Ideal Opera Co. in 1888 with Zelie De Lussan as *Marie.* Revived in 1902-03 at the Metropolitan Opera House for Sembrich, the cast including Charles Gilibert as *Sulpizio.* Produced by Oscar Hammerstein in 1909, with Tetrazzini, McCormack and Gilibert. Revived at the Metropolitan Opera House, 1917.

CHARACTERS

TONIO, a peasant of Tyrol . . . . . Tenor
SULPIZIO, Sergeant of the 21st . . . . Bass
MARIE, Vivandière of the 21st, Soprano
MARCHIONESS OF BERKENFELD
Mezzo-Soprano

The Scene is laid in the Swiss Tyrol

(The Italian name of the opera is "La Figlia del Reggimento," *Lah Feel'-yah del Red'-jee-men-toh*; the French is "La Fille du Regiment," *La Fee'-yeh d'Rezh'-ee-mong'*).

ACT I opens in a Swiss Alpine village, where trouble has long been brewing.

The *Marchioness of Berkenfeld*, clandestinely married to a young officer of inferior rank, many years before, has left her child, *Marie*, with her husband, who has since been slain in battle. The child has been discovered and reared by *Sulpizio*, the sergeant, and brought up as a vivandière,—the "Daughter of the Regiment." When the curtain lifts we see her in uniform, a lively young lady of seventeen, adored by numerous "fathers"—the gallant men of the 21st, Savoyards under Napoleon.

Marie wishes to marry *Tonio*, a young Tyrolese who has saved her from tumbling down a precipice, but who, to complicate things, is in danger of being shot as a spy, having come too near the lines for a glimpse of her. The fact that he has saved her life, however, saves his own; *Sulpizio* and the Regiment, duly consulted, give their consent to the wedding, provided *Tonio* joins the regiment—which he does.

Everything seems lovely, and the "goose to be hanging high;" but *Sulpizio* meets the *Marchioness*, who claims to be the "aunt" of *Marie*. This proud lady is horrified at the girl's betrothal to a mere peasant, having bigger plans for her. She carries her off, to her disgust, the regimental anger, and *Tonio's* despair.

The second act exhibits the *Marchioness's* salon.

Marie is living in luxury, but she still pines for her old comrades and her soldier-lover. *Sulpizio* is with her, on sick-leave after a wound. The *Mar-*

chioness counts on marrying the girl to a rich nobleman, and the marriage contract is all ready to be signed. *Marie* is half in rebellion and half in despair, when the Regiment comes to town, and with it her beloved *Tonio*, who has risen to high rank.

It is now the turn of the *Marchioness* to be gloomy; as a last resort she proclaims the truth—that *Marie* is her daughter. The girl recognizes that disobeying her mother is a serious matter; and she consents to wed the Count, her suitor. Touched by such devotion, the *Marchioness* relents, and *Marie* marries *Tonio*.

THE VICTOR RECORD

PER VIVER VICINO
(To Be Near Her) John McCormack,
    Tenor *In Italian*   6203 12-in., $2.00

BLACK LABEL RECORD

{Selection . . . . *Vessella's Italian Band*}35191 12-in., $1.25
{ *Fra Diavolo Selection* . . . . *Vessella's Italian Band*}

DONIZETTI

COPY'T FOLEY

TETRAZZINI AS MARIE

COPY'T FOLEY

McCORMACK AS TONIO

THE SHADOW DANCE

DINORAH

OPERA in three acts. Libretto by Barbier and Carré. Music by Giacomo Meyerbeer. First production Paris, *Opéra Comique*, April 4, 1859. First London production, under direction of Meyerbeer, July 26, 1859. First American production, November 24, 1864, with Cordier, Brignoli and Amodio. Sung by Ilma di Murska at Booth's Theatre in 1867. Other productions occured in 1879 with Mariman and Campanini; and in 1882 with Patti. Revived in 1892 for Marie Van Zandt; by Oscar Hammerstein in 1907 for Mme. Tetrazzini; and more recently by the Chicago Opera Company as a vehicle for the art of Mme. Galli-Curci.

CHARACTERS

HOËL, a goatherd (*Oh-ell'*)...Baritone
CORENTINO, bag-piper (*Koh-ren-tee-no*)................Tenor
DINORAH, betrothed to Hoël (*Dee-no'-rah*)...........Soprano
HUNTSMAN....................Bass
Place: Breton Village of Ploërmel

ACT I

THE homestead of *Dinorah's* father has been destroyed by storm, and the girl's lover wishes to help the stricken household. He is advised, by the village soothsayer, of a vast fortune hidden in the mountains. This can be had only by one who lives for a year in a lonesome glen, and even at that the first person to touch it will surely die. Being but a credulous goatherd, *Hoël* accepts the story, and he takes with him the half-witted bagpiper *Corentino*, hoping *he* will be the first to touch the treasure. *Dinorah* knows nothing of her lover's intentions, and becomes insane from the belief that he has deserted her. As the curtain rises, we find her in the mountains, arrayed in her bridal dress, seeking her goat. When she discovers the animal sleeping she sings a charming, if strange lullaby, "Si, carina caprettina" (Yes, My Beloved One).

This takes place near the hut of *Corentino*, and when the piper returns

89

and finds *Dinorah*, he mistakes her for an evil fairy who is said to so bewitch those who have been lost or have gone astray in the mountains, that they dance until they die. *Corentino* is scared out of his wits, and the half insane girl forces him to dance until he falls exhausted, when she disappears. *Hoël* then enters, telling the bagpiper how the wizard has instructed him to seek for a white goat which will lead him to the treasure. The bell of *Dinorah's* goat is heard and he goes off in pursuit, dragging with him the terrified *Corentino*.

ACT II

THE moon shines upon an open clearing in the woods. In its clear light is seen *Dinorah*. The moon throws a strong shadow upon the ground. Seeing her own form thus fantastically outlined, the girl regards it as a friend. She sings and dances with her shadow as with a living partner. Then is heard the world-famous "Ombra leggiera" (Shadow Song).

This delightful waltz-like coloratura aria is justly popular. The flute follows the voice through the difficult runs and vocal ornaments in a manner that clearly suggests the dancing shadow. The florid cadenza is especially effective.

The scene changes. And a violent storm arises, in the midst of which *Hoël* still seeks the treasure; but *Corentino*, having heard from *Dinorah* that he who first touches it must die, refuses to take the risk, suggesting that the demented maid of the mountains may do so in his place. As *Hoël* has no objection they go in search of her. Then a dam bursts high in the mountains and the flood carries away a bridge on which *Dinorah* is crossing a ravine. *Hoël*, rushing to her rescue, finds she is none other than his own sweetheart.

ACT III

ALL is quiet and peaceful after the storm; herders and huntsmen are gathered together. *Hoël* brings the still senseless *Dinorah*, and lays her among them. Believing her dead, he bitterly reproaches himself, in the "Sei vendicata assai" (Thou art avenged). But she revives; and with her recovery, reason returns; *Hoël*, thinking she is treasure enough, gives up his futile hunt for a mythical fortune. All ends happily as the reunited lovers go home, and the curtain descends upon the preparations for the wedding.

THE VICTOR RECORDS

(Sung in Italian)

ACT II

OMBRA LEGGIERA
(Shadow Song) AMELITA GALLI-CURCI, Soprano   6129 12-in., $2.00

Light flitting shadow, companion gay
   Go not away!
Play here beside me, dark fears betide me
When thou dost go far from me!

Each coming morn I thee would find,
Ah prithee stay and dance with me!
If thou wilt stay, nor go away,
Thou thus shalt hear me sing.

Know'st thou not that Hoël loves me?
That as his bride he claims me!
Love well hath known
Our two hearts to unite!

ACT III

SEI VENDICATA ASSAI
(Thou Art Avenged) GIUSEPPE DE LUCA, Baritone   6443 12-in., 2.00

BLUE LABEL RECORD

{Ombra leggiera (Shadow Song)......................*Olive Kline, Soprano*}55047 12-in., 1.50
{ *Lucia—Mad Scene*................................*Olive Kline, Soprano*}

90

FROM A PAINTING   SCENE FROM DON CARLOS

DON CARLOS

OPERA in four acts. Libretto by Mèry and Du Locle; music by Verdi. First produced at Paris, March 11, 1867; in London, at Her Majesty's Theatre, June 4, 1867. Although it was revised and improved by Verdi in 1883, it is seldom given nowadays. Revived at La Scala, Milan, in 1912, more recently at Monte Carlo for Ruffo. New York, 1920.

CHARACTERS

(Original Paris Cast)

PHILIP II................Obin, Bass
DON CARLOS (*Kahr'-los*) Morère, Tenor
MARQUIS DE POSA....Faure, Baritone
GRAND INQUISITOR......Belval, Bass
ELIZABETH DE VALOIS (*duh-
Val-wah*).........Sass, Soprano
PRINCESS EBOLI..Gueymard, Soprano

DON CARLOS, son of *Philip II*, King of Spain, is in love with *Elizabeth de Valois*, daughter of Henry II of France. His affection is deep and sincere, and it is returned in equal measure. For reasons of state, however, *Elizabeth* is wedded not to *Don Carlos* but to *Philip II*, and the young prince therefore finds himself in love with his own stepmother. He confides in *Rodrigo, Marquis de Posa*, who entreats him to leave the Spanish court. The two pledge friendship in the beautiful "Dio che nell' alma infondere" (Infuse Friendship Into Our Souls O Lord!). *Carlos* therefore begs the *Queen* to obtain *Philip's* permission to join the Flemings in the struggle against the Spaniards. But as the *King* is secretly in favor with the Spanish tyrants the request only

91

angers him and further estranges father and son.

Don Carlos has a dangerous admirer in *Princess Eboli*, who learns that the *Queen* has by no means ceased to love *Don Carlos* though married to his father. *Princess Eboli* allows jealousy to get the better of her and she informs *King Philip* of the condition of affairs. This maddens the *King* still further, and, on the advice of the *Grand Inquisitor*, *Don Carlos* is thrown into prison. *Rodrigo* visits the *Prince* there, and is shot by the *King's* friends, who suspect him of aiding the Flemings. He bids farewell to earth in a beautiful aria, "O Carlo, Ascolta" (O Carlos, Hear Me), repeating a theme of the friendship duet. And even before this, filled with the idea of sacrificing his own liberty for that of *Don Carlos*, he has a noble aria, the "Per me giunto è il di supremo" (The Supreme Day). *Carlos* is freed, and goes to the Monastery of St. Just to keep tryst with *Elizabeth*. The *King* surprises them there, and his anger once more aroused, he hands over *Don Carlos* to the Offi-cers of the Inquisition, who bear him away to death as the curtain falls.

THE VICTOR RECORDS
(Sung in Italian)

ACT I

DIO CHE NELL' ALMA INFONDERE

(Infuse Friendship Into Our Souls, O Lord) Enrico Caruso, Tenor and Antonio Scotti, Baritone
8036 12-in., $2.50

Giovanni Martinelli, Tenor and Giuseppe de Luca, Baritone
8047 12-in., 2.50

PER ME GIUNTO È IL DI SUPREMO

(The Day Supreme) Mattia Battistini, Baritone
6044 12-in., 2.00

Giuseppe de Luca, Baritone
6078 12-in., 2.00

ACT III

O CARLO, ASCOLTA

(O Carlos, Listen to My Plea) Giuseppe de Luca, Baritone
593 10-in., 1.50

ELLA GIAMMAI M'AMÒ!

(Her Love was Never Mine!) Feodor Chaliapin, Bass
88665 12-in., 1.50

Marcel Journet, Bass
8047 12-in., 2.50

HASSANI, MILAN   DON CARLOS AT LA SCALA, MILAN—ACT II, SCENE II

DON GIOVANNI

(DON JUAN)

(Spanish)

MOZART wrote "Don Giovanni," perhaps the greatest of his works, on a stone table in a pleasant room at Koschirz, near Prague. For once he was happy. It was in September, 1787; from his window in the house of his friend Duschek (Dussek), he could look out upon the vine-crowned hills and their clusters of purple fruit. He had rooms in Prague, where his wife stayed, but he loved the house of his friend, where he could compose or play skittles as he willed. He played much skittles—but by the end of October the opera was complete! It was produced in Prague on October 29th. The night before, the overture was still unwritten; but Mozart worked all night, kept awake by his wife with stories and with punch. He had to rest a bit, but by seven in the morning, when the music copyists came, the work was done. It is no pot-pourri of the chief airs, but a masterly work, charged with the atmosphere of the drama—a perfect introduction. When the opera was produced that night, Mozart was welcomed with a fanfare of trumpets, and the kindly Bohemian audience greeted every number with rapture. Well they might! for never has melody more fresh and spontaneous, more copious in quantity, more delicately moulded in style, greeted human ears.

Familiarize yourself with these magical melodies! So sweet and simple on the surface, they possess deeper qualities than can be fathomed at first hearing. There is perhaps no emotion of which humanity is capable, which does not find expression in Mozart's music. With his uncanny artist's intuition, he penetrated the very souls of his characters.

THE OPERA

OPERA in two acts. Libretto by Lorenzo da Ponte. Music by Wolfgang Amadeus Mozart. First produced at Prague, October 29, 1787; at Vienna, May 7, 1788; at Berlin, 1791; Paris, 1811. First London production, April 12, 1817; an English adaptation, called "The Libertine," was given in Philadelphia, December 26, 1818, with Mr. and Mrs. Henry Wallach and Joseph Jefferson (grandfather of the favorite exponent of Rip Van Winkle); produced in New York May 29, 1826. Some notable revivals occurred in 1889 at Metropolitan Opera House, with Reichmann, Kalisch, Behrens and Fischer; in 1898 with Sembrich, Nordica, Eames and Plançon; in 1900 with Sembrich, Nordica and de Reszke; and at the Manhattan Opera in 1909 with Russ, Donalda, Bonci and Renaud.

CHARACTERS

DON GIOVANNI (*Joh-vahn'-nee*), a licentious young nobleman .... Baritone

DON OTTAVIO (*Ot-tah'-vee-oh*), betrothed to Donna Anna .... Tenor

LEPORELLO (*Lep-oh-rel'-loh*), servant of Don Giovanni .... Bass

DON PEDRO (*Pay-droh*), the Commandant .... Bass

DONNA ANNA, his daughter ... Soprano

MASETTO (*Mas-set'-toh*), a peasant .... Bass

93

ZERLINA (*Tsair-lee'-nah*), betrothed to Masetto . . . . Soprano
DONNA ELVIRA (*El-vee'-rah*), a
lady of Burgos . . . . Soprano
Peasants, Musicians, Dancers, Demons

*Scene and Period: Seville, in the Middle
of the Seventeenth Century*

(The opera is also known as "Don
Juan," *Don Wahn*).

ACT I

SCENE—*The Court of the Commandant's
Palace at Seville. Night. Donna
Anna's Window is partly open*

THE stage seems wholly dark, until
we discern, among fantastic moonlight shadows, the figure of *Leporello*.
He is awaiting his master, who is within, making love to *Donna Anna*. A
scream is heard, and *Don Giovanni*
rushes into the courtyard, followed by
the lady. Her father appears, with
lamp and sword. *Don Giovanni* par-
ries with coolness each trembling pass
of the aged swordsman. He strikes
the lamp from his hand, then runs him
through. Then he and *Leporello* escape. *Donna Anna* is joined by *Don
Ottavio*. Search is hopeless. Over the
dead body of her father, *Donna Anna*
then swears vengeance.

The scene shifts to a desolate spot, by
a mountain road, with an inn. The fugi-
tives conceal themselves as a carriage
approaches. A lady is seen within, and
Don Giovanni scents adventure. To his
dismay, however, he recognizes *Donna
Elvira*, whom he has wronged. Leaving
Leporello to explain, he makes off.

Leporello's consolation to the lady is
to read over the list of his master's
former victims—in the famous "Nella
bionda" (The Fair One), often known
as the "Catalogue Song." It reveals,
for all its musical beauty, the character
of *Leporello* as an oily braggart, a coward, a lackey by nature as well as

occupation. His music differs greatly
from the suave and courtly airs of his
master. Good-natured comedy appears, none the less.

Again the scene changes—to the
grounds of *Don Giovanni's* own estate.
A wedding is in progress, and peasants
are enjoying the festivities. *Don Giovanni* is disposed to join in the fun and
make love to the bride, *Zerlina*. *Masetto*, her betrothed, interferes, but the
Don touches his sword significantly,
and the poor wretch hopelessly follows the crowd to refreshments
under *Leporello*.

Zerlina is flattered by the *Don*, who
suggests she is too beautiful to wed
the bumpkinly *Masetto*. The duet
which follows, reveals admirably the
simple character of the girl and the
evil finesse of the *Don*. It is known
as "La ci darem la mano" (Thy Little
Hand, Love,) and it nearly proves the
ruin of *Zerlina*. But *Donna Elvira*
appears, smarting under *Leporello's*
insults, and she leads away the girl.
Then *Donna Anna* and *Don Ottavio*
appear, for the extraordinary purpose
of begging aid from *Don Giovanni* in
the search for the *Commandant's*
murderer! The *Don* promises aid,
and excuses himself to look after his
guests. *Donna Anna* confides to her
betrothed that she recognizes his voice.
When the two depart, *Don Giovanni*
returns with *Leporello*, whom he commends for having escorted *Donna
Elvira* to the palace gates, declaring
to the guests that she was ill when she
endeavored to "make a scene."

Once more the visible scene shifts,
to *Don Giovanni's* garden where
Zerlina is striving to make peace with
Masetto in the lovely air, "Batti,
batti" (Scold Me, Dear Masetto),
an air that is full of natural grace and
sweetness, hence a true revelation of
the character of *Zerlina*, who really
loves her great, hulking lover.

The *Don*, however, has not made mischief enough. With another shift of the scene, he lures her away from the dance, and from *Masetto*. We are unaware of this, however, until the screams of *Zerlina*, for help behind the scenes, electrify everyone. *Donna Anna*, *Donna Elvira* and *Don Ottavio* leading, all rush in. *Don Giovanni* is cornered. He listens defiantly, then with drawn sword, fights a way through and away.

ACT II

Scene—*A Square in Seville. Donna Elvira's Residence. Moonlight*

THE *Don* is no better. This time he is enamored of *Donna Elvira's* maid. He comes to serenade her, but for safety's sake has changed costumes with *Leporello*. He finds not the maid at the casement, but *Elvira*, whom he proceeds to woo in the old fashion. Unable to resist the *Don's* blandishments, the lady descends, when she is deftly passed over to *Leporello*, dressed as the *Don*—who makes a terrible outcry. The two run away, leaving him free to serenade the maid—in one of

the most remarkable of melodies, most perfect in form and lovely in spirit.

He is interrupted by *Masetto* with armed villagers. *Masetto* boasts of the drubbing he will give *Don Giovanni*. Asking to see the weapon, the *Don* beats *Masetto* and gets away. *Leporello* is captured and brought before *Donna Anna*, *Ottavio* and *Zerlina*. The wrong man, he is permitted to go free. He is comforted in the "Vedrai Carino," (Dearest, Shall I Tell Thee). *Don Ottavio* then sings, to comfort his beloved, the "Il Mio Tesoro" (Fly With Me) one of the loveliest airs in all music—a masterpiece, too, of voice-writing, with its smooth long-drawn phrases and deft embellishments.

There is an end of all easy things. *Don Giovanni* is next rejoined by *Leporello* in a square in Seville. The moon shines upon a newly-erected statue of *Don Pedro*. *Leporello* shudders, but *Don Giovanni* speaks to it—inviting it to a banquet the following night. The statue is seen to nod reply.

The scene changes to the banquet hall, where, among festivities, *Zerlina* once again appears to beg the *Don* to

Don Giovanni: Depart! or my sword shall teach thee obedience

95

repent. After she has left, screams are heard. *Leporello* is sent to investigate, and returns, white with dread, to announce the statue. The guests flee, but the *Don* offers his hand to the strange visitor. He is once again bidden to repent. For the last time he refuses. The statue sinks, flames arise, and *Don Giovanni* is carried off by demons to his eternal punishment.

THE VICTOR RECORDS

(Sung in Italian unless otherwise noted)

ACT I

NELLA BIONDA

(The Fair One) MARCEL JOURNET, Bass
6180   12-in., $2.00

LEPORELLO:

Ev'ry country, ev'ry township, fully confesses
Those of the sex whom to his rank he presses.
Gentle lady, this my catalogue numbers
All whose charms lent my master beguiling.
'Tis a document of my compiling,
And it please ye, peruse it with me.
In Italia,—six hundred and forty;
Then in Germany,—ten score and twenty;
As for France,—double fifty seem plenty;
While in old Spain here,—we count thousands three!
Some you see are country damsels,
Waiting-maids and city ma'amselles,
Countess', duchess', baronesses,
Viscount'—ev'ry kind of *'esses.*
Womenfolk of all conditions,
Ev'ry form and ev'ry state!
First the fair one's unthinking blindness
He would dazzle with honied speeches;
Toward the dark-ey'd all pure kindness,
With the blue-ey'd he beseeches;
Winter, he prefers the fatter,
Summer, thin girls suit him better.

LA CI DAREM LA MANO

(Thy Little Hand, Love!) GERALDINE FARRAR, Soprano and ANTONIO SCOTTI, Baritone   8023   12-in.,   2.50

ACT II

SERENATA—DEH VIENI ALLA FINESTRA

(Open Thy Window) TITTA RUFFO, Baritone   818   10-in.,   1.50

ANTONIO SCOTTI, Baritone
6283   12-in., $2.00

DON GIOVANNI:

Ope, ope thy casement, dearest,
  Thyself one moment show;
Oh, if my pray'r thou hearest,
  Wave but that arm of snow.
Canst thou my ceaseless sighing
  With cold indif'rence greet?
Ah! wouldst thou see me dying
  Despairing, at thy feet?
Thy lip outvies Hymettian-honied bowers,
Virtue worthy an angel thy heart doth cherish;
Thy sigh were balm amid a heav'n of flowers;
  Oh, for one kiss, one word, the soul would perish!

VEDRAI, CARINO

(Dearest, Shall I Tell Thee) LUCREZIA BORI, Soprano   543   10-in., $1.50

IL MIO TESORO

(To My Beloved) JOHN McCORMACK, Tenor   6204   12-in.,   2.00

OTTAVIO:

Fly then, my love, entreating,
  To calm her anxious fears;
Oh, still her heart's wild beating,
  And wipe away her tears.
Tell her I'll vengeance take
  On him who slew her sire;
This arm his grave shall make,
  Or I'll by his expire.

DONNE CURIOSE—"THE CLUB," ACT I

LE DONNE CURIOSE

MUSICAL comedy in three acts; libretto by Sugana; music by Wolf-Ferrari. Produced in Munich, November 27, 1903, as *Die Neugierigen Frauen*. First production in America at the Metropolitan, January 3, 1912, with Farrar, Jadlowker, Scotti and Lambert Murphy.

CHARACTERS

OTTAVIO, a rich Venetian (*Ot-tah'-vee-oh*)....................Bass
BEATRICE, his wife (*Bay-ah-tree'-cheh*)..................Soprano
ROSAURA, his daughter (*Ro-zow-rah*)...................Soprano
FLORINDO, betrothed to Rosaura (*Floh-rin'-doh*)...........Tenor
PANTALONE a Venetian merchant (*Pahn-tah-loh'-neh*)......Baritone
COLOMBINA, Rosaura's maid (*Koh-lom-bee'-nah*)......Soprano
ELEANORA.................Soprano

Servants, Gondoliers, Men and Women of the Populace

Time and Place: Venice; the Middle of the Eighteenth Century

(The name of the opera is pronounced *Leh Don'-neh Koo-ree-oh'-seh*).

LE DONNE CURIOSE (Inquisitive Women) is pure comedy. *Beatrice, Rosaura, Eleanora* and *Colombina* plot entrance to the Friendship clubhouse, of which their husbands and lovers are members. No women are admitted. Each has her own theory as to what goes on there. The beauty of the climax is that nothing does go on, except what is right and proper. The women, by bribing servants and wheedling a key from one of the clubmen, get into the house to find the men harmlessly at dinner. Everything ends with a dance.

There is a charming air, in Act II, "Il Cor nel contento" (My Heart, How It Leaps in Rejoicing), a love-duet between *Rosaura* and *Florindo*, her fiancé, sung after she has induced him to give up his key.

97

DON PASQUALE

COMIC opera in three acts; text and music by Gaetano Donizetti. Libretto adapted from the older Italian opera *Ser Marc' Antonio*, by Camerano. First presented at the *Théâtre des Italiens*, Paris, on January 4, 1843. First production in Paris, in French, 1864; London, June 30, 1843. First New York production March 9, 1846, in English, and in 1849 in Italian. Revived at the New Theatre, New York, December 23, 1909, with di Pasquali, Bonci, Scotti and Pini-Corsi; at the Metropolitan in 1913 with Sembrich, Scotti and Rossi.

CHARACTERS

DON PASQUALE, an old bachelor
(*Don Pas-quah'-leh*)........Bass
DR. MALATESTA, his friend, a physician (*Mah-lah-tes'-tah*)...Baritone
ERNESTO, nephew of Don Pasquale
(*Ayr-nes'-toh*).............Tenor
NORINA, beloved of Ernesto
(*Noh-ree'-nah*).........Soprano
A NOTARY.................Baritone

Chorus of Valets and Chambermaids, Majordomo, Dressmaker and Hairdresser

Scene and Period: Rome; the Beginning of the Nineteenth Century

ACT I

SCENE I—*A Room in Don Pasquale's House*

THERE is a jolly overture, and the opera begins without further ado. *Don Pasquale*, advanced in years, is angry with his nephew *Ernesto*, a bit of a scapegrace who has dared to fall in love with *Norina*, an unknown but probably scandalous young Roman lady, and to refuse a wealthy and respectable mate solemnly picked out for him. *Don Pasquale* decides to disinherit the youth, and get married himself. The only trouble is, to find a bride. For this purpose, he has called in his old friend *Dr. Malatesta*, who comes in to "report progress"—in the scene, "Son nov'ore" ('Tis Nine o'clock). The *Doctor* proposes *Sophronia*, his own sister.

Now at that, the *Doctor* is no fool. He has no sister, there is no *Sophronia*; but a practical joke, he thinks, will cure the *Don's* folly and help *Ernesto* to his *Norina*. The old *Don* pipes of the wedded bliss to be: "Un fece insolite" (A Fire All Unfelt). The friends are interrupted by *Ernesto*, who is urged to give up *Norina*. He of course refuses, and is told of the *Don's* intention. Knowing that, penniless, he cannot ask *Norina* to marry him, he gives up to despair, in the scene, "Sogno soave e caste" (Fond Dream of Love). Before leaving he implores his uncle to ask *Doctor Malatesta's* advice; he is dumbfounded when he is told that the *Doctor* originally suggested marriage, and presented his own sister as a proper bride. *Ernesto*, thinking himself betrayed by his best friend, writes a farewell note to *Norina*.

SCENE II—*A Room in Norina's House*

NOW *Norina* is no fool either; what is more, she trusts the *Doctor*. We find her reading a novel, from which she quotes a passage, "Qual Garde" (Glances So Soft). It sets her thinking upon her own gifts: "So anch'io la virtu magica" (Thy Virtues Know). In this sprightly number she declares she too knows the value of a glance and a smile. Then she receives *Ernesto's* letter. What can it mean? The solution arrives in the person of *Malatesta*, who comes to tell her she must undergo a mock-marriage with the *Don*, then make things hot for him so he will yearn for the pristine peace of his bachelor days—even at the cost of *Ernesto's* marriage with herself. *Norina* proves herself a girl of spirit. She at once begins to rehearse; "Pronta io son" (My Part I'll Play!) she sings. The details are worked out in the half-giddy duet which ends the act, "Vado Corro" (Haste We!).

ACT II

SCENE—*A Richly Furnished Hall; Don Pasquale's*

THE bridegroom, youthfully arrayed, is admiring himself and awaiting the arrival of brother and sister. They arrive, the bride heavily-veiled and shy as a mouse—which interests the elderly swain. The *Don* is in love—and his judgment somewhat obfuscated. He signs over half his property to *Sophronia* and makes her absolute mistress of the house. *Ernesto* appears, and things look bad for a moment, till the *Doctor* drags him aside and whispers an explanation. He then signs the marriage-contract as a witness.

Once a wife, *Norina* "shows her disposition." She refuses to kiss the bridegroom. *Ernesto* roars with laughter. The *Don* orders him out, and *Norina* flies at the *Don* like a wildcat. She tells him he is too old and fat and feeble for a young wife. As this is perfectly true, it sears like fire. She declares she must have a cavalier, and chooses *Ernesto*. The *Don* is enraged, and *Norina*, who is quite capable, threatens to beat him. She orders in the servants, acclaims herself mistress of the house, engages fresh servants, two carriages, new furniture, and plans to spend much money. The *Don*, in querulous rage, declares, "Son Tradito!" (I am Ruined!). *Ernesto* and *Norina*, behind his back, are capering with joy.

ACT III

SCENE I—*As in Act I*

THERE is a "rag on every bush." Floor and furniture are piled with dresses and bandboxes, hats, furs and lingerie, and *Don Pasquale* is half-demented—for he is facing the bills. *Norina* enters, dressed to go out. The poor old crock makes a last bid for authority, "Signorina in tanta fretta" (Why This Haste?) and he is told in so many words to hold his tongue. The *Don* flushes, and has his ears boxed. The lady flounces out, intentionally dropping a note which asks an appointment in the garden "between nine and ten." *Don Pasquale* reads it, baa's like a sheep, and totters out after *Malatesta*, who appears, in his absence, with *Ernesto*, whom he instructs to go into the garden at nine-thirty. The *Don* returns. "Brother-in-law," exclaims he, "You see in me a dead man walking upright." *Malatesta* is all sympathy, and proposes they watch for the guilty pair. The *Don* gloats over his coming triumph: "Aspetta, aspetta, cara esposina" (Wait, Wait, Dear Little Wife!).

SCENE II—*The Garden*

THE scene is a lovely one, and *Ernesto* is moved to song, in the lovely, strange and languorous air, "Com e' gentil" (Soft Beams the Light) a wandering strain, with long sustained notes and a seductive rhythm, with frequent pauses that never disturb it. *Norina* joins her lover, and they renew their vows in an equally lovely duet. But they see the *Don* and the *Doctor*, with dark lanterns that betray their every movement. The *Don* cannot restrain himself, and he runs forth, to find *Norina* alone, *Ernesto* having vanished. He threatens divorce, which *Malatesta* discountenances, for fear of publicity. He asks

99

the privilege to settle the affair, and suggests that the bride be allowed to share the house with *Ernesto's* bride, a certain *Norina*. "*Sophronia*" protests furiously, when he suggests that she wed *Ernesto* herself. The *Don* brightens a bit—he will agree to anything to get rid of his lady-love.

Ernesto appears, and the affair is settled. It is then confessed to the *Don*, who at first is hurt, but who soon relents—as he is a good old fellow at heart, and can enjoy a good joke, even against himself; especially as there is nothing else to be done.

THE VICTOR RECORDS

(Sung in Italian)

OVERTURE—Part I and Part II
Toscanini and La Scala Orchestra
841   10-in., $1.50

ACT I

CAVATINA—QUEL GUARDO
(Glances So Soft) AMELITA GALLI-CURCI,
Soprano   6128   12-in.,   2.00

VADO CORRO
(Haste We) LUCREZIA BORI, Soprano
and GIUSEPPE DE LUCA, Baritone
8004   12-in.,   2.50

PRONTA IO SON
(My Part I'll Play) LUCREZIA BORI, Soprano and GIUSEPPE DE LUCA, Baritone   8004   12-in.,   2.50

ACT III

SERENATA—COM' E GENTIL
(Soft Beams the Light) GIOVANNI MARTINELLI, Tenor and Metropolitan Opera Chorus   734   10-in.,   1.50

COPY'T MISHKIN
BORI AS NORINA—ACT II

DULCAMARA EXPOUNDING THE ELIXIR—ACT I
(CARUSO AND DE LUCA)

ELIXIR OF LOVE

(L'ELISIR D'AMORE)
(*Italian*)

THE ancient belief in love-philtres and charms has supplied the theme for many a sparkling comedy. The present one, with its vivacity and tingle, incited Donizetti to bring forth many of his gayest and lightest melodies. Indeed, the opera has all the essentials of a first-class play in the lighter vein, the story telling of *Adina*, a lively but sensible village beauty and heiress, with whom *Nemorino*, a poor but honest peasant, is seized with a love which triumphs alike over the too-gallant *Sergeant Belcore*, and that insinuating and plausible quack, the travelling *Doctor Dulcamara*.

THE OPERA

OPERA in two acts. Text by Romani. Music by Gaetano Donizetti. First produced in Milan, May 12, 1832; Barcelona, 1833; Paris, 1839; Berlin, 1844. First London production December 10, 1836. First American production at the New Orleans Opera March 30, 1842. Given in Boston in English by the Seguins shortly afterward. The Boston Ideal Opera Company presented an English version in 1887, with the title of "Adina." Revived in 1904 at the Metropolitan with Sembrich, Caruso, Scotti and Rossi; at the Manhattan Opera in 1909, with Binkert, Bonci, Gilibert and Trentini; and in 1916 at the Metropolitan Opera, with Hempel, Caruso and de Luca.

CHARACTERS

ADINA, a wealthy and independent young woman (*Ah-dee'-nah*) .... Soprano

NEMORINO, a young peasant, in love with Adina (*Nem-o-ree'-noh*) .... Tenor

BELCORE, sergeant of the village garrison (*Bell-ko'-ray*) ...... Bass

DOCTOR DULCAMARA, a quack doctor (*Dool-kah-mah'-rah*) .... Buffo

101

A Landlord, a Notary, Peasants, Soldiers, Villagers

Scene and Period: A Little Italian Village; the Nineteenth Century

(The Italian name of the opera is pronounced *Lay-lee-seer' Dam-oh'-reh*).

ACT I

SCENE—*The Homestead of Adina's Farm*

IT is a glorious summer day. Surrounded by her friends, *Adina* sits reading a romance. From a distance the love-sick *Nemorino* gazes in a rapture that finds expression only in song—the aria, "Quant'e bella" (Oh, How Lovely!).

A burst of laughter from *Adina* startles everyone. She reads the legend of Tristan and Isolde, in which the knight wins the lady's affections by means of a wonderful elixir.

Nemorino, "sighing like furnace," can find no mirth in such a tale, and he longs, bumpkin-like, for some of the draught. He is disturbed by the sound of martial music. The dashing *Sergeant Belcore* appears with a bouquet for *Adina*, which he presents with an audacity that scares *Nemorino*. The lady, however, is not so easily won. Finding courage, *Nemorino* contrives, when the party breaks up, to obtain a word with his beloved. *Adina*, however, cares little for the doleful countenance of her lover; she tells him that while she respects him, she cannot marry him. No one can blame the girl; *Nemorino* is a worthy young fellow, but poor, and dull. If only his lover's sighs were leavened with some of the *Sergeant's* gayety! *Adina* tells him to go visit his rich uncle, who is ill at a nearby village.

Her delight in dismissing him is interrupted by a terrible rumpus. The great *Doctor Dulcamara* rides in, in his splendid carriage, with a whole trunkful of nostrums. These will cure every-thing, from apoplexy to rickets—according to the *Doctor*.

Nemorino listens open-eared, and he gazes open-eyed—and open-mouthed. He wonders if such a master-physician may not have in his possession the elixir that won Isolde for Tristan. He questions the *Doctor*, who is puzzled, but quick-witted like all of his clan. He declares he possesses it, and assures *Nemorino* it tastes just like wine. Figuring that in a few hours he will have left the village, the *Doctor* warns *Nemorino* not to expect results until the next day. His back is no sooner turned than *Nemorino* vigorously applies himself to the bottle.

Nemorino feels exalted. *Adina*, coming in, finds him singing and dancing. She is disposed to humor him, but he disregards her; he will teach her a lesson! *Nemorino's* dignity is gone; he is uproarious in a new and by no means dull fashion. In plain language, *Nemorino* is "tight."

Adina is yet more mystified. She coquets with the *Sergeant*; *Nemorino* laughs, and the indignant girl engages herself to marry *Belcore* within three days. *Nemorino* finds this a grand suggestion, and he whoops with laughter. The time is reduced to twenty-four hours. Then the *Sergeant* receives orders for departure on the morrow. *Nemorino* has a sudden chill; he sobers quickly, and pleads with *Adina*, but in vain.

ACT II

SCENE—*The Farmhouse Interior*

THERE is a great wedding-day feast. *Dulcamara*, scenting a free meal, has remained over, and he is sharing honors with the *Sergeant*. He sings a duet—the latest barcarolle from Venice—with the bride-elect. The notary arrives, and the party repairs to an inner room to sign the marriage contract. *Dulcamara* remains loyal to the table. To him comes *Nemorino*, whose uncle is dying, and whose sweetheart is marrying another. And the Elixir did not work! *Dulcamara* prescribes another bottle, but *Nemorino* has not the price. The *Doctor* places it in his pocket and walks off, declaring he will be at the inn for an hour. *Belcore* succeeds him. *Nemorino* desperately confides to *Belcore* he has no money. A thought strikes *Belcore*, and he urges him to enlist as a soldier, when he will receive twenty crowns. This colloquy takes the form of a wonderfully melodious duet, "Venti Scudi" (Twenty Crowns), in

NEMORINO:
"Night and day, in every object,
I do see and hear but thee, love!"
(CARUSO AND HEMPEL—ACT I)

which the tempter achieves an excellent stroke of business; he gets *Nemorino*, as he believes, permanently out of his way.

Nemorino makes sure of the Elixir, and the *Sergeant* of an excellent recruit. Meanwhile *Adina* develops a lachrymose fit, becoming astonishingly tearful, even for a happy bride—the more so when she sees *Nemorino*, freshly heartened by the second bottle, approaching among sixteen girls. *Adina* being only human, capitulates. *Nemorino*, seeing her tears, is convinced the Elixir has worked. He sings the lovely romance, "Una Furtiva Lagrima" (A Furtive Tear).

It now transpires that *Adina* has left the marriage-feast, cancelling her marriage with *Belcore*, from whom she has brought back *Nemorino's* discharge. She does not understand, however, the real reason why the tipsy but somehow loyal *Nemorino* has become so suddenly popular with the girls. It transpires that his uncle has left him his fortune. *Belcore*, declaring there are "other women in the world," is dismissed. The contract is made out for *Nemorino*. The Elixir is justified, and *Dulcamara* sells many bottles.

THE VICTOR RECORDS
(Sung in Italian)

ACT II

VENTI SCUDI
(Twenty Crowns) ENRICO CARUSO, Tenor and GIUSEPPE DE LUCA, Baritone   8006   12-in., $2.50

UNA FURTIVA LAGRIMA
(A Furtive Tear) ENRICO CARUSO, Tenor   6016   12-in.,   2.00
JOHN McCORMACK, Tenor 6204   12-in.,   2.00

Down her soft cheek a pearly tear
  Stole from her eyelids dark,
Telling their gay and festive cheer,
  It pained her soul to mark;
Why then her dear presence fly?
  When all her love she is showing?
Could I but feel her beating heart
  Pressing against mine own;
Could I my feeling soft impart, and mingle
  sigh with sigh,
  But feel her heart against mine own,
Gladly I then would die,
  All her love knowing!

PHOTO BYRON   SCENE FROM ORIGINAL PRODUCTION OF ERMINIE

ERMINIE

THE story of this favorite comic opera comes from the old melodrama, "Robert Macaire." Though Jakobowski has produced other comic operas—"Paolo," "The Three Beggars," "Dick," "Mynheer Jan," "A Venetian Singer," none has rivaled it in favor. The music is light and dainty, the most popular single number being the ever-delightful "Lullaby."

THE OPERA

COMIC opera in two acts. Text by Claxson Bellamy and Harry Paulton; music by Edward Jakobowski. First production at the Comedy Theatre, London, November 9, 1885. First American production at the Casino, New York, March 10, 1886, where it had the unprecedented run of more than twelve hundred performances at that house alone. The operetta has had a number of successful revivals in recent years, the names of Francis Wilson and of De Wolf Hopper being most frequently associated with the comedy rôles.

CHARACTERS

(Original American Cast)

CADEAUX (*Cah-doh'*), a thief
Francis Wilson

RAVANNES (*Rah-vahn'*), a thief
W. S. Daboll

MARQUIS DE POMVERT (*duh Pahm-vair*) . . . . Carl Irving

ERMINIE, his daughter (*Ayr'-ma-nee*) . . . . Pauline Hall

JAVOTTE (*Zha-vot'*) . . . . . Marie Jansen

EUGENE MARCEL, the Marquis' secretary . . . . Harry Pepper

CHEVALIER DE BRABAZON, Marquis' guest (*Brah-bah-zawn*)
Max Freeman

CERISE MARCEL, Eugene's sister . . . . Marion Manola

PRINCESS DE GRAMPONEUR (*Grahm-poh-nuhr*) Jennie Weathersby

VICOMTE DE BRISSAC (*Bree'-sak*) . . . . C. L. Weeks

Sergeant, Soldiers, Peasants, Acrobats, Clowns, Lords, Ladies, etc.

Time and Place: France; the Last Century

104

ERMINIE, daughter of the *Marquis de Pomvert*, is affianced to *Ernest de Brissac*, a young nobleman she has never seen. But she loves *Eugene Marcel*, the *Marquis'* secretary. She and her father have come to the inn to meet *de Brissac*,—who has been robbed and bound to a tree by two rascals, *Ravannes* and *Cadeaux*. These two arrive at the inn, where *Ravannes*, learning the circumstances, decides to pass himself off as *de Brissac*. He explains his tattered appearance as the result of highway robbery, and is taken to the castle. The true *de Brissac* arrives, and is arrested as the man who has robbed *Ravannes*.

Ravannes cannot quite live up to the rôle, and the suspicions of the *Marquis* arise. He confides them to *Erminie*, who tells him of her love for *Marcel*. Deeply touched, he informs her, nevertheless, that although, for her mother's sake, he would like her to be happy, neither he nor she can go back on the promise of betrothal. She outwardly agrees, but her true feelings are charmingly expressed in the "Lullaby." *Ravannes* gains her confidence, and she unwittingly aids him in his plan to rob the house by confessing that she is about to elope with *Marcel*. The plans of both are discovered, and *Ravannes* is arrested. *De Brissac* arrives only to explain that he is not the man *Erminie* was to marry, but a younger brother, and himself betrothed to *Cerise, Marcel's* sister. The elder *de Brissac*, the fiancé of *Erminie*, is dead. There being no further obstacle, *Erminie* and *Marcel* are duly betrothed.

THE VICTOR RECORD

LULLABY

MABEL GARRISON, Soprano with Mixed
    Chorus   6137 12-in., $2.00

DOUBLE-FACED RECORDS

{ Lullaby . . . . *Elsie Baker, Contralto* } 17345 10-in., $0.75
{ *Message of the Violet* . . . . *Olive Kline, Soprano* }

{ Selection . . . . *Victor Concert Orchestra* }
    "Soldiers' Chorus"—"Downy Jail-Birds of a Feather"—"Dream
    Song"—"Darkest the Hour"—"What the Dicky Birds Say"—"Lul- } 35583 12-in., 1.25
    laby"—Finale
{ *Chimes of Normandy Selection* . . . . *Victor Concert Orchestra* }

{ Gems from "Erminie" . . . . *Victor Light Opera Co.*
    Opening Chorus, "A Soldier's Life"—"When Love is Young All the
    World is Gay"—"Join in the Pleasure"—"What the Dicky Birds
    Say"—"Lullaby"—"Deign Pray to Cheer Each Heart"—"Marriage } 35451 12-in., 1.25
    is a Holy Union"—"Away to the Chateau"
{ *Gems from "Florodora"* . . . . *Victor Light Opera Co.* }

THE TOMB OF CHARLEMAGNE—ACT IV

ERNANI

THOUGH an early work, "Ernani" is one of the most melodious of all Verdi's operas. When first produced, it was hailed by many as an important contribution to the art of the time. London and Paris were less enthusiastic.

Its actual production was not un-eventful. In Venice the police complained of the conspiracy scene in the third act, as likely to incite volatile Italians to rebellion. An elderly noble-man complained of the hunting-horn used in the closing scene, as a desecration of music and its temple, the opera-house! A more valid objection came from Victor Hugo, who resented the fashion in which the librettist had treated his book, and the melodramatic atmosphere that had been thrown about a finely conceived written tragedy. Nevertheless the work marked

an advance in Verdi's long climb to the towering heights of "Aïda," "Falstaff" and "Otello." And Hugo must be excused if he failed to find, in occasionally bombastic passages, the strivings of a mind as tempestuous, and as ceaseless, in its efforts at genuine self-expression, as his own.

THE OPERA

OPERA in four acts. Libretto adapted by Maria Piave; from Victor Hugo's drama "Hernani"; music by Giuseppe Verdi. First performance in Venice, March 9, 1844. First London production at Her Majesty's Theatre, March 8, 1845. At its Paris *première*, January 6, 1846, the libretto was altered at Victor Hugo's request, the characters being made Italians and the name of the opera changed to *Il Proscritto*. First

106

New York production, 1846, at the Astor Place; in Boston, 1856. Produced at the French Opera, New Orleans, April 13, 1858.

CHARACTERS

DON CARLOS, King of Castile. Baritone
DON RUY GOMEZ DE SILVA, a
    Grandee of Spain (*Day Seel'-
    vah*)..................... Bass
ERNANI, a bandit chief........ Tenor
DON RICCARDO, an esquire of the
    King................... Tenor
IAGO, an esquire of Don Silva
    (*Ee-ah'-goh*)............... Bass
ELVIRA, betrothed to Don Silva
    (*El-vee'-rah*) .... Soprano
GIOVANNA, in attendance upon her
    (*Jeoh-vah'-nah*) ... Mezzo-Soprano
Chorus of Mountaineers and Bandits,
    Followers of Don Silva, Ladies of
    Elvira, Followers of the King,
    Spanish and German No-
    bles and Ladies, Elec-
    tors and Pages

Scene and Period: Aragon; about 1519

(The name of the opera is pronounced *Ayr-nah'-nee*).

ACT I

SCENE I—*The Mountains of Aragon*

ON the summit of a rocky mountain stands a solitary figure—gazing down a valley, with an expression of sadness, toward a Moorish castle, faintly visible in the blue mountain-shadows. He is Don Juan of Aragon, Duke and Count of Segorbe and Cardona; but to the district around him he is better known as *Ernani*, a chief of brigands. His father has been murdered, in cold blood, by *Don Carlos*, King of Castile, and he himself has been driven from the land of his ancestors to become nothing more than leader of a band of assassins who recognize no law but his will. One thing remains out of the past—his love for *Elvira*, who is to be married to *Don Silva*, her guardian, whose castle, in the valley, is disappearing in the night-shadows.

While *Ernani* stands pondering, his followers at the foot of the rock, make merry about the camp-fire, and their songs are heard as the curtain rises: "Beviam, Beviam" (Comrades, Let's Drink and Play). Their chief joins them. They note his melancholy appearance, and they listen in silence as he tells them how his love is to marry the elderly *Don Silva*. The story is recounted in the aria, "Come rugiada al cespite" (The Sweetest Flow'r). It is one of great tenderness and beauty, conceived in Verdi's earlier style. It has all the vocal flourish, the sustained pause-note, the clearly defined melody which characterize the Italian opera of his time; but its pathos and expressiveness are worthy of the composer at his best. The bandits pledge their service—to help prevent the wedding, and a plan is quickly formed.

SCENE II—*Elvira's Apartment in the Castle*

ELVIRA loves *Ernani*, and with equal love. She sits alone in her chamber, awaiting sacrifice. Grief-stricken, almost hysterical, she calls to her lover for aid—though he is far beyond hearing. "Ernani, Involami" (Ernani, Fly With Me), is a coloratura number, rich in vocal display, but beneath its surface, a true under-current, run the authentic accents of despair.

Young girls, bearing bridal gifts, enter to congratulate *Elvira*. She thanks them, but the tears are hard to withhold. Finally she gets rid of them—when she is amazed to discover a man in the room. It proves to be *Don Carlos*, King of Castile, not only the murderer of *Ernani's* father, but a secret admirer of her own. She pleads with him to leave.

His reply is a declaration of love—the "Da quel di che t'ho veduta" (From the Day When First Thy Beauty); and the *King* is a fiery lover. *Elvira* is terrified—the more when he threatens force. The girl draws a dagger, and threatens to slay her assailant, then herself. The *King* is about to summon his guard, when a secret panel opens in the wall, and *Ernani* appears. The men quarrel, *Elvira* trying to protect her lover. The sounds of strife attract *Don Silva*, who rushes in, astonished to find two men fighting over his bride on her wedding-eve. The aria "Infelice e tu credevi" (Unhappy One!) follows.

Heaping reproaches on *Elvira*, he summons aid, and calls for his armor and sword. Then, at the entry of one of the *King's* squires, he recognizes, for the first, just who is fighting. He cannot rebel against his own sovereign—at least not openly. He swallows down his rage, and bends his knee before *Don Carlos*, saying, "Duty to my King cancels all offences." The *King* accepts this homage in the quartet, "Verdi come il buon vegliardo" (Well I Know My Trusty Vassal), which follows, bringing the act to an end. The *King* is impressed with *Don Silva's* easy compliance, but a retainer warns him that underneath this, the old courtier nourishes a fiery and vengeful heart. *Ernani* is allowed to go, at a word from the *King*, *Elvira* urging him to fly. *Don Silva*, with smooth diplomacy, expresses delight to entertain his royal visitor. What the *King* thinks, for the present is not told. But circumstance, working against Kings as against commoners is not idle.

VAN DYCK AS ERNANI

ACT II

SCENE—*A Hall in Silva's Castle*

IT is the wedding-morn. Knights, pages and ladies-in-attendance sing praises of the noble *Silva* and his bride. All is smooth, serene; *Elvira* has been told that *Ernani* is dead.

To *Silva*, who is dressed like a Grandee of Spain, enters *Iago*, an attendant, announcing a holy man who craves hospitality. As to give this confers a blessing upon the giver, he is welcomed. Suddenly, throwing off his cloak, he reveals himself as *Ernani*. He has been hard-pressed, and defeated, by the *King*. And in desperation he has sought sanctuary with his enemy, *Don Silva*. Under the old chivalry, this is sacred, and the guest must be protected, even at the cost of life. But on learning that *Don Silva* is at last to wed *Elvira*, he begs his host to deprive him of the life he has ceased to value.

Don Silva, however, is punctiliously conscious of his duties as host. He refuses to harm a man he has voluntarily given sanctuary; the outward forms and ceremonies of life, to the old courtier, mean life itself. Suddenly word is brought that the *King* and his retainers are without. Orders are given to admit him, and *Ernani* is concealed in a secret passage. The *King* enters, demanding the outlaw, but *Don Silva* refuses, point blank, to surrender his guest. The soldiers search the castle, but vainly. The *King* threatens ("Lo vedremo") when *Elvira* begs for mercy. The *King* paints for her a bright future as his queen, and finally grants her request, but insists on taking her with him as a hostage.

PHOTO LARCHER   ELVIRA'S APARTMENT—ACT I

Scarcely have the *King* and his followers gone with *Elvira*, than *Silva's* hatred against the *King* bursts forth. Then he remembers *Ernani*, the cause of his loss; and releasing the bandit, he takes two swords from the armory and challenges him to combat: "A te scegli, seguini" (Choose Thy Sword, and Follow!). *Ernani* refuses to fight; he is taunted with fear, but both know better. He has voluntarily yielded his life to the man who has saved him from the *King* at the risk of torture. He asks, however, a last talk with *Elvira*, and is told she has gone with the *King* as hostage. The men combine against their mutual foe; but remembering his life is now *Silva's*, *Ernani* gives him a hunting-horn, and swears, by the memory of his dead father, that when the horn is blown, he shall return to yield up his life,

whenever it may be claimed of him. *Silva* accepts, and they swear vengeance upon the *King*, *Don Carlos*.

ACT III

SCENE—*A Vault in the Catacombs of Aix-la-Chapelle*

TWO figures enter, by torchlight, among the tombs of kings, one of which bears the legend, "Charlemagne." To the tomb of his ancestor, *Don Carlos*, the *King*, has come to overhear a conspiracy against his life. He has changed since the preceding events, is depressed and melancholy, and he pledges himself to better deeds should the Electors, now in session, proclaim him Emperor: "O de verd' anni miei" (Oh Bright and Fleeting Shadows), a beautiful, grave sustained cantilena, tells all. A sound is heard, and the conspirators assemble. *Ernani* is

109

chosen to assassinate the *King*. *Don Silva* begs this honor, offering for it to return the hunting-horn. *Ernani*, thinking of his father, refuses and is hailed with honor: "O sommo Carlo" (O Noble Carlos). This great ensemble is interrupted by the booming of cannon which announce that *Carlos* has been elected Emperor. At the same time the *King* appears from the tomb of Charlemagne. For a moment the conspirators believe it is the ghost of the great monarch; but they are undeceived and surrounded, and the *King* condemns them to death. *Elvira* once more pleads for mercy, and once more is successful. As an act of grace, the newly-elected *Emperor* pardons all, and even restores *Ernani* to his former rank and unites him with *Elvira*.

All glorify the new sovereign; but *Don Silva* now secretly desires vengeance against both *Ernani* and the *Emperor, Don Carlos*.

ACT IV

Scene—*Terrace of a Palace in Aragon*

THE tragedy is swiftly consummated. Another wedding scene appears—this time the wedding of *Elvira* and *Ernani*. Masquers, pages, ladies, greet the happy pair. The lovers, in bridal attire, emerge from the ball-room on their way to their own apartments. "Ferma, crudel estinguere" (Stay Thee, My Lord!).

Suddenly a blast from a horn is heard. *Ernani's* blood freezes. *Elvira* asks, "What is it?" A second time, and a third, the fatal call rings out. *Don Silva* has come to claim his debt. He offers *Ernani* the choice between a dagger and a cup of poisoned wine. *Ernani*, bound by his oath, takes the dagger, and before his bride, stabs himself. *Elvira* falls across his body, as the curtain descends upon *Don Silva's* revenge.

THE VICTOR RECORDS

(Sung in Italian)

ACT I

COME RUGIADA AL CESPITE
(The Sweetest Flow'r) GIOVANNI MARTINELLI, Tenor   737 10-in., $1.50

ERNANI INVOLAMI
(Ernani, Fly with Me) ROSA PONSELLE, Soprano   6440 12-in., 2.00
  Ernani, fly with me;
  Prevent this hated marriage!
  With thee, e'en the barren desert
  Would seem an Eden of enchantment!
  One nightless, unending day!
  One Eden of enchantment!

ACT II

LO VEDREMO, O VEGLIO AUDACE
(I Will Prove, Audacious Greybeard)
  TITTA RUFFO, Baritone 818 10-in., 1.50

ACT III

O DE' VERD' ANNI MIEI
(Oh Bright and Fleeting Shadows)
  GIUSEPPE DE LUCA, Baritone
                        6077 12-in., 2.00
  TITTA RUFFO, Baritone 6264 12-in., 1.50

THE DUEL SCENE

EUGEN ONÉGIN

PUSHKIN'S poem, written in 1833, is familiar to most Russians. The libretto, in three acts, follows it closely, the text being by Tschaikowsky and Shilowsky. The music is by Peter Iljitch Tschaikowsky. The opera never has reached perhaps, in the United States at least, the attention merited by its fine style and its dramatic moments. Scenes from it were given in New York, 1914. Walter Damrosch later gave it in concert form.

THE OPERA

OPERA in three acts. First produced at St. Petersburg, 1879, following a performance by the students of the Moscow Conservatory in March, 1879. First Berlin performance, 1888; in Hamburg, 1892. First London production in 1892; revived at Covent Garden in 1906 with Emmy Destinn as *Tatiana*. Produced, New York, 1920.

CHARACTERS

MADAM LERIN, a landed proprietress

TATIANA ⎫
OLGA   ⎬ her daughters

FILIPEVNA, a waiting-woman
EUGEN ONÉGIN, a Russian gallant
LENSKI, his friend
PRINCE GREMIN, a captain
TRIQUET, a Frenchman

Scene and Period: The Action takes place upon a Landed Estate and in St. Petersburg; Second Decade of the Nineteenth Century

(The French pronunciation is approximately *Oo-zhain Oh-nay-gheen;* Russian, *Yev-ghay'-nee Ohn-yay-gheen*).

111

ACT I

AT *Mme. Lerin's* shabby country-house near Petrograd, this lady and her daughters, *Tatiana* and *Olga*, with a servant, are making preserves. *Mme. Lerin* tells of an old romance—an officer who sang divinely but who married another. *Olga's* fiancé, *Lenski*, enters, bringing with him a friend, *Eugen Onégin. Tatiana* and *Onégin* wander off, while *Lenski* pours a love-song into the ears of *Olga. Onégin* is bored by simple *Tatiana*, who, by contrast, is delighted.

That night *Tatiana* writes to *Onégin* confessing her love, and asking a meeting. She cannot sleep. In the morning she gives the note to *Filipevna* to deliver. In the second scene she waits at the trysting place. *Onégin* appears, but is cold. He explains he is flattered but has no taste for domestic life. The girl's dream is shattered, as was her mother's.

ACT II

MME. LERIN gives a ball—for plain, bucolic neighbors, who bore *Onégin*.

Exasperated with *Lenski*, he flirts with *Olga*. Meantime a ridiculous foreigner, *Triquet*, flirts with *Tatiana*, and insists on reciting her his poems. She is compelled to listen while *Onégin* dances with her reckless sister. She can contain herself, but *Lenski* cannot. He picks a quarrel with *Onégin*, and a duel is set. The following morning, near the village mill, awaiting, he sings the strange, melancholy, but beautiful "Echo lointain de ma jeunesse" (A Distant Echo of My Youth), with its marvelously unfolding harmonies and acute climax. *Lenski* dreams of his early days, his love for *Olga*. The duel is fought in the snow and *Lenski* falls. *Onégin* realizes the folly of his acts. For jealousy he has killed his friend.

ACT III

FOR six years *Onégin* has travelled, tired of life. Returning, he attends a reception at the home of his cousin, *Prince Gremin*. In the princess he recognizes *Tatiana*, transformed into a lovely and sophisticated woman of the world. He is captivated, while *Tatiana* is strangely moved. Later he discovers her alone, weeping over the letter she had sent him. He declares his new-found passion. It is her moment for revenge, but she loves him—with the lifelong affection of a simple-minded woman. For a moment she sinks into his arms; but her sanity returns, and she tears herself loose, bids him a swift good-bye and darts from the room. *Onégin*, cheated either by himself or by Life (and who can say which?), cries out in his despair. The curtain falls.

THE VICTOR RECORDS

AIR DE LENSKI
("Echo lointain de ma jeunesse!"— Faint Echo of My Youth) ENRICO CARUSO, Tenor *In French*
6017 12-in., $2.00
GIOVANNI MARTINELLI, Tenor, *In Italian*
6195 12-in., 2.00

FORD CUDGELLING FALSTAFF, WHO IS DISGUISED AS THE OLD WOMAN OF BRENTFORD—ACT IV

FALSTAFF

THAT Verdi nearly in his eight-ieth year should have written one of the greatest of all operas in the comic vein is a matter of continual marvel. This has been more fully dis-cussed, however, in the account of "Otello."

COMIC opera in three acts. Text by Boïto, taken from Shake-speare's *Merry Wives of Windsor*. Music by Verdi. First production, Milan, March, 1893. Berlin produc-tion June 1, 1893; Vienna, 1893; Buenos Aires, 1893; Paris, 1894. First London production May 19, 1894. First North American production at the Metropolitan, New York, February 4, 1895, with Eames, Maurel, Scalchi, de Lussan and Campanari. Revived in 1909 with Scotti, Destinn, Alda, Gay, Ranzenberg and Campanari.

CHARACTERS

(Original Metropolitan Cast)

SIR JOHN FALSTAFF Baritone..Maurel
FENTON, a young gentleman
                  Tenor..Russitano
FORD, a wealthy burgher
           Baritone Campanari
DR. CAIUS, a physician Tenor...Vanni

BARDOLPH	followers	Tenor
PISTOL	of Falstaff	Rinaldini
		Bass Nicolini

MRS. ALICE FORD.Soprano....Eames
NANETTE, her daughter
            Soprano....de Lussan
MRS. QUICKLY...Contralto....Scalchi
MRS. MEG PAGE
          Mezzo-Soprano...de Vigne

ACT I

THE opera, under the loving hands of Boïto and Verdi, holds close to the Shakespearian model. The work opens at the Garter Inn, where *Fal-staff*, a potbellied, vainglorious, choleric old rogue, is with his friends *Bardolph*, *Pistol* and the innkeeper. *Dr. Caius* arrives and quarrels with him, but is thrown out. *Falstaff* then writes his extraordinary love-letters, one to *Mis-tress Page* and the other to *Mistress Ford.*

In *Ford's* garden, the two women compare the letters, finding them both alike, so with the help of *Mistress Quickly*, they plan a revenge in which the men, *Ford, Fenton*, and *Dr. Caius* give aid, together with *Bardolph* and *Pistol*,who have a bone to pick with *Fal-staff*. *Fenton* is there because he loves

113

Nanette, the daughter of *Mistress Ford* though *Nanette's* father plans to marry her to *Dr. Caius*. *Mistress Quickly* is sent to invite *Falstaff* to an interview with *Mistress Ford*, and the men arrange to have *Bardolph* and *Pistol* introduce that lady's husband to *Falstaff* under an assumed name.

ACT II

MISTRESS QUICKLY delivers her message and *Ford*, introduced as Signor Fortuna, offers money to the fat knight to intercede for him with *Mistress Ford*. *Ford* swallows his jealousy while the braggart knight is arraying

BYRON   FALSTAFF GETS IN THE BASKET—ACT II

himself for the adventure. *Falstaff* is quite ready to "intercede" for Signor Fortuna.

Falstaff arrives at *Ford's* house. He sings here the boastful "Quand' ero paggio" (When I Was Page). But *Mistress Quickly* arrives and he is compelled to hide himself behind a screen. As soon as she has departed, the men arrive, and *Falstaff* this time has to hide in a large clothes-basket, thoughtfully provided by the artful women. The men, however, hear a sound suspiciously like a kiss, and pulling down the screen, discover *Fenton* and *Nanette* in an unrehearsed love affair of their own. *Ford* is now fully

enraged, and *Fenton* is driven out in disgrace. When the men again resume the search, the "merry wives" order the clothes-basket to be thrown out into a ditch, where the escaping knight affords the crowd some gaiety.

ACT III

ONCE back at the inn, *Falstaff* receives yet another invitation through *Mistress Quickly*, the new adventure planned by the men. He is to meet a "lady" at Herne's Oak, a haunted spot in the Windsor forest. On condition that he keeps the appointment disguised as *Nanette*, *Dr. Caius* is offered the hand of that lady in marriage by *Ford*. The women, however, are determined to block this bit of enterprise, and arrange that *Fenton*, arrayed as a monk, shall upset the plans of *Dr. Caius*. *Falstaff* is superstitious and only with terror does he keep tryst at the haunted place. He and *Mistress Ford* are terrified by the declaration that the Wild Huntsman is approaching. The knight is then captured and given a sound lambasting by the men, disguised as elves and fairies. *Dr. Caius*, believing the Fairy Queen to be *Nanette*, discovers that he has been flirting with the disguised *Bardolph*. *Ford* realizes that he can no longer interfere with the will of destiny and gives his sanction to the marriage of *Nanette* with the faithful *Fenton*. All ends happily —except for the luckless *Falstaff*.

THE VICTOR RECORDS

ACT I

L'ONORE! LADRI!
(Your Honor! Ruffians!) TITTA RUFFO,
   Baritone *In Italian*   6264   12-in., $2.00

ACT II

QUAND' ERO PAGGIO
(When I Was Page) ANTONIO SCOTTI,
   Baritone *In Italian*   6283   12-in.,   2.00
TITTA RUFFO, Baritone *In Italian*
                     876   10-in.,   1.50

THE GARDEN SCENE—FAUST, MARGUERITE AND MEPHISTOPHELES

FAUST

DOCTOR FAUSTUS, the original of the dominant figure in Goethe's tragedy, was a legendary character, a metaphysician whose pseudo-logic brought him a large following among the mystical half-wits of late medieval Germany. He was a rogue, and a shrewd one, who taught philosophy with his tongue in his cheek, and who, when his casuistry approached exposure, kept the silence which was golden—from which his followers inferred that "he could an' he would."

The age was ripe for such a creature. The Reformation had broken down some of the old foundations of belief without fully establishing new ones. Artists were busy delving into pagan legends of Greece and Rome to create the Renaissance. Many kept faith with medieval Rome; others took their creed from Luther. Between these extremes were hosts of people filled with spiritual doubt and dismay, crying out for a new prophet to lead them out of the metaphysical wilderness. Such times are propitious for the upspringing of false prophets; Doctor Faustus was an unquestioned success, for people respected his alleged power over diabolical agencies. It has been said that there are always those who would rather worship the Devil in secret than God in the open. It is positive that Doctor Faustus had among these a large and believing clientele.

Many legends collected about Doctor Faustus. To most of us, today, these would only bring hilarity; but to Goethe, with his great and powerful human sympathies, they were a source of rich and splendid imagery. Poet and seer, he beheld in them the evidences of human aspiration—the ceaseless yearning, in the hearts of mankind, for some justification of life, some balance between right and wrong to which it might look for assurance of its own divinity, and its hope of salvation and happiness. The spiritual history of nine-tenths of humankind has in the past been a record of hope and of appeal to false gods and false prophets. And so, by a singular yet natural perversion, the lying Faustus, the charlatan and poseur, the impudent, brazen quack, at the hands of a man of genius became an instrument of inspiration and truth.

Now Goethe's tragedy poem, "Faustus," was built upon so vast a scale that it could not be condensed into a single opera. Gounod took, therefore, from it one single episode—that of Faust and Gretchen (Marguerite in the opera), which had previously been, because of its dramatic possibilities, the theme of many plays. From this Barbiere and Carré formed their libretto, to which Gounod wrote the greatest music he was destined to compose—producing, on the whole, the noblest opera that has yet come out of France.

Many have marvelled that Gounod, having written "Faust," should have brought forth no other opera nearly so fine. But he was peculiarly suited by training and temperament to write a work in which human passion and religious sentiment were in conflict—the same elements of war being at work within his own intelligence. He was the son of a father who was a painter, and a mother who was a musician. His father died, shortly after his birth, in 1818, and upon his mother devolved the task of bringing him up. She taught him music, but was determined he should not be a professional musician unless nature proved too strong. And nature did.

In spite of his desire, she quietly but firmly refused to permit him to go to the Conservatory until he had first graduated at the Lycée St. Louis as a "Bachelier-és-lettres," the first step toward becoming a lawyer. But in 1836 he entered the Conservatory, and three years later won the Prix-de-Rome, which entitled him to further study in Italy and marked him out as a musician with a future. In Rome he became engrossed in the religious music of Palestrina, and on returning to Paris he was appointed organist at one of the leading churches. His interest in religion widened and deepened to such a degree that he seriously thought of entering the priesthood. By natural right, therefore, he was a combination of priest and artist—a combination whose artistic validity was testified to by many a Gothic architect, many an illuminator, many a Renaissance painter. He divided his time between operatic and church music. Until "Faust" was produced, perhaps Gounod's sacred music was his best, though his operas revealed a power of sensuous melody rather startling, at times, in a man of his ecclesiastical predilections! In "Faust," however, he found the perfect vehicle for his possibly complex nature, and today it remains his masterpiece. It may, almost, like "Tannhäuser," be taken to typify the struggle between the powers of good and evil in the human soul itself.

THE PLOT

FAUST, the aged philosopher, longs for his lost youth. To regain it, he sells his immortal soul to *Mephistopheles*, an emissary of the Evil One—or as many may insist, the Evil One in person. *Mephistopheles* reveals him a vision of *Marguerite*, a lovely maiden, and the pair go in search of her. We next find them at a village festival, *Faust* appearing as a young man. *Valentine*, brother of *Marguerite*, enters on his way to the wars. He leaves his sister in charge of *Siebel*, a youth who is timidly in love with her. *Mephistopheles* contrives a meeting between *Faust* and *Marguerite;* later he throws enchant-

COPY'T BURR M'INTOSH
CARUSO AS FAUST

FARRAR AS MARGUERITE

COPY'T DUPONT
JOURNET AS MEPHISTO

ment over *Marguerite's* dwelling, allowing *Faust* and *Marguerite* to meet while he sets up a flirtation with *Martha*, her chaperon. After the lapse of time, *Marguerite* is again seen, deserted by *Faust*, who has left her with child. *Valentine* returns, and is killed by *Faust*, cursing his sister as he dies. *Marguerite*, deserted by her friends, seeks consolation in the cathedral, but the voices of demons drive her to madness, and she kills her child. She is sent to prison, where *Faust* visits her with *Mephistopheles*. At sight of the demon, who now covets her soul as well as *Faust's*, she takes refuge in prayer. As the curtain descends, a chorus of angels attends her, chanting her salvation through repentance. *Mephistopheles* drags *Faust* to the underworld to fulfil his compact.

THE OPERA

OPERA in five acts. Words by Barbier and Carré, founded upon Goethe's tragedy. Music by Charles Gounod. First produced at the *Théâtre Lyrique*, Paris, March 19, 1859. First performance in Berlin, at the Royal Opera, January, 1863; in London, June 11, 1863; in New York, November 25, 1863; at the Academy of Music, with Kellogg, Mazzoleni, Biachi and Yppolito.

Some famous American productions were in 1883, with Nilsson, Scalchi and Campanini; and the same year with Nordica (début) as *Marguerite*; in 1892 with Eames, the de Reszkes and Lasalle; and in 1913 with Caruso and Farrar. Revived at the Metropolitan in 1917, with Farrar, Martinelli and Rothier.

CHARACTERS

FAUST (*Fowst*)..............Tenor
MEPHISTOPHELES (*Mef-iss-tof' el-leez*)...................Bass
VALENTINE (*Val-en-teen*)....Baritone
BRANDER, or WAGNER.......Baritone
SIEBEL (*See'-bel*)....Mezzo-Soprano
MARGUERITE (*Mahr-guer-eet'*)Soprano
MARTHA.................Contralto

Students, Soldiers, Villagers, Sorcerers, Spirits

The Action takes place in Germany

COPY'T DUPONT
MELBA AS MARGUERITE
CHURCH SCENE

PLANÇON AS MEPHISTOPHELES

PATTI AS MARGUERITE, 1875

ACT I
The Compact

THE scene is an apartment in a medieval German house. By the expiring light of a single lamp can be seen glimpses of a student's paraphernalia—a skeleton, a retort, a shelf of parchment rolls, a number of equally curious objects. The dying flame is a symbol of the despair in the heart of *Faust*, who sits dreaming of human futility—as typified in his own lifetime of study. He is shaken with despair. "Another day," cries he, "and yet another day. O Death, come in thy pity and bid the strife be over." He raises to his lips a goblet of poison. His hand is stayed when he hears, from without, a song borne by the evening wind. Outside a happy band of farm toilers is making merry. The tune is fresh and springlike, "La Vaga pupilla" (Rise, Slumbering Maiden), and with its drone-bass and pastoral rhythm, it is in marked contrast to the gloomy and reflective polyphony of *Faust's* own music. The sage hastens to the window, and, filled with envy and despair at the sight of human happiness, he curses all things and calls upon the powers of darkness.

In a flash *Mephistopheles* appears. He is clad in courtly raiment, though it is of a brilliant crimson color throughout. His manner is cynical, debonair, blandly ingratiating. Two numbers (presented on a single record) develop the scene: "Mais ce Dieu, que peut-il pour moi" (But This God, What Will He Do For Me?) and "A moi les plaisirs" (The Pleasures of Youth).

The first of these illustrates, clearly and richly, Gounod's mastery of vocal dialogue. That which follows, in which *Faust* declares his wish for returning youth and the caresses of woman, is the very essence of youthful fire and joyous abandon. It is repeated, at the end of the scene, *Mephistopheles* echoing phrase after phrase.

In return for the boon of youth and its delights, *Mephistopheles* asks for the soul of *Faust*. The philosopher hesitates, but he is convinced when the demon vouchsafes to him a vision of the beautiful *Marguerite*. A gap is seen to open in the wall of the room, and the maiden is disclosed, sitting at her spinning-wheel. *Faust*, entranced, can only speak in wonder. "O merveille" (O Heavenly Vision), declares he, and in his declaration is heard the first promise of the famous "Garden Scene" music. It is heard in the orchestra, the tenor singing in recitative—telling how, for such loveliness, he is willing to pawn his immortal soul. Men have declared such things, with no *Mephistopheles* at hand.

It is enough! The parchment is signed in letters of fire. *Faust* drains the magic potion offered him, as the vision disappears; then, with a new spring in his step, he goes off, singing again the "A moi les plaisirs," the hand of *Mephistopheles*, his new comrade, on one shoulder.

ACT II
The Fair

IN the public square of a German town, a crowd of soldiers, students, peasants, old men, young women and matrons, has gathered to celebrate. All are drinking, talking, flirting, quarrelling. The music reveals every type of individual there and every contrasting mood. This is the so-called "Kermesse Scene." Each group contributes its distinctive melody—the rough-and-ready tune of the soldiers being in marked relief against the laughing and chattering of the women, the delicate accents of the girls, the colorless counter-tenor of the old men, and the ribaldries, it must be confessed, of the students. At the close, the different groups are combined into a six-

PAINTED BY KRELING

FAUST, AGED PHILOSOPHER, WEARIES OF LIFE

KRELING

MARGUERITE LONGS FOR FAUST'S RETURN

part chorus of cheerfully melodious polyphony.

Among the soldiers, one is reserved for an unusual fate. This is *Valentine*, brother of *Marguerite*.

When the day is over, the soldiers must depart. And *Valentine*, conscious of what may happen during his absence, bids farewell to his sister in a melody broad, noble, and of singular beauty. This is the "Dio Possente" (Even Bravest Heart), which has been the favorite operatic air of more than one fine baritone. *Valentine* speaks of his fears frankly enough, and he contemplates with affection an amulet *Marguerite* has given him as a protection against ill-fortune. This number was not originally in the score of the opera, but was written for the baritone Charles Santley in the English pro-

duction of 1864. It was first heard in the United States three years later, when Santley sang it in Philadelphia with the Caroline Ritchings Company.

The bustle of the fair scene returns. *Wagner* is singing a somewhat coarse ditty concerning a rat. *Mephistopheles* pushes through the crowd, and with an abrupt "Pardon!" volunteers a better song. Then follows the fantastic "Le Veau d'Or" (The Calf of Gold). It opens with a whistling, fiendish accompaniment in the orchestra, with odd descending chromatics in the bass and shrill semi-quavers in the treble, and it alternates between sinister gaiety and the mock-solemn, stamping chords of a diabolical hymn to Mammon. It ends with a weird dance in which *Mephistopheles* himself leads.

The crowd is vastly entertained. The stranger finds himself in the middle of an admiring circle, as he tells fortunes, reads palms, and performs bewildering feats of magic. Among others, he catches *Siebel*, and amuses the crowd by telling him that whatever flower he touches, will wither in his grasp. The simple-hearted youth is seriously disturbed, and he draws aside. *Mephistopheles* volunteers a toast. Wine is brought, and he tastes it with a grimace.

He offers to give them better, and striding over to the "Barrel of Bacchus" set above the inn-door as a sign, he strikes it with his sword. A magical wine gushes forth. Each in turn is invited to drink, and whatever wine is best to his taste, runs into his goblet. The stranger is carefully watched by some, however, including *Valentine*, whom he insults by drinking a toast, by name, to *Marguerite*. *Valentine* is amazed and hurt, but it is the desire of *Mephistopheles* to kill him and get him out of the way for *Faust*. Swords are out in a moment, but *Valentine's* is broken in his hand by the sinister touch of his enemy's. With medieval instinct, he turns the broken blade hilt uppermost, the hilt and guard forming a Cross. The demon quails to behold this sacred symbol, but, as the others advance, he draws with the point of his own weapon in the ground, a magic circle which none may pass. Behind this he shrinks away. The music here is a noble chant, with broad, sustained harmonies, magnificent in strength and simplicity. *Mephistopheles* disappears, leaving *Faust* to pursue his own fortunes, for the time, in the crowd. The popular and ever-beautiful waltz now begins.

This waltz is most interesting. Its flowing beauty, the variety and contrast of its themes, have made it a favorite among waltzes. Dramatically, its freshness and gaiety are in fine and relieving contrast to the tense mysticism and the dramatic suspense of the preceding scene. In the midst of it *Marguerite* appears, and *Faust* approaches her with a respectful greeting. To the wisdom and the craft of age, he now has added the freshness and the charm of youth; and the two are irresistible. He begs if he may not see her safely home after the Kermesse.

She declines, modestly, but her heart has been sorely fluttered. He will not be forgotten—even though she dares not hint it. Everything remains in her mind as she leaves the scene—to the diminishing strains of the waltz. She walks off like a soul in a dream— as, indeed, she is.

ACT III

The Garden Scene

VALENTINE has gone, and *Siebel*, in fulfilment of his charge, is in *Marguerite's* garden. He adores her with all the sincere and tender reverence of a first affection. He is upset, however, by the prediction of *Mephistopheles*. To test it he gathers a nosegay of flowers; but they wither away, one by one, at his touch. In this scene he sings the delightfully sweet and melodious "Le parlate d'amor" (In the Language of Love), the famous "Flower Song." It is particularly touching —especially the passage describing how the flowers fade before his eyes.

Son via · si, ahi · mè lo stre-go ma · le det · to mel di · ce · va or, ...
Tis wither'd! A-las! that dark stran-ger fore-told me What my fate must be. ...

The happy thought occurs to *Siebel* to dip them in holy water. He does, and the spell is broken. He triumphantly places them before the door of *Marguerite*, and runs off.

But the youth has been watched. *Faust* and the grinning *Mephistoph-*

PAUL BOYER & BERT   SETTING FOR GARDEN SCENE AT PARIS OPÉRA

eles step from behind the bushes. *Faust* is dreamy, quiet, distraught, for by this time he loves *Marguerite*. His demoniac companion, however, is in high glee—he is making mischief and disaster and tragedy in the world.

Faust's own worship extends, lover-like, even to the dwelling which houses his beloved. He sings to it the beautiful apostrophe, "Salut demeure" (All Hail, Thou Dwelling), a melody of exquisite tenderness, a violin obbligato wreathed about it like a living vine.

The melody is one of the loveliest in music, and one which is not easy to sing, for all of its slow and tender utterance. But while *Faust* is lost in his love-dream, the practical *Mephistopheles* has placed near the bouquet of *Siebel* a casket of jewels. His worldly wisdom knows the heart of woman as it knows that of man. Flowers against gems? Even *Faust* might

have told him that! The two hurriedly conceal themselves as the girl enters the garden.

Marguerite will never again appear as she appears now—lovely, fresh, virginal, at the mysterious threshold of womanhood, the bloom of body and mind as yet untouched. Her dreams are as innocent as those of childhood; but they center upon the handsome gallant—whose memories filter through her consciousness like strains of audible song. A lovely strain from the orchestra, in clarinets and violins, is heard at her entrance. She seats herself at her spinning-wheel, her song keeping perfect rhythm with its droning, monotonous clack. This is the song of "Le Roi de Thulé" (The King of Thulé). It is older than Gounod, being traditional; and it is surrounded with odd, quaint, yet natural-sounding archaic harmonies.

122

She cannot spin—the song breaks off in the middle—becomes vague, dreamy, until she remembers. There is another attempt, but she gives it up. The day itself is languid, dreamy, adapting itself to her mood. Half-dazed, she returns toward the house. The brilliant-hued nosegay catches her eye. *Siebel's*, of course—but look— a casket! Who could have left this? . . . perhaps the stranger. . . . .

The girl's hand goes to her heart— but it returns to the casket and the lid is thrown back.

To resist the jewels would be to re-make life. She begins to deck herself with them, at first diffidently, but confidence grows, and with it the sense of her own beauty and power. She now sings the remarkably brilliant "Air des bijoux" (Jewel Song)—one of the few instances in which a coloratura song, making the most exacting demands upon the voice, is dramatically appropriate. The swift flying scales, the dazzling *fioriture*, have none of the mechanical stiffness so often found in songs of this type, but seem indeed the exultant outpourings of a full heart— the heart of a young girl which, once awakened, speaks to the full its confidence in happiness yet to be. *Marguerite*, alone in her garden (as she believes), is at last drawn from her reserve; and she carols away like a lark in the springtime.

But patter-tongued, foolish old *Martha*, most susceptible of souls, appears upon the scene. She is in raptures over the necklace and the other treasures. But in the midst of them, the red cavalier enters—with the news that *Martha's* absent husband is dead. He behaves so graciously that she ceases to lament, and strange hopes spring up in her own foolish old heart. *Faust*, meanwhile, has busied himself with *Marguerite*, inducing her to take his arm, as the four promenade the garden. An odd but beautiful quartet here develops—mostly wrought of solo passages, but joining here and there into peals of ringing, delicious harmony. This is known as "Eh Quoi toujours seule?" (But Why So Lonely?). Then follows an equally beautiful dialogue between the lovers. *Marguerite* confides to *Faust* her loneliness, and in an exquisite passage she speaks of her little dead sister. He is all tenderness, all sympathy, and her trust in him increases. Meanwhile *Mephistopheles* has lost *Martha* in another part of the garden.

He looks on with satisfaction. His work is thriving. But it dawns on *Marguerite* that the hour is late. She flees, and *Faust* follows her. *Martha* crosses the scene, failing to see her demon-suitor, whom she now dreams of marrying. She trots off into the evening shadows; and, left alone, *Mephistopheles* proceeds to the next step. With arms extended, he sings the beautiful and solemn "Invocation" (Oh Night, Draw Thy Curtain), calling upon the night to cast over the scene its own magic, so that the lovers, beneath its witchery, shall be drawn into one another's arms. For once his satirical manner is lost; he is in deadly earnest. The music, broadly harmonic, passing through rich dignified alternations of major and minor, is weird and wonderful. As the blue darkness of the night subdues the last orange of the setting sun, the lovers again appear arm in arm, and *Mephistopheles* retires.

Then the enchantment of the night begins to work upon the souls of the lovers. *Marguerite* gently bids farewell to *Faust*, in the gentle and lovely "Tardi si fa" (The Hour Is Late), but he pleads with her. Then succeeds the soft loveliness of the "Dammi Ancor" (Let Me Gaze), which has rarely if ever been excelled in music. Saving, perhaps, the "Eternelle" which follows, no music has more perfectly expressed the sensuous beauty of human love in all its depth and sincerity. Then comes the confession of love, the avowal which, to any lovers seems the moment for which the whole of life has been waiting. Surely no lovers' litany was ever sung to music richer in emotion or more loftily conceived! Soft chords in the wood-wind, mellow tones of horns and strings blend softly with the voices of the lovers as the night, in very truth, draws its cloak about them.

Yet somewhere deep in the heart of the girl, is a sanity which protests against this ecstatic madness. She breaks away from her lover, running to the house. But on the threshold she pauses to waft him a kiss.

Faust has a promise to meet on the morrow, and already he longs for the morning to come. The woes and the pains of age are forgotten—even the wisdom of his years. He loves as youth loves — blindly, instinctively, without guile. His heart is full as he turns away. He worships *Marguerite*, and he has no thought but for her happiness.

"Wait!" cries *Mephistopheles*. "Thou dreamer, wait and hear what she tells to the stars!" "Elle ouvre sa fenêtre!" (She Opens the Window).

Marguerite indeed opens the casement, and in a stream of song she pours out to the night the full floods of her rapture—the rapture of a heart that indeed is full to overflowing. The melody, borne upward by flute and

FAUST: "ELLE OUVRE LA FENÊTRE"

MEPHISTOPHELES:
    You shall stay and hear
    That which she telleth the stars!
    See! She opens the window!

clarinet, climbs slowly but surely to its ultimate heights of ecstatic expression. She stands there, a figure of beauty. Her tremulous cry to the deaf ears of the night is heard by her lover; and *Mephistopheles*, who has held him back, releases him. Crying out her name, he rushes to the open window and clasps her in his arms, where she sinks fainting. The curtain descends to music of undying loveliness—broken only by a sardonic "Ha! Ha! Ha!" by the fiend in the garden.

ACT IV

The Desertion

THE lovely echoes of the last scene— the unearthly beauty of its music— will linger long in memory after its first hearing. It is so admirably adapted to the song-tone of the violin, that a fantasie has been built from its melodies, and played on a single record; with all the genius of Mischa Elman, it is one of the loveliest imaginable bits of violin-playing.

The drama proceeds. Love and happiness, for *Marguerite*, are at an end—at least this side the grave.

The story is an old one. A year and a half has passed, and *Marguerite* has been deserted by *Faust* and shunned by her neighbors. *Siebel* alone remains faithful. As she sits again by the spinning-wheel, he comes to her with consolation as she broods over her sorrows. Woman-like, she must brood over them, though not *Faust*, but really *Mephistopheles*, is to blame, and she, herself, except under the cruel human law, is innocent of wrong. *Siebel* talks against *Faust*, but *Marguerite*, of the guileless heart, will not hear it and the youth's own hopes die.

The scene changes abruptly, and we stand in front of the cathedral, the house of *Marguerite* on one side. Suddenly there is heard the sound of martial music—the troops are coming home victorious; the air itself seems filled with the sense of great things. *Valentine* appears among them, safe and sound, as they are greeted by their wives and sweethearts. Their welcome is voiced by the familiar "Deponiam il brando," known throughout the world, in original form and in caricature, as the "Soldiers' Chorus." *Valentine* enters his sister's house, and the stage is emptied as the others drift away.

Faust and the demon appear. *Mephistopheles* is for entering, but *Faust* is torn with grief and contrition. How much it means to his tempter is shown when, throwing back his cloak, he stations himself beneath the window, and sings a villainous and mocking serenade (Catarina, While You Play at Sleeping !).

This infernal and insulting chant, in a sinister, snarling minor mode, is a striking example of the sardonic mood in music. But least impressive is a hideous mocking laugh at the end, beginning of high G, and jumping by successive octaves to low G, where it gives way to noteless and horrible cachinnation.

Valentine rushes out, sword in hand. It is not told what has transpired in the house, but he realizes that an insult has been offered his sister. *Faust* for the first time learns his identity as *Marguerite's* own brother. *Valentine* rushes at *Mephistopheles* and shatters with his sword the mandolin which accompanied the song. "Que voulez-vous, messieurs?" (What Is Your Will With Me?) he asks.

The scene is full of brilliant, almost savage energy. Character, as always under circumstance, appears. *Valentine* is indignant, *Faust* weakly perplexed, *Mephistopheles* scornful. The

PAINTED BY KRELING

VALENTINE (*dying*):
Thy fine betrayer's sword
Hath sent thy brother home!

126

trio leads up to a fine climax, when the swords cross. *Valentine* has no chance against two adversaries, one of them a master of black magic. He is mortally wounded, and a crowd gathers.

The "Morte di Valentino" (Death of Valentine) is the next step in the tragedy. *Valentine* lies in agony, and the crowd, *Marguerite* among them, cry out with pity. But pity has been denied him—the stern law of the soldier is above the tenderer emotions. With his last breath he curses the innocent *Marguerite* as the cause of his death. The pleas of those around him, and *Marguerite's* own prayers, will not stay his tongue nor its utterances. His last syllable completes the curse.

(This and other scenes from "Faust" are vividly pictured in the paintings of Kreling which are reproduced throughout the present text. They appear through the courtesy of Mme. Sofia Romani, who lent for the purpose her collection, perhaps the only one in America).

The scene shifts again to the cathedral, where *Marguerite*, deserted and scorned in truth by her friends, has fled for consolation. But as she kneels, she hears only the voice of *Mephistopheles* and his mocking chorus of demons. On Victor Records this is distributed over three separate discs: "Scène de l'Eglise"(Church Scene) Parts I and II, and "Rammenta i lieti" (Dost Thou Remember?).

The girl, upon her knees, fearful to look up, can find no hope. Through the scene, we hear the chanting of the choir and the rolling chords of the cathedral organ, as terrible to the girl's tortured consciousness as the sound of thunder to a timorous, ignorant soul.

KRELING   MARGUERITE AT THE SHRINE

KRELING   MARGUERITE AND THE TEMPTER

127

Far from bringing hope to seal her repentance, the sounds that assail her are menacing, gloomy, sad, foreboding, as though Heaven itself added to the Tempter's mockery the condemnation of a judgment above all human measure of good or ill, eager only to punish and not to forgive.

There is a little relief for the hearer, at the end of the act, where the "Ballet Music" follows. This depicts, in music, the "Walpurgis Night," whereon the witches of earth and the demons of the underworld hold revelry on the mountain of the Brocken, in the Thuringian Hartz. *Faust*, led thither by *Mephistopheles*, for a moment sees the spectre of *Marguerite*. Through considerations of length, this scene is rarely given in the actual presentations of the opera. There are, however, Victor Records of its music, a really splendid series of orchestral recordings, brilliant, rich and varied.

ACT V
The Prison

MARGUERITE has killed her child. She is in prison, lying pale and haggard on the straw pallet of her dimly-lit cell. *Faust* and his infernal master, defying bolts and bars, have found a way within. *Mephistopheles* has warned *Faust* that if the girl is to be saved, it must be done quickly, as the gallows awaits her. The bad heart of *Faust* is melted with compassion. He calls upon her name. Hearing his voice, she responds, semi-delirious. The music is here deeply affecting. "Mon coeur est penetré d'epouvante!" cries *Faust*, (My Heart Is Torn With Grief and Repentance!).

Penetrato è il mio cor di spa-ven - to! O tor - tu ra'
My heart is torn with grief and re-pent - ance! O, what an - guish!

Marguerite sings dreamily of the Fair where she and her lover first met; the echoes of the "Kermesse Scene"

MARGUERITE *(awaking):*
'Twas not the cry of the demons;
'Tis his own voice I hear.

128

music return, phrase by phrase, with heartrending effect. Number by number, the scene develops; first the "Attends! Voici la rue" (This is the Fair), which develops the waltz music, with its echoes of a happier time. It sounds strange, ghostly, as though it had filtered into the domain of consciousness from another world or another condition of being. She repeats the first words *Faust* had addressed to her. *Faust* urges her to come away with him; but the broken mind cannot return to realities. Then the brutal "Alerte" of *Mephistopheles* opens the final superb trio, "Alerte! ou vous êtes perdus!" (Then Leave Her!).

The interruption of *Mephistopheles* for a moment brings *Marguerite* back to the world of reality. But even as she cries out in her horror, *Mephistopheles* hears in the courtyard the hoofs of the horses that are to bear him and *Faust* to the nether regions.

The tramping and the neighing of horses is suggested in the accompaniment, and the song of the "Calf of Gold" is heard in the pulsing of deep bass instruments. *Marguerite* finds the strength for prayer. Then there comes into being, like a star born suddenly into sight in a dark sky, the wonderful "Anges Pures" (Holy Angels), one of the most inspired of all operatic climaxes. The voice of *Marguerite* breaks into a wonderful, broad, noble, melodic phrase, a veritably seraphic hymn, which mounts, step by step, into higher and higher keys as to the soul of the girl is unfolded, step by step, the clear vision of Heaven and the eternal salvation that lies there alone. *Faust* and *Mephistopheles* urge her away with them, but she now is beyond earthly power, and beyond earthly hearing. She gazes upwards, as through the stony ceiling of her cell, in ecstasy. The music surges and swells around her, heavenly voices

chant. The heavens open and a company of angels gather her up in their arms and bear her away. *Mephistopheles*, with an imprecation, seizes *Faust* and bears him off into the fiery abyss.

THE VICTOR RECORDS
(Sung in French unless otherwise noted)

ACT I
O MERVEILLE
(Heavenly Vision) ENRICO CARUSO, Tenor and MARCEL JOURNET, Bass
8016 12-in., $2.50

ACT II
DIO POSSENTE
(Even the Bravest Heart) EMILIO DE GOGORZA, Baritone *In Italian*
6069 12-in., 2.00
ANTONIO SCOTTI, Baritone *In Italian* 6284 12-in., 2.00
TITTA RUFFO, Baritone *In Italian* 6429 12-in., 2.00
GIUSEPPE DE LUCA, Baritone *In Italian* 6079 12-in., 2.00

Even bravest heart may swell,
In the moment of farewell,
Loving smile of sister kind,
Quiet home I leave behind;
Oft shall I think of you,
Whene'er the wine-cup passes 'round,
When alone my watch I keep
And my comrades lie asleep
Upon the tented battleground.
But when danger to glory shall call me,
I still will be first in the fray,
As blithe as a knight in his bridal array,
Careless what fate may befall me,
When glory shall call me.
Oft shall I sadly think of you
When far away, far away.

VEAU D'OR
(Calf of Gold) MARCEL JOURNET, Bass
695 10-in., 1.50
FEODOR CHALIAPIN, Bass 960 10-in., 1.50
MEPHISTOPHELES:
Calf of Gold! aye in all the world
Incense at your fane they offer
To your mightiness they proffer,
From end to end of all the world.
And in honor of the idol
Kings and peoples everywhere
To the sound of jingling coins
Dance with zeal in festive circle,
Round about the pedestal,
Satan, he conducts the ball!

Calf of Gold, strongest god below!
To his temple overflowing
Crowds before his vile shape bowing,
As they strive in abject toil,
As with souls debased they circle
Round about the pedestal,
Satan, he conducts the ball!

SCÈNE DES EPÉES

(Scene of the Swords) PASQUALE AMATO,
Baritone, MARCEL JOURNET, Bass and
Opera Chorus   8003 12-in., $2.50

WALTZ   ERIKA MORINI, Violin
                             791 10-in., 1.50
Philadelphia Orchestra   944 10-in., 1.50

ACT III

LE PARLATE D'AMOR

(Flower Song) (Siebel's Air) LOUISE
HOMER, Contralto *In Italian*
                             678 10-in., 1.50

Each flower that you touch,
Every beauty you dote on
Shall rot and shall wither!

SALUT, DEMEURE

(All Hail, Thou Dwelling Lowly) ENRICO
CARUSO, Tenor   6004 12-in., 2.00
GIOVANNI MARTINELLI, Tenor
                            6191 12-in., 2.00
JOHN McCORMACK, Tenor *In Italian*
                            6203 12-in., 2.00
BENIAMINO GIGLI, Tenor 6138 12-in., 1.50

All hail, thou dwelling pure and lowly!
Home of an angel fair and holy,
What wealth is here, what wealth outbidding
gold,
Of peace and love, and innocence untold!
Bounteous Nature!
'Twas here by day thy love was taught her,
Here thou didst with care overshadow thy
daughter
In her dream of the night!
Here, waving tree and flower
Made her an Eden-bower of beauty and delight.

LE ROI DE THULÉ

(Ballad of the King of Thulé) GERALDINE
FARRAR, Soprano   6107 12-in., 2.00
Once there was a king in Thulé
Who was until death always faithful,
And in memory of his loved one
Caused a cup of gold to be made.

AIR DES BIJOUX

(Jewel Song) GERALDINE FARRAR, So-
prano   6107 12-in., 2.00
Oh Heav'n! what brilliant gems!
Can they be real?
Oh never in my sleep did I dream of aught so
lovely!

If I dared for a moment
But to try these earrings, so splendid!
And here, by a chance, at the bottom of the
casket, is a glass!
Who could resist it longer?

SEIGNEUR DIEU!

(Saints Above) Quartet from Garden
Scene, Part I, FARRAR, CARUSO, JOUR-
NET and MME. GILIBERT
                        10004 12-in., $3.50

EH QUOI TOUJOURS SEULE?

(But Why So Lonely?) Quartet from the
Garden Scene, Part II, FARRAR, CA-
RUSO, JOURNET and MME. GILIBERT
                        10004 12-in., 3.50

INVOCATION MEPHISTOPHELES

(Oh Night, Draw Thy Curtain!) MARCEL
JOURNET, Bass   695 10-in., 1.50
MEPHISTOPHELES:
It was high time—
See, 'neath the balmy linden,
Our lovers devoted approaching;
'Tis well! Better leave them alone,
With the flow'rs and the moon.

O night! draw around them thy curtain!
Let naught waken alarm, or misgivings ever!
Ye flowers, aid the enchanting charm,
Her senses to bewilder; till she knows not
Whether she be not already in Heaven!

LAISSE-MOI

(Let Me Gaze) (Preceded by "Il se fait
tard"—The Hour is Late!) Duet
from the Garden Scene, Part I,
GERALDINE FARRAR, Soprano and
ENRICO CARUSO, Tenor
                        8009 12-in., 2.50

ELLE OUVRE SA FENÊTRE

(She Opens the Window!) GERALDINE
FARRAR, Soprano and MARCEL JOUR-
NET, Bass   8022 12-in., 2.50
FARRAR and JOURNET 10008 12-in., 3.50

ETERNELLE

(Forever Thine!) Duet, Part II, GERAL-
DINE FARRAR, Soprano and ENRICO
CARUSO, Tenor   8009 12-in., 2.50
NOTE—*The above three numbers are from the
same scene.*

FANTASIE FROM GARDEN SCENE

MISCHA ELMAN, Violin 601 10-in., 1.50

ACT IV

SERENADE MEPHISTOPHELES

(While You Play at Sleeping) MARCEL
JOURNET, Bass   6174 12-in., 2.00
TITTA RUFFO, Baritone *In Italian*
                             819 10-in., 1.50
FEODOR CHALIAPIN, Bass 960 10-in., 1.50

KRELING   REDEMPTION OF MARGUERITE

MEPHISTOPHELES:

Thou who here art soundly sleeping,
Close not thus thy heart,
Close not thus thy heart!
Caterina! wake thee! wake thee!
Caterina! wake! 'tis thy lover near!
Hearken to my love-lorn pleading;
Let thy heart be interceding,
Awake, love, and hear!
Ha, ha, ha, ha, ha! ha! ha! ha! ha! ha!
Don't come down until, my dear,
The nuptial ring appear
On thy finger sparkling clearly—
The wedding-ring—the ring shineth clear.
Ha! ha! ha! ha! etc.
Caterina! cruel, cruel!
Cruel to deny to him who loves thee—
And for thee doth mourn and sigh—
A single kiss from thy rosy lips.
Thus to slight a faithful lover,
Who so long hath been a rover,
Too bad, I declare!
Ha, ha, ha, ha, ha!
Not a single kiss, my dear,
Unless the ring appear!
Ha, ha, ha, ha! etc.

SCENE DE L'EGLISE (I)
(Church Scene, Part I) GERALDINE FAR-
RAR, Soprano, MARCEL JOURNET, Bass
and Chorus   8021 12-in., $2.50
SCENE DE L'EGLISE (II)
(Church Scene, Part II) GERALDINE
FARRAR, Soprano, MARCEL JOURNET,
Bass and Chorus   8021 12-in., 2.50
RAMMENTA I LIETI DI QUANDO
(Dost Thou Remember?) TITTA RUFFO,
Baritone In Italian   819 10-in., 1.50

ACT V

PRISON SCENE,—PART I, MON COEUR
EST PÉNÉTRÉ D' EPOUVANTE
(My Heart is Torn With Grief) GERAL-
DINE FARRAR, Soprano and ENRICO
CARUSO, Tenor   8010 12-in., 2.50
PRISON SCENE—PART II, ATTENDS!
VOICI LA RUE
(This Is the Fair) GERALDINE FARRAR,
Soprano and ENRICO CARUSO, Tenor
                    8010 12-in., 2.50
PRISON SCENE—PART III, ALERTE!
(Leave Her) FARRAR, CARUSO and
JOURNET   10008 12-in., 3.50

BLACK LABEL AND BLUE LABEL RECORDS

Even Bravest Heart (In English)...........Reinald Werrenrath, Baritone Bohemian Girl—Heart Bowed Down........Reinald Werrenrath, Baritone	55079	12-in., $1.50
In the Language of Love (Flower Song) (In English)..Elsie Baker, Contralto Drink to Me Only with Thine Eyes(Ben Jonson)....Harry Macdonough,Tenor	35086	12-in., 1.25
Soldiers' Chorus—Made especially for School Marching........Victor Band March Religioso (Onward Christian Soldiers)...............Victor Band	35227	12-in., 1.25
Ballet Music—Cleopatra and the Golden Cup....Victor Symphony Orchestra Ballet Music—Dance of Cleopatra and Her Slaves.Victor Symphony Orchestra	35719	12-in., 1.25
Ballet Music—Dance of the Trojan Maidens and Mirror Dance Victor Symphony Orchestra Ballet Music—Dance of Phryné...............Victor Symphony Orchestra	35720	12-in., 1.25
Ballet—Dance of Nubian Slaves..................Vessella's Italian Band Ballet—Dance of Trojan Maidens.................Vessella's Italian Band	17284	10-in., .75
Prison Scene—Part III (In English)...................Victor Opera Trio Bohême-Ah,Mimi-Lambert Murphy, Tenor and Reinald Werrenrath, Baritone	45182	10-in., 1.00
Prison Scene..Vessella's Band Favorita—Fantasia...................................Vessella's Band	35449	12-in., 1.25
Waltz from Kermesse Scene...................Victor Symphony Orchestra Ballet Music—Dance of the Nubian Slaves......Victor Symphony Orchestra	35742	12-in., 1.25

132

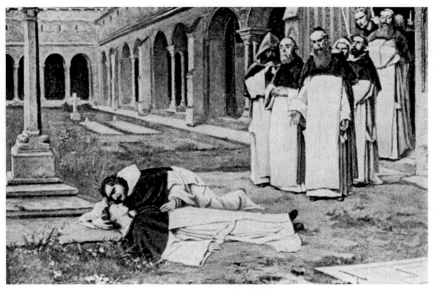

THE DEATH OF LEONORA

LA FAVORITA

THIS was about Donizetti's fifty-seventh opera, the chronological order of his sixty-four odd works not being very clear. Its plot, in comparison with the opera plots of its time and school, is almost a masterpiece of ironic tragedy. Its music is melodious, fluent, at all times without harshness.

THE OPERA

OPERA in four acts. Text by Alphonse Royer and Gustave Waez, adapted from a drama of Baculard-Darnaud, *Le Comte de Comminges*. Music by Donizetti. First produced at the *Académie*, Paris, December 2, 1840. First London production in English, 1843; in Italian February 16, 1847. First American production at New Orleans 1843. An English version was given at the Park Theatre, New York, October 4, 1848. Some later American productions were in 1895-96, with Manelli, Cremonini, Ancona and Plançon; and in 1898, at Wallack's Theatre, and in 1905 at the Metropolitan.

CHARACTERS

ALPHONSO XI, King of Castile...................... Baritone
FERDINAND, a young novice of the Convent of St. James...Tenor
DON GASPAR, the King's Minister .... Tenor
BALTAZAR, Superior of the Convent of St. James............Bass
LEONORA DI GUSMANN, the King's favorite ....Soprano
INEZ, her confidante........Soprano

Courtiers, Guards, Monks, Attendants, etc.

Scene and Period: The Action is supposed to take place in Castile, about the year 1340

(The name of the opera is pronounced *Lah Fah-voh-ree'-tah*. Its English equivalent is "The Favorite").

ACT I

SCENE—*The Monastery of St. James*

FERDINAND, or *Fernando*, a novice, is sitting with *Baltazar*, the Prior, in a quiet, grass-grown, ancient cloister. He is describing to the unworldly and somewhat scandalized old priest a beautiful girl he has seen. He speaks of her in the aria, "Una Vergine"—"Une ange, une femme inconnue" (Like an Angel).

Justly outraged, his friend and superior protests, in "Non sei tu che d'un giusto" (Know'st Thou?) an air in vigorous, dramatic, yet tuneful style, proclaiming to the youth that he is designed to succeed *Baltazar* himself as Prior. But *Ferdinand* can only reply that he loves the stranger. He is dismissed, but goes without protest, to seek, somewhere in the world, his beloved idol. At the last moment he recalls his novitiate. He would turn to *Baltazar* with outspread arms. But the *Prior* turns away.

For once the miraculous thing happens. *Ferdinand* hears from the lady, through a fair guide who leads him, with bandaged eyes, to the Isle of Leon, where *Inez*, the attendant of his unknown beloved, *Leonora*, is gathering flowers.

Leonora is the mistress of the *King of Castile*, and a most unhappy woman. Beguiled at an early age, she now is shunned by former friends. Despite the flowers and the sunshine, to her the place is a prison of torment.

Ferdinand's bandages are removed. He gazes wonderingly around him, and he begs of *Inez* the name of his unknown fair one. She smiles, declaring that only the fair one herself may tell; and in due course, the fair one appears. There is a delightful love-scene, with a constant shadow of fear, however, in the background; the *King* may arrive at any minute.

Ferdinand passionately avows his love; he is heard willingly but with distress. Finally *Leonora* commands him to leave her forever; but since miraculous things are yet to happen, she gives him a parchment which, she avers, will ensure his future. The duet "Fia vere!" (Fly From Thee!) heard here, is a dramatic but exceedingly tuneful number. He wishes to remain, when *Inez* enters, whispering that the *King* is at the villa. As *Ferdinand* leaves he recognizes the monarch, and his hopes fall. If the *King* comes to woo his mistress how can he, a recreant monk, aspire to her hand? He looks at the parchment—his commission as an officer of the *King*!

ACT II

SCENE—*Gardens of the Alcazar Palace*

THE *King* walks in his garden, recently regained from the Moors. He reflects how his victory might have been defeat, had it not been for one *Ferdinand*, a young officer who rallied the troops—an action worth reward. He is disturbed by a messenger from *Baltazar*, the *King's* father-in-law, and head of the powerful Church party. The *King* is threatened with the wrath of the church if he will not give up *Leonora;* but he is in no mood to submit to ecclesiastical authority, and he defies it.

Leonora enters. She is melancholy, and the *King* asks the cause. "Vien, Leonora," sings he (Leonora, Thou Art Alone), and he promises her wealth and honor if she will but return his love. *Leonora's* pathetic reply extends over two numbers: "Quando le soglie" (From My Father's Halls) and "Ah! l'alto ardor" (Oh Love!). She reminds the *King* that as a child she believed in his promises, but that he broke them to bring dishonor to her father. Now she dwells, in public contempt, in her island-garden, a plaything, no more.

The music here is vividly arresting; it increases in interest as *Leonora* goes on to beg the *King's* permission to leave his court, so that she may die remote from its grandeur. *Baltazar* enters, with a mandate from the Pope himself. The *King* declares he will wed *Leonora*, for a second time defying religious authority. The rejoinder is a threat, by *Baltazar*, of Divine vengeance— before which both the *King* and his favorite shrink back in terror. The music here,"Ah! paventa il furor" (The Wrath of Heaven), is one of the most impressive of the opera's concerted numbers. The curtain descends upon a dramatic tableau—*Leonora* weeping with shame, the *King* hesitating between love and fear, and *Baltazar* thundering down upon them the terrible words of the Papal curse.

ACT III

SCENE—*A Room in the Palace*

THE *King* has not forgotten his debt to *Ferdinand*. He offers to discharge it, and the young man asks the hand of the lady to whom he owes all. Her name is requested. When *Leonora* is pointed out the *King* changes his mind. He has guessed, of late, from the lady herself, the condition of her heart—so this is it! Well, why not? No pleasure the *King* might find in her, would atone for a break with the Church. And what sweeter revenge than to bestow upon this presumptuous youth a lady of tarnished honor?

In the presence of the Court, the *King* consents; the melody "A Tanto Amor" (Thou Flower Belov'd) is in bitter irony, and every word stabs like a knife-thrust the heart of *Leonora*. *Ferdinand* is oblivious of this, and he listens with respect.

Leonora, like many another woman in a false position, is a woman of character. She bids *Inez* to tell *Ferdinand* everything, but *Inez* is arrested before he can receive the message. So, then, *Leonora* prepares for the wedding. The *King* has conferred upon *Ferdinand* the title of the *Count of Zamora*.

Leonora appears, and seeing *Ferdinand* gaze at her lovingly, believes the message of *Inez* has been delivered, and that her past has made no difference. But when the pair are presented at Court, cold looks and averted eyes whisper to *Ferdinand* more than tongues. White with anger, he draws sword, and bloodshed is prevented only by the arrival of *Baltazar*, who tells the truth. The new *Count* is dumbstricken. Then he denounces the *King*. An intense scene follows, *Leonora* striving to tell of her message through *Inez*: "Orsu, Fernando" (Stay, Hear Me, Fernando). *Ferdinand* hurls at the *King's* feet his badge of honor and the pieces of his broken sword.

ACT IV

SCENE—*The Cloisters of the Monastery*

THE sun is rising over the cloister walls. The monks have assembled to welcome back *Ferdinand* from the earthly life. Heart-broken, he has asked to renew his vows, and he is returning to accept the forgiveness so freely held forth. There is first a hymn-like song of greeting, "Splendon piu belle in ciel le stelle" (In Heavenly Splendor) sung by *Baltazar* and chorus. The repentant is told to lift up his eyes from earthly things, and to contemplate the stars. Left alone a moment, he sings his farewell to the external world, the beautiful "Spirto gentil" (Spirit so Fair). The phantom of love and its illusions are left behind—only memories remain, pale, tranquil, tender and ineffably sad. As *Ferdinand* goes to the chapel, word is brought that a novice craves admittance. Unseen, the newcomer watches *Ferdinand* take the final vows, then falls before the chapel entrance. The newly-accepted monk helps the prone figure to arise; then he recognizes *Leonora*. Horrified, he bids her begone.

But love, if still of the earth, is terrible to break. *Leonora* only wishes to say farewell. There is a touching duet, "Pietoso al par d'un Nume" (As Merciful as God). Even now, the torn and wracked *Ferdinand* would go back, for the second time into the world, but she forbids him. She is seen to be very near death; and with the assurance that she and her lover will meet again, in a happier land, she sinks lifeless.

THE VICTOR RECORDS
(Sung in Italian unless otherwise noted)

ACT II

AH! L'ALTO ARDOR

(Oh, Love!) MARGARETE MATZENAUER, Contralto and PASQUALE AMATO, Baritone   8003   12-in., $2.50

VIEN LEONORA

(Leonora, Thou Alone) MATTIA BATTISTINI, Baritone   6044   12-in.,   2.00

ACT II

A TANTO AMOR

(Thou Flower Beloved) GIUSEPPE DE LUCA, Baritone   6080   12-in., $2.00

ALPHONSO:

Thou flow'r belov'd,
And in hope's garden cherish'd,
With sighs and tears refresh'd,
Both night and morn;
Fad'st from my breast,
Thine ev'ry beauty perished,
And in thy stead alone have left a thorn!

O MIO FERNANDO

(Dearest Ferdinand) GABRIELLA BESANZONI, Contralto   6047   12-in.,   2.00

ACT IV

SPIRTO GENTIL

(Spirit So Fair) ENRICO CARUSO, Tenor
6005   12-in.,   2.00

BENIAMINO GIGLI, Tenor   6139   12-in.,   2.00

EVAN WILLIAMS, Tenor   *In English*
6308   12-in.,   2.00

FERDINAND:

Spirit so fair, brightly descending,
Then like a dream all sadly ending,
Hence from my heart, vision deceiving,
Phantom of love, grief only leaving,
In thee delighting, all else scorning,
A father's warning, my country, my fame!
Ah, faithless dame, a passion inviting,
Fair honor blighting, branding my name,
Grief alone thou leav'st, phantom of love!

BLACK LABEL RECORD

{Grand Fantasia............................*Vessella's Italian Band*}
{ *Faust—Prison Scene*...........................*Vessella's Italian Band*} 35449   12-in.,   1.25

    THE METROPOLITAN CAST OF 1913

FIDELIO

BEETHOVEN'S only opera, "Fidelio," called for much revision before it satisfied the composer and his followers. It was twice condensed from its original form. At the second performance, in 1806, even the title was changed, to "Léonore." No less than four overtures were written for it, "Léonore No. 2" being the first. Then came "No. 3," then "Fidelio," which the composer himself thought too "light" for the work. Musically, "No. 3" is the grandest—a monumental work heard frequently in concert even today. It has been recorded for the Victor, on two records. The buoyant, soaring melody of its first theme is one of Beethoven's finest melodic inspirations. A striking passage for trumpet, usually played "off-stage," typifies the arrival of deliverance, in the opera,—in the person of *Don Fernando.*

THE OPERA

OPERA in two acts, adapted by Sonnleithner from Bouilly's *Léonore, ou l'Amour Conjugal.* Music by Beethoven. First produced at Vienna, November 20, 1805. Given in London May 18, 1832. In Paris at the Théâtre Lyrique, translated by Barbier and Carré, and in three acts, May 5, 1860. First American performance in New York, September 9, 1839, with Giubilei, Manvers and Poole. Other notable productions in 1858, with Mme. Caradori and Karl Formes; in 1868, with Mme. Rotter, Habelmann and Formes; at the New Orleans Opera, in Italian, December 11, 1877; the Damrosch production of 1884, with Brandt, Belz and Koegel; the Metropolitan performances in 1901 with Ternina as *Léonore;* and the revivals of more recent years.

CHARACTERS

Don Fernando (*Fair-nahn'-doh*), Minister..........Baritone
Don Pizarro (*Pee-tsar'-ro*), Governor of the State Prison.................Baritone
Florestan (*Floh'-ray-stahn*), a prisoner..................Tenor

137

LÉONORE (*Lay-oh-noh'-reh*), his
wife, known as Fidelio....Soprano
Rocco (*Roh'coh*), jailor..........Bass
MARZELLINE (*Mahr-tsay-leen'-
eh*), his daughter........Soprano
JAQUINO (*Yah-kwee'-noh*), gate-
keeper....................Tenor
Soldiers, Prisoners, People, etc.

*Place: A Spanish State Prison in the
Vicinity of Seville*

(The name of the opera is pronounced *Fee-day'-lee-oh*).

LÉONORE and *Fidelio* are one and
the same person—the wife of
Florestan, a Spanish nobleman who
has incurred the enmity of *Don
Pizarro*, Governor of the State Prison.
Pizarro has placed him in a dungeon,
and announced his death. *Léonore* refuses to believe. Disguising herself as
a lad, she makes love to *Marzelline*,
daughter of *Rocco*, the jailor, under the
name *Fidelio*, thus gaining access to
the place, where she learns of a mysterious prisoner. Hope nearly dies

when she overhears *Pizarro* plotting
with *Rocco* to have this prisoner killed.
His death has become necessary, because the harsh methods of *Pizarro*
have become known, *Don Fernando*,
Minister of the Interior, is to investigate, and "dead men tell no tales."
Fidelio is assigned the task, with
Rocco, of digging her own husband's
grave. While she is plying the spade,
Rocco brings in the prisoner, whom she
does not at first recognize, so terrible
is his condition. *Pizarro*, entering,
tries to stab the man, but *Léonore*,
now scorning disguise, throws herself
between. *Pizarro* is about to kill both
when trumpets announce the arrival of
Don Fernando. Husband and wife are
rescued, and *Pizarro* is duly punished.
The liberation of other prisoners affords opportunity for one of the most
inspiring of Beethoven's male choruses;
the "Prisoners' Chorus" (Oh, What Delight). The music throughout the opera
is of a dignified, noble character—as befits the utterance of a great composer.

BLACK LABEL RECORDS

Léonore Overture, No. 3 (Part I).............*Victor Concert Orchestra*	35268	12-in.,	$1.25
Léonore Overture, No. 3 (Part II).............*Victor Concert Orchestra*			
Léonore Overture, No. 3 (Part III).............*Victor Concert Orchestra*	35269	12-in.,	1.25
Adagio from Fourth Symphony (Beethoven).............*Vessella's Band*			
Prisoners' Chorus (Oh! What Delight)............ *Victor Male Chorus*	35576	12-in.,	1.25
The Heavens Resound (Beethoven).............*Victor Oratorio Chorus*			

REMBRANDT

SCENE FROM FIDELIO

138

THE PHANTOM SHIP

THE FLYING DUTCHMAN

(DER FLIEGENDE HOLLÄNDER)
(German)

DRIVEN by a gale, a phantom ship approaches the shore,— the ship of Van der Decken, who after trying vainly to pass the Cape of Good Hope, swore he would not quit, if he had to sail the ocean to Eternity. To punish his blasphemy, he is to sail the ocean forever, in a phantom ship with a phantom crew. Such is Heine's legend.

As in all Wagner's operas, however, there is mercy. If *The Dutchman* can find a woman who will be faithful unto death, he will go free. To find her, he is allowed to go ashore once every seven years. This is the time. The Overture itself tells the story. Above the howling of the gale is heard a motive, or theme, which signalizes *damnation*,— the *curse* motive:

There is another to balance it—the motive of *redemption*—an echo of an ancient phrase signifying "Farewell," —a phrase used by Beethoven, by Schubert, by Mendelssohn, and later on, with sublime effect, in "Lohengrin" by Wagner himself. Against the *Curse* of *The Dutchman's* own will, is the *Redemption* which will come to him through a woman's true soul. *Senta*, the daughter of *Daland*, a sea-captain, is the chosen one. But the story is best told in detail.

THE OPERA

ROMANTIC opera in three acts. Text and score by Richard Wagner. First produced at the Royal Opera in Dresden, January 2, 1843. Produced in Berlin in 1844; Zurich, 1852; Weimar, 1853; Vienna, 1860; Munich, 1864. First London production July 23, 1870, under the title

L'Olandese Dannato, the book being translated into Italian by Marchesi; and in English by Carl Rosa, October 3, 1876. In Italy, at Bologna, 1877. Another Italian version was given at Covent Garden, this time called *Il Vascello Fantasma*, June, 1877. First American production at Philadelphia, November 8, 1876, by the Pappenheim Opera Company, in Italian; first New York production, in English, January 26, 1877; in German, March 12, 1877. Given at New Orleans Opera in 1877.

CHARACTERS

DALAND, a Norwegian sea captain. Bass
SENTA, his daughter . . . . Soprano
ERIC, a huntsman . . . . Tenor
MARY, Senta's nurse . . . . Contralto
DALAND'S STEERSMAN . . . . Tenor
THE DUTCHMAN . . . . Baritone
　Sailors, Maidens, Hunters, etc.

Place: On the Coast of Norway

(The German name of the opera is pronounced *Dair Flee'-gen-deh Hol-layn'-der*).

ACT I

SCENE—*The Coast of Norway*

THE worst of the storm is over; *Daland* brings his ship to anchor off the rocky coast. As the crew furls the sails, he goes ashore to obtain his bearings. From the head of the cliff he discerns he is but seven miles from home; but as he must wait, now, for a change of wind from off-shore, he allows the crew to rest. He is weary himself after his long struggle with sea and wind, so he leaves the vessel in charge of the *Steersman* as he goes below.

The *Steersman*, to keep himself awake, sings a ballad to the South Wind—that is to bring him home to his beloved one. Nevertheless, he falls asleep, and he cannot see, gliding in silently through the darkness, the blood-red sails and the black masts of *The Dutchman's* fearful craft. The spectral crew, with their pale faces and phosphorescent eyes, furl the strange sails and drop the rusty anchor. And the *Steersman* sleeps on.

But *The Dutchman* stands alone on the rotting deck of his ship, and he sings the famous soliloquy, "Die Frist ist um" (The Term is Passed). This is a strange number, half recitative, half aria, weird, imaginative and wonderful. It expresses *The Dutchman's* hopelessness of salvation. A night or so ashore, then another seven years, then another and another and yet another, and so, possibly, throughout Eternity. What woman may be found to love such a wretch, and to remain faithful?

Daland appears on the deck of the other ship, and he is astonished to see the strange craft alongside. He wakes the *Steersman*, and the two hail her. *The Dutchman* asks for a night's shelter in the house of *Daland*, for which he offers a generous sum. He notes the Norwegian's quickness to accept, and, hearing that he has a daughter, he proposes marriage. The simple-minded captain consents, provided the girl, *Senta*, is willing. The stranger, thoughtful-looking, is nevertheless of distinguished appearance, and obviously rich. A wind springs up, the Norwegian sails for home, and *The Dutchman* promises to follow at once.

ACT II

SCENE—*A Room in Daland's House*

WOMEN, in *Daland's* house, await his arrival, spinning, singing, laughing, chatting among themselves. They sing the wonderful "Spinning Chorus," with its light tripping melody and its whirring accompaniment, for all the world like the steady rote of the spinning-wheel.

Among the girls, *Senta* sits somewhat aloof and inattentive. Her eyes are fixed upon a fanciful portrait of the

Flying Dutchman, hanging on the wall. The legend of the unhappy mariner has deeply impressed her mind. Her companions ridicule the girl, declaring her lover, *Erik*, will be jealous. She is disposed to be resentful; she objects to the spinning song, and asks that someone may sing the ballad of the *Flying Dutchman's* ship. None will. She sings it herself, the grim, fantastic, terrible "Curse" motive breaking like a raw sea-wind into the warm homelike atmosphere of the spinning party. The wind itself wails, in fierce chromatics, throughout the song.

But as the tale proceeds, this new theme of *salvation*, or *redemption* by *woman's love*, one of the tenderest and most melodious phrases in music, is heard. Half-conscious, she runs toward the portrait with outstretched arms.

The girls are amazed. Some of them rush out to produce *Erik*. The young man brings with him the news that *Daland's* ship has arrived and that of the stranger. The women-folk run to the shore with greetings; but *Erik* remains to chide *Senta*. She refuses to listen, and he goes too. Left alone, she remains in a half-dreamy state. Then the door opens, and there stands the *Flying Dutchman*, for all the world like the picture of himself that some old painter has imagined—or painted from someone's description. The girl looks at this, then at her visitor, and back again. The eyes of the pair meet, and they remain in awed silence. *Daland* is delighted at the impression his daughter and the stranger have made. He announces *The Dutchman's* proposal of marriage. The lovesick girl assents. The couple are left alone, in the strange, half mystical rapture of

their discovery. *Daland* has not recognized the original of the picture. *Senta*, before her betrothed, promises to remain faithful unto death.

ACT III

Scene—*The Harbor*

DALAND'S ship is gay with lanterns, strung out in lines of fire in the gathering gloom. The crew is merry-making—over a safe voyage, and over the wedding to be. The women bring baskets of good things to eat. The men of *Daland's* ship receive them joyously, but there is no sign from *The Dutchman's*. They turn over their baskets, and, hurt at this silent reception, they return home.

Then *Daland's* crew turn to the strange vessel. They call once more, inviting her crew to the feast. Suddenly the sea rises, the air grows icy cold, and a singular glow illumines the ship. The crew then appear, misty, spectral figures, and begin a sepulchral chant. The Norwegians are astonished and dismayed. They cross themselves in terror and run below, followed by devilish-sounding laughter. The lights burn blue and die upon the stranger's decks. And the ship and her crew disappear again into the darkness.

Senta and *Erik* arrive. The young man has heard, and he is beside himself. He kneels and begs his love to take pity on him. *Senta*, for all her love for *The Dutchman*, is human, and her pity indeed is aroused. She lets it be seen—when *The Dutchman* suddenly appears.

He cannot but believe, after his years of torture and disappointment, that his love is false. He cries out, briefly, "All is lost—farewell!"

It is the signal for action. The crews appear. *The Dutchman* declares his identity, and admits himself cursed forever. He leaps to the deck of the ship. The blood-red sails drop from the yards, and belly out beneath a wind that no man ever felt on earth. The crew set up their wild refrain, the weird St. Elmo's fires light up the mastheads, and the crazy and worm-eaten phantom ship goes off, cutting the water like a knife, irrespective of wind or tide.

Senta, in wild exultation, rushes to the shore, crying out "I am faithful unto Death!" Before a hand can stay her, she has thrown herself into the sea. As she does so, the phantom ship sinks too. But rising from the wreck can be seen the forms of the *Flying Dutchman* and his eternal bride, clasped in one another's arms. The curse has been dissolved by the love of one true woman. Legend or symbol, such is the tale.

THE VICTOR RECORD
(Sung in German unless otherwise noted)

ACT II

TRAFT IHR DAS SCHIFF
(A Ship the Restless Ocean Sweeps)
MARIA JERITZA, Soprano   (*In German*)
74776   12-in., $1.50

BLACK LABEL RECORDS

{Die Frist ist um (The Term is Past) Part I (*In German*)....*Fritz Feinhals*} 68484   12-in., $1.25
{Die Frist ist um Part II (*In German*) ....*Fritz Feinhals*}

{Spinning Chorus (*In English*)................*Victor Women's Chorus*} 35494   12-in.,   1.25
{ Lohengrin—Bridal Chorus................*Victor Opera Chorus*}

BERGER
RENAUD AS THE DUTCHMAN

DESTINN AS SENTA

HOFFERT, BERLIN
SCHUMANN-HEINK AS MARY

DON ALVARO:
Swear in this hour
That you will grant my wish!

LA FORZA DEL DESTINO

(THE FORCE OF DESTINY)

OPERA in four acts. Book by Piave; music by Giuseppe Verdi. First produced at St. Petersburg, November 11, 1862; in London, June 22, 1867; in Milan, 1869; Paris, 1876; Berlin, 1878. First New York production February 2, 1865, with Carozzi-Zucchi, Massimilliani and Bellini. It was not heard again for fifteen years, when it was produced at the Academy of Music, with the last act rewritten by the composer, the cast including Annie Louise Cary, Campanini, Galassi and Del Puente. Given in recent years in San Francisco by the Lombardi Opera Company. Revived in 1918 at the Metropolitan with Caruso.

CHARACTERS

MARQUIS OF CALATRAVA (*Kalah-trah'vah*)..............Bass

DONNA LEONORA } his { Soprano
DON CARLO } children { Baritone

DON ALVARO (*Ahl-vah'-roh*).... Tenor
ABBOT OF THE FRANCISCAN FRIARS. Bass
MELITONE, a friar..........Baritone
Muleteers,Peasants,Soldiers,Friars,etc

Scene and Period: Spain and Italy; about the Middle of the Eighteenth Century

(The name of the opera is pronounced *Lah Fort'-zah del Des-tee'-noh*)

143

THE opera has an overture, in which is given a foretaste of what is to follow. It opens with a trumpet blast, followed by an air in the minor, leading in its turn to a striking theme in the stringed instruments, which has been compared to a familiar theme in a Liszt rhapsody and one in a composition by Brahms—showing the plasticity of a simple motif in the hands of three composers of varying nationalities and temperaments. This is the theme of the "Madre Pietosa," afterwards heard with magnificent effect in the opera:

ACT I

SCENE—*Drawing Room of the Marquis of Calatrava*

DON ALVARO is a young prince of an illustrious family in India. His forbears have claimed descent from the sun itself; but this counts for little in proud Spain. Aware that her family will never permit marriage with him, *Leonora* plans to elope. *Alvaro* arrives by night, but the noise of departure awakens the household, and the aged *Marquis of Calatrava* discovers the pair. Leaping to the wrong conclusion, he ignores the protests of both. To take the blame alone, *Alvaro* throws his pistol away, intending to present his bare breast to the aged noble's sword. But the weapon is a hair-trigger affair, and in the act it goes off. When the smoke clears, the *Marquis* lies mortally wounded, cursing his daughter with his last breath.

ACT II

SCENE I—*An Inn at Hornacuelos*

IN the warm kitchen of this mountain hostelry is gathered a crowd of muleteers, soldiers, a monk, a student, a gypsy fortune-teller, and *Leonora* in male disguise. Hither she has fled from the home of an aged relative who gave her temporary shelter. Her brother, *Don Carlo*, has sworn to kill both *Leonora* and her lover; and having lost trace of *Don Alvaro* since the fatal night, *Leonora* is both alone and desperate. Her terror and despair increase when she discovers that the student, hobnobbing with a friar, is none but *Don Carlo*, who in disguise is hoping to find some trace of the man he believes the seducer of his sister and the murderer of his father. She flees the place, among the confusion caused by the announcement, from a gypsy girl, that Italy and Spain have declared war upon the Austrians.

SCENE II—*The Monastery at Hornacuelos*

LEONORA has come to the door of the monastery, where, kneeling in the moonlight, she asks the Virgin to protect her. This plea affords a very beautiful number, based on the theme, "Madre Pietosa Vergine" (Holy Mother, Have Mercy), heard previously in the overture. It begins in agitated style, but soon develops into a beautiful aria succeeded by solemn choral passages, the Venite of the monks singing in the chapel. Above these the solo voice rises with supreme power.

Still in her disguise as a man, *Leonora* seeks admission, confessing all to the *Abbot*. He procures her suitable attire, and directs her to a cave in the nearby mountainside which is shunned by the superstitious folk. The monks solemnly lay a curse upon all who may seek to learn the stranger's identity. She remains for some years in her solitary hold; but love remains alive in her heart, affording rich material for the sport of Destiny.

ACT III

SCENE—*A Military Camp near Valletri*

ALVARO, believing *Leonora* dead, has, with the outbreak of the war, enlisted with the Spanish army to fight in Italy against Austria. He bears an assumed name, but he is tormented by memories of his beloved: "O tu che in sono agli angeli" (Thou Heavenly One), he sings, in a tender and melancholy number which prays to her, believably in Heaven, to look down upon his loneliness of heart.

His reveries are interrupted. He hears a cry of distress, and goes out to find a wounded man. It is *Don Carlo*, his sworn enemy. But as the two never have met, they do not recognize one another. They become close friends. Another battle follows, and this time it is *Don Alvaro* who is wounded,—seriously, to all seeming mortally.

His new friend volunteers to administer his last wishes. *Alvaro* begs him to search in his cloak for a key and a casket of letters. These are to be burned, without opening, and *Don Carlo* is sworn to execute this office. The adjuration affords a fine duet, beautiful in melody and intense in its emotional fervor, the famous "Solenne in quest' ora" (Swear in This Hour). *Don Carlo* is torn with pity.

But, Destiny preferring to work in its own fashion, *Don Alvaro* does not die—nor does *Don Carlo* break his oath. But having accidently mentioned the name *Calatrava*, his suspicions are aroused when *Alvaro* starts at the sound of it. He does not open the casket, but otherwhere in the wounded man's effects he discovers a picture of *Leonora*. When *Alvaro* recovers, *Don Carlo* makes himself known; at the same time, unwittingly, giving his enemy to understand that *Leonora* still lives—though he does not know where. *Alvaro* is overjoyed; he in turn discloses himself, striving to convince *Don Carlo* he is guiltless of wrongdoing, and worthy of his sister. Unable to draw *Alvaro* into combat, *Carlo* threatens then to search out *Leonora*, and take her life instead. A

dramatic scene rises: "Il segreto fu dunque violato?" (Is My Secret Then Betrayed?). A duel follows, and *Alvaro* wins. Believing he has killed a second man, he decides to take holy vows and to end his days in a monastery. He cannot now go to *Leonora* with a brother's blood, as well as a father's, upon his hands.

ACT IV
SCENE—*The Monastery of Hornacuelos*

FIVE years have passed. And *Don Alvaro*, now *Father Raphael*, has become noted for his goodness of life, his compassionate kindliness toward all who suffer. But *Don Carlo* has sought,—and he has now found him— only to taunt the devoted and harmless soul with cowardice. "In Vano, Alvaro" (In Vain, Alvaro!) sings he. The friar, well schooled to ignore his own feelings, tries hard to convince *Don Carlo* that vengeance lies with God. In return he receives the most venomous insults. He endeavors, vainly, to reach a peaceful solution. In the duet, "Le minaccie, i fieri accenti" (Thy Menaces Wild), the tensity of the situation reaches the breaking point. Slowly but surely the benevolent priest becomes, again, the fiery "man of honor." A pathetic instrumental melody coupled with the broken speech of *Don Alvaro*, is exceedingly touching; but it disappears in the riot of stormier passions. The convent is no place to fight, and the two seek a hillside—the very hillside where, unknown to either, *Leonora* herself abides in misery.

ACT V
SCENE—*A Wild Spot near Hornacuelos*

PALE and worn, yet still beautiful, *Leonora* issues for the thousandth time from her cave, to implore Heaven to let her die and forget her lover.

Heaven's only reply is a storm of rain and wind and thunder which drives her back just as the two men arrive. Again *Don Carlo* is vanquished, and in fair fight. This time the wound is mortal, and the dying man begs his enemy, as *Father Raphael*, to confess him and yield absolution. This *Alvaro* cannot do, the place being under the "ban" still set upon it. But he calls the "friar" who dwells in the cave. *Leonora*, finding her brother dying, rushes to embrace him. Seeing her in the presence of *Don Alvaro*, he suspects the pair of complicity, and stabs her as her arms fold about him. The music here is impressive, "Non imprecare, umiliati" (Swear Not, Be Humble"), one of Verdi's great concerted numbers.

What is there left for *Don Alvaro*? He has been responsible, an instrument played upon by the skilful and malicious fingers of Destiny, for three deaths. What atonement is there? He casts himself from the cliff as the monks arrive singing a Miserere.

THE VICTOR RECORDS

(Sung in Italian)

ACT II

MADRE, PIETOSA VERGINE
(Holy Mother, Have Mercy)
CELESTINA BONINSEGNA, Soprano and
La Scala Chorus   6351 12-in., $2.00

LEONORA.

Oh, Holy Virgin,
Have mercy on my sins!
Send help from Heaven
To erase from my heart
That ungrateful one.
(*The friars are heard in their morning hymn.*)

O sublime song,
Which like incense,
Ascends heavenward
It gives faith, comfort,
And quiet to my soul.
I will go to the holy sanctuary.
The pious father cannot refuse to receive me.
O Lord! Have mercy on me,
Nor abandon me.
(*She rings the bell of the convent.*)

ACT III

O TU CHE IN SENO AGLI' ANGELI
(Thou Heavenly One) ENRICO CARUSO,
Tenor   6000 12-in., $2.00

SOLENNE IN QUEST' ORA
(Swear in This Hour) ENRICO CARUSO,
Tenor and ANTONIO SCOTTI, Baritone
8000 12-in., 2.50

IL SEGRETO FU DUNQUE VIOLATO?
(Is My Secret Then Betrayed?) ENRICO
CARUSO, Tenor and GIUSEPPE DE
LUCA, Baritone   8006 12-in., 2.50

ACT IV

INVANO ALVARO
(In Vain, Alvaro!) ENRICO CARUSO,
Tenor and PASQUALE AMATO, Baritone   8005 12-in., 2.50

LE MINACCIE, I FIERI ACCENTI
(Thy Menaces Wild) ENRICO CARUSO,
Tenor and PASQUALE AMATO, Baritone   8005 12-in., 2.50

PACE, PACE MIO DIO
(Peace, Oh My Lord) ROSA PONSELLE,
Soprano   6440 12-in., 2.00

BLACK LABEL AND PURPLE LABEL RECORDS

Solenne in quest' ora (Swear in This Hour) . . . . *Murphy and Werrenrath* 70103 12-in., $1.25

{Overture—Part I. . . . . *Victor Symphony Orchestra*} 35721 12-in., 1.25
{Overture—Part II. . . . . *Victor Symphony Orchestra*}

{Overture. . . . . *Arthur Pryor's Band*} 35215 12-in., 1.25
{ Orpheus Overture (Offenbach). . . . .*Arthur Pryor's Band*}

{Solenne in quest' ora. . . . . *Vessella's Italian Band*} 35512 12-in., 1.25
{ Mefistofele—Selection. *Vessella's Italian Band*}

FRA DIAVOLO

COMIC opera in three acts. Libretto by Scribe, music by Daniel François Esprit Auber. First production at the *Opéra Comique*, Paris, January 28, 1830. Presented in Vienna, 1830. London, at the Drury Lane Theatre, in English, November 3, 1831; in Italian at the Lyceum Theatre, 1857. First American production at the Old Park Theatre, New York, in English, June 20, 1833. Produced in New Orleans in 1836. It was not until 1864 that it was given in Italian in New York, at the Academy of Music, with Kellogg. Colonel Mapleson gave three performances of the opera at the Academy of Music in 1885. Zelie de Lussan made her début here in the part with the Boston Ideals in 1888. Recently revived at the Manhattan Opera and afterwards at the New Theatre by the Metropolitan forces.

CHARACTERS

FRA DIAVOLO, calling himself "Marquis of San Marco"..................Tenor
LORD ROCBURG (Lord Allcash), an English traveler....................Tenor
LADY PAMELA (Lady Allcash) his wife................Soprano
LORENZO, Chief of the Carabiniers...................Tenor
MATTEO, the innkeeper..........Bass
ZERLINA, his daughter.......Soprano
GIACOMO and BEPPO, companions of Fra Diavolo................Bass-Tenor

The Scene: Italy, in the Neighborhood of Terracina

(The name of the opera is pronounced *Frah Dee-ah'-voh-loh*).

THIS is a spirited little opera. *Zerlina* and *Lorenzo,* her soldier, are too poor to marry. The girl's father, *Matteo,* has a rich suitor all ready, and "tomorrow is the day." There is a gay time at the inn. *Lord Rocburg* and his wife, *Lady Pamela,* arrive. They have been robbed, and *Lorenzo* and his men go after the bandits. Another guest, the smooth *Marquis of San Marco,* (Fra Diavolo, the bandit,) next comes in—to flirt with *Lady Pamela,* and to gain access to the noble *Lord's* money-belt. He is distressed when *Lorenzo* returns with the jewels and news of slain robbers. The young man is given a reward which seems to make possible his marriage.

That night, the *Marquis* and two followers, *Beppo* and *Giacomo,* conceal themselves in *Zerlina's* room to rob *Rocburg* in the night. *Lorenzo* arrives; discovered, the *Marquis* makes both him and *Rocburg* believe he has been conducting affairs with *Zerlina* and *Lady Pamela.* Both men challenge him. Next morning *Zerlina* discovers *Beppo* and *Giacomo* were in her room too. *Lorenzo* arrests them, and they are forced to betray their chief. He is led into a trap and shot. Then it transpires, of course, that *Fra Diavolo* and the *Marquis* were one. All ends happily.

BLACK LABEL RECORDS

Overture to Fra Diavolo.....................*Arthur Pryor's Band* }35109	12-in.,	$1.25
Marriage of Figaro Overture (Mozart)...............*Arthur Pryor's Band*		
Fra Diavolo Selection.......................*Vessella's Italian Band* }35191	12-in.,	1.25
Daughter of Regiment Selection...................*Vessella's Italian Band*		

THE WOLF'S GLEN SCENE

DER FREISCHÜTZ

CARL MARIA VON WEBER, like others of his group—Mendelssohn, Chopin, Bellini—died before his genius had fulfilled itself. He is usually regarded as the first important operatic composer to open the new avenues of romanticism in the nineteenth century. In "Der Freischütz" he sought to escape Italian influence by discarding plots of intrigue, seeking rather, for material, the legends of his own country. He gave to German operatic music that first tinge of nationalism which developed to its ultimate in Wagner, with his monumental music dramas of Teuton mythology.

The word "Freischütz" means not so much "Freeshooter" as "Free Marksman;" it was applied to one who used charmed bullets. It plunges at once into that mystical word of legendary superstition where fact is subordinate to fancy. This opera must be enjoyed in the fairy-tale spirit, remembering that first of all it is a story. We learn, however, even in the guise of folk lore, that it is safer to put trust in the forces of right than those of evil—in whatever romantic guise.

THE OPERA

ROMANTIC opera in three acts. Words by Friedrich Kind; music by Carl Maria von Weber; completed as *Die Jägersbraut*, May 13, 1820. Produced at Berlin, June 18, 1821; in Paris (as *Robin des Bois*, with new libretto by Blaze and Sauvage, and many changes), at the Odéon, December 7, 1824. Another version, with translation by Pacini, and recitatives by Berlioz, at the Académie Royale, June 7, 1841, under the title of *Le Franc Archer*. In London as *Der Freischütz* or *The Seventh Bullet*, with many ballads inserted, July 23, 1824; in German, at King's Theatre, May 9, 1832; in Italian, as *Il Franco Arciero*, at Covent Garden, March 16, 1850 (recitatives by

148

Costa). First New York production, in English, March 2, 1825. This was followed by other versions, Charles E. Horn appearing as *Caspar* in 1827. German performances were given at the old Broadway Theatre, 1856, and by other German companies in the sixties. Produced at the Metropolitan under Dr. Damrosch in 1884, and at the Academy of Music in 1896. Revived at the Metropolitan in 1910, and in 1924 with recitatives.

CHARACTERS

PRINCE OTTOKAR, Duke of Bohemia...............Baritone
CUNO, head ranger.............Bass
MAX } two young foresters { Tenor
CASPAR } { Bass
KILIAN, a rich peasant.........Tenor
A HERMIT....................Bass
ZAMIEL, the fiend huntsman..........
AGNES, Cuno's daughter......Soprano
ANNIE, her cousin..........Soprano
Chorus of Hunters, Peasants and Spirits

Scene and Period: Bohemia, about 1750

(The name of the opera is pronounced, approximately, *Dair Frysheetz*).

A BEAUTIFUL overture sums up much of the music. A broad, low unison melody for the whole orchestra, leads to a lovely horn passage, rich with the spirit of the woodlands. The night is falling, soft and mysterious. A rushing allegro fills us with the doubts of the young hunter-hero; we hear his magic bullets fall into the melting-pot, one by one, and the terrors of the Wolf's Glen sweep down upon us. A lovely melody brings relief—picturing the tender love of the heroine, only to bring fresh dread and distress. But triumph comes at last, and the overture ends with a ringingly melodious climax.

The story is simple. *Max* a young ranger in the service of the Bohemian *Prince Ottokar*, loves *Agnes*, who has promised to marry him if he wins the shooters' contest. He fails, the prize going to a peasant, *Kilian*. *Max* bewails his misfortune in a highly dramatic air, "Durch die Wälder" (Thro' the Forest). He thinks of his beloved: "Jetzt ist wohl ihr Fenster offen" (Now Beside Her Lattice), and he works himself into rather a desperate mood. *Caspar*, a dissolute fellow-ranger, appears. *Caspar's* excesses have led him into the power of *Zamiel*, the Demon Hunter of Bohemian tradition —a kind of Mephistopheles. Any hunter who will sell his soul to *Zamiel* will receive seven bullets which will never fail their mark. For each victim he brings, the supply is extended—and his own life; but woe to him if he fails to bring a fresh one before the seventh bullet!

Caspar sees his chance in *Max*— whom he induces to meet him in the Wolf's Glen, to receive the charmed bullets.

Meanwhile, *Agnes* awaits, with alarm, her absent lover. Her cousin *Annie*, offers cheer, but vainly, so she departs. The girl, alone in her room, prays in the starlight for the safety of her lover. Her "Preghiera" (Agnes' Prayer), is the most famous air of the opera—if we except the horn passage in the overture, which has been set as a familiar hymn. The quiet dignity of the "prayer," its restful faith in Heaven, have won it the love of all true music-lovers.

Max arrives, followed by *Annie*; his manner is agitated. He declares he must go to the Wolf's Glen to bring in a stag he has shot; *Agnes*, knowing the place's reputation, begs him not to. But he insists, and the scene changes to the Glen, where, among picturesque terrors, he meets *Caspar*. Visions ar-

149

rive and pass, fiends rave, and the bullets are cast amid thunders and winds and earthquakes.

Max returns with the bullets, and the Prince asks him to shoot a dove. He does, but the bullet just misses Agnes, who has come to look for Max, among her bridesmaids. Caspar is wounded by this very bullet, which he hoped would strike Agnes and thus yield Zamiel another victim. Zamiel, however, claims Caspar and the story

is revealed. The Prince would punish Max, but opportunely a Hermit appears, showing that the prayer of Agnes has been answered, Providence using her to restore Max to truth and honor. Max is forgiven, and all ends well.

It is to be noted that, as usually produced, "Der Freischütz" is in "comic opera" form, being given with spoken dialog in places. Recitatives however, have been written for it.

BLACK LABEL RECORDS

{Freischütz—Overture—Part I..................*Victor Symphony Orchestra*}35733	12-in.,	$1.25
{Freischütz—Overture—Part II................*Victor Symphony Orchestra*}		
{Overture to Der Freischütz............................*Sousa's Band*}35000	12-in.,	1.25
{ Carmen Selection (Bizet)..............................*Sousa's Band*}		
{Leise, leise, fromme Weise (Agatha's Prayer) (*In German*) *Louise Voigt, Soprano*}68473	12-in.,	1.25
{ Tannhäuser—Dich, teure Halle (*In German*)........*Louise Voigt, Soprano*}		

PRINCE OTTOKAR PARDONS MAX—FINAL
SCENE OF THE OPERA

THE RELATIONS HEAR THE NEW WILL

GIANNI SCHICCHI

OPERA in one act; text by Gio- achino Forzano; music by Giacomo Puccini. First pro- duced at the Metropolitan Opera House, New York City, December 14, 1918, in conjunction with two other Puccini one act operas, "Il Tabarro" and "Suor Angelica."

GIANNI SCHICCHI is a shrewd, cunning, but good-hearted Tus- can peasant of the thirteenth cen- tury. He has a daughter, *Lauretta*, who loves *Rinuccio*,—whose family is much worried because a relation, *Buoso Donati*, who has just died, has left his fortune to a monastery. *Schicchi* is consulted by the disappointed relatives in the hope that he may prove clever enough to suggest a plan for getting the property. *Donati's* death not yet having been made public, *Schicchi* sug- gests that he impersonate the old man and dictate a new will, leaving the estate to *Rinuccio's* family. *Schicchi* is placed in the dead man's bed, and a notary is sent for. He takes down the new will; but *Schicchi*, after making a few minor bequests to the relatives, leaves the bulk of the property to him- self! This pleases *Rinuccio* and *Lau- retta*, since they will eventually benefit by the will. The relatives are highly indignant, but they do not dare expose *Schicchi*, as they would make them- selves liable for punishment. They keep their peace, while the opera ends happily for the lovers.

In one air *Lauretta* begs *Gianni* to help secure a part of the wealth which *Buoso* has left to a monastery, and tells her "dear daddy" that if he will con- sent she will be able to buy a handsome wedding ring. This is the "O mio bab- bino caro" (Oh, My Beloved Daddy).

THE VICTOR RECORD

O MIO BABBINO CARO
(Oh, My Beloved Daddy) FRANCES ALDA,
Soprano *In Italian*   528 10-in., $1.50

PROGRAM OF FIRST PERFORM-
ANCE (MILAN, 1876)

DESTINN AS GIOCONDA

CARUSO AS ENZO

LA GIOCONDA

LA GIOCONDA is a product of those happy days when the untrained music-lover was considered; the days before melody was banished from the opera-house in favor of uneasy harmonies and choked orchestration. Doubtless the frank "emotional appeal" of the middle nineteenth century had to suffer the general law of change in giving way to the subtleties of our own time. Those educated to the modern fashion of unresolved sevenths and augmented fifths may turn up noses today at their forefathers' simpler tastes; but even a musician of parts may today find delight in "La Gioconda"—not simply from its dramatic power, but from its music too.

Ponchielli was born at Palermo Fasolaro, Cremona, in 1834, and he died in Milan in 1886. He belongs to the halcyon days that followed Wagner's banishment of the banjo-like accompaniments and the sleep-inducing harmonies of the Italian '30's and '40's, yet preceded the hour when melody took fright before the cacophonous attacks of the "very modern." "La Gioconda" has plenty of tunes, generously embellished with interesting harmonies and with orchestrations which are generously colored.

THE OPERA

OPERA in four acts. Libretto by Arrigo Boïto; an adaptation of Victor Hugo's drama, "Angelo." Music by Amilcare Ponchielli. First presented at La Scala, Milan, April 8, 1876. Rewritten by Boïto and given at Genoa, December, 1876, and the following February at La Scala. First London production, June 7, 1883. Given in Petrograd, January 30, 1883; in Vienna April 28, 1883; in France, at Nice, December 29, 1886. First New York production, December 20, 1883,

152

with Nilsson, Scalchi, Fursch-Madi, del Puente and Novara. Revived at the Metropolitan Opera House New York, December 25, 1913.

CHARACTERS

LA GIOCONDA (*Joh-kon'-dah*), a ballad singer............Soprano
LA CIECA (*Chay'-kah*), her blind mother..............Contralto
ALVISE (*Al-vee'-zeh*), one of the heads of State Inquisition....Bass
LAURA, his wife.......Mezzo-Soprano
ENZO GRIMALDO, a Genoese noble
Tenor
BARNABA, a spy of the Inquisition
Baritone
ZUANE (*Tsoo-ahn'-ay*), a boatman.Bass
ISEPO (*Ee-zay'-poh*), public letter-writer...................Tenor
A PILOT.....................Bass
Monks, Senators, Sailors, Shipwrights, Ladies, Gentlemen, Populace, Masquers, etc.

The Action takes place in Venice, in the Seventeenth Century

There is a prelude to the opera, soft, melodic, with a fine climax. It is notable in introducing, as its chief theme, a beautiful melody from the first act, where *La Cieca*, the blind woman of Venice, accused of witchcraft by the mob and rescued by *Alvise*, offers to her protector, in gratefulness, almost her only possession—an old rosary.

ACT I

SCENE—*Street near the Adriatic Shore, Venice*

IT is the afternoon of a Spring holiday, and the Grand Courtyard of the Ducal Palace is alive with moving color —the forms of monks, sailors, dancers, shipwrights, and the people-at-large, old and young. At the rear are seen the Giant's Staircase and the Portico della Carta, with a doorway leading into the interior of the jewel-blazing Church of Saint Mark. The writing table of a public letter-writer is seen, and across-stage can be remarked one of the public "Lion's Mouths"—bearing its legend, "For Secret Denunciations to the Inquisition, Against Any Person, with Safety, Secrecy and Benefit to the State."

The spy, *Barnaba*, stands, moodily, with his back to one of the exquisite marble columns, watching the crowd. A small guitar hangs from his shoulder. He points ironically at the pavement-gratings upon which the people dance. "Dancing above their graves," says *Barnaba*, knowing the prisons of the Inquisition are underfoot.

He notices *La Gioconda*, with her blind mother, *La Cieca;* the street singer is in the bright costume of her profession; fresh and young, she brings an unpleasant hunger into the eye of *Barnaba*. Having seated her mother where she will enjoy the sun and the charity of Venice, she turns to follow the crowd, headed shoreward to watch the regatta.

But she is the last, and, save for herself, her mother and the spy, the square is deserted. Suddenly *Barnaba* steps forth and arrests her passage, declaring he loves her. She is furious, and dashes away. Believing her in danger, the blind mother screams for help.

A dastardly revenge is plotted by the man. When the people return from the regatta, "chairing" the victor, *Barnaba* tells the defeated competitor, *Zuane*, he has been bewitched by *La Cieca*, and thus defeated. The superstitious crowd attacks the old blind woman, whose screams bring *La Gioconda*, followed by *Enzo Grimaldo*, whom the girl adores. *Enzo* fights off the mob, when the *Grand Duke Alvise* and *Laura*, his wife, suddenly appear. Chiefly through *Laura*, *La Cieca* is saved; and she bestows upon the

Duchess her rosary. *Barnaba* sees a meaningful glance pass between *La Gioconda* and *Enzo*.

Presently all depart but the two men. "*Enzo Grimaldo*, Prince of Santa Fior," begins the spy, "you look thoughtful." *Enzo* is astonished that his rank is known. He is a prince proscribed, and despite his kindness to the street singer, his heart long ago was given to *Laura*, now the wife of *Alvise*. *Barnaba* tells him *Laura* will visit *Enzo's* ship that evening. *Enzo* is grateful, though the men lose no love for one another. He departs, when *Barnaba* turns to the public scribe. As he does so, the mother and daughter return, concealing themselves when the girl sees their enemy. They overhear him dictate a letter to the *Grand Duke*, warning him of the love between *Enzo* and *Laura*. Apostrophizing the stone lion for its usefulness in such matters, *Barnaba* places the missive between its jaws. All is seen by *La Gioconda*, whose passionate soul is filled with hate against *Barnaba*, against *Laura*—and against *Enzo*; for is not *Enzo* her lover? For her, too, the way of revenge lies open; but not *Barnaba's* way.

ACT II

Scene—*A Lagoon near Venice. Enzo's Ship at the Quay*

THE early moon reveals *Enzo's* ship, at anchor at an island in the Fusima lagoon. The sailors are singing and merrymaking. Disguised as a fisherman, now appears *Barnaba*, with *Isepo*, the letter-writer. He notes the number and disposition of the crew, and sends off *Isepo* for aid. He sings a merry ballad, "Ah, pescator affonda l'esca" (Fisher Boy, Thy Bait Be Throwing), which brings hearty approval from the men aboard ship. Soon *Enzo* appears, and they go below. *Barnaba* hides. Left alone, *Enzo* sings of his joy at the approaching

visit, in the beautiful aria, "Cielo e Mar" (Heaven and Ocean). It has a striking passage

Suddenly, out of the dusk, a boat appears, and *Laura* steps aboard ship. A touching love scene follows, and the pair agree to sail off as soon as the wind may rise. *Enzo* is called below, and *Laura* kneels at an altar on the deck. *La Gioconda* creeps from hiding at the bow of the ship, and advances. Her muffled curses arouse the praying woman. "Who are you?" cries *Laura*, in sudden fear.

"I am a shadow...I am Vengeance!" is the strange reply; and the girl in fury, pours out her woes. Finally she takes a dagger and points it at the breast of *Laura*—when she catches sight of the rosary, and she remembers. Her arm falls, powerless; taking the distracted *Laura*, the girl drags her to a boat alongside and puts her aboard. When *Enzo* comes on deck, crying for *Laura*, he greets the followers of *Alvise*, headed by *Barnaba*. Caught, he sets fire to the ship.

ACT III

Scene—*The House of Gold*

ALVISE is in agitation. There is a great festival at his house, where he has planned an exquisite revenge. *Laura* enters, robed for the ball. She is told that she must die. She begs for mercy, but is thrown to the floor, and dragged to an adjoining room, where she sees a funeral bier, prepared to receive her. *Alvise* gives her a goblet of poisoned wine, which she must drink before the next dance. Then he goes to receive his guests. Again *La Gioconda* appears, emptying the poisoned wine into a bottle, and replacing it with a sleep-inducing but harmless narcotic. Then begins the famous "Dance of the Hours," today one of the most popular of orchestral pieces. At the end of it, in rushes *Barnaba*, among the dancers, with *Enzo*, dragging *La Cieca*, who cries out with fright. *Barnaba* insists she was working malice, but the woman avers she was but praying for the dead. A bell is heard tolling, and *Barnaba* whispers to *Enzo* that it is for *Laura*. *Enzo* then advances upon *Alvise*, throws off his mask and lets himself be known. *Alvise* tells the story of the wrong done *Laura*, and drawing back the curtains, shows her lying, in her ball dress, on the bier. *Enzo* rushes at him but is withheld.

ACT IV

Scene—*The Orfano Canal*

STILL swooning, *Laura* is brought to a ruined palace on the island of the Giudecca, where at *La Gioconda's* command, she is placed on a couch. Near her are set a flask of poison and a dagger. The street singer has agreed with *Barnaba* to become his if he will help *Enzo* and *Laura* to escape. She sings the famous "Suicidio" (Suicide Only Remains). What is there, indeed, to live for? She is half tempted to drown the unconscious *Laura*. Then *Enzo* reappears from prison.

This is *Barnaba's* work. But when *Enzo* declares he will die at the tomb of *Laura*, *La Gioconda* mockingly declares she has removed the body. *Enzo* lifts his dagger. For a moment the girl would gladly die by his hand, so great is her infatuation; but *Laura* appears, restored. And she returns the girl her mother's rosary.

The lovers go. Then, last of all, comes *Barnaba*, to claim his reward. The girl plays upon his feelings until he cannot contain himself. He seizes her in his arms. But, more deft than he, she stabs herself with her dagger. "*La Gioconda* is thine!" she declares. *Barnaba*, stooping down, howls in her ear:

"Last night your mother offended me. I have strangled her!" But he speaks into an ear that is deaf as stone; for the girl is dead. *Barnaba* rushes back into the night.

THE VICTOR RECORDS

(Sung in Italian)

ACT II

PESCATOR, AFFONDA L'ESCA
(Fisher Boy, Thy Bait be Throwing)

TITTA RUFFO, Baritone   6265   12-in., $2.00

PASQUALE AMATO, Baritone and Metropolitan Opera Chorus   539   10-in., 1.50

CIELO E MAR

(Heaven and Ocean) ENRICO CARUSO, Tenor   6020   12-in., 2.00

GIOVANNI MARTINELLI, Tenor   738   10-in., 1.50

BENIAMINO GIGLI, Tenor   643   10-in., 1.50

ENZO:
Heaven and ocean! yon ethereal veil
Is radiant as a holy altar,
My angel, will she come from heaven?
My angel, will she come o'er ocean?
Here I await her, I breathe with rapture
The soft zephyrs fill'd with love.
Mortals oft, when fondly sighing,
Find ye a torment, O golden, golden dreams.
Come then, dearest, here I'm waiting;
    Wildly panting is my heart.
Come, then, dearest! oh come, my dearest!
    Oh come, taste the kisses that magic bliss impart!

ACT IV

SUICIDIO
(Suicide Only Remains) EMMY DESTINN, Soprano   6086   12-in., $2.00
MARIA JERITZA, Soprano 6375   12-in., 2.00

BLACK LABEL AND BLUE LABEL RECORDS

{ Prelude...*Vessella's Italian Band*} 35459   12 in., $1.25
{ Othello—Fantasia...............................*Vessella's Italian Band*

{ Dance of the Hours............................*Victor Herbert's Orchestra*} 55044   12-in., 1.50
{ Kamennoi-Ostrow (Rubinstein)................*Victor Herbert's Orchestra*

THE RUINED PALACE—ACT IV

FERD. LEEKE

SIEGFRIED:
  If you threaten my life,
  Hardly you'll win from my hand the ring!

157

GÖTTERDÄMMERUNG

(THE DUSK OF THE GODS)

MUSIC-DRAMA in three acts and a prelude. Words and music by Richard Wagner, who began composition of the music at Lucerne in 1870 and completed it in 1874. First produced at Bayreuth, August 17, 1876, with Materna and Unger. First American production at New York, January 25, 1888, with Lehmann, Seidl-Krauss, Traubman, Niemann and Fischer. Given in Italy at La Scala in 1890. Many notable productions have been made at the Metropolitan, and the work has been presented almost every year at this house.

CHARACTERS

SIEGFRIED (*Zeeg'-freed*) . . . . Tenor
GUNTHER (*Goon'-ter*) . . . . Bass
HAGEN (*Hah'-gen*) . . . . Bass
BRÜNNHILDE (*Breen-hil-deh*) . . Soprano
GUTRUNE (*Goot-troon'-eh*) . . . . . Soprano
WOGLINDA ⎱ (*Vo-glin'-de*) ⎰ Soprano
WELLGUNDA ⎰(*Vell-goon'-deh*)⎰ Soprano
FLOSSHILDE ⎰(*Floss-hil'-deh*) ⎰Contralto

(Rhine-Nymphs)

(The name of the opera is pronounced (nearly) *Gay-ter-daym-mer-oong*).

PRELUDE

WITH dawn comes the leave-taking of *Brünnhilde* and *Siegfried*, for the conqueror must go forth into the world to prove himself a hero among men. He leaves her as a love-pledge the magic Ring, the Ring taken from *Alberich* by *Wotan* to pay the giants, and taken by *Siegfried* in turn from *Fafner*, dragon-giant. In answering faith, *Brünnhilde* gives *Siegfried* her Valkyrie armor, dowers him with her protecting magic, and leads to him the horse *Grani*. Mounting, he rides away down the rocky defile, and *Brünnhilde*, watching him from a high rock, hears his horn echoing down the valley.

ACT I

SCENE—*Castle of King Gunther*

ON the banks of the Rhine is the kingdom of the *Gibichungs*, governed by *Gunther* and his sister *Gutrune*. *Gunther* has a magician adviser in *Hagen*, who is in fact a natural son of *Alberich*. When *Alberich* first renounced woman kind, he required a human agent to defeat *Siegfried*, so he bought a wife with his gold. *Hagen* tells *Gunther*, listening wide-eyed, of *Brünnhilde* and the Ring, saying that the sleeping goddess can be won only by a fearless hero who can penetrate through her curtaining veil of fire. *Siegfried* alone may bring her to *Gunther*; *Hagen* has on foot a scheme whereby with magic he may win for *Gunther* the powerful *Brünnhilde*, and wed *Gutrune* to *Siegfried*. Thus he plans to secure the ring for his father, *Alberich*.

When *Siegfried* arrives at the hall of the *Gibichungs*, he is royally welcomed. He is given to drink of a magic draught —whereby he completely forgets the unsuspecting *Brünnhilde* and falls in love with *Gutrune*, the sister of the *King*. He next swears blood-brotherhood with *Gunther*, and promises, in exchange for *Gutrune*, to bring *Brünnhilde* from her mountain of fire. By means of the *Tarnhelm* he changes himself into *Gunther's* form and goes upon his mission. *Brünnhilde* is horrified when *Siegfried*, in the visible shape of *Gunther*, seizes her. She believes this must be the last vengeance of *Wotan*. She strives to protect herself with the magic of the Ring, but as it is *Siegfried* himself appearing to her in *Gunther's* form she is dismayed to find the Ring powerless. *Siegfried* takes the Ring from her as a sign of their wedding; but remains beside her with the sword between them—in memory of his brotherhood pledge to *Gunther.*

ACT II

Scene—*The Rhine near Gunther's Castle*

HAGEN is awaiting the return of *Siegfried,* when *Alberich* appears, to discuss their plot to regain the Ring. *Hagen* swears to accomplish his purpose, and *Alberich* vanishes when *Siegfried* arrives. The hero is in his own form but wears the *Tarnhelm,* which he now places in his belt, declaring that *Gunther,* with *Brünnhilde,* is following. *Hagen* speeds to the Castle, where the retainers are called forth to celebrate the double wedding of *Siegfried* with *Gutrune* and *Gunther* with *Brünnhilde.* When *Gunther* arrives with *Brünnhilde,* the *Valkyrie* is startled to see *Siegfried,* whom she approaches tenderly. He ignores her, but she perceives the Ring upon his finger. *Gunther* is perplexed when she claims that *Siegfried* has wedded her with the Ring, and he now believes himself betrayed. *Siegfried,* still beneath the baneful effects of the drink, denies all memory of his having given *Brünnhilde* the Ring. He goes off with his new love, *Gutrune,* leaving *Brünnhilde, Gunther* and *Hagen* to plot vengeance. *Brünnhilde* tells her new companion that she has made *Siegfried* invulnerable from a frontal attack, but knowing that he will never turn his back to a foe, has taken no pains to protect him from the rear. They then plan between them to kill *Siegfried.*

ACT III

Scene I—*A Wild Valley near the Rhine*

OFF on a hunting expedition, *Siegfried* has strayed from his companions. At the banks of the Rhine,

the Rhine maidens endeavor to persuade him into giving up the Ring. He is charmed by their songs and their cajolery, but laughs at the demand for the Ring. Thereupon they warn him that this very day he will die. He treats their prophecy with lightness, forgetting it completely when *Hagen* and *Gunther* appear. Having killed nothing, he is obliged to eat of their food and drink of their wine. *Hagen* gives him yet another magic potion, by which his memory is so far restored that he tells them something of his past life, including the story of Mime and the Dragon, "Mime hiess ein murrischer Zwerg" (Mimi, Know Then, Was a Dwarf).

Plied by *Hagen,* he proceeds to tell of his communion with the birds; then, scene by scene, the whole of his past life. Much of this is given in the "Zu den Wipfeln lauscht' ich" (To the Branches Gazed I Aloft).

As he repeats to them the message of the birds, he thinks dreamily once more of *Brünnhilde, Hagen* keeping the drinking-horn well supplied. Two ravens fly overhead. "Canst read the speech of those ravens aright?" asks *Hagen,* and *Siegfried* starts at the memory of the bird who led him on his way to *Brünnhilde.* As he arises, *Hagen* plunges a spear into his back. The dying *Siegfried,* with his last breath, now recalls the kiss of *Brünnhilde* and his love. "*Brünnhilde* beckons me!" groans the hero as life dies out of him.

Scene II—*Hall in Gunther's Palace*

THE body of *Siegfried* is borne back to the Castle to the music, perhaps, of the greatest threnody ever composed, "Siegfried's Funeral March."

To the solemn rhythm of this astounding musical picture of the passage of Death, are added one by one the leading themes or "motives" of the entire Ring. We hear, as in review, the heroic motive of the *Volsungs*, the race founded by *Wotan* and ended with *Siegfried*, and then follow all the other leading motives, like the images said to be seen by drowning men; the *Compassion* of the unhappy *Sieglinde*, the love of *Siegmund* and *Sieglinde*, the *Sword*, and that of *Siegfried, Guardian of the Sword*, and that of *Siegfried* himself in its heroic form, and his love of *Brünnhilde*. The complaint of the *Rhine-maidens*, the motive of *Brünnhilde's* captivity, and the *Curse-motive* all are heard, and in the imagination we may picture the funeral procession, disappearing among the mountains into the silence of the night, a single wan beam of moonlight tragically illumining the scene.

Siegfried's body is borne majestically into the Hall of *Gunther's* Castle, where the weeping *Gutrune* clasps the dead form of her husband. *Hagen* now demands the ring, but *Gunther* refuses it. Once more the Curse works out, and *Gunther*, in his own hall, dies by *Hagen's* hand. Then, when *Hagen* approaches the dead hero to take the Ring from his finger, *Siegfried's* arm rises in warning and *Hagen* recoils in horror.

The last great moment approaches. *Brünnhilde* appears, and gazing long and sadly upon the face of *Siegfried*, commands that a great funeral pyre be set up to consume his body. The vassals obey, building a mighty pyre in sight of the Rhine waters. High upon this the body of *Siegfried* is laid. *Brünnhilde* summons the two ravens from the rocks, commanding them to summon the Fire-god.

Thus begins the great Immolation Scene, "Fliegt heim."

The ravens are sped away, to bid *Loki* burn the palace of *Valhalla*; then kindles the pile, which burns rapidly as the black-winged messengers disappear.

SETTING OF ACT II AT BAYREUTH

Commanding that the horse *Grani* be brought her, *Brünnhilde* takes from him the bridle.

She swings herself onto his broad back and rides him boldly into the burning funeral pyre, whose terrible flames partly destroy the Hall itself. The Rhine rises, however, and puts out the fire, and on its level surface are seen the Rhine-maidens, who seize the Ring from the embers. *Hagen* rushes upon them, crying: "The Ring is mine!"

But the maidens seize the creature and drag him down into the now-roaring flood. The smoke from the pyre gathers into a great bank, and the frightened *Gibichungs* note an increasing red glow appear in the midst of it high above them. *Valhalla* itself is in flames and the gods and heroes, their work accomplished, are seen awaiting their fiery doom as the flames lick about their great castle of Valhalla. Thus ends the old order, giving place to the new.

BLACK LABEL AND BLUE LABEL RECORDS

Mime hiess ein mürrischer Zwerg (Mimi, Know Thee Then, Was a Dwarf) (*In German*) ....*Carl Burrian, Tenor* Zu den Wipfeln lauscht' ich (To the Branches Gazed I Aloft) (*In German*) *Carl Burrian, Tenor*	55073	12-in., $1.50
The parting of Brünnhilde and Siegfried—Prologue, Part I *Vocalists*— Florence Austral-Tudor Davies *Symphony Orchestra—Conducted by Albert Coates* The parting of Brünnhilde and Siegfried—Prologue, Part II *Vocalists*—Florence Austral-Tudor Davies *Symphony Orchestra—Conducted by Albert Coates*	55212	12-in., 1.50
Gunther and Gutrune welcome Siegfried—Act I *Vocalists*—Tudor Davies, Robert Radford and Bessie Jones *Symphony Orchestra—Conducted by Albert Coates* Hagen meditates revenge—Act I *Vocalist*—Robert Radford *Symphony Orchestra—Conducted by Percy Pitt*	55213	12-in., 1.50
Prelude:—The Rhine-maidens scene—Act III *Symphony Orchestra—Conducted by Eugene Goossens* Brünnhilde kindles the funeral pyre—Part 1 (Act III) *Vocalist*—Florence Austral..............*Symphony Orchestra—Conducted by Albert Coates*	55214	12-in., 1.50
Brünnhilde kindles the funeral pyre—Part 2 *Vocalist*—Florence Austral *Symphony Orchestra—Conducted by Albert Coates* Brünnhilde kindles the funeral pyre—Part 3 (Act III) *Vocalist*—Florence Austral..............*Symphony Orchestra—Conducted by Albert Coates*	55215	12-in., 1.50
Siegfried's Journey to the Rhine—Part I . .*Percy Pitt and Symphony Orchestra* Siegfried's Journey to the Rhine—Part II..*Percy Pitt and Symphony Orchestra*	55167	12-in., 1.50
Siegfried's Funeral March........................*Vessella's Italian Band* Die Walküre—Ride of the Valkyries..............*Vessella's Italian Band*	35369	12-in., 1.25

GOYESCAS

OR THE RIVAL LOVERS

THIS beautiful work attracted notice at the time of its first production, not simply for its inherent charm, but for its promise of greater things to come. Enrique Granados was known only to a few as a promising composer, some piano works of his having attracted the attention of the pianist Ernest Schelling, who made them public. The scenes as well as the ideas for the four principal characters were taken from famous paintings by Goya, the Spanish painter. The composer reproduced some of the vivacity and fire of that great human satirist and much was expected of him. Such expectations, however, but served to intensify the tragedy of his loss when he and his wife, on their return journey, loaded with honors and happy with the promise of a brilliant future, went down with the ill-fated *Sussex*, torpedoed by a German submarine.

THE OPERA

TEXT by Fernando Periquet; music by Enrique Granados. The work was accepted for the Paris Opera, but war prevented a production, so Señor Granados brought it to America, personally supervising the première. It was produced for the first time on any stage at the Metropolitan, New York, January 28, 1916, and is the first grand opera to be sung in the United States at a first-class opera house in the Spanish language.

CHARACTERS AND ORIGINAL CAST

ROSARIO, a lady of rank (*Ro-zah'-ree-oh*).........Anna Fitziu
FERNANDO, her lover (*Fare-nahn'-doh*)...Giovanni Martinelli
PEPA, a notorious "maja" (*Pay'-pah*).........Flora Perini
PAQUIRO, a toreador (*Pah-kee'-roh*)...........Giuseppe de Luca
A PUBLIC SINGER.........Max Bloch
Conductor—Gaetano Baragnali

(The name of the opera is pronounced *Go-yes'-kahs*.)

Time and Place: Outskirts of Madrid, about 1800.

SCENE I

THE opera is divided into three scenes or "pictures"; the first shows a gay festival in a village near Madrid. The people of the village are making a good deal of *Paquiro*, the toreador, a swaggering ruffian. Chief among those who adore him is *Pepa*, one of the "majas," or a gay young woman of the village; but *Paquiro's* head is filled with memories of *Rosario*, a lady of high rank who has condescended to dance with him at the *baile de candil* (a low ball given in a lantern lighted barn), the lady having gone slumming in quite the modern fashion. *Rosario* arrives to keep a rendezvous with her lover, *Fernando*, and *Paquiro* audaciously invites her again to dance with him at the ball-room. She refuses, but she is overheard by *Fernando*, a young military officer of jealous disposition. He insists that she accept *Paquiro's* invitation but that she shall dance with himself alone. The toreador is affronted at this insult before all his admirers. *Rosario* tries to retreat, but *Fernando* is firm. *Pepa*, noting her toreador-admirer's angry face, admits that the young soldier has courage to take the risk of meeting *Paquiro* on his own ground.

Scene II

THE ballroom is a cheap, boisterous place, lighted by gaudy lanterns and decorated with flaring colors. Out of place in such surroundings, the aristocratic *Fernando* and *Rosario* are jeered by the crowd. In insulting language, *Paquiro* congratulates *Fernando* on his choice of a sweetheart. He provokes a quarrel, and the two men agree to meet in a duel at ten o'clock that night at the Prado, near *Rosario's* home.

Scene III

ROSARIO sits in the moonlit garden listening to the nightingale, herself singing a passionate love-song. *Fernando* arrives and they renew their vows. The clock strikes ten, and the officer strives to leave her. She begs him to stay; but unknown to her he sees the cloaked figure of *Paquiro* slipping by in the street. *Pepa* furtively follows. *Fernando* finally leaves; but with trembling steps, and as though conscious of some unnameable evil, *Rosario* trails behind. In impassiveness too deep even for contempt of the human drama, the moon looks down upon the trees. Soon comes the sound of clashing steel; then shrieks— one from *Rosario* and one from *Fernando*, mortally wounded. *Pepa* and the toreador return and pass by. Shortly afterward, *Rosario* staggers back to the garden supporting the wounded figure of her lover. In spite of her lamentations there is nothing she can do. As she sees the light of life recede from *Fernando's* eyes, *Rosario* falls fainting on his body.

Themes from the opera are included in the poetic and charmingly-colored intermezzo.

　　　　THE CHALLENGE—SCENE II

IL GUARANY

IL GUARANY contains some brilliant music and many picturesque effects. The most famous number is a beautiful duet for *Pery* and *Cecilia* in Act I. It is coloratura music of the most elaborate type, demanding both mechanical skill and finesse. The overture is characteristic, and the melodies of the Amazon Indians, which Gomez introduced to give "local color" to the work, are piquant and effective.

THE OPERA

OPERA in four acts. Text by Antonio Scalvini; music by Antonio Carlos Gomez. First produced at La Scala, Milan, March 19, 1870, and shortly afterward at Genoa, Florence and Rome. First London production, Covent Garden, July 13, 1872. Once given in New York.

CHARACTERS

Don Antonio de Maritz, a Portuguese Knight ....Bass
Cecilia, his daughter........Soprano
Pery, chief of the tribe of Guarany (*Ga-rah'-neé*) ....Tenor
Don Alvaro, a Portuguese adventurer...................Tenor
Gonzales ⎱Spanish guests of⎰Baritone
Ruy-Bento⎰Don Antonio,⎱ Tenor
Alonso ⎰adventurers ⎱ Bass
Il Cacico, chief of Aimore Tribe, Bass
Pedro, service guard of Antonio, Bass

Time and Place: Brazil, in the Neighborhood of Rio Janeiro; 1560

DON ANTONIO DE MARITZ, an early Brazilian settler of noble birth, is at war with the neighboring Indian tribes of *Aimores*, who detest the European invaders. His beautiful daughter is loved by *Gonzales*, a Spanish adventurer, but her heart is given to *Pery*, chief of the tribe of *Guarany*, a young man of lofty character, for all his despised native birth. The girl is torn between duty to her father, and love for one of his bitterest foes; and there are many dramatic scenes of rivalry between *Pery* and her admirer *Gonzales*. During the war, it is brought home to *Don Antonio* that the wrongdoing is not wholly on the side of the natives, and inspired by the genuineness of the love between his daughter and *Pery*, he resolves on a remarkable sacrifice. The climax is reached in the last act, when the *Don's* castle is besieged by the Indians. After sending *Pery* and *Cecilia* to a place of safety, the old *Don* fires the powder-magazine, destroying himself and his enemies.

As the curtain falls, the united lovers look down, from a lofty headland, upon the scene of desolation, the result of a father's self-sacrifice.

THE VICTOR RECORD

SENTO UNA FORZA INDOMITA

(An Indomitable Force)

Emmy Destinn, Soprano, and Enrico Caruso, Tenor. *In Italian*
6355 12-in., $2.00

BLACK LABEL RECORD

⎰Il Guarany Selection....................................*Pietro, Accordionist*⎰35488 12-in., $1 25
⎱ Tranquillo Overture (Pietro)........................*Pietro, Accordionist*⎰

HAMLET

TO take an opera from a Shakespeare play is to measure genius with the greatest, especially when "Hamlet" is the chosen battleground. It is not surprising that there are pages in this opera which scarcely "measure up" to the theme. But there are compensations in the music at least, and we must be grateful for many exquisite melodies. The well-known "Brindisi" is deservedly popular, a typical flash of Gallic brilliancy. *Hamlet's* song of mourning for *Ophelia*, in a directly opposite vein, is no less worthy to be cited.

The task of the librettists was hard. Opera compels few words, many tableaux and little action, many changes from the original thus being necessary. The Shakespearian must therefore be prepared to forgive much, in a French perversion of Shakespeare's verse, retranslated into libretto-English. He may find it less easy to forgive the close of the opera, where the spectre of the murdered King appears before the multitude, and, after inciting his son to kill the usurper, and committing the *Queen* to a nunnery, vanishes amid "tumultuous applause," —*Hamlet* meanwhile being placed on the throne as the curtain falls and a festive chorus gives the musical equivalent of three rousing cheers.

Such blemishes as this account for the rare production of the work. But "opera is opera;" and it does not,— and should not,—deter the world-at-large from enjoying those melodies which have won their place in the world of art through the unequivocable claims of aesthetic beauty.

PHOTO ERMINI
RUFFO AS HAMLET

THE OPERA

OPERA in five acts. Book by Barbier and Carré, based on Shakespeare's play. Music by Ambroise Thomas. First production March 9, 1868, at the Paris *Académie*, with Christine Nilsson and Faure. First London production June 19, 1869, in Italian. Produced at the Academy of Music, New York, April 20, 1872, with Nilsson, Cary, Brignoli, Barre and Jamet; in 1882, with Gerster and Ciappini; and in 1892, with La Salle and Marie Van Zandt. Revived recently by the Chicago Opera Company for Ruffo.

CHARACTERS

HAMLET . . . . Baritone
CLAUDIUS, King of
    Denmark . . . . Bass
LAERTES, Polonius'
    son . . . . Tenor
GHOST of the dead
    King . . . . Bass
POLONIUS, Chan-
    cellor . . . . Bass
GERTRUDE, Hamlet's mother, Queen
    of Denmark . . . . . . Mezzo-Soprano
OPHELIA, daughter of Polo-
    nius . . . . Soprano

Lords, Ladies, Officers, Pages,
Peasants, etc.

Scene—Elsinore, in Denmark

(In French the "H" in Hamlet is silent. The Italian name is "Amleto," *Ahm-let'-to*).

ACT I

Scene I—*A Room of State in the Palace*

KNIGHTS and nobles, Lords and retainers join in acclaiming the new *Queen* upon her wedding to *Claudius*, only two months after the death of her late husband, the present King's brother, former occupant of the throne. The absence of her son, *Hamlet*, from the festival, occasions comment. After the ceremonies he enters, in bitter mood, solemnly clothed in black. His strange musings are interrupted by the entrance of *Ophelia*, his betrothed. She has heard that *Hamlet*, disgusted at the early marriage of his mother, intends to leave the kingdom, and asks him if he has ceased to love her. The "Nega se puoi la luce" (Love Duet) is heard.

In this he reassures her, using in part Shakespeare's own words:

"Doubt that the stars are fire,
Doubt that the sun doth move,
Doubt truth to be a liar;
But never doubt my love."

COPY'T DUPONT
CALVÉ AS OPHELIA

He does not succeed, however, in wholly convincing *Ophelia*, when they are interrupted by *Laertes*, who comes to discover if *Hamlet* intends to depart with him; but *Hamlet* refuses, so *Laertes* confides *Ophelia* to his care.

Scene II—*Esplanade of the Palace. It is Night*

THE hour of midnight approaches. *Hamlet* ascends the battlements of the castle. Earlier in the day *Horatio* and *Marcellus*, two officers of the watch, have come to him with the strange story of a spectral visitant strangely like his father, the late king. Deeply moved, he seeks to find out for himself.

The clock strikes the hour of midnight, and the ghost appears. *Horatio* and *Marcellus* withdraw, leaving *Hamlet* alone with his singular guest. *Hamlet* hears the story of his father's murder, and the perfidy of the present king, who is both his uncle and his stepfather. The ghost bids him take revenge, but warns him to leave his mother's punishment to God.

ACT II

Scene—*Garden of the Palace*

IN order to watch his uncle more closely, and at the same time to avoid suspicious action, *Hamlet* decides to feign insanity. One of the first to suffer from this is *Ophelia*. The *Queen* finds the girl weeping and she soon ascertains the cause. The *Queen* is greatly disturbed, and, in a fine duet with the *King*, speaks of a vision that is haunting her too. A troupe of players arrives, and *Hamlet* plans to present a play before the *King*, so nearly in accordance with the murder as described by the spectre as to force the *King* to betray himself. By this means he seeks to verify the suspicions he has formed since seeing the ghost. In this, he reckons well.

The *King* and *Queen* are delighted at the prince's reviving interest in the festivities, and they consent to witness the play. Calling the troupe of actors about him, he instructs them in the plot he has conceived. The *Prince* then calls for wine and makes merry: The Brindisi is sung, "O vin discaccia la tristezza" (Wine, This Gloom Dispel).

This exceedingly brilliant number is deservedly popular: its bright melody and vigorous rhythm are especially attractive, especially the melody, first heard as a solo and afterward repeated by the Chorus.

In the next scene we are brought to the Palace Hall, on one side of which has been arranged a stage. The court assembles and the play opens, *Hamlet* sitting at *Ophelia's* feet, whence he can observe his uncle. As the play progresses the guilty man shows agitation, and finally in a rage orders the play to stop and the actors to begone. *Hamlet* rushes forward and denounces the murderer, but the Court believes him simply a madman. *Hamlet* has overplayed his role of simulated insanity!

ACT III

Scene—*The Queen's Apartments*

HAMLET chides himself on his lack of decision, now that he is indeed convinced of the *King's* guilt yet has so far done nothing. His thoughts find expression in the well known "Monologo," or Soliloquy.

In a fine piece of musical declamation he sings the well known passage, rather abridged to suit operatic conventions, or, rather, operatic needs:

"To be or not to be, that is the question.
To die, to sleep; perchance to dream;
Ah! were it allowed me to sever
The tie that binds me to mortality,
And seek "the undiscovered country
From whose bourne no traveler returns!"
"Ay! To be, or not to be?
To die, to sleep; perchance to dream."

His mother and *Ophelia* enter and plead with him to give up these wild imaginings. He maintains the old pose, however, half convinced *Ophelia* is involved in his mother's scheming. He treats the girl harshly ("Get thee to a nunnery, girl"), and as she departs he sternly rebukes his mother. The famous scene in which he bids her look on the two pictures of his uncle and his father is not omitted. Finally the ghost appears to *Hamlet*, but, as it is invisible to the *Queen*, she is terrified at what she simply believes a further mark of the youth's insanity.

ACT IV

Scene—*The Willow-lined Shore of a Lake*

HAMLET'S pretended madness and his harsh treatment have brought to *Ophelia* a madness that is real enough. By the shore of the lake

FROM THE PAINTING BY CZACKORSKI

HAMLET AND THE ACTORS—ACT II

she plays with a garland of flowers. This develops the "Ballata d'Ofelia" (The Mad Scene).

Ophelia turns to the shepherds and asks them to listen to her song, a strange, sad melody interrupted by wild laughter and weeping. Presently she seems to forget, and she placidly weaves wreaths of flowers, until the magical siren's song is heard luring her to the water's edge, and she plunges in, singing of *Hamlet's* vow of love as she floats to "that undiscovered country from whose bourne no traveller returns."

ACT V

SCENE—*The Churchyard*

HAMLET watches the grave diggers prepare a last resting place for *Ophelia* and he sings his beautiful song to her memory, the "Come il romito fior" (As a Lovely Flower).

The tragic pace of the rhythm and the sombre harmonies, the rich low tones and grave dignity of this number have made it deservedly popular.

Presently the cortege arrives bearing the coffin of *Ophelia*. The ghost also appears, looking reproachfully at *Hamlet*. In a tremendous scene, *Hamlet* finally rushes upon the *King* and stabs him. The ghost solemnly nominates him successor to the throne, consigns the *Queen* to a convent, and disappears as the crowd acclaim *Hamlet* King.

VICTOR RECORD
(Sung in Italian)
ACT II

O VIN DISCACCIA LA TRISTEZZA

(Brindisi) (Wine, This Gloom Dispel)
TITTA RUFFO, Baritone and La Scala
Chorus   6266 12-in., $2.00

HAMLET:

O wine! the gloom dispel,
That o'er my heart now weighs;
Come grant me thine intoxicating joy;
The careless laugh—the mocking jest!
O wine! Thou potent sorcerer,
Grant thou oblivion to my heart!
Yes, life is short, death's near at hand,
We'll laugh and drink while yet we may.
Each, alas, his burthen bears.
Sad thoughts have all;—grim thoughts and
   sorrows;
But care avaunt, let folly reign,
The only wise man he,
Who wisdom's precepts ne'er obeys!
(*The curtain falls on a scene of merriment.*)

HÄNSEL AND GRETEL

IN looking at the score of "Hän-sel and Gretel," one is reminded that Lewis Carroll, author of "Alice in Wonderland," was a university professor of mathematics; for Engelbert Humperdinck was a deeply learned musician whose scholarship is manifest on every page of this delightful ginger-bread fairy-tale opera. Not that the learning is ponderously displayed; quite the contrary. But it is there if you look for it—good, solid, workman-like counterpoint, melody and counter-melody flowing along as smooth as a lowland river, yet rich with inimitable humor, and at times exquisitely beautiful. It is said that Humperdinck wrote this little masterpiece to please his own children, without thought of publication; and it possesses just the naïve spontaneity required to give an air of probability to the legend; and as a legend, it contains the materials of delight.

THE OPERA

A FAIRY opera in three acts. Text by Adelheid Wette. Music by Engelbert Humperdinck. First produced, December 23, 1893, at Weimar. First American production at Daly's Theatre, New York, October 8, 1895. Produced at the Metropolitan 1905, with Homer, Alten, Abarbanell and Goritz.

CHARACTERS

PETER, a Broom-maker......Baritone
GERTRUDE, his wife...Mezzo-Soprano
HÄNSEL ⎱ (Hayn'-sel)..Mezzo-Soprano
GRETEL ⎰ (Gray'-tel)........Soprano
(Their Children)
THE WITCH, who eats children
            Mezzo-Soprano
SANDMAN, the Sleep Fairy....Soprano
DEWMAN, the Dawn Fairy....Soprano
Children, Angels, Peasants

ACT I

SCENE—*House of the Broom-Maker*

FATHER and mother have gone to market, leaving *Hänsel* and *Gretel* behind to do their work—*Hänsel* making brooms and *Gretel* knitting. But, as children will, they spend their time playing, and singing the old German folk-song, "Susie, What is the News?" with its nonsense about the geese going barefoot for lack of shoes—"Suse, liebe Suse" (Little Susie!)

The old nursery tune goes placidly along, the orchestra carrying on a gentle accompaniment which proves on investigation to be an independent stream of melody all its own, but ingeniously derived from the principal tune.

Hänsel's remarks interrupt but do not prevent the due recital of the story. Not keenly interested in the adventures of the geese, he wants to know when they are to eat. Very soon, however, the children grow more boisterous.

In the midst of it their mother returns, cross and tired. She has not made a penny for all her work, and there is nothing to eat in the house—except a pitcher of milk. She turns loose on the idle children, and in giving them a push knocks over the cream-pitcher. It is the last straw! She sends them out into the woods to gather strawberries, sinks down into a chair and, praying heaven to send food for her family, falls asleep. Her husband *Peter* returns with a loaded basket; and while they both have supper it grows dark. He hopes the children have not wandered into the Isenstein, the place bewitched, where an old hag entices children into her house, bakes them into gingerbread and eats them.

169

ACT II
SCENE—*In the Woods*

THE children have wandered into the depths of the forest, eating the berries fast as they pick them. Darkness soon comes, and they cling together in fright. Finally they lie down to sleep, first singing their little prayer that the fourteen angels may come and guard them. A little grey man answers. He is the *Sandman* who pours sand in their eyes as he sings his air, the beautiful "Der kleine Sandman bin ich" (I Am the Sleep Fairy)

ACT III
SCENE—*Same as Act II*

Next morning they are roused by *Dewman*, the Dawn Fairy. A mist has swept up in the night, but as it disperses it reveals a wonderful gingerbread house. The hungry *Hänsel* begins to nibble at it, and out pops the *Witch*, who does her crabbed best to cast a spell over them. Here follows the "Hexenritt und Knusperwalzer" (Witches' Dance).

The hag builds a fire in the stove for roasting *Hänsel*, who is put in the barn and fed on almonds and raisins to fatten for the repast. *Gretel* is ordered to stoke the fire while the witch rides merrily round the room to the mad melody. Clever little *Gretel* knows by now this must be the Isenstein, and pretends she cannot make the stove work. The witch pauses to examine, poking her head in the stove for a better look. The little girl gives her a good hard push, knocks her into the oven, and promptly closes the door. *Hänsel* is released and they dance around the room to a good old German waltz-tune, whose melody, for all its simpleness, really is a double-melody written with the utmost contrapuntal ease. They prepare to eat the good things they find in the house. After the witch is burned, many children who have been turned into gingerbread by the witch's magic, come to life again, and the opera ends with a joyous dance, and a final hymn of praise to the good God who takes care of little children and gives them food to eat.

THE VICTOR RECORDS
(Sung in German)
ACT I
SUSE, LIEBE SUSE
(Susy, Little Susy) ALMA GLUCK, Soprano and LOUISE HOMER, Contralto   8030 12-in., $2.50

ACT II
DER KLEINE SANDMANN
(I Am the Sleep Fairy) ALMA GLUCK, Soprano and LOUISE HOMER, Contralto   8030 12-in., 2.50

ACT III
HEXENRITT UND KNUSPERWALZER
(Witch's Dance) ALMA GLUCK, Soprano and LOUISE HOMER, Contralto
   87526 10-in., 1.25

PHOTO WHITE   THE HOME OF THE WITCH

LARCHEK   THE CHAMBER OF HEROD

HÉRODIADE

OPERA in five acts. Words by Milliet and Grémont, based on Gustave Flaubert's novelette. Music by Massenet. First production December 19, 1881, at the *Théâtre de la Monnaie*, Brussels. Produced in Paris 1884, with Jean de Reszke (his first appearance in tenor rôles), Maurel and Devriès. Revived at the *Théâtre de la Gaîté* in 1903 with Calvé and Renaud. First London production 1904, under the title *Salome*, with Calvé, Kirkby Lunn, Dalmores and Renaud, and with the locale changed to Ethiopia by the British censor's orders. First American production at the New Orleans Opera in 1892. Produced by Oscar Hammerstein at the Manhattan Opera, New York, November 8, 1909, with Cavalieri, Gerville-Réache, Duchêne, Dalmores and Renaud. Revived February, 1914, by the Philadelphia-Chicago Opera Company.

CHARACTERS

JOHN THE PROPHET............Tenor
HEROD, King of Galilee......Baritone
PHANUEL, a young Jew.........Bass
VITELLIUS, a Roman procon-
   sul ....Baritone
THE HIGH PRIEST ....Baritone
SALOME...................Soprano
HERODIAS.................Contralto
Merchants, Soldiers, Priests, Levites,
   Seamen, Scribes, Pharisees,
   Galileans, Samaritans,
   Ethiopians, Nubians,
   Arabs, Romans.

The Action takes place in Jerusalem Time, about 30 A. D.

(The name of the opera is pronounced *Ay-rohd-yadd*.)

AS the dawn casts its light upon the courtyard of the palace of *Herod*, the slaves awaken and unbar the gates, admitting many traders and merchants from all parts, laden with wares—silver and gold, and precious stones; silks, satins and sables, incense and perfumes, pistachi from Iumea, amber from Judea, attar of roses from Araby. In the huckstering that follows, however, the jovial spirit soon gives way to one of contention; the Pharisees and Sadducees begin fighting. *Phanuel*, the seer, chief adviser of *Herod the Tetrarch*, is drawn out by the sounds of conflict. He bids the people cease quarreling, and finally they disperse. *Phanuel* sadly contemplates the departing caravan. How can these weak tribes, everlastingly falling out among each other, hope to cast off the Roman yoke?

Phanuel's musings are interrupted by *Salome*, who comes from a doorway of the castle. She tells him she is seeking *John*, the Prophet whose new gospel so profoundly affects the people. In a lovely air she tells how he has saved her from the desert as a child, and how good and kind he is: "Il est doux, Il est bon" (He is Kind, He is Good).

Phanuel hearkens to this lovely, impassioned air with deep sympathy for the child,—already a woman it seems,—who has given herself so completely to one who has been to her both father and brother. He wonders if she may possibly know who her

COPY'T MISHKIN
DUFRANNE AS PHANUEL

mother is! Just as she goes out, *Herod* comes in seeking her. He has seen her but little, yet his passions are inflamed by this new beauty who lives so obscurely in the palace. His musings are stopped by *Herodias* who comes in raging and crying out for vengeance. She demands the head of *John*, saying that he has insulted her, calling her *Jezebel*. *Herod* listens impatiently, and refuses. His former favorite is amazed, and reminding him of how she has left husband, child, all, for his sake, she fights hard for her old power. As she pleads and scolds, however, *John* himself arrives, and denounces them both with such prophetic vigor that they run terrified from his presence. *Salome* comes toward him as soon as they have gone, and she confesses frankly her great love for the prophet. He listens to her kindly, understandingly; but he bids her turn to God, and dream only of that love whose fulfilment lies in heaven. *Salome* is puzzled. She does not quite make out why she should not love and be loved on the earth as well as in the promised Hereafter.

ACT II

Scene I—*Herod's Chamber*

HEROD THE TETRARCH lies restless on his couch. Before him dance the almond-eyed women whose only concern is in his pleasure and whose very lives are at the mercy of his uplifted finger. He bids them begone: for *Salome* is not among them. The fact that he has seen her so little only adds fuel unto flame; he longs for her as only a man who has everything possible may long for that which cannot be had. A serving woman brings him a cup containing a most remarkable potion,—the rays of Aurora, captured from a shrine of gold hid deep in the woods. Whoever drinks of it will see the image of the one he most loves. *Herod* yearns to drink deep of it; but he fears a trap—does death lurk at the bottom of the cup? He overcomes his fears with an effort, and, drinking down the stuff, he beholds a vision, vivid, elusive, tantalising, maddening. He sings the "Vision fugitive" (Fleeting Vision).

A world of longing lies in the surging phrases of this melody. Softly it starts, as a dream from which one fears to wake; but as the image of *Salome* takes reality, the cries of *Herod* grow more frantic. In the rushing, upward-soaring phrases one can see the bony hands of *Herod* stretching out with claw-like grasp for the fair but unattainable phantom-*Salome*.

The vision past, he tosses and turns restlessly on his couch, unable to sleep. Seeing him there, *Phanuel* muses for a moment on the man who rules a kingdom and would lose it all for a woman. *Phanuel* has come to warn him that his hold upon the populace is insecure. But even as he speaks, from without there is a great cry for *Herod*. The world of action speaks.

Scene II—*A Public Square in Jerusalem*

A DEPUTATION has come from *Herod's* allies, swearing allegiance to the death, and denouncing the power of Rome. They plan an uprising, but *Herodias* mocks their plans, warning them that Rome is fully awake. Even as she speaks, the trumpeters of *Vitellius* are heard in the distance. Soon the legionaries arrive, and *Herod* is among the first to bow the knee to *Vitellius*. His allies follow suit; but there is one who does not, and one whom the people of *Herod* greet with an odd respect. *Vitellius* wonders who this man may be, this man called *John*. *Herod* notices nothing,—his eyes are fastened upon *Salome*, following the prophet. *Herodias* sees everything. Though she watches *Herod* and *Salome* she warns *Vitellius* of the prophet's growing influence. She has no need, for *John*, with the voice of one inspired, begins to denounce Rome, fearlessly telling *Vitellius* his power is but for a day. The Canaanites surround this dangerously outspoken character, and he is lost in the crowd as *Vitellius*, *Herodias*, and the courtiers enter the palace. *Phanuel* follows with *Herod*, who comes unwillingly. His eyes are fixed upon the slight figure of *Salome*. The world of action is "abjured and forgot."

CAUTIN & BERGER
CALVÉ AS SALOME

CAUTIN & BERGER
RENAUD AS HEROD

ACT III

Scene I—*Phanuel's House*

"UNDER a wide and starry sky," *Phanuel* gazes upon the city of Jerusalem, which lies at his feet. He is thinking of *John*. "Is he man or god?" he cries to the stars, in the "Air de Phanuel" (Oh Shining Stars).

The music here possesses great dignity, though it is restless too. *Phanuel* is stirred. His cry to the stars is really a prayer, for power lies within him to read something of their eternal riddle. To hear what they may declare, even now, *Herodias* enters, in violent agitation. She longs for revenge, and bids *Phanuel* read from the firmament if her desire will be granted. He reads her horoscope, and sees nothing but blood. To her star, however, one other is inextricably linked, and it serves to remind *Phanuel* that *Herodias* has had a child in days gone by. He speaks of it to the startled woman, and strange memories stir her, for she has long since crushed down all thought of the past. She longs to see this daughter again, and *Phanuel* takes her to the window, from which are seen the gates of the Temple. As they gaze, *Phanuel* points to the figure of *Salome. Herodias* is horrified, "My daughter?" she cries. And then hatred flaming within her, "Never! She is my rival!"

Scene II—*Inner Court of the Temple*

HALF fainting, *Salome* falls before the entrance to the temple prison. She has learned that *John* has been captured, and her heart is filled with a despair that is only increased by the music of a chorus sung by invisible choirs within the temple. Here also comes *Herod*, considering the chance of using *John* as a weapon against the Romans. He stumbles on *Salome*, and all thoughts of politics vanish.

He draws close to the girl, and begins to speak,—with passion. She is at first too sick at heart to pay attention. Slowly it dawns upon her that here is *Herod*, the all-powerful, making love to her before the very gates of *John's* prison. She recoils in horror, pushing him away as she might a beast. She tells him she loves another, and *Herod*, enraged, swears to kill them both. She tells the maddened Tetrarch that she would as soon die as live, and he leaves her declaring vengeance. And *Salome*, trembling, sinks down before the Veil of the Temple that conceals the holy of holies.

ACT IV

Scene I—*Prison Cell in the Temple*

AS *John* paces up and down in prison, *Salome* appears. In his heart the prophet loves her, and her entrance seems to him almost the reply of God to his prayer. They sing a duet of infinite tenderness, *Salome* declaring her wish to die with him, though he bids her fly for her life. As they converse, the Priests come to lead the prophet to his death, and they order *Salome* to the temple. She resists desperately, but is dragged away.

Scene II—*Great Hall in the Temple*

SALOME is brought before *Herod* at a great Festival in honor of Rome. Here are gathered *Vitellius* and his centurions, and the priests and patriarchs of Jerusalem. Perfumed flower-girls dance to exotic music—women of Babylon, Phoenicia, and Egypt, and the fair-haired daughters of Gaul. Before them *Salome* is brought in and led to the steps of the throne. She begs *Herodias* to help her, saying, "If thou wert ever a mother, pity me!" The *Queen* trembles at the word, and is perhaps about to yield. But from the rear comes an Executioner with dripping sword, crying "The Prophet is dead!" At the look on the face of *Herodias*, *Salome* realizes who has caused the death of *John*. Maddened with fear and hate she draws a dagger and rushes upon the *Queen*. "Spare me!" screams the frightened woman. "I am thy mother!" A cry of astonishment goes up from the assembled multitude. *Salome* recoils in horror, then crying "If thou be my mother, take back thy blood with my life," then drives the dagger into her own breast. Her dying body falls into the arms of *Herod*, the King.

THE VICTOR RECORDS
(Sung in French)
ACT II

VISION FUGITIVE
(Fleeting Vision) EMILIO DE GOGORZA,
   Baritone   6352 12-in., $2.00
REINALD WERRENRATH, Baritone
          74610 12-in., 1.50
GIUSEPPE DE LUCA, Baritone
          6081 12-in., 2.00

ACT IV
NE POUVANT RÉPRIMER LES ÉLANS DE LA FOI
(The Power of Thy Faith Cannot be Repressed) FERNAND ANSSEAU, Tenor
          6104 12-in., 2.00

INNER COURT OF THE TEMPLE—ACT III

VALENTINE: Raoul, they will kill thee; ah, in pity stay! (Act IV)

LES HUGUENOTS

IN "L'Africaine" attention has been called to Meyerbeer's faculty for adapting his technique to his surroundings. The same faculty enabled him also to adapt his style to the peculiarities of the opera which engaged his interest. In "Les Huguenots" he had, as his biographer in Grove's Dictionary points out, to picture "the splendours and the terrors of the sixteenth century—its chivalry and fanaticism, its ferocity and romance, the brilliance of courts and the chameleon colors of artificial society, the sombre fervor of Protestantism." In this he was so completely successful as to baffle his Parisian audiences at the first production, giving them something entirely different from "Robert le Diable," which had won him so brilliant a reputation. It is hardly surprising that the opera was a failure at first; and it is less surprising that

"Les Huguenots" became eventually recognized as Meyerbeer's greatest work.

Meyerbeer's place among musicians is unique. He developed the opera through more magnificent lines than any one had before—in this respect being eclipsed by Wagner alone. His mastery of the orchestra was consummate; we are indebted to him for many novel effects. As a writer of melodies he was perhaps less successful, so many of his themes have magnificent beginnings only to tail off into insignificance. His harmonies are frequently original and arresting—and as frequently commonplace. These divergences account for the varied views of his genius during life. To some he appeared a veritable triton among minnows; others of his critics were less favorable. Not least of the latter was Wagner, who called him "a miserable

176

music-maker," and "a Jew banker to whom it occurred to compose operas." Today we know Meyerbeer to be a unique figure, one who followed his own laws and left no disciples, whose works must be judged solely on their merits; posterity, so judging, has found much that is worth hearing. And that is the final test. If there is any other, we do not know of it.

THE OPERA

OPERA in five acts. Libretto by Scribe and Deschamps. Score by Meyerbeer. First presented at the *Académie* in Paris, February 29, 1836. First given in Italy at *Teatro della Pergola*, Florence, December 26, 1841, under the title of *Gli Anglicani*. First London production in German in 1842; in Italian, July 20, 1848. First New Orleans performance April 29, 1839 (first in America). Some notable New York productions were in 1858, with La Grange, Siedenburg, Tiberini and Formes; in 1872, with Parepa-Rosa, Wachtel and Santley; in 1873, with Nilsson, Cary, Campanini and del Puente; in 1892, with Montariol, de Reszke, Lassalle, Albani Scalchi; in 1901, with Melba, Nordica, de Reszke and Plançon; in 1905, with Sembrich, Caruso, Walker, Plançon, Scotti and Journet; in 1907, with Nordica, Nielsen, Constantino and de Segurola; at the Manhattan in 1908, with Pinkert, Russ, Bassi and Ancona; and at the Metropolitan in 1913, with Caruso, Destinn, Hempel, Matzenauer, Braun and Scotti. Revived by the Chicago Opera Company 1917.

CHARACTERS

{ COUNT OF ST. BRIS (*San Bree'*)
COUNT OF NEVERS (*Nev-airz'*)
Catholic noblemen......Baritone

RAOUL DE NANGIS (*Rah-ool' day Non-zhee'*), a Protestant gentleman...............Tenor

MARCEL (*Mahr-cel'*), a Huguenot soldier and servant to Raoul. Bass

MARGARET OF VALOIS (*Val-wah'*), betrothed to Henry IV...Soprano

VALENTINE, daughter of St. Bris...................Soprano

URBANO (*Ur-bah'-noh*), page to Queen Margaret..Mezzo-Soprano

Ladies and Gentlemen of the Court, Pages, Citizens, Soldiers, Students, etc.

Scene and Period—Touraine and Paris; during the month of August, 1572

(The name of the opera is pronounced *Layz Yoogn'-noh*.)

ACT I

SCENE—*House of the Count of Nevers*

A GAY party of Catholic nobles is gathered in the magnificent salon of the *Count of Nevers*. The *Count* seems preoccupied; his guests rally him, and he tells them that he expects another guest, *Raoul*, son of the Count of Nangis. "A Huguenot!" they exclaim. The *Count* shrugs his shoulders. Everybody present knows that *Margaret of Valois* is eager to reconcile Catholic and Protestant, and that those who serve the King's betrothed are likely to win power and influence. *Raoul* arrives. He is received with ironical politeness, but he is far too frank and open by nature to be disturbed by frigid courtesy. *Nevers* toasts the ladies, proposing that each tell over some adventure with the fair sex. *Raoul* as the latest arrival, is called upon first, and he relates his rescue of an unknown beauty from some drunken revellers that very

177

morning. He does not know her, but is inflamed by her beauty.

A short recitative leads to "Piu bianca—Romanza" (Fairer Than the Lily), a melody which has long been famous among music-lovers. Its long-drawn cadences and rich vocal ornamentation never fail to please admirers of Italian Opera:

The applause which greets this romantic recital is interrupted by *Marcel*, an old servant of *Raoul*. The rugged old Protestant makes no secret of his displeasure at sight of the young man in such company. In deep distrust, he sings the Lutheran choral, "A Mighty Fortress is our God," which already has played a prominent part in the Overture, and which runs through the work as a crude sort of *leit-motiv*. The guests accept *Raoul's* apologies for his behavior, and invite the old fellow to sing. He accepts, and in sturdy defiance he trolls out a vigorous Huguenot ditty against the "snares of Rome" and the wiles of woman. "You, sirs, should know it well," he says. "It was our battle-song: you heard it at Rochelle." And with this gracious reminder of a desperate battle he sings: "Piff! Paff!" (Marcel's Air). It is almost a buffo song, in a vigorous scherzo-rhythm, its warlike quality at variance with the old man's sophisticated Parisian surroundings.

This achievement is received with applause in which there is a good deal of constraint; but the matter leaves the minds of the guests when a servant announces that a veiled lady wishes to speak to *Nevers*, who retires to an adjoining room, not without banter from his friends. Much curiosity is felt as to the lady, and *Raoul* himself is one of those who do not disdain to peep behind a curtain. It proves to be the fair one whom that morning he had rescued from ruffians. Instantly the young man's interest in her takes an opposite turn. The woman he may love is not likely to visit the somewhat unsavory *Count of Nevers* behind a sheltering veil.

COPY'T DUPONT
PLANÇON AS ST. BRIS

COPY'T DUPONT
HOMER AS THE PAGE

COPY'T MISHKIN
CARUSO AS RAOUL

Yet another diversion occurs when a young page enters, and in a lovely air known as the "Page Song," announces a message for one of the cavaliers. It proves to be for the highly puzzled *Raoul*. He has no idea who can have sent it, especially as it bears the startling request that he will go blindfold in a carriage wherever his guide will take him. He gallantly accepts the strange assignment, wondering whither it may lead. He wonders also at the singular change which comes over the guests, who suddenly begin to treat him with extraordinary respect. He is not aware that the seal on the letter is that of *Margaret of Valois*, but there are others present who are not so ignorant.

ACT II

SCENE—*Castle and Gardens of Chenonceaux*

MARGARET OF VALOIS sits on a kind of throne, surrounded by her maids of honor, rejoicing in the sunshine and the open meads of Touraine after the stress of life at court: "O, vago suol della Turenna" (Fair Land of Touraine), she sings. This is a rich and lovely melody, a moment of welcome calm before the storms so soon to break.

Among the ladies of the court is *Valentine*, daughter of the *Count of St. Bris*, who is rejoicing in the fact that her visit to the *Count of Nevers* has resulted in breaking their engagement to marry. The Queen rejoices too, having other plans for the girl. The ladies retire as *Raoul* appears, and when the bandage is withdrawn from his eyes he beholds none but *Margaret of Valois*. He offers her his sword and his service with such gallantry that she is half tempted to make love to him herself, but she finally tells him of her desire that he shall wed *Valentine*.

Possibly aware of the Queen's ambition to reconcile the Catholics and the Protestants by this union, he consents. The nobles of the Court are summoned, including those whom he has left but a short while since. When they appear, they and *Raoul* gather round the Queen and solemnly swear they will bury their differences with the union of *Raoul* and *Valentine*—whom *Raoul*, be it remembered, has not yet seen. The *Count of St. Bris* now leads in his daughter, and *Raoul* is astonished and horrified to discover her to be the lady who has that morning visited the *Count of Nevers* under such equivocal circumstances. "Perfidy! Treachery!" he cries. "I her husband? Never, never!"

A terrible scene follows. The Catholics are furious, and *Valentine* is overcome with shame. *Margaret* does her best to smooth matters over, but her plan to unite Catholic and Protestant is ruined forever. *Marcel*, the crusty old soldier-servant, alone is pleased, and as the curtain falls, the Lutheran hymn rises from the orchestra with ominous power.

ACT III

SCENE—*A Square in Paris*

NEAR the entrance to a chapel on the Seine banks, a group of Catholic students has gathered about the doors of an inn; and at another inn across the way some Huguenot soldiers are drinking and playing dice. All manner of people are passing to and fro, their variegated costumes adding color to the scene in the bright sunlight. The soldiers sing the lively "Coro di Soldati" (Soldiers' Chorus—Rat-a-plan) in which the chorus maintains a drum-like "rat-a-plan, rat-a-plan, rat-a-plan-plan-plan" against a fine sustained melody, with singularly brilliant effect.

179

This is interrupted by the arrival of a bridal procession. *Valentine* and the *Count of Nevers* are to be married. *Marcel* appears with a letter from *Raoul* to *St. Bris*, who is not to be disturbed, being in the church. Presently the wedding is over, and the *Count of Nevers* appears alone, *Valentine* having desired to spend the day in prayer before surrendering herself to a man she cannot love. After the *Count of Nevers* has passed on, *Marcel* presents his note to *St. Bris*. It proves to be a challenge. The nobles then enter the chapel.

Gradually the long day closes, but it is night when *Valentine* comes from the church. She is in deadly terror, earnestly seeking *Marcel*. During her watch in the chapel she has heard the nobles plotting to slay *Raoul*. Here follows the "Nella notte Io sol qui veglio" (Here By Night Alone I Wander).

In this lovely number, *Valentine* not only warns *Marcel* of the plot to slay *Raoul*, but shows plainly how deeply she loves the youth, despite his recent action. *Marcel* hurriedly gathers friends and proceeds to the rescue. The two parties prove to be evenly matched, and a serious fray is threatened. It is prevented by the arrival of *Margaret of Valois*, who appears just in time. She also tells *Raoul* that he has deeply wronged *Valentine*, the girl having visited *Nevers* merely to break off her engagement. *Raoul* is overcome with remorse. Too late! For already, as he gazes toward the river, a boat approaches decorated with lanterns, and gay with music. *Count of Nevers* and his bride enter the vessel and are borne away, while *Raoul* overcome with grief, seeks support in *Marcel's* arms.

ACT IV

Scene—*A Room in Nevers' Castle*

THOUGH married to *Count of Nevers*, *Valentine* can think of none but *Raoul*. Brought on the barge

CIPOLLA   THE FINAL TRAGEDY

to *Nevers'* palace, we find her brooding over her sorrows, for which even prayer can offer no comfort, "for while I pray I do but love him more." Suddenly *Raoul* himself appears, having entered the palace at risk of his life. She warns him, but he insists on remaining, and he has only time to hide behind the tapestry before *St. Bris, Nevers,* and others of the Catholic leaders arrive. Thus the young Protestant overhears the whole ghastly plot for the massacre of the Huguenots. Among them all, *Nevers* alone objects to the proposal, and, refusing to become an assassin, he breaks his sword and is led away by the guards. The conference closes with the famous "Benediction of the Swords."

The number begins with the passage sung by *St. Bris,* the father of *Valentine,* as he outlines his murderous schemes against various enemies:

This is followed by the noble strain of the *Benediction,* a broad flowing melody of impressive character:

Then comes a furious and sweeping chorus of priests and lords.

After the nobles have departed, *Raoul* slowly lifts the tapestry, looks cautiously about him, then runs swiftly to the door, hoping for time to warn his friends. On his way, however, he meets *Valentine,* who stops him. She cannot let him go when it may mean the death of her own father. But she forgets even this as love overcomes her, and he, too, is enraptured at discovering that her heart is his. *Valentine's* avowal of love is one of the finest of Meyerbeer's melodies, the "Dillo ancor" (Speak Those Words Again). Scarcely has the last cadence of this

lovely number died away than the great bell of St. Germain sounds the preliminary signal for the slaughter, and *Raoul* makes a fresh effort to go to the aid of his people. *Valentine* clings to him, but he rushes to the window and shows her that the massacre has already begun. He tears himself from her arms and leaps through the window, while she falls fainting.

In American productions, because of the great length of Meyerbeer's work, the opera usually ends with the shooting of *Raoul* by the mob as he leaps from the window; but in the original version a fifth act occurs, in which *Nevers* is killed, and *Valentine,* renouncing her faith is united to *Raoul* by *Marcel. St. Bris* and his party enter the street, and, not recognizing *Valentine,* fire upon the three and kill them. The curtain falls as *St. Bris* discovers that he has murdered his own daughter.

THE VICTOR RECORDS
(Sung in Italian except as noted)

ACT I

PIÙ BIANCA—ROMANZA
(Fairer Than the Lily) ENRICO CARUSO, Tenor 6005 12-in., $2.00

RAOUL:
Fairer far e'en than fairest lily,
Than spring morn more pure and more
 lovely and bright,
An angel of Heaven born beauty
Burst upon my ravish'd sight.
Sweetly she smiled as I stood by her side,
Sighing the love which e'en her tongue to
 speak denied;
And in her eyes the love-light gleamed,
Bidding me hope her love to gain.

PIFF! PAFF!
(Marcel's Air) MARCEL JOURNET, Bass
 In French 6173 12-in., 2.00

MARCEL:
Old Rome and her revelries,
Her pride and her lust, boys,
The monks and their devilries,
We'll grind them to dust, boys!

Deliver to fire and sword
Their temples of Hell,
Till of the black demons
None live to tell!
Woe to all defilers fair!
I ne'er heed their shrieking—
Woe to the Delilah's fair,
Who men's souls are seeking!
Refrain
Piff, paff, piff; slay them all,

Piff, paff, piff, ev'ry soul!
Piff, paff, piff; paff; piff; paff, piff, paff!
All vainly for aid or for mercy they call;
No pity for them! No they die—slay all!
No, no, no, no, no, no, no; slay all!

ACT IV
BENEDICTION OF THE SWORDS

MARCEL JOURNET, Bass, and Opera
Chorus   6173   12-in., $2.00

BLUE LABEL RECORD

{Coro di Soldati (Soldiers' Chorus)............*Metropolitan Opera Chorus*}
{ *Magic Flute—O Isis*.......................*Metropolitan Opera Chorus*} 45051   10-in., $1.00

SCOTTI AS NEVERS

IRIS' FATHER CURSES HER

IRIS

"LIGHT is the language of the eternal ones," cries Illica the librettist, in his foreword. "Hear it!" The work opens with a solemn orchestral picture of the dawn. Softly, almost inaudibly, the basses are answered by mellifluous general harmonies leading up to a climax as the sun appears to claim dominion over the earth in the choral proclamation, "I am! I am life! I am Beauty Infinite!" And an echo of this trembles throughout the whole of the work.

tanzi Theatre, Rome, November 22, 1898. Revised by the composer and produced at La Scala, Milan, January, 1899. First American production, Philadelphia, October 14, 1902, during the tour of Mascagni's own company. Two days later New York heard the same organization give the opera, but the production by the Metropolitan Opera Company did not occur until 1908, with a cast including Caruso, Eames, Scotti and Journet. Revived April 3, 1915, with Bori, Scotti and Botta in the principal rôles.

THE OPERA

OPERA in three acts. Text by Luigi Illica; music by Pietro Mascagni. First production, Cos-

CHARACTERS

CIECO, the blind man (*Tchay'-koh*).....................Bass

IRIS, his daughter (*Ee-reece*)...Soprano

183

OSAKA (*Oh-sah-kah*)...........Tenor
KYOTO, a takiomati (*Kyoh-toh*)
Baritone
Ragpickers, Shopkeepers,
Geishas, Mousmé, Laundry
Girls, Citizens, Strolling
Players

ACT I

SCENE—*The Home of Iris near the City*

BENEATH the shadow of Fujiyama, the Wistaria mountain, to which all Japanese pay that respect which is the truest reverence, *Iris* plays with her dolls among the flowers. Here this lovely Japanese girl with the Greek name,—literally "Rainbow," lives with her father *Il Cieco*. She adores him. Though she is woman grown, we find her, after the manner of her people, delighting in the sun, the semblances of living children and the exquisitely tender flowers. As the dawn wins, *Iris* turns the arms of her doll upward in salutation to the sun. She is noted by *Osaka*, dissolute nobleman, who has become enamoured with her beauty. He plots with *Kyoto*, a pander, how he may obtain her. They devise a doll show, intending to steal her away as she watches. "*Mousmés*," young girls, come to the river, and *Iris* sings her joyous song, "In pure stille" (Life is Gaily Passing).

While she thus greets the flowers in the garden, the puppet show arrives. She is interested, and joins the group of girls who surround it. She follows closely the serenade, sung by *Osaka* for one of the puppets—"Apri la tua finestra" (Open Thy Lattice Window).

As she listens to the song, three geisha girls or professional entertainers, come dancing toward her, their skirts flying higher and higher until, beneath their cover, *Iris* is carried off. *Osaka* leaves money to pay the blind old father, thereby, according to Japanese custom, leading him to believe the girl has gone voluntarily to the *Yoshiwara*. So to that singular quarter of the ancient Japanese city, the incensed old man follows her, securing two peddlers to help.

ACT II

SCENE—*Interior of a House in Yoshiwara*

THE drugged *Iris* awakens bewildered, half believing, from her luxurious surroundings, that she must be dead; but dead she cannot be, for death brings knowledge and Paradise joy, while *Iris* is weeping. *Kyoto* brings in *Osaka*, who does not quibble over the high price set upon her by *Kyoto*, but sends for adornment. *Osaka* praises her eyes, her form, her hair, her loveliness. She listens, thinking him to be the godly offspring of Amaterasu, the sun goddess. But she says his name is Pleasure, and she shrinks away, a priest having told her that pleasure and death are one. She tells *Osaka* of a certain vision of these things which came to her as a child in the Temple: this is the "Un di al tempio" (One Day at the Temple). The nobleman proceeds, but she is utterly innocent, and when at last he seizes her passionately, she weeps and asks for her father. Half weary, half afraid, *Osaka* gives her up; but *Kyoto* clothes her in richer robes, magnificent *kimono* and *obi*, placing her on the caged balcony of the *Yoshiwara* so that her beauty is visible to the pleasure-seeking passersby in the street. Once more *Osaka* returns, to plead vainly for her love.

"Iris!" It is the cry of her blind father, and wild with joy, she rushes to the edge of the balcony. But he gathers a handful of mud from the street throwing it in the direction of her voice. "There! In your face! In your forehead! In your mouth! In your eyes! *Fango!*" The girl is first dismayed, then alarmed In terror she rushes along a passage and casts herself from a window, falling into the open drain beneath.

ACT III

Scene—*A Waste Space outside the City*

FROM the bitter world of reality we pass to the realms of allegory and symbolism. By the light of the waning moon, just before the dawn, ragpickers are searching in the filth of the sewer. A ray of light from Fujiyama, the Wistaria mountain, gleams on something white in the tainted stream. Once more it flashes, and the ragpickers pull forth the body of *Iris*. They begin to strip the body of its finery but she moves, and they flee in terror. She gazes dreamily about her while voices from the invisible tell her of the world and fate.

Osaka's baffled desire; *Kyoto's* slavery to pleasure; her father's dependence upon his child,—such is life! Such is fate! Death comes softly as the girl hearkens. The sky turns rosy, and brings remembrance; she stretches out her arms to the sun with whose growing light a field of blossoms spreads about her. Into the soft depths of the flowers her body sinks as once more the song of the sun rises to blazing triumph, as in the beginning. "I am! I am life! I am Beauty Infinite!"

THE VICTOR RECORDS

(Sung in Italian)

IN PURE STILLE
(Life is Gaily Passing) Lucrezia Bori, Soprano   545   10-in., $1.50

APRI LA TUA FINESTRA
(Open Thy Lattice Window) Giovanni Martinelli, Tenor   737   10-in., 1.50
Beniamino Gigli, Tenor
                          646   10-in., 1.50

COPY'T WHITE

IRIS IN HER GARDEN (MME. BORI)

JEWELS OF THE MADONNA

LIBRETTO by C. Zangarini and E. Golisciani; music by Ermanno Wolf-Ferrari. First performed as *Der Schmuck der Madonna* at the Kurfuersten Oper, Berlin, December 23, 1911. First American production at the Auditorium Chicago, January 16, 1912. First New York performance March 5, 1912. Later included in the repertoire of the Century Opera Company.

CHARACTERS

GENNARO, in love with Maliella (*Jen-nah'-roh*)..... Tenor

MALIELLA, in love with Rafaele (*Mah-lee-el'-lah*), Soprano

RAFAELE, leader of the Camorrists (*Rah-fay-el'-leh*)..Baritone

CARMELA (*Kar-may-lah*) ..... Soprano
BIASO (*Byas-so*)............... Tenor
CICCILLO (*Tchee-chee-loh*) ...... Tenor
STELLA..................... Soprano
CONCETTA.................. Soprano
SERENA.................... Soprano
GRAZIA.................... Dancer
ROCCO........................ Bass

Vendors, Monks, People of the Streets, etc.

Time and Place: The Scene is laid in Naples, at the Present Time

(The original Italian name of the opera is "I Giojelli della Madonna," pronounced *Ee Joh-yel'-lee del-lah Mah-don-nah.*)

THE OPERA

NAPLES, that city of sunshine and loveliness under the flaming shadow of Vesuvius, has among many fortunate inhabitants its own share of the less fortunate,—those who live in squalor and in misery yet perpetually long for better things. As is usual with such people, wrongdoing and superstition walk hand in hand. There are many too, whose desperate courage exceeds their wisdom. In surroundings of this character, secret societies abundantly flourish. The *Camorristi* are perhaps the wildest of them all. And of the Camorrista, few are bolder, more attractive to the eye of a pretty girl than *Rafaele*. Small wonder that *Maliella* finds him more to her romantic liking than her foster-brother, *Gennaro*, in whom honesty is united with simplicity to the general effect of dullness. *Rafaele* has boasted that he will stop at nothing to prove his love for *Maliella*. He will even steal for her the jewels which deck the image of the Virgin! Annoyed by *Gennaro's* attentions, the girl taunts him with his lack of enterprise, and she repeats the boast of *Rafaele*. To *Gennaro* the taunt is a challenge. After a struggle with his conscience the young man summons up courage and in the dead of night he enters the church, seizes the jewels and lays them at *Maliella's* feet. At first she is fascinated; but she soon realizes the enormity of the sacrilege. In terror she flies to *Rafaele* at the inn of the *Camorristi*. But *Rafaele*, too, is shocked. He is not only shocked but jealous, and he spurns her, avowing she has sold herself for the jewels. So strangely are passion and superstition interwoven in the girl's mind that she believes herself accursed. In a moment of madness she returns the jewels to *Gennaro* and drowns herself. The unlucky youth, having naught else to live for, makes what atonement is possible, by restoring the jewels to the altar, praying for mercy, and stabbing himself with a dagger. As the outraged populace burst into the chapel to claim their vengeance they find his dead body lying at the feet of the Madonna.

The two *intermezzi* are delightful examples of the music Wolf-Ferrari has written for this rather sordid story. One is the waltz intermezzo between the second and third acts, a study in chromatics. The violins with their chatterings high in the treble are the voice of irresponsible gaiety, and in fine contrast is the lovely song of the 'cellos. The other, chiefly for harp, flute and strings, is played before Act II. The Serenade occurs in the second act. The scene is laid in

the garden of *Maliella's* house. It is evening, and from the distance are heard the strains of an old Neapolitan folk ballad, sung by a chorus afloat on the bay. This is succeeded by the tinkling of mandolins and guitars behind the wall in *Maliella's* garden. It is here that *Rafaele* and his companions come, and the reckless camorrist sings his Serenade, beginning "Apri la bella la fenestrella."

THE VICTOR RECORD
RAFAELE'S SERENADE
PASQUALE AMATO, Baritone with METROPOLITAN OPERA CHORUS *In Italian*   539   10-in., $1.50

BLACK LABEL RECORDS

{Intermezzo (Second Entr'acte)..........................*Vessella's Band*}35356   12-in., $1.25
{ Lucia Sextette (Donizetti).............................*Vessella's Band*}

{Intermezzo (Second Entr'acte)..................*Victor Concert Orchestra*}35270   12-in., 1.25
{ Merry Wives of Windsor Overture (Nicolai).......*Victor Symphony Orchestra*}

{Intermezzo 1 (First Entr'acte)......................*Victor Orchestra*}35381   12-in., 1.25
{ Danse Macabre (Saint-Saëns, Op. 40).............*Vessella's Italian Band*}

SCENE FROM JEWELS OF THE MADONNA

LE JONGLEUR DE NOTRE DAME

(THE JUGGLER OF NOTRE DAME)

THIS opera is said to owe its existence to the fact that a certain concierge, or hall porter, in Paris fell ill and took a "day off"; thereby obliging M. Massenet to collect his own mail. Otherwise, the libretto would have gone the way of hundreds of libretti continually showered upon the successful composer. It is a unique work, an experiment. It is written for men's voices only. Mr. Henry T. Finck suggests that Massenet was piqued because his critics complained of the long line of Massenet's heroines—*Thaïs, Salome, Manon*—and wished to show he could write an opera omitting the "fair sex." If so, there is irony in the fact that Mr. Hammerstein assigned the rôle of *Jean* to Mary Garden at the Manhattan production. Incidentally, the work reveals Massenet's extraordinary technical skill, reminding one that for many years he was professor of composition at the Paris Conservatoire.

THE OPERA

LE JONGLEUR DE NOTRE DAME, miracle play in three acts, text by Maurice Lena, from a mediæval miracle play, *Etui de Nacre*, by Anatol France. Music by Jules Massenet. First production at Monte Carlo, February 18, 1902, with Renaud. First Paris production May, 1904, and afterward given in all the principal cities of Europe. First American production, Manhattan Opera, New York, November 27, 1908, with Garden, Renaud and Dufranne.

CHARACTERS

JEAN (*Zhahn*), a Juggler........Tenor
BONIFACE, (*Boh-nee-fass*) cook
   of the Abbey.............Baritone
PRIOR OF THE MONASTERY.......Bass

Angels, Virgin, Monks, Cavaliers,
Citizens

Time and Place: Cluny, near Paris; Sixteenth Century.

(The name of the opera is pronounced *Luh Zhong-glur duh Noh-tr Dahm*).

ACT I

IT is May Day in Cluny, and a merry crowd is gathered before the gates of the monastery, "laughing and yelling, buying and selling," drinking a little too, and at times getting into a fight. *Jean*, "King of the Jugglers," haggard and worn from illness, and weak from lack of food, begs leave to entertain them. They scoff at his sorry appearance, but insist on hearing "The Hallelujah of Wine," a sacrilegious mock-litany for which the juggler is noted. He "obliges," regretting that his stomach is pagan while he can boast of a Christian heart. At the height of the performance, the *Prior* of the monastery appears and disperses the crowd in wrath. After threatening *Jean* with the torments of Hell, he suggests that the mountebank enter the monastery. *Jean* dislikes to give up his freedom, but the sight of *Boniface*, leading home a mule heavily laden with good things destined for the table of the brothers, is too much and he is directly converted. He enters the monastery with the *Prior* and *Boniface*, contriving to smuggle in with him the soiled fineries and the battered tools of his extraordinary trade.

ACT II

LIFE in the Abbey agrees with him physically; but *Jean's* perpetual quips and quirks and his gross delight in the things of the table, scandalize even while they amuse his fellow-monks. He strives to sing with the choir, rehearsing a Latin hymn, but the foreign language puzzles him. What should a poor juggler know of that chosen language of the saints of God? He has no sense of art, neither in painting nor sculpture, and when the monkish professors of these occupations try to teach him they quarrel among themselves as to which is the greatest of the arts, and the good *Prior* is obliged to convey them off into the chapel to study art in a spirit of prayer and contemplation. Poor *Jean*, only too conscious of his lack of all gifts but the despised art of jugglery, is grieved by his ignorance; and to console him the good cook *Boniface* tells him that anything done well is good in the sight of the Lord. To convince him *Boniface* sings the "Légende de la Sauge" (Legend of the Sagebrush).

The eyes of the old monk soften as he tells the quaint story of the rose that refused to shelter the little child Jesus from the wrath of Herod for fear of staining its lovely petals, and the humble sage-flower that undertook the task so cheerfully and became blessed among flowers. *Jean* listens open-mouthed. Is it possible that even the low gift of the juggler may be acceptable in the eyes of the Blessed Virgin?

ACT III

IN the dimlit chapel, *Jean* appears in his juggler's costume before the picture of the Virgin. To the horror of the *Prior* and his monks, he begins to perform his tricks and sing his villainous songs in the holy place. *Boniface*, noting the feverish intensity of earnestness in the juggler's manner, prevents interruption. Soon, however, *Jean* breaks into a wild dance. The *Prior* and his monks are outraged, and just as *Jean* collapses in prayer before the picture of the Virgin above the altar, the monks strive to rush upon him. But *Boniface* points to a strange glow of light upon the face of the Virgin, who slowly stretches forth her hands in benediction. "A miracle!" cries *Boniface*, and the others echo his cry and sink to their knees. They beg the wondering *Jean* to intercede for them; but he can scarcely understand. Now the chapel becomes illuminated with a mystic glow, and the face of *Jean*, the humble juggler, is transfigured. The monks pray for the passing of a soul, and from above comes the choiring of the angels chanting the *Kyrie eleison*. "At last," cries the dying juggler; "at last I can understand Latin!"

THE VICTOR RECORD

LÉGENDE DE LA SAUGE
(Legend of the Sagebrush) MARCEL JOURNET, Bass *In French*
6180 12-in., $2.00

FRENCH POSTER
DEATH OF THE JUGGLER

GALLI - CURCI
AS LAKMÉ

LAKMÉ

OF the French composers of the late nineteenth century, Léo Delibes was one of the most charming. He was born, 1836, at St, Germain du Val, and he died in Paris, where he lived most of his life, in 1891. He came beneath Wagnerian influence, and the shifting tonalities, brilliant orchestrations,—married to vivid rhythm and charming melodies,—which constitute his best gifts, reveal plainly his susceptibilities in this direction. Charm he possessed aplenty; but dramatic power seemed in great measure denied him; hence his best work is found in his admirable ballets,—"Sylvia," "Naila," "Coppelia." These survive, while his operas, all save "Lakmé," are dead. "Lakmé" survives by its melodies; the plot is unconvincing, and it obviously is indebted to "L'Africaine" for its climax. Yet the strangely exotic beauty of the music, during its really lyric moments, never is merely theatrical and never seems to lose its effect.

THE OPERA

OPERA in three acts. Book by Goudinet and Gille, taken from the story, *Le Mariage de Loti*. Music by Léo Delibes (*Deh-leeb'*). First production Paris, April 14, 1883. First London production at the Gaiety Theatre, June 6, 1885. First American performance in 1883, by the Emma Abbot Opera Company, a version that can hardly be taken seriously. First adequate production March 1, 1886, at the Academy of Music, by the American Opera Company, under Theodore Thomas, with Pauline L'-Allemand in the title rôle. Produced at the Metropolitan Opera House, April 2, 1890, with Patti; and again on April 22, 1892, with Marie van Zandt and de Reszke. Revived in 1906 for Sembrich; in 1910 by the Chicago Opera Company, for Tetrazzini; in 1916 at the Metropolitan, with Barrientos, Martinelli and de Luca; and in 1917, at Chicago for Galli-Curci.

CHARACTERS

GERALD } officers of the British army in India } Tenor
FREDERIC } Baritone
NILAKANTHA (*Nee-la-kun-thah*) a Brahman priest.............Bass
HADJI (*Hud-jee*), a Hindoo slave Tenor
LAKMÉ (*Lak-may*), daughter of Nilakantha.............Soprano
Hindoos, English Officers and Ladies, Sailors, Bayaderes, Chinamen, etc.

Scene and Period: India at the Present Time

ACT I

SCENE—*A Garden in India*

IN a flower-decked garden of India there stands a small temple, half concealed by the trees. The figure of the Lotus is sculptured over the door, and nearby is a statue of Ganesa, the God of Wisdom, a creature with a human body and the head of an elephant. Behind the temple, the light of dawn reveals a small river, forming a barrier on one side of the garden, which is enclosed otherwise in a light fence of bamboo. Near this sacred spot lives *Nilakantha*, its Brahman guardian. Before the shrine are gathered many Hindoo worshippers, and *Nilakantha* exhorts them to have courage and await the day when the English invaders shall be driven from their land. Even as he speaks, the voice of a maiden is heard in prayer, "O Durga! O Shiva! Mighty

Ganesa, created by Brahma!" it runs, and the worshippers echo it devoutly. *Lakmé* is praying, the daughter of *Nilakantha*, so lovely she is regarded, even by her father, with a sort of dread. To-day *Nilakantha* has to go on a journey, and he leaves *Lakmé* in charge of her attendants, warning them that if any foreigner dares trespass within the holy garden, his life is forfeit.

Lakmé and her attendant sing a lovely greeting to the flowers—the jasmine and roses—which cluster about the temple, before leaving in the little boat that has been kept among the reeds by the river. As they float away the sounds of light laughter and conversation are heard. A party of English officers and ladies are sight-seeing and they have wandered hither. Against the advice of an officer, *Frederic*, they break down the frail fence and make a way into the garden. *Gerald*, another officer, is charmed by the spot, and he is disposed to belittle the danger—of which his friend is more conscious. "These trees and lovely flowers can hide no harm," avows one of the girls, gathering a white blossom. "Those are *daturas*," answers *Frederic*, "they are dazzlingly beautiful—and deadly poisonous!" *Frederic* tells them of *Nilakantha* and his daughter, *Lakmé*, and the romantic *Gerald* is much interested—despite the presence of his fiancé, *Ellen*, daughter of the English Governor. Presently they come on some jewels left by *Lakmé*, and decide to leave a spot where they are so obviously trespassing. *Frederic*, however, insists on sketching the design of the jewels, which has caught his fancy. Left alone, he contemplates them with pleasure in the "Fantasie aux divins mensonges" (Idle Fancies). It is a charming melody, its interjectural phrases highly typical of a poet's wayward fancy.

Despite his happiness, he is subtly aware of danger. He decides to leave without completing the sketch, and he is about to depart when he hears the voice of *Lakmé* from the approaching boat. He conceals himself, and watches her and her attendants place votive blossoms at the foot of the image of Ganesa. Her attendants go into the stream to bathe, but *Lakmé* hesitates—conscious of a strange sense of rapture, singing the "Pourquoi dans les grands bois" (Why Love I Thus to Stray?).

Suddenly she beholds *Gerald*. She knows he is one of the race she is sworn to hate, but she cannot dislike this good-looking stranger. She knows perfectly well that a word from her would bring guards from the temple, but she is powerless to utter the summons that would mean instant death to the youth, so frankly charmed at her presence. Dismayed, she bids him begone. His answer is a rhapsody of love, which, far from arousing fury, affects her deeply. But she remembers that at any moment her father may return. Finally she does get rid of *Gerald*, just as *Nilakantha* comes back, to find the fence broken where the strangers have entered. He declares, before the terrified *Lakmé*, the intruder must die.

ACT II

Scene—*A Street in an Indian City*

IN the bazaar, the native shopping district, of an Indian town may be discovered people of many races, of all ages and both sexes, official and nonofficial, rich, poor, and those indifferently blessed with wealth. In the crowd, *Nilakantha* and *Lakmé* are free to mingle with little chance of recognition by any but their friends. The Brahman knows that in the bazaar today are the same English people who wandered into his grounds so recently, and he is determined to single out the man who has dared address himself to *Lakmé*. It does not occur to the man,

192

a high-caste Brahmin, of the old school, that she herself may not desire vengeance upon the intruder. He conceives that if the stranger should see *Lakmé* or hear the priestess's voice he could not fail to betray himself. He orders her, therefore, to sing the legend of the Pariah's daughter, the well-known "Où va la jeune Hindoue" or "Bell Song."

The music of this is in one sense that of a coloratura air—certainly it makes most exacting demands upon the voice; but its peculiar oriental quality, the use of bells, the appropriateness of the context to the situation, give it an emotional quality far beyond that of most such arias. The classical story of the Indian maid beloved by a god is so much like *Lakmé's* own that the effect is strangely moving.

A crowd gathers, but *Gerald* is not among those present. The disappointed *Nilakantha* thereupon orders her to sing it a second time; and scarcely has she begun when *Gerald*, attracted by her singing, draws near and betrays himself by his expression. *Nilakantha* now is convinced that the gods have made his daughter the divine instrument of the officer's doom. He accordingly contrives to have him cut off from his friends. But *Lakmé* manages to warn him, and bids him flee. *Gerald* will not go—he feels this to be unworthy of his rank as an officer. She pleads in vain, for they are surrounded, and *Nilakantha* himself rushes up, drives a knife into the soldier, and makes his escape. *Lakmé* is in despair, but soon finds that, although her lover who lies at her feet, has swooned away, he is not mortally hurt.

She has him taken to a hut in the forest where she may nurse him back to safety and perhaps win his love! Torn between this hope and her sacred duty, she chooses, womanlike, with unwisdom. Time will show!

ACT III

SCENE—*An Indian Forest*

GERALD lies on a bed of leaves, *Lakmé* watching over him with loving care. He wakes and greets her with rapture, in the "Vieni al contento profondo" (In Forest Depths).

His awakening consciousness recalls the events of the past, and his eyes fasten upon *Lakmé* in adoration. As *Gerald's* strength steals back, he appears to forget all else but his love for *Lakmé*, who is deliriously happy.

One morning a group of young men and maidens pass on their way to drink at a sacred spring. Lovers who drink thereof may be sure of retaining one another's love, for they are blessed

PHOTO WHITE
MARTINELLI AND DE LUCA IN LAKMÉ

of the gods. *Gerald* questions *Lakmé* and eagerly she consents to go and bring some of the water. While she is away, *Frederic*, who has followed the trail of blood into the forest, appears, and reminds the wounded man of his duty. *Gerald* agrees to go back when he hears that the troops have been ordered out to put down an uprising but he secretly dreams of remaining with *Lakmé*. After *Frederic's* departure, the girl returns, quick to discover a subtle change in her lover. With sickening dread she notes how *Gerald* starts at the sound of a distant bugle. She drinks some of the sacred water, and gives some to her patient. As he drinks it down, *Gerald* hears the sound of drums and fifes, and the song of soldiers on the march. He starts up eagerly, and *Lakmé* knows now that her hold is broken. Unobserved she gathers some of the *datura stramonium* flowers whose innocent milky-white petals conceal a rank poison.

Nilakantha suddenly appears in rage at finding them both together. But the now dying *Lakmé* warns her father that *Gerald* has drunk from the sacred spring, and is therefore blest of the gods; to harm him would be sacrilege. Thus *Lakmé* saves his life once more. With her last breath she thanks her lover that he has given her that intermingled agony and delight which the heart of humanity calls love. She dies in his arms, and the curtain descends.

THE VICTOR RECORDS

ACT I

POURQUOI DANS LES GRANDS BOIS
(Why Do I Thus Love to Stray) Lucrezia Bori, Soprano *In French*
1009   10-in., $1.50

ACT II

OÙ VA LA JEUNE HINDOUE
(Bell Song) Mabel Garrison, Soprano
In French   6135   12-in.,   2.00
Amelita Galli-Curci, Soprano *In Italian*   6132   12-in.,   2.00

Lakmé:
Down there, where shades are glooming,
What trav'ler's that, alone, astray?
Around him flame bright eyes, dark depths illuming,
But on he journeys, as by chance, on the way!
The wolves in their wild joy are howling,
As if for their prey they were prowling;
The young girl forward runs, and doth their fury dare.
A ring in her grasp she holds tightly,
Whence tinkles a bell, sharply, lightly,
A bell that tinkles lightly, that charmers wear!
(*She imitates the bell*)
Ah! Ah! Ah! Ah!
While the stranger regards her
Stands she dazed, flush'd and glowing,
More handsome than the Rajahs, he!
* * * * * *

And to heaven she soars in his holding,
It was Vishnu, great Brahma's son!
And since the day in that dark wood,
The trav'ler hears, where Vishnu stood,
The sound of a little bell ringing,
The legend back to him bringing.

DANS LA FORÊT
(In the Forest) Frances Alda, Soprano
In French   533   10-in., $1.50

ACT III

VIENI AL CONTENTO PROFONDO
(In Forest Depths) John McCormack,
Tenor *In Italian*   3029   10-in.,   2.00

Gerald:
I too recall,—still mute, inanimate,—
I saw you bent o'er my lips; while thus lying,
My soul upon your look was attracted and fastened;
'Neath your breath life awoke and recovery hastened.
O my charming Lakmé;
Through forest depths secluded,
Love's wing above us has passed;
Earth-cares have not been intruded,
And heaven on us falls at last.
These flow'ring vines, with blooms capricious,
Bear o'er our pathway scents delicious;
Which soft hearts, with raptures beset,
While all else we forget!

THE LILY OF KILLARNEY

ROMANTIC opera in three acts. Text by Oxenford and Boucicault, founded on the latter's romantic drama, "The Colleen Bawn." Music by Sir Julius Benedict. First production at Covent Garden, London, February 8, 1862.

Time and Place: Killarney, Ireland; Nineteenth Century

IN the hall of Torc Cregan a wedding party is held to celebrate the forthcoming union of *Hardress Cregan* with *Anne Chute*, the lovely heiress. The party, as might be expected, ends in a wager concerning two horses. The guests issue forth to run the race by moonlight, and no sooner are they gone than *Corrigan* appears. He is a smooth adventurer, who, by mortgage, holds the *Cregans* in his power. To ensure payment he asks either that a written guarantee shall be given that *Hardress* will marry *Anne Chute*, or else that *Mrs. Cregan* shall herself become *Mrs. Corrigan*. *Mrs. Cregan* is somewhat puzzled by the first of these conditions until she learns that *Hardress* is secretly married to *Eily O'Connor*, the "Colleen Bawn." In proof of this, he and *Mrs. Cregan* conceal themselves and watch *Hardress* signal across to an island in the lake, where *Eily* is concealed.

On the island itself *Eily* awaits her husband; but he comes only to beg her to give him up. Her old adviser *Father Tom*, however, makes her promise not to part with her "lines," and a former lover of hers, *Myles Na Coppaleen*, keeps faithful watch over her. In the meantime, *Hardress Cregan* learns of *Corrigan's* alternative, and he longs to be rid of *Eily*. His hunchback boatman, *Danny Mann*, offers to do away with her if he will but let him have his glove to lure her away from the cottage.

This, of course, *Hardress* refuses, but the boatman, bent on murder, goes to *Mrs. Cregan* and without giving a reason, he secures from her one of her son's gloves. This he presents to *Eily*, declaring her husband wishes to see her at a cave in the "Divil's Island." *Danny*, fortified with drink, is a bad guide, but *Eily's* faith in her husband is strong and she goes. At the cave, however, *Danny* demands her marriage certificate; refused, he throws her into the water. *Myles*, her former lover, who is in the habit of shooting otters for a living, takes a pot-shot in the darkness at what he believes to be legitimate prey. In reality it is *Danny*, who is mortally wounded. *Myles* comes forward in time to rescue *Eily*, clinging to a rock. He conveys her to his cabin.

Word having gone out that both *Eily* and *Danny* are dead, *Hardress* is stricken with remorse. On the very day of his wedding to *Anne Chute* he confesses his marriage with *Eily*. No sooner has he done so than, at *Corrigan's* instigation, *Hardress* is arrested as an accessory to the murder of *Eily*. When he denies the charge, his glove is offered in proof. His mother screams at the sight of it, insisting that she alone is guilty. Just then, however, matters are set right by the appearance of *Eily* herself. *Hardress* is overjoyed to see her, and we are led to infer that the generous *Anne Chute* comes to his aid with money and eliminates *Corrigan*.

The best-known melody is the duet sung by *Hardress* and *Danny Mann*, "The Moon Has Raised Her Lamp Above."

THE VICTOR RECORD

THE MOON HAS RAISED HER LAMP ABOVE
  JOHN McCORMACK and REINALD WERRENRATH *In English*
3024   10-in., $2.00

LINDA DI CHAMOUNIX

OPERA in three acts. Words by Rossi; music by Donizetti. First production in Vienna, May 19, 1842; in Paris, November 17, 1842; in London, June, 1843; in New York, at Palmo's Theatre, January 4, 1847, with Clotilda Barili. Given at the Academy of Music, March 9, 1861, with Clara Louise Kellogg. Revived April 23, 1890, at the Metropolitan, with Patti, Fabbri, Bauermeister, Marescalchi and Carboni. A gala performance was given some years ago in Milan before the King and Queen and a distinguished audience. De Luca was specially engaged to sing *Boisfleury*.

CHARACTERS

MARQUIS DE BOISFLEURY (*Mar-kee duh Bwah-flur-ee*)................Baritone

CHARLES DE SIRVAL, his son (*Sharl duh Sur-vahl*)......Tenor

THE PARISH PRIEST..........Bass

ANTONIO LOUSTOLOT, a farmer (*Loos-toh-loh*).........Bass

MADELINE, his wife (*Mad-a-layn*)..........Mezzo-Soprano

LINDA, their daughter (*Lindah de Sha-moo-nee*)....Soprano

Time and Place—Chamounix and Paris, 1760, during the reign of Louis XV

IN the valley of Chamounix, beneath the shadow of the French Alps, live the aged couple *Loustolot* and *Madeline* with their daughter *Linda*. They are heavily in debt, but the *Marquis de Boisfleury* assures them he will not press the mortgage. His secret object, in this unusual kindness, is to possess himself of *Linda*, who is very much in love, however, with a young painter, *Charles*. Her affection is charmingly expressed in a well known air, the "O luce di quest'anima" (Guiding Star of Love).

Their love is a charming idyl, but it is soon to be interrupted. The *Prefect* of the village acquaints the girl's parents of the *Marquis's* designs against her, and *Linda* is sent off to Paris, to live with the *Prefect's* brother. On arriving she learns this personage is dead, and she soon is in difficulties. *Charles* has followed her. He tells her he is in reality the *Marquis's* own nephew and the son of the *Marchioness de Sirval*. He installs her in a palatial house of her own, and he then goes off to ask his mother's consent to marry her. While he is away, the girl's father arrives, having been compelled by the extortionate *Marquis* to give up his farm. Finding *Linda* in suspiciously fine circumstances, he leaps to the worst possible conclusion and he curses his own daughter. In the meantime, the *Marchioness* has refused consent to the wedding, and threatens to put *Linda* in prison unless *Charles* proves willing to marry, instead, a lady of her own choice. The young man consents—temporarily. But as *Linda* knows nothing of his secret intention to be true to her alone, she accepts his denial as final; and this, added to her father's cruelty, drives her insane.

In the last act we are back in Rome, *Linda* having gone to friends. At last winning the consent of the *Marchioness*, *Charles* comes in pursuit of her. He sings to her the old song of their early courtship, and by this means restores her mental balance.

THE VICTOR RECORD
ACT I
(Sung in Italian)

CAVATINA—O LUCE DI QUEST' ANIMA (Guiding Star of Love) AMELITA GALLI-CURCI, Soprano   6357 12-in., $2.00

FERD. LEEKE

LOHENGRIN:
Thy life I spare:
May'st thou in peace repent!
(Lohengrin, Act I)

197

LOHENGRIN

WAGNER completed the score of "Lohengrin" in Dresden, in 1847, the year he was banished from Germany for complicity in the popular uprising. Before his ten years of exile he had heard only the last chorus of the first act in his new opera, which he rightly believed to be his greatest achievement to that time. In his extremity, he turned to Liszt, and to that musician of genius and man of profound generosity he owed the first production of "Lohengrin." No one at the present time can imagine the moral courage necessary for a man like Liszt to sponsor a work of Wagner's. Liszt was courted of kings, the greatest living pianist, acknowledged on all sides, and as usual in such cases, the target of endless criticism. Wagner was a political exile, and practically unknown. The letters he and Wagner exchanged during the period of preparation and rehearsal are worth reading. Liszt's respect for the work was profound, and he, the foremost musical power of his day, sits at the feet of Wagner like a disciple before his master.

By this means "Lohengrin" was not only launched, but given the proper artistic attention its undoubted beauty warranted.

In the days of its production, "Lohengrin" was at once over- and underestimated. In these days we need do neither. As music, it contains some of Wagner's finest inspirations, some of the greatest music of all time. This is true, for instance, of the Prelude with its ethereally divided strings. The "Swan" music, Elsa's "Dream," and many other lovely passages are unsurpassably beautiful. Generations of couples seem unwilling to proceed down the nuptial aisle to any music but the "Lohengrin Wedding March." To us the beauty of this music is familiar enough, but in the day of its origin it must have seemed like a new language. To the musty academics Wagner was an iconoclast; to men of younger blood he was a prophet, a guiding star. He was a little of both, like all men of true genius. And no one better realized it, perhaps, than Wagner himself.

If your heart is still young enough to accept a fairy story of a shining prince and a golden-haired princess; if you would permit the intoxication of sweet sounds to possess your very soul, then by all means see and hear "Lohengrin" as it really is—one of the most beautiful of all operas, and one of the most inspired.

THE OPERA

OPERA in three acts. Words and music by Richard Wagner. First produced at Weimar, Germany, August 28, 1850, under the direction of Liszt. Produced at Wiesbaden, 1853; Munich and Vienna, 1858; Berlin, 1859; Bologna, 1871. First London production in German, 1875, and also, in Italian, at Covent Garden, the same year. First production in English at Her Majesty's, in 1880. Given at St. Petersburg, 1875; Paris, 1887. First American production in German at Stadt Theatre, in New York, April 3, 1871; in Italian, March 23, 1874, with Nilsson, Cary, Campanini and Del Puente; in German in 1885, with Brandt, Krauss, Fischer and Stritt—this being Anton Seidl's American début as a conductor. First New Orleans production, in Italian, December 3, 1877; in French, March 4, 1889. More frequently given since than any other opera of Wagner's.

CHARACTERS

HENRY THE FOWLER, King of
  Germany.....................Bass
LOHENGRIN (*Lo'-hen-grin*).....Tenor
ELSA OF BRABANT...........Soprano
DUKE GODFREY, her brother
                Mute Personage
FREDERICK OF TELRAMUND (*Tel'-rah-moond*), Count of Brabant
                   Baritone
ORTRUD (*Ohr'-trood*), his wife
              Mezzo-Soprano
THE KING'S HERALD............Bass
Saxon, Thuringian and Brabantian
Counts and Nobles, Ladies of Honor,
    Pages, Attendants

ACT I

SCENE—*Banks of the Scheldt, near Antwerp*

ON the green banks of the river, seated upon a raised throne beneath the Oak of Justice, sits *Henry the Fowler*, King of Germany. On one side of him are gathered the knights and nobles of the Saxon Arriére-ban. Opposite to them are the Counts and Nobles of Brabant, headed by *Frederick of Telramund*, his wife *Ortrud* beside him.

The *King* has come to gather an army together but he finds the people of Brabant torn in dissension. The trouble is due to the disappearance of young *Duke Godfrey* of Brabant, who with his sister *Elsa*, lived under the charge of *Telramund*, who was to have married the girl. *Telramund*, however, charges that *Elsa* herself has killed the boy, hoping to succeed to his estates. *Telramund* has been led to believe this by *Ortrud*, whom he has married after being assured of *Elsa's* guilt. *Ortrud* is the daughter of Radbod, the last of her race, and her faith is still with the ancient gods, Wotan and Freia. She practices the black art of magic, and it is she, in fact, who has caused *Godfrey's* disappearance.

Telramund is a knight of proven courage. Indeed, he has saved the life of the *King* himself in a fight against the Danes. Yet *Henry the Fowler* is loth to believe the monstrous charge of fratricide against the girl *Elsa*. He commands that she shall be brought before him. She approaches as one in a dream, a mystic look in her deep blue eyes, the pale gold of her hair gleaming in the sunlight. Her women attend-

HOMER AS ORTRUD

EAMES AS ELSA

SCHUMANN-HEINK AS
ORTRUD

ants accompany her, but remain respectfully at the outer edge of the circle of justice. *Telramund* makes his charge in a clear, ringing voice, and the *King* declares that justice shall be done through the ancient ordeal by battle. *Elsa* is asked to name her champion, but she at first declines. When pressed she tells of a dream she has had, in which a knight in shining armor comes to protect her. This is the wonderful "Elsa's Traum" (Elsa's Dream). The soft, ethereal music of the Grail suffuses this lovely number, its shifting harmonies seeming, in their visionary opalescence, to be of the very texture of dreams.

The *King* is greatly moved, and he invokes the judgment of God. Four trumpeters blow a summons to the four points of the compass, and the Herald calls, "Who will do battle for *Elsa of Brabant?* Let him appear." There is no answer, and *Elsa* sinks to her knees in fervent prayer. A second call is sounded and a challenge given. This time the men nearest the river bank suddenly descry a strange figure. Lo! a knight in shining armor, such as *Elsa* described, approaches in a boat drawn by a swan, to whose neck is attached a long golden chain. The nobles crowd to the river bank. The knight arrives and is greeted warmly by the crowd. He pauses, however, to bid farewell to the swan which has brought him here. "Nun sei bedankt, mein lieber Schwan!" (My Trusty Swan!) sings he. The mystical beauty of this number, its exquisite tenderness, its mood of profound, almost religious reverence, give it a unique place in the field of opera music.

The *King* offers to this mysterious champion a grave and lordly welcome, saying he believes he may know from whence he arrives. *Elsa* welcomes him with shy, adoring eyes. He tells her that he has come at her summons, and he asks if she will accept him as her betrothed. When she humbly accepts him he offers to fight for her and wed her, insisting, however, upon one thing.

COPY'T MISHKIN

WITHERSPOON AS THE KING

COPY'T MISHKIN

DALMORES AS LOHENGRIN

GADSKI AS ELSA

PANEL BY HUGO BRAUNE
ELSA RELATING HER DREAM

FROM AN OLD PRINT
ORTRUD KNEELING TO ELSA

On no account must she ask his name, rank or station. Her trust must be absolute. Twice he repeats the condition, and *Elsa* wholeheartedly accepts.

Then the *King* summons the knights to combat, first calling solemnly upon heaven to judge the right. This is the famous "Mein Herr und Gott—Königs Gebet" (King's Prayer).

There are few bass airs in opera which have the majestic breadth and stateliness of this fine inspiration. The broad, full, opulent harmonies of the accompaniment are typically Wagner.

The nobles warn *Telramund* that he may not hope to break such a heaven-protected champion, but the knight's courage is more commendable than his judgment. He elects to fight. A field of battle is measured off by three Saxons for the stranger and by three Brabantians for *Telramund*. They solemnly stride forward and plant their spears,

to form a complete circle. The *King* beats three times with his sword upon his shield, which hangs upon a tree, and the fight begins.

The innocence of *Elsa* is soon proven. The white knight strikes *Telramund* to earth, but mercifully spares his life. Amid cheering crowds *Elsa* plights her troth to the stranger. *Telramund* drags his stricken body to the feet of *Ortrud*, in whose deep eyes gleams a light that promises harm to the innocent.

ACT II

Scene—*Court of the Palace*

IT is night. The moon precipitates gloomy shadows off the battlements of the great castle in Antwerp. On the steps of the chapel, *Telramund* and *Ortrud* crouch dejectedly, clad in the habiliments of disgrace. Outcasts both, they suffer each in some individually poignant way. *Telramund* is querulous, irritably blaming his wife for misleading him. *Ortrud* is defiant. She is the stronger of the two, and she skilfully works upon his superstitious feelings. This strange knight, she claims, has won by magic; if he could be compelled to divulge his name and state, his power would cease. *Elsa* alone has the way to compel that secret! Possessed of it, *Telramund* can freely fight him again, for the first loss of blood will weaken him for ever. *Telramund* listens breathlessly. All, then, is not lost.

Presently *Elsa* comes to the window, to sing to the wandering breezes, beneath the white moon, the new joy of her life. In a rapturous soliloquy she pours out her love for the stranger and her gratitude for her own vindication. But she hears her name called in the darkness and she ceases in wonder. *Telramund* has spoken, but *Ortrud* bids him begone. Then, with smooth guile the witch-woman, called to *Elsa's* side, first feigning repentance, implants in the girl's heart the insidious seeds of doubt. She hints of mystery and magic —things easily believed in in the circumstances of the case. Outwardly *Elsa* rejects all suspicion. Her song of faith in her lover and defender uprises in pure triumph. But *Ortrud* has accomplished her work, nevertheless.

The light of day is welcomed by a castle trumpeter, his ringing dawn-call answered by another trumpeter from a distant turret. It is *Elsa's* wedding day. Servitors pass to and fro in the bustle of preparation. Knights and nobles cross the court, arrayed in festive attire, the sharp glitter of their steel accoutrements, and the blaze of their multi-colored robes making brave their pageantry in the clear sunlight. A Herald proclaims the banishment of *Telramund*, the recreant knight, and the leadership of the mysterious champion who will not accept the Dukedom, but calls himself the "Guardian of Brabant." The wedding procession commences; ere long *Elsa* herself appears, marching in stately fashion across the courtyard. Just as she is about to enter the chapel, however, *Ortrud* springs up before her—a very different *Ortrud* from the suppliant of the night before, now demanding priority over the bride-elect of a nameless knight. Her stormy harangue raises some commotion, and soon the *King* and *Elsa's* champion appear. *Telramund* steps out from behind a buttress, and a stormier scene ensues. The beaten man charges the knight with sorcery, demanding his name and station, claiming his mysterious arrival upon the swan-drawn boat as evidence of magic. But the *King* will not listen, the couple are ignominiously driven forth, and the procession is continued after *Elsa* has renewed her vows of faithfulness. Her mind is filled with questionings, nevertheless.

ACT III

Scene I—*The Bridal Chamber in the Palace*

BEFORE the opening of this Act the orchestra plays the gorgeous "Epithalamium" prelude so beloved of concert-goers. The joyous burst of strings, wood-wind and brass, the crash of cymbals, the masculine strength of the tremendous theme for trombones are familiar to all music lovers, no less than the charming feminine grace of the middle section. Never has wedding festival been more happily, riotously expressed in music!

As the curtain rises upon the bridal chamber, the strains of the wedding music continue, but in softer mood. The great doors at the rear fly open, and the bridal procession enters—the ladies leading *Elsa* and the *King*, the nobles conducting the bridegroom. They sing the familiar "Bridal Chorus."

As this comes to an end the *King*, nobles and ladies retire, leaving the bride and bridegroom together. Then it is that *Elsa* first shows the doubt that is in her heart.

"How sweet my name as from thy lips it glided!
Canst thou deny to me the sound of thine?"

The stranger knight reproves her with gentleness. He sings his beautiful air reminding her of her faith in the vision, the "Atmest du nicht mir sussen Düfte?" (Dost Thou Breathe the Incense Sweet?). It is an exquisite melody, familiar to music lovers.

Elsa scarcely hears; the poison injected into her mind by *Ortrud* is working and fermenting there. She grows more and more insistent, her curiosity strengthening by her lover's own protests. As the scene moves to a climax *Telramund* suddenly leaps into the chamber, close-followed by four associates with drawn swords. *Elsa* swiftly hands her husband his own sword, and with the weapon he strikes the assassin dead. The four men promptly kneel at the champion's feet. But the noise of the fight brings others to the chamber, and the victor commands that the dead body of *Telramund* be carried to the Oak of Justice. He may no longer keep his identity secret, and he is going to yield to *Elsa's* demand.

SCENE II—*Same as Act I*

STRANGELY perturbed, the *King* waits beneath the Oak of Justice. Soon he beholds *Elsa*, pale as one already dead; behind her is the stranger knight, his countenance drawn and stern. He easily justifies the slaying of *Telramund* and, in a few words, he reveals how *Elsa* has broken her promise. Then comes one of the most touching of scenes, in which the stranger knight proclaims himself to be none other than *Lohengrin*, the son of Parsifal of Monsalvat, a knight of the Holy Grail.

After the amazing "Lohengrin's Narrative" (In Distant Lands), which is received in sad wonder, *Elsa* is deeply affected. " 'Tis dark around me! Give me air! Oh, help, help! oh, me, most wretched!" During her lamentations the swan is seen approaching and *Lohengrin* prepares to go. He bids an af-

PHOTO BYRON   THE KING DENOUNCING TELRAMUND—ACT II

203

fecting farewell to his bride, saying that had she trusted him for a year, her vanished brother *Duke Godfrey* would have been returned to her. He leaves behind his horn, his sword, and his ring to be given to the boy should he ever return. Meantime the swan with the boat has reached the river bank. And *Lohengrin* steps aboard. No sooner has he done so than a sudden cry of triumph is heard. It is *Ortrud*, who claims that after all her magic is superior. " 'Twas I that wound the golden band around the neck of yonder swan; he is the true heir of Brabant!" But *Ortrud* speaks prematurely. Her words are heard by *Lohengrin*, who is seen by the excited onlookers to be kneeling in the boat, and earnestly praying. All

eyes are fixed upon him. The white dove of the Holy Grail flutters down from above. *Lohengrin* perceives it, and with a grateful look rises swiftly and loosens the chain from the swan, which immediately sinks. From the depths of the water *Lohengrin* then raises *Godfrey*, a fair boy in shining silver raiment, and lifts him to land. "Behold the ruler of Brabant!" cries he. The boy rushes into *Elsa's* arms, while the dove mysteriously draws the boat on its course to Monsalvat. *Lohengrin* is seen once more ere he is lost to view, with head bent sorrowfully, leaning upon his shield. "My husband! My husband!" cries *Elsa*, sinking lifeless to the ground. But *Lohengrin* is gone forever.

THE VICTOR RECORDS
(Sung in German except as noted)

ACT I

ELSAS TRAUM
(Elsa's Dream) MARIA JERITZA, Soprano
6172 12-in., $2.00

ELSA:
Oft when the hours were lonely,
I unto Heav'n have pray'd,
One boon I ask'd for only,
To send the orphans aid;
Away my words were wafted,
I dreamt not help was nigh,
But One on high vouchsaf'd it,
While I in sleep did lie.
(*with growing enthusiasm*)
I saw in splendor shining,
A knight of glorious mien,
On me his eyes inclining,
With tranquil gaze serene.
A horn of gold beside him,
He leant upon his sword,
His words so low and tender,
Brought life renew'd to me.
(*with rapture*)
My guardian, my defender,
Thou shalt my champion be.

NUN SEI BEDANKT, MEIN LIEBER SCHWAN!
(My Trusty Swan) ORVILLE HARROLD,
Tenor 74813 12-in., 1.50

LOHENGRIN:
I give thee thanks, my faithful swan!
Turn thee again and breast the tide,

Return unto that land of dawn
Where joyous we did long abide,
Well thy appointed task is done!
Farewell! farewell! my trusty swan!
(*to the King*)
Hail, gracious sov'reign!
Victory and honor be thy valor's meed!
Thy glorious name shall from the land
That chose thee ruler, ne'er depart.

MEIN HERR UND GOTT—KÖNIGS GEBET
(King's Prayer) MARCEL JOURNET, Bass
915 10-in., 1.50

KING HENRY:
O King of kings, on Thee I call;
Look down on us in this dread hour!
Let him in this ordeal fall
Whom Thou know'st guilty,
    Lord of pow'r!
To stainless knight give strength and might,
With craven heart the false one smite;
Do Thou, O Lord, to hear us deign,
For all our wisdom is but vain!

ACT III

PRELUDE—THE WEDDING MARCH
BOSTON SYMPHONY ORCHESTRA
547 10-in., 1.50

LOHENGRIN'S NARRATIVE
(In Distant Lands) EVAN WILLIAMS,
Tenor   *In English*   6314   12-in., $2.00

LOHENGRIN:

In distant land, by ways remote and hidden,
There stands a mount that men call Monsalvat;
It holds a shrine, to the profane forbidden;
More precious there is nought on earth than that,
And thron'd in light it holds a cup immortal,
That whoso sees from earthly sin is cleans'd;
'Twas borne by angels thro' the heav'nly portal,
Its coming hath a holy reign commenc'd.
Once every year a dove from Heav'n descendeth,
To strengthen it anew for works of grace;
'Tis called the Grail, the pow'r of Heav'n attendeth
The faithful knights who guard that sacred place.

He whom the Grail to be its servant chooses
Is armed henceforth by high invincible might;
All evil craft its power before him loses,
The spirits of darkness where he dwells take flight.
Nor will he lose the awful charm it blendeth,
Although he should be called to distant lands,
When the high cause of virtue he defendeth:
While he's unknown, its spell he still commands.
By perils dread the holy Grail is girded.
No eye rash or profane its light may see;
Its champion knight from doubtings shall be warded,
If known to man, he must depart and flee.
Now mark, craft or disguise my soul disdaineth,
The Grail sent me to right yon lady's name;
My father, Percival, gloriously reigneth,
His knight am I, and Lohengrin my name!

BLACK LABEL AND BLUE LABEL RECORDS

{ Bridal Chorus (*In English*) . . . . *Victor Opera Chorus* { *Flying Dutchman—Spinning Chorus* (*In English*) . . . . *Victor Women's Chorus*	35494	12-in.,	$1.25
{ Introduction to Act III (Wedding March) . . . . *Herbert's Orchestra* { *Wedding March (Mendelssohn)* . . . . *Herbert's Orchestra*	55048	12-in.,	1.50
{ Coro delle nozze (Bridal Chorus) (*In Italian*) . . . . *La Scala Chorus* { *Tannhäuser—Pilgrims' Chorus* . . . . *Pryor's Band*	16537	10-in.,	.75
{ Lohengrin Fantasie . . . . *Rosario Bourdon, 'Cellist* { *Souvenir (Drdla)* . . . . *Maximilian Pilzer, Violinist*	35399	12-in.,	1.25
{ Selection, No. 1 . . . . *Sousa's Band* { *Flower Song (Blumenlied) (Lange)* . . . . *Rosario Bourdon, 'Cellist*	35114	12-in.,	1.25

FRAGMENT OF THE BRIDAL CHORUS IN
WAGNER'S OWN HANDWRITING

The Trio *from* I Lombardi

I LOMBARDI

(THE LOMBARDS)

I LOMBARDI is one of Verdi's earlier operas. It is rarely heard, though it contains some lovely music, which Verdi afterwards used to some extent in his "Jerusalem," brought out at the *Academie*, Paris, November 26, 1847. It is typically Verdian.

THE OPERA

OPERA in four acts; words by Solera. Music by Verdi. First produced at La Scala, Milan, February 11, 1843. Produced in London, at Her Majesty's Theatre, March 3, 1846; Paris, *Théâtre Italien*, January 10, 1863. First New York production March 3, 1847, by an Italian Opera Company, under the management of Signor Sanguinico Patti (father of Adelina Patti), and Signor Pogliani.

CHARACTERS

PAGANO (*Pah-gah'-noh*), a bandit, brother to Arvino..............Bass
ARVINO (*Ar-vee'-noh*), a nobleman of Lombardy...............Tenor
PIRRO (*Pee'-roh*), an accomplice of Pagano....................Bass
ACCIANUS (*At-chan-nus*), King of Antioch....................Tenor
ORONTES (*Oh-ron'-tayz*), son of Accianus...................Tenor
VICLINDA, wife of Arvino.....Soprano
GISELDA (*Jee-zel'-dah*), her daughter.......................Soprano
SOPHIA, mother of Orontes..Contralto

Time and Place: Lombardy and Antioch in the Holy Land, Eleventh Century

(The name of the opera is pronounced *Ee Lom-bar'-dee.*)

206

BEFORE the rising of the curtain, *Pagano* and *Arvino*, sons of *Folco*, the Lombard, have fallen in love with *Viclinda*. *Pagano* is a man of storms and passions, and his hatred is awakened when the girl prefers his younger brother, and marries him. *Pagano* then attempts to kill *Arvino*, and, compelled to fly for his life, becomes leader of a gang of brigands.

The opera begins in the square in front of the Cathedral Church of St. Ambrose at Antioch. *Arvino* has been elected a captain in the first Crusade against the Saracens. The seemingly repentant *Pagano* has returned and been forgiven, but the air is dark with suspicion, and justly; for with the aid of *Pirro* he again attacks *Arvino* and attempts to kidnap *Viclinda*. By mistake, however, he slays his father, *Folco*, and in despair he then flies to the wilderness.

After many years we find *Viclinda* dead, and her daughter *Giselda* a captive of the Saracens. *Giselda* has been placed in the harem of a Saracen prince, *Orontes*, who loves her and whom she loves dearly. *Orontes*, however, obeys his mother's command that they shall not marry until both are of the same religion. *Arvino*, meanwhile, with a Crusaders' company, seeks a hermit who dwells in a cave above Antioch, hoping to learn from him the whereabouts of his daughter. The repentant *Pirro*, who aided *Pagano* in the attack on *Arvino*, is now in Antioch with the Saracens. Through him the mysterious *Hermit* contrives to have a gateway left open by night. The Crusaders enter the city, and *Arvino* rescues his daughter. But *Giselda*, almost insane, believing *Orontes* dead, is so palpably distressed at sight of her father that he becomes greatly angered. *Orontes*, however, is not dead, and he soon comes to her at risk of his life. She flees with him, but he is wounded, and the pair find refuge in the cave of the *Hermit*. Through his influence, the dying *Orontes* becomes a Christian. The remarkable trio at this point has been recorded, the "Qual volutta" (With Sacred Joy). Comparatively little else is heard today, from this opera.

Orontes begins the trio with a lovely flowing melody, and this is followed by duet passages between *Giselda* and the priest and later with her wounded lover. The terzetto grows more impassioned as it proceeds, the three voices combining into a splendid climax at the end.

After the death of *Orontes*, the *Hermit* conveys *Giselda* to her father, and by his inspiration enables her to find happiness in the religious life. For this both father and daughter are profoundly grateful. The *Hermit* takes a highly active part in the fighting against the Saracens, and is mortally wounded. Almost with his last breath he confesses to *Arvino* and *Giselda* that he is none other than *Pagano*. He dies forgiven by the brother whom he twice has tried to kill.

THE VICTOR RECORD

QUAL VOLUTTA
(With Sacred Joy) FRANCES ALDA, Soprano, ENRICO CARUSO, Tenor and MARCEL JOURNET, Bass. *In Italian*
10010 12 in., $3.50

LOUISE

OPERA in four acts. Words and music by Gustave Charpentier. First presented at the *Opéra Comique*, Paris, February 2, 1900. First American production at the Manhattan Opera, 1908.

CHARACTERS

LOUISE..................... Soprano
HER MOTHER............. Contralto
HER FATHER.............. Baritone
JULIEN, an artist.............. Tenor
  Girls at the Dressmaking Establishment, Street Peddlers, People, etc.

Scene and Period: the Present Time

CHARPENTIER'S first opera, "Louise," is a romance of Bohemian Paris. The story tells of *Louise*, a beautiful young girl employed in a dressmaking establishment. *Julien*, a romantic artist, falls in love with the maiden, and soon finds his love returned. The mother and father of *Louise* disapprove of the gay young artist, but *Julien* will not give up his sweetheart, and he implores her to leave her hard work and go with him to a little home. *Louise* at first refuses, knowing how her parents would grieve, but *Julien* persists. He tempts her with visions of a bright future, and at last, unable to resist, the young girl consents.

She falls in with a merry company of true Parisian Bohemians, who crown her as the Queen of Revels. In the midst of a gay party her mother appears, begging her to return to her father, who is ill. *Louise* is filled with remorse and returns to her home, trying all the while to forget the gay, happy life she has left at Montmartre. Her father reproaches her for her conduct, and *Louise* remembering only the kindness and tenderness of *Julien*, rushes out into the night and hastens back to the protection of her lover.

The lovely "Depuis le jour," is sung by *Louise* in the garden at Montmartre in Act III. The young girl tells *Julien* how happy she has been since they have come to the cottage, comparing her life with the dreary one she has left.

The melody of this number, one of the most beautiful in the whole range of modern opera, is so simple that almost anyone might have written it. But it only occurred to Charpentier. It is a remarkable instance of the fact that a composer of creative power may be able to weave the simplest melodic forms into a thing of beauty far outranking the more ambitious works of an inferior mind. The "Depuis le jour" is probably the most popular lyrical number in any French opera of a generation younger than Gounod, Bizet and Saint-Saëns.

THE VICTOR RECORDS

(Sung in French)

DEPUIS LE JOUR
  (Ever Since the Day) NELLIE MELBA,
    Soprano   6216 12-in., $2.00
  ALMA GLUCK, Soprano 6145 12-in., 2.00
DEPUIS LONGTEMPS
  (For a Long Time) ORVILLE HARROLD,
    Tenor and EVA GAUTHIER, Soprano
                     6151 12-in., 2.00

THE SEXTETTE

LUCIA DI LAMMERMOOR

A SCOTCHMAN named Izett, wandering afield in search of fortune, discovered it in Italy, where he took to himself the prefix of "Don," thus acquiring for his children the name "Donizetti." Such was the ancestry, according to report, of Gaetano Donizetti, composer of "Lucia di Lammermoor," and some sixty-two other operas. Donizetti was born at Bergamo, November 25th (Dr. Hugo Riemann says November 29th), 1797, and he died there April 8, 1848, much taking place in the intervening half century. His father intended he should become a teacher, and to avoid this he enlisted in the army, where, if history serves, he spent most of this time writing music—which art he had studied in Naples and Bologna. His first opera, "Enrico di Borgogna," was produced in Venice, 1818, while he was quartered there,

and two others followed. But his "Nozze in Villa," Rome, 1822, won military exemption with honors, for he was carried through the streets in triumph and crowned at the citadel. From that time on he devoted himself to music, more particularly to opera. He was a prolific and a rapid worker. In 1836, while he was in Naples, a certain theatre was in imminent risk of bankruptcy, and the *prima donna* came to him for help. He had no libretto, but one was gotten somehow, and in nine days, it is said, "the libretto was written, the music composed, the parts learned, the opera performed, and the theatre saved." He is also said to have composed the whole of the last act of "La Fille du Regiment" (Act IV), except the aria, "Ange si Pur," and the slow part of the duet, in three or four hours. Not only could Donizetti boast great musical ability, but also considerable literary skill. He is known to have designed and written the last acts of both "La Favorita" and "Lucia di Lammermoor."

Donizetti's musical career, which began, so far as a reputation was concerned, with "Anna Bolena," produced at Milan, 1830, and which later gave the world such masterpieces as "Lucia di Lammermoor," "Daughter of the Regiment," "Linda di Chamounix," "La Favorita," "Lucrezia Borgia" and "Elixir d'Amore," ended some-

what sadly. During his last years Donizetti was subject to fits of melancholia. In 1845 he had a stroke of paralysis, and in 1847 he returned to Bergamo in time to die. He was buried some little distance outside the town, and lay in peace until September 12, 1875, when his body was disinterred and given the belated distinction of burial in the church of Santa Maria Maggiore, where a monument by Vincenzo Vela does honor to his memory. He has not been forgotten, however, elsewhere. For his works live.

THE OPERA

OPERA in three acts. Text by Salvator Cammerano, derived from Scott's novel, "The Bride of Lammermoor." Music by Gaetano Donizetti. First production at Naples, September 26, 1835. Performed in London, at Her Majesty's, April 5, 1838; Paris, 1839; New Orleans, December 28, 1841; New York, in English, at the Park Theatre, November 17, 1845; and in Italian, November 14, 1849. Notable revivals occurred April 7, 1890, at the Metropolitan, with Patti; April 26, 1894, at the Metropolitan, with Melba; November 20, 1900, American Theatre, with Yvonne de Treville.

CHARACTERS

HENRY ASHTON, of Lammermoor..................Baritone
LUCIA, his sister (*Loo-chee'-ah*)
    (Lucy)................Soprano
SIR EDGAR, of Ravenswood....Tenor
LORD ARTHUR BUCKLAW......Tenor
RAYMOND, chaplain to Lord
    Ashton....................Bass
ALICE, companion to Lucy
    Mezzo-Soprano
NORMAN, Captain of the Guard
    at Ravenswood..........Tenor

Ladies and Knights related to the Ashtons; Pages, Soldiery, and Domestics in the Ashton Family

Scene and Period: The Action takes Place in Scotland, close of the Sixteenth Century

ACT I

SCENE I—*A Wood near Lammermoor*

A STRANGER is seen lurking about the grounds of Lammermoor. This is disquieting, for *Sir Henry Ashton*, who through black treachery has recently acquired the neighboring Ravenswood estates, has many enemies, not least of them *Sir Edgar of Ravenswood*. When the curtain rises, therefore, we find *Norman, Sir Henry Ashton's* Captain of the Guard, directing his men to search the vaults beneath the ruins of the old Ravenswood tower, whose grey battlements are visible above the tree-tops. Hardly have the men gone than *Sir Henry* himself appears, followed by the chaplain, *Raymond*. He is troubled over the strange visitant, troubled over his own fate, and troubled over his sister *Lucy*, who has been behaving curiously since her mother's death, and who has formed the habit of going daily to visit her grave. From *Norman, Sir Henry* learns that on these visits, *Lucy* has been meeting the stranger, and furthermore, that this mysterious personage has rescued her from an angry bull by shooting the beast. As they speak of these things, the retainers come back, telling of a man who has met them near the ruined tower, "pale and mute, with aspect daring," clad in black and mounted upon a black charger. This is *Edgar of Ravenswood.*

SCENE II—*A Park near the Castle*

AT the daily trysting place near a fountain in the park *Lucy* waits for *Edgar.* She is accompanied by her maid, *Alice.* *Lucy* is pale and distraught. She looks with dread at the fountain, and she tells *Alice* a gruesome legend of a Ravenswood who stabbed his sweetheart beside it.

She vows that she herself has seen, in the dark waters, an apparition of the murdered woman, who has warned her against her present lover. This is told in the "Regnava nel silenzio" (Silence O'er All).

There is probably more of wistfulness than fear in this pathetic melody, which clearly foreshadows the mood of *Lucy's* tragic "Mad Scene" at the end.

Meanwhile she turns away from these memories to the anticipations of happier things, and in the second part of the aria, "Quando rapida in estasi" (Swift as Thought), she chants the ecstasy of love.

This number is bright and joyous as anyone might wish—a loving woman's dreams of a love that shall be "all in all."

Edgar arrives, a sombre figure with his melancholy attire, his black-plumed cavalier hat, his cloak of sable. It is to tell her that this is their last meeting,

PHOTO WHITE   ACT II, SCENE II, AT THE METROPOLITAN OPERA

for he has been ordered to France. He begs permission to go to her brother, to volunteer to forget and forgive, and to claim her hand in marriage; but *Lucy* knows this impossible. And why? he asks, answering himself; because her brother still nourishes hatred in his bosom, even though he has killed *Edgar's* father and usurped his estates. *Lucy's* lover is inflamed with passion, and she tries vainly to check it; but he tells how his love for her has made him give up all dreams of vengeance. The two of them chant their lovers' litany, the "Verrano a te sull'aura" (Borne on the Sighing Breeze).

The swaying rhythm of this melody lends a swift glint of sunshine and a breath of summer wind to a soon-developing tragedy.

Edgar tears himself from *Lucy's* arms, leaving the half-fainting girl to be consoled by the sympathetic *Alice*.

ACT II

SCENE I—*An Anteroom in the Castle*

IN supposing that *Henry Ashton's* opposition is a matter of hatred, *Edgar* is wrong. As a matter of fact, *Henry Ashton* is in desperate straits because of the part he has taken in a rebellion against King William I. His only chance of escape is to wed *Lucy* to *Lord Arthur Bucklaw*, beneath whose domination he now lives. To make *Lucy* break off her connection with *Ravenswood* he has resorted to guile. He reads all the correspondence that passed between the lovers, and he now has a letter forged in *Ravenswood's* hand-writing which seems to prove beyond doubt that *Lucy* is betrayed, her lover having deserted her. The girl is almost dumbstricken. And *Henry* then tells her he will be disgraced and ruined unless she consents to wed *Lord Arthur*. The discussion between them takes the form of a highly dramatic duet, the "Se tradirmi, tu potrai" (I'm Thy Guardian).

The unequal struggle between them is the more unequal, because with *Henry Ashton* haste is necessary. Preparations for the wedding ceremony are already made, *Lord Arthur* approaching while *Lucy* is kept helpless by reason of the forged note. She miserably consents to the sacrifice.

SCENE II—*The Great Hall of the Castle*

IN a great hall of the castle, where walls are hung with the trophies of hunt and battle, a great concourse of people is assembled to witness the wedding of *Lucy of Lammermoor* with *Lord Arthur Bucklaw*. The knights and ladies sing a gay chorus of welcome but the bride is so pale and agitated that their gaiety rings false. *Sir Henry* excuses her conduct to *Lord Arthur* on the ground that she still mourns for her mother. *Lucy* is escorted to a table where the notary is preparing the marriage papers. Pale to the lips and almost fainting, she is supported by her maid, *Alice*, and the chaplain, *Raymond*. With trembling hand she signs the document which makes her *Lady Arthur Bucklaw*. No sooner has she set down the pen, than a stranger enters the room. All eyes are turned upon him, in fear and amazement. *Edgar of Ravenswood*, sword in hand, pistol in belt, stalks boldly toward the table.

Such a dramatic moment might have inspired a far less powerful composer than Donizetti to produce a masterscene, but he has made it ever-memorable with his immortal sextette, "Chi me frena" (What Restrains Me).

To attempt to describe this Sextette is superfluous; only music may express music. Its flowing melody, majestic rhythm and gorgeous harmonies and soaring climax are known to all; but few realize how magnificently it expresses in sound the conflicting emotions of this dramatic scene.

After it reaches its climax and dies out in lingering tones, others find voice, and many bid the stranger begone. There follows the quartet, "T' allontana, sciagurato" (Get Thee Gone!).

Henry Ashton faces his enemy with drawn sword, and the two are ready for life or death. *Raymond* restrains them, bidding both in Heaven's name sheathe their weapons. Coldly *Ashton* asks *Ravenswood* the reason of the visit, and he displays the marriage contract. *Ravenswood*, refusing to believe his senses, then turns to *Lucy* for confirmation. With her eyes fixed upon him she tremblingly nods her head in assent. In a furious rage, *Edgar of Ravenswood* seizes the paper, tears it to pieces, flings it at the horror-stricken girl, and rushes from the castle. *Lucy* stares after him with unseeing eyes. What is left the girl?

ACT III

SCENE I—*The Tower of Ravenswood Castle*

THAT night as poor *Ravenswood* broods over his misfortunes, a horseman rides up, dismounts and enters the tower. It proves to be *Sir Henry*, who brings a challenge. They agree to fight to the death when morning arrives, and in a duet they pray that the night may hasten away, and the dawn bring vengeance. This is "O sole piu rapido" (Haste, Crimson Morning).

Henry Ashton departs, and *Ravenswood* wanders to the burial ground of his ancestors, where, beside the grave of his murdered father, he finds consolation in the thought that death, on the morrow, may claim him, too.

SCENE II—*Hall in Lammermoor Castle*

MEANTIME at the castle, the lights burn in the windows, and the peasants and domestics make

RAYMOND ANNOUNCING THE TRAGEDY—ACT III

merry. Suddenly the laughter ceases and the song dies upon their lips. *Raymond* tells them that *Lucy* has gone insane, and that she stands in the bridal chamber with a bloody sword above the corpse of her husband. "O qual funesto avvenimento" (Oh! Dire Misfortune), sing they. Scarcely has the full story been heard by the guests when *Lucy* herself appears, pale and lovely, robed in white, her hair loose upon her shoulders. In her eyes there is seen a strange unnatural light, and her face wears the tender, half-puzzled expression of one who strives to recall a dream. Exactly as the nerves become paralyzed when pain is inflicted beyond the bearing point, so, too, the tortured brain refuses to suffer an agony too prolonged. *Lucy* is mad indeed, but she is happy in her madness, for she believes herself with her lover. Then comes the famous "Mad Scene."

Heard apart from the opera, this number seems hardly more than an unusually brilliant coloratura aria. But in its proper setting, carolled out by the demented *Lucy* amid the startled retainers, it takes on an ironic character quite its own. The scales and *fiorituri* seem what they are, the audible wanderings of a mind distraught. The very happiness of the music adds only to its grim pathos. *Lucy*, in this strain, reënacts the wedding-scene of the day before, and the memories come flooding back. She falls insensible, and is carried to her room by *Alice* and *Raymond*, as the curtain descends.

SCENE III— *The Tombs of the Ravenswoods*

BUT as the night wears on, the lights still winking gaily from the castle at Lammermoor, convey to the silent watcher who stands amid the graves of the Ravenswoods, no knowledge of these tragic events. The young man's despair is revealed in a lovely number, the "Fra poco a me ricovero" (Farewell to Earth).

The tragic pathos of the situation has penetrated through the conventional form of the opera. The "dulcet strains" of the music move like the clock, and as inexorably. Time will neither postpone the end, nor hasten it. The set musical speech of the stage *Edgar*,—if it is not Life, it is Fate.

Edgar's only desire is to find peace in the grave, and he calls upon "that faithless woman" to give it a thought as she passes by leaning on the arm of her husband. Yet even as he, in self-pity, heaps reproaches upon the absent *Lucy*, he remarks a train of mourners coming from the castle. His intention had been to cast himself upon his adversary's sword, but he soon learns that *Henry*, filled with remorse, has left Scotland never to set foot again upon its unhappy shores. Then he is told of *Lucy's* madness and of her love for himself. She lies, they tell him, in the castle, at the point of death. And even as they rehearse the story, the sound of a tolling bell brings word that *Lucy's* gentle soul has passed. As the dawn comes, *Edgar of Ravenswood* sings his own dying prayer—that *his* soul may join that of his beloved in realms remote from the gloomy halls of Lammermoor. "Tu che a Dio spiegasti l'ali" (Thou Hast Spread Thy Wings to Heaven), sings he, in a melody of wonderful pathos, which deepens as it proceeds.

There is none of that momentary hope, that disbelief in misfortune, which withholds many a man, similarly circumstanced, from putting hands to his life. The tolling bell has not lied.

Edgar Ravenswood draws a dagger from his belt, and despite the efforts of *Raymond* to prevent him, stabs himself, and so speeds forth his soul to that eternity from whence beckons his beloved *Lucy*.

THE VICTOR RECORDS

(Sung in Italian except as noted)

ACT II

SEXTETTE—CHI MI FRENA

(What Restrains Me) TETRAZZINI, CA-
RUSO, AMATO, JOURNET, JACOBY and
BADA   96201 12-in., $2.50
GALLI-CURCI, EGENER, CARUSO, DE
LUCA, JOURNET and BADA
              10000 12-in., 3.50

ACT III

IL DOLCE SUONO

(Mad Scene) (With Flute Obbligato)
LUISA TETRAZZINI, Soprano
              6337 12-in., 2.00
NELLIE MELBA, Soprano 6219 12-in., 2.00
AMELITA GALLI-CURCI, Soprano
              6129 12-in., 2.00

Lucy:
I hear the breathing of his tender voice,
That voice beloved sounds in my heart forever.
My Edgar, why were we parted?
Let me not mourn thee;
See, for thy sake, I've all forsaken!
What shudder do I feel thro' my veins?
My heart is trembling, my senses fail!
(*She forgets her trouble and smiles.*)
Come to the fountain;
There let us rest together,

Ah me! see where yon spectre arises,
Standing between us! Alas! Dear Edgar!
See yon phantom rise to part us!
(*Her mood again changes.*)
Yet shall we meet, dear Edgar, before the altar.
Hark to those strains celestial!
Ah! 'Tis the hymn for our nuptials!
For us they are singing!
The altar for us is deck'd thus,
Oh, joy unbounded!
'Round us the brilliant tapers are shining,
The priest awaits us,
Oh! day of gladness!
Thine am I ever, thou mine forever!

SPARGI D'AMARO PIANTO

(Cast on My Grave a Flower) (Mad
Scene—Part 2) AMELITA GALLI-CURCI,
Soprano   634 10-in., $1.50

FRA POCO A ME RICOVERO

(Farewell to Earth) JOHN McCORMACK,
Tenor   6196 12-in., 2.00
GIOVANNI MARTINELLI, Tenor
              6189 12-in., 2.00

TU CHE A DIO SPIEGASTI L'ALI

(Thou Hast Spread Thy Wings to
Heaven) GIOVANNI MARTINELLI,
Tenor   6189 12-in., 2.00
JOHN McCORMACK, Tenor
              6196 12-in., 2.00

BLACK LABEL AND BLUE LABEL RECORDS

{Mad Scene (*In Italian*)............................*Olive Kline, Soprano*} 55047 12-in., $1.50
{ Dinorah—Shadow Song (*In Italian*)................*Olive Kline, Soprano*}

{Sextette (*In Italian*)................................*Victor Opera Sextette*} 55066 12-in., 1.50
{ Rigoletto Quartet (*In Italian*).......................*Victor Opera Quartet*}

{Sextette (Trancription) *Pianoforte*.........................*Himmelreich*} 35223 12-in., 1.25
{ Caprice Español (*Moszkowski*) *Pianoforte*...........*Charles G. Spross*}

{Sextette...*Vessella's Italian Band*} 35356 12-in., 1.25
{ Jewels of the Madonna—Intermezzo...............*Vessella's Italian Band*}

{Sextette...................................*Hurtado Bros. Marimba Band*} 35559 12-in., 1.25
{ Aïda Selection (*Verdi*)....................*Hurtado Bros. Marimba Band*}

{Verranno a te sull'aura (*In Italian*)................*Pereira and Salvati*}
{ Quartetto, T'allontana, sciagurato (Get Thee Gone!) (*In Italian*)   } 68454 12-in., 1.25
{   *Pereira, Maggi, Bettoni and de Gregorio*}

{Prelude (Act I, Scene II)....................*Francis Lapitino, Harpist*} 17929 10-in., .75
{ Norma—Fantasie..........................*Francis Lapitino, Harpist*}

215

LUCREZIA BORGIA

OPERA in three acts; text by Felice Romani, from Victor Hugo's novel. Music by Donizetti. First production La Scala, Milan, 1834; given at the *Théâtre Italien*, Paris, October 27, 1840. First London production, June 6, 1839; in English, December 30, 1843. Produced in New Orleans, April 27, 1844; in New York, Astor Place Opera House, 1847, and September 5, 1854, with Maria Grisi; given in 1855 at the Boston Theatre, with Grisi and Mario, this being the first Italian Opera Company to sing at the present Boston Theatre; in May, 1855, Steffanone, Brignoli and Vestvali appeared in the opera at the Boston Theatre; and later a long list of popular singers appeared in Boston as *Lucrezia*, among them La Grange, Parodi, Medori, Carozzi-Zucchi, Parepa Rosa, Lavielli, Tietjiens and Pappenheim; given in New York in 1876, with Tietjiens and Brignoli, and not again until Colonel Mapleson gave a production at the Academy of Music, October 30, 1882. The next production did not occur until 1904 with Caruso, de Macchi, and Scotti.

CHARACTERS

LUCREZIA BORGIA (*Loo-kray'-tz-yah Bor-jah*).........Soprano
MAFFIO ORSINI (*Maf'-fee-oh Or-see'-nee*)............Contralto
GENNARO (*Jen-nah'-roh*).......Tenor
IL DUCA ALFONSO (*Eel Doo'-kah Al-fon'-soh*)....Baritone
LIVEROTTO, VITELLOZZO, PETRUCCI, GAZELLA, Young noblemen

Scene and Period: Italy; the Beginning of the Sixteenth Century

ACT I

SCENE—*In Venice*

LUCREZIA BORGIA, now *Duchess of Ferrara*, has had a son by a former marriage, but has concealed the fact from her husband, the child having been raised by a fisherman without knowledge of his parents,—save that good fortune has attended him through the mysterious influence of a mother unknown to him, yet whom he adores. Overcome by a desire to see her son, *Lucrezia* has secretly come from Ferrara to Venice, is followed, unsuspecting, by her husband's spies.

At the rise of the curtain, *Gennaro*, with his sworn friend *Orsini*, are among those of a merry party. *Gennaro* however, is tired, and when *Orsini* begins to express hatred and dread of the Borgias, he drops off asleep. The others depart, and as they do, *Lucrezia* herself appears, and gazes upon the slumbering *Gennaro*. She kisses his hand and thus awakes him. He makes love to her but, moved by impulse, tells her of his love for his unknown mother. *Lucrezia* listens, deeply touched, until unknown to her, *Orsini* and his companions have returned. *Lucrezia* weeps,—withdrawing the mask from her face to dry her eyes. She is recognized by *Orsini* as the dreaded *Borgia*, the poisoner of his brother, who has murdered his brother's sister. All, including *Gennaro*, though powerless to harm a woman of her rank denounce her. She is maddened at their insults, and plans revenge upon all save her son.

ACT II

SCENE—*In Ferrara*

ORSINI, *Gennaro* and their companions are part of an embassy appointed from Venice to Ferrara. They hate the Borgias. *Don Alfonso*, Duke of Ferrara, is aware of his wife's interest in *Gennaro* without divining the cause, and he is naturally jealous. Unhappily, *Gennaro* in his contempt for the Borgias deletes the letter B from

216

the name above the palace gate, and *Lucrezia*, stung by the insult, demands instant death for the miscreant. This furnishes the *Duke* opportunity for vengeance. The bitterness of his feeling is expressed in a well known aria: "Vieni, la min vendetta" (Haste Thee, for Vengeance).

The *Duke* has *Gennaro* arrested, and great is *Lucrezia's* horror on discovering that the man whose death she commands is her own son. She pleads with the *Duke*, but only to learn of his jealousy. She is told *Gennaro* must die by dagger or by the famous Borgia wine, a poisonous vintage. She selects the wine, and she is compelled to administer it while the *Duke* offers *Gennaro* his liberty with fair promises. Secretly, however, she gives him an antidote which counteracts the poison and permits him to escape.

ACT III
Scene—In Venice

RELEASED from the grip of the Borgia, *Gennaro* returns to his own home. Around the gates are a group of bravos who have been set to watch for him. They make merry while they wait, singing the chorus, "Rischiarata e la finestra" (Yonder Light is the Guiding Beacon).

Unexpectedly, however, *Gennaro* falls in with his friend *Orsini*, who persuades him that the attempt on his life is a trick of *Borgia's* to win his gratitude and so make him her tool. Against his better judgment, *Gennaro* is also persuaded to attend a banquet that night. Once there, all is gaiety. Wine is handed round to the guests and made the subject of the fine Brindisi, or

drinking song, "It is Better to Laugh."

While the feast is at its height, a bell tolls, and there is heard the sound of a chant for the dead. The lights fade out. Hooded monks file into the room and behind them a company of armed men followed by *Lucrezia Borgia*. She reminds them of their deadly insults in Venice, and she informs them they have made merry on Borgia wine. As a reminder of its potency, curtains are flung back, disclosing five narrow coffins. To her horror, however, *Gennaro* steps forward and demands a sixth. As the dying guests leave to enter the curtained room, *Lucrezia* desperately offers her son the phial with the last drop of the antidote. Not being enough to save his friends also, he refuses, even though she makes known to him that she is his mother. It is but to accord him the privilege of dying in her arms. When the *Duke* enters a few moments later it is to find that she also has taken the fatal draught, and lies beside her son.

THE VICTOR RECORDS

VIENI LA MIA VENDETTA
(Haste Thee, for Vengeance) Jose Mardones, Bass. *In Italian* 6456 12-in., $2.00
BRINDISI
(It Is Better to Laugh) Ernestine Schumann-Heink, Contralto. *In German* 6278 12-in., 2.00
Sophie Braslau, Contralto. *In Italian* 550 10-in., 1.50
Margarete Matzenauer, Contralto. *In Italian* 999 10-in., 1.50

It is better to laugh than be sighing.
When we think how life's moments are flying;
For each sorrow Fate ever is bringing,
There's a pleasure in store for us springing.
Tho' our joys, like to waves in the sunshine,
Gleam awhile, then are lost to the sight,
Yet, for each sparkling ray
That so passes away,
Comes another as brilliant and light.

PINKERTON'S JAPANESE HOME

MADAME BUTTERFLY

EARLY in 1900, an American producer needed a play with which to save a rather disastrous season, and finding possibilities in the story, fashioned "Madame Butterfly" in considerable haste. It was a success. The all-night vigil was especially attractive. The play then went to London, where it was seen by the stage manager of the Covent Garden Opera. Knowing Puccini needed a successor to "La Tosca," he wired the Italian composer, who came on immediately, and fell in love with "Madame Butterfly," though he did not at this time, it is said, understand a word of English.

The opera, "Madame Butterfly" was produced at La Scala, February 17, 1904. Strange to say it was a fiasco. It is hard to account for this save on the ground that Italian audiences are notoriously parochial in operatic matters. They did not seem to have relished the Japanese setting. *Viva Italia!* The opera was withdrawn, and Puccini made a few changes, notably omitting the all-night vigil which had been so successful in the play. Three months later, the work was given a new production at Brescia, this time with success. After a trial performance in Washington, D. C., an English version ran for several months at the Garden Theatre, New York, under the management of the Savage Opera Company, and a Metropolitan performance, of course in Italian, was given February 11, 1907. Since then it has become one of the most popular of all operas.

While much of this success is due to the dramatically-conceived play, much more is due to Puccini's music, which attains a quality not exceeded by any of this composer's works, and perhaps equalled only in "La Bohème." The composer makes free use of Japanese themes, but he is frankly Italian, as a rule, in the emotional parts. And in these he is more than successful.

THE OPERA

OPERA in two acts, a Japanese lyric tragedy, founded on the book of John Luther Long and the drama by David Belasco, with Italian libretto by Illica and Giacosa. Music by Giacomo Puccini. First produced at La Scala, Milan, in 1904, it proved a failure. Revived the following year in slightly changed form with much success. First American presentation (in English) occurred in October, 1906, in Washington, D. C., by Savage Opera Company. Produced in English at the New Orleans Opera, January 9, 1907, and in French January 6, 1912. First representation in Italian at Metropolitan Opera House, February 11, 1907, with Farrar, Caruso, Homer and Scotti, and from six to eight performances have been given each season since that time.

CHARACTERS

MADAME BUTTERFLY (Cho-Cho-San) .... Soprano
SUZUKI, Cho-Cho-San's servant .... Mezzo-Soprano
B. F. PINKERTON, Lieutenant in the United States Navy .... Tenor
KATE PINKERTON, his American wife .... Mezzo-Soprano
SHARPLESS, United States Consul at Nagasaki .... Baritone
GORO, a marriage broker .... Tenor
PRINCE YAMADORI, suitor for Cho-Cho-San .... Baritone
THE BONZE, Cho-Cho-San's uncle .... Bass
TROUBLE, Cho-Cho-San's child, Cho-Cho-San's relations and friends—Servants
At Nagasaki, Japan—Time, the Present

ACT I

SCENE—*Exterior of Pinkerton's House at Nagasaki*

IT is all vastly amusing! This match-box of a house and its sliding panels, convertible rooms, neat and ingenious devices; and ridiculously inexpensive! *Pinkerton* is charmed and amused as the self-important *Goro* shows him over the little house he is to share with his "Japanese wife" during a not-too-prolonged stay in Japan. Presently *Sharpless*, United States Consul, turns up. *Pinkerton* tells him delightedly about the whole thing and plans the "wedding." The consul has a dim suspicion that the experiment may turn out more seriously than the sailor anticipates, but *Pinkerton* will not listen to hints of tragedy. They argue the matter in a magnificent duet; the "Amore o grillo" (Love or Fancy?)

Pinkerton's share of this music is a splendid melody which grows in life and energy until a sudden modulation shifts the tonality from B flat to D flat, and it is repeated a minor third higher in pitch, in a region calling for the most brilliant of tenor tones. *Sharpless*, as becomes his greater age and dignity, is given a more dignified part. The voices combine at the end for a brilliant climax, when, having filled their glasses, they drink to "folks in America," and to the time when *Pinkerton* will have a "real" wedding back there in "God's country."

As the two men are looking out over the glorious scenery, they see a group of girls approaching. Among them is *Cho-Cho-San* — "Madame Butterfly" herself.

The warmth and freshness of her first melody, the entrance of *Cho-Cho-San*, fully express the girl's youth and the awakening of springtime in her heart. Curious successions of harmonies (mostly augmented fifths) lead to a melody which is to be heard again in the finale of the act, in much nobler form. The throbbing of the orchestra perfectly symbolizes her meaning as she tells her girl companions how she has hastened here at the call of her own beating heart.

Madame Butterfly is duly introduced. She vastly entertains her American lover with the stories of her relations; an awkward moment is achieved when she speaks of her dead father and the grinding poverty of her lot since the misfortune of his loss. A very pathetic melody used here is heard in "Ieri son salita," in a beautifully augmented form.

Swarms of relatives now arrive and the amused *Pinkerton* signs the wedding papers—by which, for the paltry sum of one hundred yen, he acquires the deliciously attractive little maiden who has come to him, arrayed in white like a real American bride. During the formalities she entertains him by withdrawing from her capacious sleeves her small possessions—silk handkerchiefs, a pipe, a tiny silver buckle, a fan, a jar of carmine, and—with great solemnity—the sheath of a dagger. The laughing *Pinkerton* is slightly puzzled by the last, and seeing that it is evidently of great importance to the girl he asks *Goro* for information. It had contained a knife sent to her father by the Mikado. Something in *Goro's* manner induces *Pinkerton* to pursue the topic. "And her father?" —"Was obedient!" is the grim answer. *Pinkerton* is thus suddenly reminded that he is in a land given to seppuku, or "hara-kiri," a condemned gentleman's privilege to die by his own hand. Not all is tea and incense and chrysanthemums.

The girl also brings from her capacious sleeves her *ottoke*—images of her forefathers—which the young officer examines curiously. He does not take

VICTROLA BOOK OF THE OPERA

THE MARRIAGE SCENE—ACT I

them very seriously. It is then, however, that the girl confides in him the fact that she has been to the Mission and has adopted the Christian religion.

This is the "Ieri son salita" (Hear Me). The melody is an expanded form of that which is heard softly and tenderly during her mention of her father. In it she pours out from her full heart, her confession of surrender to her American lover. She promises him, with infinite pathos, that she will "try to be frugal," remembering that he has paid for her the vast sum of a hundred yen. Almost, she declares, she can forget her own race and kindred for his dear sake.

Pinkerton, we cannot help observing, does not realize, even remotely, the power of her devotion. To him it is simply a charming if casual adventure. His chief concern is to get rid of the relatives, for which purpose he plies them with *saki* and cakes. As they are about to leave, however, *Madame Butterfly's* uncle rushes in, violently enraged. He asks *Madame Butterfly* what she has been doing at the Mission. Guessing that she has forsworn her religion, he and her relatives are indignant beyond measure. Her mother intervenes, but is pushed angrily aside.

Finally they disown her altogether. The girl stands petrified.

Having not the faintest idea what the turmoil is all about, *Pinkerton* resents the intrusion; he eventually dismisses the whole gathering. He is perhaps somewhat amused; but it is plain that *Butterfly* is deeply perturbed. He comforts her, and now that they are alone, he makes ardent love. Her delightful, shy coquetry fascinates him. Well is she named "*Butterfly*." The name, however, reminds the girl that she has heard how, in America, butterflies are sometimes caught and a needle driven through their struggling bodies; is that true? *Pinkerton* admits it gaily, and says he has now captured his little butterfly and she is his forever, no matter how she may struggle.

In a fashion that perhaps only the East may know, they talk on, far into the afternoon, until the sun sets and its gold and scarlet fires die out and are replaced by the soft glow of moonlight. They sing the "O quanti occhi fisi" (Oh Kindly Heavens).

The chief melody of this passionate love-duet is a fuller and richer variant of the melody suggested at the entrance of *Cho-Cho-San*. It is a full-throated song of love, soaring upward to a magnificent mid-climax, which ultimately quiets down till the voices almost cease. Then, very softly, as the curtain descends, we hear the tender melody used at the mention of *Butterfly's* father, and used again in "Ieri son salita." It is the melody of *Butterfly's* sacrifice, the quintessence of her love for the man who, with such light-hearted gaiety, goes on to amuse himself with a Japanese wife, in a little match-box of a house, in a ridiculously charming land of tea and chrysanthemums.

ACT II

Scene I—*Interior of Butterfly's Home— at the back a Garden with Cherries in Bloom*

THREE years have now elapsed since the wedding of *Cho-Cho-San; Pinkerton* has long been back in America! He does not know that there is now a little son in the match-box house, nor is he aware that the money he left is almost gone. *Butterfly* remembers how he promised to return "when the robins built their nests"; so far he has not come, though the robins have built thrice. *Suzuki,* the maid, insists that she never heard of a foreign husband who returned to his Japanese bride; *Madame Butterfly* at once flies into as royal a rage as Japanese house-etiquette permits. At length she quiets down somewhat, and compels the maid to say "he will come"; but the tears in *Suzuki's* eyes sadden her beyond words. And yet somehow they serve in the end to strengthen her faith in his return. This finds new expression in by far the most famous air in the opera; the "Un bel di vedremo" (Some Day He'll Come).

This melody, with its peculiar step-by-step descent from a high G flat curiously wavering before each long note, is one of the most haunting of Puccini's many haunting melodies, and surely the one most strongly associated with this opera. There are many which might easily belong to either "Bohême," "Tosca" or "Butterfly"—possessing a certain family resemblance which undoubtedly blurs memory; but this is not so with "Un bel di vedremo." It is *Madame Butterfly's* own tune!

Sharpless comes in while the women are discussing their affairs. He has a difficult task to perform. He has received a letter from *Pinkerton* informing him that there is now an American Mrs. Pinkerton and that *Butterfly* is free to seek a Japanese divorce. His methods must be delicate, for *Butterfly* has faith in her husband. She asks her visitor how often the robins nest in America, and the embarrassed consul is obliged to confess that he is no ornithologist. The question is overheard by *Goro,* who laughs outright. *Madame Butterfly,* for all her affection, begins to waver at *Pinkerton's* faithlessness. *Goro,* however, presents *Yamadori,* a wealthy but elderly Japanese who swears he is dying for love of *Butterfly.* She is more surprised than flattered; *Yamadori* has had many "consorts." *Goro* withdraws with the discomfited love-seeker, and *Sharpless* renews his efforts to read the letter. This leads into the "Ora a noi!" (Letter Duet).

After a brief introductory passage the orchestra takes up a melody having a distinctive rhythmic accompaniment soon to be heard again during the all-night vigil. The two converse to musical phrases cleverly worked into the tonal scheme with great ease and naturalness.

Everything *Sharpless* reads is perverted by *Butterfly* into a happy assurance that her husband is soon to return. So he is obliged, at last, to tell her bluntly enough, that *Pinkerton* wants no more to do with her. She is furious, and she sends out for *Suzuki* to show this impudent man the gate. Her natural politeness returns, and with it perhaps, a glimmering doubt of *Pinkerton*. When *Sharpless* asks her what she will do if he fails to return she says, gravely, that there are two alternatives: one is to go back and entertain, as a professional geisha, her friends with songs and games; the other is to kill herself. *Sharpless* is horrified, and he advises her to marry *Yamadori*. This restores her faith in her husband, and to convince *Sharpless* she orders *Suzuki* to bring *Trouble* —the name she has bestowed on her little son. The consul receives a second shock to learn that, unknown to *Pinkerton*, there is a child. The worst of it is, *Pinkerton* is about to return to Nagasaki with his American bride.

Madame Butterfly now sings a pitiful little air to her child, the "Sai cos' ebbe cuore" (Do You Know My Sweet One).

She enjoins little *Trouble* not to believe the bad man who says her husband would leave her, forcing her to wander through the streets for a living. *Sharpless* is badly upset. He goes away wondering what the outcome will be. Soon after he has gone a cannon shot is heard booming over the water, announcing an American warship in the bay. With the help of a telescope, *Butterfly* discovers it is *Pinkerton's* ship. With difficulty she makes out the vessel's name, the "Abraham Lincoln."

So, then, the agony of waiting is over! He has come with the robins— her lover, her husband, her adored one! In a moment the two women are feverishly rushing to the garden to gather cherry blossoms to deck the house. They sing the joyous "Tutti i fior" (Duet of the Flowers).

The feverish abandon and exultation of this number make it memorable. It throbs with excitement from start to finish.

Butterfly hastens to put on the wedding dress she wore that day so long ago, so that she may greet her lover as he first knew her. It is white, the color worn only for love and death.

But night is falling, and as it is un-

COPY'T DUPONT
THE LETTER FROM PINKERTON,
ACT II (GERALDINE FARRAR)

COPY'T MISHKIN
DESTINN AS BUTTERFLY

COPY'T MISHKIN
MARTIN AS PINKERTON

likely *Pinkerton* will come before the morrow, *Butterfly*, *Trouble*, and the maid *Suzuki* take their places at the window and the long night vigil commences. As it begins, the waiting motive (a sustained melody with a peculiarly haunting rhythmic accompaniment) is heard in the orchestra, together with distant voices of the sailors on the vessel in the harbor. This music is included in the recorded "Fantaisie" by Victor Herbert's Orchestra.

SCENE II—*Same as in Preceding*

IT is daybreak. *Suzuki*, exhausted, is sleeping, but *Butterfly* still watches the pathway leading up the hill. The maid awakens, and insists that her mistress take some rest. She promises to call her when the Lieutenant arrives. While *Butterfly* sleeps, however, her husband comes with *Sharpless*. *Pinkerton* is deeply touched at finding that *Butterfly* has been faithful, and that a child has been born.

Suzuki beholds a lady in the garden, wearing European dress, and she learns that it is *Pinkerton's* American wife, *Kate*. She is horrified and she justly dreads the effect of this news upon her mistress. Weeping, she goes to *Butterfly's* chamber, while the friends are left to their bitter reflections. These find expression in a powerful duet, "Ve lo dissi?" (Did I Not Tell You?) It is in semi-recitative, an admirable example of modern musical dialogue, made intimate with rich harmonies and fluent counterpoint. *Pinkerton* seems a broken man, and the Consul again reminds him to beware lest the heart of *Butterfly* suffer likewise.

Suzuki returns, and the duet leads into a fine trio, "Lo so che alle sue pene" (Naught Can Console Her).

Here the accompaniment is fuller and more melodic, and the three singers converse in especially tuneful phrases.

Pinkerton is conscious of the decorations, the cherry-blossoms so lavishly scattered about the little match-box house where he had found so much happiness in days gone by. But they leave before *Butterfly* comes, and instead of *Pinkerton* she meets *Kate*.

The introduction of *Kate* into this act has been somewhat criticised, and her rôle is usually omitted in French productions. She is kindly and sympathetic, and she offers to adopt *Trouble* if *Butterfly* so wills it. *Butterfly* learns that *Pinkerton* has been married a year, and she is sure now, that *Pinkerton's* love for her is dead.

With this fact certain, and with the welfare of her child made certain, the conviction slowly dawns upon the mind of the wretched *Butterfly* that she, and she alone, stands in the light of *Pinkerton's* complete happiness. There is therefore only one thing she can do. She takes down the dagger with which her father has fulfilled the iron law of his race, and she reads the inscription written upon its blade: "To die with honor when one can no longer live with honor." Then comes the grand "Finale Ultimo" (Butterfly's Death Scene).

This affords a wonderful end. In the orchestra, American motives are strangely mingled with Japanese themes, notably the theme usually associated with *Butterfly's* mystical fear of her ancestors. At the close, however, a stern Japanese melody, thundered out in octaves by the whole orchestra, with occasional chords to fix the tonality, gains the day. The final chord of the opera is arresting to an extraordinary degree. Many music-lovers are curious regarding it, and they may be interested to know it is simply a first inversion of the submediant chord of the prevailing key, B minor. Instead of the chord, B, D,

PHOTO BYRON   (Homer)   (Farrar)

MADAME BUTTERFLY—ACT II, SCENE II

F sharp the ear has learned to expect, it hears B, D, G, the G making all the difference.

The end of the opera soon is told. *Butterfly* seats her child on a little cushion, giving him a doll and an American flag to play with while she gently bandages his eyes. She then goes behind a screen from which hangs a long white veil. The knife is heard to fall, and the veil disappears. A moment later and *Butterfly* with the veil about her neck, drags herself toward her child. As she reaches him with a last effort of her failing strength, *Sharpless* and *Pinkerton* rush in. With a feeble gesture the dying *Butterfly* points to the child and expires. *Pinkerton* kneels beside her stunned with horror, and *Sharpless* takes to his knees the child, still playing contentedly with the American flag. Then, as that stupendous Japanese melody rings out from the orchestra, the curtain falls. *Pinkerton* has learned.

THE VICTOR RECORDS
(Sung in Italian except as noted)

ACT I

AMORE O GRILLO
(Love or Fancy?) Enrico Caruso, Tenor and Antonio Scotti, Baritone
8014 12-in., $2.50

ENTRANCE OF BUTTERFLY
(Ancora un passo) Geraldine Farrar, Soprano   616 10-in., 1.50
Frances Alda, Soprano   528 10-in., 1.50

IERI SON SALITA
(Hear What I Say) Geraldine Farrar, Soprano   616 10-in., 1.50

O QUANTI OCCHI FISI
(Oh Kindly Heavens) Geraldine Farrar and Enrico Caruso
8011 12-in., 2.50
Frances Alda and Giovanni Martinelli   8002 12-in., 2.50

ACT II

UN BEL DI VEDREMO
(Some Day He'll Come) Geraldine Farrar, Soprano   6110 12-in., 2.00

225

FRANCES ALDA, Soprano 6037 12-in., $2.00
FRANCES ALDA, Soprano 8044 12-in., 2.50
AMELITA GALLI-CURCI, Soprano
6130 12-in., 1.50

ORA A NOI
(Now at Last) (Letter Duet) GERALDINE
FARRAR,Soprano and ANTONIO SCOTTI,
Baritone 8039 12-in., 2.50

SAI COS' EBBE CUORE
(Do You Know, My Sweet One)
GERALDINE FARRAR, Soprano
617 10-in., 1.50

TUTTI I FIOR
(Duet of the Flowers) FRANCES ALDA,
Soprano and SOPHIE BRASLAU, Con-
tralto 8044 12-in., $2.50

VE LO DISSI?
(Did I Not Tell You?) ENRICO CARUSO
and ANTONIO SCOTTI 8014 12-in., 2.50

LO SO CHE ALLE SUE PENE
(Naught Can Console Her) MARTIN,
FORNIA and SCOTTI 87503 10-in., 1.25

BUTTERFLY'S DEATH SCENE
(L'ultima scena) GERALDINE FARRAR,
Soprano 617 10-in., 1.50

BLACK LABEL AND BLUE LABEL RECORDS

{ Madame Butterfly Selection, No. 1 . . . . *Pryor's Band* }
{ *Bartered Bride Overture* (*Smetana*) . . . . *Pryor's Band* } 35148 12-in., 1.25

{ Madame Butterfly Selection, No. 2 . . . . *Pryor's Band* }
{ *Tannhäuser Selection* (*Wagner*) . . . . *Pryor's Band* } 35331 12-in., 1.25

{ Madame Butterfly Fantasie . . . . *Rosario Bourdon, 'Cellist* }
{ *La Bohème Selection* (*Puccini*) . . . . *Vessella's Italian Band* } 35353 12-in., 1.25

{ O quanti occhi fisi (Oh! Kindly Heavens) . . . . *Olive Kline, Soprano* }
{ Paul Althouse, Tenor } 55058 12-in., 1.50
{ *Aida—Fuggiam gli ardori* (*Verdi*) . . . . *Marsh-Althouse* }

{ Madame Butterfly Fantasie . . . . *Victor Herbert's Orchestra* }
{ "Some Day He'll Come"—"Waiting Music," Act II—"Indeed, My }
{ Friend, You're Lucky," Act I—Duet, Act I—"Oh, Kindly Heavens" } 55094 12-in., 1.50
{ *A Dream of Love* (*Liszt*) . . . . *Victor Herbert's Orchestra* }

{ Some Day He'll Come (*In English*) . . . . *Agnes Kimball, Soprano* }
{ *Martha—Spinning Wheel Quartet* . . . . *Victor Opera Quartet* } 55114 12-in., 1.50

PHOTO BYRON
FARRAR AND HOMER IN ACT II

226

MADELEINE DINES WITH HER MOTHER

MADELEINE

LYRIC opera in one act. Text by Grant Stewart, based upon a short French play, *Je dine chez ma Mère*, by Decourcelles and Thibaut, long a standard work on the French stage. Music by Victor Herbert. First performance at the Metropolitan Opera House, New York, January 24, 1914.

CHARACTERS AND ORIGINAL CAST

MADELEINE FLEURY (*Mah-duh-layn' Fluh-ree*), prima donna Frances Alda
NICHETTE (*Nee-shet'*), her maid
Leonora Sparkes
CHEVALIER DE MAUPRAT (*duh Moh-prah*)......Antonio Pini-Corsi
FRANÇOIS (*Frahn-zwah*), Duc d'Esterre...........Paul Althouse
DIDIER (*Dee-dee-ay*), a painter
Andrea de Segurola

Time and Place: Salon of Madeleine's House, Paris; New Year's Day, 1770

THE OPERA

CONTINUING the policy, begun in 1900, of making an annual production of an opera by an American composer, the management of the Metropolitan Opera House brought out on January 24, 1914, this new one-act opera by Victor Herbert. Mr. Stewart's English text is familiar in Mrs. Burton Harrison's playlet, frequently given by amateurs.

Nichette, the maid, is in high spirits as she receives the many gifts for *Madeleine*, for today is New Year's day, which all good French people spend at home. She and the lackeys arrange the presents, but scuttle out when *Madame* herself appears with that ancient beau, the *Chevalier de Mauprat*. *Madeleine* admires the beautiful bracelet he has made for her, and she begs him to dine. But alas! it is impossible. Today he dines with his mother.

Good naturedly the prima donna accepts the excuse, for nothing can alter his decision,—not even a quail with truffles and fresh asparagus. As he bows himself out, she asks *Nichette* if *Didier*, the artist, has yet brought the picture of her mother which he has been restoring. He has not. *Madeleine* is disappointed, but she is very happy. She doubles the servants' wages. A commotion outside announces her lover, *François*, with a gift of four high-stepping English thoroughbreds. *Madeleine* is enraptured, and begs *François* to dine with her. But *François*, too, must dine at home. *Madeleine* is distinctly annoyed; her invitations to dine are not usually so treated. But *François* is firm. She insists, threatening to close the door upon him forever if he will not dine with her today. Gravely he declines, for today is sacred. He loves her. Tomorrow morning he must fight a duel for her sweet sake with the *Baron de Fontanges*, but today he dines with his mother. Now fairly enraged, *Madeleine* bids him begone, vowing she will invite the *Baron* and wish him luck for the morrow. No sooner does *François* go than she writes her letter. But even the *Baron* declines, for the same reason that the others gave. The singer is now determined to have somebody dine with her, and she invites *Nichette*. The trembling maid, however, reminds her that today of all days it is impossible, *Madame* has given her leave, and her parents are expecting her. *Madeleine* grows almost hysterical. She dismisses the maid, she dismisses all her servants who stand helplessly about as she walks to and fro like the proverbial caged panther. In the midst of all, *Didier* arrives with the picture of her mother. The now weeping *Madeleine* confides her sorrows to this old friend of her youth. Treating her like a child, he finally assuages her tears. But of course he cannot accept her invitation to dine, as today he dines at home. Will she not dine with him? Eagerly she accepts. *Nichette* enters in tears to say good-bye, but *Madeleine* reinstates her, reinstates all the servants. She borrows one of *Nichette's* dresses, for she must not appear too grand before *Didier's* peasant parents. As she does, she realizes it is unfair to intrude on *Didier's* humble abode under false pretences at such a time. She decides she will dine at home. *Nichette* returns to say that she has told the circumstances to her mother, who gives her permission to dine with *Madame*. But the now radiant *Madeleine* sends her home again, reaffirming her intention to double the salaries of her servants. She kisses *Didier* a tender good-bye, and sits down at the table, placing the restored portrait in front of her. She, too, will dine with her mother! And tomorrow she will forgive *François*. As she sits there alone, a last ray of the waning sun strikes through the window upon the portrait, and lovely strains of soft music from the orchestra make us feel what is in the heart of this spoiled yet altogether lovable child.

The noted composer has given us some characteristically charming melodies in this opera, notably *Madeleine's* air, "A Perfect Day." But there are others, too, in abundance.

THE VICTOR RECORD

A PERFECT DAY

FRANCES ALDA, Soprano   6370   12-in., $2.00

THE GREAT INVOCATION SCENE

THE MAGIC FLUTE

MOZART wrote and produced "The Magic Flute" in 1791, the year of his death. He wrote it to help Schickaneder, an actor-manager-musician of highly mingled virtues and vices, who yet had the gift of winning friends. This musical extravaganza (for that is what it really is) was highly successful, and it relieved Schickaneder from his financial straits. It is the more extraordinary, therefore, that this managerial upstart could not see his way to help Mozart in his distress; for while the cheery people of Vienna flocked nightly to see the amazing "show" and to hear the master's incomparable music, Mozart lay dying in deepest poverty. Within a few hours of his last breath he wished he might conduct another performance of the work, and he smiled when, at his request, somebody sang *Papageno's* air. Yet Mozart was laid in a pauper's grave, which has never since been located, while Schickaneder waxed fat. So humanity conserves chaff and throws the wheat to the four winds of Heaven.

THE OPERA

OPERA in two acts. Libretto by Schickaneder, adapted from a tale by Wieland, "Lulu; or the Magic Flute." Music by Wolfgang Amadeus Mozart. First produced in Vienna, September 30, 1791, Mozart directing. First Paris production as "*Les Mystères d'Isis,*" August 20, 1801. First London production, in Italian, in 1811; in German, 1833; in English, 1838. First New York production April 17, 1833, at the Park Theatre, in English, and not again until November 21, 1859, when it was given at the German Theatre in Italian. Later productions included that of 1876, with Carlotta Patti; at the Grand Opera House, with di Murska, Lucca and Ronconi; and at the Academy with Gerster.

The latest revival was at the Metropolitan in 1912, with Destinn,

229

Hempel, Homer, Slezak and Lambert Murphy.

CHARACTERS

SARASTRO (*Sahr-ass'-troh*), High Priest of Isis.....................Bass
TAMINO (*Tah-mee'-noh*), an Egyptian Prince...........Tenor
PAPAGENO (*Pap-ah-jay'-noh*), a bird-catcher..........Baritone
THE QUEEN OF NIGHT.......Soprano
PAMINA (*Pam-ee'-nah*), her daughter..............Soprano
MONOSTATOS (*Moh-noh-stat'-oss*), a Moor, chief slave of the Temple..........Baritone
PAPAGENA (*Pap-ah-jay-nah*)..Soprano
Three Lady Attendants of the Queen; Three Boys belonging to the Temple; Priests and Priestesses; Slaves; Warriors; Attendants, etc.

The Action occurs at the Temple of Isis at Memphis, about the Time of Rameses I

ACT I

INTO a rocky territory, a mysterious region which supplies a foreground to the Temple of the *Queen of Night*, the Japanese prince *Tamino* has been chased by a huge serpent. Separated from his friends, alone with this dreadful creature, amid such ominous surroundings, and desperately fatigued, he falls into a faint. Three maidens from the castle, veiled attendants of the *Queen*, slay the serpent and depart. When *Tamino* recovers, he finds the serpent dead, and no one near; yet from the rocks there comes the piping of a syrinx. *Tamino* hides, to see the performer, who is none other than the bird-catcher, *Papageno*, picturesquely arrayed in birds' feathers. In a merry song this odd-looking creature describes his calling, and *Tamino*, gathering courage, steps forth to make his acquaintance. *Papageno* is not of a

nature to deny his own importance and he indicates that he has slain the serpent. He is somewhat dismayed, therefore, by the sudden return of the veiled ladies, who berate him for boastfulness, and lock up his loose mouth with a huge padlock. To *Tamino*, however, they are all smiles. They let him see a miniature portrait of *Pamina*, the lovely daughter of the *Queen of Night*, who has been taken off by *Sarastro*, the Priest of Isis, here represented as a most evil being. *Tamino* falls in love with the picture, and offers to restore *Pamina* to her mother. A burst of thunder, which nearly kills off the muzzled *Papageno*, announces the *Queen of Night*, who promises that if *Tamino* is successful his reward shall be the princess. As *Papageno* wishes to adventure with his new friend, in the hope of finding a suitable mate for himself, the padlock is removed, and he is given a magical chime of bells to help him on his dangerous journey. At the same time, *Tamino* is presented with the Magic Flute, whose music endows him with rather more than the powers of that Orpheus whose music made the very trees bow their heads. In addition three *genii*, lovely boys who are "young, beautiful, pure and wise," are told off to act as hidden yet powerful guardians. It is these three youths who are so unceremoniously made over into servants of *Sarastro* in the next act, without notice being served on the opera's hearers. Thus armed and equipped, the two set off. The interesting quintette in which these doings are told is said to have been planned by Mozart during a game of billiards, to which it appears he was at least as fond as was the philosopher Herbert Spencer.

The scene changes to a room in the Castle of *Sarastro*, where *Pamina* is in charge of the Moor, *Monostatos*.

This gentleman has been placed in solemn wardship over the girl by the High Priest, but he breaks faith by making love to *Pamina*, who lies in chains, weeping. Just as the Moor is about to woo her, however, *Papageno* enters. The Moor is as scared by the feathered man of the woods, as the bird-catcher is by the Moor's black face. They run from one another. But *Papageno*, first recovering spirits, returns to comfort *Pamina* with the tale of *Tamino's* quest, and his deep love for her. They then sing a charming duet, "La dove prende" (Smiles and Tears). This delightful number, with its grace and inimitable gaiety, introduces the melody of an old song, "Bei Männern."

Meantime the three *genii* lead *Tamino* into a beautiful grove, where are three temples dedicated to Wisdom, Nature and Reason. Admonished to be "steadfast, patient and silent," he is left alone in this sacred and mysterious place. He then knocks at each of the temple doors. Entrance is sternly denied him at the first two. From the Temple of Wisdom, however,

steps an aged priest, from whom he learns that he is at the abode of *Sarastro,* and that admission is refused anyone whose heart entertains hatred or the desire for vengeance. He remonstrates, but is told that he has been deceived by a woman of evil omen, and that *Pamina* has been removed for her own good. He cannot even learn if the girl is living, for the priest is bound to silence by an oath. Voices from the temples, however, answer his question in the affirmative, he learns that he may be admitted only by solemn initiation. Beginning, in his delight, to play upon his magic flute, he soon draws about him the strange creatures of the wood. *Papageno* comes with *Monostatos*, but they are set upon by *Pamina* and her slaves. *Papageno*, by his magic chime, compels the girls to dance, and leads them away. Thus *Pamina* and *Tamino* meet. Solemn strains of music are heard, and soon the High Priest, *Sarastro* himself, appears. He agrees to unite them but only after they have been proven worthy. They kneel before him, their heads are veiled,

GADSKI AS PAMINA

PAPAGENA AND PAPAGENO

PAPAGENO

and they are ushered into the Temple of Probation as the curtain descends.

ACT II

BEFORE a great gathering of the Elect, in a forest before the Temple of Wisdom, the lovers are initiated. The priests assemble, and *Sarastro* sings the magnificent "Invocation" (Great Isis), praying the gods Isis and Osiris to give strength to the neophytes.

The stately melody, with its solemn harmonies, enhanced by the sombre coloring of the deeper-toned orchestral instruments of the orchestra, affords an indeed impressive number.

The priests accept them, their promotion being announced by three trumpet calls like those heard in the Overture. *Papageno* is also admitted, as a probationer. *Tamino* and his comrade are solemnly warned against the deceitfulness of women, and their trials begin. They are left alone but a short while when the *Queen of Night* magically appears with her three veiled attendants. She thinks to terrify them with stories of the priests. *Papageno*, at least, is affected. Voices from within, however, proclaim the sanctity of the temple, and the ladies disappear. *Pamina* also is tempted by the *Queen of Night*, who rises from the earth and gives her a dagger, telling her that she must slay *Sarastro* if she will have *Tamino*. *Pamina* hesitates, and her mother threatens vengeance upon all, in the terrifyingly dramatic "Aria della Regina" (The Queen's Air).

This is famous not only for its beauty but for its extreme technical difficulty, more especially for its remarkable range. It was specially composed by Mozart for his sister-in-law, who first played the rôle.

The *Queen* is confronted by the entrance of *Sarastro*, who declares that in punishment her daughter shall marry *Tamino*. He then sings a noble air, justly considered one of the finest of basso numbers, the "Qui sdegno non s'accende" (Within These Sacred Walls).

Meantime the probationary trials of *Tamino* and *Papageno* continue. They are taken into a large hall and told to keep silent till they hear a trumpet call. The bird-catcher begins chattering with an old woman, but a thunder-clap reduces him to terrified silence. The three *genii* bring a table of food, and the flute and bells, and he is at once restored. The hardest trial for *Tamino* is when *Pamina* is suffered to pass through, and, unaware of his compulsory silence, is led to believe that he has ceased to care for her. She expresses her grief in a pathetic little air: "Ach ich fühl's, es ist verschwunden" (My Happiness Has Flown). The girl is distressed; she tries to kill herself, but she is prevented by the three *genii*, who, by order of *Sarastro*, assure her that all will end well. Other trials await the neophytes, a lion appears, but is tamed by *Tamino's* flute; the youth is condemned to walk for a space through flood and flame, for which he enters a subterranean cave, guarded by two men in armor; and there is much more fantasy of the pantomimic order, accompanied by divinely beautiful music. In the end, however, the lovers are united in the sacred temple. The *Queen* and her accomplices try to prevent the ceremony, but the scene suddenly changes to the Temple of the Sun, where *Sarastro* is seen on his throne with *Tamino* and *Pamina* beside him, while the baffled *Queen* sinks into the earth. *Papageno* also is made happy, when the old woman he talked with is magically changed into the charming *Papagena*, arrayed in bird-feathers like himself. Out of this farrago is built a magnificent opera.

THE VICTOR RECORDS
(Sung in Italian unless noted)

ACT II

INVOCATION
(Great Isis) POL PLANÇON, Bass
(Piano acc.)   6371 12-in., $2.00

MARCEL JOURNET, Bass *In French*
    699 10-in., 1.50

Great Isis, great Osiris!
  Strengthen with wisdom's strength this tyro
    pair;
Ye who guide steps where deserts lengthen,
  Brace theirs with nerve, your proof to bear!
Grant them probation's fruit all living;
  Yet, should they find a grave while striving,
Think on their virtues, gracious gods,
  Take them elect to your abodes!

BLACK LABEL AND BLUE LABEL RECORDS

O Isis und Osiris (Chorus of Priests, "Grand Isis!") (*In German*)
                             Metropolitan Opera Chorus
 Huguenots—Coro di Soldati (Soldiers' Chorus) (*In Italian*)   45051 10-in., $1.00
                             Metropolitan Opera Chorus

Magic Flute Overture—Part I . . . .*Victor Symphony Orchestra*
Magic Flute Overture—Part II . . . .*Victor Symphony Orchestra* 18951 10-in., .75

PHOTO WHITE THE HIGH PRIEST BLESSING THE LOVERS

FARRAR
AS MANON

MANON

MUCH of this opera was composed by Massenet in the summer of 1882, in the very room in which the Abbé Prévost had lived in The Hague. "His bed," Massenet remarks, "a great cradle shaped like a gondola, was still there." No doubt these surroundings aided him to create *Manon*, one of the loveliest and most pathetic figures in all opera, as she is in French literature. There is so much natural, spontaneous girlishness and grace about her that the misfortunes which befall the girl, even though they come about by her own self-indulgence, seem like enormous crimes. In the eyes of the moralist there was no excuse for *Manon*, yet she was none the less beautiful. Her siren-loveliness led men to their destruction, yet no man could quarrel with her. *Des Grieux* not only loved her, but understood her. He knew that she loved pretty things to wear, sparkling gems, silks and satins, better than she loved him, yet he sinned, as men so often sin, for her sake bringing down disgrace upon himself and ruin upon others. And the charm of her held him to the last. He offered her gold for her silver, reckless love for petty affection which was all she was capable of giving. Tragedy followed.

Possibly alone among modern composers could Massenet deal with this modern Helen of Troy. In his subtly-wrought score she stands forth, frail and lovely as in the Abbé's novel. We do not need his reminiscences to tell us that he long desired to write an opera about her. He was born to the task.

The opera remains one of his greatest achievements; and it is pleasant to think that he reaped from it some benefit during his lifetime. In his memoirs, written shortly before his death, he refers to the 763rd performance of the work. Surely a remarkable record!

Massenet and his librettist departed considerably from the details related by the Abbé Prévost, notably in having *Manon* die in the arms of *Des Grieux* in Havre instead of in that impossible, dry "vast plain" so unceremoniously dumped into the swamps of Louisiana. In such a work as this, though, mechanics matter little. It is *Manon* alone that counts. The external mechanisms of the plot are merely designed to reveal her character, and Massenet, seeing this, wisely adapts them to the modern theatre. Massenet has his critics, but none denies to him that acute dramatic sense which seems to be every Frenchman's natural birthright.

THE OPERA

OPERA in four acts. Words by Meilhac and Gille, after the novel of Abbé Prévost. Music by Jules Massenet. First production at the *Opéra Comique*, Paris, January 19, 1884; at Brussels, March 15, 1884. First London production May 7, 1885; in English by the Carl Rosa Company, at Liverpool, January 17, 1885. In French at Covent Garden, May 19, 1891; in Italy at Milan, October 19, 1893. First American production at New York, December 23, 1885, at the Academy of Music, with Minnie Hauk, Giannini and Del Puente. First New Orleans production January 4, 1894. Some notable revivals were: in 1895 with Sybil Sanderson and Jean de Reszke; in 1896, with Melba and de Reszke; in 1899 with Saville, Van Dyk, Dufriche and Plançon; in 1909, at the Metropolitan, with Caruso, Farrar, Scotti and Note; and in 1912, with Caruso, Farrar, Gilly and Reiss.

CHARACTERS

CHEVALIER DES GRIEUX (*Day Gree-uh*)..................Tenor

COUNT DES GRIEUX, his father.... Bass

LESCAUT (*Les-koh*), Manon's cousin, one of the Royal Guard........................Baritone

GUILLOT MORFONTAIN (*Mohr-fon-tahn*), a roué, Minister of France......................Bass

DE BRÉTIGNY (*Duh Bray-teen'-ye*), a nobleman...........Baritone

MANON (*Mahn'-on*), a school girl......................Soprano

People, Actresses and Students

Time and Place: 1721; Amiens, Paris, Havre

ACT I

SCENE—*Courtyard of an Inn at Amiens*

IN this age of the railway, we are prone to forget how great a part in the life of the people of the past was played by the inn. It was the gathering place of the convivial, the depot for travellers and the meeting place of friends. Among the crowd gathered to meet the coach in the Inn Courtyard is *Lescaut*, who has come to meet his cousin *Manon*, and to escort her to a convent. *Lescaut* is a soldier, and a good deal of a rascal. He is pleasurably surprised to find his cousin as charming as she is unsophisticated. He accepts her proffered lips in cousinly greeting, and he hastens within to engage rooms.

No sooner has he gone than the old roué *Guillot* trots out and begins to pay court to the girl. *Manon* is amused and a trifle flattered. Others of the crowd make game of the old libertine, who is not easily thwarted. He is called away, however, by *Brétigny*, his travelling companion. Among those who remark *Manon* are three girls of doubtful character, beautifully costumed. Their fine apparel is not lost upon *Manon*, who thinks between sighs and tears of her own sad lot, and her approaching gray life in a convent. Her musings are interrupted by *Des Grieux*, who now approaches and pays his own addresses. The famous duet follows, "Et je sais votre nom" (If I Knew Your Name). The two quickly become acquainted, and in the passionate climax it is evident their attraction is to be a strong one. The story continues in the "Non, votre liberte ne sera pas ravie" (You Shall Remain Free).

A carriage previously placed at the disposal of the young girl by the infatuated *Guillot* unexpectedly draws near; intoxicated with her new-found love, she suggests they fly together to Paris. *Des Grieux* joyfully agrees and in their second duet, the "Nous vivrons à Paris" (We Will Go to Paris), they carol rapturously of their life together. Presently *Manon* hears the voice of her cousin, *Lescaut*, and the two jump into the carriage and depart.

Lescaut comes out of the inn grumbling. He has lost his money. He is soon to learn that he has lost his cousin also. *Guillot* appears, and the angry soldier accuses him of having taken off *Manon*. A crowd assembles to watch the fun, but the innkeeper tells them that *Manon* has departed with a young man. "Listen!" he says, and faintly they hear the rattle and the galloping hoof-beats of the departing coach.

ACT II

SCENE—*Apartment of Des Grieux and Manon in Paris*

DES GRIEUX is writing at a desk while *Manon* is looking over his shoulder. He is writing to his father and trembles for fear the old man may read in anger what he writes from his heart. "Afraid?" says *Manon*. "Ah well, then we'll read it together." Then follows the well-known "On l'appelle Manon" (She Is Called Manon). It is a charming duet, beginning with a simple and charming melody.

Some little glint of *Manon's* weakness is visible in her answer to his glowing phrase, "In her eyes shines the tender light of love." "Is this true?" asks *Manon*. *Des Grieux* is soon to ask himself that same question. As he passes to go out, he remarks a bouquet of flowers mysteriously left for *Manon*. She returns only an evasive answer to his questions. The servant declares that two soldiers are without, dressed in guardsman's uniforms. As *Des Grieux*, somewhat perturbed by the sight of the flowers, opens the door to leave, the two soldiers enter. One is *Lescaut*, the other *Brétigny*, who has been at the Inn at Amiens and has noticed *Manon's* beauty. *Lescaut* loudly demands satisfaction of *Des Grieux* for the abduction of his cousin. *Des Grieux* takes him off, and shows him the letter to his father, as proof of his honorable intentions. *Brétigny*, left with *Manon*, makes the best of his time. He tells her that *Des Grieux* is to be carried off by his own father that night, and he urges her to fly with him. Knowing that *Brétigny* can give her the pretty things for which her heart so longs, *Manon* hesitates—and is lost. *Lescaut* again becomes vociferous, but this time over his pretended satisfaction at *Des Grieux's* intentions toward the girl. He departs with *Brétigny*.

Des Grieux also goes out to mail his letter. *Manon*, left to herself, struggles with the temptation that has come to her but the struggle is brief, as her pathetic little song reveals: "Adieu notre petite table" (Farewell, Our Little Table) sings *Manon*. Farewell to her love of a day—off with the old love and on with the new! The peculiar wistful charm of this melody, the play of light and shadow between the major and minor harmonies of its accompaniment, make it a typical Massenet aria, French in form and content.

COPY'T MISHKIN

DE SEGUROLA AS LESCAUT

COPY'T DUPONT

ALDA AS MANON

CLEMENT AS DES GRIEUX

Tears come into *Manon's* eyes, but at the return of *Des Grieux* she tries to hide them. He sees them, none the less, and tries to comfort her. He sings the familiar "Il sogno"—"Le Rêve" (The Dream).

Very tenderly, to a soft, murmurous accompaniment, he describes the little home he plans to share with her. But a knock at the door halts the dream, and *Manon* starts guiltily. "Oh Heaven," she cries, "already they have come for him." She tries to prevent her lover from opening the door, but he insists, and before *Manon's* suddenly repentant eyes he is captured and borne off. She gives way freely to her grief and despair.

ACT III

SCENE I—*A Street in Paris on a Fête Day*

A BIG crowd of holiday-makers, with the usual peddlers, and small-fry entertainers, are in the streets. *Lescaut* enters, and later *Manon*, accompanied by *de Brétigny*. Her beauty is remarked by the people about her, and the flattery goes to her foolish head. She is in a gay mood, reckless, daring, but always delightful. She sings a fine vocal gavotte, "Obeissons quand leur" (Hear the Voice of Youth).

A stranger approaches. He proves to be an old friend of *Brétigny*, and a gentleman of some significance to *Manon*. It is the *Comte de Grieux*, father of *Manon's* erstwhile lover. He vouchsafes the information that his son is about to enter a monastery. *Brétigny* is incredulous, and begs him to explain. "Heaven attracts him," says the *Count* with a shrug. *Manon* knows better. She determines to go and see him, and calls *Lescaut*, bidding him take her there. Puzzled, he demurs; but *Manon*, petulant, repeats that he is to take her to St. Sulpice. And to St. Sulpice this singular couple go.

SCENE II—*Reception Room at St. Sulpice*

THE *Count* is before her. He does his utmost to persuade the boy to give up his notion of a holy life. Is he to tell the people at home that they have a "saint in the family?" He pleads, he grows bitter, he grows cynical; he is everything but impolite, and that he cannot be. But it is all to no purpose. *Des Grieux*, left alone, sings a melody of altogether haunting loveliness, the "Ah! fuyez, douce image!"— "Dispar, vision!"(Depart, Fair Vision!). The consciousness of *Manon* obsesses the youth even here, where the soul within him cries out for peace.

Des Grieux leaves the reception-room for the quiet of his own cell, but scarcely has he gone when *Manon* appears, delicately shuddering at the gloomy walls and wondering if her lover has quite forgotten her. She sends the porter in search of him. Somewhere in the place a choir is heard practicing a Magnificat, and *Manon*, always affected by her surroundings, begins to pray also. By the time *Des Grieux* arrives she has worked herself up into a fine mood of repentance. He is surprised to see her. "Toi! Vous!" (Thou Here!) exclaims he.

Des Grieux chides her for her perfidy, but he asks Heaven for strength to resist her pleadings. He well may; for her mood of repentance is no less charming than all her other moods, and *Des Grieux*, monk or no monk, is a young man in love. The more he resists the more she pleads. "N'est-ce plus la main?" (Is it Not My Hand?) signalizes the real climax of their meeting, and it works into a fine frenzy of passion. *Des Grieux* can resist no longer. "Ah! *Manon!*" he cries. "No longer will I struggle against myself!" And they depart together. Love is stronger than determination, and impulse stronger than reason. Fate is stronger than all.

ACT IV

SCENE—*A Gambling Room in Paris*

IN a gambling-house in Paris, *Guillot* and *Lescaut* are playing amid a mob of croupiers and fellow-punters. But everything stops when *Manon* enters with *Des Grieux*. He is sad, and *Manon* rallies him. She responds to the peculiar environment of the gambling-den as readily as she did to that of the monastery, and now she is all seduction. *Des Grieux* is tempted. Elusive as quicksilver ordinarily, never was *Manon* more soft, more siren-like than tonight. As ever, he is compelled to yield and he soon engages *Guillot* in a game for heavy stakes. He wins, and they play again. Always, with *Manon* to help him, he beats his rival, who soon comes to believe that he is being cheated. There is a great scene; but finally *Guillot* leaves. *Manon* desires to go, too, but *Des Grieux* insists that if they go now it may seem as though *Guillot's* charges are true.

Soon there is a knocking at the door, and the police enter with *Guillot*, who gives in charge both *Manon* and *Des Grieux*. Nor is that all, for among those who come with the police is the *Comte des Grieux*, the young man's father, shocked beyond measure at the sight of his son in such circumstances, so soon after he had left him at the priory.

ACT V

SCENE—*On the Road to Havre*

THROUGH the influence of his father, *Des Grieux* has been released. Indeed, he appears to be guiltless, for Massenet's librettists are more merciful than the Abbé Prévost and the *Des Grieux* of the opera does not degenerate into the common cheat of the novel. The only result is to make the deportation of *Manon* a trifle unconvincing. Apparently, however, her other misdemeanors are enough. She is convicted as an abandoned woman,

and she is sentenced to be deported to the French province of Louisiana. When the curtain rises *Des Grieux* and *Lescaut* are on the Havre road, awaiting the soldiers and the prisoners for the ship to America. He has conceived a mad plan to effect a rescue: "Manon, la catena" (Manon in Chains!) declare they. But *Des Grieux* learns from *Lescaut* that there are no "men fully armed" hiding in ambush to leap out at his command. The soldiers approach, singing; *Des Grieux* is for attacking them bare-handed, but *Lescaut* knows a better way. He waits till they draw up, thirsty with song, and begging their sergeant to let them get a drink. The sergeant is inclined to do so; he finds little glory in escorting "les demoiselles sans vertu." He inquires as to the prisoners and learns that one is ill, almost dead. "Heavens!" cries *Des Grieux*, "Manon!" *Lescaut* bids him be silent. *Lescaut* comes forward with money, and tells the sergeant that the sick girl is of his family. The sergeant is not so hard, but he is willing to be bribed into permitting a half-dead girl to see her cousin. *Manon* is in the village behind, *Des Grieux* takes the place of *Lescaut*, so that he may at least bid her farewell. The duet follows, "Manon? Tu piangi?" (Manon, Thou Weepest) and "Si maledico ed impreco" (With Remorse and Contempt).

In a magnificent finale, *Manon*, remembering all those who worshipped at her peculiar shrine, begs and receives the forgiveness of the one man who really loved her,—*Des Grieux*, who had sacrificed everything—money name, honor,—for but a part of her love. He is content that she should die in his arms, though his despair is touching as he sees her young beauty fade at the silent call of death. He gives a great cry and falls upon her dead body as the curtain descends.

THE VICTOR RECORDS

(Sung in French, unless noted)

ACT II

ON L' APPELLE MANON
(She is Called Manon) GERALDINE
FARRAR, Soprano and ENRICO CARUSO,
Tenor   8011   12-in., $2.50
ADIEU NOTRE PETITE TABLE
(Farewell, Our Little Table) GERALDINE
FARRAR, Soprano   6111   12-in.,   2.00
LUCREZIA BORI, Soprano 1009   10-in.,   1.50
LE RÊVE
(The Dream) EDMOND CLEMENT, Tenor
          6062   12-in.,   2.00

JOHN McCORMACK, Tenor *In Italian*
          767   10-in., $1.50
TITO SCHIPA, Tenor *In Italian*
          828   10-in.,   1.50

ACT III

GAVOTTE—OBÉISSONS QUAND
LEUR VOIX APPELLE
(Hear the Voice of Youth) GALLI-
CURCI   1018   10-in.,   1.50

AH! FUYEZ, DOUCE IMAGE!
(Depart, Fair Vision!) ENRICO CARUSO,
Tenor   6020   12-in.,   2.00

LANDE   ANTEROOM OF ST. SULPICE—METROPOLITAN OPERA SETTING

THE BURIAL OF MANON—ACT IV

MANON LESCAUT

NOT often in modern times do two composers go to the same source for inspiration, as they did in the days of Händel and Gluck, when the same Greek legends appeared over and over again. It is somewhat unusual, therefore, that Puccini should have selected the Abbé Prévost's book, "Manon Lescaut," as a theme for an opera nine years after the production of Massenet's similar work. It was a bold step, for Massenet's reputation was safely established by the time Puccini began his "Manon Lescaut," while the Italian had to his credit only the immature one-act opera "Le Villi" and the confessed failure "Edgar." Puccini, moreover, was thirty-five years old when "Manon Lescaut" was produced, his genius having flowered slowly. Yet he was quite sure of himself, and he was convinced the failure of "Edgar" was due to an impossible libretto—as indeed it was. With the help of a few friends, he made his own libretto from the Abbé's novel, thus safeguarding himself against a second failure. He followed the French author somewhat more faithfully than Massenet, even to the end, the final scene of his opera, like that of the book, being laid in "a vast desert plain" near New Orleans!

Puccini and Massenet were not alone in having selected this work for operatic setting. Halévy wrote a ballet upon the same subject in 1830, and other settings followed, by Balfe, 1836, Auber in 1856, and Massenet in 1884. Puccini's music does not surpass Massenet's, but it has a full right to existence upon its own merits. His "Manon Lescaut" is somewhat a forerunner giving promise of the genius so abundantly fulfilled in his next operatic venture, three years later, with "La Bohême." It won the composer some considerable reputation, just the same, and frequent performances testify strongly enough to the excellence of the work as a whole.

THE OPERA

OPERA in four acts. Music by Giacomo Puccini, the libretto (founded on Abbé Prévost's novel) being mainly the work of the composer and a committee of friends. English version by Mowbray Marras. First presented at Turin, February 1, 1893, with Cremonini, Ferrani and Moro. Produced at Covent Garden, May 14, 1894; at Trieste, June 10, 1893; at Hamburg, November 7, 1893. First performance in France at Nice, March 19, 1906 (not given at Paris until 1910); at Madrid, November 4, 1893. First performance in the Americas at Buenos Aires, June 9, 1893; in the United States at Grand Opera House, Philadelphia, in English, August 29, 1894, with Selma Kronold and Montegriffo. Given in French by a small travelling company at Wallack's Theatre, May 27, 1898, and at the Tivoli Opera House, San Francisco, in 1905. Produced at Wallack's Theatre, New York, May 27, 1898, by the Royal Italian Grand Opera Company. First important New York production, January 18, 1907, with Caruso, Cavalieri and Scotti, under the direction of the composer, who then visited America for the first time. Given by the Philadelphia-Chicago Company in 1912, with White, Sammarco and Zenatello.

CHARACTERS

MANON LESCAUT (*Mahn-on Leskoh'*)....................Soprano
LESCAUT, sergeant of the King's Guards.................Baritone
CHEVALIER DES GRIEUX (*day Gree-uh'*)...................Tenor
GERONTE DE RAVOIR, Treasurer-General (*day Rah-vwah'*).....Bass
EDMUND, a student...........Tenor
An Innkeeper, a Dancing-master, a Sergeant, a Captain, Singers, Beaux and Abbés, Girls, Citizens, Students, People, Courtesans, Sailors

Scene and Period: Paris and Vicinity; Second Half of the Eighteenth Century

ACT I

SCENE—*A Street in front of an Inn at Amiens*

THE scene is laid in a spacious square near the Paris Gate, beside the inn. It is gay with students and citizens, women, girls and soldiers. A group of students, headed by the poet *Edmund*, ridicule *Des Grieux*, who stands somewhat apart and who does not seem any too interested in the girls. Readers of Prévost's novel may remember that the *Des Grieux* of this period was rather a serious young man. He rallies sufficiently, however, to sing a gallant song, ostensibly of flattering purport, but not quite free from irony. This is the "Tra voi belle brune" (Now Among You).

It is a typical Puccini melody, broad, full, hauntingly sweet. As though considering some secret ideal, he asks if among the maidens before him there may be gleaming his own "fair star." His subtlety is lost upon the girls, who assume that he is making game of them as they turn away to seek new excitement.

This is provided by the arrival of a diligence, containing *Manon Lescaut*. Her brother is with her, and a chance acquaintance, the elderly *Geronte*, who is "all eyes" for the girl. *Manon* is indeed beautiful, and *Des Grieux* sees in her the ideal of his romantic dreams. He takes the liberty to speak while her brother and *Geronte* are in the inn arranging for quarters. *Manon* responds shyly, but without fear; already we detect that fatal softness of character

242

which causes her to yield so easily to temptation, yet which, by its very frailty, but charms the more. *Des Grieux* is an immediate victim, and he is properly horrified when she tells him her brother is taking her to a Convent. Soon, however, her brother calls her to the inn, and the pensive youth gazes after her a prey to her beauty—and his own emotions. "Donna non vidi mai" (A Maiden So Fair), which sums them up in music, is a lovely melody, luminous with the fires of youth. "Manon Lescaut, they call me!"—he repeats her phrase to himself, wringing out of memory every last inflection of her low, tender voice. His comrades rally *Des Grieux*, but he is in no mood for their japes, and he quietly goes indoors. Meantime, the rascally *Lescaut*, *Manon's* brother, already counting on a road to *Geronte's* purse by way of his sister's charms, is attracted by a group of soldiers playing cards. *Geronte* himself, seeing *Lescaut* absorbed in the game, orders the landlord to have ready a swift horse and carriage; with these he designs to abduct *Manon*. The observant *Edmund*, however, overhears the plot, and he informs *Des Grieux*. *Des Grieux* decides to save *Manon* from the restrictions of convent life on one side, and the amorous attentions of her elderly *beau*, on the other. His methods are simple; he will abduct her himself. It is (alas!) no difficult matter to persuade *Manon*. When *Geronte* is all ready to fulfil his own plans, the pair have gone. He is furious, but the fertile-minded *Lescaut* reminds him that a student's purse is never too full, and they will be found in Paris. He even hints, with charming grace, that if *Geronte* will include him in the family he will use his influence to get her away from *Des Grieux*. Of *Manon* he thinks little; what is a sister for, if not to fill a gallant soldier's pockets once in a while? Poor *Manon!* Her only sin is beauty!

ACT II

SCENE—*An Apartment in Geronte's House*

TIME flies fast in Grand Opera. *Lescaut* has already been so far successful that *Manon* has been installed in the home of *Geronte*. She is at her toilet, preparing for a party in her honor, surrounded by every luxury. She is dealing with a hairdresser, a dancing-master, maids and attendants. Her brother comes in, and she asks after *Des Grieux*,—only to learn that, disconsolate over her loss, he is gambling hard in hope to have her back. *Manon* confesses she still loves him; but her enjoyment of her new luxuries is pretty evident. Then, since confessions are in order, she confesses she is weary of *Geronte*. Here is heard the lovely "In quelle trine morbide" (In these soft silken curtains).

She is interrupted by a group of singers, sent by the devoted old gallant for her entertainment. They sing the Madrigal, "Sulla vetta del monte" (Speed O'er Summit), a quaint conception, a rather knowing pseudo-pastoral, which celebrates the amorous adventures of Phyllis and Phaon. The composer has cleverly caught the old-time style. The accompaniment suggests the lute.

Geronte, who has brought with him some of his cronies, (old *beaux* in their dotage), applauds the singers, and they watch delightedly when the dancing-master steps forward to teach *Manon* the minuet. Other visitors come in, loading *Manon* with flowers and compliments. But soon the party is over; *Geronte* and his guests leave; *Manon* is to follow later. She completes her toilet, and is about to go when *Des Grieux* appears. He chides her for deserting him, but, weak as ever, yields to her pitiful appeals and soon they sing a passionate duet. This is followed by a song in which *Des Grieux* reproaches her for her weakness, her love of silks and satins, of jewels and precious things, soft to the touch and dazzling to the eye. As well reproach a kitten for enjoying warmth!

Into the midst of this pleasant scene, enter *Geronte!* He has come to see what has delayed *Manon* at the party. He is enraged, his is a cold rage—and a deadly one, the polished anger of one who knows the world. *Manon*, deceived by his ironical civility, goes a bit too far. She has the bad grace to put a mirror before him and before *Des Grieux*, laughing at the comparison. It is the last merriment she is destined to know for some considerable time. *Geronte* leaves them, apparently in cynical indifference. *Manon*, womanlike, possibly indifferent too, lets him go. A little time later, in flies *Lescaut* with a warning that the police are at hand. There is time for escape, and both *Des Grieux* and *Lescaut* urge the girl to hasten. Her love of finery, in this as in so much else, proves her undoing. She stops to gather her jewels, her pretty dresses and possessions. When *Des Grieux* rushes her to the alcove it is to find the way barred by police. *Geronte*, quiet, keen and as cold as ice, has her borne away.

ACT III

Scene—*The Harbor of Havre*

WE are spared the prison scenes of Prévost's novel. Banished from France, as an abandoned woman, *Manon* is to embark for the French prov-ince of Louisiana. By bribing the sentinel, *Des Grieux* and *Lescaut* nearly succeed in rescuing the girl from prison, where she awaits the ship. They are interrupted, however, by the arrival of the man of war's captain. As a last resort, *Des Grieux* begs the captain to take him also to America. To his overjoyed surprise, the bluff old skipper consents, and the strangely-assorted pair, with some hopes of fresh fortunes, embark for the New World.

ACT IV

Scene—*A Desolate Spot in Louisiana*

MANON'S flamelike beauty having won her, in the New World, the unwelcome attentions of yet one more importunate, the French official commander, the lovers have had to flee into the wilderness. *Manon's* strength is failing, and her companion is powerless to help. The musical last farewell of the pair culminates, of course, in the death of *Manon*. In her lover's arms she dies—a harmless, helpless soul whose only crime is her beauty. *Des Grieux* chants his misery to the desolate waste, and he falls senseless across her dead body as the curtain shuts out the scene.

THE VICTOR RECORDS

(Sung in Italian)

DONNA NON VIDI MAI

(A Maiden So Fair) ENRICO CARUSO, Tenor 505 10-in., $1.50

GIOVANNI MARTINELLI, Tenor 738 10-in., 1.50

MARITANA

LIKE John Field, like Arthur William Balfe and like Victor Herbert, William Vincent Wallace, composer of "Maritana" and of many delightful minor works, was born in Ireland. Though, unlike these three gentlemen, he was not born in Dublin, he went there at an early age from Waterford, his birth-town. He was an accomplished organist, and a violinist of notable powers. He toured the greater part of the civilized world, giving concerts and meeting many interesting adventures. "Maritana," first given in London, held the stage for many years, by virtue of its simple and melodious character throughout.

THE OPERA

OPERA in three acts. Libretto by Edward Fitzball. Music by William Vincent Wallace. First produced at Drury Lane, London, November 15, 1845. First American production at the Bowery Theatre, New York, May 4, 1848, by the Seguins. Other notable productions: In 1854 at the old Broadway Theatre, New York, with Louise Pyne and Sims Reeves; in 1857 by the Pyne and Harrison Opera Company, with the composer conducting; in 1865 by the Harrison English Opera Company, at Niblo's, with Theodore Thomas conducting; in 1868 by the Caroline Richings Opera Troupe, and in 1870 by the Parepa-Rosa English Opera Company. More recent revivals by the Metropolitan English Opera Company, Gustave Hinrichs and Henry W. Savage.

CHARACTERS

CHARLES II, King of Spain....... Bass
DON JOSE DE SANTAREM, his
   Minister................. Baritone
DON CAESAR DE BAZAN........ Tenor
MARQUIS DE MONTEFIORI...... Bass
LAZARILLO.......... Mezzo-Soprano
MARITANA, a gypsy singer....Soprano
MARCHIONESS DE MONTEFIORI
                     Soprano

Time and Place: The Scene is laid in Madrid, at the Time of Charles II

CHARLES II of Spain is hated by his minister, *Don Jose*, who formerly loved the Queen. Disguised in Madrid during Holy Week celebrations, he meets *Maritana*, a gypsy singer. *Don Jose* observes, and he decides to use the girl in his plots. *Don Caesar de Bazan*, an old friend, gets into a brawl protecting *Lazarillo*, an armorer's apprentice, who has tried to drown himself. He fights the captain of the guard, and is sentenced to be hanged for duelling in Holy Week. *Don Jose* visits *Don Caesar* in prison, and tells him that if he will marry a certain veiled woman, he will arrange that he shall die a gentleman's death by shooting instead.

Lazarillo unexpectedly brings in the *King's* pardon, but gives it to *Don Jose*, who decides to produce it for his "grand effect" when the time comes. The veiled lady is duly married to *Don Caesar*, while *Lazarillo* takes the bullets from the rifles of the firing party.

The *Marquis Montefiori* gives a ball, during which shots are heard, as though for the execution of *Don Caesar*. *Don Jose*, who holds the *Marquis* under obligation, tells him he is to receive a visit from his "niece," the *Countess de Bazan*. Believing *Don Caesar* has been shot, the puzzled *Marquis* consents. The *King* enters, disguised, then *Maritana*, believing she is to meet her promised husband—promised by *Don Jose*. Incognito, the *King* tries to make love to *Maritana*; she resents it, and he departs, making way for *Don*

Caesar, who, disguised as a monk, demands his wife of the startled *Don Jose*. *Don Jose* meets the situation by having the heavily veiled *Marchioness* appear as *Don Caesar's* wife. *Don Caesar* is horrified; *Don Jose* offers him a pension to get out of Madrid, and he consents. Ready to go, he hears the voice of his beloved singing in the next room. He demands his wife. *Maritana* enters and asks who the stranger may be. *Don Jose* has them arrested and they go off, the girl to a villa where she is to be used as a bait for the *King*, and *Don Caesar* to prison.

Maritana still mourns her unknown husband; *Don Jose* brings to her the *King*, disguised, telling her this is her husband. She repudiates his love. *Don Caesar* meanwhile has been released. *Lazarillo*, placed by him on guard, shoots at a man who climbs in the window of *Maritana*. The *King* is suspicious of this entry. *Don Caesar*, not revealing himself, demands his wife again. He is equally curious regarding the stranger, whom he asks his identity. The *King* replies "*Don Caesar de Bazan*," sorely puzzling the *Don*. *Lazarillo*, horrified at having pot-shotted at his benefactor, whispers to him that he is in the presence of the *King*. "Who are *you?*" asks the monarch of *Don Caesar*, who replies, "*The King of Spain*." The *King* is amused, explanations follow. *Maritana* returns, to be united with her husband, *Don Caesar*, who later kills *Don Jose* when he finds him in the Queen's apartment. As the *King* cannot object to this duel, he appoints *Don Caesar* governor of Valencia.

THE VICTOR RECORD

THERE IS A FLOWER

JOHN McCORMACK, Tenor   775   10-in., $1.50

NANTEUIL   DON CAESAR, THE HERO OF "MARITANA"

PAINTED BY BECKER   MARRIAGE OF FIGARO AND SUSANNA

THE MARRIAGE OF FIGARO

(LE NOZZE DI FIGARO)

(Italian)

THE MARRIAGE OF FIGARO is the second of a trilogy of "Figaro" comedies by Beaumarchais—from the first of which Rossini derived his "Barber of Seville." Though Mozart's work precedes Rossini's by thirty years, it is taken from the second of the three comedies. It will be recollected, however, that the Italian, Giovanni Paisiello composed a "Barber of Seville" in 1780—six years previous to Mozart's setting of a Beaumarchais comedy.

Beaumarchais deliberately aimed in his "Figaro" comedies to expose the moral complacency—and the intellectual futility—of the aristocrat of his time. Performance of this very comedy,"The Marriage of Figaro,"was forbidden in Paris, not on moral grounds but on political. Modern audiences are accustomed to comedies in which the

servant is exalted and the noble lord assigned to a comedy rôle, but in those days it savored of lèse majesté. The play was written only a scant decade before the French Revolution; and government officials, already conscious of gathering storms, made out that such a production, at such a time, could serve less as a warning to a Court apparently bent on riding to its destruction, than as a simple means of developing resentment against a cynical and a scienceless aristocracy. The inevitable happened; "The Marriage of Figaro" took on the charm of forbidden fruit. In place of the public performances, private "rehearsals" were given, at which no less a personage than Marie Antoinette (always liberal in matters of art) condescended to be present.

It was an instant success. One of the singers in that memorable production has left record of the event. This authority, Kelly, who took the double roles of *Basilio* and *Don Curzio*, tells us that "Never was anything more complete than the triumph of Mozart and his 'Nozze di Figaro', to which numerous overflowing audiences bore witness. Even at the first full band rehearsal, all present were roused to enthusiasm, and when Benucci came to the fine passage, 'Cherubino, alla vittoria, alla gloria militar,' which he gave with stentorian lungs, the effect was electric, for the whole of the performers on the stage, and those in the orchestra, as if actuated by one feeling of delight,

vociferated 'Bravo! Bravo, Maestro! Viva, viva, grande Mozart!' Those in the orchestra I thought would never have ceased applauding by beating the bows of their violins against the music desks. And Mozart? I never shall forget his little animated countenance, when lighted up with the glowing rays of genius; it is as impossible to describe it as it would be to paint sunbeams."

It is pathetic to remember that all this glory brought no grist to the mill, and even after the success of "Figaro" Mozart still had to struggle on for mere existence—a struggle which hastened his death only five years later.

THE OPERA

OPERA in four acts. Text by Lorenza da Ponte, founded on a comedy by Beaumarchais. Music by Mozart. First production Vienna, May 1, 1786, with Mozart conducting. In Paris as *Le Mariage de Figaro*, in five acts, with Beaumarchais' spoken dialogue, at the Academie, March 20, 1793; at the Theatre Lyrique, as *Les Noces de Figaro*, by Barbier and Carré, in four acts, May 8, 1858. In London, in Italian, at the King's Theatre, June 18, 1812. First American production in 1823, in English. Some notable revivals were—in the '70s, with Hersee, Sequin and Parepa-Rosa; in 1889, with Nordica, Eames, and de Reszke; in 1902, with Sembrich, Eames, de Reszke and Campanari; and in 1909, with Sembrich, Eames, Farrar and Scotti, and in 1917 with Hempel, Farrar and de Luca.

CHARACTERS

FIGARO (*Fee'-gahr-roh*), the Barber, valet to the Count........Bass
COUNT ALMAVIVA (*Al-mah-vee'-vah*), a Spanish noble......Baritone
COUNTESS ALMAVIVA, his wife Soprano

SUSANNA, maid of the Countess, betrothed to Figaro........Soprano
CHERUBINO (*Kay-ruh-bee'-noh*), page to the Countess......Soprano
MARCELLINA (*Mar-chel-lee'-nah*), servant to Bartolo.......Contralto
BARTOLO, a rejected lover of Susanna....................Bass
BASILIO (*Bah-zee'-lee-oh*), a busybody......................Tenor
Servants, Country People, Guards

Scene and Period: Seville; the Seventeenth Century. The Action is a direct continuation of the Barber of Seville

The opera is preceded by an Overture, which, without drawing directly upon the music of the following scenes, is admirably alive with the spirit of comedy in which the work was conceived.

The chattering violin-figure in octaves at the opening is famous. No less charming is the second subject, in which the laughter in the treble provokes a response from the bass—an ascending figure for basses and bassoons.

248

CALVÉ AS CHERUBINO

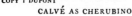

"What is this feeling makes me so sad?
What is this feeling makes me so glad?"—Act II.

"Play no more, boy, the part of a lover
Nor about beauty foolishly hover."
—Act I.

ACT I

SCENE—*A Room in the Chateau, only Half Furnished*

FIGARO, in high spirits, is preparing the room assigned to him and *Susanna* by *Count Almaviva*. His spirits are dashed, however, when *Susanna* points out the proximity of the room to the *Count's* own, and suggests that the *Count* has not paid her dowry for nothing. *Figaro's* rage at his master finds expression in a famous air, the "Se vuol ballare, Signor Contino" (Will You Dance?), in which he expresses his fears with some little directness.

But other troubles are to beset the erstwhile Barber of Seville. Old *Dr. Bartolo*, whom he outwitted in former days, yet bears a grudge against him. *Bartolo* discovers that in a weak moment *Figaro* has promised to marry the aged *Marcellina*, and that the old dame seeks to force him to fulfil the contract. *Susanna* overhears their plotting, some of which is levelled against herself.

Bartolo departs and *Susanna* and *Marcellina* exchange a few cattish remarks, in which the younger girl comes off rather best. *Marcellina* departs; in her place there appears the adolescent *Cherubino*, deeply in love, if you please, with no less a personage than the *Countess* herself. He describes his emotions to the amused *Susanna*, in the "Non so piu cosa son" (Oh What Feelings!).

Rarely has music more subtly swayed to the mingled emotions of a youth in the throes of his first love. Mozart's ineffable genius has captured one of the most difficult moods in the whole realm of emotion. This air will repay many hearings, for it does not reveal itself to the full at the first performance. This is characteristic of Mozart, the past-master of the art that conceals art beneath a deceptive and always charming simplicity.

The *Count* suddenly knocks at the door, and *Cherubino* hastily conceals himself behind a large arm-chair. When

249

the *Count* enters, it is to exclaim against *Cherubino*, whom he suspects of paying court to his *Countess*. Yet even as he speaks another knock is heard. The *Count* hastily hides behind the same chair as *Cherubino*, the page darting out to the front and concealing himself in the depths of a chair covered with one of *Susanna's* dresses. This time it is *Basilio*, an odious busybody, who first taunts *Susanna* with flirting with the *Count*, and then twits her concerning *Cherubino*. The feelings of the pair in hiding may be imagined. As soon, however, as *Basilio* mentions *Cherubino's* name in conjunction with that of the *Countess*, *Almaviva* can stand it no longer. He appears and indignantly demands an explanation of all this talk. *Count Almaviva* then tells how but a short while ago he discovered the boy flirting with *Basilio's* cousin, *Barbarina*, *Cherubino* being concealed under the table. To show how he found him under the table-cloth, the *Count* reaches *Susanna's* dress from the arm-chair and so discovers—*Cherubino!*

The *Count* is so enraged, he threatens then and there to have the boy killed; but *Figaro* enters and pleads for him; so the *Count* is satisfied to give the lad a commission as Captain in his own regiment, where he may expend some of his energies on the field of honor.

ACT II

SCENE—*Apartment of the Countess*

SUSANNA has confided to the *Countess* the unwelcome attentions of the *Count*, and the two women are in despair. The *Countess* sings her lovely appeal to Cupid, the "Porgi amor" (Love, Thou Holy Impulse).

The resourceful *Figaro* enters and describes his plan to make the *Count* jealous—by letting him discover a note making an assignation between the *Countess* and a lover in the garden. It is planned to send *Marcellina* in the *Countess'* place, and *Cherubino*, dressed as *Susanna*, to meet the *Count* in *Susanna's* place. It is hoped that through ridicule the *Count* will be persuaded henceforth to stick to his *Countess*. With this plan settled, *Figaro* leaves. *Cherubino* comes, charmed at the prospect of seeing his beloved *Countess* before joining the army. He sings his devotion to her in a delightful air, the "Voi che sapete" (What Is This Feeling?).

The noted critic Otto Jahn has pointed out that *Cherubino* is not expressing his emotions directly, but indirectly in a romance, directing his shy but ardent glances toward the *Countess* in all the bashfulness of youth. The guitar-like accompaniment of the strings is filled out by solo wind-instruments which seem to express delicate suggestions of the boy's inner feelings.

The women dress up the page to represent *Susanna*. They have no sooner done so than the *Count* knocks. *Cherubino* is concealed in the closet; and the *Count*, observing his wife's confusion, and hearing the sound of a falling chair, (clumsily upset by the terrified youth), demands entry. *Susanna*, concealed in an alcove, hears the *Countess* refuse to open the door—on the ground that her maid is dressing within. The suspicious *Count*, however, goes out for a crowbar to break down the door, and insists on taking the *Countess* with him. As soon as they have gone *Cherubino* emerges, and escapes through the window—a twenty-foot drop!—and *Susanna* quickly hides in the cabinet in his place. When the *Count* returns, prepared to batter a way, the *Countess* finally confesses that *Cherubino* is within. She is therefore as startled as her husband when *Susanna* suddenly appears! The *Count* quickly concludes he is the victim of a joke, and is almost penitent when a half-drunken gardener arrives and complains that somebody has dropped on his flower-bed from the window, and smashed a valued flower-pot. Quickly the *Count's* suspicions reawaken, but *Figaro* now opportunely turns up and, grasping the situation, promptly announces that it was he who jumped through the window. The gardener produces a paper dropped by the runaway, and the thoroughly perplexed but highly suspicious *Count* tells *Figaro* that he will believe him if he will tell what the paper contains. Through a quick whisper of *Susanna's*, *Figaro* learns it is *Cherubino's* commission! The situation looks hopeless, but *Figaro*, ever-resourceful, declares that the commission lacked a seal, and he had it in his pocket for attention. As the commission actually does lack a seal, the day is saved. But *Figaro* now has to face a worse situation. *Marcellina* now enters with her lawyer, and demands that *Figaro* shall keep his promise and marry her. The *Count*, disposed to vengefulness, avers he will look into this; assuredly the *Count* will!

ACT III

SCENE—*A Cabinet in the Count's Residence*

COUNT ALMAVIVA plans to force *Susanna* to accept his attentions by threatening to make *Figaro* wed the ancient *Marcellina*, but *Susanna*, unexpectedly entering, and wishing to further the plans of her mistress, seems to surrender. The *Count* goes forth happy in the conviction that his ends are gained. But he overhears *Susanna* explain to *Figaro*, who enters as he leaves, that "our cause is victorious." He at once grows suspicious, resolving to deal with *Susanna* in his own time, but to punish *Figaro* at once.

Figaro, however, is concerned with another matter, having discovered some clues which appear to suggest he is a man of noble birth. As he is explaining, *Marcellina*, with *Bartolo*, the *Count* and her lawyer, come to inform *Figaro* that he must wed or pay damages. He probably will be rich enough to pay the damages, but as he is

SUSANNA, COUNTESS AND CHERUBINO IN ACT I
(HEMPEL, MATZENAUER AND FARRAR)

explaining this, *Marcellina* suddenly asks him if he has a spatula mark upon his right arm. He has. By this she knows him to be her long-lost son. The *Count* finds his plans badly disarranged. Mother and son embrace—and are so discovered by *Susanna*, who

CHERUBINO'S BALLAD

is much distressed until explanations are forthcoming. Since there is no further obstacle, preparations for the wedding of *Figaro* and *Susanna* are begun.

Susanna now seeks the *Countess* and tells her of the success of their plan. The mistress then dictates a letter in which *Susanna* is to appoint a time and a place for the meeting. This results musically in the "Che soave zeffiretto" (Letter Duet—Song to the Zephyr).

It is a remarkably simple, fluent duet conversation, full of melody. The *Countess* dictates, and *Susanna* takes

down the message, the orchestra allowing ample time for the writing—a fine exhibition of Mozartian craftsmanship.

The letter is sealed with a pin, which the *Count* is to return as a sign that he will keep the appointment. In the next scene, *Figaro* and *Susanna* are married, and *Susanna* contrives during the ceremony to slip the note to the *Count*. Some amusement is caused when the *Count*, engaged in the task of bestowing a seignorial kiss upon some of the village maidens, unexpectedly kisses *Cherubino*, still in woman's clothes. The page is discovered, and condemned to marry *Barbarina*.

ACT IV

Scene—*The Garden of the Chateau*

IT is night. *Figaro*, having discovered the note of *Susanna* to the *Count*, at the place of assignation, soliloquizes upon the fickleness of women. He then conceals himself, just as the *Countess*, disguised as *Susanna*, and *Susanna*, disguised as the *Countess*, enter. The mistress hides, too, and the maid, awaiting the *Count*, and knowing that her husband is listening, sings her famous soliloquy addressed to her imaginary lover. This is with a view to harrowing *Figaro*.

Cherubino, having an appointment with *Barbarina*, suddenly appears on the scene, and seeing the *Countess*, whom he believes to be *Susanna*, he attempts to kiss her. The *Count* arrives, just in time to see this, and steps between them, unexpectedly receiving the kiss himself. He gives the boy a violent box on the ear, and the youngster flies, his head ringing. The *Count* then proceeds to make ardent love to his wife, believing her *Susanna*. He presents her with a diamond ring.

Figaro, mad with rage, unexpectedly meets *Susanna*, whom he of course believes to be the *Countess*. He accordingly tries to awaken her jealousy. *Susanna*, however, reveals herself, and the *Count*, seeing *Figaro* apparently embracing the *Countess*, promptly forgets the supposed *Susanna*, and seizing *Figaro*, calls for help. Explanations now follow, and the *Count*, perceiving himself outwitted, begs his wife's forgiveness and promises to be a model husband. *Cherubino* and *Barbarina* appearing, the curtain falls upon three happy couples, about to re-enter the palace to take part in the marriage festivities.

THE VICTOR RECORDS

(Sung in Italian)

ACT I

SE VUOL BALLARE, SIGNOR CONTINO

(Will You Dance?) GIUSEPPE DE LUCA,
Baritone   596 10-in., $1.50

NON SO PIU COSA SON
(I Know Not What I'm Doing)
AMELITA GALLI-CURCI, Soprano
634 10-in., 1.50

ACT II

VOI CHE SAPETE

(What Is This Feeling?) NELLIE MELBA, Soprano   6219 12-in., 2.00

CHERUBINO:
What is this feeling makes me so sad?
What is this feeling makes me so glad?
Pain that delights me,—How can it be?
Pleasure that pains me!—
Fetter'd though free!
Whence, too, these yearnings,
Strange to myself?
Tell me their meaning, spirit or elf!

ACT III

CRUDEL PERCHE FINORA

(Too Long You Have Deceived Me)
GERALDINE FARRAR-ANTONIO SCOTTI
8039 12-in., 2.50

ACT IV

DEH VIENI, NON TARDAR?

(Ah, Why Delay So Long?) LUCREZIA
BORI, Soprano   6049 12-in., 2.00

BLACK LABEL RECORD

{Overture.................................... *Arthur Pryor's Band*} 35109 12-in., $1.25
{ *Fra Diavolo Overture (Auber)*.................... *Arthur Pryor's Band*}

THE FAIR SCENE

MARTHA

ARTHA (in Italian "Marta"), perhaps of all operas most deserves the appellation of an "old favorite." Friedrich von Flotow, possibly as much as von Weber, deserved Beethoven's censure, as knowing the "art of pleasing"; had Beethoven lived, he would have placed him in the same category, as regarded his effect upon the "popular mind."

Flotow was of noble birth; he was a son of Baron von Flotow of Mecklenburg, who designed him for a diplomatic career. He was born in 1812, and he was not so very old, perhaps, when the Baron sent him to Paris for study; for the boy loved music. His first opera was "Pierre et Catharine," followed by "Stradella"; the overture to the latter work is a concert favorite, even today.

Many great *prime donne* have sung the rôle of *Martha*—Patti, Nilsson, Gerster, Richings, Parepa-Rosa—not to speak of the present generation, in which Sembrich and Hempel have excelled. The opera, though it belongs to the "coloratura" class, is composed under the German tradition. Melody and harmony are vigorous, never too "fleshly," and at times they reach heights, if not too exalted heights, of inspiration, and depths, if not too profound depths, of musical knowledge. The work is a lively one.

THE OPERA

OPERA in four acts. Libretto by St. George and Friedrich. Music by Friedrich von Flotow. The opera is an elaboration of "Lady Henrietta," a ballet-pantomime, with text by St. George and music by Flotow, which was presented in Paris in 1844. "Martha" was first produced at the Court Opera, Vienna, November 25, 1847, with Anna Kerr and Carl Formes. First London production July 1, 1858, at Covent Garden, in Italian, and at Drury Lane in English. First Paris production 1858. In Italy, at Milan, April 25, 1859. Given in 1865 at the *Théâtre Lyrique,* Paris, with Patti. First American production 1852, in German.

254

First New Orleans production January 27, 1860, with Mlle. Dalmont. A notable New York production occurred in 1887 with Patti, Guille, Del Puente and Scalchi. Later Metropolitan performances were in 1896; 1897 (sadly memorable because of the death of Castelmary on the stage in the second act); 1900, in English; the brilliant revival of 1906, with Caruso, Sembrich, Homer and Plançon. In 1916 another production was made with Caruso, Hempel, Ober and de Luca.

CHARACTERS

LADY HARRIET DURHAM, Maid-of-
    honor to Queen Anne. . . . Soprano
NANCY, her friend. . . . Mezzo-Soprano
SIR TRISTAN MICKLEFORD, Lady
    Harriet's cousin. . . . . Bass
PLUNKETT, a wealthy farmer. . . . Bass
LIONEL, his foster-brother, after-
    wards Earl of Derby. . . . . . Tenor
THE SHERIFF OF RICHMOND. . . . . Bass
Chorus of Ladies, Servants, Farmers,
    Hunters and Huntresses,
        Pages, etc.

The Scene is laid, at first, in the Castle of Lady Harriet, then in Richmond

ACT I
SCENE I—*Boudoir of Lady Harriet*

LADY HARRIET, a maid-of-honor to Queen Anne, has grown weary of the elaborate monotony of court life. She has admirers without number —dresses and jewels and flowers, social position, all the assurances and all the distractions, in short, all the average woman craves. Her faithful maid, *Nancy*, discovers her weeping. "Why do you weep?" she is asked, and the reply is one familiar to all races and generations of humanity. It is the expected one—"I don't know!"

Harriet has a cousin, *Tristan*, a gay but rather tottery old beau. Skilled in the ways of women, he now proposes a new list of diversions; but *Harriet* rejects them all, and she "rags" the gentleman unmercifully. Hearing through the open window, the song of the servant maids on their way to Richmond Fair, *Harriet* has a characteristic inspiration—she will go with them! *Nancy* and *Tristan* demur, but she orders them along with her.

The women go off dressed as servant girls, and the aristocratic *Tristan* as a farmer.

SCENE II—*The Fair at Richmond*

THE fair is in full swing—crowded mostly with men and maidens in search of work; for it was the old custom for farmers to seek their hired "help" at the fair. Two young farmers, *Lionel* and *Plunkett*, appear in the crowd. *Lionel* is an orphan, and *Plunkett's* adopted brother. *Lionel's* father, on his deathbed, it appears, has bequeathed to *Plunkett* a ring, which he has been instructed to present to the Queen if he ever gets into trouble.

The two men sing of this circumstance in the familiar "Solo, Profugo" (Lost, Proscribed), an air which has become in truth "universally popular." It has been reset to various poems, including a familiar hymn:

So lo, pro - fu - go, re jet - to, Di mia vi ta 'sul mat - tin..
Lost, pro - scrib'd, a friend-less pil - grim, Sink ing at your cot tage door.

Plunkett, in the course of it, reaffirms his life-long affection for his foster-brother. Soon the disguised ladies appear, with the harassed *Tristan*, who considers the whole affair in monstrous poor taste. The farmers see the two girls, and, attracted by their obvious good looks, they offer to hire them. Carried off by the spirit of their prank, the two "servants" accept. They take the money proffered them, not knowing that by this they are legally bound to serve their masters for a year. *Tristan* protests, but he is hooted off the grounds, and the now terrified girls are led away by the two farmers. Work threatens.

ACT II

Scene—*A Farmhouse*

AS the curtain rises, the two men enter, dragging with them the new members of their household. Then follows the first of the beautiful quartets for which this act is especially famous, the "Siam giunti, o giovanette" (This is Your Future Dwelling). It is followed, at once, by the second, the "Che vuol dir cio" (Surprised and Astounded!). *Harriet*, asked her name, gives it as *Martha*. *Nancy* becomes *Julia* for the time being.

Mistress and maid recover their breath; when they realize that nothing very frightful is going to happen to them, their temptation to plague their employers becomes irresistible. It begins in earnest when the young men endeavor to instruct them in their new duties. *Plunkett* shows them the door of their room. They are eager to escape and talk things over; but halfway there, *Plunkett* stops them. The man is hungry; who is going to cook for him? He gives them his hat and coat to hang up, and *Harriet* throws them on the floor.

The men are mystified. Such insubordination is not in their philosophy. They ask the girls to exhibit their skill at spinning. Then follows the beautiful "Presto, Presto" (Spinning Wheel Quartet). The girls cannot spin, and their employers, melting, volunteer to teach them. At the end of the quartet, *Nancy* overturns her wheel and runs out, pursued by *Plunkett*, who quickly loses his temper. *Lionel* follows the beautiful *Martha*,

with whom he already is head over heels in love. The girl laughs at him, but there is an odd little catch in her laughter; he is a good-looking and manly youth, with an air of distinction she is not quite able to account for. Suddenly he asks her to sing for him, and, taking the rose from her bosom, she sings for him the familiar "Last Rose of Summer," which every soprano of the last seventy-five years, almost, has sung at some time or other.

This air, as is now generally known, is not by Flotow, but is an old Irish air, "The Groves of Blarney," to which Thomas Moore fitted the poem. First criticised by musicians as an obvious bid for popular favor, it is probably the best known of all "operatic" numbers even today.

At the end of the song *Nancy* returns, followed by the bleating but exasperated *Plunkett*. The farmers now realize they have engaged a couple of "problems." They bid the girls good-night in the exceedingly beautiful "Quartetto notturno," or "Goodnight Quartet."

The farmers retire. The girls peep out from their room, and seeing no one near, they whisper their chances of escape. Outside, they suddenly detect the soft call of *Tristan's* voice. A carriage awaits them, and they slip away home. They sleep profoundly.

ACT III

Scene—*A Hunting Park in Richmond Forest*

THE young farmers, more mystified than ever at the defection of their servants, have come to watch the Queen and her train at the hunt—in the hope, thereby, to forget the bright eyes and the bad manners of the two girls. The act opens with a very masculine and very spirited apostrophe to Porter, which is an obsolete drink

256

somewhat resembling beer, but darker in color and somewhat sweeter to the taste. *Lionel* attributes to porter the leonine strength of the British empire. The farmers disperse, leaving *Lionel* alone—to sing, forgetting even porter, his famous "M'appari" (Like a Dream), a singularly melodious air, telling, with genuine feeling, of his seemingly hopeless passion for the unknown *Martha*.

In the midst of the song, enters *Lady Harriet*. Though the young man is amazed at seeing her in the dress of a lady, he is frank enough to declare his love, and he still is young enough and unworldly enough to plead it. *Lady Harriet* is forced to call the hunters, to whom she declares *Lionel* must be insane. Poor *Lionel* is nearly distracted, *Plunkett* administering vain consolation. A beautiful finale brings the scene to an appropiate close.

ACT IV

SCENE I—*Plunkett's Farm House*

PLUNKETT is alone, musing on the unhappy plight of his foster-brother, who, since his rejection by *Harriet*, is not to be appeased. His mind is clouded, and nothing can be done for him. *Nancy* enters, and she, being of common birth, is able to patch up peace with the young man—a peace which, if it does not pass understanding, at least develops into it. The pair decide to present *Lionel's* ring to the Queen, and thus clear up the mystery surrounding him.

SCENE II—*A Representation of the Richmond Fair*

LIONEL'S ring has been duly shown to the Queen, when it transpires that he is really the son of the banished Earl of Derby. He refuses, nevertheless, to accept his rightful rank, and he continues to brood over the insult offered him in the forest. Being the

son of an earl, things are now arranged for him—the most important being a complete reproduction of the scene at Richmond Fair, into which *Harriet* is introduced, in her servant's dress. *Lionel* is led in by *Plunkett*, and his mind at once clears. He embraces *Harriet*, *Plunkett* embraces *Nancy*, and there is a general time of embracing, when the curtain drops.

THE VICTOR RECORDS
(Sung in Italian unless noted)

ACT I
SOLO, PROFUGO
(Lost, Proscrib'd) ENRICO CARUSO, Tenor and MARCEL JOURNET, Bass
8016 12-in., $2.50

ACT II
SIAM GIUNTI, O GIOVINETTE
(This Is Your Future Dwelling) FRANCES ALDA, Soprano; JOSEPHINE JACOBY, Contralto; ENRICO CARUSO, Tenor and MARCEL JOURNET, Bass
10002 12-in., 3.50

CHE VUOL DIR CIO
(Surprised and Astounded) FRANCES ALDA, JOSEPHINE JACOBY, ENRICO CARUSO and MARCEL JOURNET
10002 12-in., 3.50

PRESTO, PRESTO
(Spinning Wheel Quartet) FRANCES ALDA, JOSEPHINE JACOBY, ENRICO CARUSO and MARCEL JOURNET
10003 12-in., 3.50

LAST ROSE OF SUMMER
LUISA TETRAZZINI, Soprano *In English*
6343 12-in., 2.00
AMELITA GALLI-CURCI, Soprano *In English*
6123 12-in., 2.00
MISCHA ELMAN, Violinist 608 10-in., 1.50

'Tis the last rose of summer,
Left blooming alone;
All her lovely companions
Are faded and gone;
No flower of her kindred,
No rosebud is nigh
To reflect back her blushes,
Or give sigh for sigh!

I'll not leave thee, thou lov'd one,
To pine on the stem;

Since the lovely are sleeping,
Go sleep thou with them.
Thus kindly I scatter
Thy leaves o'er the bed—
Where thy mates of the garden
Lie scentless and dead!

QUARTETTO NOTTURNO

(Good Night Quartet) FRANCES ALDA,
JOSEPHINE JACOBY, ENRICO CARUSO
and MARCEL JOURNET 10003 12-in., $3.50

ACT III

CANZONE DEL PORTER

(Porter Song) MARCEL JOURNET, Bass
698 10-in., 1.50
TITTA RUFFO, Baritone 876 10-in., 1.50

PLUNKETT:
I want to ask you, can you not tell me,
What to our land the British strand
Gives life and power? say!
It is old porter, brown and stout,
We may of it be justly proud,
It guides John Bull, where'er he be,
Through fogs and mists, through land and sea!
Yes, hurrah! the hops, and hurrah! the malt,
They are life's flavor and life's salt.
Hurrah! Tra, la, la, la, la, la, la, la!
And that explaineth wher'er it reigneth

Is joy and mirth! At ev'ry hearth
Resounds a joyous song.
Look at its goodly color here!
Where else can find you such good beer?
So brown and stout and healthy, too!
The porter's health I drink to you!

M'APPARI

(Like a Dream) ENRICO CARUSO, Tenor
6002 12-in., $2.00
GIOVANNI MARTINELLI, Tenor
6193 12-in., 2.00
BENIAMINO GIGLI, Tenor 6446 12-in., 2.00

LIONEL:
Like a dream bright and fair,
Chasing ev'ry thought of care,
Those sweet hours pass'd with thee
Made the world all joy for me.
But, alas! thou art gone,
And that dream of bliss is o'er.
Ah, I hear now the tone
Of thy gentle voice no more;
Oh! return happy hours
Fraught with hope so bright.
Come again sunny days of pure delight!
Fleeting vision cloth'd in brightness,
Wherefore thus, so soon depart;
O'er my pathway shed thy lightness once again,
And glad my heart.

BLACK LABEL AND BLUE LABEL RECORDS

{Overture to Martha.........................*Victor Symphony Orchestra*} {Overture to Martha.........................*Victor Symphony Orchestra*}	35735 12-in., $1.25
{Overture to Martha...............................*Pryor's Band*} { *Nocturne in E Flat (Chopin) (Piano acc.)* ....*Victor Sorlin, 'Cellist*}	35133 12-in., 1.25
{Last Rose of Summer (*In English*)..................*Elizabeth Wheeler*} { *Tannhäuser—The Evening Star* ....*Rosario Bourdon, 'Cellist*}	16813 10-in., .75
{Good Night Quartet (*In English*)..........................*Lyric Quartet*} { *Madrigal from " The Mikado" (Gilbert-Sullivan)*.............*Lyric Quartet*}	17226 10-in., .75
{Spinning Wheel Quartet...........................*Victor Opera Quartet*} { *Madame Butterfly—Some Day He'll Come*.........*Agnes Kimball, Soprano*}	55114 12-in., 1.50
{Last Rose of Summer..................... *Lucy Isabelle Marsh, Soprano*} { *My Ain Countrie*.......... .... *Lucy Isabelle Marsh, Soprano*}	45183 10-in., 1.00
{Last Rose of Summer (*Violin*).........................*Samuel Gardner*} { *Believe Me If All Those Endearing Young Charms*......*Samuel Gardner*}	17871 10-in., .75

EAMES AS AMELIA

CARUSO AS RICHARD

DE SEGUROLA AS SAMUEL

THE MASKED BALL

(BALLO IN MASCHERA)
(Italian)

THE history of "Un Ballo in Maschera" is a stormy one, at least in its beginnings. This work was written for the San Carlo Opera House in Naples during a period of great political stress. It was just after the attempt of Orsini upon Napoleon III, and as it was first called "Gustavo III," after an assassinated Italian monarch, and included in its plot a similar murder, it not unnaturally attracted unwelcome attention from the police. Verdi was told outright to adapt his music to fresh words. He of course refused. He was then sued for 200,000 francs damages by the manager of the San Carlo—for breach of contract. When this became known, together with the fact that the San Carlo manager had not sought permission to give the work as Verdi intended, a riot ensued which nearly amounted to revolution. The episode was turned to political account. Crowds of Italians, angered against Austria, gathered under Verdi's window or followed him through the streets shouting "Viva Verdi!"—an innocent pastime in itself until the letters forming the composer's name are taken as initials of the phrase "*V*ittorio *E*mmanuele *R*e *D'I*talia." In this crisis, Jacovacci, a Roman impresario, offered to produce the work in the Eternal City, making arrangements with the Roman police, and undertaking all responsibilities. Verdi gratefully accepted this offer, and the work was given a Roman début, February 17, 1859. It proved a great success; but in order to meet the police requirements the names of the characters and the *locale* of the plot incidents were altered so that *Gustavo III* became *Richard*, "*Count*" of *Warwick* and "*Governor*" of *Boston*.

THE OPERA

OPERA in three acts. Text by M. Somma, music by Verdi. First produced in Rome at the Teatro Apollo, February 17, 1859; at Paris, *Théâtre des Italiens*, January 13, 1861. First London production June 15, 1861. First New York production February 11, 1861. Some notable Metropolitan revivals occurred in 1903 with de Reszke; in 1905, with Caruso, Eames, Homer, Scotti, Plançon and Journet; and in 1913, with Caruso, Destinn, Hempel and Amato.

CHARACTERS

RICHARD, Count of Warwick
    and Governor of Boston......Tenor
REINHART, his secretary......Baritone
AMELIA, wife of Reinhart.....Soprano
ULRICA, a negress astrologer. Contralto
OSCAR, a page..............Soprano
SAMUEL } enemies of the Count { Bass
TOMASO }   { Bass

The Scene is laid in Boston, U. S. A., at the end of the Seventeenth Century.

(The Italian name of the opera is pronounced *Bahl-loh in Mahs'-keh-rah*).

ACT I

SCENE I—*A Hall in the Governor's House*

THE hall of the *Governor's* audience chamber is filled with people—officers, deputies, gentlemen—who have come to transact their sundry affairs at the beginning of the day. They sing the *Governor's* praises, but not all are his friends; for among the many most loyal followers are *Samuel* and *Tomaso*, his bitter enemies. The *Governor* enters and is warmly greeted. A list of names of those invited to the ball is given and he is delighted to find *Amelia's* name on the list. His greeting to his followers, and his joy over *Amelia* find expression in the delightful quartet and chorus, "La rivedra nell' estasi" (I Shall Behold Her).

The people unite in a chorus of praise. *Tomaso* and *Samuel* decide to wait for some better occasion before attempting the *Governor's* life. A judge enters, with a paper to be signed condemning *Ulrica*, a negro witch, accused of sorcery. *Richard* laughs at the charge, and refuses to sign; he invites his friends to go with him in disguise to hear the woman prophesy.

SCENE II—*The Hut of Ulrica*

ULRICA'S hut is crowded with people who have come to hear their fortunes. The sorceress stands over a cauldron, chanting incantations and invoking the powers of darkness to aid her. The *Governor* arrives, dressed as a sailor, his companions with him, including the vengeful *Tomaso* and *Samuel*. All are dismissed, however, from the witch's presence, to admit a mysterious lady visitor. *Richard*, nevertheless, conceals himself. To his amazement he hears *Amelia* beg the old dame for something that will yield her peace of mind—by driving from her heart her love for *Richard, Count of Warwick and Governor of Boston*, for she is (and she desires to remain) the loyal wife of his friend *Reinhart*. *Richard's* feelings may well be imagined. The witch tells her that there is a certain herb, but to make potent it must be gathered at night by the one who suffers the pangs of love; and it grows only where the moon shines upon a gallows where men have actually been hanged. Here there is an interesting trio, the "Della citta all 'occaso" (Hard by the Western Portal).

The frightened girl consents to go, and *Richard* secretly vows that he shall be there. When she has gone, the crowd reënters the hut, and *Richard* asks the witch his fortune. In his character as sailor he sings a barcarolle, a song of the sea:"Di' tu se fedele" (The Waves Will Bear Me).

This ballad is full of humor, the *staccato* passages toward the end indicating the *Governor's* impatience to learn the future. He openly banters the woman, asking if he will meet with storms on his next voyage.

But *Ulrica* finds nothing to ridicule. She warns him that he is soon to die, not sword in hand as men desire, but by the dagger of a friend—and that that friend shall be the next one who is to take him by the hand. This involves the fine quintet and chorus, "E scherzo, od e follia" (Your Prophecy Absurd!)

The *Governor* scoffs at the notion, and promptly offers his hand to all his friends present. They refuse it in dread, *Tomaso* and *Samuel* being especially uneasy.

Suddenly, however, *Reinhart* enters, in some anxiety over his chief. Glad to find all well with him, he shakes him warmly by the hand, addressing him by name, to the astonishment of those who did not know the *Governor* was among them. *Richard* tells the witch she is a poor fortune-teller for this is the best friend he ever had. Nevertheless, he pardons *Ulrica*, declaring she has nothing to fear from him, and he throws her a fat purse of money. His bravery and his gallant action win fresh applause of the people, who kneel and sing a hymn to his honor, "O figlio d'Inghilterra" (Oh, Son of Glorious England).

ACT II

Scene—*On One Side a Gallows*

UNDER the shadow of the gallows, the frightened *Amelia* seeks the magic herb—in the "Ma dell'arido stelo divulsa" (Yonder Plant Enchanted). A shadowy figure terrifies her, but it resolves itself into *Richard*, who now makes himself known. The unhappy girl confesses she loves him, but she begs him to go away. A duet follows, "Ah! qual soave brivido" (Like Dew Thy Words Fall).

In this remote spot, the last person on earth they wish to see suddenly appears—*Reinhart*. He has come to warn *Richard* that his life is in danger. *Richard* refuses to escape down an available sidepath, but *Amelia* threatens to make herself known if he refuses. As *Reinhart* does not know who the veiled lady is, the threat is effective, and *Richard* consents to escape provided *Reinhart* will give her his protection back to the city without speaking or making any attempt to learn her identity. This *Reinhart* promises, and we have the Boccaccio-like situation of a husband escorting his own wife home from a meeting with her lover. As the *Governor* leaves however, his would-be murderers appear. Discovering that *Reinhart* is not *Richard* they tear the veil away from the lady's face, and thus *Reinhart* discovers *Amelia*! The great finale to the act now occurs, the "Ve'se di notte qui con la sposa" (Ah! Here by Moonlight).

Protesting her innocence, the unhappy woman almost faints with shame. *Reinhart* bitterly upraids her, denouncing his false friend *Richard*. The conspirators depart, anticipating a sensation on the morrow when the city shall learn of the incident; but before they go *Reinhart* makes an appointment with them for the morning. He then tells *Amelia* that he will escort her to the city—but in such tones as make her tremble for her life. As the curtain goes down, a sensitive audience can easily share in the poor soul's forebodings. There is tragedy in the air.

ACT III

SCENE I—*A Room in Reinhart's House*

IN a terrible scene, *Reinhart* pours down upon the unhappy *Amelia* the full flood of his anger. Finally in an access of fury he bids her prepare for instant death. The frightened woman swears she is innocent, begging on her knees for a chance to bid farewell to her child—their child. This is the solemn and tender "Morro, ma prima in grazia" (I Die, Yet First Implore Thee). It sobers *Reinhart*, for the time at least, and he grants her request. Left alone, he repents his intention, reserving his wrath and his vengeance for *Richard* in the remarkable "Eri tu" (Is It Thou?)

This is the greatest air allotted to *Reinhart*, and perhaps the most famous in the entire opera. At its close, *Samuel* and *Tomaso* enter, doubtful of their reception. *Reinhart* proves by a paper that he is aware of their plan to attack the *Governor*, and as they cower back expecting arrest he unexpectedly tells them that he, too, seeks revenge. To convince them he offers his own son in hostage. They are delighted to secure so influential an ally. His only stipulation is that his own hand must deliver the blow. They refuse this, but consent to draw lots. Just as soon as these have been prepared, however, *Amelia* enters announcing *Oscar*, the *Governor's* messenger. The crazed *Reinhart* looks on her as an instrument of Fate, and he forces her to draw the scraps of paper. It is her hand therefore that, by drawing a slip bearing *Reinhart's* name, condemns *Richard* to death. With her woman's instinct, she divines it. The page enters with invitations to the *Governor's* ball. And the conspirators withdraw after deciding on the password, and upon the costumes to be worn. The frightened *Amelia*

overhears a word or two and all doubt dissolves as to the quality of the men's intentions. They are bent on murder.

SCENE II—*The Governor's Private Office*

MEANTIME, *Richard* decides upon a beautiful sacrifice. By sending *Reinhart* and *Amelia* back to England can he avoid the peril of betraying his friend. He sings the pathetic romanza, "Ma se m'e forza perdeti" (Forever to Lose Thee), a recitative, closely followed by a lovely air. A page brings a note from an unknown lady, warning him that an attempt will be made upon his life at the ball. Remembering, however, that his absence might be construed into cowardice, he decides to go.

SCENE III—*The Grand Ball Room in the Governor's House*

REINHART in vain seeks the *Governor* among the masked guests. At last he meets the page *Oscar*, who, however, taunts him, in the sprightly "Saper vorreste" (You Would Be Hearing).

This singularly felicitous little *scherzo* is grossly out of tune with the vengeful *Reinhart's* mood. He tells the page harshly enough, that affairs of state, make it imperative he should know the *Governor* on sight. He is told that *Richard* is dressed in black with a red ribbon on his right breast.

Amelia, in the meanwhile, has contrived a meeting with *Richard* in order to say farewell, and to warn him against her husband's vengeance. As the two are mournfully parting, *Reinhart* rushes in and stabs the *Governor* in the back. The dying man, supported by friends, now tells *Reinhart* that *Amelia* is guiltless; that he himself has planned, for her happiness and *Reinhart's*, to send them both back to England out of harm's way. With his dying breath he forgives his friend, and declares him innocent of harm.

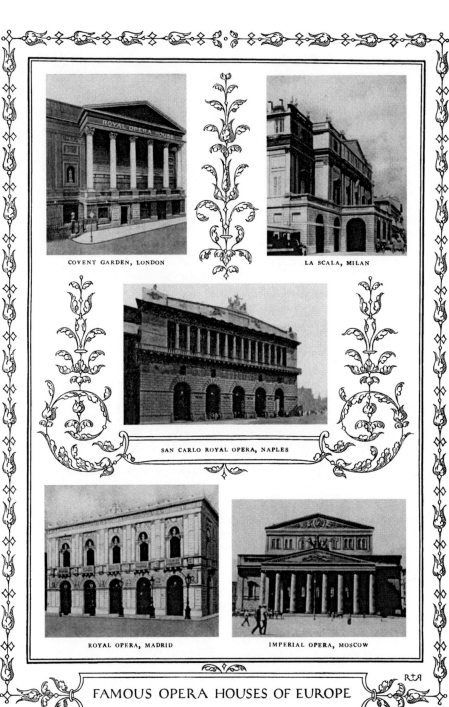

COVENT GARDEN, LONDON

LA SCALA, MILAN

SAN CARLO ROYAL OPERA, NAPLES

ROYAL OPERA, MADRID

IMPERIAL OPERA, MOSCOW

FAMOUS OPERA HOUSES OF EUROPE

THE VICTOR RECORDS

(Sung in Italian unless otherwise noted)

ACT I

LA RIVEDRA NELL' ESTASI

(I Shall Behold Her) ENRICO CARUSO, Tenor, FRIEDA HEMPEL, Soprano, LEON ROTHIER, Bass, A. PERELLO DE SEGUROLA, Bass; and Chorus
10005   12-in., $3.50

DI' TU SE FEDELE

(The Waves Will Bear Me) ENRICO CARUSO, Tenor, and Metropolitan Opera Chorus   512 10-in., 1.50
GIOVANNI MARTINELLI, Tenor
732 10-in., 1.50

RICHARD:
Declare if the waves will faithfully bear me;
If weeping the lov'd one from whom I now tear me,
Farewell, to me saying, my love is betraying.
With sails rent asunder, with soul in commotion,
I go now to steer thro' the dark waves of ocean,
The anger of Heav'n and Hell to defy!
Then haste with thy magic, the future exploring,
No power have the thunder or angry winds roaring,
Or death, or affection my path to deny!

QUINTETTE—E SCHERZO, OD È FOLLIA

(Your Prophecy Absurd) ENRICO CARUSO, Tenor, FRIEDA HEMPEL, Soprano, LEON ROTHIER, Bass, A. PERELLO DE SEGUROLA, Bass, MME. DŪCHENE, Soprano, and Metropolitan Chorus
10005   12-in.,   3.50

ACT III

ERI TU CHE MACCHIAVI

(Is It Thou?) EMILIO DE GOGORZA, Baritone   6068 12-in.,   2.00

PASQUALE AMATO, Baritone
6040   12-in., $2.00
TITTA RUFFO, Baritone
6266   12-in.,   2.00
GIUSEPPE DE LUCA, Baritone
6078   12-in.,   2.00

MA SE M'È FORZA PERDERTI— ROMANZA

(Forever to Lose Thee) (Preceded by the recitative, "Forse la soglia") (This Affair Must End) ENRICO CARUSO, Tenor   6027 12-in.,   2.00

RICHARD:
Haply I have decided, finding peace of mind.
Reinhart will return to his country,
His wife, submissive, will follow him.
Farewells unspoken, the broad ocean will divide us.
If compelled to lose thee now
To part from thee forever:
My burning thoughts will fly to thee,
Though fate our lot may sever.
Thy memory still enshrined shall be
Within my inmost heart.
And now, what dark forebodings
Around my soul are thronging?
When, once more to behold thee,
Seems like a fatal longing!

SAPER VORRESTE

(You Would Be Hearing) LUISA TETRAZZINI, Soprano   6341 12-in.,   2.00

OSCAR:
You would be hearing, what dress he's wearing
When he was bidden, the fact be hidden?
I know right well but may not tell
Tra la la la, la la la!
Of love my heart feels all the smart,
Yet watchful ever, my secret never
Rank nor bright eyes shall e'er surprise!
Tra la la la, la la la!

PHOTO BYRON

SCENE FROM MEFISTOFELE (ACT III)

MEFISTOFELE

ARRIGO BOÏTO was a man of unusual genius, but one whose achievements, perhaps, did not quite reach his natural possibilities. He was as much poet as musician, and he was the author of a novel, some remarkable poems and opera libretti, including "La Gioconda," and Verdi's "Falstaff" and "Otello." In addition he was a composer. He was born at Padua, 1842, and died in 1918. His father was Italian, but his mother was Polish, and perhaps this northern strain in his blood may account for his philosophical bent. His elder brother, an architect of note, suggested Goethe's "Faust" to the boy as an opera theme long before Gounod's work was produced; and even in his student days he had the work in hand. The failure of "Mefistofele" at its first production was partly due to technical conditions —the rôle of *Faust* being assigned to a baritone—and the scenes tending to discursiveness. But it was also due, in part, to a lack of understanding by enthusiastic but unphilosophical artists and producers. And misconceptions of the work were certainly induced by

discussion. In a revised form, far more practical but perhaps less distinctively original, "Mefistofele" was again brought forward at Bologna in 1875— and this time with success.

Boïto's opera is never likely to be popular, yet it is a landmark in music— especially in Italian opera. He has sought to give the whole of Goethe's "Faust" and not merely the Faust-and-Marguerite incident employed by Gounod and others. So gigantic a poem cannot readily be condensed into a four-hour opera without suffering a diffusiveness highly perplexing to those unfamiliar with Goethe's masterpiece. Full appreciation of Boïto's "Mefistofele" calls for familiarity with the operatic score supplemented by much quiet study of Goethe's poem. It is a really significant work, in no sense popular, yet one which has strongly influenced many of the best of latter-day Italian composers. Verdi himself cherished the greatest veneration for Boïto's genius, and there is no question that Boïto influenced the later masterpieces of the composer who wrote "Otello" and "Falstaff" as well as "Trovatore" and "Aida."

THE OPERA

OPERA in four acts. Text and music by Arrigo Boïto; a paraphrase of both parts of Goethe's "Faust." The first production at La Scala, Milan, 1868, was a failure. Rewritten and given in 1875 with success. First London production July 6, 1880. First American production at the Academy of Music, November 24, 1880, with Campanini, Cary and Novara. Given at the New Orleans Opera in 1881, in Italian, and in 1894, in French. Some notable American productions were in 1896, with Emma Calvé; in 1889, in German, with Lilli Lehmann; and in 1901 with McIntyre, Louisa Homer and Pol Plançon; in 1904 with Caruso and Emma Eames; in 1907, for Chaliapin; in 1906 at the Manhattan Opera; the Chicago opera revival for Titta Ruffo; and the recent Metropolitan production with Caruso, Emmy Destinn, Frieda Hempel and Pasquale Amato.

CHARACTERS

MEFISTOFELE.................Bass
FAUST......................Tenor
MARGARET..................Soprano
MARTHA..................Contralto
WAGNER....................Tenor
HELEN....................Soprano
PANTALIS................Contralto
NEREUS ....Tenor

Celestial Phalanxes, Mystic Choir, Cherubs, Penitents, Wayfarers, Men-at-arms, Huntsmen, Students, Citizens, Populace, Townsmen, Witches, Wizards, Greek Chorus, Sirens, Naiads, Dancers, Warriors.

PROLOGUE

SCENE—*The Regions of Space*

IN the realms of space, invisible angels and cherubim, accompanied by celestial trumpets, are singing in praise of the Ruler of the Universe. As in Goethe's drama, *Mefistofele*, representing the Evil One, converses with the

FARRAR AND MARTIN IN ACT II

PHOTO NUMA BLANC FILS, MONTE CARLO
MELBA AS HELEN

266

Almighty, expressing his contempt for "that small God of Earth who, like the grass-hopper, pokes his head among the stars only to fall back trilling into the grass." The mystical choirs answer, "Is *Faust* known to thee?," much as in the Book of Job, which Goethe followed with some faithfulness in this scene. *"The Lord said unto Satan, Hast thou considered my servant Job, that there is none like him in the earth, a perfect and an upright man, one that feareth God and escheweth evil?"* And as God, in the Biblical narrative, permitted Satan to influence Job, so *Mefistofele* is permitted to wager with Heaven that he can lure *Faust* to his destruction.

ACT I

SCENE I—*A Square in Frankfort— Easter Sunday*

THE aged philosopher, *Faust*, and his pupil *Wagner*, while mingling with the crowd, remark a Grey Friar. *Faust* shortly observes that he "moves slowly on in lessening circles; and with each spiral, comes ever nearer and nearer. Oh! as I gaze," he continues, "I see his footsteps marked in fire!" To *Wagner* this sounds like madness; he can see nothing but a mendicant friar.

Dramatic necessity no doubt obliged Boïto to substitute a friar for Goethe's "pudel," and in a note Boïto justifies the change on the ground that in the old *Faust* legends it is a friar and not a "water dog."

SCENE II—*The Studio of Faust*

RETURNING to his studio, *Faust* does not see the friar slip in behind and conceal himself in an alcove. The aged philosopher delivers his soliloquy, "Dai campi, dai prati" (From the Green Fields), in which peaceful and serene melody he speaks of his contentment, his love of God and his fellow man. The melody is simple but expressive throughout; the middle section is distinctly pastoral in character.

The friar suddenly stands forth, and throwing off his disguise, he reveals himself as *Mefistofele*, arrayed as a cavalier. He offers his services to the philosopher on the same terms as in Gounod's work. But it is no mere passion for *Margaret* that so allures *Faust*. Boïto follows Goethe. The terms of the compact are that *Mefistofele* binds himself to *Faust's* service *here* without restraint. *Below*, the conditions will be reversed. *Faust*, always in pursuit of greater knowledge, is willing to sacrifice immortality to win it; but he, too, imposes a condition:

If it chance that I say to the fleeting atom:
Stay! thou art beautiful! then may I die!

By this it will be seen that *Faust* undertakes to maintain his philosophic disinterestedness in the quest of Truth no matter into what temptations of love and ambition—of *Desire*—his journey with *Mefistofele* may lead. Failing in this, he is willing to sacrifice eternity. The bargain is made, and the two set forth on their adventures.

ACT II

SCENE I—*The Garden of Margaret*

FAUST, now a handsome young man known as *Henry*, strolls in the garden with *Margaret*. *Mefistofele*, as in Gounod's version, makes ironic love to *Martha*, who here appears as *Margaret's* mother. As with Goethe, the young girl wonders why so magnificent a young man deigns to notice her. *Faust* wishes to see the girl alone, and hearing that she sleeps with her mother he gives her a sleeping draught for the old lady. He assures her this is harmless. Then as the scene closes, *Margaret* surrenders to her love for *Faust*. "I love thee! I love thee!" he cries as the innocent girl surrenders.

Scene II—*The Summit of the Brocken*

MEFISTOFELE now conducts Faust to a wild spot in the Brocken mountains, where, beneath the moonlight, he may behold the people over whom his companion reigns as king. The wind is shrilling weirdly, and flames dart forth from the jagged rocks at each step as they climb. Once at the summit, *Mefistofele* summons forth his infernal subjects—demons, witches, wizards, goblins, imps—who acclaim him as King. They dance in joy when he shatters a crystal globe to symbolize his power over the earth.

To this Saturnalia, *Faust* pays little heed. He beholds a vision of *Margaret*, on her way to prison for the murder of her babe and her mother. He is especially horrified by a red stain about her neck, like a crimson thread—the mark of the headsman's axe. But *Mefistofele* bids him away. The act closes with an orgy, in which, however,

KRELING

THE VISION OF MARGARET

Faust takes no part. There is nothing in this to tempt him to say "Thou art beautiful!"

ACT III
Scene—*The Prison of Margaret*

AS in Gounod's opera, *Faust* and his guide visit *Margaret*—in prison for drowning her babe and poisoning her mother in a fit of madness. *Faust* is torn with pity as the doomed girl recalls the scenes of their love-making. She believes the newcomers are her jailers, come to take her to the scaffold. *Faust*, however, reassures her, and urges her to fly with him. In this scene is heard the remarkable "Lontano, lontano" (Far Away).

Mefistofele, who has left them together to make arrangements for the girl's escape, now returns and *Margaret* is frantic with terror to behold him. She refuses to leave the prison, where she dies in *Faust's* arms. *Mefistofele* cries out "She is judged!" but a chorus of celestial beings announces salvation. *Faust* and his companion leave, just as the headsman and jailers come to conduct the girl to the scaffold. This climax ends, by the way, Part I of Goethe's poem.

ACT IV
The Night of the Classical Sabbath

THE next episode is the meeting of *Faust* with *Helen* of Troy in the classic groves of Greece. The scene reveals an enchanting spot on the banks of the Peneus, the moon shedding a golden light upon *Helen*, *Pantalis* and groups of Sirens. *Faust* and his demon-friend now enter, but *Mefistofele* is uncomfortable amid such scenes of loveliness and he steals away to the Brocken. The meeting of *Faust* and *Helen* has a deeper significance than the mere temptation of *Faust*. "Helen and Faust," Boïto tells us, "represent Classic and Romantic Art gloriously wedded, Greek beauty and Germanic beauty gleaming under the same aureole, glorified in one embrace, and generating an ideal poesy, eclectic, new, powerful."

EPILOGUE

SCENE—*Faust's Studio*

WITHERED and feeble, *Faust* has returned to his studio. *Mefistofele* stands behind him. "O songs! O memories!" the philosopher cries, looking back on his past. "Thou hast desired, enjoyed, and desired again," says *Mefistofele*, "nor hast yet said to the fleeting atom: '*Stay, thou art beautiful!*'" But *Faust* is lost in his own thoughts: "Reality was grief; and the Ideal but a dream!" Yet to the last he seeks the Ideal, and his swan-song is a yearning desire to be "King of a peaceful realm," where under wise laws he may give happiness and fecundity to the people. This finds expression in a famous epilogue, the "Giunto sul passo" (Nearing the End of Life).

As he sings, the celestial throngs gather near, and the vision of heaven becomes brighter with the approach of death. As in the Prologue, celestial Phalanxes cry their *Aves* to the Lord, and bear upward to realms on high the soul of the departed *Faust*. A shower of roses falls upon the dead body. Roses, too, are showered upon *Mefistofele*, stifling him with their purity and perfume. He disappears as the tri-

umphant host cry out their Hallelujahs against the strong, clear notes of silver trumpets. So "the ideal hymn is chanted in heaven."

NOTE—"*Mefistofele*" *quotations are made from the Ditson libretto, by permission. (Copyright, 1880, Oliver Ditson Company.)*

THE VICTOR RECORDS

(Sung in Italian)

PROLOGUE

AVE SIGNOR
(Hail, Sovereign Lord) FEODOR CHALIA-
PIN, Bass   981 10-in., $1.50
MARCEL JOURNET, Bass   915 10-in., 1.50

ACT I

DAI CAMPI, DAI PRATI
(From the Green Fields) BENIAMINO
GIGLI, Tenor   644 10-in., 1.50
FAUST:
From the meadows, from the valleys, which lie bathed in moonlight,
And where paths silent sleep, I come returning; my soul filled
With calmness, mysterious and deep,
The passions, the heart rudely trying,
In quiet oblivion are lying;
My spirit knows only its love for its fellows;
Its love for its God!

ACT III

L'ALTRA NOTTE
(They Threw My Child Into the Sea)
FRANCES ALDA, Soprano 6353 12-in., 2.00
LONTANO, LONTANO
(Away From All Strife) GERALDINE FARRAR,
Soprano and EDMOND CLEMENT, Tenor
                              8020 12-in., 2.50
GIUNTO SUL PASSO ESTREMO
(Nearing the End of Life) BENIAMINO
GIGLI, Tenor   644 10-in., 1.50

BLACK LABEL RECORD

{ Mefistofele—Selection . . . . *Vessella's Band* }
{ *Forza del Destino—Solenne in quest'ora* . . . . *Vessella's Band* } 35512 12-in., $1.25

WALTER:
> The maid Elysian
> I saw in vision,
> She whom my heart doth choose!
> (Meistersinger, Act III.)

DIE MEISTERSINGER

(THE MASTERSINGERS)

DIE MEISTERSINGER differs from Wagner's other works—all of them except the immature "Rienzi"—in the circumstance that the characters in the play all are human. In fact, they are historical personages. For once there are no gods, no fairies, no magic potions, no superhuman interference in men's affairs. *Eva* and *Walter* naturally fall in love with each other without requiring any magical draught to awaken their emotions as in the case of *Tristan* and *Isolde*. And in the end, *Walter* wins with his prize-song by sheer merit, both in composition and presentment; and he defeats *Beckmesser* fair and square. In this he more likely gains the sympathy of Anglo-Saxon audiences than in *Lohengrin*, (say), whose victory over *Telramund*, thanks to the magic of *Monsalvat*, is a foregone conclusion. American audiences are prone to cherish a sneaking sympathy for the villainous *Telramund* in such an uneven combat. The same holds true with the young *Siegfried*, rather a dubious "hero" without his magic assets.

The idea of a "high-born" hero with magical embellishments is rather a Teutonic than an Anglo-Saxon conception, but in *Walter* (despite his knightly descent) we at least have an all-human hero, and one, also, who commits an occasional mistake. But it is *Hans Sachs*, the chief of the Mastersingers, who is the real hero. He is an historical personage, as indeed was *Beckmesser* also, and Wagner beheld in him the last of the Mastersingers, the true poet and musician, the real and even sorrowful arbiter between Classicism and Romanticism.

Mastersingers, it may be explained, were the medieval successors to the Minnesingers, and the Minnesingers (of whom *Tannhäuser* was one) were knightly poets and musicians analogous to the troubadours of France. When Minne-singing fell into decay, the burghers of the cities took up the good work with their Guilds in which singers worked up their way as "Scholars," "Schoolmen," "Singers," "Poets" and finally "Masters." The purpose of the Guilds was to train the minds of the young, to sustain the highest standards of art, and encourage the development of genius. This was an excellent purpose in itself, but not unnaturally, the Mastersingers' Guild in time arrogated itself an undeserved importance. The "rules" grew irksome, and they were too pedantically enforced.

This is the condition Wagner satirizes in the opera, using the good *Hans Sachs* to typify the true artist's conception, in which a sane respect for systematized principles really is balanced by an open-minded tolerance of new developments. It is easy to see that *Hans Sachs* is (as it were) Richard Wagner himself, and *Beckmesser* the personification of his critics and of those composers who are tangled hopelessly in the barbed wires of pedanticism. The score is woven with a richness of counterpoint which the scholastic followers of Richter and Jadassohn could not have equalled, had they sought to produce such polyphony as an end in itself; yet to Wagner this elaborately interwoven musical texture is merely a means of expression. How openly he laughs at the tricks of the scholars when, as an exhibition of that much-vaunted contrapuntal device, "Diminution of the theme," he diminishes the broad, pompous theme of the Mastersingers by having it played four times as fast, and thus makes it do duty as a theme for the "pert apprentices!"

THE OPERA

OPERA in three acts. Text and music by Wagner. First production in Munich, June 21, 1868. Vienna, 1870; Berlin the same year; Leipsic, 1872; Milan, 1890. The first performance in England took place at Drury Lane, May 30, 1882; an Italian version was given at Covent Garden in 1889, and an English production by the Carl Rosa Company at Manchester in 1896. In 1888 it was given for the first time at Bayreuth; and the first American production took place at the Metropolitan Opera House, New York, January 4, 1886, with Fischer, Staudigl, Kemlitz, Krämer, Krauss and Brandt. Some notable American productions occurred in 1901, with de Reszke, Gadski, Schumann-Heink, Dippel and Bispham; in 1905, with Van Rooy, Acte and Burgstaller, and some forty Metropolitan performances under Gatti-Casazza, with various fine casts.

CHARACTERS

Die Meistersinger (*My-ster-zing-er*), or Master-Singers—

HANS SACHS, cobbler .... Bass
POGNER, goldsmith .... Bass
VOGELGESANG, furrier .... Tenor
NACHTIGAL, buckle maker .... Bass
BECKMESSER, town clerk .... Bass
KOTHNER, baker .... Bass
ZORN, pewterer .... Tenor
EISSLINGER, grocer .... Tenor
MOSER, tailor .... Tenor
ORTEL, soap boiler .... Bass
SCHWARZ, stocking weaver ...... Bass
FOLZ, coppersmith .... Bass
SIR WALTER VON STOLZING, a
  young Franconian knight .... Tenor
DAVID, apprentice to Hans
  Sachs .... Tenor
EVA, Pogner's daughter ...... Soprano
MAGDALENA, Eva's nurse ..... Soprano

Burghers of all Guilds, Journeymen, Apprentices, Girls and People.
Scene: Nüremberg in the Middle of the Sixteenth Century

ACT I

SCENE—*Interior of St. Katherine's Church*

THE good people of Nüremberg are gathered in the church on the festival of St. John's day. Among them are *Eva*, the daughter of the wealthy goldsmith *Pogner*, and her maid *Magdalena*. They are engaged in singing the last verse of the last hymn, and, as usual in German choirs, there is a brief musical interlude between the lines of the verse. Under cover of this, the young knight, *Walter von Stolzing*, is secretly making an appointment with *Eva*, with whom he is deeply in love. Wagner has cleverly adapted the music between the stately lines of the hymn to picture the lover's mood. When the service is over, and the congregation leaves, *Walter* for the first time learns that *Eva's* father has a singular plan in view: he intends to give his daughter as bride to the winner of the song-contest on the morrow, making it a rule that none but a Master of the guild may compete.

Walter promptly decides to become a Master and win the contest, though he has not the faintest idea what may be the processes involved. *Magdalena* is called in to assist, and she in turn calls upon *David*, the young apprentice, who on pain of his sweetheart's displeasure, is to try and instruct *Walter* in the rules of the Guild-master's art. As there is to be a test immediately, *David* begins instruction at once, while his brother apprentices are arranging the body of the church for the Guild meeting. His efforts make an amusing feature, ill-calculated to help the ardent *Walter*.

In due course the Masters arrive, and, while they are surprised at his boldness, they agree to give *Walter* a hearing. A "Marker" is appointed. This is none other than *Beckmesser*, the Town Clerk. *Beckmesser* himself is eager to wed *Eva.* He is a formidable stickler for rules, and the result may be imagined. The uninstructed *Walter* is allowed to sing, but he is interrupted by the scratching of the pencil on the slate as the Marker notes down his errors. At the end of the rambling first verse the Masters refuse to hear any more. *Hans Sachs* alone is willing to go further. *Sachs,* himself a Master of true worth, has detected in the song a touch of genuine inspiration. He admits that it may disregard the "rules" of the Guild, but he suggests that it may be governed by other rules justifying its character. He is shouted down, however, and the indignant young knight is dismissed amid the jeers of the 'prentices. Thus is innovation received in the arts. But the youthful *Walter,*— once more a type of Wagner's own life and his struggles against classical and scholastic pedantry, is not beaten, only for the moment. He will go far beyond his critics.

ACT II

A Street in Nüremberg. The Houses of Pogner and Hans Sachs Separated from each other by a Narrow Alley, but both Facing the same Broader Street, which is shown Sectionally on the Stage

IT is night in the city. The 'prentices are putting up the shutters. They are disposed to ridicule *David,* who has suffered *Magdalena's* ire as a result of *Walter's* failure. *Sachs* drives them away, whooshing *David* off to his bed, but he first has his workman's bench so placed that at the same time he can work and watch the street. He settles down to a long soliloquy. He has been greatly moved by *Walter's* song, for which he half suspects the inspiration. This affects him the more, since, as a middle-aged widower, he dreams of winning *Eva* himself. In this mood *Eva* appears. Despairing to change her father's determination and win *Walter* for a husband she half suggests that *Sachs* might be a welcome suitor. She has known and loved him from childhood, and is well aware of his essential worth. But *Sachs* understands in his heart that she loves *Wal-*

OTTO GORITZ
AS HANS SACHS

BECKMESSER'S SERENADE

COPY'T DUPONT
FISCHER AS SACHS IN FIRST
AMERICAN PRODUCTION, 1886

273

ter, and she leaves him. He shakes his wise head over the turn of events; he observes *Eva* and *Walter* talking together, and he half reveals his knowledge by means of a song whose words have a meaning for the lovers alone. They decide to elope, but *Sachs* "accidentally" places his lamp where the light will fall upon them, and they are deterred by fear of being seen. While they debate, however, a stranger appears and they draw back into the shadow. It is *Beckmesser,* who has come to serenade his mistress with the song he hopes to sing on the morrow. *Sachs,* hearing him tinkle on his lute, breaks in with a lusty song of his own, and *Beckmesser* is greatly discomfited. He pretends he has come to inquire about a pair of shoes, and *Sachs,* the cobbler, declares he is working on them. In the meanwhile, *Magdalena,* wondering what has happened to her mistress, appears at the window, and *Beckmesser* thinking her to be *Eva,* wishes to sing,— worse than ever. He pretends that he wants *Hans Sachs* to criticise the song, and *Sachs* agrees to act as "Marker,"

hammering on the shoe for every mistake. In this way, *Beckmesser* proceeds. In his agitation, however, his song runs wild, and *Sachs* hammers loudly. The thumping becomes more and more vehement as the mistakes of *Beckmesser* increase. The disturbance arouses the neighbors. *David* also is awakened, and seeing the Town Clerk apparently serenading *Magdalena,* who is still at the window, he vows vengeance. Dashing out, club in hand, he proceeds to beat *Beckmesser.* Soon the apprentices are out and the different guilds—clothiers, furriers, goldsmiths and what-not—are having a grand free-for-all fight. During the disturbance *Hans Sachs* draws *Walter* into the cobbler's shop, and *Eva* slips away home. The joyous riot lasts till the approach of the Night-Watchman, who arrives after the traditional manner of the police, when the show is all over. Finding the street quiet, he gravely announces the hour and bids the people sleep in peace. The sound of his horn is distantly heard as he wanders off, staff and lantern, calling the hour.

COPY'T DUPONT
HOMER AS MAGDALENA

COPY'T MISHKIN
WITHERSPOON AS POGNER

COPY'T DUPONT
GADSKI AS EVA

ACT III

SCENE I—*Interior of Sachs' Workshop*

NEXT morning *Sachs*, still brooding over the song and very conscious of his fading romance, does not notice when *David* enters with a basket of eatables. *David* has patched it up with *Magdalena* and he is in consequence happy; only *David* is fearful that his part in last night's disturbance will bring down a beating from his Master. He begins to explain, declaring the night before was just a "polterabend" —a night of merrymaking on the festival of St. John. *Sachs* appears not to notice; but suddenly he bids the wondering youth sing the song of the day— a carol of St. John. This tells the quaint story of the child of a woman of Nüremberg christened in the River Jordan by Johannes, the saint, for whom he was named; but on his return to Nüremberg the name was abbreviated to "Hans," and the festival is therefore the name-day of *Hans Sachs* himself. *Sachs*, though still preoccupied, understands the 'prentice's hopes and desires, and he dismisses him kindly.

Scarcely has he gone than *Walter*, who has just awakened, enters from another room. He is full of a wonderful dream he has had in which a marvellous poem and melody have sung their way into his heart. *Sachs* desires to hear it. He is struck with amazement at its beauty and inspiration, and he tactfully instructs the young poet-composer in the technical requirements necessary to make it satisfactory to the judges. These instructions, by the way, are so excellent that they are seriously quoted by Sir Charles Stanford in his book on musical composition, as a valuable exposition of Wagner's own methods.

After they have written down the poem, they leave the room. *Beckmesser* enters, and believing the song to be by *Hans Sachs* himself, after the manner of plagiarists the world over, pockets it, intending to make use of it himself. When *Sachs* returns, the Town Clerk scolds him for planning to enter the contest. *Sachs* denies this so *Beckmesser* produces the manuscript, and *Sachs*, perceiving the man's mistake, does not undeceive him. On the contrary, he divines the fact that *Beckmesser* desires the poem, and knowing the Town Clerk incapable of making good use of it, he gives it to him, promising not to make known the real author. *Beckmesser* leaves in high glee.

Eva next enters, in festival attire. Her shoe pinches, and *Sachs*, knowing well what is in her heart, fusses and fumes in trying to adjust it. She raises her pretty foot on a low stool, and while *Hans Sachs* bends over it, *Walter* enters. *Sachs* pretends not to see. *Walter*, spellbound, gazes at his adored one, and then softly sings the last verse of his prize-song. *Sachs* is deeply moved, and when it is over he gravely gives the two his blessing. *Eva*, weeping for joy, falls into his arms and the kindly man comforts her as her own father could not hope to. During this moment of mingled tears and laughter, *David* and *Magdalena* enter, also in gala attire. *Hans* invites them to a christening—he seeks to name *Walter's* song, a witness is needed, and as a 'prentice will not suffice, the kindly cobbler, with twinkling eyes, gives *David* his freedom by making him a full journeyman-cobbler, thus opening the way to his marriage with *Magdalena*. The boy can hardly believe his ears, and the curtain goes down on a scene of blent pathos and comedy.

SCENE II—*A Field on the Shores of the River Pegnitz*

IN an open meadow on the banks of the river, a great crowd of people is assembling for the song-contest. There is much merriment and jesting, which

DAVID: "Forgive me, Master, and pardon the slip."

EVA AND SACHS—ACT II

ceases, however, as *Eva*, in bridal array attended by many maidens, arrives on a gaily decked barge. *Sachs*, in an air of nobility, announces to the various Guilds the terms of the contest and the contest begins then and there, with exceeding pomp and circumstance. Because of his years, *Beckmesser* is given first opportunity. Still sore from his beating of the previous night, grievously flustered, with his stolen song only half-learned, he attempts to wed the poem to his own serenade-melody. The result is a hopeless jumble—which first excites the wonder, then the derision of the audience. *Beckmesser*, enraged, declares the song is not his own but is the work of *Hans Sachs*. The Masters believing this a spiteful joke, call upon *Sachs* for an explanation. He then insists that the song is a good one if properly sung, and persuades them to let it be interpreted by the young knight, *Walter von Stolzing*. After some argument, the young man, whose handsome appearance at once wins the favor of the crowd, is permitted to sing his great "Preislied," or Prize Song.

The beauty of this melody beggars description. To an intense degree it reflects all that is best in Wagner's most inspired moments.

Eva, who has listened with rapt attention, now advances to the edge of the platform and places on the head of *Walter* a wreath of laurel and myrtle, then leads him to her father, before whom they both kneel. *Pogner* extends his hands over them in benediction and presents the emblem of the Master's guild to the young knight. But *Walter*, remembering his reception of the day before, and conscious also of his noble birth, refuses the honor. There is consternation for a moment, but *Hans Sachs*, grasping *Walter's* hand, bids him not to disparage the Master's ways, but to show respect for art. In a splendidly dignified passage he bids the young man forget his noble birth, since he has fairly won his Mastership by his gifts as a poet and musician. *Walter* consents, and he leans on one side of *Sachs* with *Eva* on the other, while *Pogner* kneels as if in homage before the group. And thus the cobbler-musician and the two lovers become symbols of Art and Life, enshrined among music of incomparable splendor.

THE VICTOR RECORDS

PRIZE SONG
 (Preislied) JOHN McCORMACK, Tenor
 6209 12-in., $2.00
 EVAN WILLIAMS, Tenor 6314 12-in., 2.00
 MISCHA ELMAN, Violin 6090 12-in., 2.00

WALTER (*who has ascended to the platform with firm and proud steps*):

Morning was gleaming with roseate light,
 The air was filled
 With scent distilled
 Where, beauty-beaming,
 Past all dreaming,
A garden did invite.
Wherein, beneath a wondrous tree
With fruit superbly laden,
In blissful love-dream I could see
The rare and tender maiden,
Whose charms beyond all price,
Entranced my heart—
Eva, in Paradise!

Evening fell and night closed around;
 By rugged way
My feet did stray
 Towards a mountain,

Where a fountain
Enslaved me with its sound;
And there beneath a laurel tree,
With starlight glinting under,
In waking vision greeted me
A sweet and solemn wonder;
She dropped on me the fountain's dews,
That woman fair—
Parnassus's glorious Muse!

(*With great exaltation*):

Thrice happy day,
To which my poet's trance gave place!
That Paradise of which I dreamed,
In radiance before my face
 Glorified lay.
To point the path the brooklet streamed:
 She stood beside me,
 Who shall my bride be,
The fairest sight earth ever gave,
My Muse, to whom I bow,
So angel—sweet and grave.
I woo her boldly now,
Before the world remaining,
By might of music gaining
Parnassus and Paradise.

BLUE LABEL AND PURPLE LABEL RECORDS

{Prize Song.......................... ....*Beatrice Harrison, Violoncellist*}55067 12-in., $1.50
{ *Ave Maria* (Schubert).......................*Beatrice Harrison, 'Cellist*}

Prize Song *In German* *Lambert Murphy, Tenor* 70080 12-in., 1.25

{Meistersinger—Overture—Part I......*Albert Coates and Symphony Orchestra*}55171 12-in., 1.50
{Meistersinger—Overture—Part II.....*Albert Coates and Symphony Orchestra*}

FIRST PROGRAM OF MEISTERSINGER,
MUNICH, 1868

MIGNON

CHARLES LOUIS AMBROISE THOMAS, born at Metz in 1811, came honestly by his creative genius, as he was the son of a musician. He wrote numerous operatic and other works. Like Gounod, he was an artist, poet, writer in general, a man of unusual and arresting versatility. His musical style is easy, fluent, brilliant at times in the extreme. To many persons "Mignon" is his masterpiece. Its overture, known the world over for its grace and delicacy, is a concert-piece which few orchestras do not return to from time to time. It is a typical example of that grace and ease so characteristic of the French school of operatic music, and by summing up the chief themes of the opera, including *Filina's* dashing "Polonaise," it presents, in brief form, some of the most significant utterances that school has made to the world of music.

THE OPERA

OPERA in three acts. Text by Barbier and Carré, based upon Goethe's *Wilhelm Meister*. Music by Ambroise Thomas. First production at the *Opéra Comique*, Paris, November 17, 1866. In London at Drury Lane, 1870. First New York production November 22, 1872, with Nilsson, Duval and Capoul. Revived at the Metropolitan in 1900, with de Lussan, Adams, Selignac and Plançon; by Oscar Hammerstein in 1907, with Bressler-Gianoli, Pinkert, Bonci and Arimondi, and at the Metropolitan in 1908, with Farrar, Jacoby, Abott, Plançon and Bonci.

CHARACTERS

MIGNON, a young girl stolen by gypsies (*Meen'-yohn*)
Mezzo-Soprano

FILINA (*Fil-lee'-nah*), an actress..................Soprano

FREDERICK, a young nobleman................Contralto

WILHELM, a student .... Tenor

LAERTES, (*Layr'-tayz*), an actor Tenor

LOTHARIO (*Loh-tah'-ree-oh*), an Italian nobleman, Basso Cantante

GIARNO (*Jahr'-noh*), a gypsy ....Bass

Townsfolk, Peasants, Gypsies, Actors and Actresses

The Scene of Acts I and II is laid in Germany; of Act III in Italy

ACT I

SCENE—*Courtyard of a German Inn*

AMONG the wine tables, at which a number of people are merrily drinking, an old man wanders, harp in hand, singing strange songs. It is *Lothario*, an Italian nobleman whose memory has left him so that he knows not even his own name. His condition is told in the "Fuggitivo e tremante" (A Lonely Wanderer).

Though he has forgotten her, he is the father of *Mignon*, a young girl who was stolen from her home in childhood by gypsies and who is now forced by the mercenary *Giarno* to dance in the streets for a living. The gypsy band appears, and *Mignon*, a singular, half-boyish-looking figure, rebels when she is bidden to dance for a troupe of actors in the balcony of the inn and for the casual throngs in the courtyard. She refuses and her master threatens to beat her. *Lothario* intervenes but the old man is powerless. Suddenly, however, *Wilhelm* enters, and, grasping the situation, he forces *Giarno*, with a pistol, to release the girl. For this he is applauded by the actors, and one of them is sent by *Filina* with the request that he shall visit them. *Filina* is an actress of designing temperament, who succeeds in attracting *Wilhelm's* attention,—much to the jealousy of *Frederick*, a young nobleman. For the present, however, *Wilhelm* is curious about the girl he has rescued, and he questions her regarding her childhood. She remembers nothing, except that she was captured by gypsies in a country she describes with such eloquence that *Wilhelm* guesses it must be Italy. She tells of it in the "Connais-tu le pays?"—"Kennst du das Land?" —"Non conosci il bel suol?" (Knowest Thou the Land?). The opening passage:

gives an idea of the melody, one of the loveliest in the entire range of opera. The passionate longing of the orphan child for the home of her infancy is expressed in a superb climax:

Moved to pity, *Wilhelm* offers *Giarno* money to "buy" the girl, and he goes into the inn to complete the bargain. *Lothario*, drawn by some subtle bond of parenthood, comes to bid her farewell, saying that he must go south, following the swallows. A sprightly duet ensues, "Les Hirondelles",—"Leggiadre Rondinelle," (Song of the Swallows).

Filina is invited to go to the castle of *Prince Tieffenbach* with the troupe of players and any guests she may care for. She promptly invites *Wilhelm*, whom she desires to captivate, and he is included as playwright of the company. *Wilhelm* plans to leave *Mignon* behind, being somewhat embarrassed by his "purchase", but she begs so

hard to go with him that finally she is permitted to, disguised as a servant. The gypsy girl is infatuated with her new "master", and she causes him no little uneasiness. His respectful attitude toward her, only makes her love him the more deeply.

ACT II

Scene I—*A Boudoir in the Tieffenbach Castle*

FILINA sits at her mirror, considering her charms and laying on cosmetics. She is thinking of *Wilhelm*, who really has made a "great impression". Presently he enters. With him, however, comes *Mignon*, who is greeted by the actress with civil yet subtly "cattish" remarks. The poor girl does not resent this, however, and she apparently goes to sleep. Yet she observes, under half-closed lids, that *Wilhelm* is paying court to the actress, to whom he has given a bouquet of blooms presented to him by *Mignon* herself. Presently *Filina* and *Wilhelm* leave and *Mignon*, dreaming that she may equal the actress's charm, powders her face and "tries on" one of *Filina's* manifold gowns. At the entrance of *Wilhelm*, followed by *Frederick*, however, she scurries into hiding. The two men quarrel over *Filina*. Swords are drawn, but *Mignon* intervenes, and they separate. Finally, left alone with *Mignon*, *Wilhelm*, in the "Addio, Mignon" (Farewell, Mignon), tells her he must leave her.

Mignon begins to weep, refuses the money, and is about to say farewell. At this juncture, however, enters *Filina*. Observing the girl decked out in borrowed raiment, she utters a few things which raise a flush of anger in *Mignon's* cheeks. The girl dashes into an inner cabinet, where she tears off the dress, reappears in her own gypsy clothes, and finally runs out of the room.

SCENE II—*The Gardens of the Castle*

THE despairing *Mignon*, believing her love for *Wilhelm* to be without hope, decides to drown herself. She is about to jump into the lake, when she is stopped by *Lothario*, who listens sympathetically to the angry girl's talk of her desire for vengeance, and her wish that fire and thunderbolts might descend from heaven and burn the castle. The half-crazed minstrel starts curiously at the word "fire" and goes off muttering to himself.

In the meantime, the performance in the theatre having ended, the actors and actresses and guests appear in the garden. *Filina* has made a brilliant success of it, and, still flushed with triumph, she sings her dashing and showy *Polonese* or *Polacca* (French *Polonaise*), an exceptionally difficult and showy coloratura soprano air, in somewhat different mood from that with which Chopin invested his wonderful polonaises for the piano.

"Io son Titania"(I'm Fair Titania!) sings she. Her brilliant and exacting melody, with its fiery energy of rhythm is a great favorite, not only in the opera house but on the concert platform too.

Mignon, arrives on the scene, and *Filina*, enraged at sight of her, sends the girl into the house to find a bouquet she has lost. As *Filina* knows the bouquet is made of flowers gathered by *Mignon* for *Wilhelm*, there is malice enough in her request; yet *Mignon* goes without complaint. No sooner has she gone, however, than the word "Fire!" springs from everybody's lips. The half-witted *Lothario* has interpreted *Mignon's* wild talk only too literally, and set fire to the castle. Instantly there is great commotion. *Wilhelm*, realizing that *Mignon* is in danger, rushes off to her rescue. He reappears with her in his arms as the curtain descends. He places the un-conscious girl on a grassy bank, and she lies there still clasping the bunch of withered flowers.

ACT III

SCENE—*Count Lothario's Castle in Italy*

HEADING south, as if indeed with the instinct of the swallow, *Lothario* has brought *Mignon* to the neighborhood of an old castle in Italy, which *Wilhelm* is half inclined to purchase. *Wilhelm*, who now realizes that he loves *Mignon*, has followed them hither. The young girl is recovering from a dangerous illness, and as *Lothario* watches, outside her sickroom he sings a beautiful berceuse or lullaby, "Ninna nanna". Lullabies for bass voices are rarities, and this is a notable and delightful exception.

Wilhelm takes *Lothario's* place as watcher, and tells of his new-found affection in a beautiful air, "Elle ne croyait pas" (Pure as a Flower).

Mignon comes, with feeble step, to the balcony, and seeing *Wilhelm*, she becomes greatly agitated, fearing *Filina* may be with him. He soothes her, but she insists that only *Lothario* loves her. Meantime, however, a strange thing has happened. Having returned to his home by some strange instinct of the blind, *Count Lothario's* memory is restored, and he now reappears in his rightful character. His only regret is the loss of his daughter, *Sperata*. At sound of that name, the floodgates of memory are opened in *Mignon's* perturbed consciousness, and when *Lothario* shows her the jewels and prayerbook of his lost daughter she not only recognizes them but she unconsciously begins to sing the prayers of her early childhood. In this way, father and daughter are restored and reunited, and *Wilhelm* admitted to the family circle, so that all ends happily.

THE VICTOR RECORDS

ACT I

CONNAIS-TU LE PAYS?

(Knowest Thou the Land?) GERALDINE FARRAR-FRITZ KREISLER, Violin. *In French*   8024   12-in., $2.50

ERNESTINE SCHUMANN-HEINK, Contralto. *In German*   6367   12-in.,   2.00

EMMY DESTINN, Soprano. *In German*   6085   12-in.,   2.00

MIGNON:

Knowest thou yonder land where the orange grows,
Where the fruit is of gold, and so fair the rose?
Where the breeze gently wafts the song of birds,
Where the season round is mild as lover's words?
Where so calm and so soft, like Heaven's blessing true,
Spring eternally reigns, with the skies ever blue?
Alas, why afar am I straying, why ever linger here?
'Tis with thee I would fly!
'Tis there! 'Tis there! my heart's love obeying,
'Twere bliss to live and die!
'Tis there my heart's love obeying,
I'd live, I would die!

LES HIRONDELLES

(Song of the Swallows) GERALDINE FARRAR, Soprano and MARCEL JOURNET, Bass. *In French*   8022   12-in., $2.50

ACT II

POLONAISE, "IO SON TITANIA!"

(I'm Fair Titania!) AMELITA GALLI-CURCI, Soprano. *In Italian*   6133   12-in.,   2.00

FILINA:

Yes; for to-night I am queen of the fairies!
Observe ye here, my sceptre bright;
(*Raising the wand*)
I'm fair Titania, glad and gay,
Thro' the world unfetter'd I blithely stray.
With jocund heart and happy mien,
I cheerily dance the hours away,
Like the bird that freely wings its flight.
Elfin sprites around me dance;
For I'm fair Titania!
My attendants ever sing,
The achievements of the god of Love!
On the wave's white foam,
'Mid the twilight grey, 'mid flowers,
I blithely do dance!
Behold Titania, glad and gay!

GAVOTTE

MAUD POWELL, Violinist   803   10-in.,   1.50
Philadelphia Orchestra   944   10-in.,   1.50

BLACK LABEL RECORDS

Overture—Part 1 . . . . *Victor Concert Orchestra*	17909	10-in.,	$0.75
Overture—Part 2 . . . . *Victor Concert Orchestra*			
Gems from Mignon . . . . *Victor Opera Co*			
"Away Ye Friends"—"Polonaise"—Barcarolle, "Now On We Sail"	35337	12-in.,	1.25
"Pure as a Flower"—"Dost Thou Know"—Finale			
Gems from "Tales of Hoffmann" . . . . *Victor Opera Co*			

SCENE FROM MIKADO

THE MIKADO

COMIC opera in two acts; text by W. S. Gilbert; music by Sir Arthur Sullivan. First produced at the Savoy Theatre, London, March 14, 1885. First American production at the Museum, Chicago, July 6, 1885, followed by the production at the Union Square Theatre, New York, July 20, 1885. All star revival by Messrs. Shubert and William A. Brady at the Casino Theatre, May 30, 1910. Revived at the Majestic Theatre by the Gilbert and Sullivan Festival Company, 1913. The most popular of all the Gilbert and Sullivan operettas.

CHARACTERS

MIKADO of Japan............Baritone
NANKI-POO, his son, disguised as a minstrel, in love with Yum-Yum...............Tenor
KO-KO, Lord High Executioner of Titipu...........Comedian
POOH-BAH, Lord High Everything Else.................Bass
PISH-TUSH, a noble lord.....Baritone
YUM-YUM, PITTI-SING, PEEP-Bo, wards of Ko-Ko.....Soprano
KATISHA, an elderly lady, in love with Nanki-Poo...Contralto
Schoolgirls, Nobles, Guards and Coolies

Time and Place—The Scene is laid in Japan; Present Time

SO far as the plot is concerned, the whole trouble begins with *Nanki-Poo*, the son of the Japanese Mikado, who has fled from the court, disguised as a wandering minstrel, to avoid matrimony with *Katisha*, a lady of equivocal age but unequivocal temper. *Nanki-Poo* arrives in Titipu, where *Ko-Ko* is Lord High Executioner and *Pooh-Bah* is Lord High Everything Else. He has the temerity to fall in love with the ward of *Ko-Ko*, the lovely *Yum-Yum*. As *Ko-Ko* intends to marry her himself, however, his wooing is not a success. About this time, the Mikado sends a note to *Ko-Ko* complaining of the lack of executions in

282

Titipu, and adding that unless somebody is beheaded during the next month, *Ko-Ko* will lose his position. *Pooh-Bah* happens to come upon *Nanki-Poo* as he is about to hang himself for love of *Yum-Yum*. He persuades the young man to consent to be beheaded instead, his terms being a month of wedded bliss with *Yum-Yum*. To this he agrees, and *Ko-Ko* is forced to add a somewhat grudging consent.

At the opening of the second act, *Yum-Yum* is preparing for the ceremony, but a hitch occurs. It seems, that according to law, when a married man is executed, his wife also is buried alive, and *Yum-Yum*, though she loves *Nanki-Poo* dearly, objects to "such a stuffy death." *Ko-Ko* is at first elated, but news is brought that the *Mikado* himself is approaching,—to see why his orders are unobeyed. *Pooh-Bah* then ventures that as *Nanki-Poo* insists on killing himself unless he weds *Yum-Yum*, he had better be allowed to marry her and depart with his bride on condition that he consents to be the "hero" of a wholly fictitious execution,—to be described to the *Mikado* in great detail. *Nanki-Poo* has no objection to this and a story is appropriately "cooked up." The *Mikado* duly arrives, with *Katisha* in his train. He is delighted with the account of the execution, but the lynx-eyed *Katisha* has made out that *Nanki-Poo*, the supposed victim, is none other than the *Mikado's* heir. To save themselves from "boiling in oil, or something lingering" the miscreants are obliged to confess that the execution has never taken place. This involves another form of not-too-sudden death for deceiving the *Mikado*, but eventually, that great monarch, made happy by the rediscovery of his son, consents to pardon everybody, even *Ko-Ko*,—except that this very gentle Lord High Executioner is condemned to marry the formidable *Katisha*, a circumstance which evokes from him the ever-memorable lines:

"The flowers that bloom in the spring, tra-la,
Have nothing to do with the case;
I've got to take under my wing, tra-la,
A most unattractive old thing, tra-la
With a caricature of a face."

BLACK LABEL RECORDS

Gems from "The Mikado"—Part I . . . . *Victor Light Opera Co.* Quartet, "Behold the Lord High Executioner"—Solo and Chorus "The Flowers that Bloom in the Spring"—Women's Trio, "Three Little Maids"—Solo, "Tit-Willow"—Duet and Chorus, "He's Gone and Married Yum Yum"—Chorus, "With Joyful Shout" Gems from "The Mikado"—Part II . . . . *Victor Light Opera Co.* Chorus, "Gentlemen of Japan"—Solo, "A Wandering Minstrel"— Solo and Quartet, "A Song of the Sea"—Solo, "Moon Song"— Duet, "Emperor of Japan"—Solo and Chorus, "My Object All Sublime"—Chorus, "We Do Not Heed"	35551	12 in.	$1.25
Madrigal—Brightly Dawns Our Wedding Day . . . . *Lyric Quartet* Martha—Good Night Quartet . . . . *Lyric Quartet*	17226	10 in.	.75
Mikado Selection No. 1 . . . . *Victor Concert Orchestra* Entrance of Mikado, "Mi-Ya-Sa-Ma"—"A Wandering Minstrel" "Moon Song"—Quintet, "Youth Must Have Its Fling"—Trio, "The Criminal Cried" Mikado Selection No. 2 . . . . *Victor Concert Orchestra* "Tit-Willow"—"Three Little Maids"—"He's Going to Marry Yum Yum"— "The Flowers that Bloom in the Spring"—"Here's a State of Things"—Finale, "With Joyful Shout" (arr. by Tobani)	18191	10-in.	.75

MIREILLE

(MIRELLA)

MIREILLE—ACT I

MIREILLE, which came later than "Faust" in order of production, is a pastoral romance based on "Mirèio," a poem by that beloved poet of Provence, Frederic Mistral. Gounod has drawn freely upon Provençal folk-songs. The plot, therefore, is less significant than the "atmosphere," and the work indeed is but a tale of simple peasant life.

The scene opens in a mulberry grove, where the village girls are teasing *Mirella* over her hopeless love for *Vincent*, a poor basket-maker. *Tavena*, the fortune-teller, warns her that *Ramon*, the girl's father never will consent to the union. *Mirella* accepts the woman's help, but soon forgets her when *Vincent* arrives. The two have a passionate love scene, and they arrange to meet at a distant shrine if anything goes wrong.

Mirella learns that her father plans to marry her to the wild herdsman, *Ourrias*, but when he arrives, *Mirella* refuses him, and avows her love for *Vincent*. *Vincent's* father attempts to gain the consent of *Mirella's* father to the union, but the latter charges mercenary motives. A quarrel ensues, and *Mirella's* plans seem spoiled forever. She therefore starts on the journey across the desert to the distant shrine.

The journey proves almost too much, even though *Tavena* overtakes her and assures her *Vincent* will be there. She arrives so exhausted that her death seems imminent. *Vincent* attempts to revive her but without success. Her father *Ramon*, however, who has followed, is so overcome by her distress that he finally consents to the marriage and *Mirella* recovers—so that all ends happily—even under operatic law.

OPERA in five acts. Words by M. Carré, from *Mirèio*, Provençal poem by Mistral; music by Gounod. First version given at Saint Rémy-de-Provence, under the direction of the composer, in 1863. Produced in Paris March 19, 1864. Reduced to three acts, with the addition of the waltz, and reproduced December 15, 1864. In London, in Italian with five acts, as "Mirella" July 5, 1864. The first performance in America was given by Mapleson, at the Brooklyn Academy, December, 1884, with Nevada, Scalchi and Vicini. Given at the New Orleans Opera, January 29, 1885, in Italian. April 23, 1885, given at the Academy of Music, New York, with Patti in the cast. Revived at the Metropolitan Opera House, New York, March 8, 1919.

VICTOR BLACK LABEL RECORD

{Mirella Overture—Allegro......................*Vessella's Italian Band*} 68471 12-in., $1.00
{ Puritani Quartet (Bellini). ....*Vessella's Italian Band*} 68471 12-in., $1.25

WHITE   THE DAGGER DANCE—ACT II

NATOMA

NATOMA, the work of an American composer and librettist, with an American setting and an American first production in English, may be regarded as one of the most successful American operas this country has yet known. For this reason alone it is a notable achievement; at the same time, its intrinsic merits ensure it the high regard of music lovers of all races.

THE OPERA

OPERA in three acts; text by Joseph D. Redding; music by Victor Herbert. First produced by the Philadelphia-Chicago Opera Company, at the Metropolitan Opera House, Philadelphia, February 25, 1911. First New York production February 28, 1911.

CHARACTERS

(With the Original Cast)

Don Francisco de la Guerra, a noble Spaniard. . Bass (Huberdeau)
Barbara, his daughter
              Soprano (Grenville)

Natoma (*Nah-toh'-mah*), an Indian girl . . . . . . Soprano (Garden)
Paul Merrill, Lieutenant of the U. S. Brig "Liberty"
              Tenor (McCormack)
Juan Alvarado, a young Spaniard . . . . Baritone (Sammarco)
José Castro, a half-breed
              Baritone (Preisch)
Father Peralta, Padre of the Mission Church . . . Bass (Dufranne)
Pico; Kagama, Comrades of Castro . . . . (Crabbé) (Nicolay)

American Officers, Nuns, Convent Girls, Friars, Soldiers, Dancers, etc.

Scene and Period: California, under the Spanish régime, 1820

ACT I

Scene—*Hacienda of Don Francisco on the Island of Santa Cruz*

FROM his island home by the blue waters of the Pacific, gazing toward the mountains of California, faintly penciled against a cloudless sky, *Don Francisco* waits for the coming of his

285

daughter, *Barbara*, whose school-days at the convent are over. But there is another watcher with less reputable purpose. Aware that *Barbara* will inherit her mother's vast estates, her cousin, *Alvarado*, hopes to marry her, and he, too, looks forward to her arrival.

This expectancy is shared, if with varied feelings, by the island, for the lovely young girl is very popular. None loves her more, however, than *Natoma*, the Indian girl, within whose veins is to be found the royal blood of distant Aztec ancestors. *Natoma* is deeply in love with *Lieutenant Paul Merrill*, of the U.S. Brig "Liberty," which lies at anchor in the bay. He and she are sitting on a hilltop overlooking the sea, and *Paul* regards with interest an amulet of abalone shell, which *Natoma* wears about her neck. She tells him of its proud history, and then proceeds to tell with loving pride of *Barbara*, whom she loves so dearly. *Paul* is charmed with this beautiful Indian maid, whom he calls his "wildflower."

PHOTO WHITE
McCORMACK AS PAUL

With the arrival of *Barbara*, *Alvarado* at once urges forward his suit. The young girl regards him with disdain, however, for her heart is already given to *Paul*. Her cousin at once plots with *Castro*, a half-caste, to carry *Barbara* off to the mountains the next day, when there is to be a *fiesta* in honor of the girl's coming of age and her accession to the estates. The plot is overheard by *Natoma*. That night, after the guests depart, *Barbara* comes to the porch, where under the blue light of the southern moon she breathes to the stars her love for the young American. *Paul* joins her, and soon his arms are about her. But they are not unobserved, for *Natoma* from her window sees all, and she learns that the man she loves is not for her. Long into the night she battles with herself. A word from her, and the plot to kidnap *Barbara* may be thwarted and *Barbara* saved—for *Paul!* Silence on her part, and her only rival is lightly removed.

ACT II

Scene—*Plaza at Santa Barbara*

IT is dawn. The Spanish soldiers raise the national flag in the Plaza beside the mission Church, while trumpeters and drummers yield it a full salute. Hither creeps *Natoma*, her problem still unsettled. She prays alternately to the Great Spirit of whom *Padre Peralta* has taught her, and to Manitou, the Mighty. Soon the vaqueros and rancheros arrive and the *fiesta* begins. With the arrival of *Don Francisco* and his daughter the ceremonies reach their height. The old nobleman places upon his daughter's head a woof of royal Castilian lace, —a pretty Spanish custom. *Barbara*, full of love and happiness, sings the delightful "Spring Song"—(I List the Trill of Golden Throat).

After this rich melody, with its modern harmonies and delicate orchestration, *Paul* arrives with a company of armed sailors, to do official honor to the representative of the race which is responsible, through Columbus, for the discovery of his own land. The "Panuelo" or "dance of declaration" follows, in which each man places his hat upon the head of the girl he loves. *Alvarado* places his upon *Barbara's*, but she gaily flicks it into the crowd. The Spaniard is infuriated, and the act excites comment. *Castro*, remembering the plan to kidnap *Barbara*, distracts attention by loudly demanding that somebody shall dance with him the fiery dagger dance. He plunges his dagger into the ground and dares any girl to throw another beside it. Suddenly making up her mind, *Natoma* responds, and throwing a similar blade to the earth, she leaps into the ring beside him. They dance, to a wild and barbaric rhythm, the now famous "Dagger Dance."

The crowd watches so intently that nobody but *Natoma* sees *Alvarado*, with an Indian follower to help him, suddenly throw a serape over *Barbara's* head. Snatching one of the daggers, *Natoma* wildly rushes past *Castro* and plunges the knife into the heart of *Alvarado*. Instantly the startled crowd demands her blood, but *Paul*, with his sailors, intervenes. In this crisis the good *Padre* appears, holding a cross on high. At sight of him the people kneel in reverence, and *Natoma*, dropping her weapon, staggers toward the steps of the church and falls at the good man's feet. The right of sanctuary is claimed and implied. Beneath the Father's protection the girl remains trembling as the curtain falls.

ACT III

SCENE—*Interior of the Church*

NATOMA is seen kneeling at the altar, invoking the Great Spirit to yield her vengeance. The old *Priest*, with wonderful penetration, at last finds the "responsive chord" in her heart—her love for *Barbara*. He leaves her kneeling at the altar. A word to an acolyte and the *Priest* dons his vestments; the church slowly fills with people, including *Paul* and *Barbara* in opposite pews. The *Priest* ascends the pulpit, and the air is filled with the chanting of monks and nuns. *Natoma* remains kneeling. Presently the singing stops, and the music of the organ dies down to a pedal-note. The air is tense with expectancy. *Natoma* rises and walks down the aisle. Moved by some strange impulse, *Paul and Barbara* kneel in her path. From her neck, *Natoma* takes the amulet of abalone shell, and places it upon *Barbara*, whom she loves so dearly,— a sign of renunciation. Then with uncertain steps she slowly makes her way toward the convent garden, and the *Priest* raises his hands in benediction as the doors of the cloister shut behind her. Natoma will not leave them again.

THE VICTOR RECORD

SPRING SONG
(I List the Trill of Golden Throat)
ALMA GLUCK, Soprano   6147   12-in., $2.00

NORMA (*proudly*): Then fulfil thy fate, and follow him ! (Act I.)

NORMA

BELLINI'S opera, "Norma", came the year after "La Sonnambula" had won exceptional favor, and it was no less successful. The technique of the work is that of the older Italian Opera School, in which airs and ensemble numbers, based on the simplest harmonic and melodic architecture, are plentiful enough. This does not mean, however, that emotional quality is absent, or even meager; and such numbers as "Casta Diva" or the duet in the final scene are remarkable for their sincerity of emotional expression, notwithstanding their clear simplicity of style. Those who weary of declamatory modern opera, in which the music is constantly changing in agreement with the most swift and subtle moods that emotion throws upon the stage, at the expense of clearly defined melody, will have no quarrel with the simplicity of "Norma."

THE OPERA

OPERA in two acts. Book by Felice Romani, founded on a French tragedy by Soumet, pro-duced at the Théâtre Français, at Paris, about a year before the opera. Score by Vincenzo Bellini. First production December 26, 1831, at Milan. First London production at King's Theatre, in Italian, June 20, 1833. In English at Drury Lane, June 24, 1837. First Paris production, Théâtre des Italiens, 1833. First Vienna production, 1833; in Berlin, 1834. First New York production, February 25, 1841, at the Park Theatre. Produced at the New Orleans Opera, December 31, 1842. Other American productions: September 20, 1843, with Corsini and Perozzi; October 2, 1854, with Grisi, Mario and Susini, at the opening of the Academy of Music; and December 19, 1891, at the Metropolitan, with Lehmann. Recently revived by the Boston Opera Company.

CHARACTERS

NORMA, High Priestess of the Temple of Esus..........Soprano
ADALGISA, a Virgin of the Temple....................Soprano
CLOTILDE, Norma's attendant, Soprano

288

POLLIONE, a Roman proconsul
  commanding the legions of
  Gaul .... Tenor
FLAVIO, his lieutenant .... Tenor
OROVESO, the Arch-Druid,
  father of Norma .... Bass
Priests and Officers of the Temple,
Gallic Warriors, Priestesses and Virgins
of the Temple, two children of Norma
and Pollione

*Scene and Period: The Scene is laid in
Gaul, shortly after the Roman Conquest*

ACT I
SCENE—*Sacred Grove of the Druids*

THE opera has an overture, which
has been recorded. The first scene
is laid beneath the sacred Oak of Irmin-
sul, at the foot of which is a great Dru-
idical stone. It is night, and from behind the distant trees there sparkle the
torches of the Gallic army, which is
coming in procession to this rough altar.
They are followed by a procession of
priests, headed by *Oroveso*, the father of
Norma, the High Priestess. It is their
hope the prophetess *Norma* will bid
them rise against their Roman conqueror, and they plan to reassemble at
the altar within a short time. For the
present they disperse, and *Pollione*
enters cautiously with his lieutenant,
Flavio; these two Romans are enveloped
in their togas. *Pollione,* the secret lover
of *Norma* and the father of her two
children, now confides that he has
ceased to love her, as he longs for another maid, the Virgin Priestess, *Adalgisa,* whom he hopes now to meet.

The sacred Bronze is heard sounding,
and the two men withdraw as the Gauls
return singing a familiar march. *Norma*
appears in solemn state, warning her
followers against war with the Romans,
and dismissing them after the ceremony of cutting the mistletoe. She
then invokes peace in the exquisite
"Casta Diva" (Queen of Heaven).

Pollione tempts *Adalgisa* to fly with

him to Rome, and the distraught girl,
not knowing of his previous romance,
carries her trouble to the High Priestess, *Norma*. *Norma* is disposed, in
memory of her own love, to release the
young priestess from her vows, but
when she asks the name of the lover,
she is confronted with *Pollione*, for
whom she herself has betrayed her gods.

Norma's soul is filled with the desire
of vengeance. Nearly frantic with
rage, she thinks to kill her husband and
children, and expiate upon the funeral
pyre her secret marriage with the natural enemy of her race, for death is the
punishment laid upon any priestess
who dares break her vows of chastity.

ACT II
SCENE—*Interior of Norma's Dwelling*

THE children of *Norma* lie sleeping
on a Roman couch covered with
bearskins. The crazed mother advances
upon them with uplifted dagger; but
the sight of her unsuspecting victims is
too much, and, with a piercing cry, she
falls upon her knees before them. Her
maid *Clotilde* enters, and *Adalgisa* next
is summoned. *Norma* then confides
her children to her rival, vowing that
she will die on the funeral pyre and
permit *Adalgisa* to wed *Pollione*. The
younger girl, deeply affected, pleads
with her not to seek this desperate end,
promising she will persuade *Pollione* to
return to his first love. Her generous
impulse is nobly expressed in an air
familiar to all opera-goers, the "Mira O
Norma" (Hear Me, Norma).

The effort is futile. *Pollione* refuses
to return to *Norma* and against her will
he attempts to seize *Adalgisa*. The
now infuriated *Norma* summons her
followers, to rouse them to battle with
the Romans. No sooner are the men
assembled than *Pollione* is discovered
in their midst, a spy. *Norma* claims
the right to kill him, and advances
against him with blade uplifted. She

has not the strength, however, to take away the life of the man she continues to love, and, declaring she wishes to question the prisoner, she bids the guards depart. She then tries to persuade him to give up his guilty love for *Adalgisa*, death being the alternative. This leads to the duet, "In mia mano" (In My Grasp).

As *Pollione* continues to refuse, *Norma* strikes the sacred shield, and again summons her hosts. Before them she confesses a priestess has violated her vows of chastity and that she must suffer death. *Pollione* believes she is about to denounce *Adalgisa*. But *Norma* now is bent upon confession for herself, and to the astounded gathering, of whom her own father, *Oroveso*, is one, she reveals her own fault and claims purification by death upon the sacrificial pyre. Moved by her devotion, *Pollione* finds his love returning, and begs leave to share the flames. The wish is granted. *Norma* confides the two children to her father's care, and the lovers, reunited, go out to meet their death as the curtain falls.

BLACK LABEL RECORDS

{Mira o Norma (Hear Me Norma)............*Francis Lapitino, Harpist*}	17929	10-in.,	$0.75
{ Lucia—Prelude............*Francis Lapitino, Harpist*}			
{Overture............*Arthur Pryor's Band*}	35166	12-in.,	1.25
{ Oberon Overture (*Weber*)............*Arthur Pryor's Band*}			

NORMA: Now, for your judgment, a new victim is offered—I am guilty! (Act II, Scene III.)

THE ENCHANTED FOREST—ACT I

OBERON

OR THE ELF-KING'S OATH

WEBER'S peculiar gift was to interpret, through the opera, the romance and beauty of the Fairyland myths with which German literature is so enriched. In "Oberon" he is especially successful, and especially in this opera's Overture. From the opening horn-call, answered by the fairy-like tripping measure of the wood-wind, to the very end, which refers to the famous air in the opera, "Ocean, Thou Mighty Monster," we are transported to the never-never land of magical beauty which the most sophisticated among us longs for in secret. Weber took us there by melodies, harmonies and orchestral effects absolutely new in style at the time he wrote them. His pioneer-work, in this direction, has affected all the leading German composers; without it Mendelssohn would never have given us the "Midsummer Night's Dream Overture" in its present form. Wagner, especially, was indebted to Weber, and in his great works, based on myths and legends, he is the earlier composer's natural successor. To anyone with a musically historical sense, the importance and beauty of Weber's works cannot be exaggerated, and it has been well said that "the historian of German music in the 19th century will have to make Weber his starting-point."

THE OPERA

ROMANTIC fairy opera in three acts. Text by James Robinson Planché; music by Carl Maria von Weber. First produced at Covent Garden, London, April 12, 1826, in English, under the personal direction of the composer. Translated into German by Theodor Hell, and given in Leipsic, December, 1826; Vienna, March 20, 1827; Berlin July 2, 1828. First Paris production in German, in 1830, was a comparative failure. Revived at the Théâtre Lyrique, translation by Nuitter, Beaumont and Chazot, with success, February 27, 1857. Revived in London, December

7, 1878. First American production, New York, October 9, 1827. Revived at the Academy of Music, March 29, 1870, in English, with Parepa-Rosa and Mrs. Seguin. The opera was first sung in Italian at Her Majesty's, London, July 3, 1860, with recitatives by Benedict, and this version was given in Philadelphia in 1870. Revived in New York in 1912 and 1918.

THE opera opens in Fairyland, where elves are dancing about the form of the sleeping *Oberon*, their King. *Oberon* has quarreled with his Queen, *Titania*, who vows never to be reconciled with him until he shall have found two mortal lovers who remain constant through trial and temptation. *Oberon's* "tricky spirit," *Puck*, believes he has met with such a pair in *Sir Huon de Bordeaux* and *Rezia*, daughter of *Haroun* of Bagdad.

Sir Huon has killed the son of Charlemagne, and he has been condemned to travel to Bagdad to slay the person who sits at *Haroun's* left hand, and claim *Rezia* as his wife. Having been permitted by *Oberon* to see *Rezia* in a vision, *Sir Huon* at once falls in love with her. He is presented with a magic horn, which, when sounded, will bring the forces of Fairyland to his aid; thus armed, he sets upon his difficult mission. *Sir Huon* is transported to Bagdad accomplishing his purpose and carrying off *Rezia*. But trials await the lovers. They are tossed about in a storm raised by *Oberon* and then shipwrecked upon a desert island. *Rezia* is abducted by pirates and sold to the *Emir of Tunis*, while *Sir Huon*, believing her dead, is left on the beach. He is transported by good fairies, however, to Tunis, where he enters the very harem in search of *Rezia*. The two are captured, and sentenced to be burned alive. In this desperate crisis *Huon* sounds the fairy horn and *Oberon*, with *Titania*, comes to his rescue. The *King of the Fairies* transports them to the court of Charlemagne, where *Huon* is pardoned. *Titania*, recognizing the devotion of *Sir Huon* and *Rezia*, forgives *Oberon*. All ends happily.

THE VICTOR RECORD

OVERTURE—Parts I and II

Mengelberg and New York Philharmonic
Orchestra   6224   12-in., $2.00

BLACK LABEL RECORD

Oberon Overture......................................*Pryor's Band*	35166	12-in., $1.25
Norma Overture (Bellini)..............................*Pryor's Band*		

LANDE   ELYSIUM—ACT II

ORPHEUS AND EURYDICE

THOUGH produced in Vienna, before Gluck's memorable pilgrimage to Paris as the prophet of a new order of opera, "Orpheus and Eurydice" was a forerunner of the ideals which culminated in "Iphigenie." "Orpheus" was composed among a group of ballets and similar works written for the lively court of Vienna. "Orpheus", however, contains so many lovely airs that it was a truer success, winning for its composer an annuity of 6,000 francs from Marie Antoinette, Dauphiness of France—a former pupil of his and his most powerful supporter in Paris.

THE OPERA

OPERA in four acts. Book by Ramieri De Calzabigi; music by Gluck. First production in Vienna October 5, 1762, Gluck conducting. First Paris production, 1774, when the rôle of *Orpheus* was transposed for high tenor. Revived at Paris 1859, when Pauline Viardot restored the Italian contralto version. First London production, Covent Garden, 1860. Some notable revivals were during the Winter Garden season of 1863; in 1885 (in German), by the Metropolitan Opera; the English production in 1886 by the National Opera Company; the Abbey revival in Italian in 1892; and the Gatti-Casazza production of 1910, with Homer, Gadski and Gluck.

CHARACTERS

ORPHEUS (*Or-fay-us*)......Contralto
EURYDICE (*U-ree-dee'-chay*)...Soprano
LOVE....................Soprano
A HAPPY SHADE.............Soprano
Shepherds and Shepherdesses, Furies and Demons, Heroes, etc. ·

THE story concerns the Greek poet *Orpheus*, who grieves so deeply over the death of his wife *Eurydice* that he finally declares he will enter the realms of *Pluto* and search for her among the spirits of the departed. The god of *Love* appears and promises to aid him, on condition that when he has found *Eurydice* he will return to earth without once looking at her.

The music accompanying this scene is exquisite and the most familiar part of it is the beautiful melody to be found

293

in the "Ballet Music" on Victor Records. In the orchestral number there is a flute solo of the most profound pathos.

Orpheus now journeys to the Gates of Erebus, where he so softens the hearts of the Demon guards by his grief and by the exquisite playing of his lyre, that he is permitted to enter. He finds *Eurydice* and, without looking at her, takes her by the hand and bids her follow. She obeys, but, failing to understand his averted gaze, upbraids him for his apparent coldness and asks that he shall look at her.

Orpheus, knowing that to cast a single look at his loved one means death, at first keeps his face averted, but finally, unable to endure longer the reproaches of his wife, he clasps her in his arms, only to see her sink down lifeless. This scene includes the great "Che faro senza Euridice" (I Have Lost My Eurydice).

"What have I done! Into what gulf has my fatal love cast me?" cries the hapless youth, and breaks into his lovely and pathetic lamentation. Of the many beautiful numbers in Gluck's drama this lovely aria of mourning is the most familiar. *Orpheus* is about to kill himself when *Love* appears. *Eurydice* is miraculously restored. The spirit of the beautiful old tale is violated, but the work reaches a happy end.

THE VICTOR RECORDS

MELODIE
(From "Ballet Music") MAUD POWELL, Violin   807   10-in., $1.50
MISCHA ELMAN, Violin   6090 12-in., 2.00

DANCE OF THE SPIRITS
("Ballet Music") PHILADELPHIA ORCHESTRA   6238 12-in., 2.00

CHE FARO SENZA EURIDICE
(I Have Lost My Eurydice) LOUISE HOMER, Contralto *In Italian*   6165 12-in., 2.00

ORPHEUS:
I have lost my Eurydice
My misfortune is without its like.
Cruel fate! I shall die of my sorrow.
Eurydice, Eurydice, answer me!
It is your faithful husband.
Hear my voice, which calls you.
Silence of death! vain hope!
What suffering, what torment, wrings my heart!

HOMER AND GADSKI AS ORPHEUS AND EURYDICE

OTHELLO AND DESDEMONA

OTHELLO

SIXTEEN years after "Aida" had seemed to be the crowning glory of Verdi's long musical career, the great composer astonished the musical world with "Othello." At the age of seventy-four he showed, past all doubt, that the fierce creative spirit which burned within him was not only alive, but, if anything, brighter than ever. In that sixteen-year interval Verdi had kept close touch with the development of modern music. "Othello," therefore, is essentially modern in spirit and technique. The characterization is marvellous, there are no set airs and ensembles, the scenes fusing into each other without a break. Its power and almost youthful energy, set upon a lifetime of practical musical and dramatic experience, give the work a unique place in music. Verdi, greatly daring, measured skill with Shakespeare himself, and he accomplished a success the Elizabethan dramatist would have been the first to applaud.

Six years later—when Verdi was in his eightieth year—this incredible composer produced another great Shakespearian work in "Falstaff," triumphantly bringing forth the most difficult of all musical composition—inspired comedy. Almost any gifted composer may, with a few gloomy chords, achieve the semblance of tragedy, but comedy, utterly devoid of burlesque, and of Shakespearian breadth and humanity, is quite another matter. The heart somehow goes out to this intrepid old soul, bidding good-bye to a world in which he had had his full share of triumph and failure, with the strong laughter of "Falstaff" as his Requiem.

THE OPERA

OPERA in four acts. Text by Arrigo Boïto. Music by Verdi. First production February 5, 1887, at La Scala, Milan, with Tamagno. First London production May 18, 1889; in English 1893. First American production April 16, 1888, with Campanini as *Othello*. Notable revivals occurred in 1894, with Tamagno and Maurel; in 1902, with Eames, Alvarez and Scotti; in 1908 at the Manhattan, with Melba, Zenatello and Sammarco; and in 1910 at the Metropolitan Opera.

CHARACTERS

OTHELLO, a Moor, general in the Venetian army (*Oh-tel-loh*)...Tenor
IAGO (*Ee-ah'-goh*), his ensign..Baritone
CASSIO (*Cass'-ee-oh*), his lieutenant
    Tenor
RODERIGO (*Roh-der-ee'-goh*), a Venetian gentleman..............Tenor
LODOVICO (*Loh-doh-vee'-koh*), ambassador of the Venetian Republic. Bass
MONTANO, predecessor of Othello in the government of Cyprus.....Bass
DESDEMONA, wife of Othello..Soprano
EMILIA (*Ay-mee'-lee-ah*), wife of Iago
    Mezzo-Soprano
Soldiers and Sailors, Venetians, Cyprians, an Innkeeper

Scene and Period: End of the Fifteenth Century; a Seaport in Cyprus

ACT I

SCENE—*Othello's Castle in Cyprus*

A STORM rages and the angry sea is visible in the background. A number of Venetians and soldiers watch the vessel bearing the victorious *Othello* as it struggles in the storm. They include *Cassio*, *Othello's* lieutenant, the villainous *Iago*, and his co-conspirator, *Roderigo*. *Iago* privately expresses the hope that the landing will never be made. But he is doomed to disappointment, for the Moor, *Othello*, is brought ashore in a small boat, and he announces a complete victory over the Turkish fleet, which has been sunk. *Othello* enters his castle, to greet there his beloved wife, *Desdemona*.

The soldiers begin drinking. *Iago*, bent on his plan to regain the power which has fallen to *Othello*, induces *Roderigo* (who desires *Desdemona*) to help in plying *Cassio* with wine. *Cassio* at first refuses, knowing his own particular weakness; but when *Iago* toasts *Desdemona*, he is obliged to respond. He soon is hopelessly befuddled, *Iago* helping on the process at the Brindisi, "Inaffia l'uoglia" (Drinking Song).

In this vigorous yet subtle air, the shrewd cunning of *Iago* is remarkably portrayed. *Cassio* becomes hilarious, finally quarrelsome. *Iago* who has watched every phase of the process with feline cunning, now forces him, adroitly enough, to pick a quarrel with *Montano*. Swords are drawn, *Montano* is wounded, and *Iago* fans the disturbance into a small riot. This is put down by the appearance of *Othello* himself, enraged that the sleep of *Desdemona* should be disturbed by the troops. The Moor deprives *Cassio* of his command, exactly as *Iago* has foreseen. It is the first step toward the downfall of *Othello*.

ACT II

SCENE—*A Room in the Castle*

IAGO plays subtler still upon foolish *Cassio*. He advises him to beg *Desdemona* to intercede with *Othello* to give him back his command. *Cassio* goes in search of her, and, well satisfied with his work, *Iago*, gazes after him. He then sings his superb "Credo" (Iago's Creed).

This is a free adaptation of *Iago's*

last speech with *Cassio* in Shakespeare. Verdi has, with remarkable skill, made his music reflect the vain and cynical character of *Iago*. *Iago* affirms his faith in a cruel God who intended him for evil, and he declares his belief that life ends with death.

As soon as *Iago* sees *Cassio* in conversation with *Desdemona*, he seeks out *Othello* and sows in the heart of the Moor the first seed of jealousy, when he bids him watch his wife. The Moor, much troubled, finds *Desdemona* and questions her. As she at once begins to plead *Cassio's* cause, his suspicions are more fully awakened; and when she

LANDE
THE MURDER OF DESDEMONA (ALDA AND SLEZAK)

seeks to wipe his perspiring brow with a handkerchief that was his own first gift, he tears it from her. It is picked up by *Emilia*, *Desdemona's* maid and *Iago's* wife. While *Othello* roughly berates his alarmed *Desdemona*, *Iago* forces *Emilia* to give him the kerchief.

After the scene with *Desdemona*, *Othello* grows more jealous and suspicious than ever. He lets this be known in a bitter soliloquy, the "Ora e per sempre addio" (And Now, For-

ever Farewell)—farewell to peace of mind, to ambition, to the glory of conquest and to the love of *Desdemona*. He cannot but believe his wife guilty.

Iago now appears to pour fuel on the flame of jealousy by avowing that he has seen *Desdemona's* handkerchief in *Cassio's* home. He also declares he has heard the sleeping *Cassio* speak of her in his dreams. *Othello* becomes frantic with rage, and the act closes with the great scene in which *Iago* offers to help him to vengeance. They swear an oath never to pause until the guilty shall be punished. This is the "Si pel ciel" (We Swear by Heaven and Earth). It is a bit of tragedy.

ACT III

SCENE—*The Great Hall of the Castle*

THE arrival of a galley bearing the Venetian ambassador, *Lodovico*, is announced to *Othello*; but he has no interest in anything now but his own insane jealousy. He seeks his wife, and he contrives an excuse to borrow the handkerchief. She evades him, sadly puzzled both to account for its loss and to comprehend the suspicious attitude of the sullen husband she adores. After she has gone, *Cassio* enters, bent only upon forgiveness through the kindness of *Desdemona*. Bidding *Othello* hide behind a pillar, *Iago* contrives with devilish ingenuity to keep up a half audible conversation with the demoted officer, taking care that the remarks overheard by *Othello* shall be of a kind to inflame the Moor's suspicions. *Cassio* also, in all innocence, produces the fatal handkerchief, saying he has found it in his room. Aside, to *Othello*, *Iago* jokes over it. *Cassio*, too, laughs. After this, *Othello* goes mad with rage. He asks *Iago* to procure him poison wherewith to kill *Desdemona*, swearing he will himself attend to *Cassio*. *Iago*, not wishing to be involved, suggests that she had better be strangled in the bed she has dishonored, and *Othello* grimly accepts the task.

The Venetian ambassador, *Lodovico*, arrives in great pomp, informing *Othello* that he has been called to greater honors in Venice, while *Cassio* is appointed Governor of Cyprus in his stead. *Desdemona* also is present, but every remark brings a rebuke from *Othello* which does not escape the wondering attention of *Lodovico*. *Othello* announces his departure on the morrow, but unable to contain his smouldering anger, he publicly insults *Desdemona* and flings her to the ground. Overcome with his feverish emotion, he, too, falls to earth in a fit. Meantime, the public outside, hearing that greater honors have fallen to their hero, rush in shouting "Hail to Othello!" But *Iago*, standing erect, points with horrible triumph to the prostrate Moor, and cries, "Behold your Lion of Venice!"

ACT IV

Scene—*Desdemona's Bedroom*

ATTENDED by *Emilia*, the heartbroken *Desdemona* prepares to retire. She tells the wondering woman of an old, sad song of her childhood, the song of a maiden who waited in vain for the return of her lover, and she sings the pathetically beautiful "Salce, Salce" (Willow Song).

Too little known to the general public, this number is really a little masterpiece, not too deep but always simple and obvious. Its tuneful phrases, though they come haltingly, are exquisitely beautiful, perfectly expressing the sadness of despair which is deepening in the soul of *Desdemona*.

The faithful *Emilia* leaves her mistress, who kneels before the image of the Madonna, and sings yet another air, the "Ave Maria" (Hail, Mary).

Scarcely has this wonderful melody, in its turn, died away, than the final scene commences. *Othello* enters. Finding his wife asleep, he stands for a moment brooding over her couch. She wakes, and he again charges her with intriguing with *Cassio*. Denial is useless. When *Desdemona* bids him bring *Cassio* himself in witness, *Othello* declares the man's tongue has been silenced forever. Overcome with horror the unhappy woman cries out for aid as *Othello* takes her by the throat. *Emilia* hears and knocks at the door. She is admitted, but too late. In reply to her shrieks, the people rush in, *Iago* among them. *Othello* then denounces the woman he has killed. Others demur and he exhibits the handkerchief in proof, but *Emilia* tells how this murderous emblem of false evidence was taken from her by *Iago*, and *Othello* thus learns of his false friend's duplicity. The Moor is torn with remorse. Gazing at the body of *Desdemona*, now lovely in death, he sings his last air, the "Morte d'Otello" (Death of Othello).

Unseen by the mystified watchers, *Othello* takes from his girdle a hidden dagger. He stabs himself, then with a last effort, strives to embrace the woman he has so cruelly wronged. But death comes, and the miseries of *Othello* are done.

THE VICTOR RECORDS
(Sung in Italian)

ACT I

BRINDISI—INAFFIA L'UGOLA
(Drinking Song) Antonio Scotti,
Baritone   6283 12-in., $2.00

ACT II

CREDO
(Iago's Creed) Pasquale Amato,
Baritone   6042 12-in., 2.00
Titta Ruffo, Baritone 6267 12-in., 2.00
Titta Ruffo, Baritone 8045 12-in., 2.50

ORA E PER SEMPRE ADDIO
(And Now, Forever Farewell) Enrico
Caruso, Tenor   505 10-in., 1.50

ERA LA NOTTE
(Cassio's Dream) TITTA RUFFO, Baritone   6267 12-in., $2.00

SI PEL CIEL
(We Swear by Heaven and Earth)
ENRICO CARUSO, Tenor, and TITTA
RUFFO, Baritone   8045 12-in., 2.50

BLACK LABEL RECORD

{Fantasia (Brindisi—Morte d'Otello)................*Vessella's Italian Band*}35459 12-in., $1.25
{ *Gioconda—Prelude (Ponchielli)*.................*Vessella's Italian Band*}

COPY'T MISHKIN
SCOTTI AS IAGO

LE THEATRE　　　　ARRIVAL OF THE PLAYERS—ACT I

PAGLIACCI

(PAILLASSE)
(*French*)

(THE PLAYERS)
(*English*)

PAGLIACCI was one of the operas submitted in the same operatic prize contest won by Mascagni's "Cavalleria Rusticana." It was disqualified, it is said, because it was in two acts instead of the required one. Nevertheless, the publisher Sonzogno recognized its possibilities and produced it at a time when the success of Mascagni's work had created a demand for brief operatic works of a direct and passionate nature. Its success has been overwhelming, and it is usually presented in conjunction with Mascagni's masterpiece to make up an evening's entertainment, the two works having an underlying kinship with each other from the similarity of the root idea in both works—the vengeance of a jealous husband.

"Pagliacci" was composed, one might say, in a fit of temper. Leoncavallo, who had had good music training at the Conservatory of Naples, had rather a hard time in the world. An early opera failed production because the impresario ran away with the funds and left Leoncavallo in poverty. He managed to exist by teaching and by playing in cafés, but he arose out of this drudgery as a concert pianist. While touring over Europe, he outlined a vast trilogy which was to do for Italian music what Wagner's "Ring" had accomplished for German. The outline was accepted by a publisher and Leoncavallo completed the score of the first of the three dramas in a year. No production followed, however, and the composer waited for three years. It was while enraged at this treatment that he wrote "Pagliacci" for the rival publisher's contest, impetuously completing the whole work, libretto and all, in five months. With the success of "Pagliacci" the way was open for his trilogy, but the first opera failed, and he never completed the other two parts. So long as Leoncavallo lived there was always hope that he might produce another such masterpiece as "Pagliacci" but the divine fire that had flamed in his blood when he wrote this work afterwards seemed to flicker and burn low. His subsequent works, such as "Chatterton" (1896),"Bohême" (1897),"Zaza" (1900) and "Roland" (written at the invitation of Kaiser Wilhelm to celebrate the Hohenzollerns, 1904) came into varied success, but it is doubtful if even the recently-revived "Zaza" possessed the compelling force of "Pagliacci."

Leoncavallo, the son of the Chevalier Vincont, an Italian magistrate, was born at Naples, 1858, and died in 1919. He combined literary gifts with his musical abilities, not only writing his own libretti but even, like Boïto, occasionally fulfilling that office for others. The "play within a play" which gives "Pagliacci" its peculiarly ironic quality, is not new, and, as a dramatic idea, is at least as old as Shakespeare's "Hamlet." Other plays similar to "Pagliacci" in theme have also appeared, one by Catulle Mendes, entitled "La Femme du Tabarin," being so much like it that the author attempted to enjoin the performance of "Pagliacci" at Brussels on the ground that Leoncavallo had stolen his plot. The Italian composer, however, had no difficulty in proving that many French and Spanish dramas existed along similar lines, and he claimed also that "Pagliacci" was based on an actual incident of Italian village life which came to his father's official notice while serving as magistrate.

Musically speaking, Leoncavallo had a very pretty talent for striking but brief melodies, treating them with the resources of modern harmony and instrumentation, one of his principal resources being a trick of startling modulation or change of keys. This is an admirable expedient in a brief work like "Pagliacci," but as other composers, including Edvard Grieg, have proven, repeating the same tune in a new and unexpected key is not the same thing as genuine thematic development in which a melodic germ undergoes a great number of symphonic evolutions in the style Wagner used so effectively. Hence the failure of Leoncavallo to achieve the sustained interest necessary for long works, and the breakdown of his ambitious but futile dream of rivalling Wagner.

THE OPERA

DRAMATIC opera in two acts; libretto and music by Ruggiero Leoncavallo. First performed at the Teatro dal Verme, Milan, on May 21, 1892; in Vienna, September 17, 1892; in London, May 19, 1893; Dresden, January 23, 1893; Paris, in French December 17, 1902. First New York production June 15, 1894, with Kronold, Montegriffo and Campanari. Some famous casts of recent years at the Metropolitan and the Manhattan opera: Caruso, Farrar, Stracciari—Alvarez, Scheff, Scotti—Farrar, Bars, Scotti—Cavalieri, Rousseliere, Scotti—Deveyne, Martin, Campanari, etc.

CHARACTERS

CANIO (*Kah'-nee-oh*) (in the play "*Pagliaccio*" [*Punchinello*]), master of the troupe.........Tenor
NEDDA (*Ned'-dah*) (in the play "*Columbine*"), his wife.....Soprano
TONIO (*Toh'-nee-oh*) (in the play "*Taddeo*"), the clown......Baritone
PEPPE (*Pep'-pay*) (in the play "*Harlequin*").............Tenor
SILVIO (*Sil'-vee-oh*), a villager..Baritone
Villagers and Peasants.

The Scene is laid in Calabria, near Montalto, on the Feast of the Assumption.

(The Italian name of the opera is "Pagliacci," *Pahl-yat'-chee*; the French name is "Paillasse," *Pah-yass*).

THE plot of "Pagliacci" owes much dynamic force to its simplicity of construction. *Canio*, head of a group of traveling players in Italy, discovers his wife, *Nedda*, in the arms of *Silvio*, planning an elopement for that night, *Nedda* having been betrayed by the clownish hunchback *Tonio*, himself a base admirer of *Nedda*, who has scorned him. *Canio*, however, fails to recognize *Silvio*, or to force his wife to betray his identity. That night, by chance, the players give a play based on the very same situation, *Canio* playing the rôle of a jealous husband, who taxes his wife (in the rôle assumed by *Nedda*) with her perfidy, and demands the name of the other man. She happens to repeat in the play the phrase he has overheard her speak to her lover of the morning, and this so enrages *Canio* that he stabs her in the hope she may cry out the name of her lover. The dying girl calls for *Silvio*, who leaps to her defense from his seat in the audience. The jealous husband, however, slays him with the same knife that killed *Nedda*, yielding himself to justice with the bitterly ironic comment, "The comedy is finished." This classic phrase, of course, is Dante's, and is also said to have been almost the last speech of Beethoven ("*Plaudite, amici, comedia finita est!*").

THE PROLOGUE

LEONCAVALLO adopted an old theatrical custom, dating back to Greek drama,—that of having a "prologue," one of the characters, step forward before the curtain and remind the audience that the players are of like flesh and blood with themselves, sharing their joys and sorrows, their angers and jealousies, their love and laughter. It is a charming touch when *Tonio* steps from between the curtains to sing his dramatic introduction, worked into the orchestral prelude, the familiar "Prologo" (Prologue).

The first, or orchestral, part of the Prologue is in itself a miniature overture, containing the three themes most associated with the primary events of the drama: The first is the motive which always accompanies the appearance of the players, or *pagliacci:*

FARRAR AS NEDDA

GLUCK AS NEDDA

CARUSO SINGING
"VESTI LA GIUBBA"

302

The second theme represents *Canio's* jealousy, a sombre strain suggesting revenge:

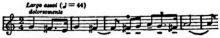

The third represents the guilty love of *Nedda* and *Silvio:*

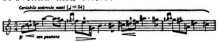

This theme frequently appears throughout the drama, not only in the love-duet but in the last act when *Nedda*, even at the point of death, refuses to betray her lover.

The statement of these themes is followed by the appearance of *Tonio*, who in the traditional clown's costume now peeps through the curtains. He pleads for a hearing, and speaks of the author's inspiration.

The beautiful *andante* which follows this, a melody in broad, sweeping style, is the most admired portion of the aria, and it is indeed a noble strain.

The curtain now lifts and the orchestra resumes the *Pagliacci* theme.

ACT I

SCENE—*The Entrance of a Village, where two Roads meet.*

THE Italian sun smiles on a small village of Calabria, where the people, determined to make the most of the Feast of the Assumption, are in holiday attire. They yield a special welcome to the troupe of players, headed by *Canio*, which comes down the road, with its little tent, in a donkey-cart. At the back of the cart is *Nedda* in the gay costume of a Columbine; her husband. *Canio*, wears the familiar Pierrot costume of Punchinello. The crowd sings its welcome to the merrymakers in a lively chorus: Opening Chorus —"Son qua!" (They're Here!).

The brisk rhythm and the changes of key in this brilliant number are quite familiar. We need but to quote the opening phrase:

The little troupe comes to a halt, and the noise redoubles. *Canio* is given a particular welcome as he bows acknowledgment from the top of the cart, while *Peppe*, the Harlequin, and *Tonio*, the misshapen clown, make hideous music with a cracked trumpet and a bass drum. *Canio* announces the performance will be at seven that evening, and turns away to assist his wife from the cart. *Tonio*, the clown, however, is before him, and the crowd laughs heartily at his maneuver. This does not please the jealous *Canio*, who, under the semblance of jest, gives the fool a heavy blow. The crowd rocks with laughter as *Tonio* slinks off, vowing vengeance. Fine sport, this! think the laughing villagers.

Canio and *Peppe* go off with one of the peasants for a friendly glass, and the leader of the troupe calls *Tonio* to go with them. But the clown declares he must rub down the donkey. A villager remarks:

> Careful, Pagliaccio!
> He only stays behind thee
> For making love to Nedda!

Canio makes a wry smile, but his temper is going, and he shouts back a caution to the jesters: "The stage and life—they are different!" *Nedda*, with her guilty conscience, understands only too well the black looks of her husband. "What does he mean?" she asks. The villagers, too, are somewhat puzzled and they ask if he is serious. With an effort, however, he rouses himself, saying lightly, "Not I—I love my wife most dearly," kissing her on the forehead.

From the distance is heard the

wailing of bagpipes (the oboe), and *Canio* leaves to join in the merrymaking. Then follows the famous "Coro della campane" (Chorus of the Bells), sometimes called the "Ding Dong Chorus," because of the chiming bells which mingle with it so effectively. The measure dies away as the people wander off to the village.

Left alone, *Nedda* falls to brooding over *Canio's* jealous temper, wondering if the man really suspects her. She shakes off her gloom, however, and gradually waking to the brightness of the afternoon and the joyfulness of the holiday spirit, she sings her delightful ballatella, "Che vol d'augelli!" (Ye Birds Without Number!). It is notable for a tremolo in the strings, the piping of birds and rustling of soft leaves in musical onomatopœia. *Nedda* sings, though, of her mother, who was skilled in interpreting bird-songs and the sounds of nature.

The number is really a sort of modernized coloratura song, set against an exquisite orchestral accompaniment. It serves to make us better acquainted with *Nedda*, and to understand better, too, the jealousy of *Canio* and the love of *Silvio*, to say nothing of the groundling passion of *Tonio*, who now injects himself into the scene. He begins his lovemaking in a fashion that would justify any woman's scorn. The scene includes the "So ben che deforme" (I Know That You Hate Me).

The more *Tonio* persists, the louder his inamorata's laughter. At last, driven to madness by her beauty, *Tonio* seizes *Nedda* and fights to kiss her. She leaps away, striking him across the face with her whip.

No sooner has *Tonio* gone, than a new and more welcome lover approaches by a secret path, lightly vaulting over the wall and greeting her with a laugh. It is *Silvio*, one of the villagers, whom *Nedda* has met before on previous visits and found much to her liking. She is alarmed at the sight of *Silvio*, but he reassures her by telling how he has left *Canio* with *Peppe* at the tavern, where they are drinking, and likely to remain.

Nedda tells *Silvio* of the clown's threats, bidding him be cautious; but the young villager laughs at her fears, and consoles her after the manner of lovers the world over. He asks her to fly with him, and the pair sing an impassioned duet, the "De toi depend mon sort" (My Fate is in Thy Hands). *Nedda* remains fearful, however, and she is so charming when she implores him not to tempt her, that he only grows worse. He reproaches the young woman for her coldness, until at last, throwing discretion to the winds, she yields herself to the bliss of the moment and consents to go. The music leads into the "Pourquoi ces yeux" (Why Those Eyes).

It leads to its climax in another lovely number, the music of which is based on the melody first heard in the orchestral Prelude. This is the "Nulla scordai!" (Naught I Forget!).

At this climactic moment the lovers are far too absorbed to remark the approach of *Canio*, who has been warned by the too-observant clown. He now rushes forward, having heard *Nedda's* parting words. He has not, however, seen *Silvio's* face, and when the lover makes a swift flight over the wall, *Nedda* bars the way. *Canio* thrusts her aside in fierce anger, and leaps over the wall in pursuit. He is too late, for *Silvio* knows a path hidden by the brush, and *Canio* cannot find it. *Tonio* laughs in glee, and *Nedda* rewards him with a scornful "Bravo! Bravo! Well done, *Tonio!*" The clown promises to do better next time. *Canio* returns, out of breath, exhausted, but maddened with anger. From the orchestra we hear the ominous motive of vengeance and jealousy, the "Ride, Pagliaccio!":

The outraged husband commands his wife to pronounce the name of her lover, but she proudly refuses. Clean beside himself, *Canio* rushes upon her with upraised knife, but he is withheld by the others. "Restrain yourself," cries *Peppe*, playing for time, "the fellow will come back!" He warns them it is time to dress, *Nedda*, glad of an excuse, disappears in the dressing tent, while *Peppe* and *Tonio* also go on about their business. *Canio* is left thinking, and the stage, for the time, is his alone.

With bowed head, worn out by passion and jealousy, *Canio* remains to consider his betrayal, fanning, moment by moment, the fires of vengeance now at work in his soul.

The act closes with the "Vesti la giubba" (On With the Play).

ACT II

Scene—*Same as Act I*

WE have an odd situation. *Nedda* is loved by *Canio*, who as her husband has a right to love her; by *Silvio*, who has no right to love her but does so anyhow; and by *Tonio*, the clown, whose love is something less than love. And now we are to behold the situation closely paralleled in the play set forth before the peasants.

When the curtain lifts, we find the audience assembling, *Tonio* beating a big drum at the entrance, and drowning the chatter of the men and women from the village. *Silvio* arrives, to feast his eyes on *Nedda*, greeting his

CANIO SURPRISES THE LOVERS—ACT II

friends as he takes his place near the footlights. The orchestra sympathetically reflects the bustle of the occasion in a merry tripping measure:

Soon the play begins. On the little stage, *Nedda* appears as Columbine. She rises and looks out of the window, announcing that her husband will be late this evening. From beneath the window comes the sound of a guitar, cleverly imitated by the violins, *pizzicato*, and we hear the voice of Harlequin (the *Silvio* of the play interpreted by *Peppe*) in the extravagant "Serenata d'Arlecchino" (Harlequin's Serenade). Before Harlequin can enter, however, Taddeo enters (the clownish rôle of Taddeo being rightly enacted by *Tonio*) bearing a basket. He sings a pompous greeting, which brings a roar from the assembled villagers: "E dessa!" (Behold Her!).

Columbine's reply is to demand the chicken he had been sent for, and *Tonio* kneels before her, holding up the fowl in grotesque devotion.

His buffoonery is cut short by Harlequin, who enters and leads him out by the ear—to the high delight of the village audience. In departing, the clown leaves the lovers a mock benediction: "Versa il filtra nella tazza sua!" (Pour the Potion in His Wine) advises he.

With the clown banished the "lovers" now make merry. Harlequin gives his Columbine a little vial, saying:

Take this little sleeping-draught,
'Tis for Pagliaccio!
Give it him at bedtime,
And then we'll fly!

Columbine assents, but suddenly the clown reappears, bawling out in mock alarm:

Be careful! Pagliaccio is here!
Trembling all over, he seeks for weapons!
He has caught you, and I shall fly to cover!

The lovers simulate the greatest alarm, the spectators applauding lustily. Harlequin leaps from the window, and Columbine continues the scene by repeating the lines which, by a strange coincidence, are the very words she has spoken to *Silvio* earlier in the day, overheard by her husband:

This is almost too much for *Canio*, who swears, forgetting for a moment his rôle of Punchinello as he enters upon the scene. In the lines of the play, he charges her with having had a man with her; but she insists that it was only Taddeo, the clown, who, concealed in a closet, cries out "Believe her, sir, she is faithful!" Punchinello forgets his part for a moment and becomes *Canio*: "Ah, they could never lie, those lips . . . . !"

The audience applauds enthusiastically, for the unhappy man touches realism, condemned, as he is, to play a rôle in public all-too-like that decreed for him by the real events of the afternoon. Forgetting his part, he turns fiercely on the woman, demanding her lover's name. *Nedda*, still as Columbine, protests, but in alarm cries, "Pagliaccio! Pagliaccio!" This reminder of his actor's rôle only maddens the jealous actor, and he finally throws off all disguise, becoming now the jealous husband: "No, Pagliaccio non son!" (No, Punchinello No More!) cries he.

The audience applauds heartily, still unaware that anything more than comedy is going on before them. For a moment *Canio* recovers himself, but not for long. He is no longer an actor but a man quite probably honest and sincere, if only in hate, whose feelings have been outraged. His passion yields to a softer strain when he speaks of his love for *Nedda*, his faithfulness and sacrifice for her sake. Then comes the finale to the opera.

The audience, not knowing that this has no part in the play, cries "Bravo!" Some of the women begin to weep in sympathy. *Nedda* is by this time white with fear, but she courageously faces her husband, striving with all her power to continue the play. *Canio's* appearance now is alarming.

As she sings we hear the love motive in the orchestra, triumphantly sounding above her voice:

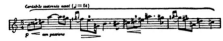

This theme, heard at such a moment, is reminder enough that the thought of *Silvio* is in her heart, and that fears and all, she will keep faithful unto death.

Canio suddenly hits upon the idea that if he could but stab his wife, she might call out the name of her lover. He springs at her, knife in hand. *Peppe* and *Tonio* rush forward to restrain him, and the audience crowds to help. The shrieking women, struggling from their seats, knock down the benches, only hindering the men from getting at the stage. The two actors are powerless to hold *Canio*. He breaks away, and stabs *Nedda*:

> Take that!
> Perhaps in death's last agony
> You will speak!

Nedda falls, and with a last faint effort calls, "Oh help me, *Silvio*!" With drawn dagger, *Silvio* goes forward, but *Canio*, crying "Ah, 'twas you!" stabs him too. Out of the orchestra rises the tragic motive of vengeance, jealousy and death, booming forth with terrible significance. *Canio*, as if stupefied, lets drop the knife and surrenders. Then, with bitter irony, he declares, "La Commedia e finita!"—the Comedy is ended. Down go both the curtains.

LE THEATRE   THE COMEDY IS ENDED!

THE VICTOR RECORDS

(Sung in Italian unless noted.)

ACT I

PROLOGO

(Prologue) PASQUALE AMATO, Baritone
6039 12-in., $2.00
EMILIO DE GOGORZA, Baritone
899 10-in., 1.50

Ladies and gentlemen!
Pardon me if alone I appear.
I am the Prologue!
Our author loves the custom of a prologue to
his story,
And as he would revive for you the ancient
glory,
He sends me to speak before ye!
But not to prate, as once of old,
That the tears of the actor are false, unreal,
That his sighs and the pain that is told,
He has no heart to feel!
No! our author to-night a chapter will borrow
From life with its laughter and sorrow!
Is not the actor a man with a heart like you?
So 'tis for men that our author has written,
And the story he tells you is true!

PROLOGO

(Prologue) (Complete in two parts)
Part 1—Si puo? (A Word) TITTA RUFFO,
Baritone 6268 12-in., 2.00
RENATO ZANELLI, Baritone
881 10-in., 1.50
Part 2—Un nido di memorie (A Song of
Tender Memories) TITTA RUFFO,
Baritone 6268 12-in., 2.00
RENATO ZANELLI, Baritone
881 10-in., 1.50

A song of tender mem'ries
Deep in his list'ning ear one day was ringing;
And then with a trembling hand he wrote it,
And he marked the time with sighs and tears.
Come, then;
Here on the stage you shall behold us in human
fashion,
And see the sad fruits of love and passion.
Hearts that weep and languish, cries of
rage and anguish,
And bitter laughter!
Ah, think then, sweet people, when ye look
on us,
Clad in our motley and tinsel,
For ours are human hearts, beating with
passion.
We are but men like you, for gladness or
sorrow.

Will ye hear, then, the story,
As it unfolds itself surely and certain!
Come, then! Ring up the curtain!

BALLATELLA, "Che volo d'augelli!"
(Ye Birds Without Number!) LUCREZIA
BORI, Soprano 6048 12-in., 2.00
ALMA GLUCK, Soprano 6148 12-in., 2.00
NEDDA:
Ah, ye birds without number!
What countless voices!
What ask ye? Who knows?
My mother, she that was skillful at telling
one's fortune,
Understood what they're singing,
And in my childhood, thus would she sing me.

VESTI LA GIUBBA
(Air de Paillasse) (On With the Play)
ENRICO CARUSO, Tenor 6001 12-in., 2.00
GIOVANNI MARTINELLI, Tenor
736 10-in., 1.50
EDWARD JOHNSON, Tenor
64840 10-in., 1.00
BENIAMINO GIGLI, Tenor 643 10-in., 1.50
CANIO:
To play! When my head's whirling with mad-
ness,
Not knowing what I'm saying or what I'm
doing!
Yet I must force myself!
I am not a man,
I'm but a Pagliaccio!
The people pay you, and they must have their
fun!
If Harlequin your Columbine takes from you,
Laugh loud, Pagliaccio,
And all will shout, well done!

* * * * * *

Laugh Pagliaccio, for the love that is ended!
(Sobbing):
Laugh for the pain that is gnawing your heart!

ACT II

SERENATA D'ARLECCHINO
(Harlequin's Serenade)
TITO SCHIPA, Tenor 828 10-in., $1.50

NO, PAGLIACCI NON SON!
(No, Punchinello No More!) ENRICO
CARUSO, Tenor 6001 12-in., 2.00
CANIO:
No, Pagliaccio, I'm not!
If my face be white,
'Tis shame that pales it
And vengeance twists my features!

* * * * * *

I am that foolish man
Who in poverty found and tried to save thee!
He gave a name to thee,
A burning love that was madness!
(Falls in a chair overwhelmed.)

CANIO (*recovering himself*):
  All my life to thee I sacrificed with gladness!
  Full of hope and believing far less in God than
    thee!

Go! Thou'rt not worth my grief,
O thou abandoned creature!
And now, with my contempt,
I'll crush thee under heel!

BLACK LABEL AND BLUE LABEL RECORDS

Prologue (*In Italian*)....................*Reinald Werrenrath, Baritone*
Carmen—Chanson du Toreador (*In French*)........*Reinald Werrenrath and Victor Chorus* 55068   12-in., $1.50

Vesti la giubba (On With the Play) (*In Italian*).......*Paul Althouse, Tenor*
Tosca— E lucevan le stelle (*The Stars Were Shining*)..*Paul Althouse, Tenor* 45055   10-in.,   1.00

Vesti la giubba (On With the Play)................*Pietro, Accordionist*
Cavalleria Rusticana—Intermezzo..............*Pietro's Accordion Quartet* 17941   10-in.,   .75

Gems from "Pagliacci"...............................*Victor Opera Co*
  Bell Chorus, "Ding Dong"—Solo, "This Evening at Seven"—Solo,
  "Ye Birds Without Number"—Solo, Pagliacci's Lament—"Vesti
  la giubba"—Duet, "Just Look, My Love"—Chorus, "See, They
  Come"
Gems from Cavalleria Rusticana......................*Victor Opera Co* 35343   12-in.,   1.25

THE TEMPLE OF THE GRAIL

PARSIFAL

PARSIFAL has long occupied a singular position in the world of music, partly because of its inherently semi-religious, mystical character, partly because of its sheer musical beauty.

Its history is interesting. As everybody knows, Wagner, after a long career of tribulation, found at the court of Ludwig II of Bavaria the sympathy and encouragement which were rightly his due. At Bayreuth he fashioned his own theatre, producing his works in a manner befitting their worth, permitting free play to his marvellous and imaginative skill in stage craft; for in addition to his being critic, poet, conductor, master-composer, who revolutionized the development of the opera, this astounding man was also a stage-manager and producer who exercised a profound influence upon the theatre of our own time. "Parsifal" was the last of his works. He began to compose the music in his sixty-fifth year, (1878) the poem, long planned, already having been completed. Interrupted by illness, the work was not finished and produced until 1882, a year before Wagner's death. It was therefore his swan-song. During these years of Wagner's life, Bayreuth became the Mecca of musicians and music-lovers the world over, but after his death his disciples were to be found in all countries, and performances of "The Ring," "Tristan," "Meistersinger" were given in all the leading operatic centres, not infrequently better than at Bayreuth itself. Actuated partly by sentimental reasons, his prudent and remarkable widow,

Frau Cosima Wagner, daughter of Franz Liszt, beheld in "Parsifal" a means of maintaining the Wagnerian tradition and the prestige of Bayreuth. By simply enforcing the copyright law, performances of the work were forbidden anywhere but in Bayreuth, Frau Wagner's justification being in Wagner's known wishes.

The Grail legend, which is said to have originated in pre-Christian Wales, became known to Wagner through a medieval poem by Wolfram Von Eschenbach. The legend itself is a Christian adaptation of a very ancient talismanic myth. The "Grail" is usually identified with the chalice used at the Last Supper, also the basin said to have received Christ's blood from the Cross. It is analogous to the cup of Hermes of the Egyptians, the basket of the Greek, Dionysia, the vase or basin of the Druid's used to contain the blood of the sacrificial victim, and similar European or Oriental mystical vessels. Similarly the Holy Spear of *Amfortas*, supposed to be the spear with which Christ was wounded on the Cross in Christian legend, has been identified with the "bloody spear" of the Celts, upon which they swore hatred and eternal enmity to their persecutors. The tendency of the primitive Church to adapt the myths of pagan converts to its own purposes is familiar to students of Christian symbolism and heathen mythology.

Wagner's philosophy, which is taken very seriously by some, and reduced to terms of bathos by others, fundamentally is the doctrine of renunciation. In the opera "Parsifal" (as in the legend) the wounded *Amfortas*, who typifies suffering humanity, can be redeemed only by a "guileless fool," *Parsifal*, who resists the temptations of the sorceress *Kundry* (a reincarnation of Magdelena, Herodias, Gundryggia—for the lady figures in many myths under various names). *Parsifal*, after many privations and considerable self-sacrifice, becomes the head of that mystical body of knights who perpetuate the observances of the Last Supper in the legendary domain of Monsalvat. In his music-drama, Wagner draws obviously upon the rites of the Last Supper, the Mass of the Apostolic Church, and the ceremonies of the Christian Masonic Order of Knights Templars in the second scene of the first act. There is also a thinly veiled reference to the life of Christ, in the baptizing of *Kundry* in the last act. To some, this employment of religious themes for dramatic purposes may savor of open sacrilege, but it was the essence of Wagner's teaching that the Stage should be restored to its place beside the Church in the exposition of religion and ethics. The quasi-religious character of "Parsifal" has been partly responsible for the awe in which the work has so long been held in Europe.

As regards the music, for a time, this opera was held as Wagner's masterpiece, even by the most discerning of critics. Modern commentators, however, less blinded by partisanship, detect in it, they declare, a note of senility. The score is even more complicated than those of his previous musical works, but has behind it less, perhaps, of the driving inspiration of "Die Meistersinger", "Tristan" and "Siegfried." Some of the vocal parts are practically unsingable,—which was rarely the case in the most difficult of his earlier works. Wagner seems always lucid in these even when most complicated; but here, it is changed, he often is needlessly obscure. Nevertheless, there are passages of unequivocal grandeur, especially in those themes, so familiar to orchestra concert goers, represented in the Prelude and in the "Good Friday Music." Here at least, Wagner's genius is supreme. It is interesting to compare this last and most mature work of the great composer with the earlier "Lohengrin." He now has won complete mastery over the means of expression for which he was striving in the earlier "Grail" opera. He does not disdain to quote some of the "Swan" music in the later work, but references to "Lohengrin" have been scant, from the contradictions in the two works. *Lohengrin*, we learn, in the earlier work is the son of *Parsifal*, who is necessarily childless

in "Parsifal"! The theme which Wagner borrowed from the Dresden "Amen" (an old ecclesiastical cadence) and used tentatively in "Tannhäuser" and "Lohengrin," here appears as the "Grailmotiv." It is developed with stupendous skill, both in the Prelude and later in the second scene of the first act. The orchestration is superb, and the work as a whole must be conceded to be a towering achievement even in the life of a master accustomed as Liszt said, to accomplishing the impossible. If ever, it has been done here.

THE OPERA

FESTIVAL drama in three acts. Music and libretto by Richard Wagner; based on the famous Grail Legend. First produced at Bayreuth, July 28, 1882, but not elsewhere until 1903, when the work was given at the Metropolitan Opera, in spite of the determined opposition of Mme. Wagner. A production in English was afterward given by Henry W. Savage. The copyright expired in 1913 and productions at Berlin, Paris, Rome, Bologna, Madrid and Barcelona followed.

CHARACTERS

TITUREL, a Holy Knight (*Tee-too-rel*)..................Bass

AMFORTAS, his son (*Ahm-for-tas*)..................Baritone

GURNEMANZ, a veteran knight of the Grail (*Goor-neh-mantz*)....................Bass

PARSIFAL, a "guileless fool" (*Pahr'-see-fahl*)..........Tenor

KLINGSOR, an evil magician (*Kling-sohr*)..............Bass

KUNDRY (*Koon-dree*)........Soprano

Knights of the Grail; Klingsor's Fairy Maidens

ACT I

SCENE I—*A Forest near Monsalvat*

IN the "world of long ago" there stands a dream-citadel, its pinnacles rising high from a mountain top, surrounded by gardens of trees and flowers that cannot fade because they are watered by the tears of repentant sinners. Within the Citadel is the shrine of the Holy Grail, that blessed cup in which flowed the Blood of the Saviour. Night and day it is guarded by the knights of the Grail, and once every year there descends a dove from heaven giving these a new spiritual strength to carry on their task. For many years the chief of these knights was *Titurel*, but old age has claimed him, so that he can no longer conduct the sacred rites and the charge has fallen upon his son *Amfortas*.

There is a recreant knight, a kind of Satan expelled from this earthly Paradise, an evil genius and magician known as *Klingsor*, who covets the power of *Titurel*. He has built a castle over against Monsalvat, where, with his magic, it is a pastime of his to entice the Grail Knights to their destruction. In his gardens of beauty

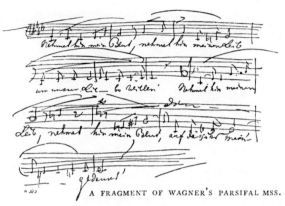

A FRAGMENT OF WAGNER'S PARSIFAL MSS.

there lurk strangely wonderful damsels, who so tempt the knights with their peculiar charms that the strength of these becomes as water. One woman, in particular, is a creature of ineffable beauty, a reincarnation of the great temptresses of the past. She is known as *Kundry*. With her aid the magician once lured *Amfortas* to his gardens, and when the knight weakly surrendered himself to the lure of the temptress, *Klingsor* stole from him the Sacred Spear, that which was held by Longis, the Roman soldier who pierced the side of Christ upon the Cross. Rousing himself, *Amfortas* sought to do battle with *Klingsor*, but the magician smote him with the spear. *Amfortas* returned to Monsalvat grievously stricken with a wound which could not be healed except at the touch of the Sacred Spear. The Spear, so ran the rede, could be recovered only by a "guileless fool," a young man without wisdom, without sin, who should withstand the temptations of *Klingsor's* bower, and with pity and self-denial atone for the sin of *Amfortas*.

For many years, *Amfortas*, deeply repentant, has suffered untold agonies, and his knights ransack the world for healing herbs and ointments, but without success. *Kundry*, who after the tempting of *Amfortas* loathes the tasks imposed upon her by the magician *Klingsor*, is wont to appear in the grounds of Monsalvat as a strange woman who asks humbly to serve the knights. But even she can find no cure.

As the curtain rises upon the gardens of Monsalvat, we find *Gurnemanz*, an old knight of the Grail, with two novices who sleep under a tree until the time shall come to assist *Amfortas* in the daily bath with which he seeks to cleanse his wound and assuage his intolerable sufferings. A trumpet call from the castle announces the coming of *Amfortas*, and after kneeling in prayer the two squires proceed to their task. Two knights who enter, report that the ointment brought by Sir Gawaine has failed to heal the wound, and *Gurnemanz*, who alone knows what the cure must be, shakes his head. The squires beg for information, but he bids them tend the bath.

They note a horseman wildly riding toward them. It is *Kundry*, a gypsy-like creature, her dark eyes blazing between the locks of her wild black hair, and her garments gathered about her waist with a long snakeskin. She brings yet another lotion for the wound of *Amfortas*. A procession enters, bearing *Amfortas* upon a litter. He stops to receive the ointment,

313

COPY'T PACH BROS. PARSIFAL, KUNDRY AND GURNEMANZ ENTERING THE CASTLE—ACT III

groaning with the pain of his wound, for which he thanks *Kundry*, who now rests wearily upon the ground, stirring uneasily at his words. The procession passes on, and the squires seek to drive *Kundry* away, but *Gurnemanz* bids them leave the strange woman alone. Her ways are strange, but harm always comes to Monsalvat when she is absent. The youths depart to tend *Amfortas*.

A dead swan with an arrow in its breast, falls at the feet of *Gurnemanz*, who is outraged at this wanton work, the deed, it transpires, of a youth who now appears. It is *Parsifal*, but in answer to *Gurnemanz's* questions he is unable to give either his name or his origin. He lives with his mother alone in the woods, and he has followed a train of knights to the hill. *Kundry* supplies information. He is the son of a knight slain shortly before his birth, and his mother has now died for grief at her son's departure.

Believing that here at last may be the "guileless fool" so long desired, *Gurnemanz* bids the youth come with him.

The scene now miraculously changes to the interior of the castle; it is effected in the opera by a scene moving behind *Gurnemanz*, so that the two seem to be walking slowly along, at first through the forest, then into a rocky gallery which ascends to the Castle. This device was first used at Bayreuth and afterward used in the American representations.

Scene II—*The Castle Hall*

THE two arrive at last in a great hall, so high that the dome through which streams the illumination is lost to view. Bells are heard. At the back of the hall is a couch spread beneath a gorgeous canopy. Around the sides is the table where the knights are seated during the ceremonies, its long surface bearing cups or chalices. In the centre is an altar-like table with

314

GURNEMANZ'S HERMITAGE—ACT III

a marble top. The Knights of the Grail enter in solemn procession, the bells pealing from the heights above the dome, and the Knights and Squires chanting solemn liturgies. *Parsifal* gazes upon the scene with wonder.

Soon the Holy Vessel is produced. It is draped in purple-red cloth. *Amfortas* then is borne in upon a litter and laid upon his couch. In an agony of suffering he begs to be spared the task of consecration, but the voice of the aged *Titurel* from a tomb-like chapel beyond, bids him continue. *Amfortas* then proceeds, and a blinding light miraculously streams in from the dome, as the knights partake of the Wine and the Bread. As the ceremony progresses, *Amfortas* attains to a certain rapturous exaltation which subsides as the light fades. Then the wound breaks out afresh. He is borne off in the litter, and the knights depart. *Gurnemanz*, believing that *Parsifal* is a mere dolt, opens a side door and turns him out. "Thou art nothing but a Fool," declares the Knight: "Begone.......

Leave all our swans in future alone, and seek thyself, gander, a goose."

ACT II

Scene—*Klingsor's Magic Castle*

ON the ramparts of his castle sits the magician *Klingsor*, awaiting the approach of *Parsifal*. He gloats over the boy's arrival, knowing his destiny, and believing that by enticing him with the flower-damsels, he may at last win the coveted office. He lights a brazier of incense, which immediately fills the lower part of the castle with a bluish vapor, amid which can be seen the necromantic implements of his calling. He summons *Kundry*, who arises ghostlike from the mist, and who utters a dreadful wail, as if she had been awakened from a deep sleep into unimaginable horrors. Her master informs her that one more task of seduction awaits, and she vainly protests against it. He reminds her that whoever spurns her in reality sets her free, and he bids her try her fate with the approaching youth *Parsifal*.

315

With a last cry of anguish *Kundry* returns into the vapor. The tower itself sinks beneath the earth, and the scene is transported, as it were, to *Klingsor's* magic garden. Marvellous flowers and plants arise in the sunlight. On the wall of the garden stands *Parsifal*, looking down with astonishment upon the strange scene. From all sides, from the garden and the palace, the beautiful denizens of the place come forth, first singly, then in numbers. Their robes are hastily flung about them as if they had been awakened from sleep. They are in alarm, having discovered that some of their lovers have been slain by an unknown foe. They accuse *Parsifal*, who admits victory, declaring, in all innocence, that had he not conquered he never could have approached their lovely domain.

They soon accept him as a friend; they dance about him, touching his cheeks with their soft hands, and seeking to arouse him to a sense of their beauty. But one greater and more lovely than any of them now approaches. Beholding *Kundry*, fair beyond the dreams of men, they depart, laughing gently, as *Parsifal* grows angry and tries to flee. But *Kundry* calls, "Parsifal, tarry," and the astonished boy remembers that once when dreaming his mother had called him by that name. *Kundry* tells him that she it was who gave him that name, an inversion of the Arabian "Fal parsi," or "guileless fool." She further tells him of his father, the knight Gamuret, of his mother, Herzeleide, or "Heart's Affliction," and of the mystery of his birth and life in the woods. This is the number "Ich sah das Kind" (I Saw the Child).

Parsifal is greatly affected, his resistance melts, and he sinks in distress at *Kundry's* feet. She embraces him tenderly, seeking ever to conquer him with her feminine charm. *Parsifal* thinks it is again his mother whose gentle embraces he is receiving. Believing that he is fast becoming enslaved *Kundry* presses her lips upon his mouth.

But the kiss has a startling effect. It thrills him indeed, but not with the pangs of love. He starts up suddenly with a gesture of terror; his face is filled with a look of anguish and he presses his hands to his heart as if in pain. "Amfortas!" he cries. "The spearwound—the spearwound!" With heart of pity he suffers the mortal anguish of the Knight of the Grail and recalls the solemn festival held before his wondering eyes in the citadel of Monsalvat. He feels for a moment the sensuous thrill of love-longing, but he conquers it, and finally in an agony, sinks to his knees in despair.

He pushes *Kundry* away, and the woman, knowing that he has discovered her, makes one last terrible effort to awaken Desire in his heart. But he repels her with growing firmness, and as she seeks once more to embrace him, thrusts her away.

"Hither!" she cries at last in despair. "Hither! Oh help! Seize on the caitiff! Oh help!" *Klingsor* approaches in haste and the damsels rush forth in terror. *Klingsor* cries out in scorn.

He flings the Holy Spear of *Amfortas* at the youth, but lo! a miracle happens. The Spear leaps from his hand, but stays in mid-air, halted in the blank above *Parsifal*. The youth seizes it, and makes with it the sign of the Cross.

As with an earthquake, the castle falls to ruins, the flowers are consumed and the garden withers like a desert; the damsels lie like shrivelled blossoms strewn upon the ground. *Kundry* sinks to the earth with a dreadful cry, and *Parsifal* departs quickly. Before he leaves, however, he turns to the temptress, saying enigmatically:

"Thou know'st—
Where only we shall meet again!"

ACT III

SCENE—*A Spring Landscape in the Grounds of Monsalvat. At the back a Small Hermitage*

MANY years elapse before we again find ourselves at Monsalvat. *Gurnemanz*, now an aged man, dressed as a hermit but still wearing the tunic of a Knight of the Grail, emerges from his hut and listens. He goes to a thicket and finds *Kundry* there, seemingly dead, but she revives under his ministrations. *Kundry* appears as in Act I, and she proceeds as before to take up, about the grounds, the humble tasks of a serving maid.

A knight in black armor, bearing a spear, is now discovered. *Gurnemanz* warns him that no armed warrior is allowed in the sacred environs of Monsalvat, especially on this day, Good Friday. Without a word, however, the knight plunges the spear in the ground; then removing his helmet, he kneels in prayer. Only then does *Gurnemanz* recognize him and point him out to *Kundry*. *Parsifal* rises, and gazing calmly around, he recognizes *Gurnemanz*, and puts forth a hand in greeting. He is questioned well. On learning of his wanderings, *Gurnemanz* at length is assured it is *Parsifal*, the redeemer of sins to the Grail brotherhood. He informs the young knight how *Amfortas* yet suffers, and that *Titurel* has just died. Gloom reigns at the citadel, and the knights long for his return and their own deliverance. *Parsifal*, believing these misfortunes due to his long delay, is deeply affected. He staggers and would fall but for the hermit's support. He finally sinks down on a grassy knoll, where *Kundry* bathes his tired feet and dries them with her long hair. *Parsifal* asks *Gurnemanz*, who by his pure life has become worthy, to anoint him with the water of purification, and the contents of the golden vial, which *Kundry* produces from her bosom. *Gurnemanz* then performs his devotional act, bestowing on *Parsifal* the title of Prince and King of the Grail. *Parsifal* now looks with deep compassion upon *Kundry*, baptising her.

COPY'T MISHKIN
MATZENAUER AS KUNDRY

PHOTO MATZENE
WHITEHILL AS AMFORTAS

COPY'T MISHKIN
WITHERSPOON AS GURNEMANZ

Then comes the wonderful "Charfreitagszauber," or Good Friday Spell.

Gurnemanz explains that the beauty of the woods and fields is caused by the fact it is Good Friday, and that the flowers and trees, watered by the tears of repentant sinners, express in their luxuriousness the redemption of mankind. *Kundry*, who has sat with bowed head, now looks up beseechingly upon *Parsifal*, who in great compassion, kisses her upon the brow.

Distant bells are heard, pealing softly at first but gradually swelling into majestic power. Wagner here uses the same famous bell-motiv heard in the first act but in minor mode as befits the hour's greater sadness and solemnity. The moment has come, and the old hermit places upon *Parsifal* a coat of mail and the mantle of a Grail-Knight. As before, the landscape gradually changes, and *Parsifal*, grasping the Sacred Spear, follows *Kundry* and *Gurnemanz*. Once more the woods disappear, and as they approach the rocky galleries, a procession of Knights in mourning garb is seen. Here develops, to the deep tones of the bells of Monsalvat, the "Processional of the Knights of the Holy Grail."

At last the whole immense hall reappears as in the first act, but without the tables. The light is faint. From the doors on one side, Knights appear, bearing the coffin of *Titurel*. From another door *Amfortas* is borne on his litter, preceded by the covered shrine of the Grail. The bier is erected

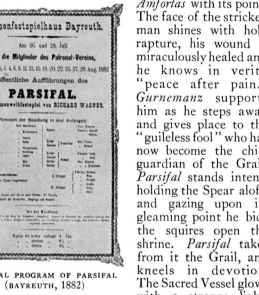

ORIGINAL PROGRAM OF PARSIFAL
(BAYREUTH, 1882)

in the centre of the hall; behind it is the canopied couch where *Amfortas* is set down. Then is heard Amfortas' Gebet, "Mein Vater!" (Amfortas' Prayer, "My Father").

All have shrunk back in awe, and *Amfortas* stands alone in fearful ecstasy. *Parsifal*, accompanied by *Gurnemanz* and *Kundry*, has entered unperceived. He now steps forward with the Spear, and before the wondering knights, he touches the wound of *Amfortas* with its point. The face of the stricken man shines with holy rapture, his wound is miraculously healed and he knows in verity "peace after pain." *Gurnemanz* supports him as he steps away and gives place to the "guileless fool" who has now become the chief guardian of the Grail. *Parsifal* stands intent, holding the Spear aloft, and gazing upon its gleaming point he bids the squires open the shrine. *Parsifal* takes from it the Grail, and kneels in devotion. The Sacred Vessel glows with a strange light, and a halo of glory pours down from above. *Titurel*, for the moment restored to life, raises himself from his coffin, lifting his hands in benediction. From the dome descends a white dove, which hovers above the head of *Parsifal*, who lifts the Grail for the adoration of the Knights. *Kundry*, her task accomplished, and her redemption assured, sinks in death to the ground. *Amfortas* and *Gurnemanz* kneel in homage before *Parsifal*, and the curtain falls upon this most extraordinary of all operatic works.

THE VICTOR RECORDS

(Sung in German)

ACT II

ICH SAH DAS KIND

(I Saw the Child) MARGARETE MATZENAUER, Contralto

6327 12-in., $2.00

KUNDRY:

I saw the child upon its mother's breast;
Its infant lisping laughs yet in my ear:
Though filled with sadness,
How laughed then even Heart's Affliction,
When, shouting gladness,
It gave her sorrow's contradiction!
In beds of moss 'twas softly nested,
She kissed it till in sleep it rested:
With care and sorrow
The timid mother watched it sleeping;
It waked the morrow
Beneath the dew of mother's weeping.
All tears was she, encased in anguish,
Caused by thy father's death and love:
That through like hap thou shouldst not languish,
Became her care all else above.
Afar from arms, from mortal strife and riot,
Sought she to hide away with thee in quiet.
All care was she, alas! and fearing:
Never should aught of knowledge reach thy hearing.
Hear'st thou not still her lamenting voice,
When far and late thou didst roam?
For days and nights she waited,
And then her cries abated;
Her pain was dulled of its smart,
And gently ebbed life's tide;
The anguish broke her heart,
And—Heart's Affliction—died.

ACT III

CHARFREITAGSZAUBER

(Good Friday Spell—Part II) (Du siehst, das ist nicht so,) HERBERT WITHERSPOON, Bass

6330 12-in., $2.00

GURNEMANZ:

Thou see'st, that is not so.
The sad repentant tears of sinners
Have here with holy rain
Besprinkled field and plain,
And made them glow with beauty.
All earthly creatures in delight
At the Redeemer's trace so bright
Uplift their pray'rs of duty.
To see Him on the Cross they have no power:
And so they smile upon redeemed man,
Who with dread no more doth cower,
Through God's love made clean and pure:
And now perceives each blade and flower
That mortal foot to-day it need not dread;
For, as the Lord in pity man did spare,
And in His mercy for him bled,
All men will keep, with pious care,
To-day a tender tread.
Then thanks the whole creation makes,
With all that flow'rs and fast goes hence,
That trespass-pardoned Nature wakes
Now to her day of Innocence.

AMFORTAS' GEBET, "MEIN VATER."

(Amfortas' Prayer, "My Father") CLARENCE WHITEHILL, Baritone

74406 12-in., $1.50

AMFORTAS (*raising himself on his couch*):

My father!
Highest venerated hero!
Thou purest, to whom once e'en the angels bended!
Oh! thou who now in Heavenly heights
Dost behold the Saviour's self,
Implore Him to grant that His hallowed blood,
He pour upon these brothers.

SEVERAL KNIGHTS (*pressing forward*):

Uncover the shrine!
Do thou thine office!

AMFORTAS ((*in a paroxysm of despair*):

No!—No more!
I bid ye to slay me!
(*Tears open his dress.*)
Behold me!—the open wound behold!
Here is my poison—my streaming blood.
Take up your weapons!
Kill both the sinner and all his pain:
The Grail's delight will ye then regain!

BLUE LABEL RECORD

{ Charfreitagszauber (Good Friday Spell-Part I) Mein erstes Amt verricht' ich so........................*Karl Jörn, Tenor, Jean Müller, Bass*
{ Charfreitagszauber (Good Friday Spell-Part II) Du siehst, das ist nicht so *Jörn-Müller* } 55061 12-in., $1.50

319

BUNTHORNE AND THE LOVE-SICK MAIDENS

PATIENCE

COMIC opera by Gilbert and Sullivan. First produced at the Opéra Comique, London, April 23, 1881. First American production at the Standard Theatre, New York, September 23, 1881.

PATIENCE is Gilbert's famous satire on the esthetic craze of the early '80s, which did not long survive the witty ridicule this gifted librettist aimed at it.

In the first act twenty love-sick maidens are singing plaintively of their love for *Bunthorne*. *Patience*, a buxom milkmaid, ridicules them, telling them the *Dragoon Guards* are expected shortly; but though the maidens doted upon the *Dragoons* a year ago they scorn them now. The *Guards* arrive, also *Bunthorne*, followed by the fair twenty, who pay no attention whatever to the *Dragoons*—who leave in a rage. *Patience* appears, and the poet makes love to her. She is frightened and runs to *Lady Angela*, who tells her it is her duty to love some one. *Patience* thereupon declares she will not permit the day to go by without falling in love.

Grosvenor, the idyllic poet, and an old playmate of *Patience*, enters, and she promptly falls in love with him, but he remains indifferent. *Bunthorne*, unable to decide between the maidens, puts himself up as the prize in a lottery, but *Patience* interrupts the drawing and announces that she will be his wife. She is accepted, whereupon the fickle maidens transfer their affections to *Grosvenor*.

In the second act we see a rather ancient damsel, *Jane*, mourning because of the maidens' desertion of *Bunthorne*, who is content with a milkmaid. *Grosvenor*, followed by *Patience*, who tells him that she still loves him, and *Bunthorne*, with *Jane* clinging to him, enters. Finally, *Bunthorne* in a jealous rage at *Patience's* regard for the rival poet, exits with *Jane*. Now the maidens grow tender to the *Dragoons*, and the poets quarrel. *Bunthorne* asks *Grosvenor* how to make himself less attractive, and he is told to dress himself in a more commonplace manner. When the maidens find he has given up esthetics they find suitors among the *Dragoons; Patience* deserts *Bunthorne* for *Grosvenor*, and *Jane* goes over to the *Duke,* leaving *Bunthorne* disconsolate.

SCENE FROM ACT II AT THE METROPOLITAN

PESCATORI DI PERLE

(LES PECHEURS DES PERLES)
(French)

(THE PEARL FISHERS)
(English)

NOT until the success of "Carmen" did the world ask, too late for him to hear, what other operas this brilliant composer might have produced. "The Pearl Fishers" had previously met with little success, but once disinhumed, it revealed a wealth of unregarded, almost unsuspected beauty. Based on an oriental theme, it is picturesque and colorful, even though it lacks the electric thrill, the dash and the tragic sense of "Carmen." The melodies in it are lovely, and they are coming into the better appreciation they deserve. In especial, Bizet's gifts as a composer for the orchestra are well revealed in the beautiful Prelude.

THE OPERA

OPERA in three acts. Text by Carré and Cormon. Music by Georges Bizet. First production at the Théâtre Lyrique, Paris, September 29, 1863. First London production, entitled "Leila," at Covent Garden, April 22, 1887; and as *Pescatori di Perle*, May 18, 1889. Recently revived at Covent Garden for Tetrazzini. First performance in America occurred at Philadelphia, August, 1893, in English. First New York production (two acts only) January 11, 1896, at the Metropolitan Opera House, with Calvé. Revived at the Metropolitan in 1916, with Caruso, Hempel and de Luca. It is interesting to recall that Caruso and de Luca sang together in this opera twenty years ago in Genoa, at the very beginning of their operatic careers.

CHARACTERS

LEILA, a priestess (*Lay'-lah*)...Soprano
NADIR, a pearl fisher (*Nah-deer*) Tenor
ZURGA, a chief (*Zoor'-gah*)...Baritone
NOURABAD, high priest (*Noo-
rah-bad*) ....Bass
Priests, Priestesses, Pearl Fishers,
Women, etc.

*Scene and Period: Ceylon; Barbaric
Period*

(The original French name of the opera is pronounced *Lay Pay-shur-day Pairl;* the Italian, *Pes-kah-toh'-ree dee Pair-leh*).

ACT I

SCENE—*The Coast of Ceylon*

THE time has come to select a new chieftain in the little world of the Cingalese fishermen, who gather together for a ceremonial dance and festival, before their ancient pagoda. The choice falls on *Zurga*, who accepts the office. Scarcely has he been inaugurated than a long lost friend of his youth appears, *Nadir*. They greet each other with affection, and speak of the days when they were foolish enough to quarrel over a beautiful girl, a priestess in the temple of Brahma, known to them as *Leila*. Of her they sing the duet "Del tempio al limitar" (In the Depths of the Temple), one of Bizet's finest inspirations. It is begun by *Nadir*, who describes the scene impressively. Believing themselves now cured of their old infatuation, they swear eternal friendship, pledging themselves to remain blood-brothers to the end.

A fisherman announces the arrival of a mysterious veiled priestess whose custom it is to come once a year, in a boat from the sea, to pray for the success of the fishermen, who look upon her as their guardian. No one dares approach the place of her devotions,

upon the rocks above the village, but all treat her with veneration. She invariably comes among them close-veiled, and as she goes toward the temple the folk sing a chorus of prayer in which she herself joins,—the "Brahma gran Dio" (Divine Brahma).

Before she enters the temple, *Zurga* adjures her to pray for the people night and day, promising that if she keeps her oath of chastity she shall receive a pearl of great price. If she breaks it, however, death will be her portion. She is about to swear when, with a start, she observes *Nadir*. The High Priest, *Nourabad*, reminds her that even now she may revoke her vows, if she desires it, but she refuses, entering the temple. *Nadir*, left alone, is shaken by the discovery that the veiled woman is none other than *Leila;* more than this, he realizes he still loves her. In a lovely air, he recalls his memories of the first time he beheld her, the "Mi par d'udire ancora" (I Hear as in a Dream).

Nadir decides he must tell *Zurga.* Meanwhile, he is somewhat weary, and, throwing himself on the ground he falls asleep. As he lies there, returning priests build a fire on the rocks, where *Leila* sings a song of prayer to Brahma. *Nadir* awakens, and calls to her softly. She subtly answers in her song without awakening the suspicions of the priests. Under cover of the growing darkness, *Nadir* forgets *Zurga*, hastening to the side of his lost love.

ACT II

SCENE—*A Ruined Temple*

NEAR an ancient, ruined temple, *Leila* begins her lonely watch, *Nourabad* reminding her of her oath —her renunciation of marriage and her devotion to her people. She tells him of a vow she made when a child to protect a fugitive, who implored her to save his life. Even though a dagger was held to her breast by his enemies, she kept her vow, and he escaped, leaving her, as remembrance, a golden chain. This story is told in the number "Siccome un di caduto" (A Fugitive, One Day).

The priest reminds her of the punishment which is certain to overtake her should she now violate her oath. "Shame and death shall be thy portion!" warns the harsh and bitter old man. So she is left alone with her thoughts, the mysterious night-sounds of the jungle for her only companionship. Bound by her oath, yet conscious of her love for *Nadir*, she sinks down in an agony of despair. She is roused by the voice of her lover, who comes to the Temple, his heart awake in passionate longing. *Nadir* sings the beautiful "De mon amie" (My Love).

Rushing to her, the priestess's lover implores her to defy the priests, her oath to Brahma, and to fly with him. She refuses, but the love in her heart is too strong, and she soon finds herself in his arms. Then follows the "Non hai compreso un cor fedel" (You Have Not Understood).

Now begins the tragedy. Unknown to the lovers, *Nourabad* has been watching. He alarms the people, telling them *Leila* has proven faithless. The fishermen advance toward the couple with drawn knives, demanding death as their punishment. *Zurga* steps forward, and orders them to begone. As they go, *Nourabad* tears the veil from the girl's face, and thus reveals to the astonished *Zurga* that she is none other than *Leila*, the woman *Nadir* has sworn with him to forget forever. Enraged at what he regards as his friend's betrayal, he orders both to death. *Nadir* is carried off in chains, and the priests lead away *Leila*.

ACT III

SCENE I—*The Camp of Zurga*

BEFORE the tent where *Leila* is held under guard, *Zurga* stands brooding over the impending death of his friend and of the woman he loves. *Leila* comes to the entrance of the tent, and calls softly. She begs him to dismiss the guards and talk to her awhile, and he does so. Then *Leila* pleads for *Nadir* in an aria of great dramatic power, the "Temer non so per me" (I Fear Not).

Zurga declares his love, and openly reveals his jealousy of *Nadir;* but the girl scorns him; she is too proud to sue for her own life. Her refusal angers him. *Nourabad* comes to announce the forthcoming sacrifice, and to him she gives the chain of the fugitive, imploring him to send it to her mother.

SCENE II—*The Place of Execution*

IN a wild part of the jungle, the funeral pyre has been set up,—and hither are brought *Leila* and *Nadir*. As they mount the pyre a red glow is seen in the sky, which is heralded by the people as the dawn. Then *Zurga* enters to warn them that what they have seen is not the dawn, but the red glow of their burning homes, and they fly to save their children and their household goods. The two prisoners and *Zurga* remain, secretly watched by *Nourabad*, who thus hears *Zurga* explain that he has kindled the fire to save them both. With a great battle-axe, *Zurga* smashes the chains that bind them. They speak their gratitude in a splendid trio, "Fascino etereo."

The lovers praise the generosity and greatness of *Zurga*, who for the sake of friendship has done a deed which may cost him his own life. They depart as the voices of the enraged Indians, returning for vengeance, draw nigh. With his knife, *Zurga* holds them off until *Nadir* and *Leila* are seen from afar, high among the rocks. *Zurga* then is overpowered, and forced to mount the funeral pyre. As the flames roar about him, it is seen that the forest itself is on fire, and reading in this last catastrophe the anger of Brahma himself, the people prostrate themselves, as the flames envelop them too. In this tremendous "suttee" the community perishes with the lovers.

In this fashion is consummated one of the most remarkable tragedies in French opera, a tragedy set to music of extremely high and original power.

THE VICTOR RECORDS
(Sung in French unless otherwise noted)
ACT I
DEL TEMPIO AL LIMITAR
(In the Depths of the Temple) ENRICO CARUSO, Tenor and MARIO ANCONA, Baritone *In Italian* 8036 12-in., $2.50
EDMUND CLEMENT, Tenor and MARCEL JOURNET, Bass 8017 12-in., 2.50
JE CROIS ENTENDRE ENCORE
(I Hear as in a Dream) ENRICO CARUSO, Tenor 6026 12-in., 2.00
DMITRI SMIRNÓV, Tenor *In Italian* 6105 12-in., 2.00
ACT II
DE MON AMIE
(My Love) ENRICO CARUSO, Tenor 513 10-in., $1.50
COMME AUTREFOIS
(As in Former Times) AMELITA GALLI-CURCI, Soprano 6124 12-in., 2.00

ZURGA:
"Hold you! Mine alone is the right to judge!"—Act II

LA PERLE DU BRÉSIL

(THE PEARL OF BRAZIL)

LYRICAL drama in three acts. Words by Gabriel and Sylvain Saint Étienne; music by Félicien David. First produced at the Théâtre Lyrique, Paris, November 22, 1851. Revived at the same theatre March, 1858, with Mme. Miolan-Carvalho; and at the Opéra Comique, 1883, with Emma Nevada.

CHARACTERS
(With the Original Cast)

ZORA....................Mlle. Duez
LORENZ, her lover.............Soyer
ADMIRAL SALVADOR.........Bouché
Sailors, Brazilians, etc.

LA PERLE DU BRÉSIL, (*Pairl du Breh-zeel'*) was David's first dramatic work. It is the story of *Lorenz*, a sailor, and *Zora*, a young girl found by *Admiral Salvador* in Brazil, and whom he intends to educate and eventually to marry.

They set sail from South America, but *Salvador* soon finds that *Zora* has a lover, *Lorenz*, a young lieutenant, who has disguised himself as a sailor and is on board in order to be near his sweetheart. A storm arises and the ship is compelled to seek shelter in a harbor of Brazil. The natives attack the ship and almost overpower the sailors, when *Zora* chants a hymn to the Great Spirit, and the Brazilians, recognizing their compatriot, make peace. In gratitude for the young girl's act, which has saved the lives of all on board, the *Admiral* gives his consent to her marriage with *Lorenz*.

The "Charmant oiseau" is, perhaps, the most beautiful number in David's opera. It is one of the most famous of coloratura airs, and one of which sopranos are very fond, as it exhibits their art to perfection, especially in the duet with the flute.

THE VICTOR RECORDS
(Sung in French)

CHARMANT OISEAU
(Thou Charming Bird) With Flute obbligato. LUISA TETRAZZINI, Soprano
6343 12-in., $2.00
AMELITA GALLI-CURCI, Soprano
6124 12-in., 2.00

Delightful bird of plumage glowing
With sapphire and with ruby dyes,
'Mid the shade his rare beauty showing
Before our wonder-stricken eyes;
When on the branch with blossoms trembling,
He poises swinging gay and bright,
His checkered pinions' gleams resembling
A many-colored prism of light.
How sweet is he, the Mysoli!

When day appears his joyful singing
Awakes the dawn's enchanted rest;
When evening falls his notes are ringing,
While fiery day fades from the west.
A-down the grove the silence doubles,
As now his plaintive dulcet lay,
That breathes of love's ecstatic troubles,
From out the tulip tree dies away.
How sweet is he, the Mysoli!

From Ditson edition—Copy't Oliver Ditson Co.

H. M. S. PINAFORE

OR THE LASS THAT LOVED A SAILOR

RECENT revivals of this opera have proven that it has lost nothing of its original charm and wit, though both librettist and composer have passed away, together with the noble lord satirized by *Sir Joseph Porter*. Strangely, this most successful of all light operas was not accepted with favor at its first production in London. It owed its success to Americans who found it a genial satire upon English officialdom which could be applied to human nature generally. Sullivan's sparkling melodies soon were universally whistled and the American success was repeated in London, actually leading up to the establishment of the Savoy Theatre and a long string of delicious operettas such as "The Mikado," "The Pirates of Penzance" and "Patience." W. S. Gilbert's death, which occurred in 1911, was a Gilbertian affair in itself, the librettist, well advanced in years, leaping into a shallow ornamental lake to save a lady from drowning, of which in fact she was in no danger! Sullivan's "Pinafore" music was composed while the composer was suffering acute gastric trouble, much of it being written in bed. At that, its humor—and brilliancy—did not suffer a whit.

THE OPERA

COMIC opera in two acts. Text by W. S. Gilbert; music by Sir Arthur Sullivan. First produced at the Opéra Comique, London, May 28, 1878. First American performance occurred in New York in 1878, but was unauthorized, and was followed by the first important production at the Boston Museum, in November, 1879. Successfully revived in New York in 1911 and again in 1912.

CHARACTERS

RT. HON. SIR JOSEPH PORTER, K. C. B., First Lord of the Admiralty.........Baritone
CAPTAIN CORCORAN, Commanding "H. M. S. Pinafore"................Baritone
RALPH RACKSTRAW, able seaman...................Tenor
DICK DEADEYE, able seaman.....Bass
BILLY BOBSTAY, boatswain's mate...................Bass
BOB BECKET, carpenter's man

TOM TUCKER, midshipmite
SERGEANT OF MARINES
JOSEPHINE, the Captain's daughter...............Soprano
HEBE, Sir Joseph's first cousin...........Mezzo-Soprano
LITTLE BUTTERCUP, a bumboat woman...........Contralto
First Lord's Sisters, his Cousins and Aunts, Sailors, Marines.

Time and Place: The Scene is laid on the Quarterdeck of "H. M. S. Pinafore" Time, 1878

ACT I

THE sailors on "H. M. S. Pinafore" are busy scrubbing the decks for the expected arrival of *Sir Joseph Porter, K. C. B.* The ship is in the harbor, and Portsmouth is seen in the distance. *Little Buttercup*, a bumboat woman who is by no means as small as her name would imply, comes aboard with the stock of "snuff and tobaccy and excellent jacky," not to mention the "excellent peppermint drops." It transpires that a handsome young sailor, *Ralph*, is in love with the *Captain's* daughter, *Josephine*, and aside from the difference in their station, *Josephine* is to be betrothed to *Sir Joseph Porter*, who duly arrives, attended by his "sisters and his cousins and his aunts." In the meantime, *Ralph* plans to elope with *Josephine*, the crew assisting. The plot is overheard by *Dick Deadeye*, the lugubrious boatswain.

ACT II

CAPTAIN CORCORAN, in disgrace for using a "big, big D" in public, sings to the moon, (accompanied by a mandolin) and *Little Buttercup* reveals her affection for him. He tells her, however, that he can only be her friend, and she hints darkly that a change is in store for him—"Things are seldom what they seem." *Sir Joseph* then enters complaining that *Josephine* does not favor his suit, when the *Captain* comforts him by averring she is awed by his lofty station, and

suggesting that he plead his cause on the ground that love levels all rank. *Josephine* does not respond, being naturally determined to marry *Ralph*. *Dick Deadeye* now reveals the elopement plans and he and the *Captain* lie in wait for the crew, "Carefully on tip-toe stealing." The elopers are captured, and the *Captain* is so exasperated that he actually swears, using a "big, big D" which is overheard by *Sir Joseph Porter*. For this serious breach of morals, a horrible example of depravity before the whole crew, the *Captain* is ordered to his cabin. Affairs are interrupted by *Little Buttercup*, who discloses her secret, telling how the *Captain* and *Ralph* had been accidently exchanged while they were both babies. Whereupon, *Sir Joseph*, revealing the crowning absurdity of Gilbert's plot, sends for *Ralph*, giving him command of the ship and reducing the *Captain* to *Ralph's* humble grade of "able seaman." *Sir Joseph* nobly consents to the marriage of *Ralph* and *Josephine*, and the *Captain* consoles himself with *Little Buttercup*.

BLACK LABEL RECORDS

Gems from "Pinafore" (Part I)..............*Victor Light Opera Company*
   Opening Chorus, "We Sail the Ocean Blue,"—"A Maiden Fair to
   See"—"I am Monarch of the Sea"—"I'm Called Little Buttercup"—
   "Captain of the Pinafore"—Finale, "His Foot Should Stamp"
Gems from "Pinafore" (Part II)..............*Victor Light Opera Company*
   "The Gallant Captain of the Pinafore"—"When I Was a Lad"—
   "The Merry Maiden and the Tar"—"Carefully on Tip-Toe Stealing"
   "Baby Farming"—"Farewell, My Own"—"For He is an Englishman"
	35386 12-in.; $1.25

Pinafore Selection (Part I)........................*Victor Concert Orch.*
   "Now Give Three Cheers for the Sailor's Bride"—"A Maiden Fair
   to See"—"We Sail the Ocean Blue"—"I'm Called Little Butter-
   cup"—"Admiral's Song"—"When I Was a Lad"
Pinafore Selection (Part II)................ ....*Victor Concert Orch.*
   "Fair Moon"—"Carefully on Tip-Toe Stealing"—"Refrain, Auda-
   cious Tar"—"He is an Englishman"
	18176 10-in., .75

PIQUE DAME

(THE QUEEN OF SPADES)

OPERA in three acts. Text by Modeste Tschaikowsky, the composer's brother, taken from Puschkin's novel of the same name. Music by Peter Ilyitsch Tschaikowsky. First production at St. Petersburg, December, 1890; in Vienna, under Gustav Mahler, 1902; at La Scala, Milan, 1905-6; Berlin, 1907, with Destinn, Goetz, Griswold and Grüning. First American production at the Metropolitan Opera House, New York, March 5, 1910, in German, under Mahler, with Destinn, Slezak and Alma Gluck. This was the first production in America of any of Tschaikowsky's operas, an odd fact in view of the great popularity of his concert music, although "Eugen Onégin" had previously been given in concert form.

Time and Place: St. Petersburg; Eighteenth Century

THE story of "Pique Dame" is a melodramatic story, filled with superstition and tragedy. The *Queen of Spades* (*Pique Dame*), is an elderly countess who possesses the secret of the three fateful cards which bring luck at the gaming table. Her granddaughter, *Lisa*, betrothed to *Prince Jeletski*, is deeply in love with *Hermann*, a young officer, who is seeking a way to make a fortune that he may marry the young girl. *Lisa* gives her lover the key to her grandmother's rooms, where he goes at night in an effort to extract from the old *Countess* the secret of the three cards. The *Countess* will not listen to his pleadings and she orders him from her apartment. When he draws his pistol in an effort to compel her to reveal to him the names of the cards, she falls dead from terror.

The next scene shows *Hermann* in his barrack room. As the funeral of the *Countess* passes the barracks, a gust of wind blows the window open, and the ghost of the *Queen of Spades* appears, declaring, "Your fate is sealed! These are the cards—ace, seven, three." She vanishes, and the officer goes out to meet *Lisa*, who is waiting for him on the banks of the Neva. The young girl fails in her effort to prevent *Hermann* from carrying out his determination to go to the gambling house, and as he leaves her she throws herself into the Neva. In the last act *Hermann* is gambling madly with the *Prince*. He has won on the first two cards, but when the third card, the queen of spades, turns up, he loses all. The spectre of the *Countess* appears, and *Hermann*, imagining she has come for his life, stabs himself.

Tschaikowsky has written much beautiful music for this work, but the gems of the opera are probably the delightful duet for *Lisa* and *Pauline* in the second scene of Act I, which reminds one somewhat of the lovely Tales of Hoffman "Barcarolle"; the solo of *Lisa* in Act III, given as she waits on the banks of the Neva for her lover *Hermann;* and the duet from the Carnival Scene, Act II, sung by *Daphnis* and *Chloe* in the little pastoral given for the amusement of the guests.

THE VICTOR RECORDS

ACT II

O VIENS MON DOUX BERGER
(My Dear Shepherd) EMMY DESTINN, Soprano and MARIA DUCHENE, Soprano *In French* 8017 12-in., $2.50

THE PIRATES OF PENZANCE

COMIC opera in two acts. Text by Sir W. S. Gilbert; music by Sir Arthur Sullivan. First performance on any stage, New York, December 31, 1879, under the supervision of the authors. Produced at the Opéra Comique, London, April 3, 1880. Occasional amateur productions.

Time and Place: The Scene is laid on the Coast of Cornwall; time 1879

THIS little opera is a satire on British respectability and the exaggerated moral sense of the Victorian era. In this it is a triumph. In Act I, the *Pirates* celebrate the twenty-first birthday of *Frederic*, whose apprenticeship is ended. He wishes to give up his calling, though he has to berate the *Pirates* for a softhearted lot,—through their tenderness with orphans. Being orphans themselves, they feel compelled to be kind to other orphans, and, as the fact is known, all their victims claim exemption upon the ground of common orphanhood. *Ruth*, a "female pirate," *Frederic's* nurse in childhood, who got him into this scrape by binding him 'prentice to a pirate instead of a pilot, expects now to marry him. *Frederic* never has seen any other woman, and consents, while suspecting that younger women may have more charm. His suspicions are confirmed when *General Stanley's* daughters arrive. He conceals himself behind a rock, but as the ladies decide to paddle in the water his modesty obliges him to step forth when each of the girls has removed one shoe. He thus meets *Mabel*, who consents to reform him from his piratical ways. The *Major-General* himself arrives, just as the *Pirates* capture the girls. In order to save them and himself he tells them he is an orphan, and the tender-hearted *Pirates* are compelled to release their captives.

In the second act, the *General* laments his deception as to his having been an orphan, and he is brooding in misery beside the tombs of his ancestors, whom he feels he has disgraced. *Frederic* tries to console him with the thought that he only bought the place a year ago, ancestors and all. But the *General* is not convinced; he bought the ancestors along with the place, and no matter whose ancestors they were, they are now his! The *Police* arrive to help *Frederic* "jug" the *Pirates*, and *Frederic* bids *Mabel* goodbye. The *Pirate King* and *Ruth*, however, interfere with his plans by informing him that he was bound apprentice to the *Pirates* until his twenty-first *birthday*, and since he happened to be born on the 29th of February, he has yet had but five birthdays and consequently is still a member of the band for some sixty-four years. His sense of duty compels him to return to the *Pirates*, and to inform them that the *General* was not really an orphan after all. The *Police* attack the *Pirates* and are defeated. The *Police*, however, arrest them in the name of Queen Victoria, and at the mention of this august monarch the *Pirates* reverently yield themselves up. It is discovered, then that the *Pirates* are themselves all English noblemen gone wrong, and the *Police* at once respectfully release them, on condition that they give up their piracy. They willingly do so, and *Frederic* is thus free to marry *Mabel*.

PRINCE IGOR DEPARTS FOR THE WAR—ACT I

PRINCE IGOR

ALTHOUGH Borodin wrote many symphonic works, "Prince Igor" was his only opera, and even this was not finished when he died in 1887, although begun twenty years earlier. It was completed by the composer's friends, Rimsky-Korsakoff and Glazounoff. The Italian version, written by Antonio Lega and Giulio Setti, was used in the American production. The music is wild, free, and whether completed by Borodin or his friends, it is highly original. The ballet music frequently has been danced by the Ballet Russe and its successors.

THE OPERA

OPERA in a prologue and three acts. Libretto by the composer and his friend, Vladimir Stassoff, based on "The Epic of the Army of Igor," an old historical Russian chronicle, supposed to have been written by a literary monk in the twelfth century. Music by Alexander Porphyrievich Borodin. First production at Imperial Opera House, St. Petersburg, October 23, 1890. First American production in New York, December 30, 1915, with the cast given below.

CHARACTERS

PRINCE IGOR SVIATOSLAVITCH
 (*Ee-gohr' Svee-aht-oh-slav'-itch*)
 Pasquale Amato
PRINCESS JAROSLAVNA, his wife
 (*Ya-roh-slav-nah*)...Frances Alda
VLADIMIR IGOREVITCH, his son
 (*Ee-gohr-ay'-vitch*)..Paul Althouse
PRINCE GALITZKY AND KONTCHAK
 (*Gah-litts-kee and Kohnt-chak*)
 Adamo Didur
KONTCHAKOVNA, his daughter
 (*Kohnt-cha-kohv'-nah*)
 Flora Perini
OVLOUR (*Ohv-toor*)....Pietro Audisio
SCOULA (*Skoo-lah*).Andrea de Segurola
EROCHKA (*Ay-roch-kah*)..Angelo Bada
A YOUNG GIRL..Raymonde Delaunois

IN the Prologue, which takes place in a square in Poutivle, *Prince Igor* and his expedition are about to depart for battle with an Oriental tribe. An eclipse occurs, which overawes the people, but *Igor* refuses to heed the warnings of his wife and departs with his son *Vladimir*, after entrusting the care of his wife to his brother, *Prince Galitzky*, whose ambition it is to usurp *Igor's* place, and who bribes the rogues, *Scoula* and *Erochka*, deserters from *Igor's* army, to give him their support.

Act I shows feasting and carousing in the courtyard of *Galitzky's* house. Young girls bewail the fact that one of their number has been abducted and is kept a prisoner in *Galitzky's* hold. They ask for her return, but the *Prince*, who is actually the abductor, frightens them and they run away. *Jaroslavna*, brooding over the absence of her husband, is appealed to by the girls, but on the appearance of *Galitzky* they flee in terror. *Jaroslavna* reproaches her brother, but he defies her. Worse troubles are in store for her, however, as a delegation of Boyars appears to tell the *Princess* that *Igor* is wounded and a prisoner, together with his son, in the enemy's camp. Distant flames are seen, and the people cry that the enemy is advancing.

As the curtain rises on the second act it is evening in the enemy's camp, where *Prince Igor* and *Vladimir* are prisoners. A chorus of girls is singing, among them *Kontchakovna*, daughter of *Kontchak*, the Oriental chief. *Prince Vladimir*, who has fallen in love with *Kontchakovna*, enters and tells the young girl that *Igor* disapproves of his attachment to the daughter of his enemy, but she says that her father will consent to their union. *Igor* appears, lamenting his predicament, but when *Ovlour*, who is on guard, offers him a horse as a means of escape, he refuses. *Kontchak* promises *Igor* his freedom if he will agree never to fight again. The slaves are ordered to dance for his diversion, and the act ends with a ballet.

The third act shows another part of the enemy's camp, where *Kontchak's* triumphs over the Russians are being celebrated. *Igor* is supposed to make his escape, while *Kontchak* orders his soldiers not to pursue.

The last act shows the city walls and public square in Poutivle. *Jaroslavna*, grieving for her absent husband, suddenly sees two horsemen approaching, and is overjoyed to recognize her husband and *Ovlour*. *Jaroslavna* and *Igor* go into the citadel, while the rascals, *Scoula* and *Erochka*, who have been drinking, enter and sing a song ridiculing *Igor* and praising *Galitzky*. Suddenly they perceive *Igor* in the door of the citadel, and tremble for fear of punishment. "Ring the town bell," says the resourceful *Scoula*, and they pull the rope lustily. This brings the townspeople, who greet their king with much rejoicing. And all ends well.

THE VICTOR RECORD

ACT I
SONG OF PRINCE GALITZKY
FEODOR CHALIAPIN, Bass 558 10-in., $1.50

BLUE LABEL RECORD

Coro di donne (Chorus of the Tartar Women, Act II) (*In Italian*) *Metropolitan Opera Chorus* Coro e Danza (Chorus of Slaves, Act II) (*In Italian*) *Metropolitan Opera Chorus*	45133 10-in., $1.00

SCHUMANN-HEINK
AS FIDÈS

LE PROPHÈTE

(THE PROPHET)

THIS opera was one of the last of Meyerbeer's works, representing therefore the final change of style in a curiously changeable composer. Meyerbeer seems to have applied a special method for each work. The general public, expecting another "Huguenots," was at first somewhat disappointed; but "Le Prophète" soon established itself, for all its gloomy and tragical character, the gorgeous pageantry of the Cathedral scene, the brilliant ballet and excellent music serving to compensate for the lack of love-interest and the mixed character of the "hero"—who redeems himself at the end only by blowing up a castle with himself and his enemies. A thin but tragic love-romance gleams through the work, but the chief love-interest really is that of a mother for her son, a most unusual main theme in opera. The plot is based on the uprising of the Anabaptists of the sixteenth century. This was a semi-religious, semi-social movement characteristic of the early Renaissance period. It knew some qualities which appealed to the downtrodden masses, but it was badly marred by the charlatanry of its leaders, including John of Leyden, whose character appears to be the foundation for the *Prophet* of the present work. The music was completed with most lavish care by Meyerbeer, and it includes some of his best-known arias and concerted numbers, such as "Ah, mon fils," and the familiar "Coronation March"—the latter still recognized as one of the great processional marches and frequently used in European state functions, not to speak of its popularity among us here in the United States.

THE OPERA

OPERA in five acts. Text by Scribe. Music by Giacomo Meyerbeer. First presented in Paris, April 16, 1849. First London production July 24, 1849. First American production at the New Orleans Opera, April 2, 1850. First New York production November 25, 1854. Revived in 1898 at the Metropolitan with Brema, de Reszke and Lehmann; in 1903 with Alvarez and Schumann-Heink; in 1909 at the Manhattan Opera with d'Alvarez, Lucas and Walter-Villa; and in 1918 with Caruso, Muzio, Matzenauer and Didur.

CHARACTERS

JOHN OF LEYDEN (*Ly'-den*), the Prophet, chosen leader of the Anabaptists .... Tenor

BERTHA, his sweetheart...... Soprano

FIDÈS (*Fee'-dayz*), mother of John of Leyden ... Mezzo-Soprano

COUNT OBERTHAL, ruler of the domain about Dordrecht ... Bass

ZACHARIAH	three	Bass
JONAS	Anabaptist	Tenor
MATHISEN	preachers	Bass

Nobles, Citizens, Peasants, Soldiers, Prisoners

Scene and Period: Holland and Germany; in 1543, at the Time of the Anabaptist Uprising

(The original French name of the opera is "Le Prophète," *Leh Pro-feht*; the Italian, "Il Profeta," *Eel Pro-fay'-tah*).

ACT I

SCENE—*A Suburb of Dordrecht*

JOHN OF LEYDEN is the son of *Fidès*, a widowed innkeeper of Leyden, a man of strange mystical character. He is about to wed *Bertha*, an orphan girl of great beauty. But as the girl is a vassal of *Count Oberthal*, and her home in Dordrecht, *Bertha* is obliged to seek the *Count's* consent to her wedding. She and *Fidès* go to the castle at a moment when a group of peasants, armed with sticks and staves, are about to start a riot, invoked by the preaching of three Anabaptists. The trouble is easily suppressed on the appearance of the *Count*, his followers, and his soldiers, who tend to make merry over it. The *Count* hears the girl's plea, but is so impressed with her beauty that he desires her for himself, and he has her and *Fidès* cast into the dungeons of his castle. Such was ancient justice.

ACT II

SCENE—*The Inn of Fidès in the Suburbs of Leyden*

DRIVEN from the castle, the three Anabaptists enter the inn of *Fidès*, where they meet *John*. They are much struck with his resemblance to the portrait of the guardian saint, David, at Munster, and recognizing him as a possible tool, who might pass with the crowd as a reincarnation, they try to persuade him into becoming a leader in their movement. He tells them of a dream he has had. In this he was venerated by a crowd of people in a great cathedral; the Anabaptists eagerly strive to use this dream to work upon *John's* feelings. But he refuses because of his approaching marriage to *Bertha*. The girl herself, however, having escaped from the castle, suddenly appears with news of the *Count's* dastardly act. She is concealed by *John* as the *Count's*

CARUSO AS THE PROPHET

CARUSO AND MATZENAUER AS JOHN AND FIDÈS

soldiers rush in to recapture her. *John* refuses to betray her. He is told that unless he yields her up, his own mother will suffer death. In the struggle between two desires, his filial loyalty prevails, and he yields his betrothed. *Fidès* is released and sings her gratitude in one of the most pathetic of airs, the "Ah, mon fils!"— "Ach, mein Sohn!" (Ah, My Son!).

Left by his mother to his bitter reflections, *John* now hears the Anabaptists in the distance, and he resolves to join them as a means of vengeance against the *Count*. A compact with the three conspirators is soon made, and they depart, leaving bloodstained garments to make *Fidès* believe her son has been slain by the *Count's* assassins.

ACT III
Scene—*Camp of Anabaptists*

AIDED by *John's* mystical zealotry and his resemblance to the saint, the Anabaptists have no difficulty in persuading the rabble that he is indeed the Prophet. Under his leadership, the uprising has been partly successful, and the rebels now stand before the walls of Munster. An attempted attack on the city has failed, and the rebels are for the moment out of hand. *John's* vigorous preaching, however, restores them. He makes them kneel and pray for victory. They chant the *Miserere*, and *John* sings his noble hymn: "Re del cielo e dei beati" (Triumphal Hymn, "King of Heaven").

ACT IV
Scene I—*A Public Square in Munster*

THE insurgents have captured the city, but the Prophet is received with mixed feelings, some denouncing him as an impostor, despite the plain fact his leadership has won victory. *John* is in fact weary of the bloodshed

he has caused. He has led the insurgents mainly because he has known *Bertha* is in the city. Now, for his part in the fighting, *John* is to be solemnly crowned King. But on the same day his mother, in beggary, arrives at Munster intending to buy masses to be said for the soul of the son whom she believes dead. She meets *Bertha*, and tells her that *John* is dead. *Bertha* believes that his death was caused by the Prophet and goes out swearing vengeance on the Prophet himself!

Scene II—*The Munster Cathedral*

GLITTERING pageantry, gorgeous decoration, supplemented by pealing of bells, solemn chants and the stately Coronation March, have made justly celebrated this scene of *John's* enthronement.

As *John*, in processional pomp, is led into the church, *Fidès* appears from behind a pillar and, in a transport of joy, greets him as her son. To acknowledge this would be to deny the divine origin imputed to the Prophet, and *John* is compelled to repudiate it. To save her from death, he pronounces his mother insane and obliges her to kneel before him; then standing over her with hands upraised and magnetic fire in his eyes he bids the soldiers slay him if she should answer to his question that she *is* his mother. Poor *Fidès*, alarmed for him, at once answers "no," and all exclaim, "a miracle," believing her miraculously cured of her insanity. *Fidès* is then carried away to prison, and *John* regains his power.

ACT V
Scene I—*The Crypt of the Palace*

BEING certain that her son will contrive to see her, the old woman awaits *John* in her prison cell. She at first denounces the "Prophet's" conduct. but later, with magnificent elo-

COPY'T WHITE JOHN:
"May God the choice determine!
Upon your head fall the lightning of his curse!"

quence, prays for his penitence and redemption. This, of course, is the great "Prison Scene."

An officer enters, announcing the arrival of the Prophet, and her sorrow is transformed to joy. When *John* enters, *Fidès* denounces the bloody deeds of the Anabaptists, and she calls on her son to repent and put off his false robes. His hands are reeking with the blood of those he has deceived by his blasphemous assumptions. He acknowledges the truth of what he is hearing, and just as a faithful officer enters to tell him that his associates have betrayed him to the Emporer's forces, he renounces his apostacy and kneels to receive the blessing of his mother. The Emperor's troops are marching on the city.

In a moment, *Bertha* enters through a secret passage revealed to her by her grandfather, once keeper of the palace. She is bent on slaying the Prophet. But on discovering him to be her former betrothed, she is torn between irreconcilable emotions. Unable to bear the strain of love and hate combined, she stabs herself, collapsing into the arms of *Fidès*. *John* plans a terrible vengeance, in which all shall go to death together, including himself.

SCENE II—*The Great Hall of the Palace*

AFTER the Emperor's troops have forced an entrance, *John* orders the gates closed. *Count Oberthal*, the source of all his troubles and one of the leaders of the Emperor's forces, now comes to him saying, "You are my prisoner." But *John* answers "Nay, ye are all *my* captives!" He has secretly had the cellars filled with gunpowder, and even as he speaks a terrific explosion takes place; the walls fall and flames leap on every side. Amid the lurid scene of death and destruction, a woman with dishevelled hair rushes through the ruins into *John's* arms. "My mother!" he cries. She has indeed come to pardon him and to share his death. "Welcome, sacred

336

flame," they chant together as the fire mounts about them and the curtain falls.

THE VICTOR RECORDS

ACT II

AH, MON FILS!
(Ah, My Son!) ERNESTINE SCHUMANN-HEINK, Contralto *In French*
6279 12-in., $2.00

FIDÈS:

Ah, my son! Blessed be thou!
Thy loving mother to thee was dearer
Than was Bertha, who claim'd thy heart!
Ah, my son! For thou, alas,
Thou dost give for thy mother more than life,
For thou giv'st all the joy of thy soul!
Ah, my son! now to heav'n my pray'r ascends for thee;
My son, blessed be forever more!
From Operatic Anthology, by permission of G. Schirmer, (Copy't 1899)

ACT V

PRISON SCENE—PART II
ERNESTINE SCHUMANN-HEINK,
Contralto *In French* 6279 12-in., $2.00

FIDÈS (*alone*):

O! my cruel destiny! Whither have you led me?
What, the walls of a prison! they arrest my footsteps.
I am no longer free.
Bertha swore my son's death, he denied his mother;
On his head let the wrath of Heaven fall!
(*Her wrath subsides.*)
Though thou hast abandoned me,
But my heart is disarmed,
Thy mother pardons thee.
Yes, I am still a mother.
I have given my cares that thou may'st be happy,
Now I would give my life,
And my soul exalted, will wait for thee in Heaven!

FIDÈS (*joyfully*):

I shall see him, delightful hope!
Oh, truth! daughter of heaven,
May thy flame, like lightning,
Strike the soul of an ungrateful son.
Celestial flame restore to him calmness!
Restore, bless'd Heaven, his guardian angel!

BLACK LABEL RECORDS

{Coronation March	*Vessella's Italian Band*	35610	12-in., $1.25
{ Carmen Selection (*Bizet*)	*Vessella's Italian Band*		
{Coronation March	*Arthur Pryor's Band*	35683	12-in., 1.25
{ Wedding March (*Sousa*)	*Sousa's Band*		

JOHN DENYING HIS MOTHER—ACT IV

337

I PURITANI

(THE PURITANS)

I PURITANI was the last of Bellini's operas, and with it his all-too-brief career came to a glorious end. Bellini, like Chopin, Mendelssohn, Weber, Mozart and Schubert, died in "the fatal thirties" (1801-1835), being but thirty-four when attacked by an insane delirium on a visit to England shortly after "I Puritani" had been the success of the London season. His biographer asserts that his end was hastened by his habit of sitting at the piano playing feverishly day and night until he was "obliged forcibly to leave it." The actual cause of death was probably hastened by the privations of a life which, despite his many successes, really was spent in hardship and poverty. He received pitifully small sums for his numerous operas.

COPY'T VICTOR GEORG

GALLI-CURCI AS ELVIRA

Directly after his death, on the eve of his funeral, "I Puritani" was produced in Paris. Not many hours after this successful but dolorous event the singers were repeating the melodies but using the words of the Catholic service for the dead. As this is not, perhaps, a cheerful introduction to the opera, we may point out, not without thankfulness, that "I Puritani" departs from the usual run of operas in its having a happy end.

The music of the work is essentially melodious, and the "mad scene" especially vies in popularity with that of Donizetti's "Lucia." Perhaps, however, the best airs are written for the tenor rôle, but these lie so high that few can sing them effectively. They were designed for Rubini, a tenor with an exceptional range. And most of them died with Rubini.

THE OPERA

OPERA in three acts. Book by Count Pepoli; music by Vincenzo Bellini. First presented at the *Théâtre Italien*, Paris, January 25, 1835, with a famous cast—Grisi, Rubini, Tamburini and Lablache. First London production, King's Theatre, May 21, 1835, under the title of *Puritani ed i Cavalieri*. First New York production, February 3, 1844. Produced at the New Orleans Opera, March 3, 1845; and at the Metropolitan Opera in 1883 with Sembrich. Revived in 1906 at the Manhattan Opera, with Pinkert, Bonci and Arimondi; in 1908 with Tetrazzini, Constantino and de Segurola; Galli-Curci at the Chicago Opera; and at the Metropolitan in 1918, with Barrientos, Lazaro and de Luca.

Scene and Period: England, near Plymouth, in the Reign of Charles I

(The Italian name of the opera is pronounced *Ee Poo-ree-tah'-nee*).

ACT I

SCENE I—*Exterior of a Fortress, near Plymouth*

IT is a time of Civil War in England, when the conflict of Puritans and Cavaliers has arrayed brother against brother, father against son, and shattered even the ranks of the nobility upon the rocks of divergent ideas. We find ourselves in the grounds of the Fortress held at Plymouth by the Puritans. *Sir Richard Forth* has learned that his adored *Elvira* has no mind to marry him; and rather than urge her into a union she does not desire, her father has consented to her marriage with *Lord Arthur Talbot*, one of the hated Cavaliers. He is so torn with anguish and jealousy that he little heeds the invitation of *Bruno* to become one of the Puritan leaders.

Scene II—*Elvira's Room in the Castle*

MEANTIME, *Elvira*, the daughter of *Lord Walton*, the Puritan Governor-General, learns from her uncle, *Sir George*, that he has persuaded her father to consent to her marriage with the man of her choice. Trumpets sound a shrill blast of welcome, and to her surprise, entrance is permitted her Cavalier lover for the express purpose of the marriage. She greets *Lord Arthur* rapturously when he enters, attended by squires and pages.

Scene III—*A Vast Armory of Gothic Architecture*

THE wedding festivities are hastened. Already the pages bring in the nuptial gifts, including a splendid white veil, which is soon to play an important part in the drama. Villagers and soldiers arrive and toast the betrothed pair, after which *Elvira*, *Arthur*, *Sir George* and *Lord Walton*, sing the famous quartet, "A te o cara" (Often, Dearest).

A somewhat mysterious lady is introduced to *Lord Arthur*, who subsequently discovers, in a brief scene alone with her, that she is the widow of Charles I, *Queen Henrietta*, under sentence of death. As a loyal Cavalier,

he is naturally horrified, and seeks a way to aid her escape. At this moment *Elvira* enters, in all her charm and gaiety. She is already dressed in bridal array, wearing the veil given her by *Lord Arthur*, and in sport she insists on placing the veil over the head of the unhappy prisoner, who smiles wanly. To *Lord Arthur* this opens a way of escape, and when *Elvira* leaves the room, he suggests that under cover of the veil, the *Queen* may depart with him from the castle. To carry out the plan will mean the sacrifice of his marriage to *Elvira*, but to the royalist Cavalier this is nothing more than honorable. The *Queen* is persuaded, and they are about to leave when *Sir Richard Forth* enters, bent on vengeance. Swords are drawn, but the *Queen* intervenes. In doing so her veil is disarranged, and *Forth* recognizing her and guessing the plan of escape, bids them depart, perceiving that the union of *Elvira* and *Lord Arthur* at once becomes impossible.

The escape is soon discovered, and *Lord Arthur* is denounced. The effect on the unhappy *Elvira*, who supposes her lover has deserted her on her wedding day, is madness.

ACT II
Scene—*The Pilgrim Camp*

IN the camp of the Puritans, *Sir George Walton* announces that Parliament has decreed the death of *Lord Arthur* for his part in aiding the escape of the *Queen*. *Elvira* enters, a pathetic figure, to sing her famous air, somewhat resembling the "Mad Scene" in "Lucia," "Qui la voce" (In Sweetest Accents).

Her father and *Forth* try vainly to appease *Elvira*, and her uncle, hoping that the sight of her lover may restore her, begs *Forth* to pardon the young man. *Forth* consents provided *Arthur* comes helpless—and at his own peril—to the camp; but if he comes bearing arms against the Puritans he must die. *Sir George* agrees to this and they pledge themselves to fight together for their country.

ACT III

SCENE—*A Garden near Elvira's House*

IN accordance with the plan, *Arthur*, fleeing from the enemy, enters the grounds of the castle in hope to see *Elvira* before leaving England forever. She issues from the castle, pensively singing an air which he himself has sung to her in days gone by. The young man is touched to the heart. She recognizes *Arthur*, and better than this, comprehends his explanation that his acts were inspired by loyalty to his *Queen*. She is overjoyed and, temporarily at least, sane. They sing the lovely duet, "Vieni fra queste braccia" (Come to My Arms).

COPY'T WHITE
SIR GEORGE AND SIR RICHARD—I PURITANI

Forgetting present danger, they think only of their love and the consciousness they are once more in each other's arms. But the sound of a drum reawakens the delirium which afflicts *Elvira*. She cries out for help, believing in her madness that *Arthur* wishes to leave her. Her cries have an evil result. Soldiers rush in, *Arthur* is recognized, captured and sentenced to death on the spot.

Just as the execution is about to take place, however, a messenger arrives, bearing news that the Stuart forces have been defeated, and that Cromwell has granted pardon to all captives. *Elvira's* reason at last returns, and the lovers are united. In this case, all is well.

Few operas end so happily, a circumstance well worth remembering in a day of numerous operas.

THE VICTOR RECORDS
(Sung in Italian)

ACT I

AH PER SEMPRE
(To Me Forever Lost) GIUSEPPE DE LUCA, Baritone   6080 12-in., $2.00
O TE, O CARA, AMOR TALORA
(To Thee, Oh Dearest) MIGUEL FLETA, Tenor   948 10-in., 1.50
POLONAISE—SON VERGIN VEZZOSA
(With Joy My Heart is Bounding) AMELITA GALLI-CURCI, Soprano
          6432 12-in., 2.00

ACT II

QUI LA VOCE
(In Sweetest Accents) AMELITA GALLI-CURCI, Soprano   6128 12-in., 2.00

ELVIRA:

It was here in accents sweetest,
He would call me—he calls no more!
Here affection swore he to cherish,
That dream so happy, alas! is o'er!
We no more shall be united,
I'm in sorrow doomed to sigh,
Oh, to hope once more restore me,
Or in pity I die! (*Her mood changes.*)
'Tis no dream, by Arthur, oh, my love!
'Ah, thou art smiling—thy tears thou driest,
Fond Hymen guiding, I quickly follow!
(*Dancing toward Richard*)
Come to the altar!

BLACK LABEL RECORD

{Quartet from Puritani.........................*Vessella's Italian Band*} 68471 12-in., $1.25
{ *Mirella Overture—Allegro (Gounod)*...............*Vessella's Italian Band*}

REGINA DI SABA

(THE QUEEN OF SHEBA)

MOSENTHAL'S story tells of the struggle of *Assad*, a courtier of *Solomon*, against fleshly temptation, and of his final victory which involves the sacrifice of the happiness of his betrothed, *Sulamith*.

For this text Goldmark has written some of the most beautiful and original music in the entire range of opera, and it is an interesting detail that after he had finished his work and had submitted it to the Imperial Opera, Vienna it was not accepted on the ground that it was too "exotic"! Later, through the influence of Princess Hohenlohe, it was presented, and it became a success.

THE OPERA

OPERA in four acts. Text by Mosenthal, founded upon the Biblical mention of the visit of the Queen of Sheba to Solomon. Music by Goldmark. First production 1875, in Vienna. In New York, December 2, 1885, with Lehmann and Fischer. English version given by the National Opera Company in 1888. Given November 29, 1889, at the Metropolitan with Lehmann, which was the last New York production until the revival in 1905, with Walker, Rappold, Knote and Van Rooy.

CHARACTERS

KING SOLOMON . . . . Baritone
HIGH PRIEST . . . . Bass
SULAMITH (*Soo-lah-mit*), his
    daughter . . . . Soprano
ASSAD (*Ahs-sadd*), Solomon's
    favorite . . . . Tenor
QUEEN OF SHEBA . . . . . Mezzo-Soprano
ASTAROTH (*Ahs-ta-roht*), her
    slave (a Moor) . . . . Soprano
Priests, Singers, Harpists, Bodyguards, Women of the Harem, People.

SCENE—*Jerusalem and Vicinity.*

THE wisdom and fame of *Solomon* having reached even distant Arabia, the *Queen of Sheba* decides to visit him, and a favorite courtier, *Assad*, has been sent to meet her and escort her to the city. When *Assad* arrives with the *Queen*, his betrothed, *Sulamith*, is astonished to find him pale and embarrassed, and trying to avoid her. *Assad* afterward confesses to *Solomon* that he has met a beautiful woman at Lebanon and has fallen in love with her. When the *Queen of Sheba* arrives and removes her veil, *Assad* is astounded to recognize in her the mysterious woman who has captured his senses. Involuntarily he rushes toward her, but she coldly repulses him and passes on with the *King.*

In Act II, the *Queen* discovers that she loves *Assad*, and seeing him in the garden, bids her maid attract his attention with a weird Oriental song. *Assad* starts when he hears the mysterious air, as it seems to bring back memories of the night at Lebanon. He sings his beautiful air, "Magiche note" (Magic Tones!)

The *Queen* and *Assad* soon meet and confess their love for each other, but are interrupted by the arrival of the night guard.

In the next scene the Court assembles for the wedding of *Sulamith* and *Assad*, but *Assad* insults his bride and declares his love for the *Queen*. He is banished from Jerusalem and finally dies in the arms of *Sulamith*, who is crossing the desert on her way to a convent. This is a fascinating opera.

THE VICTOR RECORD

MAGICHE NOTE
    (Magic Tones) ENRICO CARUSO, Tenor
      In Italian   520 10-in., $1.50

SOLOMON RECEIVING THE QUEEN—ACT I

LA REINE DE SABA

(QUEEN OF SHEBA)

LA REINE DE SABA is one of the four operas which Gounod composed between his "Faust" (1859) and "Romeo" (1867). Text by Jules Barbier and Michel Carré. Music by Gounod. First performed at the Operá, Paris, February 28, 1862. An English version called *Irene*, by Farnie, was given in London at the Concert Palace, August 12, 1865. First American production at the New Orleans Opera, January 12, 1889.

CHARACTERS

KING SOLOMON.................Bass

BALKIS (*Bahl-kees*), Queen of
   Sheba...............Soprano

ADONIRAM   (*Ah-don-ee-rahm*),
   a sculptor..............Tenor

BENONI (*Ben-ohn-ee*), his assistant.....................Tenor

PHANOR		Baritone
AMRU	workmen	Tenor
METHUSALL		Bass

SARAHIL, maid to the Queen. Contralto

SADOC.....................Soprano

The Action takes place in Jerusalem

ACT I

THE curtain rises, disclosing the sculptor at work on an important group of statuary. *Benoni* enters and informs him that the *King* desires his presence, as the *Queen of Sheba* is expected to arrive at any moment. As *Adoniram* prepares to leave the studio his workmen demand higher wages, but he refuses them and they go out muttering threats.

Adoniram, said to be descended from a divine race, the "Sons of the Fire," holds in contempt all earthly greatness, and treats the *King* as the son of a shepherd.

342

The works which earned for *Solomon* the surname "the Wise" are supposed in reality to have been executed by *Adoniram*.

The *Queen* arrives and is welcomed by *King Solomon* and the people. The *Queen* has promised to marry *King Solomon*, and gives him a ring. When *Adoniram* is presented to her as one of Palestine's great artists, she seems greatly impressed by the handsome young sculptor, and begins to regret her engagement. To please her *Adoniram*, by sorcerer's signs, collects a vast army of workmen from every point in the city, and his great influence alarms even the *King* himself.

ACT II

KING SOLOMON and the *Queen* have promised to come and see the final casting of *Adoniram's* masterpiece, and he is preparing for this event singing the "Prête moi ton aide" (Lend Me Your Aid), invoking the spirits of his forefathers to bless the work, when *Benoni* enters hurriedly and reveals a plot of the workmen who have stopped the channels so that the melted bronze cannot flow. His information comes too late, and the molten mass overflows, apparently ruining the statue.

ACT III

ADONIRAM meets the *Queen of Sheba* and she soon confesses her love for him. He is at first inclined to repel her advances, but soon falls under the spell of her fascinations and clasps her in his arms. He tells her that he also is of her race, the Nimrod. The faithful *Benoni* hurriedly enters in search of *Adoniram*, telling him that despite the plot of the workmen, the statue has been successful.

ACT IV

ADONIRAM is received by *Solomon* and the Court and he is proclaimed the greatest sculptor of the time. All leave the hall except *Solomon* and the *Queen*, who gives a sign to her maid, *Sarahil*, to bring a draught which she presents to *Solomon*. He soon falls asleep at the feet of the *Queen*, who takes the ring from his finger and leaves the Palace.

ACT V

ADONIRAM and the *Queen* have planned to fly together. They already approach the meeting place, when three of *Adoniram's* discontented workmen, bent on revenge, inform *Solomon* of the secret meetings between *Adoniram* and the *Queen*, and he decrees that the sculptor must die. As they set out together for Jerusalem they are overtaken by the messengers of the *King*, who set upon and stab *Adoniram*. The *Queen* hurries to his side and falls on his body, cursing his murderers and *Solomon*, while the dying man offers a last protestation of his love, and expires in her arms.

THE VICTOR RECORD

PRÊTE-MOI TON AIDE

(Lend Me Your Aid) ENRICO CARUSO, Tenor *In French*   6035 12-in., $2.00

Lend me your aid, Oh race divine,
Fathers of old to whom I've pray'd,
Spirits of pow'r, be your help mine,
Lend me your aid, Fathers of old
To whom I've pray'd, O lend your aid!
Oh grant that my wild dream be not vain,
That future time shall owe to me
A work their bards will sing in their strain,
Tho' Chaos still an iron sea!
From the caldron the molten wave
Soon will flow into its mould of sand,
And ye, O sons of Tubal Cain,
Fire, Oh fire my soul, and guide my hand!
Lend me your aid, Oh race divine,
Fathers of old to whom I've pray'd,
Spirits of pow'r, be your help mine,
Lend me your aid!

FERD. LEEKE

FASOLT:
Should we not find
The Rheingold fair and red,
Freia is forfeit!
(Rheingold, Act I.)

344

DAS RHEINGOLD

(THE RHINEGOLD)

MUSIC-DRAMA in four scenes. Words and music by Richard Wagner. First produced at Munich, September 22, 1869. First American production January 4, 1889, with Fischer and Alvary. Annual performances given at the Metropolitan in recent years with many famous artists: Soomer, Reiss, Jörn, Goritz, Burrian, Ober, Fremstad, Ruysdael, Witherspoon, Matzenauer, Homer, etc.

CHARACTERS

Gods

WOTAN (*Vo'-tahn*)..........Baritone
DONNER (*Dohn'-ner*)...........Bass
FROH (*Froh*).................Tenor
LOGE (*Loh'-geh*)..............Tenor

Giants

FASOLT (*Fah-zohlt*).............Bass
FAFNER (*Fahf'-ner*)............Bass

Nibelungs (Gnomes)

ALBERICH (*Ahl'-ber-ich*)......Baritone
MIME (*Mee'-meh*).............Tenor

Goddesses

FRICKA (*Frik'-ah*)..........Soprano
FREIA (*Fry'-ah*)............Soprano
ERDA (*Air'-dah*)...........Contralto

Nymphs of the Rhine

WOGLINDE (*Vog-lin-deh*)......Soprano
WELLGUNDE (*Vell-goon'-deh*)..Soprano
FLOSSHILDE (*Floss-hill'-deh*).Contralto

(The name of the opera is pronounced *Dass Rine'-goldt*).

THE OPERA

SCENE I—*The Bottom of the Rhine*

WITH extraordinary skill, Wagner makes a listener feel that the Rhine is the source of all German legend. Wishing to picture this mighty giant of rivers in a peaceful mood, symbolical of the quiet that reigned before the rape of the Gold, he gives us a prelude which begins on a single note—a low E flat (usually supplied by a pipe-organ), above which the chord of E flat is allowed to grow in wave-like rhythms with gradually increasing intensity for a long period. The chord is in fact maintained for 136 bars, the only case on record of a chord held so long without monotony. When the curtain rises we behold a strange world below the surface of the water, where in the submarine gloom the three Rhine maidens swim about the huge rock on which the gold is stored, singing their quaint and beautiful song.

MOTIVE OF THE RHINE MAIDENS

They have a visitor in *Alberich*, a hideous dwarf of the race of Nibelungs or gnomes, who dwell in the dark caves beneath the mountains. *Alberich* passionately desires the maidens, who swim elusively into his grasp and away before he can seize them. Suddenly, a beam from the rising sun pierces the waters, making the gold shine with a singular glow (marvellously portrayed in the music), and *Alberich* learns that whosoever will renounce the love of women, and fashion some of the gold into a ring, can be master of the world. The maidens believe that the lovesick dwarf is so amorously inclined that the gold is in no danger; but, knowing that he is powerless to win their love, he suddenly changes love into ambition, and renouncing Woman forever, he seizes the gold and bears it away. The maidens bewail their loss with harmonies of incredible pathos, swimming

345

half-blindly now in the green darkness which follows the loss of the treasure. The dwarf's mocking laughter is their only reply.

Scene II—*A Mountain Top, Showing the Castle of Walhalla*

MEANWHILE, there is trouble in the heavens. Egged on by *Loge*, the god of fire, *Wotan*, the father-god of all, has had the giants, *Fafner* and *Fasolt*, build for him, in a single night, the great castle of Walhalla. The price of this is to be *Freia*, the goddess of youth and beauty, from whose garden the gods must each day eat an apple lest they perish. The darkness of the previous scene is gradually illumined till we discover ourselves near a grassy eminence, where *Wotan* and his wife, *Fricka*, lie sleeping. In the distance is the towering new castle. *Wotan* awakens rejoicing; but *Fricka* is alarmed for *Freia*. *Wotan* tries unsuccessfully to calm her, telling how he has sent *Loge* to earth, in hope to find a substitute there. Suddenly *Freia* enters in deep distress, followed by the giants, and by her brothers *Donner* and *Froh*. The giants demand pay for their labor. *Wotan* tries vainly to laugh them out of it, uneasily "playing for time" till *Loge* shall return. After a long discussion, *Loge* appears. He has scoured the earth, and has found but one soul willing to renounce the love of women for the sake of treasure. That is *Alberich*, who now rules the underworld by virtue of the ring he has fashioned from the *Rhinegold*. The giants at length consent to accept the treasure in place of *Freia*. They take *Freia* away as hostage, and the gods, deprived of their golden apples, at once become languid and faint. *Wotan* then proceeds with *Loge* to the domain of *Alberich*, passing through the sulphurous crevices of the rocks. The dwarf must be made to pay.

Scene III—*Alberich's Cave*

NOW master of the underworld, *Alberich* develops into a tyrant. With a scourge he forces *Mime* to make him a magic cap or helmet, known as the *Tarnhelm*, which has the property of making invisible him who wears it, or of converting him into some other animal at will. *Mime* has hoped to wear it himself and thus escape his cruel master, but *Alberich* is too quick and too powerful through the magic aid of the Ring, so he places the helmet on his own head. Now unseen he administers to *Mime* a terrific beating, and he departs, chuckling, to terrify his workers afresh with the fear of an invisible master, forever watching over them. While he is absent, *Wotan* and *Loge* appear, and *Loge* soon learns from *Mime* of the *Tarnhelm's* magic properties, represented by a "leit-motiv" or theme in the music:

Alberich soon returns, and through the flattery of *Loge* is persuaded to exhibit the powers of the magic helmet. *Loge*, also, has his leit-motiv, a strangely flickering chromatic passage, typifying fire. First, for the entertainment of his visitors, *Alberich* converts himself into a huge serpent, whereat *Wotan* and *Loge* simulate fear. Asked if he can turn himself into a small animal also, *Alberich* becomes a frog. *Wotan* quickly puts his foot on the frog and seizes the helmet. Thus robbed, *Alberich* returns to his normal shape but remains in the power of the gods. As the price of his freedom they demand the *Rhinegold*. And *Alberich* pays. Later, the rest of his world shares in the payment. A strange story, strange in music and action, unfolds.

SCENE IV—*Same as Scene II*

WOTAN and *Loge* bring the hapless dwarf into the upper world, and they hold him fast while his myrmidons bring forth the treasure gold of his caves. *Alberich* entreats to be set free, but *Wotan* demands the Ring also. And he is inexorable. Before yielding the Ring, however, the dwarf lays a frightful curse upon it, predicting that it will bring misery and death to each new possessor until it comes back again to the Nibelungs. The "curse" theme plays a great part in the subsequent dramas, combining with others, indeed, to make new themes.

Wotan wastes little attention upon the curse, putting on the Ring, and gazing at it with admiration. The giants, who have taken *Freia* as hostage for the treasury, now demand payment, stipulating that the gold shall be piled about her until she is completely covered. The gold is stacked until only a small chink remains, through which she still is visible. This can be filled only by the ring itself, and *Wotan*, knowing its magic properties, refuses to part with it, desiring it for himself and fearing its power in the hands of the giants. *Fafner* and *Fasolt* seize *Freia* once more, and *Erda*, the goddess of the earth, arises from the slumbering valley to warn *Wotan* of danger if he persists in refusing. *Fricka* "nags" too, and *Wotan* is compelled to yield it. No sooner do the giants take the Ring than the Curse begins to work. They fight over the treasure, and *Fasolt*, to the horror of the gods, is slain by *Fafner*, who departs with the gold. *Donner* then, in a great storm (which is marvellously suggested in the music), makes a rainbow bridge to the castle of Walhalla and the gods then enter in state, the Walhalla theme being heard in all its glory:

WALHALLA-MOTIVE

BLUE LABEL RECORDS

GALLI - CURCI
AS GILDA

RIGOLETTO

GREATLY desiring a new libretto for the Venice Opera, Verdi requested Piave to adapt Victor Hugo's play, "Le Roi s'Amuse," which, in spite of its morals, was recognized by the composer to possess operatic possibilities. A libretto was soon written, the suggestive French title being changed to "La Maledizione." The work was urgently needed, and dismay followed the flat refusal of the police to grant permission for the performance of a work in which a king was shown in such dubious character. It will be remembered that Venice was then in Austrian hands, and but a short time previously, 1848-49, there had been an Italian insurrection. As Verdi refused to consider any other plan, the management was in despair. Help arrived from an unexpected quarter, for the Austrian police chief, Martello, was an ardent musical and dramatic enthusiast, and a great admirer of Verdi. He perceived that by substituting the *Duke of Mantua* for *Francois I*, and by changing the title to "Rigoletto" and arranging that all the curses should fall upon the duke of a small town, the work could be presented without any material changes in the original dramatic situations. Verdi was reasonable over all but fundamental things, and accepted the changes. He went to Busseto, near his birthplace in the mountains, and came back within six weeks with the completed score. The situation was saved, and a brilliant success was the result.

Though it precedes "Il Trovatore" and "La Traviata" by two years, "Rigoletto" is generally classed with them as representing one, if not the final, high water mark in the master's development. These works established Verdi's European reputation as an operatic composer of the first rank, for they possessed beauties of melody, harmony and orchestration, and subtleties in the presentment of character, somewhat beyond his previous works.

They would have established him "for all time," even though they had not been succeeded by such achievements as "Un Ballo in Maschera," "La Forza del Destino," "Don Carlos," and the tremendous "Aïda,"—not to mention his greatest works of all, "Otello" and "Falstaff," the fruit of his old age.

THE OPERA

OPERA in three acts. Text by Piave, adapted from Victor Hugo's drama *Le Roi s'Amuse*. Music by Giuseppe Verdi. First produced in Venice, March 11, 1851. First London production at Covent Garden, May 14, 1853; at the *Italiens*, Paris, January 19, 1857. Produced at the New Orleans Opera March 19, 1860, and in New Orleans on February 6, 1861, Patti sang in the opera for the first time. First New York production November 2, 1857, and since that time the opera has seldom been absent from the American stage. Clara Louise Kellogg made her début in opera, February 26, 1861, as *Gilda*, at the old Academy of Music, New York; Maretzek was the conductor and Theodore Thomas played first violin in the orchestra. A notable performance occurred November 23, 1903, at the Metropolitan Opera House, when Caruso made his American début. November 4, 1912, Ruffo made his début in the United States at the Metropolitan Opera House, Philadelphia, as *Rigoletto*.

349

FARRAR AS GILDA

COPY'T DUPONT
CARUSO AS THE DUKE

COPY'T MISHKIN
RENAUD AS RIGOLETTO

CHARACTERS

RIGOLETTO (*Ree-goh-let'-toh*), a hunchback, jester to the Duke.................Baritone

DUKE OF MANTUA, a titled profligate....................Tenor

GILDA (*Jeel'-dah*), daughter of Rigoletto...............Soprano

SPARAFUCILE (*Spahr-ah-foo-chee-leh*), a hired assassin........Bass

MADDALENA (*Mad-dah-lay'-nah*) his sister..............Contralto

COUNT MONTERONE (*Mon-ter-oh'-nay*)...............Baritone

COUNT CEPRANO (*Chay-prah'-noh*).Bass
Courtiers, Pages, Servants

Scene and Period: Mantua and Vicinity; Sixteenth Century

ACT I

SCENE I—*Ballroom in the Duke's Palace*

A FÊTE is in progress at the Ducal Palace, where the cynical and licentious *Duke* confides to a courtier that he is pursuing a lovely unknown whom he has seen in church, every Sunday during the past three months. She lives in a remote part of the city, where a mysterious man visits her nightly. His interest in this romantic adventure, however, does not prevent him from admiring the *Countess Ceprano*, who is dancing near them. His listener warns him that the *Count* might hear, but the *Duke* shrugs his shoulders indifferently. He gives vent to his philosophy of such matters in his first air: "Questa o quella,"—"Qu'une belle" (Mid the Fair Throng).

It is a smooth, flowing melody which in itself is a clue to the *Duke's* character. It is gay, yet there flows through it an undercurrent of irony.

The *Duke* dances with the *Countess*, but is watched by *Ceprano*; the fervent manner in which he kisses her hand is not lost upon the jealous husband. Nor does it escape the hunchback *Rigoletto*, who discharges a bit of raillery at *Ceprano's* expense. The *Duke* goes off, and *Ceprano* follows. *Rigoletto* also disappears, and the courtiers listen to the gossip *Marullo*, who tells them *Rigoletto* is in love, and that he pays nightly visits to his sweetheart. There is much laughter over the hunchback, pander to the Ducal romances, turned Cupid. The *Duke* returns with *Rigoletto*, *Ceprano* still following, and something like a scene develops as *Rigoletto*, under cover of the *Duke's* protection, talks satirically of *Ceprano*.

The courtiers long have chafed, as it

350

happens, under the immoralities of the *Duke*, abetted by *Rigoletto*, and so *Ceprano* plans vengeance. Matters come to a head, however, with the entrance of *Monterone*, an aged courtier whose wife was first a victim of the ducal passions, and afterwards his daughter. He protests with such vigor that *Rigoletto* steps between him and the *Duke*, with the flippant "Ch'io le parli" (I Will Speak to Him).

Rigoletto coarsely ridicules the old man, which enrages him beyond all reason. He utters a fearful curse, a father's malediction, against the *Duke* and his hunchback. This creates a profound sensation among the courtiers. Even the *Duke* is scared, so he orders the man arrested. The old *Count* is taken out, but *Rigoletto* in his own turn, is genuinely terrified. Like many of no conscience he is profoundly superstitious, where his daughter is concerned; for the "sweetheart" *Marullo* speaks of is in truth his own child, whom he keeps secluded against harm. He is, above all, suspicious of the *Duke*. And well he need be, for the girl whom the *Duke* has remarked at Church is none other than *Gilda*, the hunchback's beautiful daughter.

SCENE II—*A Street. Rigoletto's Cottage on one side, opposite the Palace of Count Ceprano*

THE jester steals away to the house where *Gilda* lives concealed. He is deeply oppressed by *Monterone's* malediction. In the street he is accosted by *Sparafucile*, a professional bravo, who offers to make him rid of the enemy, if he has one. The assassin confides that his method of work is to lure people to his home on the outskirts of the town, through his charming sister, there to make away with them with his trusty knife. *Rigoletto* promises to bear the rascal in mind. He dilates to himself on the re-

semblance of their two methods, for while *Sparafucile* stabs men with a dagger, *Rigoletto* uses, with equal skill, his poisonous tongue, and it is hard to say which is the more deadly. This soliloquy is the famous "Monologo—Pari siamo" (We Are Equal),—Rigoletto's Monologue.

Rigoletto's affection for *Gilda* seems the one redeeming feature in his black character. When he enters the courtyard of his house, the girl runs out to meet him, and the scene between them is touching in its display of genuine affection. *Gilda*, who is lonely, and knows nothing of her origin, asks him of her mother, and a pathetic duet follows, the "Deh non parlare al misero" (Recall Not the Past).

Rigoletto embraces her tenderly, but recalling the curse, he solemnly enjoins her to remain strictly within the house and never to venture into the town. He even questions her to know if anybody has followed her to church, but *Gilda* keeps silent regarding the man whom she has met there. Even while they converse, the *Duke*, disguised as a student, slips into the courtyard under cover of the increasing darkness and hides behind a tree, throwing a purse to *Giovanna*, the maid.

Soon as *Rigoletto* has departed, the *Duke* comes forward. *Gilda*, alarmed, bids him begone; but he knows well how to calm her fears, and soon a love-duet is heard,—the "E il sol dell'anima" (Love is the Sun).

After a tender farewell, the *Duke* leaves her, first declaring his name is Walter Malde. *Gilda* remains pensive, and when he is gone, she dreams of her wonderful lover in an air that will always remain a favorite,—the "Caro Nome" (Dearest Name).

This lovely melody, with its delicate accompaniment and flute passages, is one of the most exacting of coloratura arias, calling for extraordinary skill if its *fioriture* are to be performed with the grace they demand.

But while she is yet singing, there is a conspiracy at work. Night has fallen, and a band of masked courtiers, led by *Ceprano*, sets out for vengeance. *Rigoletto*, unexpectedly returning, runs across them. He is much alarmed to find them in his neighborhood. His fears, however, are somewhat calmed when they declare they are bent on stealing *Ceprano's* wife, for their good friend, the *Duke*. He points out *Ceprano's* house, and offers help. They insist that he must be disguised, and they contrive to give him a mask which covers his eyes and ears. Then they lead him in a circle to his own balcony, giving him the ladder to hold. *Gilda* is seized, her mouth is gagged with a handkerchief, and she is carried away. Left alone, *Rigoletto* suddenly becomes suspicious, and, tearing off his mask, he finds himself at his own balcony. On the ground he sees *Gilda's* kerchief. Frantic with fear he rushes into the house, finds his daughter gone, and falls in a swoon as the curtain descends. "Ah!" he cries, "The curse!"

ACT II

Scene—*A Hall in the Duke's Palace*

AFTER leaving the house of the hunchback, the *Duke* returns only to find the bird flown. He is now back at the palace, mourning for her with such eloquence that we are almost disposed to pity.

The *Duke's* melancholy musings are changed to joy, however, when the courtiers enter and apprise him they have captured *Rigoletto's* "mistress." He is amused at the details of the capture, laughing at the brilliant idea that makes *Rigoletto* himself a party to the abduction. He learns that *Gilda* is in the next room, and he hastens to her. No sooner has he gone than *Rigoletto* enters, pitifully striving to conceal his deep distress under a laughing exterior.

"Povero Rigoletto" (Poor Rigoletto!) sing the courtiers, enjoying his discomposure at the loss of one they still believe to be only his mistress. A page enters, but is told the *Duke* cannot be disturbed. The Jester hunchback, all attempts at concealment

MONTERONE DENOUNCES THE JESTER—ACT I

352

breaking down, declares the girl his daughter. He attempts to force an entrance, but the courtiers bar his efforts. Then follows one of the most remarkable scenes in any opera, the "Cortigiani, vil razza dannata" (Vile Race of Courtiers). Giving way freely, he rages like a mad man among the *Duke's* followers. Soon follows abjectness, collapse, abasement. The courtiers first laugh, then they grow indifferent. Into the midst of this enters *Gilda*. The courtiers, now somewhat abashed, leave the hunchback and his daughter together, and she then tells of the lover who followed her from church: "Tutte le feste al tempio" (On Ev'ry Festal Morning).

Rigoletto does his best to comfort the ruined girl, clasping her to his bosom with a tenderness and love that does much to atone for his vileness. Then follows the very beautiful "Piangi fanciulla" (Weep, My Child).

By a singular chance, *Count Monterone* passes through the hall, under guard. He pauses before the *Duke's* portrait, exclaiming, "No thunder from Heaven yet hath burst down to strike thee!" As he passes on, *Rigoletto* watches him grimly. Her father's stern demeanor frightens the girl, and he vows a terrible vengeance upon the *Duke*.

ACT III

SCENE—*A Ruined Inn at a Lonely Spot on the River Mincio*

FROM the luxurious grandeur of the Ducal Palace to this desolate harbor of crime, leads on the story of *Rigoletto's* vengeance. We are taken to the abode of *Sparafucile*, the assassin. It is an ancient inn, so ruined that one may see the broken staircase which leads to the loft from the ground floor, and even a couch within the loft itself. Near the inn rolls the river; beyond, the towers of Mantua reach toward the scudding clouds. *Sparafucile* is indoors seated by the table polishing his belt, unconscious that *Rigoletto* and his daughter are without, the latter dressed as a young cavalier, for it is her father's intention that she shall leave the city disguised as a boy.

The hunchback asks *Gilda* if she still dreams of the *Duke*, and she is obliged to confess that she still cherishes in

THE ABDUCTION OF GILDA

353

her heart her love for the student who came to her so full of romantic protestations. He startles her by leading her to the inn. The *Duke* appears, disguised as a soldier, calling loudly for wine. While *Sparafucile* is serving him he sings one more song of the love of women. *Gilda* learns her lover's true character at first hand. This song is the well-known "La donna e mobile" (Woman is Fickle).

The air needs only a brief quotation to be readily recognized:

La don-na è mo-bi - le qual piu-ma al ven - to, mu-ta d'ac - cen - to e di pen sie - ro
Wom-an is fick - le, false al-to-geth-er, Mov'd like the feather borne by the bree-zes

It portrays, clearly as words and music may, the indolently amorous young noble and his views of women kind,—whom he charges all and sundry with his own worst failings.

The murderous innkeeper brings the wine and knocks upon the ceiling, when his young sister descends. She laughingly evades the caresses of the *Duke.*

All this is part of *Rigoletto's* plan for vengeance, as *Sparafucile* has been engaged to kill him.

Then follows the Quartet, which with the "Sextet from Lucia," enjoys the greatest popularity of all operatic concerted pieces,—"Bella figlia dell'amore" (Fairest Daughter of the Graces).

Those who love this masterpiece for the sheer charm of its melody, the blending of the voices, the masterly development of the climax, have only a slight conception of its true beauty. It expresses, simultaneously, the rapture of the *Duke,* the sensuous charm of the girl who coquets with him, the dismay of the heartbroken *Gilda,* who now sees with her own eyes the perfidy of her seducer, and lastly the lust for vengeance of *Rigoletto,* who beholds, at last, the *Duke* within easy grasp.

Rigoletto bids his daughter observe what is going on within.

The *Duke* ascends the rickety stairs to his bedroom and is soon asleep. *Rigoletto* bids his daughter go with all

THE QUARTET—ACT III

speed to Verona, where he plans to follow. Once gone, he pays *Sparafucile* half his assassin's fee, the remainder being due when the *Duke's* body is delivered to the hunchback at midnight.

Rigoletto would have done better had he listened more closely to the *Duke's* plaint that "women are fickle," for no sooner does *Rigoletto* vanish than the assassin's sister, *Maddalena*, who has fallen in love with the *Duke*, delicately suggests he should kill *Rigoletto* instead. The honor said to exist among thieves apparently includes murderers too, for *Sparafucile* declares that he has never yet failed in his duty toward an employer. *Maddalena* pleads, however, and finally he agrees that if another guest shall arrive before midnight, he will slay him instead of the *Duke*, so that *Rigoletto* will at least have a corpse for his money.

A storm bursts, adding to the tragedy the wailing of the winds and the long rush of rain. As the first drops fall, *Gilda* creeps back to the inn, for she would learn more of what is going on. The storm develops, and its characteristic number is sung,—the "Tempesta—Somiglia un Apollo" (He's Fair as Apollo). The tragedy moves on.

While *Gilda* expresses horror, *Maddalena* sings in praise of her Apollo-like lover. *Sparafucile* bids her repair the sack which is to hold the dead man's body. Add to this the wailing of a chorus behind the scenes, humming in parallel minor thirds chromatically up and down the scale to suggest the winds, and you have the contents of an impressively dramatic record!

Gilda, hearing the extraordinary agreement of brother and sister, sees a way to preserve her lover and to end her own sorrows at one blow. Summoning up her last despairing courage, she knocks at the door, and thus receives the assassin's stroke.

Rigoletto returns. He pays off the assassin and receives the sack with its gruesome contents. The murderer, fearing discovery, offers to throw the body into the river; but this is to be the revengeful Jester's own special privilege. He bids *Sparafucile* begone.

Left alone he gloats horribly over his vengeance:

He is there, pow'rless! Ah, I must see him!
Nay, 'twere folly! 'tis he surely! I feel his spurs
    here.
Look on me now ye courtiers!
Look here, and tremble,
Here the buffoon is King!

He is about to drag the body to the

SPARAFUCILE'S DEN—ACT III

river, when he hears a sound that makes his blood run cold. It is the voice of the *Duke*, in the inn, making fresh love to the charming *Maddalena*. At once he begins to tear at the sack, and, holding wide his mouth, he discovers the crumpled form of *Gilda*.

Though unconscious she is not yet quite dead, and she revives under the night air, just enough to bid him a last farewell. The duet which closes this strangely powerful work is a noble piece of music,—the "Lassu in cielo" (In Heaven Above).

THE VICTOR RECORDS

(Sung in Italian unless noted)

ACT I

QUESTA O QUELLA
('Mid the Fair Throng) ENRICO CARUSO, Tenor   500   10-in., $1.50
GIOVANNI MARTINELLI, Tenor
                                     731   10-in., 1.50
JOHN McCORMACK,Tenor 767   10-in., 1.50
DUKE:
'Mid the fair throng that sparkle around me,
 Not one o'er my heart holds sway;
Though a sweet smile one moment may charm me,
 A glance from some bright eye its spell drives away.
All alike may attract, each in turn may please;
 Now with one I may trifle and play,
Then another may sport with and tease—
 Yet all my heart to enslave their wiles display.

MONOLOGO—PARI SIAMO
(We Are Equal) TITTA RUFFO, Baritone
                                    6263   12-in., $2.00
RIGOLETTO:
Yon assassin is my equal—
He stabs in darkness,
While I with a tongue of malice
Stab men by daylight!
(*He thinks of Monterone's curse.*)
He laid a father's curse on me....
(*Continuing in a burst of rage.*)
Oh hideous fate! Cruel nature!
Thou hast doom'd me to a life of torment.
I must jest, I must laugh,
And be their laughing stock!
Yonder the Duke, my master,
Youthful and brilliant, rich and handsome,
Tells me, between sleeping and waking:
"Come, buffoon, I would laugh now!"
Oh shame, I must obey him!
Oh life accursed! How I hate ye,
Race of vile and fawning courtiers!

CARO NOME
(Dearest Name) LUISA TETRAZZINI,
 Soprano   6344   12-in., $2.00
NELLIE MELBA, Soprano 6213   12-in., 2.00
AMELITA GALLI-CURCI, Soprano
                                     6126   12-in., 2.00
GILDA:
Carv'd upon my inmost heart
Is that name forevermore
Ne'er again from thence to part,
Name of love that I adore,
Thou to me are ever near,
Ev'ry thought to thee will fly,
Life for thee alone is dear,
Thine shall be my parting sigh!
(*Gilda enters the house, but reappears on the balcony.*)
Oh, dearest name!
(*She disappears, but can still be heard.*)
Oh! name beloved!
Dear name, within this breast,
Thy mem'ry will remain!
My love for thee confess'd,
No power can restrain!
Carved upon my inmost heart
Is that name forevermore.
Ev'ry thought to thee will fly,
Thine shall be my parting sigh,
Oh Walter mine!

ACT II

PARMI VEDER LE LAGRIME
(Each Tear That Falls) ENRICO CARUSO,
 Tenor   6016   12-in., $2.00
POVERO RIGOLETTO
(Poor Rigoletto) PASQUALE AMATO,
 Baritone with BADA, SETTI and
 Metropolitan Opera Chorus
                                     6041   12-in., 2.00
CORTIGIANI, VIL RAZZA DANNATA
(Vile Race of Courtiers) PASQUALE
 AMATO, Baritone   6041   12-in., 2.00

RIGOLETTO:
Race of courtiers, vile rabble detested,
Have ye sold her, whose peace ye molested?
Where is she? do not rouse me to madness—
Though unarm'd, of my vengeance beware,
For the blood of some traitor I'll pour!
(*Again making for the door.*)
Let me enter, ye assassins, stand back!
That door I must enter!
(*He struggles again with the courtiers but is
repulsed and gives up in despair.*)
Ah, I see it—all against me—have pity!
Ah, I weep.before ye, Marullo, so kindless?
Others' grief never yet saw thee mindless,
Tell, oh tell where my child they have hidden,
Is't there?—say in pity—thou'rt silent! alas!
(*In tears.*)
Oh, my lords, will ye have no compassion
On a father's despairing intercession?
Give me back my belov'd only daughter,
Have pity, oh give me back my child,
In pity, oh hear me implore!

TUTTE LE FESTE AL TEMPIO
(On Every Festal Morning) AMELITA
GALLI-CURCI, Soprano 6432 12-in., $2.00

PIANGI FANCIULLA
(Weep, My Child) AMELITA GALLI-
CURCI, Soprano and GIUSEPPE DE
LUCA, Baritone 3027 10-in., 2.00

ACT III

LA DONNA È MOBILE
(Woman is Fickle) ENRICO CARUSO,
Tenor 500 10-in., 1.50

GIOVANNI MARTINELLI, Tenor
733 10-in., $1.50
MIGUEL FLETA, Tenor 948 10-in., 1.50

DUKE:
Woman is fickle, false altogether,
Moves like a feather borne on the breezes;
Woman with guiling smile will e'er deceive you,
Often can grieve you, yet e'er she pleases,
Her heart's unfeeling, false altogether;
Moves like a feather borne on the breeze,
Borne on the breeze, borne on the breeze!
Wretched the dupe is, who when she looks
kindly,
Trusts to her blindly. Thus life is wasted!
Yet he must surely be dull beyond measure,
Who of love's pleasure never has tasted.
Woman is fickle, false altogether,
Moves like a feather, borne on the breeze!

QUARTETTE—BELLA FIGLIA DELL'
AMORE
(Fairest Daughter of the Graces)
AMELITA GALLI-CURCI, FLORA PERINI,
ENRICO CARUSO and GIUSEPPE DE
LUCA 10000 12-in., 3.50

LUCREZIA BORI, Soprano; JOSEPHINE
JACOBY, Mezzo-Soprano; JOHN MC-
CORMACK, Tenor; REINALD WER-
RENRATH, Baritone 10006 12-in., 3.50

PARAPHRASE DE CONCERT
(Liszt) ALFRED CORTOT, Pianist
6064 12-in., 2.00

BLACK LABEL AND BLUE LABEL RECORDS

{Rigoletto Quartet.............................*Victor Opera Quartet*}55066 12-in., $1.50
{ Lucia Sextette.................................*Victor Opera Sextette*

{Rigoletto Quartet........................*Kryl's Bohemian Band*}35239 12-in., 1.25
{ Trovatore Selection (Home to Our Mountains).............*Vessella's Band*

{Rigoletto Quartet *Accordion*......................................*Pietro*}35367 12-in., 1.25
{ Light Cavalry Overture *Accordion*.............................*Pietro*

{Rigoletto Quartet........................*Brown Bros. Saxophone Sextette*}18217 10-in., .75
{ Passion Dance (C. M. *Jones*).............*Brown Bros. Saxophone Sextette*

{E il sol dell'anima (Love is the Sun)...........*Pereira and de Gregorio*}67135 10-in., .75
{Deh non parlare (Recall not the Past)................*Pereira and Maggi*

{Comme la plume (Woman is Fickle) (*In French*)...*Leon Campagnola, Tenor*}45118 10-in., 1.00
{Qu'une belle (Mid the Fair Throng) (*In French*)....*Leon Campagnola, Tenor*

{Gems from "Rigoletto"...........................*Victor Opera Company*}
{ "Pleasure Calls Us"—"Carved Upon My Heart"—"Sun of the Soul"— }35731 12-in., 1.25
{ "Woman is Fickle"—Quartet, "Fairest Daughter"—"Away Disturber." }
{Gems from "Faust"............................*Victor Opera Company*}

RINALDO

OPERA in three acts. Text by Adam Hill; Italian text by Rossi, founded on the episode of *Rinaldo* and *Armida* in Tasso's *Gerusalemme Liberata*. Music by George Frederick Händel.

"Rinaldo" was produced at a time when Italian music had become the fashion in London, and the composer followed the plan then in vogue, to write the dialogue in recitative form. This opera was written by Händel in the amazingly brief time of fourteen days, and first performed at Queen's Theatre, February 24, 1711. The work was put on to signalize the coming of Händel to London, and it was a magnificent production for that period. Only the year before, the composer had been induced to leave the Court of Hanover for that of England; and upon his arrival in London, Mr. Aaron Hill, the enterprising manager of the new Haymarket Theatre, engaged him to supply an Italian opera. Hill planned "Rinaldo," Rossi wrote the Italian libretto and Händel hurriedly dashed off the music.

The opera ran for fifteen consecutive nights—an unprecedented feat for that age—and it was mounted with a splendor then quite unusual. Among other innovations, the gardens of *Armida* were filled with living birds, a piece of realism hardly outdone even in these days.

CHARACTERS

RINALDO, a knight (*Ree-nahl'-doh*)................Soprano
ARMIDA, an enchantress (*Ahr-mee'-dah*) ....Soprano
ALMIRENA, Godfrey's daughter (*Ahl-mee-ray'-nah*) ......Soprano
ARGANTE, a Pagan king (*Ahr-gahn'-teh*)................Bass
GODFREY, a noble..............Bass
EUSTAZIO (*Yoo-statts'-ee-oh*) ......Alto

The Action takes place in Palestine at the Time of the Crusade

RINALDO is a Knight Templar who loves *Almirena*, daughter of *Godfrey*. The enchantress, *Armida*, also loves *Rinaldo*, and in a jealous rage seizes *Almirena* and conceals her in a magic garden. *Armida's* lover, a Pagan King named *Argante*, complicates matters by himself falling in love with *Almirena*. *Rinaldo* finally rescues *Almirena*, and the sorceress and her lover are captured and converted to Christianity.

Among the many arias of great beauty with which the score abounds is the "Lascia ch'io pianga", in which *Almirena* laments her capture by the sorceress. This air is one of the finest bequeathed to us by the grand old composer of "The Messiah." Händel liked it so well that he used it in no less than three of his works. It appears first as a Sarabande, used as a dance to accompany some Asiatics in the ballet scene in the last act of "Almira." "Almira" was the first of Händel's operas, and was produced in Hamburg, 1795, the composer then being only nineteen years of age. Later the melody was used in "Il Trionfo del Tempo," and finally as "Lascia ch'io pianga" in another opera, "Rinaldo."

THE VICTOR RECORD

LASCIA CH'IO PIANGA
(My Tears Shall Flow) GIUSEPPE DE LUCA, Baritone *In Italian*
6081 12-in., $2.00

ROBERT LE DIABLE

(ROBERT THE DEVIL)

OPERA in five acts; words by Scribe; music by Meyerbeer. First presented in Paris, November 22, 1831; in London, in English, at Drury Lane, 1832; in Italian, May 4, 1847 (first appearance of Jenny Lind). First American production, New York, April 7, 1834. Revived at the Astor Place Theatre, 1851, and 1857, with Formes in the cast; and in 1875 with Ilma di Murska. The first Metropolitan production occurred in the '80s under Henry E. Abbey's management.

ROBERT, Duke of Normandy, who was called *Robert the Devil* because of his courage in battle and his successes in love, is banished by his subjects and goes to Sicily, where he continues to struggle with an Evil Spirit, which seems to tempt him to every kind of excess. *Alice*, his foster sister, suspects that his supposed friend *Bertram* is in reality this evil influence. At the close of Act I *Robert*, led on by *Bertram*, gambles away all his possessions, and failing to attend the Tournament, loses the honor of a knight and greatly displeases the *Lady Isabella*, whom he loves.

The second act shows the entrance to the Cavern of Satan, and a company of Evil Spirits. Then is heard the "Valse Infernal," "Ecco una nuova" (I Have Spread My Toils) when *Bertram* promises the Demons that he will complete the ruin of *Robert*. The fiends rejoice at the prospect of adding another soul to their company.

Alice, who has come to the vicinity of the cave to meet her lover, overhears this infernal bargain and determines to save him. *Robert*, dejected over the loss of his wealth and honor, meets *Bertram*, who promises that all shall be restored if he will have the courage to visit the ruined abbey and secure a certain magic branch, which has the power to convey wealth, power and immortality. The next scene shows the ruins, where *Bertram* invokes the aid of the buried nuns. The spectres arise, and when *Robert* appears they dance around him and lead him to the grave of St. Rosalie, where he is shown the branch. Overcoming his fears, he grasps it, and by its power defeats the demons. In the next scene *Robert* uses the branch to become invisible, and he goes to *Lady Isabella's* room to carry her off. But moved by her entreaties, he breaks the branch, thus destroying the spell.

In the last act *Bertram* renews his efforts to induce *Robert* to sign an eternal contract. Tired of life, he is about to yield when *Alice* appears and tells him of the last words of his mother warning him against the *Fiend*,—who is in reality *Robert's* father. The clock strikes twelve, and the baffled *Fiend* disappears, while the cathedral door opens displaying the *Princess* waiting for the reformed *Robert*.

THE VICTOR RECORDS

VALSE INFERNAL—ECCO UNA NUOVA PREDA
(I Have Spread My Toils) MARCEL JOURNET, Bass, with Opera Chorus
In French   6176 12-in., $2.00

ACT III

INVOCATION—NONNES, QUI REPOSEZ
(Ye Slumb'ring Nuns) POL PLANÇON, Bass. *In French*   6371 12-in., $2.00

PHOTO WHITE   SCENE FROM ROBIN HOOD—ACT II

ROBIN HOOD

COMIC opera in three acts. Libretto by Harry B. Smith; music by Reginald de Koven. First performance in Chicago, June 9, 1890, by the Bostonians, who sang the opera more than four thousand times.

CHARACTERS
(With Original Cast)

ROBERT OF HUNTINGTON, known as
Robin Hood..Edwin Hoff, Tenor
SHERIFF OF NOTTINGHAM
Henry Clay Barnabee, Bass
SIR GUY OF GISBORNE, his ward
Peter Lang, Tenor
LITTLE JOHN, outlaw
W. H. Macdonald, Baritone
WILL SCARLET, outlaw
Eugene Cowles, Bass
ALLAN-A-DALE, outlaw
Jessie Bartlett Davis, Contralto
FRIAR TUCK, outlaw
George Frothingham, Bass
LADY MARIAN, afterwards Maid
Marian.... Marie Stone, Soprano
DAME DURDEN, a widow
Josephine Bartlett, Contralto
ANNABEL, her daughter
Carlotta Maconda, Soprano

Villagers, Milkmaids, Outlaws, King's Foresters, Archers and Peddlers

Time and Place: Nottingham, England, in the Twelfth Century

AT the beginning of the opera a merrymaking is in progress at the marketplace in Nottingham. The three outlaws *Little John, Will Scarlet* and *Friar Tuck,* enter and sing of their free life in the Forest of Sherwood, and finally the handsome, dashing *Robin Hood* appears, declaring that he is the *Earl of Huntington,* and demanding that the *Sheriff* shall so proclaim him. The *Sheriff,* however, protests that the youth has been disinherited by his own father, who before the birth of *Robin Hood* was secretly married to a peasant girl, who died when her child was an infant. The child is *Sir Guy of Gisborne,* the rightful heir to the earldom and the *Sheriff's* ward, whom he is planning to marry to *Lady Marian,* ward of the Crown. However, the young girl and *Robin* already are deeply in love and exchanging vows of eternal faith—to the indignation of *Sir Guy. Lady Marian* protests against her marriage, hoping that on the return of the *King* from the Crusades she will be released, while *Robin Hood* plans with the help of the *King* to prove his right to the earldom. The outlaws sympathize with the pair and invite *Robin Hood* to join them, promising him he shall be their king and rule them under the Greenwood Tree—to which proposal *Robin Hood* at length agrees.

In the last act the dashing king of the outlaws brings the message saving *Maid Marian* from *Sir Guy*, and the opera ends amid general rejoicings at the triumph of *Robin Hood* and the gentle *Maid* over the plotting *Sheriff* and his ward. The finale is lively.

THE VICTOR RECORD

OH, PROMISE ME
LOUISE HOMER, Contralto
680 10-in., $1.50

BLACK LABEL RECORDS

Gems from "Robin Hood"—Part I...............*Victor Light Opera Co.* "Hey, for the Merry Greenwood"—"Brown October Ale"—"Come Dreams So Bright"—"Tinkers' Chorus"—"Oh, Promise Me"— "Come Away to the Woods" Gems from "Robin Hood"—Part II...............*Victor Light Opera Co.* "Ho, Ho, Then for Jollity"—"Ye Birds in Azure Winging"—"Armorer's Song"—"A Hunting We'll Go"—"Ah! I Do Love You"— "Sweetheart, My Own Sweetheart"—"Love, Now We Never More Will Part"	35413	12-in.,	$1.25
Oh, Promise Me.............................*Elsie Baker, Contralto* In the Gloaming................................*Elsie Baker, Contralto*	17806	10-in.,	.75
The Cross Bow....................................*Imperial Male Qt.* Way Down Yonder................................*Imperial Male Qt.*	17873	10-in.,	.75
Oh, Promise Me.............................*Lewis James, Tenor* Sing Me to Sleep...........................*Elsie Baker, Contralto*	16196	10-in.,	.75
Oh, Promise Me.............................*Alan Turner, Baritone* Dearie......................................*Elsie Baker, Contralto*	17189	10-in.,	.75
Oh, Promise Me ....*Violin-'Cello-Harp Venetian Trio* Silver Threads Among the Gold.....................*Neapolitan Trio*	17816	10-in.,	.75
Favorite Airs from the Opera........................*Pryor's Band* Prince of Pilsen Selection (*Luders*).................*Sousa's Band*	16919	10-in.,	.75
Armorer's Song...........................*Wilfred Glenn, Bass* Till The Sands of the Desert Grow Cold............*Wilfred Glenn, Bass*	17268	10-in.,	.75

PHOTO WHITE   SCENE FROM ROBIN HOOD—ACT III

LE ROI DE LAHORE

(THE KING OF LAHORE)

THIS is an early work of Massenet's, though it is highly characteristic. It is especially noted for its brilliant ballet, which deals with an Eastern paradise.

THE OPERA

OPERA in four acts. Libretto by Jules Gallet; music by Jules Massenet. First produced Grand Opera, Paris, April 27, 1877; Covent Garden, Royal Italian Opera, June 28, 1879; New York, February 29, 1924.

CHARACTERS

ALIM, King of Lahore (*Ah-leem, Rwah du Lah-ohr*) . . . . Tenor
SCINDIA, his minister (*Seen-dee-ah*) . . . . Baritone
TIMUR, a priest (*Tee-moor*) . . . . . . Bass
INDRA (*In-drah*) . . . . Bass
SITA (*See-tah*) . . . . Soprano
KALED, confidant of the King (*Kah-led*) . . . . Mezzo-Soprano

Time and Place: India; the Eleventh Century, during the Mussulman Invasion

SITA, niece of the high priest and the namesake of a Brahmanical goddess, is beloved by *Alim*, King of Lahore. His own minister and rival, *Scindia*, accuses her of profaning the Temple. She is condemned to death, but she is saved by the *King*, who asks her hand in marriage. *Alim*, at war with the Mussulmans, is betrayed by his false minister, who seizes the throne and carries away *Sita*.

Alim is transported to the heavens, but he is not contented, and he begs the gods, headed by *Indra*, to permit him to return to earth. He is granted the power, provided he does not resume his rank, and that he returns when *Sita* dies. On his return he discovers the true condition of affairs. He declares himself but is denounced as an impostor. He takes flight, *Sita* with him, and as they are about to be captured she kills herself. *Alim*, fulfilling his vow, perishes also, and the lovers are united in celestial realms. A mystical feeling prevails throughout.

One of the most famous of all the opera's numbers is the beautiful "Promesse de mon avenir," in Italian "O Casto Fior," and in English "Oh, Promise of a Joy Divine." This is sung by *Scindia* when, his evil victory accomplished, he dreams of the beautiful *Sita*. It is a marvellous aria.

THE VICTOR RECORDS

ACT IV

O CASTO FIOR
(Oh, What Promise of a Joy Divine!)
TITTA RUFFO, Baritone *In Italian*
6265 12-in., $2.00
MATTIA BATTISTINI, Baritone *In Italian*
6046 12-in., 2.00

SCINDIA :
The Sultan's barb'rous horde, who had so
gladly riven
From us fair Lahore,
By our own might have from the field been
driven.
From care my people free,
Loudly sound forth my praises!
O promise fair of joy divine, Sita,
Thou dream of all my life,
O beauty torn from me by strife,
At last, thou shalt be mine! O Sita!
O fair one, charm my loving heart,
And ne'er again from me depart!

* * * * * * * * * * * *

Sita, my queen thou soon shalt be!
To thee the world its glory offers,
To thee a king his crown now proffers;
Come, Sita, O come! ah! be mine!

(From the English translation by Dudley Buck, from the Schirmer "Operatic Anthology" (Copyright, G. Schirmer), given here by permission).

THE STATUE OF SAINT CORENTIN WARNING KARNAC—ACT II

LE ROI D'YS

Opera in three acts and five tableaux; text by Édouard Blau; music by Édouard Lalo. First production at the Opéra Comique, Paris, May 7, 1888. The opera made a great success and was awarded the *Acâdemie* prize. It had its hundredth representation in 1889, and is still in the repertory of the Opéra Comique. First American production at the New Orleans Opera, January 23, 1890, with Furst, Balleroy, Geoffroy, Rossi, Leavinson and Beretta.

CHARACTERS

THE KING OF YS (*Luh Rwah Deece*)
MARGARET; ROZENN, his daughters
MYLIO, a Knight
PRINCE OF KARNAC, at war with the King
People, Soldiers, Gentlemen of the Court, Ladies, Horsemen, Retainers

Time and Place: Armorica (Ancient Brittany); Middle Ages

Blau's libretto is based on an old legend about the flooding of the ancient Armorican city of Is, or, as Blau called it, "Ys." *The King of Ys* is at war with his neighbor, the *Prince of Karnac*. His daughters, *Margaret* and *Rozenn*, both have loved a Knight *Mylio*, but he is supposed to have died in battle. The *King* has bargained with *Karnac*, proposing that he shall wed *Margaret*, and thus end the exhausting war. The *Princess* does not relish the thought of this alliance, and when *Mylio* proves to be still alive she decides to wed him even at the cost of her father's kingdom. *Karnac* is enraged at the insult and challenges *Mylio* to a duel. The *King* agrees to give his other daughter, *Rozenn*, to the victor. *Mylio* wins and *Margaret*, furious that her sister should possess *Mylio*, induces *Karnac* to flood the city by opening the sluice-gates which keep out the sea. When the water begins rising the *King* and his family flee to high ground, *Karnac* taking the reluctant *Margaret* with him. As they watch the floods begin to destroy the city and drown the inhabitants, the *Princess*, remorseful, confesses her guilt and precipitates herself into the flood. Her sacrifice saves the city, however, as Saint Corentin rises from the sea and commands the waters to recede.

THE VICTOR RECORD

VAINEMENT, MA BIEN AIMÉE
(In Vain, Beloved) EDMOND CLEMENT,
  Tenor *In French*   6062 12-in., $2.00
BENIAMINO GIGLI, Tenor *In French*
                        906 10-in., 1.50

FARRAR AS JULIET

GALLI-CURCI AS JULIET

ALDA AS JULIET

ROMEO ET JULIETTE

(ROMEO AND JULIET)

AFTER "Faust," "Romeo and Juliet" is the most popular of Gounod's many operas, the most of them forgotten. It has been called, and not unjustly, "a love duet with occasional interruptions," and it contains many melodies of great beauty, the most famous of which is the waltz, in the first act. The opera follows very closely the action of Shakespeare's drama, though the interruption of the balcony scene will come as a surprise to many. What artistic purpose is served by this is doubtful; at any rate it serves the practical purpose of lending variety, increasing "suspense" and giving the singers a chance to breathe. Several of the Shakespearian personages have been omitted from the opera cast by the librettists, and a new one added —the page, *Stephano*, who precipitates the fight in the third act. These changes, however are but natural. It takes longer to sing through a drama than it does to talk, and a play so lavish with words as Shakespeare's must needs go through some process of reduction. As far as possible the authors appear to have stuck to Shakespeare's text, but here again operatic necessities have had to be considered. The steady metre of Shakespeare's verse had to be cut up to afford the composer a supply of lyrics, and a variety of rhythms; otherwise he would scarcely have escaped monotony. If it is borne in mind that Shakespeare's English first had to be turned into French, the French turned into Opera-librettese, and that again translated into English so as to fit Gounod's music, it is likely that the verses used in the English libretto of the work will offer a few

FROM A PAINTING

ROMEO AND JULIET IN THE FRIAR'S CELL

THE MARRIAGE

surprises to the Shakespearian student. Those who desire, however, a more poetic version of the world's greatest love-drama know well where to find one!

THE OPERA

OPERA in five acts. Words by Barbier and Carré, after Shakespeare's drama. Music by Charles Gounod. First produced at the *Théâtre Lyrique*, Paris, April 27, 1867. First London production July 11, 1867. First Milan production at La Scala, December 14, 1867. Presented in America, 1868, with Minnie Hauk.

Some famous American productions: 1890, with Patti, Ravelli, del Puente and Fabri; 1891, with Eames (début), the de Reszkes and Capoul; 1898, with Melba, Saleza, de Reszke and Plançon; more recently with Galli-Curci as *Juliet;* New York, 1922.

CHARACTERS

JULIET, daughter of Capulet..Soprano
STEPHANO (*Stef'-ah-noh*), page
    to Romeo..............Soprano
GERTRUDE, Juliet's nurse
        Mezzo-Soprano

ROMEO......................Tenor
TYBALT (*Tee-bahl'*), Capulet's
    nephew..................Tenor
BENVOLIO   (*Ben-voh'-lee-oh*)
    friend of Romeo..........Tenor
MERCUTIO (*Mer-kew'-shee-oh*)
    friend of Romeo........Baritone
PARIS (*Pah-ree'*), Capulet's
    kinsman...............Baritone
GREGORIO, Capulet's kinsman Baritone
CAPULET(*Cap-u-leh'*), a Veronese noble................Basso
FRIAR LAURENCE...............Bass
THE DUKE OF VERONA........Bass
Guests, Relatives and Retainers of the Capulets and Montagues.

The Action takes place in Verona

(The original French name of the opera is "Romeo et Juliette," *Zhoo-lee-et'*; the Italian is "Romeo e Giulietta," *Joo-lee-et'-tah*).

ACT I

SCENE—*Ballroom in Capulet's House*

CAPULET, a Veronese noble, is giving a masked ball in honor of his daughter *Juliet's* entrance into society. The young girl is presented to the guests by her father, and he calls on his guests to make merry. They leave for the banqueting-hall, *Juliet* leaning on the arm of *Paris*, to whom she has been betrothed at the wish of her father, and *Tybalt*, who is also her admirer and a friend of *Paris*.

No sooner are they gone than *Romeo* and a half dozen of his friends enter,—including *Mercutio*. As representing the rival house of *Montague*, their visit is a bit of audacity likely to cost their lives. While they are laughing over their prank, however, *Juliet* returns and they scarcely have time to hide before she appears, calling for her nurse, *Gertrude*. When *Gertrude* has gone, *Juliet* gives expression to her happiness in the charming "Valse" (Juliet's Waltz-Song).

She is about to return to the banquet, when *Romeo* enters. It is a case of love at first sight, which is not so rare as many might suppose. *Juliet* with delicious coquetry refers to his costume which is that of a pilgrim or palmer. The duet "Ange adorable" (Lovely Angel), ensues. Love travels fast. But the tete-a-tete is interrupted by the entrance of *Tybalt*, who is indeed a hot-headed member of the *Capulet* faction. He recognizes *Romeo* through his mask, and denounces him. There is a scene of course, as some of the other guests enter. *Romeo* is for drawing sword, but an open quarrel is avoided by the entrance of *Capulet*, who is loath to have the festivities spoiled. *Romeo* and his friends are permitted to go in peace.

ACT II
Scene—*Capulet's Garden; Juliet's Apartment Above*

IT is night. With a rope-ladder, *Romeo* ascends to the balcony where *Juliet* waits, and the long love-duet begins. The scene is taken almost as it stands from Shakespeare, save that

Gregorio and a company of servants, warned of a trespasser in the grounds, enter and make a search for the invader. *Romeo* is well concealed, and they depart vowing vengeance on the person who sent them on such a wild-goose chase. Nothing now interrupts the lovers, who soon are breathing their ecstasy to the stars. There is another lovely duet, "O nuit divine, je t' implore" (Night All Too Blessed).

It is interrupted by *Juliet's* nurse, who calls to them the hour grows late, so they indulge the sweet sorrow of parting with a lingering farewell, "Ne fuis encore" (Linger Yet a Moment).

ACT III
Scene I—*The Cell of Friar Laurence*

THE secret marriage of *Romeo* and *Juliet* takes place in the cell of *Friar Laurence*, who sees in the union a chance to reconcile the futile enmity of the *Montagues* and the *Capulets*. *Juliet* returns home with *Gertrude*.

Scene II—*A Street in Verona*

ROMEO'S impudent page, *Stephano*, having come in search of his master, sings an impertinent song before the *Capulet* house, which brings out *Gregorio*. Soon there is a fight, and things begin to look bad for the venturesome youth; but he is joined by others of the *Montagues*, including *Mercutio*, while *Tybalt* comes to the aid of *Gregorio*. *Mercutio* and *Tybalt* quarrel. Coming suddenly upon them *Romeo* tries to stop the fighting; it is impossible to quarrel now with the relatives of his bride. He is unsuccessful, however, and the fight is resumed. The *Capulets* and *Montagues* swarm out on either side and the trouble becomes general. *Mercutio* is wounded. Believing him dead, *Romeo* can no longer refrain from avenging his friend, and he sets-to against *Tybalt*. *Tybalt* is mortally wounded, and falls into the arms of *Capulet* himself. *Tybalt's* last prayer is for vengeance, and the head of his house now swears that vengeance shall be done.

Suddenly the *Duke of Verona* enters. On learning the cause of the trouble, he sentences *Romeo* to instant banishment, sparing his life only because he has fought honorably.

ACT IV

SCENE—*Juliet's Room*

ROMEO finds a way into *Capulet's* house, at imminent risk of death, bent on saying farewell to his bride and winning her pardon for the death of *Tybalt*. This is readily granted. After a tender farewell he departs. *Friar Laurence* enters, to tell the girl that it was *Tybalt's* dying wish that she should marry *Paris*, and that the wedding is to be hastened. *Juliet* is in despair, but *Friar Laurence* counsels patience. He then gives her a potion, telling her to drink it when the

marriage ceremony is about to commence. It will throw her into a death-like trance for forty-two hours, after which she may escape from her tomb and fly with *Romeo*.

With the departure of the kindly priest, *Capulet* enters with *Paris*, and the wedding is about to take place. She therefore drinks the potion, and sinks, apparently dead, before them.

ACT V

SCENE—*The Tomb of Juliet*

IN the silent vault of the *Capulets*, *Juliet* lies pale as marble in her trance. Having failed to receive *Friar Laurence's* message, *Romeo* forces in the door,—to gain one last glimpse of the bride he believes dead. After a tender farewell he drinks in turn a deadly poison. No sooner has he swallowed it than he is startled to behold signs of life in the body of *Juliet*. Too late! They have but time to say farewell. On learning that he has

DEATH OF THE LOVERS

slain himself, *Juliet* upbraids him for drinking all the poison:

Ah! thou churl
To drink all! No friendly drop
  thou'st left me
So I may die with thee!

She has, however, a dagger concealed among her grave-garments, and with this she stabs herself. Well content to face eternity together, *Romeo* and *Juliet*, in one another's arms, enter into their eternal sleep.

THE VICTOR RECORDS
(Sung in French except as noted)

ACT I
VALSE
(Juliet's Waltz Song) LUISA TETRAZZINI, Soprano *In Italian*   6345   12-in., $2.00
LUCREZIA BORI, Soprano   542   10-in.,   1.50
AMELITA GALLI-CURCI, Soprano
                        6133   12-in.,   2.00

JULIET:
Song, jest, perfume and dances.
Smiles, vows, love-laden glances
All that spells or entrances
In one charm blend
As in fair dreams enfolden
Born of fantasy golden,
Sprites from fairyland olden,
On me now bend.
Forever would this gladness
Shine on me brightly as now,
Would that never age or sadness
Threw their shade o'er my brow!

ANGE ADORABLE
(Lovely Angel) GERALDINE FARRAR, Soprano, and EDMOND CLEMENT, Tenor   8020   12-in., $2.50

ACT II
AH! LÈVE-TOI SOLEIL
(Arise, Fair Sun) FERNAND ANSSEAU, Tenor   6348   12-in.,   2.00

AH! NE FUIS PAS ENCORE!
(Ah! Linger Yet a Moment) LUCREZIA BORI, Soprano and BENIAMINO GIGLI, Tenor   3027   10-in.,   2.00

BLACK LABEL RECORD

Romeo and Juliet Selection......................*Arthur Pryor's Band*
  Introduction to Act I, "The Capulets' Ball"—Interlude, Act IV—   35234   12-in., $1.25
  Capulet's Solo, "The Altar is Prepared"—Ballet—Nuptial Procession.
Samson and Delilah Selection (Saint-Saëns)..........*Arthur Pryor's Band*

BENQUE, PARIS
JEAN AND EDUARD DE RESZKE AS ROMEO AND FRIAR LAURENCE

DELILAH: Come, dear one, follow me.
To Sorek, the fairest of valleys!

SAMSON AND DELILAH

DESPITE his extraordinary brilliance and the early success of his first works as a composer, Saint-Saëns had some difficulty in finding a way for his biblical opera, "Samson and Delilah." These difficulties were largely due to factional disturbances in musical Paris, springing up largely around the then revolutionary musical doctrines of Richard Wagner. Men of the older generation prized their authority; and in fighting tradition, Saint-Saëns but shared the lot of Massenet, Bizet, Chabrier, Godard and others. It is interesting to note, by the way, that Saint-Saëns relinquished some of the opinions he held at that time, himself growing more conservative as the years increased. In the seventies of the last century, however, he was regarded as quite an iconoclast. With the completion of "Samson and Delilah," a powerful friend came to his aid in the person of generous Franz Liszt, who never missed an opportunity to give genius a hearing. The young man was invited to Weimar, where the work was produced with a success which made other productions inevitable, and today it is regarded as one of the great classics of the opera stage. Saint-Saëns has composed many operas, none of which

SAMSON (*Caruso*):
 Lord, thy servant remember now,
 For one moment make him strong!
 (*Softly, to the boy*)
 Toward the marble columns,
 My child, guide thou my steps!
         (Act III)

PHOTO WHITE　　　　　　　　DANCE OF THE PHILISTINE MAIDENS

has equalled it in popular esteem, the nearest approach to it being "Henry VIII." No doubt a work bearing so closely upon the history of his race made its own special appeal. The score is a magnificent piece of work, with its Hebrew chants vividly contrasted with the sensuous music of the pagan Orient, and reaching its highest levels in the ever popular air of Delilah, "Mon coeur s'ouvre a ta voix," and in the Bacchanal music. The opera deserves to live.

THE OPERA

OPERA in three acts. Text by Ferdinand Lemaire; music by Camille Saint-Saëns. First production at Weimar under Liszt, December 2, 1877. In France at Rouen, 1890. Performed at Covent Garden in concert form, September 25, 1893. First American production at New Orleans, January 4, 1893, with Renaud and Mme. Mounier. First New York production February, 1895, with Tamagno and Mantelli (one performance only). Revived by Oscar Hammerstein, November 13, 1908, and again in 1911, with Gerville-Réache, Dalmores and Dufranne. Produced at the Metropolitan in 1915, with Caruso, Matzenauer and Amato.

CHARACTERS

DELILAH..............Mezzo-Soprano
SAMSON......................Tenor
HIGH PRIEST OF DAGON......Baritone
ABIMELECH, Satrap of Gaza First Bass
AN OLD HEBREW........Second Bass
PHILISTINE MESSENGER........Tenor
Chorus of Hebrews and Philistines

Time and Place: 1150 B. C.; Gaza in Palestine

(The original French name of the

371

opera is "Samson et Dalila," *Sahn-sohn'* (nasal) *ay Da-lee-lah*).

ACT I

Scene—*A Public Square in Gaza*

THE opera has no overture; we are plunged at once into the great scene where the Hebrews mourn in bondage, before the very gates of the temple of Dagon in Gaza. *Samson*, in the fervor of religious prophecy, bids them find new courage; but without arms, without leadership, they are despondent. *Abimelech*, the satrap of Gaza, enters with many warriors behind him, imperiously mocking the captive Israelites. *Samson*, exasperated, attacks him. With heaven-born strength he seizes *Abimelech's* sword and lays him dead, warding off the hosts that press against him. It is the signal for revolt, and the fight becomes general. The Philistines are pressed back by the Israelites under the fanatical leadership of *Samson*, and soon the stage is empty but for the body of *Abimelech*, slain by his own law of violence.

The gates of Dagon's Temple are thrown open, and the *High Priest* steps forth, attended by guards and followers. He bids his men avenge the stricken *Abimelech*, but their blood is turned to water. Messengers come announcing the defeat of the Philistines, and in despair, the *High Priest* curses the Israelites. He and his followers are forced to flee with the body of *Abimelech*, as the victorious Hebrews return headed by their aged men, chanting hymns of praise. It is *Samson's* great hour, and his followers enjoy their deliverance.

Once more the gates of the temple of Dagon are flung apart, but for a different scene. *Delilah* comes at the head of a company of women, bearing garlands of flowers for the victors. She is lovely, and her wisdom is not that of the temple, but of the world. Conscious of her power and charm, she approaches *Samson*, singing the beautiful "Je viens celebrer la victoire" (I Come to Celebrate Victory).

"I come to celebrate the victory of him who reigns in my heart," coos *Delilah* to the conqueror of the Philistines—soft words upon her lips but guile in her fair bosom. *Samson* prays for divine power to resist her, but in spite of himself he is forced to gaze at the beautiful creature as she dances with her maidens. An old man among the Hebrews warns him. But in the hands of *Delilah*, *Samson's* will is water. The three voices each pleading its own cause, *Delilah* and the old man with *Samson*, and *Samson* with his God, blend in rich harmony in this trio. As the young girls dance, *Delilah* sings to *Samson* the lovely song of Spring, "Printemps qui commence"—"Der Frühling erwachte" (Delilah's Song of Spring).

So in the hour of his triumph, as it is written, the heart of *Samson* is shaken within him, and as the curtain falls, he is *Delilah's* and *Delilah* knows it.

ACT II

Scene—*Delilah's Home, Valley of Sorek*

NIGHT is descending upon the valley, and *Delilah*, more sumptuously clad than ever, waits outside her dwelling for the approach of *Samson*. She calls upon Love to aid her, in another lovely song, the "Amour viens aider" (Love, Lend Me Thy Might).

The *High Priest of Dagon* comes to *Delilah*, enjoining her not to fail in her purpose. After he has gone, *Samson* himself appears, impelled by irresistible temptation, past principle, past conscience, past hope. Fearing she may even now have lost him, *Delilah* exercises her peculiar powers to the limit, in the "Mon coeur s'ouvre a ta voix" (My Heart at Thy Sweet Voice).

During this exquisite melody a storm has gathered, the swift pattering of the

COPY'T WHITE

SAMSON: Sore my distress, my guilt and anguish,
Have pity, O Lord, in misery I languish!
(Act III)

rain being suggested in the accompaniment. *Delilah* strives her utmost to persuade *Samson* to betray his plans, the increasing fury of the storm serving as the appropriate background for the turmoil of emotions. *Delilah* is anxious, imperative; *Samson*, drawn toward her, yet resisting. He finally refuses, praying for strength with a vehemence that threatens *Delilah's* own safety. She leads him into the house and calls for help. Her cry is answered by the Philistines, who rush in· and overpower *Samson*, just as the storm reaches a climax with a violent crash of thunder.

ACT III

SCENE I—*A Prison at Gaza*

SIGHTLESS and chained, his heavy locks shorn away, the mighty

Samson slowly and painfully treads round and round, a heavy mill which is grinding corn for the Philistines. Near by is a group of Hebrew captives. Out of the depths of his misery, *Samson* calls upon the Lord to pity him, offering his "poor, bruised soul" to the Almighty whose mandates he has disregarded for the sake of the false *Delilah*. His prayer is echoed by the wretched prisoners, a few of whom, however, are pitilessly scornful. "Vois ma misere helas" (Sore My Distress, Alas!), sings the broken hero.

SCENE II—*A Magnificent Hall in the Temple of Dagon*

THE *High Priest* and the Philistines are having a great feast, and rejoicing over the downfall of their enemies. This is a wonderful scene, with a remarkable "Chorus and Bacchanale."

They send for *Samson* to provide sport. When he appears, *Delilah* approaches him, to taunt the man with his weakness. She offers him wine, and with malignant irony she repeats to him sensuously cruel words of love. *Samson* cannot reply. He prays with bowed head. When all have wearied of their sport he begs a youth to lead him to the great pillars which uphold the Temple. He offers a last prayer for strength to overcome the wretches, then straining at the roof pillars, he overthrows them. The Temple crashes down amid shrieks and groans.

THE VICTOR RECORDS
(Sung in French except as noted)

ACT I

JE VIENS CÉLÉBRER LA VICTOIRE

(I Come to Celebrate Victory) ENRICO CARUSO, Tenor, LOUISE HOMER, Contralto and MARCEL JOURNET, Bass
10010 12-in., $3.50

PRINTEMPS QUI COMMENCE

(Delilah's Song of Spring) ERNESTINE SCHUMANN-HEINK, Contralto *In German* 6280 12-in., 2.00
LOUISE HOMER, Contralto 6164 12-in., 2.00

DELILAH:

Spring voices are singing,
Bright hope they are bringing,
All hearts making glad.
And gone sorrow's traces,
The soft air effaces
All days that are sad.
The earth glad and beaming,
With freshness is teeming.
In vain all my beauty:
I weep my poor fate!
(She gazes fondly at Samson.)
When night is descending,
With love all unending,
Bewailing my fate,
For him will I wait.
Till fond love returning,
In his bosom burning
May enforce his return!

ACT II

AMOUR VIENS AIDER

(Love, Lend Me Thy Might) LOUISE HOMER, Contralto 6165 12-in., $2.00

DELILAH:

O Love! in my weakness give power!
Poison Samson's brave heart for me!
'Neath my soft sway may he be vanquished;
Tomorrow let him captive be!

Ev'ry thought of me he would banish,
And from his tribe he would swerve,
Could he only drive out the passion
That remembrance doth now preserve.
But he is under my dominion;
In vain his people may entreat.
'Tis I alone that can hold him—
I'll have him captive at my feet!

MON COEUR S'OUVRE A TA VOIX

(My Heart at Thy Sweet Voice) LOUISE HOMER, Contralto 6164 12-in., $2.00
JULIA CULP, Contralto 568 10-in., 1.50
GABRIELLA BESANZONI, Contralto *In Italian* 541 10-in., 1.50
ERNESTINE SCHUMANN-HEINK, Contralto *In German* 6280 12-in., 2.00

DELILAH:

My heart at thy sweet voice opens wide like the flower
Which the morn's kisses waken!
But, that I may rejoice, that my tears no more shower,
Tell thy love still unshaken!
O, say thou wilt not now leave Delilah again!
Repeat thine accents tender, ev'ry passionate vow,
O thou dearest of men!
(Copy't 1892, G. Schirmer.)

ACT III

VOIS MA MISÈRE HÉLAS

(Sore My Distress, Alas!) ENRICO CARUSO, Tenor and Metropolitan Opera Chorus 6026 12-in., $2.00

SAMSON:

Look down, look down on me, have pity on me,
Have mercy, Lord, have mercy upon me!
I turned away from Thy most righteous path
And now I suffer justly from Thy wrath.

My poor bruised soul to Thee now do I offer,
I who deserve but the jeers of the scoffer.
On sightless eyes doth the light of day fall,
Now is my soul steeped in bitterness and gall.

CHORUS:
Samson, why hast thou betrayed thy brethren?

SAMSON:
Alas; Israel, still in chains!
From heav'n God's vengeance descending

Ev'ry hope of return now ending,
Now only suffering remains.
Grant us again, Lord, the light of Thy favor,
Deign but once more, Lord, Thy people to aid.
Withhold Thy wrath, though Thou hast been betray'd,
Thou art our God and Thy love doth not waver.

BACCHANALE
Philadelphia Orchestra   6241   12-in., $2.00

BLACK LABEL RECORDS

Spring Flowers (*In English*)....................*Victor Women's Chorus*	17624	10-in., $0.75
Trovatore—Anvil Chorus (*In English*)............*Victor Male Chorus*		

Samson and Delilah Selection.............................*Pryor's Band*		
"The Breath of God," Act I—Chorus of the Philistines, Act III—	35234	12-in., 1.25
"My Heart at Thy Sweet Voice," Act II		
Romeo and Juliet Selection (*Gounod*).....................*Pryor's Band*		

My Heart at Thy Sweet Voice ....*Michele Rinaldi, Cornet*	17216	10-in., .75
Farewell to the Forest (*Mendelssohn*).............*Victor Brass Quartet*		

COPY'T MISHKIN
GERVILLE-RÉACHE AS DELILAH

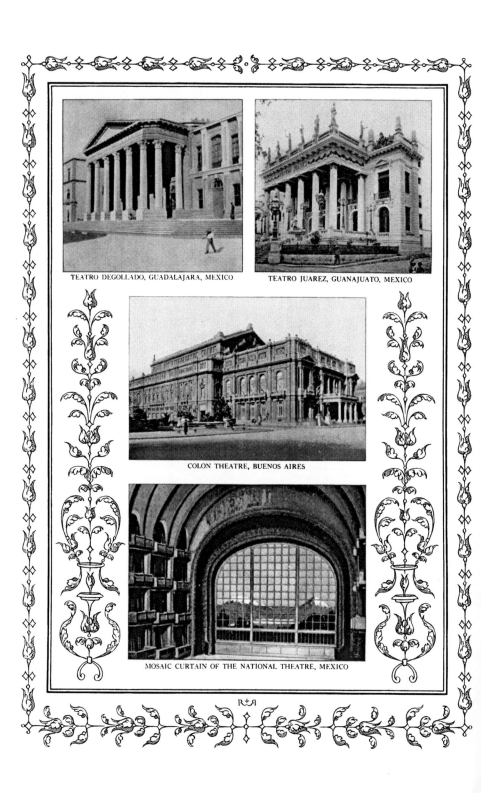

TEATRO DEGOLLADO, GUADALAJARA, MEXICO

TEATRO JUAREZ, GUANAJUATO, MEXICO

COLON THEATRE, BUENOS AIRES

MOSAIC CURTAIN OF THE NATIONAL THEATRE, MEXICO

SEMIRAMIDE

SEMIRAMIDE is perhaps the finest of Rossini's serious operas, but although it was a great success in its day, its splendid overture and the brilliant *Bel raggio* are about the only reminders of it which remain.

The story is based on the classic subject of the murder of *Agamemnon* by his wife, called *Semiramis* in the Babylonian version. It is a work which the composer completed in the astonishingly short time of one month, but which exhibits his peculiar art at its ripest and best.

THE OPERA

TRAGIC opera in two acts. Text by Rossi; music by Gioachino Antonio Rossini. It is founded on Voltaire's tragedy *Semiramis*. First produced at the Fenice Theatre, Venice, February 3, 1823; in London at the King's Theatre, July 15, 1824. In French, as *Semiramis*, it appeared in Paris, July 9, 1860, First American production occurred in New York, April 25, 1826. First New Orleans production May 1, 1837. Some notable American revivals were in 1855 with Grisi and Vestvali; in 1890 with Adelina Patti as *Semiramide;* and in 1894 with Melba and Scalchi.

CHARACTERS

SEMIRAMIDE (*Say-mee-rah'-mee-day*) or SEMIRAMIS, Queen of Babylon................... Soprano

ARSACES or ARSACE (*Ahr-sah'-chay*) commander in the Assyrian army, afterward the son of Ninus and heir to the throne
Contralto

THE GHOST OF NINUS or NINO (*Nee-noh*)................. Bass

OROE, chief of the Magi........ Bass

ASSUR, a Prince of the blood royal Bass

AZEMA, Princess of the blood royal................... Soprano

IDRENUS, of the royal household. Tenor

MITRANES, of the royal household................... Baritone

Magi, Guards, Satraps, Slaves

THE action takes place in Babylon; *Semiramide*, the Queen, assisted by her lover *Assur*, has murdered her husband, *King Ninus*, who, in the second act, rises in spirit from the tomb and prophesies the *Queen's* downfall.

The *Bel raggio*, a favorite cavatina with all prima donnas, and a brilliant and imposing air, occurs in the first act. Its particular scene shows the Temple of Belus, where a religious festival is in progress. *Semiramide* is about to announce a successor to the throne and has secretly determined to elect *Arsaces*, a young warrior, with whom she has fallen in love, unaware that he is in reality her own son.

BLACK LABEL RECORDS

{Semiramide—Overture—Part I ....*Victor Symphony Orchestra*}	18927	10-in.,	$0.75
{Semiramide—Overture—Part II ....*Victor Symphony Orchestra*}			
{Overture.....................................*Police Band of Mexico City*}	35167	12-in.,	1.25
{ Marche Slave (*Op. 31*) (*Tschaikowsky*)............*Arthur Pryor's Band*}			

SIEGFRIED AND THE DRAGON

SIEGFRIED

MUSIC-DRAMA in three acts. Words and music by Wagner. First produced at Bayreuth, August 16, 1876. It was given in French at Brussels, June 12, 1891, and subsequently at the Opéra in Paris. In London (in English) by the Carl Rosa Company, in 1898. First American production in New York, November 9, 1887, with Lehmann, Fischer, Alvary and Seidl-Kraus.

CHARACTERS

SIEGFRIED (*Zeeg'-freed*)........Tenor
MIME (*Mee'-meh*).............Tenor
THE WANDERER (WOTAN) (*Voh'-tan*)
Baritone
ALBERICH (*Ahl'-ber-ich*).....Baritone
FAFNER (*Fahf'-ner*)............Bass
ERDA (*Air'-dah*)...........Contralto
BRÜNNHILDE (*Bruen-hill'-deh*)
Mezzo-Soprano

ACT I

Scene—A Forest. At One Side a Cave

THE birth of *Siegfried* has been followed by the death of his mother *Sieglinde*, and the child has been brought up by *Mime*, who has hoped, through him, to win back the treasure of the Nibelungs. But *Mime* has undertaken no light task, for *Siegfried* has grown into a fearless young hero, a magnificent creature, powerful and beautiful, with nothing but contempt for the wretch who has undertaken to play both father and mother. *Mime* is now at work upon a sword for his master, certain it will be no more enduring than the last.

Suddenly *Siegfried* himself appears, in forest dress, a horn hung about his young neck, leading a huge bear with a halter. With this he terrifies *Mime* half to death, laughing aloud as the hideous and cowardly dwarf shrinks away. This pleasantry over, he frees the bear, and seizes the new sword *Mime* has forged. He beats it on the anvil, where it breaks, the pieces flying about. *Siegfried* complains bitterly of "this silly switch." *Mime*, who has fled, protests, from a distance, against this ingratitude. He finally brings food, however, as a peace-offering; but *Siegfried* still grumbling over the sword, declares he will get his own meals. *Mime* appears to be hurt, wailing loudly as he speaks of his wasted efforts to please. *Siegfried*, somehow wondering why he so dislikes the dwarf when every other living thing in the forest is his friend, questions *Mime* about his birth, and thereby learns, for the first time, of *Sieglinde* his dead mother. He also hears of the shattered sword of *Siegmund*, his father, and commands *Mime* to repair it. He then runs off into the woods.

While *Mime* is still brooding over this impossible task, *Wotan* appears disguised as a *Wanderer*. *Mime* is appalled as the one-eyed warrior with his huge spear, looms above him, especially when the *Wanderer* carelessly touches the earth with his long spear and a soft crash of thunder follows. The *Wanderer* offers to answer at the price of his life any three riddles *Mime* can propound. After successfully answering three questions regarding the Nibelungs, the giants and the gods, he asks three himself at the same price. *Mime* successfully answers the first two, regarding the birth of *Siegfried;* but is terrified when the last question is asked as to how the sword may be repaired. This is, of course, the one thing he desires to know—believing that with the sword *Siegfried* will slay *Fafner*, who guards the treasure of the Nibelungs, when his own wits may cozen the treasure from *Siegfried;* but as he cannot reply to the *Wanderer*, his life is forfeit. The *Wanderer* then tells him that the sword can be repaired only by one who knows no fear. He then departs.

Siegfried returns demanding his sword, is told that it can be repaired only by one who knows no fear. He is much interested in this new thing, fear. What is Fear? *Mime* tries to explain by describing the dragon *Fafner*, and *Siegfried*, growing impatient to see the creature, essays to mend the sword himself. Before *Mime's* wondering eyes he forges it anew, and once whole to the dwarf's terror and amazement, he strikes with it a mightly blow upon the face of the anvil, which splits in pieces. *Siegfried* swings his weapon as the curtain falls.

ACT II

SCENE—*The Dragon's Cave in the Forest*

FAFNER, the "giant-who-is-now-a-dragon," drowses over his wealth in Hate-Cavern, while *Alberich*, hoping yet for a chance to secure the ring, watches nearby. The *Wanderer* cautions *Alberich* that *Siegfried*, with no other aid than his own youthful strength, will overcome the dragon and win the gold. But *Alberich* has a plan of his own, and he warns the dragon of *Siegfried's* approach. *Fafner* makes light of the danger. As the day dawns, *Mime* creeps out behind with *Siegfried*, and leaving the hero, girt with the sword, at the dark entrance of Hate-Cavern, reconnoitres awhile, returning to describe the beast to *Siegfried*, who laughs at him for his pains. While *Mime* is absent, *Siegfried* listens to the murmurings of the trees and the awakening of life about him, and is disappointed when he fails to reproduce the song of the birds on a pipe which he cuts from a reed with his own new sword. In this scene occurs some of the loveliest nature-music in existence.

Fafner is aroused; and his lizard-like form proceeds from the cave to a spot near *Siegfried*. He utters a thunderous yawn, which fails to frighten *Siegfried*, who replies with laughter. Soon the combat begins when *Siegfried* succeeds in driving the sword, *Nothung*, into the heart of the dragon. The dying *Fafner*, realizing that the *Curse of Alberich* has descended upon him too, endeavors to warn *Siegfried* with his dying breath. *Siegfried* pays little heed. He draws the sword, *Nothung*, from the breast of the monster, and in doing so its blood soils his hands. Instinctively, he licks the blood away, when at once he becomes aware that he has thus gained a mystical power to understand the language of birds. The lovely woodland music returns, and from his new friends he learns that he must seize the ring and the Tarnhelm, which he does, ignoring the rest of the treasure. He does not know the value of his possessions.

Mime now steals forth, doing his best to wheedle *Siegfried* into giving him the Ring and the Tarnhelm; *Alberich* looks on amused. *Siegfried* watches *Mime* tolerantly enough, but after a time he grows annoyed, for his new power makes clear to him the inner purpose of *Mime's* deceitful talk. He makes one pass at him with his sword, and *Mime* falls dead. He throws the corpse into the cave, stuffing up the entrance with the body of *Fafner*. Then his friends the birds tell him of a marvellously beautiful woman who lies sleeping behind a mysterious veil of fire, and who can be won only by a man who knows no fear. *Siegfried* laughs with delight, saying, "Why, this stupid lad who knows not fear—it is I!" So saying he follows the bird, which flies ahead, guiding him, turn by turn and slope by slope, to *Brünnhilde's* sleeping-place.

ACT III

Scene—*A Wild Region at the Foot of a Rocky Mountain*

IN the meantime, the *Wanderer, Wotan*, doubtful of the future, goes to consult his earth-wife, the earth-goddess *Erda*, hoping to learn if deliverance may come, for the gods, through the union of *Siegfried* and *Brünnhilde*; but *Erda* is puzzled. She can give him no determinate answer, and she asks to be allowed to sleep. *Wotan* fears that with the coming of *Siegfried* his power must end, and with it, forever, the power of the gods.

Siegfried approaches, his bird-guide having disappeared. He demands right-of-way from the stranger who bars his path. *Wotan* questions him good-humoredly and learns of the death of *Fafner*. He asks, too, whence comes the sword, and *Siegfried* answers he has forged it from a broken weapon. And whence come the broken pieces? pursues *Wotan*. But *Siegfried* answers that he cares not since a broken sword is useless until it is repaired. *Wotan* again laughs, but *Siegfried* becomes insistent to know the way to the fiery couch of *Brünnhilde*, the bird that directed him thither having flown. He is insistent, being young, sans fear. *Wotan* then confesses that he himself has driven off the bird, and he tells *Siegfried* how the spear he holds has shattered the sword in the grasp of his father. *Siegfried* at once decides that this fierce-looking one-eyed warrior must be his father's enemy, and so his own. The spear of *Wotan* confronts him, but with a mighty blow he severs the haft in twain. *Wotan* knows now that he is beaten by the son he has reared to save himself, and that destiny pursues him for his wrong-doing. The end of the gods is near. He makes way for *Siegfried*. Soon a great fire surrounds the young hero, who, nothing daunted, pursues his way, assured at last that he is on the right track. The flames vanish, and the smoke they leave behind lifts clear, so that all is fresh and spring-like. Upon a grassy mound, covered with a great shield, lies a human form. *Siegfried* takes the shield, and removes the armor and stands wondering before the sleeping *Brünnhilde*. With a kiss he awakens her. Love stirs within him, so that the blood in his veins runs feverish. *Brünnhilde* slowly revives. Manhood comes to the young hero, and the path of destiny opens before him as the curtain descends upon the third of the dramas of The Ring. With the last one, Destiny awaits its fulfilment, the Twilight of the Gods being at hand. Its premonitions, to those who know the music, are heard in it.

Introduction:—Wotan invokes Erda (Act III) *Vocalist*—Clarence Whitehill / *Symphony Orchestra—Conducted by Albert Coates* / Siegfried's ascent to the Valkyrie rock (Act III) *Vocalists*—Clarence Whitehill and Tudor Davies.. *Symphony Orchestra—Conducted by Albert Coates*	6436	12-in., $2.00
Siegfried forges the broken sword—Finale, (Act I) *Vocalist*—Tudor Davies / *Symphony Orchestra—Conducted by Albert Coates* / The forest bird warns Siegfried—(Act II) *Vocalists*—Tudor Davies, Sydney Russell, Florence Austral / *Symphony Orchestra—Conducted by Eugene Goossens*	55209	12-in., 1.50
Siegfried follows the forest bird—Finale, (Act II) *Vocalists*—Tudor Davies and Bessie Jones..... *Symphony Orchestra—Conducted by Albert Coates* / Brünnhilde hails the radiant sun—(Act III) *Vocalists*—Florence Austral and Tudor Davies...... *Symphony Orchestra—Conducted by Percy Pitt*	55210	12-in., 1.50
Brünnhilde recalls her Valkyrie days (Act III) *Vocalists*—Florence Austral and Tudor Davies *Symphony Orchestra—Conducted by Albert Coates* / Brünnhilde yields to Siegfried—(Finale of Opera) *Vocalists*—Florence Austral and Tudor Davies..... *Symphony Orchestra—Conducted by Albert Coates*	55211	12-in., 1.50
Forest Murmurs—Part I.............. *Percy Pitt and Symphony Orchestra* / Forest Murmurs—Part II .... *Percy Pitt and Symphony Orchestra*	55168	12-in., 1.50

SISTER ANGELICA

OPERA in one act. Text by Gioachino Forzano; music by Giacomo Puccini. First production at the Metropolitan Opera House, New York, December 14, 1918.

CHARACTERS
(With Original Cast.)

SISTER ANGELICA (*An-jay-lee-kah*)
　　　　　　　　　　Geraldine Farrar
THE PRINCESS, her Aunt. . Flora Perini
THE ABBESS . . . . Rita Fornia
THE SISTER MONITOR, Marie Sundelius
THE MISTRESS OF THE NOVICES
　　　　　　　　　　　Cecil Arden
SISTER GENOVEVA (*Jen-oh-vay-vah*)
　　　　　　　　　　　Mary Ellis
SISTER OSMINA (*Os-mee-nah*)
　　　　　　　　　Marguerite Belleri
SISTER DOLCINA (*Dol-chee-nah*)
　　　　　　　　　Marie Mattfeld

Scene and Period: An Italian Convent; Seventeenth Century

SISTER ANGELICA, daughter of a Florentine noble, was forced by her family to enter a convent after a youthful love affair. Seven years have elapsed, when the *Abbess* announces a visitor, who proves to be the *Princess*, *Sister Angelica's* aunt. She has come for the signature of her niece to a legal document, necessary before the marriage of a younger sister. The *Princess* tells *Angelica* of the death of her boy two years before, and, unmoved by the grief of the girl, tells her that her only course is one of long expiation. In despair the girl swallows poison, and as she is dying the Virgin appears on the threshold of the church, leading a little child. She gently pushes the boy into his mother's arms, and as the choir of nuns and angels chant, forgiveness, *Sister Angelica* passes away. By reason of its shortness, the opera is frequently given with "Il Tabarro."

IL TABARRO

(THE CLOAK)

OPERA in one act. Text by Giuseppe Adami, based on Didier Gold's "La Houpplande"; music by Giacomo Puccini. First production, Metropolitan Opera House, New York, December 14, 1918. Usually given with preceding opera.

THE scene of "Il Tabarro" is *Michele's* barge on the Seine. *Michele* suspects that his young wife, *Giorgetta*, is in love with *Luigi*, his assistant. He discovers that she is planning to meet *Luigi* that night, and he decides to lay in wait for him. When *Luigi* appears he is attacked by the husband, who forces a confession of his love for *Giorgetta*, and then strangles him. Hearing his wife approaching, *Michele* conceals the dead body under his cloak and when she appears, terrified at the sounds of the scuffle, she asks if he does not want her to come rest under his cloak. He throws open the garment, and she screams in horror as the body of her dead lover rolls at her feet. The opera, though brief, is conceived in genuinely tragic spirit.

382

SNEGOUROTCHKA

SNEGOUROTCHKA (The Snow Maiden), abounds in picturesque scenes, representing Winter and Spring, and the poetic little story is supposed to take place in the happy country of Berendey, an unknown province of an imaginary Russia, ruled by a benevolent old *Czar* who has devoted his life to the happiness of his people, governing his kingdom by the law of love.

THE OPERA

OPERA in four acts and a prologue. Text by Ostrovsky, based on the old folklore tale of the *Snow Maiden*. Music by Nicolai Andreyevich Rimsky-Korsakoff. First production St. Petersburg, March, 1882. Produced at the Private Opera, Moscow, 1911. In Paris, at the *Opéra Comique*, June, 1908. Metropolitan Opera, 1922.

CHARACTERS

SNEGOUROTCHKA, the Snow Maiden
  (*Snyay-goo-rotch-kah*)....Soprano
MISGUIR, her lover........Baritone
SHEPHERD LEHL (*Layl*)....Contralto
CZAR BERENDEY.............Tenor
BOBY......................Bass
BOBYLYCKA, his wife.......Soprano
KOUPAVA, betrothed to Misguir
                        Contralto

The Scene is laid in Berendey, an Imaginary Province of Russia

THE beautiful, unknown *Snegourotchka*, daughter of old *Winter* and the fairy *Spring*, is found one cold morning by some villagers, abandoned in the forest, and the old drunkard, *Boby*, and his wife, *Bobylycka*, adopt her without knowing her parentage. *Misguir*, a merchant, falls in love with her, abandoning his sweetheart, *Koupava*, but *Snegourotchka*, as her name indicates, is made of ice, and her coldness and indifference discourage all the young men who are infatuated with her beauty. Even the handsome *Shepherd Lehl*, who sings such wonderful songs, gives up in despair and offers his heart to *Koupava*. The old *Czar* is grieved that this coldness has entered his kingdom, and offers the hand of the *Snow Maiden* and a handsome gift besides to any one who can win her love. *Snegourotchka* finds it impossible to love, and appeals to her mother, the fairy *Spring*, who invokes the aid of the flowers—the carnation lending its grace, the rose its heart and the jasmine its languor. This influence gradually touches the heart of the *Snow Maiden*, and she finds herself falling in love with the handsome *Misguir*. They both attend the festival of lovers and present themselves to the good *Czar* as a betrothed couple. But, alas, at the first kiss from her lover the little snowflake melts and disappears, while *Misguir*, in despair, throws himself into the river.

THE VICTOR RECORDS

PROLOGUE—JE CONNAIS, JE CONNAIS, MA MÈRE
(I Know the Song of the Lark) LUCREZIA BORI, Soprano *In French*
                        542 10-in., $1.50

ACT III

ALLER AU BOIS
(Go to the Forest) ALMA GLUCK, Soprano *In French*   647 10-in., 1.50

DANCE OF THE TUMBLERS
STOKOWSKI and Philadelphia Orchestra
                        6431 12-in., 2.00

SONG OF THE SHEPHERD LEHL
ALMA GLUCK, Soprano *In English*
                        647 10-in., 1.50

COVENT GARDEN, LONDON

LONDON OPERA HOUSE

FAMOUS OPERA HOUSES OF EUROPE

LA SONNAMBULA

(THE SOMNAMBULIST)

OUR grandfathers and grandmothers regarded this opera with the greatest favor, and as one reviews its tuneful melodies, its simple, natural story, one grows disposed to congratulate them on their good sense. The opera was much beloved among débutantes, both Albani and Adelina Patti using it for their first appearances in England. In the 30's it was a novelty by a young and gifted composer; by 1850 it was part of every opera season, shining through a halo of great casts—Malibran, Pasta, Jenny Lind, Gerster, Campanini, Grisi,—and it continued to be popular until the Wagnerian era brought a revulsion of feeling against the simplicities of the Bellini school. Early in the twentieth century, however, this very simplicity proved its charm once more, and came as a refreshing draught from the bubbling spring of "pure" melody in an operatic era which was to culminate with the "Salome" of Richard Strauss, and even more complex works.

THE OPERA

OPERA in three acts. Libretto by Felice Romani; music by Vincenzo Bellini. Produced at the *Teatro Carcano*, Milan, March 6, 1831; Paris, October 28, 1831; and at the King's Theatre, London, July 28th of the same year. At Drury Lane in English, under the Italian title, May 1, 1883. First performance in New York in English, at the Park Theatre, November 13, 1835, with Brough, Richings and Mr. and Mrs. Wood. First New Orleans performance, January 14, 1840. First performance in Italian in New York, Palmo's Opera Company, May 11, 1844. Revived in 1905 at the Metropolitan with Caruso, Sembrich and Plançon; at the Manhattan Opera, 1909, with Tetrazzini, Trentini, Parola and de Segurola.

CHARACTERS

COUNT RUDOLPH, lord of the village......................Bass
TERESA (*Tay-ress-sah*), milleress..............Mezzo-Soprano
AMINA (*Ah-mee'-nah*), orphan adopted by Teresa, betrothed to Elvino........Soprano
ELVINO (*El-vee'noh*), wealthy peasant..................Tenor
LISA (*Lee-sah*), inn-keeper, in love with Elvino.........Soprano
ALESSIO (*Al-les-shee-o*), peasant, in love with Lisa............Bass
Peasants and Peasant Women

The Scene is laid in a Swiss Village

(The name of the opera is pronounced *Lah Son-nahm'-boo-la*).

ACT I

SCENE—*A Village Green*

THE charming *Amina* is about to marry *Elvino*, and the friendly villagers have made the event an occasion to celebrate. This is not agreeable to *Lisa*, who had hopes of winning *Elvino* herself; her bitter reflections find voice in a melodious air.

Alessio offers himself to *Lisa* for consolation, but she is not receptive. They are interrupted when *Amina* and her friends enter, followed by *Elvino*, for the signing of the marriage contract. *Elvino* places a ring on the finger of his future bride as a sign of their betrothal, and they sing a charming duet, "Prendi l' anel ti dono" (Take Now This Ring).

The celebrations are interrupted by the sound of horses' hoofs, and a handsome and distinguished stranger arrives, asking the way to the castle. Finding it some distance off, he decides to remain at the inn. He looks around him, seeming to recognize the scene, and he sings the air: "Vi ravviso" (As I View These Scenes).

Inquiring the reason for the festivities, the stranger is introduced to the pretty bride, in whom he is much interested—rather to *Elvino's* annoyance. He tells the peasants that in his childhood he lived with the lord of the castle, and he now brings news of the lord's only son, who disappeared some years since.

The night approaches, and *Amina's* mother, *Teresa*, declares it is time to go indoors lest the "phantom" appear. The stranger is told of a spectre that has much been seen of late, and when he scoffs at the story, the peasants describe the ghostly visitant in the chorus "Ah! fosco ciel!" (When Daylight's Going).

The stranger, desiring rest, retires to his room. *Amina* and *Elvino* remain; the young man reproaches his sweetheart for her unseemly interest in the guest. At sight of her tears, however, he repents of his jealous temper, and begs forgiveness, the act closing with a duet by the reconciled lovers.

ACT II

SCENE—*The Apartment of the Stranger*

THE guest reflects that he might have done worse than stay at this little inn—the people are courteous, the women pretty, and the accommodations quite good. *Lisa* enters to see if he is comfortable, addressing him as "my lord," and thus betraying the fact that the villagers suspect him of being *Count Rudolph.*

The *Count* takes it in good part, in spite of being somewhat annoyed by his recognition, but his mood changes into amusement when he tries to flirt with the buxom landlady, and she coyly slips away,—dropping her veil in the process.

A surprise is now in store for him. *Amina* calmly walks in through the window, saying "*Elvino*, dost thou remain jealous? I love but thee." The *Count* quickly perceives that she is walking in her sleep. *Lisa* peeps into the room, and runs off scandalized, for the unconscious *Amina* has by now begun to disrobe. The embarrassed *Count* not knowing quite what to do, finally goes out by the window. *Amina*, however, repeats in her dream the marriage ceremony of the afternoon, entreating *Elvino* to believe that she loves him. She finally throws herself on the bed.

By the time *Lisa* arrives with *Elvino* and the villagers, they find her calmly sleeping in the *Count's* room. She wakes at the noise, bewildered, and runs to *Elvino*, but he repulses her roughly. She is met with cold looks on all sides, and she sinks down in despair, weeping bitterly. Rousing herself, she again protests her innocence, but *Elvino* spurns her, and none will believe her except her mother, to whose arms she flies as *Elvino* rushes in anger, out of the room.

ACT III

SCENE I—*A Shady Valley near the Castle*

BELIEVING that the *Count* alone may clear her good name, *Amina* goes there with her mother. On the way they meet *Elvino*, and they again plead with him. But they meet only reproaches, and in his bitterness *Elvino* roughly takes the betrothal ring from the girl's finger and departs.

SCENE II—*A Street in the Village*

LISA is informed that *Elvino* has transferred his affections to her, and is therefore overjoyed. When

Elvino himself arrives, they depart for the church. But on their way they are met by the *Count*, who assures them of *Amina's* innocence. *Elvino* flatly refuses to listen, bidding *Lisa* follow him. He is stopped once more, however, by *Teresa*, who, having heard of his proposed marriage, now shows him *Lisa's* veil, found in the *Count's* room. "Deceived again!" cries the thoroughly perplexed bridegroom, asking if any women are to be trusted. The *Count* again assures him of *Amina's* innocence. "But where is the proof?" cries *Elvino* "There!" cries the *Count* suddenly.

He points toward the roof of the mill, upon which, to everybody's astonishment, *Amina* is seen in her night-dress, carrying a lamp, and quite evidently walking in her sleep. All watch, breathlessly, fearing she will fall. She climbs down to the bridge, over the wheel, and descends the stairs. As she makes the hazardous descent, she sings the lovely air, "Ah! non credea mirarti" (Could I Believe).

It opens with a tender cantabile in minor key, its pathos fully in keeping with *Amina's* plight, discarded by her lover, doubted by her friends, and mourning for her short-lived dream of happiness.

Elvino can restrain himself no longer, and he rushes toward the girl. She wakes to find him kneeling at her feet, and uttering a cry of delight, she raises him and falls into his arms. Since there is nothing now to mar their happy union, and even the mystery of the "ghost" has become clear, the opera closes with a joyous, bird-like air, in keeping with the pastoral scene and the mood of innocent happiness. This is the "Ah, non giunge" (Oh, Recall Not One Earthly Sorrow).

THE VICTOR RECORDS

(Sung in Italian)

ACT I

COME PER ME SERENO

(Oh! Love, for Me Thy Power) Amelita Galli-Curci, Soprano 6125 12-in., $2.00

SOVRA IL SEN

(While My Heart its Joy Revealing) Amelita Galli-Curci, Soprano
633 10-in., 1.50

VI RAVVISO

(As I View These Scenes) Feodor Chaliapin, Bass 981 10-in., 1.50

ACT III

AH! NON CREDEA MIRARTI

(Could I Believe) Amelita Galli-Curci, Soprano 6125 12-in., 2.00

Amina:
　Ah! must ye fade, sweet flowers,
　　Forsaken by sunlight and showers,
　As transient as lover's emotion
　　That lives and withers in one short day!
　But tho' no sunshine o'er ye,
　　These tears might yet restore ye,
　But estranged devotion
　　No mourner's tears have power to stay!
　　　—From the Ditson Edition

AH! NON GIUNGE

(Oh, Recall Not One Earthly Sorrow) Luisa Tetrazzini, Soprano
6345 12-in., 2.00

Amina:
　Do not mingle one human feeling
　With the rapture o'er each sense stealing;
　See these tributes, to me revealing
　My Elvino, true to love.
　Ah, embrace me, and thus forgiving,
　Each a pardon is now receiving;
　On this bright earth, while we are living,
　Let us form here a heaven of love!

STRADELLA

COMIC opera in three acts. Libretto adapted from Bonnet-Bourdelet's *Histoire de la Musique et de ses Effets*, published in Paris in 1715. Music by Friedrich von Flotow. First written as a lyric drama, "Stradella" was produced at the Palais Royal, Paris, in 1837, but was subsequently rewritten and given at Hamburg, December 30, 1844. Slight changes were made in the English version by Bunn, and the opera brought out in London, June 6, 1846, as *Alessandro Stradella*. Produced at Niblo's Garden, New York, in 1856; at Academy of Music, December 8, 1860; at the German Opera House on Broadway, September, 1864; at Mrs. John Wood's Olympic, February, 1867; revived at Thalia Theatre, 1887; at the Metropolitan Opera House, February 4, 1910, with Gluck, Slezak, Goritz and Reiss.

CHARACTERS

ALESSANDRO STRADELLA, singer
(*Ahl-lay-sahn'-droh Strah-del'-lah*)..................... Tenor
BASSI, a wealthy Venetian
(*Bahs'-see*)............... Tenor
LEONORA, his ward (*Lay-oh-noh'-rah*)................... Soprano
BARBARINO ⎱ bandits ⎰ .... Tenor
MALVOLIO ⎰ ⎱ .... Baritone

Pupils, Peasants, etc.

Time and Place: Venice and the Vicinity of Rome; about 1658

IN the opera *Stradella*, having come to Venice to write music, takes for a pupil the ward of a rich Venetian. He falls in love with, and finally elopes with her. *Bassi*, the girl's guardian, intending to marry her himself, is furious when he discovers the affair. Bent on revenge, he secures the services of two bandits, *Malvolio* and *Barbarino*. These worthies conceal themselves in the singer's home, while *Stradella* and *Leonora* are on their way to the church to be married. On their return the groom sings such a charming ballad that the bravos decide to spare his life.

Bassi, however, when he learns that his rival still is alive, calls them cowards, and by increasing the amount of the reward, induces them to consent to carry out the plot. The three conspirators go to the home of their victim to await his return. *Stradella* appears and begins to rehearse a hymn which he is to sing at church on the morrow. As he commences the bandits steal out to stab him, but are so affected by his singing of the beautiful hymn that they are overcome with repentance, and fall at his feet imploring forgiveness. When *Leonora* appears *Bassi* blesses their union, as the people arrive to pay homage to *Stradella*.

The Overture is one of the most appreciated works of Flotow, and it seems to have taken a permanent place among the "standards."

BLACK LABEL RECORDS

⎧ Stradella Overture............................. *Vessella's Italian Band* ⎱
⎨   *Morning, Noon and Night in Vienna Overture (von Suppé)* ⎬ 35276 12-in., $1.25
⎩   *Vessella's Italian Band* ⎭

⎧ Stradella Overture............................. *Pietro, Accordionist* ⎱ 35345 12-in., 1.25
⎩   *Bridal Rose Overture (Lavallée)*..................... *Pietro, Accordionist* ⎭

LEGEND OF KLEINZACH

TALES OF HOFFMAN

(CONTES D'HOFFMANN)
(French)

"MAKE haste, make haste to mount my piece," cried the dying Offenbach to Carvalho the producer, "I am in a hurry and have only one wish in the world— to see the *premiere* of this work." No doubt M. Carvalho did his best, but he was too late, the composer dying before he was ready. Offenbach (whose real name was Levy), was born at Offenbach-on-Main, 1819, the son of a Jewish cantor. Like our own foremost composer of light opera, Victor Herbert, he began his career as a 'cellist, but soon gave it up to write light operas, many of which he produced himself. He was not a profound musical scholar, but he had a pretty gift for melody and a sense of rather ironic humor, by which he rose into great popularity. It may be remembered what a *furore* attended his visit to America in 1875. It was said of him that he had more wit than knowledge (le savoir-faire vaut mieux que le savoir), and Grove's Dictionary solemnly laments that of his works "nothing will remain." This is premature, for "The Tales of Hoffman" has regained some of its former popularity and the Barcarolle will, apparently, never be forgotten. The "Tales" was his greatest work, and he lavished many years upon it in the intervals of his busy career. Unhappily he died before he had completed even the scoring and the work was revised and finished by Guiraud. Offenbach died of cardiac gout, at Paris, on October 5, 1880, and "The Tales of Hoffman" was only produced there February 10, of the following year, so he missed by four months the fulfilment of his wish.

THE OPERA

OPERA in three acts, with prologue and epilogue. Text by Jules Barbier. Music by Offenbach. First performance in Paris, February 10, 1881. First United States production October 16, 1882, at Fifth Avenue Theatre, by Maurice Grau's French Opera Company on their first appearance in America. Revived at the Manhattan Opera House, New York, November 27, 1907, and by the Metropolitan Opera Company in 1911, with Hempel, Bori, Fremstad, de Segurola, Ruysdael and Rothier.

CHARACTERS

THE POET HOFFMAN..........Tenor
NICLAUS, his friend..........Soprano
OLYMPIA, GIULIETTA, ANTONIA,
STELLA—the various ladies
with whom Hoffman falls
in love................Sopranos
COPPELIUS }
DAPERTUTTO }his opponents...Baritone
MIRACLE }
(These three rôles are usually
sung by the same artist)
LUTHER, an innkeeper..........Bass
SCHLEMIL, Giulietta's admirer....Bass
SPALANZANI, an apothecary.....Tenor
COUNCILLOR CRESPEL, father of
Antonia..................Bass

THE PROLOGUE

SCENE—*Interior of the Tavern of Martin Luther in Nüremberg*

A GROUP of noisy students are drinking quantities of light beer, at the tavern of one facetiously named *Martin Luther*, who shares, however, few of the characteristics of the great reformer. Weary of their own stale jokes, they are glad to welcome *Hoffman*, a poet who has many gay songs at the tip of his tongue. For their entertainment he sings the "Legende de Kleinzach" (Legend of Kleinzach).

It is a merry song, but it is not completed, the poet falling off into dreamland. A woman he has seen that night at the theatre has awakened old memories. His companions rally him, but the lights go out. In comes *Martin Luther* with a flaming bowl of punch, over which the students make merry. They soon fall to sentimentalising over their own love affairs, when

Hoffman breaks in on them, by telling of his own three loves. Scenting a story, they gather around the poet, who, sitting on the corner of the table, begins, "The name of the first was Olympia......"

The curtain falls, and we see enacted the story of his first love.

ACT I

SCENE—*A Physician's Room, Richly Furnished*

HE tells of one *Spalanzani*, a wealthy and rather malicious citizen with a mania for making automatons, marvellous mechanical dolls so lifelike that one is almost deceived into believing them human. One of these, named *Olympia*, he pretends to be his daughter. *Hoffman*, it seems, has been provided by him with a pair of magical glasses, and to the amusement of his comrades he falls in love with *Olympia*, thinking her genuine flesh and blood "C'est elle" ('Tis she!) he sings.

His friend *Nicholas* endeavors his best to prevent *Hoffman* from making a fool of himself. But the guests, who politely marvel at the wonder, are thought by *Hoffman* to be in earnest, and when he can snatch a word with the doll, in private, he is thrilled by the automatic "yes" that issues from her clock-work throat.

The great event of the evening is when *Olympia* is made to dance for the guests' amusement. As she dances, also she sings,—to the wonder of the company and the enravishment of *Hoffman:* "Doll Song—Les oiseaux dans la charmille." In this clever number the rigid rhythm admirably suggests the stiff movements of the doll and there is a touch of comedy introduced when she "runs down" with a life-like gasp and has to be rewound!

She dances and *Hoffman* dances with her. Unfortunately she pirouettes out of the room. In the excitement

THE VENETIAN SCENE AT THE METROPOLITAN OPERA

Hoffman's glasses are knocked off, so that when he, with the excited inventor rush into the room where she had gone he sees but a broken doll. "An automaton!" he cries in despair, while the guests roar with laughing at his disillusion.

ACT II

SCENE—*Venice, a Room in a Palace on the Grand Canal*

TO the radiant beauty of Venice we are transported on the swaying rhythms of the Barcarolle,—the "Belle Nuit" (Oh Night of Love).

The exquisite loveliness of this melody, its enchanting rhythm and rich orchestration (in which the 'cellos superbly ring out), will never be forgotten.

From Ditson Edition—Copy't 1909

To the soft swaying of this melody comes the *Lady Giulietta*, a Venetian coquette who is next, in the work of Fate, to capture the heart of the amorous *Hoffman*. No magic spectacles pervert the poet's gaze this time, and he boasts to his friend *Nathaniel* that neither is he to be blinded by any mist of romance whatsoever. His boast is overheard by *Dapertutto*, the lady's lover,—and the malignant influence which prevails in all three romances, appearing as *Spalanzani* in the first episode and *Dr. Miracle* in the third. *Dapertutto* lays a wager with *Hoffman* that he, too, will fall a victim to the charms of *Giulietta* as *Schlemil*, another young man, has fallen. In token of conquest he is to give the girl his reflection from a mirror! *Giulietta* practices her art with such success that when, a little later, *Dapertutto* shows him a mirror which fails to reflect his visage he is astonished. But he is too deeply enmeshed now to care, an easy victim to *Dapertutto's* designs. *Giulietta* is made to advise him that *Schlemil* has the key to her room, and that he has but to secure it to win her. *Schlemil* appears and the two men fight; *Schlemil* is killed. But when *Hoffman* looks for *Giulietta* he sees her sailing off in a gondola in the arms of *Dapertutto*. *Nathaniel*, the ever-present protective influence, warns him the police approach. Once more he is disillusioned!

ACT III

SCENE—*Munich: the Home of Antonia*

IN the humble home of *Crespel,* a magic influence works. The wife of *Crespel* has been done to death by the vampire-like *Dr. Miracle,* and now he seeks the daughter, *Antonia,* though the father is striving his utmost to shield her. The poor girl is consumptive, yet she possesses a marvelous voice—which she can use only at the cost of her vitality. *Hoffman* comes to see her, enamoured once more, and she sings for him, greatly weakening her little store of energy. Then *Dr. Miracle* appears, and after mesmerizing her father commands her to sing yet again. The dying girl protests, but the portrait of her mother miraculously becomes suffused with light, and the spirit voice commands her to sing: Her response is the "Romance—Elle a fui" (The Dove Has Flown!)

With this number the unfortunate maiden literally sings herself to death. Her father endeavors to prevent her. *Hoffman* rushes in and *Crespel,* beside himself, desires blood for her pale cheeks when *Dr. Miracle* pronounces her dead. He rushes at *Hoffman,* knife in hand, but once more *Nathaniel* arrives in the nick of time. So ends the third romance.

THE EPILOGUE

SCENE—*Same as Act I, the Various Characters in same Position as at end of Act I*

"THERE is the history of my loves," cries the poet *Hoffman,* still seated on the table. The students applaud vigorously at the dramas-within-a-drama which reveal the disillusionment, in turn, of the worship of mere beauty, sensuous passion, and the affection that springs from the heart, with *Olympia* smashed, *Antonia* dead and *Giulietta*......?

"Oh for her," laughs *Hoffman,* "the last verse of the song of Kleinzach." So the party ends in merriment, and the students leave. But *Hoffman* does not go with them. He sits in a dream, and presently a vision comes to him of his poetic Muse, appearing in an aureole of light. She alone is faithful and her alone must he, the poet, serve with all his heart and soul. She disappears. *Stella,* the woman at the play who had stirred his old memories comes in and finds him

asleep. "No," says his friend *Nicholas,* "dead drunk. Too late, madame!" She goes off with the counselor *Lindorf,* an admirer, but as she goes she stops

GARRISON AS THE DOLL

to look at *Hoffman,* throwing at his feet a flower from her bouquet. The sleeping poet pays no heed.

More sweet than love, more acceptable than fame, is oblivion.

THE VICTOR RECORDS

(Sung in French except as noted)

ACT II

DOLL SONG—LES OISEAUX DANS LA CHARMILLE

MABEL GARRISON, Soprano
6135 12-in., $2.00

ACT III

BARCAROLLE—BELLE NUIT
(Oh, Night of Love) GERALDINE FARRAR,
Soprano and ANTONIO SCOTTI, Baritone
3025 10-in., 2.00

ALMA GLUCK, Soprano and LOUISE HOMER, Contralto
3010 10-in., 2.00

JOHN McCORMACK, Tenor and FRITZ KREISLER, Violinist *In English*
3019 10-in., 2.00

Beauteous night, O night of love,
Smile thou on our enchantment;
Radiant night, with stars above,
O beauteous night of love!
Fleeting time doth ne'er return
But bears on wings our dreaming,
Far away where we may yearn,
For time doth ne'er return.
Sweet zephyrs aglow,
Shed on us thy caresses—

ACT IV

ROMANCE—ELLE A FUI
(The Dove Has Flown) LUCREZIA BORI,
Soprano 6049 12-in., 2.00

BLACK LABEL AND BLUE LABEL RECORDS

{Barcarolle—*In English* ....*Lucy Marsh and Marguerite Dunlap*} { *Naughty Marietta—Italian Street Song*..................*Lucy Marsh*}	45181	10-in., $1.00
{Gems from "Tales of Hoffman" ....*Victor Opera Company*} Chorus, "Our Good Host"—Solo, "Song of Olympia"—Chorus, "Hear Him His Tales Disclose"—Solo, "Ah, Now Within My Heart" Barcarolle, "Oh, Night Divine"—Chorus, "See She Dances"— Finale, "Fill Up Our Glasses" { *Gems from "Mignon"*.........................*Victor Opera Company*}	35337	12-in., 1.25
{Barcarolle—Waltz (For Dancing)..................*Victor Military Band*} { *Passing of Salome—Waltz*.......................*Victor Military Band*}	35383	12-in., 1.25
{Barcarolle.........................*Victor Concert Orchestra*} { *Cavalleria Rusticana—Intermezzo*... ....*Victor Concert Orchestra*}	17311	10-in., .75
{Venetian Scene with Barcarolle..................*Vessella's Italian Band*} { *Slavonic Dance (Dvořák)*.......................*Vessella's Italian Band*}	35507	12-in., 1.25
{Barcarolle.........................*Shannon Quartet*} {Mighty Lak' a Rose...............................*Shannon Quartet*}	18375	10-in., .75

TANNHÄUSER AND VENUS

TANNHÄUSER

THE characters in this great opera are not wholly imaginary. There was a Landgrave of Thuringia, named *Hermann*, who held court in the Wartburg. *Wolfram von Eschenbach* was a minstrel knight who wrote the "Quest of the Holy Grail" from which Wagner took the story of "Parsifal." *Tannhäuser* himself derives, in part, from a knight-minstrel of that name who served at the court of Duke Frederick II of Austria, early in the thirteenth century, dying a penitent after a somewhat too hilarious life. He has been the subject of many folk-ballads of Germany, and of a carnival play by Hans Sachs (of Meistersinger fame). *Tannhäuser* was a Minnesinger (or knight-minstrel) while the bourgeois Hans Sachs was a Meistersinger (or burgher minstrel) and many find a connection between Wagner's two operas owing to this circumstance, combined with a song-contest with a maiden's hand in marriage as the prize. The *Elizabeth* in the present opera seems to be a Wagnerian adaptation of the original St. Elizabeth, of Austria, estimable lady who is also the heroine of Liszt's oratorio of the same name, which was unsuccessfully presented as an opera a few years ago. The contest of song in which participated most of the knightly minstrels mentioned in the above cast, also is historical, and one Heinrich von Ofterdingen (whom some writers identify with *Tannhäuser*) was saved from a violent death by the Landgravine Sophia, who threw her cloak over him. This provides Wagner with the chief incident of his second act. Many popular ballads recount the story of *Tannhäuser* and the *Venus* of the Wartburg, also that of the Pope's refusal to give absolution to the penitent sinner and the subsequent flowering of the papal staff, as a mark of divine pardon.

"Tannhäuser" was produced at Dresden while Wagner, as Hofkapellmeister, was enjoying comparative luxury on a salary of about twelve hundred dollars a year. His "Rienzi" and "Flying Dutchman" had already given him a reputation of sorts, but "Tannhäuser" was not wholly successful in Dresden. "You are a man of genius," said Mme. Schroeder-Devrient, the *Venus* of the occasion, "but you write such eccentric stuff it is hardly possible to sing it." The march in the second act was admired, but critics found fault with its "lack of form," and the Intendant of the Theatre, like a modern movie-impresario, objected to the unhappy ending—"why shouldn't *Tannhäuser* marry *Elizabeth?*" he querulously asked. Nevertheless, the work attracted attention. Liszt, prompt as ever in the recognition of genius, had the overture performed at Weimar, 1848, and he produced the entire work four months later; and other leading German opera houses followed. The comments of contemporary musicians make sport for the present generation. Spohr, an older composer, disposed to admire the newcomer, nevertheless wrote, "The opera contains much that is new and beautiful . . . also several ugly attacks on one's ears." Moritz Hauptmann, a great man in his day, pro-

nounced the overture (now the most popular of all overtures) "quite atrocious, incredibly awkward, long and tedious." Mendelssohn, then in his heyday, patronizingly admired "a canonical answer in the adagio of the second finale" which "had given him pleasure." The generous and warm-hearted Robert Schumann, however, wrote to Dorn, "I wish you could see 'Tannhäuser;' it contains deeper, more original, and altogether an hundred-fold better things than his previous operas—at the same time a good deal that is musically trivial. On the whole Wagner may become of great importance and significance to the stage." Thus prophesied the musician whose judgment again revealed itself a little later when he hailed the young Brahms with his memorable "Hats off; a genius!"

To many persons "Tannhäuser" is the greatest of all operas. It represents a period in Wagner's life before he had abandoned the opera-form for the music-drama. Its music is of noble character throughout. It does not, like the "Ring of the Niebelungen", deal chiefly with the sins and the weaknesses of pagan gods, but with those of aspiring, suffering, self-defeated humanity. To those who look for the "moral lesson" in a work of art, there is no disappointment; for the whole opera, with its magnificence of structure and its richness of detail, at bottom only typifies the struggle between the good and the baser elements in the human soul.

THE OPERA

OPERA in three acts. Words and music by Richard Wagner. First presented at the Royal Opera, Dresden, October 19, 1845; at the *Opéra*, Paris, March 13, 1861; in Italy, at Bologna, 1872. First London production at Covent Garden, in Italian, May 6, 1876. First American production at the Stadt Theatre, New York, April 4, 1859, in German. First production in Italian at the New Orleans Opera in 1877.

CHARACTERS

HERMANN, Landgrave of Thuringia.....................Bass

TANNHÄUSER (*Tahn'-hoy-zer*) — Tenor

WOLFRAM VON ESCHENBACH (*Vohl-frahm*) — Baritone

WALTHER VON DER VOGELWEIDE — Tenor

BITEROLF — Bass

HEINRICH DER SCHREIBER — Tenor

REINMAR VON ZWETER — Bass

{ Minstrel Knights }

ELIZABETH, Niece of the Landgrave.................Soprano

VENUS....................Soprano

A Young Shepherd.........Soprano

Four Noble Pages...Soprano and Alto

Chorus of Thuringian Nobles and Knights, Ladies, Elder and Younger Pilgrims, Sirens, Naïads, Nymphs, Bacchantes

Scene and Period: Vicinity of Eisenach; Beginning of the Thirteenth Century

THE Overture to "Tannhäuser," which has been recorded, sums up in miniature the whole story of the opera, and really its whole theme. It contrasts the solemn and beautiful "Pilgrims' Chorus" with the weird abandon of the Venusberg music. It is so complete in form and so rich in material that it has become, through the long passage of years, perhaps the best-beloved of all operatic overtures. Liszt called it a "poem upon the same subject as the opera," and he considered it, in its way, just as comprehensive. It contains enough musical ideas to keep busy a score of lesser composers for the whole of their respective lifetimes.

It begins with the "Pilgrims' Chorus"

PHOTO GERLACH
GADSKI AS ELIZABETH

COPY'T MISHKIN
WITHERSPOON AS THE LANDGRAVE

PHOTO GERLACH
FARRAR AS ELIZABETH

itself, in horns and deep woodwinds, softly at first, but repeated with a growing fortissimo, against a smashing triplet-rhythm.

The chant returns very softly, breaking off before the first voluptuous rushings of the Venusberg music:

This flying motive is developed and redeveloped with ever-increasing vehemence. At its climax, it gives way before the knightly, swinging "Hymn to Venus," later sung by *Tannhäuser* in the opera. The hymn never ends twice in the same fashion. Heard twice in the overture, the first time it dissolves, after a series of abortive half-climaxes, into the Venusberg music, as if beneath some new spell of the goddess,— whose most exquisite love-motive next is heard, very softly, first in the clarinet against shimmering strings.

The hymn is repeated, this time with a triumphant end, before the tale is again swallowed up in the riot of the bacchanale music. The "Pilgrims' Chorus" returns, this time in 4/4 time, thundered out majestically by trombones and trumpets, the strings working against it a new, swift, subtle Venusberg theme, very softly, as though the last echoes of the place were dying out. Near the close there is a high horn counter-melody which is one of the finest inspirations, perhaps, in the whole overture.

There are two versions of "Tannhäuser." In the original, the overture comes to an end and the first act begins as a separate musical entity. In the so-called "Paris" version, revised to meet the demands of the French Grand Opera for ballet music, the overture does not close, but rushes directly into the music of the first scene.

ACT I

SCENE I—*Within the Hill of Venus— Nymphs, Sirens, Naïads and Bacchantes Dancing or Reclining Luxuriously upon Undulating Banks. In a Distant Lake, Naïads are Bathing*

IN the foreground of this scene, in which the attendants of *Venus* are disporting themselves, *Venus* reclines upon a couch, gazing at *Tannhäuser*. The minstrel knight is in a dejected attitude, weary of this life of the senses which, now that experience has brought repletion, has grown so revolting. *Venus* chides him, when he rouses himself to sing her praises anew. But his words are forced, and in the end he confesses that he yearns once more for the earth he has left. The outraged *Venus*, after vainly striving to recall him from himself, finally bids him begone, predicting his ultimate return. The scene miraculously changes. *Venus* and her host have disappeared, and *Tannhäuser* suddenly finds himself in a beautiful sunlit valley.

SCENE II—*A Valley*

IN this lovely vale, whose calm and sunny serenity is in such contrast with the scenes he has just left, *Tannhäuser* finds himself near a wayside shrine, before which he kneels in prayer and repentance. From a nearby hill a shepherd pipes his lay, and the tinkling of sheep-bells is heard. A company of Pilgrims pass, singing their chant as they journey to Rome, and the shepherd ceases piping to beg that they shall say a prayer for him. The scene is one of extraordinary beauty, and has been recorded.

The beauty and the peace of the earth brings balm to the soul of the erring but repentant knight, and, falling to his knees, he gives thanks to the

Almighty in a splendid noble phrase. While he is thus engaged, the *Landgrave* and his minstrel-knights enter, and perceiving a strange knight so devoutly at his orisons, are moved to wonder. They recognize him with astonishment, and call him by the name by which he was formerly known to them, "Henry!" At first they are in doubt as to whether his visit is friendly or otherwise, but *Wolfram*, his old friend and minstrel rival, comes to him with outstretched hands. He gives indirect replies to their wondering questions as to where he has been during the past years. The *Landgrave* urges him to come back with him, and as an inducement, *Wolfram* tells how much *Elizabeth*, the niece of the *Landgrave*, longs for the return of the knight whose minstrelsy has won their trophies in the past. *Tannhäuser* joyfully consents to return and promises to compete in the forthcoming Tournament of Song, the prize for which is to be the hand of *Elizabeth*. The remainder of the *Landgrave's* hunting train arrives in time to greet the minstrel knight, and the curtain closes upon grand finale.

ACT II

Scene—*The Great Hall of Song in the Castle of Wartburg*

OVERJOYED at the return of *Tannhäuser*, *Elizabeth* greets the hall of song with a rapturous hail to the memories of the minstrel's former triumphs there. This is the "Dich teure Halle" (Hail, Hall of Song).

Tannhäuser enters and kneels at the feet of *Elizabeth*, who in confusion bids him arise. A long scene follows between the lovers; in the midst of it *Wolfram* enters, only to realize that his own hopes of *Elizabeth* are done. His grave and dignified self-forgetfulness form a curious contrast to the rapture of *Tannhäuser* and *Elizabeth*.

It is the day of the Contest, and the

BRAND, BAYREUTH   THE HALL OF SONG—ACT II

398

Minstrels and Courtiers enter to a great processional march, acclaiming the *Landgrave* and wishing him a happy reign. The *Landgrave* replies with beautiful dignity, and the contest begins. Four pages, who have drawn lots from a cup, announce that *Wolfram* will sing first upon the subject of Love. He sings with power and eloquence of a Love that is pure and free from stain. *Tannhäuser*, with memories of his life in the Venusberg, shows impatience at this praise of a love that is chaste but tepid. He at length breaks in to exalt a more earthly type of love. Comment and dismay follow, and *Biterolf*, a hot-headed knight, rises and challenges to mortal combat the unfortunate *Tannhäuser*, who as excitedly returns that such a grim wolf as *Biterolf* knows little of the delights of love. In wild exultation, he then breaks into his blasphemous "Praise of Venus." All is confusion, and the knights rush from their seats with drawn swords.

Elizabeth, who has listened with horror and amazement to her lover's impious chant, now casts herself between the knights and *Tannhäuser*. She now begs for his life, in phrases, and in music, of sublime beauty. The *Landgrave* pronounces judgment, declaring *Tannhäuser* banished from the realm. He suggests that the knight may journey to Rome with a band of Pilgrims about to start for that city. In the distance is heard the "Pilgrims' Chant," and the strains thrill the penitent soul of the erring knight. "To Rome," he cries, "to Rome!" and so leaves the despairing but pitying *Elizabeth*.

ACT III

Scene—*The Valley Beneath the Wartburg. At one side a Shrine*

IT is a year later. *Elizabeth* waits at the shrine for the returning Pilgrims. Hardly daring to hope for *Tannhäuser's*

return, she kneels in prayer. Certain that he will find her before the shrine, *Wolfram* approaches down a woodland path. He notes with grief her changed appearance and muses on his own hopeless love. The song of a band of Pilgrims is heard in the distance, and when they draw near, *Elizabeth* eagerly scans their faces for that of the missing *Tannhäuser*. He is not among them, and the despairing maid kneels again at the shrine, offering her prayer to the Virgin. This is the wonderful "Elisabeths Gebet" (Elizabeth's Prayer).

Its solemn and pathetic beauty has made it familiar to all music lovers; it often is heard in the concert-room.

For a long time she remains kneeling, then rises as one entranced. *Wolfram* now approaches. She bids him by gesture not to speak, but he begs leave to escort her safely homeward. *Elizabeth* again, by a beautiful gesture, signifies that her way leads to Heaven alone. She slowly ascends the height and disappears from view.

Night draws its soft veil about the scene, but *Wolfram*, lost in his dream, lingers beside the shrine. His harp is near, and taking it in hand he begins to preludize upon it. The evening star appears, and his mood finding inspiration in its pale lustre, he sings the tender and beautiful "O du mein holder Abendstern" (The Song to the Evening Star).

Yet even while *Wolfram's* fingers still pluck idly at the strings, a stranger appears clad in the raiment of a Pilgrim, his face wild and drawn. It is *Tannhäuser*, who supports his weary limbs with a Pilgrim's staff. *Wolfram* greets him with profound emotion, and learns that he has failed to win the forgiveness of the Pope, who vowed never to forgive him till the barren papal staff should again put forth leaves and blossoms. In despair, *Tannhäuser* is determined to return to the Venusberg;

as he voices the old desire, once more are heard the wild strains of the Venusberg music. The mountainside opens, the *Goddess* herself appears as in a vision,—beautiful, open-armed, singing her delirious and seductive melody. *Wolfram* struggles for a long time with *Tannhäuser;* finally it occurs to his tormented consciousness to mention the name of *Elizabeth.* The unhappy *Tannhäuser,* in sudden repentance, sinks to his knees. As the dawn slowly disperses the darkness, minstrels are seen approaching. They carry between them a bier upon which lies the body of *Elizabeth,* whose prayers have saved the soul of the repentant sinner at the cost of her own life,—for even while *Tannhäuser* kneels beside her body, a procession of Pilgrims is seen on the heights above, announcing how, shortly after *Tannhäuser* had left, the papal staff had miraculously brought forth green leaves. *Tannhäuser* has been redeemed through the prayers of *Elizabeth.* Supported by *Wolfram,* he looks once upon her face, and while the Pilgrims sing their praises to the Lord, he kneels beside her body and gives up the ghost.

THE VICTOR RECORDS

ACT II
DICH, TEURE HALLE

(Oh, Hall of Song) MARIA JERITZA, Soprano *In German* 688 10-in., $1.50
OVERTURE—Parts I and II
STOKOWSKI and Philadelphia Orchestra
6244 12-in., 2.00
OVERTURE—Part III
STOKOWSKI and Philadelphia Orchestra
74768 12-in., 1.50

ACT III
ELISABETHS GEBET

(Elizabeth's Prayer) EMMY DESTINN, Soprano *In German* 6085 12-in., 2.00
MARIA JERITZA, Soprano *In German*
6172 12-in., 2.00

ELIZABETH:
Oh, blessed Virgin, hear my prayer!
Thou star of glory, look on me!
Here in the dust I bend before thee
Now from this earth, oh, set me free!
Let me, a maiden pure and white,
Enter into thy kingdom bright!
If vain desires and earthly longing
Have turn'd my heart from thee away,
The sinful hopes within me thronging,
Before thy blessed feet I lay;

I'll wrestle with the love I cherish'd,
Until in death its flame hath perish'd.
If of my sin thou will not shrive me,
Yet in this hour, oh grant thy aid!
Till thy eternal peace thou give me,
I vow to live and die thy maid.
And on thy bounty I will call,
That heav'nly grace on him may fall!

O DU MEIN HOLDER ABENDSTERN

(The Evening Star) EMILIO DE GOGORZA, Baritone *In German* 6352 12-in., $2.00

WOLFRAM:
Like Death's dark shadow, Night extendeth
Her sable wing o'er all the vale she bendeth;
The soul that longs to tread yon path of light,
Yet dreads to pass the gate of Fear and Night,
I look on thee, oh, star in Heaven the fairest,
Thy gentle beam thro' space thou bearest;
The hour of darkness is by thee made bright,
Thou lead'st us upward by pure light.
O ev'ning star; thy holy light
Was ne'er so welcome to my sight,
With glowing heart, that ne'er disclos'd;
Greet her when she in thy light reposed;
When parting from this vale of vision,
She rises to an angel's mission.
(*He continues to play, his eyes raised to Heaven*)

BLACK LABEL RECORDS

{Tannhäuser—Overture—Part I .... *Victor Symphony Orchestra*} 35727 12-in., $1.25
{Tannhäuser—Overture—Part II .... *Victor Symphony Orchestra*}

{Tannhäuser—Overture—Part III .... *Victor Symphony Orchestra*} 35728 12-in., 1.25
{Tannhäuser—Fest March—Act II .... *Victor Symphony Orchestra*}

{Lied und Chor der Pilger (Shepherd's Song and Pilgrims' Chorus) (Part I)
{   (*In German*) .... *Gertrude Runge and Nebe Quartete* } 68352 12-in., 1.25
{Lied und Chor der Pilger (Part II) ......*Gertrude Runge and Nebe Quartete*}

Selection from Tannhäuser......................... *Arthur Pryor's Band* *Madame Butterfly Selection, No. 2* .... *Arthur Pryor's Band*	}35331	12-in., $1.25
The Evening Star.......................... *Rosario Bourdon, 'Cellist* *Last Rose of Summer*...................... *Elizabeth Wheeler, Soprano*	}16813	10-in., .75
The Evening Star (*In English*)...................... *Alan Turner, Baritone* *The Rosary (Nevin)*.......................... *Alan Turner, Baritone*	}17446	10-in., .75
Pilgrims' Chorus..*Pryor's Band* *Lohengrin—Coro delle nozze (Bridal Chorus) (In Italian)....La Scala Chorus*	}16537	10-in., .75
Pilgrims' Chorus............................... *Victor Brass Quartet* *Don Carlos—Grand March (Verdi)*........................ *Sousa's Band*	}17133	10-in., .75
Pilgrims' Chorus (*In English*)..................... *Victor Male Chorus* *Trovatore—Anvil Chorus (In English)*.............. *Victor Male Chorus*	}17563	10-in., .75
Dich, teure Halle (Hail, Hall of Song) (*In German*)....*Louise Voigt, Soprano* *Freischütz—Leise, leise, fromme Weise (Agatha's Prayer) (In German)* *Louise Voigt, Soprano*	}68473	12-in., 1.25
Fantasia on Tannhäuser (Dream of Wagner)................ *Pryor's Band* Prelude, Act II—Air for Venus, Act I—Duet, Elizabeth and Tannhäuser, Act II—Bacchanale, Act I—Tannhäuser's Air, Act I *Reminiscences of Verdi*................................*Sousa's Band* *Excerpts from "Rigoletto"—"Trovatore"—"Traviata"*	}35230	12-in., 1.25

LANDE   SETTING OF ACT III AT THE METROPOLITAN

THAÏS

THIS opera was composed by Massenet with a view to provide the American singer, Sybil Sanderson, with a rôle worthy of her talents. After its successful production in Paris, the composer went to Milan to supervise the performance at La Scala, where, as he records in his memoirs, he for the first time met Enrico Caruso. Since the Hammerstein production, "Thaïs" has been perhaps the most popular of Massenet's works in America, largely due to the beautiful Meditation.

THE OPERA

OPERA in three acts. Libretto by Louis Gallet, based on the novel of Anatole France; music by Jules Massenet. First production at the Opéra Comique, Paris, 1894, and the opera has since been given in nearly every music capital of Europe. First American production November 25, 1908, at the Manhattan Opera House, New York. Revived at the Metropolitan Opera House, 1917.

CHARACTERS

THAÏS, actress and courtesan
　(*Tah-ees'*) . . . . .Soprano
ATHANAEL, a Cenobite monk.Baritone
NICIAS, a wealthy Alexandrian . .Tenor
PALEMON, an aged Cenobite monk.Bass
ALBINE, an abbess . . . .Mezzo-Soprano
CROBYLE ⎱slave girls . . . . . . .Sopranos
MYRTALE ⎰
　Monks, Nuns, Citizens, Servants, Dancers, etc.

Time and Place: Alexandria and the Egyptian Desert. Early Christian Era

ACT I

SCENE I—*The Camp of the Cenobites near the Nile*

IN a time when Alexandria is wrapped in luxury and profligacy, *Thaïs*, a priestess of Venus, is recognized as the loveliest of all women. *Athanael*, a Cenobite monk, who has been to the city in an effort to preach the gospel, returns to his devout associates with strange stories of Alexandria's subtle wickednesses. Wearied from his journey, but stirred by his own recital, he falls asleep, when a vision comes to him of *Thaïs* herself, posing in the Alexandrian Theatre before a great throng which is in rapture over her beauty. He is determined to "reform" her, and against the advice of the good *Palemon*, he sets out upon this mission.

SCENE II—*The House of Nicias at Alexandria*

IN Alexandria, *Athanael* has a friend of his former unregenerate days in *Nicias*, whose palace occupies a commanding situation in Alexandria. As *Athanael* looks down from the terrace upon the wonderful yet wicked city beneath him, he reflects, in a mysterious air, upon its alluring but unhallowed beauty: "Voila donc la terrible cité" (That Awful City I Behold).

Nicias greets his old friend with courtesy, but is moved to laughter at his apparently whimsical notion of reforming the lovely *Thaïs*, upon whom *Nicias* himself has squandered a fortune. Willing to help for old time's sake, however, he has his household slaves array *Athanael* in rich robes, concealing his monkish habit. When at last *Thaïs* herself arrives she is at first repelled by this austere visitor, but her curiosity is awakened, none the less. *Athanael* tells her that he has come to bring her to the only God, whose humble but jealous servant he stands before her. *Thaïs's* reply is characteristically pagan—she believes in the joy of living; but she is none the less impressed. *Athanael* leaves, shocked by the preparations for an orgy, which he beholds going on about him.

ACT II

Scene I—*The Apartments of Thaïs*

IN her room lies *Thaïs*, weary of her world, for the moment wearied with luxury, and stirred to an unusual soberness by memories of the monk who has come to reform her. Nearby is a figure of Venus, whose priestess and votarist *Thaïs* remains; before it burns incense. The floor is covered with precious rugs of Byzantium, and many an exotic odor is blown in from the rich blossoms in vases of agate. *Athanael* comes to her, and she answers his singular admonitions lightly. But one fear lurks in the heart of *Thaïs;* she knows that in time her beauty must fade as the blooms around her. Yet *Athanael* speaks to her of life everlasting, of an eternal beauty of the spirit. Gradually the vision of a new and higher life comes to the pagan priestess, half frightened, half defiant. *Athanael* leaves her, confident she must repent. "On thy threshold till dawn I shall await thy coming," declares the inexorable *Athanael*, who longs to lead her to a convent in the desert.

Scene II—*A Street in Alexandria*

TRUE to his word *Athanael* maintains vigil. Sounds of revelry come to him from an adjacent house, where *Nicias* keeps the night hours. Towards dawn, *Thaïs* appears, worn and repentant after a night of emotion, ready now to follow her holy guide into the wilderness. She leaves everything behind her, only begging that she may bring with her a small statue of Eros (Cupid) which has been given her by *Nicias*. This *Athanael* casts to the ground, shattering it into a thousand fragments. He then goes into her palace to set fire to her manifold treasures. *Thaïs* accepts her sacrifice without demur. As soon as they are gone, *Nicias* appears, having won heavily at the games. He orders fresh dancing, wine and music, and a scene of luxury is revealed in the awakening day. *Thaïs* enters, in the robes of a penitent, followed by her lamenting women, and accompanied by the stern monk. The attendants of *Nicias* are enraged at the prospective loss of *Thaïs*, and the firing of the palace. They seek to hang *Athanael*. To save him, *Nicias* throws gold coins among them, and as the crowd scrambles for the money, *Athanael* and *Thaïs* depart for the desert and a life of repentance.

ACT III

Scene I—*A Desert Oasis*

TORTURED by lack of water, and weary with her long journey, *Thaïs* almost faints—though the end of the journey is in sight. *Athanael* remorselessly drives her on, and she goes willingly. But the monk is moved to pity as he notes her sufferings. He permits her to lie down while he bathes her feet, and he gives her fruit and water. An exquisite scene follows, "D'acqua aspergimi" (With Holy Water Anoint Me).

Thaïs now seems uplifted, beyond the dominion of flesh, into great spiritual exaltation; she is glad when the *Abbess Albine* and the *White Sisters* come to lead her to a cell in the convent, a short way off. At last she has found that peace for which her soul has craved. Only *Athanael* is troubled.

Scene II—*The Cenobites' Camp*

BACK among the brethren, *Athanael* is compelled to confess to the aged *Palemon* that he has saved *Thaïs* at the cost of his own soul. Passionately, raging at himself, he strives to cast out of his mind the memories of her human weakness and of her intoxicating beauty. He longs for her, and cannot now put down the desires that have sprung up within his tortured and struggling consciousness. In sleep, a vision comes to him of *Thaïs*, lovely,

ATHANAEL: "Courage, oh, my sister!
The dawn of rest begins."
(Act II, Scene II)

self-sure, mocking, as he first beheld her in Alexandria; then the vision changes and he sees her differently, her face illumined with the white fervor of religious mysticism as she lies dying in the convent. Awakening in terror

he rushes out into the darkness to seek her retreat.

SCENE III—*The Convent of the White Sisters*

THAÏS, worn with repentance and self-denial, is dying; upon her worn eyelids there falls, in truth, the "peace that passeth understanding." *Athanael* comes to her, shaken and distraught. He implores her to return with him to Alexandria. There is no reply. She sees the gates of Heaven before her and hears the sweet and powerful beating of angels' wings as the life slips away. *Athanael*, cheated by himself, falls to the ground in despair.

The lovely "Meditation" symbolizes the conversion of *Thaïs*, "Thy word has remained in my heart as a balm divine." It is first heard between the acts, a violin solo accompanied by harp and strings. But it recurs again in the scene in the oasis of the desert, and is at last triumphantly heard at the end, as *Thaïs* lies dying, enriched, ennobled, and with the melodies sung by the repentant sinner and the concurrent voices of the orchestra.

THE VICTOR RECORDS

INTERMEZZO
(Méditation Religieuse) (Te souvient-il du lumineux voyage) GERALDINE FARRAR, Soprano *In French*
6111 12-in., $2.00
FRITZ KREISLER, Violinist 6186 12-in., 2.00
MISCHA ELMAN, Violinist 6100 12-in., 2.00

BLACK LABEL RECORD

{ Intermezzo (Meditation)...............*Maximilian Pilzer, Violinist* }
{ *Humoresque* (Dvořák)...............*Maximilian Pilzer, Violinist* } 35306 12-in., $1.25

TOSCA AND SCARPIA—ACT II

TOSCA

AFTER the romantic charm of "La Bohême," Puccini turned to the gruesome play of Sardou for a source of inspiration. "La Tosca" was the fifth of his works, coming between "Bohême" and "Butterfly." The story is "tense" and even sensational, so much depending upon the action that Puccini's musical opportunities were limited. "Tosca" has been called a play with incidental music, but this hardly does justice to the skilful characterization which he reveals throughout, especially with *Scarpia*. The opera might as well have been called "Scarpia" as "Tosca," for this sinister gentleman dominates the whole of the action.

OPERA in three acts. Text by Illica and Giacosa after Sardou's drama. Music by Giacomo Puccini. First produced at the Constanzi Theatre, Rome, January 14, 1900. First London production at Covent Garden, July 12, 1900. Given in Constantinople and Madrid in 1900. During 1901, brought out in Odessa, January 1st; Lisbon, January 29th; Santiago, July 29th; Cairo, November 26th. First in Germany at Dresden, October 21, 1902; in France, at Paris, October 13, 1903, in French, and October 31, 1904, in Italian. Given at Budapest, May 10, 1906; Berlin, January, 1907; Vienna, October 26, 1909. First production in the Americas at Buenos

Aires, June 16, 1900; in the United States, February 4, 1901, at the Metropolitan, the cast including Ternina, Cremonini, Scotti and Gilibert. Also produced in English by Henry W. Savage. The opera has become a fixture in the American opera repertoire, and more than fifty performances have been given at the Metropolitan since 1908, besides those by the Chicago Opera Company and various traveling companies.

CHARACTERS

FLORIA TOSCA (*Floh'-ree-ah Toss'-kah*) a celebrated singer . . Soprano
MARIO CAVARADOSSI (*Mah'-ree-oh Cav-a-rah-doss'-ee*) a painter, Tenor
BARON SCARPIA (*Scar'-pee-ah*) chief of the police . . . . Baritone
CESARE ANGELOTTI (*Chay-zahr'-ay Ahn-jel-lot'-tee*) . . . . Bass
A SACRISTAN . . . . Baritone
SPOLETTA (*Spo-let'-tah*) a police agent . . . . Tenor
SCIARRONE, a gendarme (*Shar-rohn'-nay*) . . . . Bass
Judge, Cardinal, Officer, Sergeant, Soldiers, Police Agents, Ladies, Nobles, Citizens

Scene and Period: Rome, June, 1800

ACT I

SCENE—*Interior of the Church of St. Andrea*

THERE is no overture or prelude. As the curtain rises we hear the three chords of *Scarpia* thundered out, and we behold the high-vaulted interior of the church. *Angelotti* enters, pale, dishevelled, panic-stricken, in prison garb. He looks hurriedly around, soon discovering the key of the Attavanti chapel hidden for him by his sister. The escaped prisoner has barely had time to conceal himself before the *Sacristan* appears, with *Cavaradossi's*

paint-brushes, which he has been cleaning. As the *Sacristan* approaches the platform on which the painter has been standing to decorate the church, the Angelus is heard and he sinks to his knees. In this reverent position he is found by *Cavaradossi*, returning to work. *Cavaradossi* has been painting a fair-haired, blue-eyed Madonna, using for his model an unknown worshipper in the church, whose beauty has amazed him. She is the sister of his friend *Angelotti*, but he is not aware of it. His interest in the portrait is purely artistic, as we learn from the charming melody in which he discusses the more or less technical question of its contrasted colors. This is known as "Recondita armonia" (Strange Harmony).

Eager to continue work, he dismisses the *Sacristan*, who departs after a covetous glance at a neglected basket of food for the painter, which has been left on the platform. *Cavaradossi* has said he is not hungry, but the *Sacristan* does not share his lack of appetite. Scarcely has the man left him than the painter is startled to hear the sound of a key, turning sharply the lock of the chapel-door. *Angelotti* appears, wild-eyed at the sight of a stranger. His look changes to one of relief as he recognizes an old friend, *Cavaradossi*. He makes known his condition, and the painter promises every aid. Giving him the basket of food, he advises him to hide in the chapel, as the voice of a woman is heard without, calling to *Cavaradossi*, "Mario! Mario!" This is *La Tosca*, the beautiful singer, the betrothed of *Cavaradossi*. With a few hurried directions, the painter dismisses *Angelotti*, who takes with him a woman's dress, belonging to his sister, who has left it in the church along with the key.

When *Tosca* enters, she is enraged that *Cavaradossi* has kept her waiting.

LE THEATRE · · · · · TOSCA AND MARIO IN THE CHURCH—ACT I

She is suspicious of his confusion, too, believing she has heard him talking to a woman. The painter consoles her jealousy in lover-like fashion, but her anger breaks out afresh when she discovers that he is painting a fair-haired Madonna. Her own hair is dark and her eyes coal-black. He again quiets her jealous fancies, and she departs, arranging to meet him again that evening after the brief part she has to take in a cantata to be sung to the queen.

After *Tosca* has gone *Angelotti* returns. He is directed to a place of escape, to await *Cavaradossi* later. Even as the men converse the sound of cannon is heard booming out the announcement that a political prisoner has escaped. *Angelotti* rushes off in a frenzy of fear, knowing that his implacable enemy, the chief of police, *Scarpia*, already has taken up the trail. *Mario* goes with him to point a further way to escape.

The *Sacristan* returns, is surprised to find *Mario Cavaradossi* has gone. With him are members of the choir, brought to prepare for a festival, news of Bonaparte's defeat having arrived. The excitement is hushed, however, when the dreaded *Scarpia* with his assistant *Spoletta* and the police enter the church, infuriated at *Angelotti's* escape. The prisoner has been traced to the sacred building, and *Scarpia* savagely questions the *Sacristan*. The empty food-basket and the key to the chapel are discovered, and a fan belonging to *Angelotti's* sister. Hearing that *La Tosca* has been to the church, *Scarpia* resolves to use the fan to arouse her jealousy, as Iago used Desdemona's kerchief in his plot against Othello. Still doubting her lover, *Tosca* returns, and *Scarpia* loses little time in setting his plan into effect. He approaches her, courteously enough, in the familiar aria, "Tosca Divina" (Divine Tosca!).

407

THE TE DEUM—ACT I

At first she ignores his man's attentions, but *Scarpia*, with considerable skill, insinuates that she is not like other women who come to the church to distribute their favors. Then he exhibits the fan. The excitable singer soon is wrought to a high pitch of jealousy regarding *Mario*. She leaves the church weeping, just as the procession enters for the festival Te Deum in honor of the victory. *Scarpia* bows low to the *Cardinal*, concealing beneath an attitude of respectful reverence, a spirit busy with ugly and manifold plans. There is then heard the "Te Deum" which has been recorded.

The tolling of the bells, and the chanting of the choir above a groundbass in the orchestra, form a striking background for *Scarpia's* monologue.

ACT II

SCENE—*A Room in Scarpia's Apartments in the Farnese Palace*

ABOVE the apartments of the queen in the palace are *Scarpia's* own chambers. The table is laid for supper,

but the chief of police is too restless and excited to eat. He awaits with impatience the reports of his men regarding *Cavaradossi* and *Angelotti*. Hearing *Tosca's* voice in the apartment below, where the cantata is in progress, he sends her down a message declaring he has received word of her lover. He knows only too well what the effect will be. He exults over his imminent conquest, for he desires even above worldly power to make *Tosca* his victim. In a famous soliloquy he repeats his creed of life. *Scarpia* loves such a victory as this—no tender vows by moonlight for him! Whatever *Scarpia* desires, he wins for himself by force; when wearied he is ready for more. God has made divers wines and many kinds of beauty, and he intends to enjoy them all.

Spoletta returns with the exasperating news that *Angelotti* is still in concealment. *Scarpia* blazes with anger; he is consoled, however, by the news that *Cavaradossi* has been taken. The painter is brought before him, but

408

when questioned he refuses all information. He is consigned to the torture-chamber adjoining—just as *Tosca* appears.

Then begins that tremendous scene where *Scarpia*, soft as a cat with a mouse, plays upon the girl's emotions to find out where *Angelotti* is hidden. He greets her with horrible courtesy, and, when he thinks the time is ripe, lets her know bluntly that her lover is undergoing torments next door, and that for every denial he makes a twist is given to the wire about his head. She hears *Mario* steadily refuse, and *Scarpia* opens the door to the chamber so that she may hear his stifled cries. He even permits her to look in and see her lover's anguish. Even the hardened *Spoletta* gives utterance to a horrible prayer at sight of such abominable double-torture. A scream of pain from *Cavaradossi* at last weakens the girl's resolution and she tells *Scarpia* where *Angelotti* is hidden. *Cavaradossi* is brought in and placed, fainting, on a couch. "Did I betray

him?" he asks in anguish; and *Tosca* answers "No." But he hears *Scarpia* whip out directions to his men, and he knows that *Tosca* has given up the information. Weak, faint, like to die, he denounces the singer.

News now arrives that the reported victory over Napoleon is a mistake, and that Bonaparte has won the battle of Marengo. *Scarpia* stands abashed, but *Cavaradossi*, weak as he is, lets forth with a cry of Victory, a hail of freedom from the tyrannical *Scarpia*. *Tosca* does everything she can to withhold her lover, but in vain. The words pour forth, and the maddened *Scarpia* finally orders *Cavaradossi* to prison—and to death.

When *Cavaradossi* has been taken away, the chief of police resumes his lovemaking. He tells the singer he has long adored her, and sworn to possess her. This declaration is made in the famous "Cantabile Scarpia" (Scarpia's Air).

It is notable for a curious accompaniment in a rhythmic figure which

FARRAR AS TOSCA

COPY'T DUPONT
CARUSO AS MARIO—ACT I

COPY'T DUPONT
EAMES AS TOSCA

persists beneath long-drawn veritably "Cantabile" phrases and heroic high notes, somehow suggesting both the uprise of *Scarpia's* anger at news of Napoleon's victory and the unholy passion that now rages in his heart.

Tosca's spirit is broken, and she pleads with him, weeping for shame. She tells, in the beautiful "Vissi d'arte e d'amore" (Love and Music), how her life has been devoted to art and to music.

What has she done, she asks, that Heaven should so forsake her? The melody is infinitely tender, sympathetic harmonies in minor key murmur a soft accompaniment. But *Scarpia* stands unmoved. The drums, ordering out the escort for the condemned prisoner, break in ominously upon *Tosca's* pleading, and at last she yields, stipulating, with bowed head, that she and *Mario* shall the next day be given a safe-conduct. *Scarpia* is overjoyed. He informs her that a mock execution is necessary, and summoning *Spoletta*, he gives this worthy some instructions which he understands only too well.

When *Spoletta* has gone, *Scarpia* returns to his desk to write. The exhausted *Tosca* fills a glass of wine, and drinks it. She sees a sharp knife on the table, seizes and conceals it. *Scarpia* advances, inflamed with passion—and the consciousness of triumph. He takes her in his arms. But in that first unholy embrace the now maddened *Tosca* drives the knife into his body. Thus, she cries, will *Tosca* yield her kisses.

As the life passes out of *Scarpia*, she washes her hands in a bowl on the table, and with strange reverence lays out the body, placing candles at the head and a cross upon the bosom. Thus she leaves him. As the curtain descends, we hear once more the ominous three chords usually associated with *Scarpia*.

ACT III

SCENE—*A Terrace of San Angelo Castle, Outside the Prison of Cavaradossi. A View of Rome by Night*

A MOVING picture of the awakening dawn is presented by the orchestral Prelude.

An accompaniment of bells is heard; first but the sheep-bells of the distant hillsides, but afterward the giant clang of those in the church-tower.

THE MURDER OF SCARPIA—ACT II

Mario is brought out from his cell, and shown the official death-warrant, being told that he has but an hour to live. He sings a touching farewell to his dreams of art, and of the loved one he never hopes to see again. This is known as "E lucevan le stelle" (The Stars Were Shining).

Mario recalls the former meetings of the lovers on starlight nights in quiet gardens, crying out his passionate agony in a melodic phrase that strikes poignantly to the heart of the most indifferent listener.

Mario receives a shock when *Tosca* herself comes, bringing joyful news. She tells him of the death of *Scarpia*, and he commends the gentle hands that struck the blow, however much regretting they should have to foul themselves with a scoundrel's blood. He sings the lovely "O dolci mani" (Oh, Gentle Hands).

Tosca then explains that his execution is to be a mock affair. She directs him to fall when the volley is fired, and she exhibits to him the officially-sealed safe-conduct to a haven of safety and a future with some promise in it: "Amaro sol per te m'era il morire" (The Bitterness of Death).

As their love duet closes, the soldiers enter. The shots are fired and *Mario* falls. *Tosca*, waiting till the firing party has gone, bids him rise. "Now, Mario, all is safe," she cries, but he does not answer. She rushes to him, only to find that the dead hand of *Scarpia* has struck back. The firing squad had done its work, and *Mario* is no more. She throws herself upon his body in an agony of grief, but is roused by *Spoletta*, who, with the soldiers, comes rushing in with the news of *Scarpia's* murder. They attempt to arrest the girl, but she still has one alternative. She leaps from the castle wall to freedom—and death.

THE VICTOR RECORDS
(Sung in Italian)
ACT I

RECONDITA ARMONIA
(Strange Harmony) Enrico Caruso, Tenor   511   10-in., $1.50
Giovanni Martinelli, Tenor
    731   10-in.,   1.50
Beniamino Gigli, Tenor 646   10-in.,   1.50

ACT II

CANTABILE DI SCARPIA
(Scarpia's Air) Antonio Scotti, Baritone   6284   12-in.,   2.00
VISSI D'ARTE E D'AMOR
(Love and Music) Nellie Melba, Soprano   6220   12-in.,   2.00
Geraldine Farrar, Soprano
    6110   12-in.,   2.00
Emmy Destinn, Soprano 6086   12-in.,   2.00
Frances Alda, Soprano 6037   12-in.,   2.00
Maria Jeritza, Soprano 687   10-in.,   1.50

ACT III

E LUCEVAN LE STELLE
(The Stars Were Shining) Enrico Caruso, Tenor   511   10-in.,   1.50
Giovanni Martinelli, Tenor
    733   10-in.,   1.50
Beniamino Gigli, Tenor 942   10-in.,   1.50
O DOLCI MANI
(Oh, Gentle Hands) Beniamino Gigli, Tenor   942   10-in.,   1.50

BLUE LABEL RECORD

{ E lucevan le stelle................................*Paul Althouse, Tenor* } 45055   10-in., $1.00
{ *Pagliacci—Vesti la giubba*........................*Paul Althouse, Tenor* }

FARRAR AS VIOLETTA—ACT III

LA TRAVIATA

OPERA in three acts. Text by Piave, founded on Dumas' "Lady of the Camellias," but the period is changed to the time of Louis XIV. Score by Giuseppe Verdi. First presented in Venice, March 6, 1853; London, May 24, 1856; Paris, in French, December 6, 1856; in Italian October 27, 1864. First American production December 3, 1856, with Brignoli and La Grange. Recent productions at the Metropolitan with Caruso, Melba, Tetrazzini, Lipkowska, McCormack and Sammarco. Many notable productions in America in recent years, among the most recent being the Metropolitan production of 1905, for Caruso and Sembrich; that of 1908 (début of Amato) and 1909 (début of Lipkowska); the Hammerstein revivals for Tetrazzini and Melba; and the recent Metropolitan production with Hempel. Always considered a "test" opera for coloratura sopranos.

CHARACTERS

VIOLETTA VALERY, a courtesan
(*Vee-oh-let-tah Vah-lay-ree*), Soprano

FLORA, friend of Violetta
Mezzo-Soprano

ANNINA, confidante of Violetta
Soprano

ALFREDO, (ALFRED) GERMONT, lover of Violetta (*Ahl-fray-do Zhair-mon'*) .... Tenor

GIORGIO GERMONT, his father (*Jor-jo*) .... Baritone

GASTONE, Viscount of Letorieres (*Gahs-tohn*) .... Tenor

BARON DOUPHOL, a rival of Alfred (*Doo-fohl*) .... Baritone

DOCTOR GRENVIL, a physician... Bass

GIUSEPPE, servant to Violetta (*Joo-zep'-peh*) .... Tenor

Chorus of Ladies and Gentlemen, Friends of Violetta and Flora.

Mute Personages: Matadors, Picadors Gypsies, Servants, Masks, etc.

Scene and Period: Paris and Environs about the year 1700

(The name of the opera is pronounced *Lah Trah-vee-ah'-tah*).

412

ACT I

Scene—*Drawing-Room in the House of Violetta*

THE salon of the coquettish *Violetta* is the meeting place of the gayer element of Parisian society. To-night a lively entertainment is taking place. *Alfred* has been introduced to *Violetta* as another one of her admirers, and at her own request he sings a jovial drinking song, in which *Violetta* joins, and the guests in chorus. This is the famous "Libiam nei lieti calici" (A Bumper We'll Drink).

The energy and rhythmic beauty of this number place it among the finest of the many operatic drinking-chorus ensembles.

The dance begins and all go into the ballroom. But *Violetta* is attacked with a sudden faintness, an ominous forewarning of consumption. She begs the guests to proceed; more concerned for their own amusement than for the welfare of a somewhat notorious lady, they do—all except *Alfred*. *Violetta* is more than touched by this anxiety for her well-being and in the beautiful duet, "Un di felice" (Rapturous Moment) their mutual love is told.

After the guests have gone and *Alfred* has followed them, *Violetta* dreams of the new influence this love has brought into her life. It is expressed in the "Ah, fors e lui" (The One of Whom I Dreamed) and the "Sempre libera" (The Round of Pleasure).

These two (really one) of the most brilliant of coloratura arias, appear in the repertoire of every singer gifted with a voice capable of interpreting brilliant vocal display passages. It is preceded by the soliloquy "E Strano" ('Tis Strange) in which she is wonderstruck at finding herself the object of pure love.

ACT II

Scene I—*Interior of a Country House, near Paris*

SO sweet is this new love, that *Violetta* yields herself up to it wholly, going with *Alfred* to a little home near the city. Poet that he is, *Alfred* is enraptured by his good fortune in finding in *Violetta* a true mate after his somewhat wild youth. He tells her so in the "Dei miei bollenti spiriti" (Wild My Dream).

But the practical affairs of life insist upon obtruding, and *Alfred* is much astonished to learn from the maid that *Violetta* has quietly sold all her jewels to maintain the little *ménage* in the city. He is deeply ashamed, as he ought to be. Then, without warning, *Violetta* departs for Paris to obtain funds.

Returning to the little home she is surprised to find him absent. She is more surprised when she is visited by *Germont*, the father of *Alfred*. The older man has been greatly distressed at what he conceives to be a boyish entanglement, and he is none too polite in his greetings. *Violetta*, however, maintains such dignity that he is both charmed and abashed, especially when he learns that, far from being dependant upon *Alfred*, she has sold her property to support him. He abandons his former attitude, and throws himself wholly upon her mercy. *Alfred* has, it seems, a younger sister, whose marriage to a young noble will be jeopardised if *Alfred's mésalliance* is made known. Her character is described in "Pura siccome un angelo" (Pure as an Angel). *Violetta* at first refuses to give up *Alfred*, but realizing that her character has been destroyed, and that this must ultimately react to *Alfred's* disadvantage, she finally yields. Two numbers continue the scene: the "Dite alla giovine" (Say to Thy Daughter), and "Imponete" (Now Command Me).

In these *Violetta*, having resolved upon the sacrifice, places herself unreservedly at *Germont's* commands. He is deeply grateful, and he weeps as he enfolds the girl in his arms.

Soon as *Germont* has gone, the unhappy *Violetta* writes a note of farewell to *Alfred* and makes ready to leave for Paris. *Alfred* returns, mystified by her confusion. But she contrives to get away, bidding him farewell with such tenderness that he is deeply moved. He awaits his father, when a servant, however, brings him *Violetta's* note. Just as he sees *Germont* approaching him in the garden, he learns that *Violetta* has left him forever.

Alfred's despair is dreadful; he is not to be aroused, even when his father enters and vainly strives to console him. He sits down at a table, covering his face with his hands. It is then that *Germont* endeavors to stir him with the memories of his home—by singing the ever-lovely "Di provenza il mar" (Thy Home in Fair Provence).

In this touching appeal he asks his son to return to his home—and to his father's heart.

The appeal is not successful. Believing *Violetta* has wilfully duped him *Alfred* rushes past *Germont*, and he is soon on his way to Paris. *Violetta*, though not forgotten, is put, as nearly as may be, out of memory.

GALLI-CURCI AS VIOLETTA

SCENE II—*A Richly Furnished Salon in Flora's Palace*

AFTER leaving *Alfred*, *Violetta*, it becomes known, has gone to Paris and attached herself to her admirer, *Baron Douphol*. She is expected with this new admirer at a gambling party given by her friend *Flora*. She is ill, physically and spiritually worn, disinclined for such a life, but she knows it is the only way to convince *Alfred* their ways divide, and she has taken it to fulfil her agreement with *Germont*.

To this party now comes *Alfred*, who remarks with assumed indifference that he knows nothing of *Violetta's* whereabouts. He begins to gamble, winning heavily. When *Violetta* arrives with the *Baron*, she is horrified to see *Alfred*, but he pretends not to remark her, and he challenges the *Baron* to a game. He wins extravagantly, and the excitement runs high. Supper is announced, however, and all leave the room. *Violetta* returns, followed by *Alfred*. She implores him to leave the house, now horrified at the prospect of a duel between the two men. He refuses, bitterly, and charges her with falseness, asking her if she loves the *Baron*. Poor *Violetta*, remembering her promise to *Germont*, is compelled to answer yes, and *Alfred* then loses self-control. He flings wide the folding doors and summons back

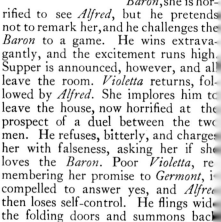

414

the astonished guests, who crowd into the room. Before them all he denounces her in the "Questa donna conoscete" (Know Ye All This Woman?).

He completes the insult by throwing at her feet a small portrait of herself which she has given him, together with the money he has won. *Violetta* faints in the arms of *Flora* and a *Doctor* who is present. At this moment, *Germont* enters, to be horrified at his son's scurvy treatment of the woman whose self-sacrifice he has himself brought about. Then follows the great finale, "Alfredo, di questa core" (Alfred, Thou Knowest Not).

ACT III

Scene—*Violetta's Apartment. She is Asleep on the Couch*

THIS act has a prelude. Then the story resumes.

The illness with which *Violetta* has been afflicted from the first, has been intensified by these new developments, and she now lies upon what is to be her death-bed. The *Doctor* comes with reassuring words, but they do not deceive her, and the *Doctor* confesses to the maid that she has not long to live. Left alone, she again reads a letter she has received from *Germont:*

"You have kept your promise. The duel took place, and the Baron was wounded, but is improving. Alfred is abroad. Your sacrifice has been revealed to him by me, and he will return to you for pardon. Hasten to recover; you deserve a bright future."—Germont.

"Alas! it is too late," is her comment, and she sings her beautiful and pathetic farewell, "Addio del passato."

She has not long to wait for *Alfred,* who arrives in repentance. He is speedily forgiven, and *Violetta,* forgetting, or seeming to forget her illness, plans with him to leave Paris forever. For the moment, like so many others in the shadow of disaster, they are happy. They sing the "Parigi O cara" (Far From Gay Paris).

The shock of their meeting, however, is too much for *Violetta's* strength. The end is very near now, and she collapses into her lover's arms. Noting her pallor, he sends for the doctor. *Germont* enters with the physician. The scene is an affecting one, and *Germont* blames himself for having brought all the troubles upon his son and *Violetta.* But *Violetta* no longer feels pain. She rouses herself with a strange accession of strength. "Ah! Yes!" she cries, "I live! I have again returned to life." And with this she falls back upon the couch—dead.

THE VICTOR RECORDS

(Sung in Italian unless noted)

ACT I

LIBIAM NEI LIETI CALICI

(A Bumper We'll Drain) ALMA GLUCK, Soprano, ENRICO CARUSO, Tenor and Metropolitan Opera Chorus
3031 10-in., $2.00

AH, FORS' È LUI

(The One of Whom I Dreamed) AMELITA GALLI-CURCI, Soprano 6126 12-in., 2.00
LUISA TETRAZZINI Soprano
6344 12-in., 2.00
NELLIE MELBA, Soprano 6213 12-in., 2.00

How wondrous!
His words deep within my heart are graven!
No love of mortal yet hath moved me.
Shall I dare disdain it,
And choose the empty follies that surround me?
Ah, was it he my heart foretold, when in the throng of pleasure,
Oft have I joy'd to shadow forth one whom alone I'd treasure.
He who with watchful tenderness guarded my waning powers,
Strewing my way with flowers,
Waking my heart to love!
What folly! what folly!
For me there's no returning!
In ev'ry fierce and wild delight.
I'll steep my sense and die!

SEMPRE LIBERA

(The Round of Pleasure) AMELITA GALLI-CURCI, Soprano 627 10-in., 1.50

ACT II

DEI MIEI BOLLENTI SPIRITI
(Wild My Dream of Youth) GIOVANNI
MARTINELLI, Tenor   6212 12-in., $2.00

DITE ALLA GIOVINE
(Say to Thy Daughter) AMELITA GALLI-
CURCI, Soprano and GIUSEPPE DE
LUCA, Baritone   8025 12-in., 2.50

IMPONETE
(Now Command Me) AMELITA GALLI-
CURCI, Soprano and GIUSEPPE DE
LUCA, Baritone   8025 12-in., 2.50

DI PROVENZA IL MAR
(Thy Home in Fair Provence) PASQUALE
AMATO, Baritone   6042 12-in., 2.00
GIUSEPPE DE LUCA, Baritone
    6079 12-in., 2.00

GERMONT:
From fair Provence's soil and sea,
Who hath won thy heart away?
From thy native sunny clime,
What strange fate caus'd thee to stray?
Oh, remember in thy woe
All the joy that waits for thee,
All the peace thy heart would know.

ACT III

ADDIO DEL PASSATO
(Farewell to the Bright Visions)
LUCREZIA BORI, Soprano
    543 10-in., $1.50
AMELITA GALLI-CURCI, Soprano
    627 10-in., 1.50

VIOLETTA:
Farewell to the bright visions I once fondly
    cherish'd,
Already the roses that deck'd me have per-
    ish'd;
The love of Alfredo is lost, past regaining,
That cheer'd me when fainting, my spirit sus-
    taining.
Pity the stray one, and send her consolation,
Oh, pardon her transgressions, and send her
    salvation.
The sorrows and enjoyments of life will soon
    be over,
The dark tomb in oblivion this mortal form
    will cover!

PARIGI O CARA
(Far From Gay Paris) LUCREZIA BORI,
Soprano and JOHN McCORMACK, Tenor
    10006 12-in., 3.50

BLACK LABEL AND BLUE LABEL RECORDS

{ Ah, fors' è lui (One of Whom I Dreamed).........*Lucy Marsh, Soprano* }
{ *Parla valse* (*Arditi*).......................*Lucy Marsh, Soprano* } 55107 12-in., $1.50

{ Gems from "Traviata," Part I....................*Victor Opera Co.* }
{ Chorus, "Drinking Song"—Duet, "The One of Whom I Dreamed"— }
{ (Ah, fors' è lui)—Solo, "Thy Home in Fair Provence"(Di Provenza)— }
{ Solo, "I'll Fulfill the Round of Pleasure" (Sempre libera)—Chorus of }
{ Matadors }
{ Gems from "Traviata" Part II....................*Victor Opera Co.* } 35433 12-in., 1.25
{ Chorus of Matadors—Duet, "May He Be Spared the Anguish"(Cono sca }
{ il Sacrifizio)—Solo, "Farewell to the Bright Visions" (Addio)—Duet, }
{ "Far from Gay Paris" (Parigi o cara)—Chorus, Finale }

{ Traviata Selection............................*Arthur Pryor's Band* }
{ "Bacchanal Chorus"—"Far from the Busy Throng," Finale—"Death } 35076 12-in., 1.25
{ of Violetta" }
{ *Trovatore Selection*..........................*Arthur Pryor's Band* }

{ Prelude.....................................*Victor Symphony Orchestra* } 35717 12-in., 1.25
{ Casse Noisette (Waltz of the Flowers)..........*Victor Symphony Orchestra* }

TRISTAN AND ISOLDE

Opera in three acts. Words and music by Richard Wagner. First presented in Munich, June 10, 1865. First London production June 20, 1882. First American performance in New York, December 1, 1886, with Lehmann, Brandt and Fischer. Produced at the New Orleans Opera December 21, 1895. Some notable American productions were: in 1895 with Sucher, Alvary, Brema and Fischer; in 1896 with the de Reszkes, Nordica and Brema; in 1901 with Ternina and Van Dyck; and in 1910 with Homer, Fremstad, Knote and Van Rooy, this being Gustav Mahler's American début as a conductor.

CHARACTERS

TRISTAN, a Cornish knight, nephew of King Mark (*Triss'-tan*) . . . . Tenor
KING MARK of Cornwall. . . . . Bass
ISOLDE, Princess of Ireland (*Ee-sohl'-deh*) . . . . Soprano
KURVENAL, Tristan's devoted servant (*Koor'-vee-nahl*) Baritone
MELOT, one of King Mark's courtiers . . . . Tenor
BRANGÄNE, Isolde's friend and attendant(*Brahn-gay-neh*)Soprano
A Shepherd, a Steersman, a Sailor Lad; Chorus of Sailors, Knights, Esquires and Men-at-Arms

Time and Place: Legendary Cornwall

TRISTAN has been sent to Ireland by *King Mark of Cornwall* to fight *Morold*, a recalcitrant knight who refuses to pay tribute, and to bring back *Isolde* as the *King's* bride. *Morold* is slain and *Tristan* badly wounded. He is nursed by *Isolde*, *Morold's* betrothed, who does not know it is he who has slain *Morold*.

Tristan, however, is loyal to *King Mark* and brings her with him to Cornwall. During the voyage, he keeps clear of *Isolde*, but as they approach the coast, the anguished *Isolde*, longing for vengeance and death, and loathing her fate, begs him to drink with her a cup of poison. *Tristan*, knowing that he owes his life to her nursing, is honorably disposed to yield her the life she has spared, and he takes the potion with her. The maid, *Brangäne*, however, has substituted in its place a love-philtre, so that, as the ship comes to anchor, the two are lovers in each other's arms. The all-over-powering love of the pair causes them to meet after *Isolde* is married to the Cornish *King*. Their tryst is suspected by *Melot*, himself in love with *Isolde*. He warns the *King*, and the guilty couple are discovered. *Tristan*, who fights but half-heartedly, is wounded and he departs to his castle in Brittany. There, in mortal agony, he yearns for *Isolde*, and *King Mark*, having learned about the love-potion, brings her to him, forgiving all; but it is too late. She arrives just as *Tristan* expires, and after singing her marvellous "Death-Song" she, too, dies beside him.

The Prelude, which has been recorded, is founded on the following theme, which is used continuously throughout the opera, in various forms, to express the love and longing, and the suffering of the two lovers:

It will be noticed that the theme in the upper stave is "two-voiced," the upper notes being used to suggest love and longing, and the lower ones to indicate pain and suffering. Some-

ISOLDE:
    Tristan! Traitor beloved!
TRISTAN:
    Isolde! Woman divine!
    (Tristan and Isolde, Act I.)

times heard together, sometimes separate, and in all manner of forms they
recur again and again. A peculiarity
of the Prelude also, is that it contains
no "cadence" or halting-place where
dissonant chords resolve into con-
sonance. Though for concert-use the
Prelude comes to an end, in the opera
it continues right through to the
lifting of the curtain and beyond.
There is in fact no full "cadence"
until the end of the Act, the hearer's
attention being kept continually at
high pitch and his expectancy led on
by dissonances that do but resolve
into fresh dissonances. The same
principle obtains through the following
acts, and it is typically Wagnerian.
The various themes of the work are
made to recur in countless different
forms and the whole score becomes
really symphonic in its intricacy.
This accounts for the fact that a first
performance attempted in Vienna was
abandoned after fifty-four rehearsals
between November, 1862, and March,
1863, the work being regarded as
"impossible." In spite of its elabora-
tions, however, the music is surpris-
ingly lucid, and the simple amateur,
provided he loves good music, can
yield himself up to it in perfect
certainty that, with a reasonable
knowledge of the plot, he can follow the
themes and realize to the full the
depth and beauty of the tale, and
the varied qualities of human emotion
that furnish it material.

In concert performances, it is cus-
tomary to follow up the yearning
Prelude with the ecstatic "Liebestod"
(Love-Death) at the end, and the
available Victor records make this
course possible with the Victrola. It
will be noted how the "yearning"
theme at the opening of the Prelude
is heard at the very last in extended
form, resolving exquisitely into perfect
consonant harmony.

ACT I

SCENE—*On Board the Vessel, nearing
the Cornish Coast*

ON the deck of a great ship has
been set up a pavilion richly
hung with tapestry. Within it *Isolde*
lies on a couch, her face buried in
cushions. Her maid, *Brangäne*, holding open a curtain, peers over the side
of the vessel. The voice of a young
sailor is heard from the masthead
trolling out a sea-song. It is a bold
tune, yet it strangely suggests the
lonesomeness of the ocean. The
words, however, bear upon the present
voyage, and *Isolde*, looking up suddenly
from her couch, construes them as
an insult. She calls *Brangäne*, who
reports that land is already in sight.
The passionate *Isolde* gives way to fear
and anger; this frightens the maid and
she is compelled to open the pavilion
for air. The whole length of the ship is
seen, clear to the stern, where *Tristan*
stands apart among his knights while his
henchman *Kurvenal* reclines at his feet.

The sight of *Tristan* brings back to
Isolde a flood of recollection. He has
remained aloof from her during the
voyage, determined to bring her safely
to his uncle, *King Mark*. She attributes this to her undeclared lover's
cowardice and her love for him is
turned to hatred. She bids *Brangäne*
go fetch him, and the maid, unwilling
enough, departs. Always solicitous
for his charge, *Tristan* receives her
courteously enough. But he excuses
himself on the ground that they are nearing shore and it is his duty to attend the
ship. *Kurvenal*, a sturdy soldier, a plain-
spoken man of no diplomacy, finds this
a good time to gloat over *Tristan's* victory over *Morold*,—killing the Irish
knight, and bringing Ireland's tribute
to Cornwall, and *Isolde* to boot.

His vainglorious song is loudly
taken up by the knights. *Isolde* is

inflamed with anger. Alone with *Brangäne*, the curtain again drawn tight, her wild brain repeats the story of *Tristan's* "treachery," how she nursed him without recognizing him under the pseudonym of "Tantris," how she found a piece of the sword which slew *Morold*, her betrothed, exactly fitted the wounded man's weapon; how she took the sword and sought to slay the knight in his bed; how his weakness and suffering brought pity to her heart; how she nursed him back to health; and how, finally, he had repaid her kindness by bringing her aboard this ship as the bride of the hereditary enemy of her race, and one whom she had never seen, *King Mark of Cornwall!* Images of these scenes inflame the wild brain of *Isolde* and lend greater wildness to her speech.

Brangäne, much astonished at this recital, tries to comfort her mistress with the notion that *Tristan* seeks to repay her by making her a queen, but *Isolde* only cries upon Death to ease her sufferings. The horrified maid seeks to dissuade her, but is commanded to bring a certain mysterious casket of herbs and drugs. *Brangäne* tries to induce *Isolde* to take a soothing balm, but *Isolde* chooses something of known deadly qualities. At this moment cries to reduce sail indicate that the journey's end is near and *Kurvenal*, entering boisterously, bids them prepare to land. *Isolde*, with open scorn, bids him direct *Tristan* to attend her. In due course the hero enters, pausing respectfully at the doorway. After taking him to task for his ill manners in remaining away so long, *Isolde* offers him the cup. *Tristan*, who has kept a chivalrous aloofness throughout, accepts the cup, knowing well the contents are deadly. He tries to drink it to the dregs, but *Isolde* snatches it from him, determined to end her own life too.

The effect is not what they expected. They stand for a long time facing each other, dazed, but with growing wonder. Unknown to them, *Brangäne* has substituted a love potion for the death draught, and the hatred of *Isolde* and the indifference of *Tristan* are turned to overpowering love. They fly to each other's arms, while *Brangäne*, wringing her hands, looks on in despair. She at last arouses them to the fact that *King Mark's* followers are near at hand. *Isolde* puts on her royal robe. The curtains of the pavilion are thrown back, so that the officers and crew are seen pointing to the shore, and heard shouting their loyal greetings: "Hail to King Mark! Cornwall, hail!"

ACT II

SCENE—*A Garden before Isolde's Chamber: Summer Night*

SINCE *Isolde's* marriage to *King Mark*, her beauty has attracted *Melot*, a knight of the court, whose

TRISTAN AND ISOLDE

ISOLDE: "Ah, look again! it hath the grace of dawn, the stars are flushed with crimson, and the sky holds some new light I know not!" (Tristan and Isolde—Act II)

suspicions, quickened by jealousy, arise round *Tristan* and *Isolde*. He persuades *King Mark* to pretend to go off on a night hunt with the hope that, returning unexpectedly, they may find the guilty lovers together.

When the curtain rises, there are heard the horn calls of the departing huntsmen, blended with the music of *Isolde's* longing, against the enchanting tone-picture of a warm and lovely summer evening. A lighted torch burns before *Isolde's* chamber, warning *Tristan* not to approach until it is put out. *Brangäne* is suspicious, but *Isolde*, after a lengthy talk with her, finally seizes the torch and throws it to the ground, waving her kerchief as a signal to her lover to come to her. He appears, like one in a dream.

The long duet follows, setting forth with amazing musical eloquence the passionate ecstasy of the lovers, their joy and faith in each other. Throughout the night they rest in one another's arms, oblivious of all things save only the magic spell of their love. *Brangäne* has confessed to the love potion, but heedless alike of honor and of danger, they glory in her mistake.

They do not hear *Brangäne's* warning, even when, with a piercing cry, she announces the return of the huntsmen. *Kurvenal* rushes in with his master's sword, but is followed almost immediately by *King Mark*, *Melot* and their followers who regard the scene astounded. *Tristan* makes no move, only to draw his cloak about the girl in his arms. Dawn breaks, and *Tristan* notes that "the dreary day its last time comes." *Melot* grows voluble; he has proven his charges. *King Mark*, deeply moved and with trembling voice, then addresses the pair. His utterances to his trusted friend and nephew, the bravest knight of his court, on his black treachery, are full of dignity and nobility,

especially where he reminds *Tristan* that it was upon *his* counsel that *Isolde* was brought from Ireland. He offers *Tristan* banishment with *Isolde* who is only too willing to follow. But such leniency does not suit *Melot* who rushes forward sword in hand. *Tristan* draws in turn, and reproaches *Melot*. But *Tristan* has no real intention of fighting; he only seeks death with honor, so he drops his guard and receives a terrible stroke from his adversary. *Isolde* throws herself upon the breast of her wounded lover, and the *King* restrains *Melot* as the curtain descends. What next will follow?

ACT III

SCENE—*In the Garden of Tristan's Castle in Brittany, overlooking the Sea*

TRISTAN lies delirious, *Kurvenal* beside him bowed with grief. From beyond comes the strange and melancholy piping of a shepherd boy, who, when he has finished comes to *Kurvenal*. Other peasants appear, to look with sadness upon their stricken lord. They depart shaking their heads. *Kurvenal* bids the shepherd scan the horizon for a sail, for he knows that

COPY'T DUPONT
GADSKI AS ISOLDE

none can cure his master save the "lady-leech" who has been the cause of his plight. The shepherd sees no sail, but he promises to play a livelier strain should one appear upon the golden horizon.

Tristan comes back to momentary consciousness, and *Kurvenal* tells him how he has been brought hither. The wounded man soon relapses into delirium, pining for *Isolde.* The scene is a prolonged one, but at length the shepherd's pipe takes a joyful turn. *Kurvenal,* crying out that *Isolde* is at hand, rushes off. *Tristan* is overcome with joy, and in his feverishness he rises to his feet, tearing away the bandages from his wounds, and madly rejoices to see the red blood flow. He staggers forward, but the effort is his last and soon he crashes to the ground. *Isolde* arrives, but too late! The dying *Tristan* can but turn eloquent eyes upon her before he expires and *Isolde* sinks senseless upon her lover's body.

King Mark and his followers follow hard behind, the *King* all forgiveness, having learned of the fatal love-potion. *Kurvenal* does not know this, and seeing *Melot* he draws his sword and slays the man. But he is himself mortally stricken in the process.

All of these painful scenes only lead on—to the sublime and terrible climax of the work.

Isolde returns to consciousness.

Then begins that marvellous, ecstatic Liebestod, or "Love-Death," which brings the drama to its close. The following is the melody upon which the music is based:

This "theme" is carried through a prolonged and exquisitely beautiful series of modulations, or changes of key, the sequences rising and falling and rising again until from them is evolved with almost superhuman skill the great crescendo which leads to *Isolde's* ecstatic death. Words cannot convey the extraordinary effect of this crescendo, rising ever higher and higher in pitch, semitone by semitone. On the basis of an impassioned melody, Wagner builds a mighty climax of bitter-sweet dissonances which seem ever about to resolve into restful harmony, yet which never rest until they reach at length their gloriously impassioned climax. Without question this is the greatest, the most ecstatic love-song in the whole realm of music. As *Isolde* falls at length upon the body of her lover, the orchestra, with heavenly serenity after long storm and stress, plays an extended form of the unutterably sweet theme of longing with which the Prelude commenced, now resolving at the last into a concord of almost intolerable beauty.

BLACK LABEL AND BLUE LABEL RECORDS

{Isolde's Liebestod (Isolde's Love-Death)......... *Victor Herbert's Orchestra*			
{ Träume (Dreams) (*Wagner*)................. *Victor Herbert's Orchestra*	}55041	12-in.,	$1.50
{Prelude.. *La Scala Orchestra*			
{Isolde's Love-Death............................. *La Scala Orchestra*	}68210	12-in.,	1 25

IL TROVATORE

(THE TROUBADOUR)

NEARLY two years after "Rigoletto," "Il Trovatore" was produced at Rome, and a month later "La Traviata" at Venice. "Il Trovatore" was a success from the first, and it has been popular ever since. Naturally!—for it is full of melody from start to finish, and the action, if blood-curdling, is swift and plentiful. There are more technical things that are equally admirable. The harmonies are rich and varied, though a little trite in comparison with the newer style already coming into vogue with Berlioz, Liszt and Wagner. The orchestration is masterly—rich and sonorous. There is even considerable character-analysis in the role of *Azucena*, who, to many, is, in truth, even more human and convincing than the Wagnerian Brünnhilde, the gradual wane of her vindictive fury as death approaches, and the last flare of vengeance being especially touching. "Il Trovatore" preaches no moral and it cloaks no muddy philosophy. It aims only to tell a thrilling story of a gypsy's vengeance in straightforward fashion, and the most hardened playgoer cannot deny that it succeeds admirably.

THE OPERA

OPERA in four acts. Words by Salvatore Cammanaro, the story being suggested by a Spanish drama of the same name. Music by Giuseppe Verdi. Produced at the Teatro Apollo, Rome, January 19, 1853; at the *Théâtre des Italiens*, Paris, December 23, 1854; at the *Opéra*, Paris, as *Le Trouvère*, January 12, 1857; at Covent Garden, London, May 17, 1855; in English as *The Gypsy's Vengeance*, Drury Lane, March 24, 1856. First New York production, in Italian, April 30, 1855, with Brignoli, Steffanone, Amodio and Vestvali. First Philadelphia production at the Walnut Street Theatre, January 14, 1856, and at the Academy of Music, February 25, 1857. Produced at the New Orleans Opera, April 13, 1857. A German version was given at the Metropolitan Opera House in 1889. Some notable revivals occurred in 1908, with Caruso, Eames and Homer; and again, in 1914, with Destinn, Ober, Martinelli, Amato and Rothier.

CHARACTERS

LEONORA (*Lay-oh-noh'-rah*), a noble lady of the Court of an Aragon Princess...........Soprano
AZUCENA (*Ahz-you-chay'-nah*), a wandering Biscayan gypsy
       Mezzo-Soprano
INEZ (*Ee'-nez*), attendant of Leonora....................Soprano
MANRICO (*Man-ree'-koh*), a young chieftain under the Prince of Biscay, of mysterious birth, and in reality a brother of Count di Luna.....Tenor
COUNT DI LUNA (*dee Loo'-nah*), a powerful young noble of the Prince of Aragon.........Baritone
FERRANDO, a captain of the guard and under di Luna.......Bass
RUIZ, a soldier in Manrico's service....................Tenor
AN OLD GYPSY..............Baritone
Also a Messenger, a Jailer, Soldiers, Nuns, Gypsies, Attendants, etc.
Scene and Period: Biscay and Aragon; Middle of the Fifteenth Century

ACT I

SCENE I—*Vestibule in Aliaferia Palace*

AT the outset we plunge into an atmosphere of mystery and romance. The retainers of *Count di Luna*, awaiting the arrival of their master, are beguiled by *Ferrando* with the history of the *Count's* childhood, and the supposed loss of his brother. The brother, as a baby, came under the evil eye of a witch, condemned to the stake. This woman, however, had a daughter who was determined to avenge her mother's death. After the capture of her mother the child disappeared. Nothing was absolutely known of its fate, but among the charred embers about the stake where the witch-woman had been burned were discovered the bones of a child. Such is the circumstance that *Ferrando* tells in the "Abbietta zingara" (Swarthy and Threatening). The story is set to a melody with a strong, almost fierce rhythm that gives it peculiar force.

The hearers are much affected; in their comments they declare the witch appears in ghostly shape. They are interrupted by the clock, striking twelve, and they disperse with cries of "Cursed be the witch infernal!"

SCENE II—*The Garden of the Palace*

IT is evening. In the garden of the Palace, *Leonora*, a noble lady of great beauty, is walking with her faithful companion, *Inez*, to whom she confides her interest in an unknown knight she has seen at a Tournament. This unknown hero has since serenaded her —hence his descriptive title, "*Il Trovatore—The Troubadour.*" She sings of him in the "Tacea la notte placida" (Peaceful Was the Night).

The melody has a wistful tenderness that is actually grateful after the stormy first scene.

The ladies go into the house, just as the *Count di Luna*, himself bent on serenading the lovely *Leonora*, comes to her window. But he has barely taken his station before the mysterious *Troubadour* appears upon the same errand. The *Count* hides, and listens to the song of *Manrico*, which is so effective that *Leonora* comes out to greet her lover. She is met by the *Count*, too; and the *Count* is in a fine rage. *Manrico* defies

COPY'T DUPONT
MARTIN AS MANRICO

COPY'T MC INTOSH
HOMER AS AZUCENA

COPY'T MISHKIN
SLEZAK AS MANRICO

him, and unable to restrain their jealous passions, the two men rush at one another with drawn swords. *Leonora*, fearing the death of her lover, swoons away as the curtain descends. What is to be the next development?

ACT II

SCENE I— *A Gypsy Camp in the Biscay Mountains*

THE sun rises upon a gypsy encampment, where the men are already beginning the business of the day, hammering lustily as they sing the familiar Anvil Chorus: "La Zingarella."

The swinging tune, accompanied by blows on the anvil swelling the rough voices of the men, is justly famous. The rhythm is broad and sweeping, and there are few who listen to it without being carried away.

Among these workers, however, is a wild woman of fierce aspect and violent passions, *Azucena*. It was she who stole the infant, as told by *Ferrando*, and she now repeats the story for the benefit of *Manrico*, who is supposed to be her son. He was wounded in the duel with the *Count*, but she has nursed him back to health. The story is told in the "Stride la vampa" (Fierce Flames Are Soaring).

In this wild air, so well adapted to its grim recital,—through which the changing tones of the contralto voice are so powerfully brought into play,— *Azucena* lives over again the dreadful scene of her mother's burning at the stake. Questioned by *Manrico*, she tells how her mother's last unearthly cry for vengeance led her to steal the child of the present *Count di Luna's* father, intending to throw it on the flames which had consumed her mother. She discovered, however, that in her frenzy she had destroyed her own infant, preserving the child of her enemy.

The story sets *Manrico* thinking. "If your son perished," he asks, "whose

child am I?" But the gypsy woman, with a born instinct for prevarication, avoids the question, claiming him as her son. She changes the subject by reminding him how she had nursed him back to life after the almost fatal wound received in the duel with the *Count*. *Manrico* at once tells of his violent struggle with his rival, in which, by an irresistible impulse, he had spared the man's life after felling him to the ground in the first rush.

The air, "Mal reggendo all'aspro assalto" (At My Mercy Lay the Foe), is in martial vein, yet smooth and flowing. *Azucena* brings a more agitated feeling into the music as she bids her foster-son never to allow an enemy to escape, but to kill without hesitation. This leads to a powerful, intensely rhythmic climax, in which both voices are strikingly blended.

SCENE II—*The Cloister of a Convent*

SINCE the duel, *Leonora* has heard no more of her Troubadour lover, and she believes him dead. She now decides to enter a convent. *Count di Luna*, however, is determined that before this may happen he will carry her away by force, and so has come to the walls of the convent with a body of troops. His deep love for her finds expression in a remarkable number, the "Il balen del suo sorriso" (The Tempest of the Heart). It is a genuine and heartfelt tune, one of the finest in the operatic baritone anthology.

As its last cadenza comes to an end, the convent bell is heard tolling as a signal for the final rites which will remove *Leonora* from the outward world. The *Count*, in a passion, declares she must be taken before she reaches the altar. This gives way to the vigorous "Per me ora fatale" (This Passion that Inspires Me). The *Count* and his followers conceal themselves among the trees, and the chanting of the nuns is heard, the "Ah! se l'error t'ingombra" ('Mid the Shades of Error).

The women sing in pure, sweet harmonies of *Leonora's* abstraction from the world of desire and unhappiness. From their place of hiding the *Count* and his men discuss their coming triumph.

The nuns issue from the chapel, escorting the penitent. They are terrified when the *Count* and his troops rush forward to seize *Leonora*. But just as they are about to carry the girl away, they are confronted by *Manrico*, who manages to protect her, and gain at least a short-lived victory. His followers contrive to fend off the followers of the baffled *Count*. *Leonora* is saved.

ACT III

Scene I—*The Camp of di Luna*

AZUCENA has fallen into the hands of a scouting party sent out by the *Count*, and she is led before him as a possible spy: "Giorni poveri vivea" (In Despair I Seek My Son), she sings, vainly enough.

Questioning brings out the story of her past life, and her connection with the episode of the *Count's* childhood. *Ferrando* swears she is the murderess of *di Luna's* long-lost brother. *Azucena* in her extremity, cries out the name of *Manrico*, and the *Count*, on finding she claims the *Troubadour* as her son, vows upon her a double vengeance. She is bound and dragged away.

Scene II—*Manrico's Castle*

BEFORE the final catastrophe, *Manrico* and *Leonora* enjoy a brief respite in which to avow their love. An attack by the *Count di Luna* is hourly expected, and *Manrico* is forced to sing a tender farewell before departing to repel the assault. This is the "Ah, si ben mio" (The Vows We Fondly Plighted). It is a lyrical number, ten-

der and wistful, a relief from the stormy scenes that have passed, and a preparation for that which is to come.

The quiet of the lovers is interrupted by news of *Azucena's* capture. Already the faggots are being piled about the stake at which she is to be burned, as her mother was before her. *Manrico* still believes the gypsy woman to be his own mother, and he is maddened by the news. He prepares to rush to her aid and sings a fiery air, the "Di quella pira" (Tremble, Ye Tyrants).

This is led up to by a powerful introductory passage, and the high notes at the end, delivered in robust tones, and rising to the high tenor C, never fail of their musical and dramatic effect.

ACT IV

Scene I—*Exterior of the Palace of Aliaferia*

DEFEATED by *Count di Luna* and his men, *Manrico* has been taken captive, and he is languishing in a dungeon with *Azucena*. To the castle, *Leonora* also wanders, and outside its frowning battlements sings the first plaintive melody of what may almost be considered the greatest scene in Italian opera,—the "D'amor sull'ali rosee" (Love, Fly on Rosy Pinions).

As she sings, the chanting of the priests is heard, and a solemn bell tolls out announcement of her lover's impending doom. She hears, too, the voice of *Manrico*, from his prison. This is set forth in the ever-famous "Miserere" (I Have Sighed to Rest Me).

Quite apart from its dramatic significance, the music of this scene is extraordinarily impressive. It begins with the chanting of priests. This leads to a strange accompaniment for the orchestra, shuddering chords in slow but irresistible reiterated rhythm which sound like the veritable approach of doom. Then comes a lovely, passion-

426

LEONORA: What voices of terror!
For whom are they praying?

ately sorrowful minor melody for *Leonora*.

In upon this breaks the exquisite air of *Manrico*, from within the prison walls, followed by a joyful cry from his beloved.

These passages, heard separately at the beginning, are combined and interwoven into the marvellously impressive ensemble which makes the scene perhaps, the best-known and the best-beloved of all operatic situations. It comes to an end when the *Count* approaches to enter the castle. *Leonora* begs mercy for *Manrico*, but he refuses, almost gloating over his triumph. As a last resource she offers to marry the *Count* if her lover may go free, though she never intends, in her heart, to be his actual bride. His manner changes, and *Leonora* so far forgets her own fate as to rejoice over the safety assured *Manrico:* "Vivra! Contende il giub-lo" (Oh, Joy, He's Saved), cries his beloved one.

The *Count's* rapture is well expressed in this number, and he does not hear the words of *Leonora*, as the scene

changes and she proceeds to enter the tower and set free *Manrico:* "Thou shalt possess but a lifeless bride."

SCENE II—*The Prison Cell of Manrico*

AZUCENA lies on a pallet of straw. With the second-sight of her race she is predicting her own end. *Manrico*, believing her his mother, strives to comfort her, and they sing an exquisite duet, the "Ai nostri monti" (Home to Our Mountains).

No longer is *Azucena* a wild and vengeful gypsy; she is but a poor old woman very near to death, longing for that peace and rest which only the hills of her childhood may restore.

Into this touching scene comes *Leonora* with the news of *Manrico's* freedom. His joy at the news, however, is turned to desperation as he learns the price to be paid. In a sudden frenzy he accuses *Leonora* of betraying his love: "Ha quest' infame" (Thou Hast Sold Thyself), he shouts.

In this vivid number, *Leonora* protests to *Manrico*, and *Azucena*, who cares nothing for their love, counsels

427

flight, singing her everlasting "Home to Our Mountains" through the music of the lovers. But the end comes. *Leonora* has already taken, from its concealment in a finger-ring, the poison which is to be her bane, and she falls at the feet of her lover, who now realizes the full degree of her sacrifice. He is all contrition, and he pleads for the forgiveness the dying girl is only too willing to give.

At this juncture, *Count di Luna* enters. Perceiving that *Leonora* has cheated him by dying, he orders *Manrico* to instant execution.

The guards at once lead him out. *Azucena*, half-mad with excitement, drags the *Count* to the window where he sees his own sentence carried out. Now is the moment of the gypsy's final vengeance before she too must die. With her ancient fire, the last effort of her passionate soul, she shrieks, "You have killed your brother!" *Di Luna*, with a wild cry, falls at her feet. The gypsy at least has had revenge!

FROM AN OLD DRAWING
THE DEATH OF LEONORA

428

THE VICTOR RECORDS

(Sung in Italian unless noted)

ACT I

ABBIETTA ZINGARA

(Swarthy and Threatening) MARCEL
JOURNET, Bass   6176   12-in., $2.00

FERRANDO:

With two sons, heirs of fortune and affection,
Liv'd the Count in enjoyment;
Watching the younger for his safe protection
A good nurse found employment.
One morning, as the dawn's first rays were
    shining,
From her pillow she rose,—
Who was found, think ye, near the child re-
    clining?
(*Impressively*)
Sat there a gypsy-hag, witch-like appearing;
Of her dark mysteries, strange symbols wear-
    ing.
O'er the babe sleeping—with fierce looks
    bending,
Gaz'd she upon him, black deeds intending!
Horror profound seized the nurse;
And the dark intruder was soon expelled.
Soon they found the child was failing,
The hag's dark spell enthrall'd him!
(*All appear horrified.*)
Sought they the gypsy, on all sides turning,
Seiz'd and condemn'd her to death by burning.
One child, accursed, left she remaining,
Quick to avenge her, no means disdaining.
Thus she accomplished her dark retribution!
Lost was the Count's child; search unavailing;
But on the site of the hag's execution
They found, 'mid the embers,
The bones of a young infant,
Half consumed and burning!

ACT II

TRIDE LA VAMPA

(Fierce Flames Are Soaring) LOUISE
HOMER, Contralto   678 10-in., $1.50
GABRIELLA BESANZONI, Contralto
                        541 10-in., 1.50
MARGARETE MATZENAUER, Contralto
                        999 10-in., 1.50

Upward the flames roll; the crowd presses
    fiercely on,
Rush to the burning with seeming gladness;
Loud cries of pleasure from all sides re-echoing!
By guards surrounded—forth comes a woman!
While, o'er them shining, with wild, unearthly
    glare,
Dark wreaths of flame curl, ascending to
    heaven!

MAL REGGENDO ALL' ASPRO ASSALTO

(At My Mercy Lay the Foe) LOUISE
HOMER, Contralto   and   ENRICO
CARUSO, Tenor   8013 12-in., $2.50

IL BALEN DEL SUO SORRISO

(The Tempest of the Heart) EMILIO DE
GOGORZA, Baritone   6069 12-in., 2.00
GIUSEPPE DE LUCA, Baritone
                       593 10-in., 1.50

COUNT:
Of her smile, the radiant gleaming
    Pales the starlight's brightest reflection,
While her face with beauty beaming,
    Brings me fresh ardor, lends to my affection.
Ah! this love within me burning,
    More than words shall plead on my part,
Her bright glances on me turning,
    Calm the tempest in my heart!

ACT III

AH, SI BEN MIO

(The Vows We Fondly Plighted) ENRICO
CARUSO, Tenor   6002 12-in., $2 00

MANRICO:
'Tis love, sublime emotion, at such a moment
Bids thy heart still be hopeful.
Ah! love; how blest our life will be
Our fond desires attaining,
My soul shall win fresh ardor,
My arm new courage gaining.
But, if, upon the fatal page
Of destiny impending,
I'm doomed among the slain to fall,
'Gainst hostile arms contending,
In life's last hour, with fainting breath,
My thoughts will turn to thee.

DI QUELLA PIRA

(Tremble, Ye Tyrants) ENRICO CARUSO,
Tenor   512 10-in., 1.50
ENRICO CARUSO, Tenor   3031 10-in., 2.00
GIOVANNI MARTINELLI, Tenor
                       732 10-in., 1.50

MANRICO:
Ah! sight of horror! See that pile blazing—
Demons of fury around it stand gazing!
Madness inspiring, Hate now is raging—
Tremble, for vengeance on you shall fall.
Oh! mother dearest, though love may claim me,
Danger, too, threaten, yet will I save thee;
From flames consuming thy form shall
    snatch'd be,
Or with thee, mother, I too will fall!

ACT IV

D'AMOR SULL' ALI ROSEE

(Love, Fly on Rosy Pinions) LUISA
TETRAZZINI, Soprano   6346   12-in., $2.00

LEONORA:
In the dark hour of midnight
I hover round thee, my love!
Ye moaning breezes round me playing,
In pity aid me, my sighs to him conveying!
On rosy wings of love depart,
Bearing my heart's sad wailing,
Visit the prisoner's lonely cell,
Console his spirit failing.
Let hope's soft whispers wreathing
Around him, comfort breathing,
Recall to his fond remembrance
Sweet visions of his love;

But, let no accent reveal to him
The sorrows, the griefs my heart doth move!

MISERERE

(Pray that Peace May Attend a Soul)
ENRICO CARUSO, Tenor, FRANCES
ALDA, Soprano and Chorus of the
Metropolitan Opera   8042   12-in., $2.50
EMMY DESTINN, Soprano, GIOVANNI
MARTINELLI, Tenor and Metropolitan
Opera Chorus   6190   12-in.,   2.00

AI NOSTRI MONTI

(Home to Our Mountains) LOUISE
HOMER, Contralto and ENRICO
CARUSO, Tenor   8013   12-in.,   2.50
ERNESTINE SCHUMANN-HEINK, Con-
tralto and ENRICO CARUSO, Tenor
8042   12-in.,   2.50

BLACK LABEL RECORDS

Trovatore Selection................................*Arthur Pryor's Band* Introduction, Act III—"Fierce Flames," Act II—Introduction, Act I—"At My Mercy," Act II Traviata Selection..............................*Arthur Pryor's Band*	35076	12-in.,	$1.25
Miserere (*In English*)......*Olive Kline, Soprano; Harry Macdonough, Tenor and Victor Chorus* Home to Our Mountains *Marguerite Dunlap, Contralto; Harry Macdonough*	35443	12-in.,	1.25
Anvil Chorus (*In English*)...........................*Victor Male Chorus* Tannhäuser—Pilgrims' Chorus (*In English*)..........*Victor Male Chorus*	17563	10-in.,	.75
Anvil Chorus (*In English*)...........................*Victor Male Chorus* Samson and Delilah—Spring Flowers.............*Victor Women's Chorus*	17624	10-in.,	.75
Anvil Chorus....................................*Arthur Pryor's Band* Forge in the Forest (*Michaelis*)..................*Arthur Pryor's Band*	17231	10-in.,	.75
Home to Our Mountains......................*Vessella's Italian Band* Rigoletto Quartet—(*Verdi*).....................*Kryl's Bohemian Band*	35239	12-in.,	1.25
Tempest of the Heart (*In English*)................*Alan Turner, Baritone* Carmen—Toreador Song (*In English*)............*Alan Turner, Baritone*	16521	10-in.,	.75

DIE WALKÜRE

(THE VALKYRIE)

MUSIC-DRAMA in three acts. Text and music by Richard Wagner. Completed in 1856 but not given until June 25, 1870, at Munich. First London production, in English, at Covent Garden, October 16, 1895. First New York production at the Academy of Music, April 2, 1877, with Mme. Pappenheim, Canissa, Listner, Bischoff, Blum and Preusser. Not heard again in New York until January 30, 1885, when Dr. Leopold Damrosch revived the work at the Metropolitan, with Brandt, Schott and Materna. Since that time the work has seldom been absent from the Metropolitan. Among the artists who have appeared in the opera during the past thirty years may be mentioned the following: as *Sieglinde*—Fremstad, Ternina, Nordica, Morena, Saltz-mann-Stevens, Osdorn-Hannah; as *Brünnhilde*—Ternina, Gadski, Walker, Leffler-Burckhard, Matzenauer, Nordica, Litvinne, Weidt; as *Siegmund*—Burrian, Burgstaller, Dalmores, Urlus, Kraus; as *Wotan*—Van Rooy, Griswold, Whitehill, Feinhals and Goritz.

CHARACTERS

SIEGMUND (*Zeeg'-moond*) . . . . Tenor
HUNDING (*Hoond'-ing*) . . . . Bass
WOTAN (*Voh'-tahn*) . . . . Baritone
SIEGLINDE (*Zeeg-lin'-deh*) . . . . . Soprano
BRÜNNHILDE (*Bruen-hill'deh*) . Soprano
FRICKA (*Frik'-ah*) . . . . Soprano
VALKYRIES—Gerhilde, Ortlinde, Waltraute, Schwertleite, Helmwige, Siegrune, Grimgerde, Rossweise.

(The name of the opera is pronounced *Dee·Vahl-kuer-reh*).

THE OPERA

ACT I

*Interior of Hunding's Hut in the Forest
—a Large Tree rises through
the Roof*

A TERRIBLE storm is raging. *Siegmund*, weaponless, wounded, spent, finds his way into the house of *Hunding*, where he is received and comforted by *Sieglinde*. When *Hunding* returns he perceives an extraordinary likeness between the two, and learns that the stranger was brought up by his father *Wolsung* in the woods, whither they had fled after their home had been ravaged, and his infant sister carried off by the Neidungs. Knowing now that he entertains a mortal enemy, *Hunding* out of hospitality permits *Siegmund* to remain for the night, but declares that on the morrow, he shall die. *Sieglinde* is dismissed, but she glances significantly at the ash-tree, the pillar of the hut, where the hilt of a sword is visible. She mixes with *Hunding's* night-draught a potion to make him sleep soundly. When all is quiet she returns to *Siegmund*, telling him of the sword, which has been stuck into the tree, at the time of her wedding, by a one-eyed warrior, whom *Siegmund* recognizes to have been his own father, *Wolsung*. The storm clears, and when the door is opened a wonderful spring-night is revealed. The two compare stories, and find that beside being lovers they are also brother and sister. Their love-song is one of the most beautiful of melodies.

The mating of *Siegmund* with *Sieglinde* has awakened bitter criticism. But it is well to remember such mat-

431

BRÜNNHILDE BEARING A WOUNDED WARRIOR TO WALHALLA

ings are common in mythology—Oriental, Greek, Roman, as well as Teutonic, and it is absolutely essential that the race founded by *Wotan* shall be of immortal strain through earthly parents. It supplies one of the greatest love-scenes in music. Toward its close *Siegmund*, with a mighty effort, draws the sword *Nothung* from the tree and the lovers escape into the woods. The sword-theme, which plays such an important part in this scene, is heard frequently in subsequent dramas. Derived from the Rheingold-Fanfare, it will make new themes in turn:

ACT II

Scene—*A Wild and Rocky Pass*

WOTAN, the one-eyed father-god chief of the immortals, the Jupiter of Rome, the Zeus of the Greeks, and the Indra of Brahmanism, confers with his daughter *Brünnhilde*, commanding her to protect *Siegmund* in the forthcoming combat. *Brünnhilde* is one of nine daughters of *Wotan* and *Erda*, goddess of the earth, whose mission is to bring the souls of heroes to Walhalla for protection against *Fafner*. The Valkyrie warns him that his plan will offend his wife *Fricka*, the protector of the Neidungs and the goddess who specially protects the marriage institution. Arrayed from head to foot in armour, and mounted on her steed Grani, *Brünnhilde* then goes off shouting her weird battle-cry: "Ho, yo, to, ho!" (Brünnhilde's Battle-Cry).

This wild and technically difficult number is founded on the battle-cry which plays so significant a part in the "Ride of the Valkyries" from the third act. It is hard to sing with the required force and accuracy, from the leaping width of its intervals and the unusual harmonies upon which it is founded. It ascends to "high C."

PHOTO MATZENE
WHITEHILL AS WOTAN

COPY'T DUPONT
GADSKI AS BRÜNNHILDE

PHOTO BERT
JOURNET AS WOTAN

WOTAN'S FAREWELL

434

No sooner is *Brünnhilde* gone than *Fricka* approaches on her chariot drawn by two rams. She is furious at the injustice done to *Hunding*, in the illicit union of *Siegmund* and *Sieglinde*. *Wotan*, for once no god but only a husband, explains his purpose, when *Fricka* shrewdly points out that his children are in fact himself, and that his protection virtually amounts to a breach of his contract with *Fafner*—which may lead to the downfall of the gods. Forced to agree, he finally swears that *Siegmund* shall be punished. *Fricka* then triumphantly recalls *Brünnhilde*, who is dismayed when *Wotan* revokes his order. *Wotan* explains, at great length of the circumstances told in "Das Rheingold," and she departs to warn *Siegmund* of his approaching doom. *Wotan*, at parting, enjoins obedience.

Brünnhilde discovers *Siegmund* and *Sieglinde* still fleeing from *Hunding* and his hounds. While *Sieglinde* sleeps, the Valkyrie warns *Siegmund* of his fate, and in some of the noblest music ever conceived, she promises him happiness in Walhalla. When *Siegmund* learns, however, that *Sieglinde* may not join him there, he spurns all hope of it, defying *Wotan* himself. *Brünnhilde* is deeply moved. She knows that *Wotan* loves these fearless children of his, and she herself is struck with *Siegmund's* indomitable courage. The scene grandly unfolds. *Brünnhilde*, more than half human, disobeys the divine command, promising help to *Siegmund* in the forthcoming struggle. *Hunding* arrives, and the fight takes place, *Brünnhilde* hovering above the hero, who trusts fearlessly in the sword from the ash-tree. But *Wotan* has learned of *Brünnhilde's* disobedience and through the riven skies he comes raging upon his wild steed. He fends off the sword with his own spear, shattering it into fragments. *Siegmund* is felled by *Hunding*; then the outraged god, having accomplished the will of *Fricka*, contemptuously slays *Hunding* with a motion of the spear. *Brünnhilde* has already escaped with *Sieglinde*, but *Wotan*, bent on punishment, rides into the skies in full pursuit.

ACT III

Scene—*The Summit of a Rocky Mountain*

THE meeting place of the Valkyries, and their wild ride through the skies is pictured by Wagner in an orchestral prelude of thrilling power, the so-called "Ride of the Valkyries."

This is possibly the most imaginative of all orchestral compositions; certainly nothing approaching it for wild and savage energy has ever been written into any opera. Several themes work out simultaneously; a trilling theme, the neighing of the Valkyries' horses; a "snorting" theme over the musical interval of a fourth; a gallop-theme, and the motive of the "Walkürenrittes," or the ride itself, bandied about, like a minor bugle-call, between trombones and trumpets, finally emphasized by the tuba. In the midst of it appears the Valkyries' shout, later sung by the eight Valkyries in their heroic garb, with great winged helmets, shields and spears. As the Valkyries one by one alight upon the great rock where they congregate, they behold *Brünnhilde*, their favorite sister, careering toward them, bearing not a dead hero but a woman at her saddle-bow. Alighting, she runs from one to the other, asking protection, but none dares offer it. *Brünnhilde* gives to *Sieglinde* the pieces of the broken sword, bidding her flee to the woods where *Fafner* dwells; there she may give birth to her child—who shall become the inheritor of the world.

The Valkyries hurriedly conceal *Brünnhilde* in their midst as the out-

FERD. LEEKE   BRÜNNHILDE:
Was it so shameful, what I have done,
That for my deed I am scourged?
(Walküre, Act III)

raged *Wotan* springs from his horse. *Brünnhilde* is compelled to come forth. The other Valkyries separate with cries of woe. Left alone, *Brünnhilde* pleads with *Wotan*. Was it such a dreadful thing to do,—knowing his love for his mortal children, and the deceit practiced on poor *Siegmund* with the sword? She pleads with tender eloquence, and *Wotan* is deeply moved. But he remains inexorable. She must lose her power as a goddess, put off divinity and lapse into a mere earthly woman; she must sleep, to become the bride of any one who awakens her. The shame of this rouses *Brünnhilde*, and she pleads at least that she be surrounded with fire so that only a hero may break through. This is granted her, and *Wotan* bids her farewell in music of unexampled power and almost heartbreaking pathos, the great "Wotan's Abschied" (Wotan's Farewell).

Brünnhilde sinks rapt and transfigured upon *Wotan's* breast, and he holds her in a long embrace. She throws her head back, gazing with solemn emotion into her father's eyes.

As *Wotan* kisses her godhood away, *Brünnhilde* sinks back into her long sleep. He assists her to lie upon a low, mossy bank, closes her helmet and covers her over with her great steel shield. Slowly moving off, he touches a rock with his magic spear, and summons *Loge*, the God of Fire. A stream of answering flame issues from the rock, surrounding *Wotan* and leaping wildly and touching the skies to a red volcanic glow. This scene is the thrilling "Magic Fire Spell."

It begins with the end of "Wotan's Farewell," and develops one of the most amazing passages of tone-painting ever imagined by mortal musician. The leaping, whistling flames writhe up before one's very eyes, subsiding as peace enfolds the sleeping woman.

There is heard the motive of the Twilight of the Gods—a kind of premonition; *Brünnhilde's* godhood lost, others will inevitably follow, through the working out of the Curse placed by *Alberich* upon the stolen gold of the Rhine. The farewell is heartrending —but sorrow, like all sorrow, is deeper and finer than joy. The cruelty of this parting seems dramatically unnecessary; but as its consciousness steals over the listener, there is heard as *Wotan* disappears, the stern three-note motive of the Decree of Fate—it is Fate working, Fate which is stronger than life or death, stronger than joy or suffering, Fate which was stronger yet than the will of the gods. This is one of Wagner's sublimest scenes. As with the "Ride of the Valkyries," a number of motives are worked out together: almost the last is the heroic theme of *Siegfried* Guardian of the Sword, or, as many call it, *Siegfried* the Inheritor of the World, which trumpets magnificently through the dying mazes of the Fire-music. Had Wagner never written another scene, this would have sufficed to yield him place among the greatest three composers of the modern world.

THE VICTOR RECORDS

(Sung in German)

ACT II

HO, YO, TO, HO!
(Brünnhilde's Battle Cry) EMMA GADSKI,
  Soprano   904   10-in., $1.50

BRÜNNHILDE:
Ho-yo-to-ho! Ho-yo-to-ho! Hei-aha!
But listen, father! care for thyself;
For a storm o'er thee will break;
Fricka, thy busy wife, approacheth in her ram-
    impelled car.
Ha! how she swings her golden whip!
The frighten'd goats are fainting with fear,
Wheels rattling and rolling whirl her here to
    the fight.
At such a time away I would be,
Tho' my delight is in scenes of war!
Take heed that defeat be not thine,
For now I must leave thee to fate!

ACT III

RIDE OF THE VALKYRIES

Philadelphia Orchestra 6245 12-in., $2.00
OLGA SAMAROFF, Pianist 6270 12-in., 2.00

FORT DENN EILE

(Fly Then Swiftly) MARGARETE MATZEN-
AUER, Contralto 904 10-in., 1.50

BRÜNNHILDE:
Fly then swiftly, and speed to the east!
Bravely determine all trials to bear.
The highest hero of worlds hidest thou, O
wife,
In sheltering shrine!
(*She produces the pieces of Siegmund's sword
and hands them to Sieglinde.*)
For him these shreds of shattered sword-blade;
From his father's death-field by fortune I saved
them:
Anon renewed this sword shall he swing;
And now his name I declare—Siegfried, of
vict'ry the son!

WOTAN'S ABSCHIED

(Wotan's Farewell, Part I) CLARENCE
WHITEHILL, Baritone 64278 10-in., 1.00
Parts 1 and 2 CLARENCE WHITEHILL
and Symphony Orchestra
In English 6435 12-in., 2.00

WOTAN:
Farewell, my brave and beautiful child!
Thou once the light and life of my heart!
Farewell! Farewell! Farewell!
Loth I must leave thee; no more in love
May I grant thee my greeting;
Henceforth my maid no more with me rideth,
Nor waiteth wine to reach me!
When I relinquish thee, my beloved one,
Thou laughing delight of my eyes,
Thy bed shall be lit with torches more brilliant
Than ever for bridal have burned!
Fiery gleams shall girdle the fell,
With terrible scorchings scaring the timid
Who, cowed, may cross not Brünnhilde's
couch
For one alone freeth the bride;
One freer than I; the god!

WOTAN'S FAREWELL AND MAGIC FIRE MUSIC

STOKOWSKI and Philadelphia Orchestra
6245 12-in., $2.00

Finale of Opera CLARENCE WHITEHILL
and Symphony Orchestra
In English 74857 12-in., 1.50

BLACK LABEL AND BLUE LABEL RECORDS

Ride of the Valkyries.............................*Vessella's Italian Band*	35369	12-in., $1.25
Götterdämmerung—Siegfried's Funeral March.............*Vessella's Band*		
Magic Fire Spell (Feuerzauber)....................*Vessella's Italian Band*	35387	12-in., 1.25
Rienzi Overture (Wagner)........................*Arthur Pryor's Band*		
Magic Fire Spell (Feuerzauber).............*Julius L. Schendel, Pianist*	35448	12-in., 1.25
Rustle of Spring (Sinding) (2) Papillon (Grieg).........*Julius Schendel*		
Siegmund's Love Song..................*Violin-'Cello-Piano Tollefsen Trio*	17749	10-in., .75
Romance (Rubinstein).................*Violin-'Cello-Piano Tollefsen Trio*		
Prelude:—Siegmund seeks shelter from the storm—Act I		
Symphony Orchestra—Conducted by Albert Coates	55204	12-in., 1.50
Siegmund sees the sword hilt in the tree—Act I *Vocalist*—Tudor Davies		
Symphony Orchestra—Conducted by Eugene Goossens		
Siegmund greets the Spring night—Act I *Vocalist*—Tudor Davies		
Symphony Orchestra—Conducted by Eugene Goossens	55205	12-in., 1.50
Siegmund draws out the sword—Finale, Act I *Vocalist*—Tudor Davies		
Symphony Orchestra—Conducted by Eugene Goossens		
Introduction:—Brünnhilde's battle cry—Act II *Vocalists*—Florence Austral		
and Robert Radford...*Symphony Orchestra—Conducted by Albert Coates*	55206	12-in., 1.50
Wotan warns Brünnhilde not to disobey—Act II *Vocalists*—Florence Austral		
and Robert Radford.*Symphony Orchestra—Conducted by Eugene Goossens*		
Brünnhilde foretells Siegmund's death—Act II *Vocalists*—Florence Austral		
and Tudor Davies.....*Symphony Orchestra—Conducted by Albert Coates*	55207	12-in., 1.50
Introduction:—Ride of the Valkyries—Act III		
Symphony Orchestra—Conducted by Albert Coates		
Brünnhilde gives Sieglinde the broken sword—Act III		
Vocalists—Florence Austral, Edith Furmedge and Edward Halland		
Symphony Orchestra—Conducted by Albert Coates	55208	12-in., 1.50
Brünnhilde implores the protection of fire—Act III		
Vocalists—Florence Austral and Robert Radford		
Symphony Orchestra—Conducted by Eugene Goossens		

WERTHER

LYRIC drama in four acts and five tableaux. Libretto by Edouard Blau, Paul Milliet and George Hartman, founded upon Goethe's story of his own life, *The Sorrows of Werther*. Music by Massenet. First produced Imperial Opera House, Vienna, February 16, 1892, with Van Dyck and Renard. Paris, Opéra Comique, January 16, 1893, with Mme. Delna. Milan, December, 1894. New Orleans Opera, November 3, 1894. First American production, the Metropolitan Opera House, April 20, 1894, with Eames, Arnoldson and Jean de Reszke. Revived at the New Theatre by the Metropolitan Opera Company, 1910, with Farrar, Clement, Gluck and Dinh-Gilly; Boston Opera, 1913.

CHARACTERS

WERTHER (*Wair-tair*)......... Tenor
ALBERT, the bailiff......... Baritone
SCHMIDT } his friends { .... Bass
JOHANN } .... Tenor
CHARLOTTE, his daughter.... Soprano
SOPHIE, her sister..... Mezzo-Soprano

Time and Place: In the Vicinity of Frankfort, Germany, 1772

CHARLOTTE, surrounded by her brothers and sisters, is preparing the noonday meal. *Werther*, a serious-minded and romantic young man, comes to the house with *Albert*, who is betrothed to *Charlotte*. *Werther* falls in love with the young girl. *Charlotte* returns his affection, but feels it her duty to marry *Albert* to fulfill a promise made to her mother, and so begs *Werther* to leave the village.

After *Charlotte* and *Albert* are married *Werther* tells *Charlotte* that he still loves her. She entreats him to spare her and go away forever. *Werther* then writes to *Albert*, telling him he has resolved to go on a long journey, and asking him for his pistols. *Charlotte*, alarmed, follows *Werther*. It is Christmas Eve, nearing midnight, and the snow almost blinds her. The scene changes to a tiny room, and reclining on a chair in the lamplight is *Werther*, mortally wounded. *Charlotte* arrives too late, and he dies in her arms. Overcome with grief, she faints on the body of her lover, while the pealing of bells and the joyous voices of little children singing Christmas carols are heard in the distance. The gem of the opera is *Werther's* love-dream, "Do Not Waken Me."

THE VICTOR RECORDS

AH! NON MI RIDESTAR!
POURQUOI ME RÉVEILLER (*French*)
(Why Awake Me?) MATTIA BATTISTINI, Baritone *In Italian* 6045 12-in., $2.00
GIOVANNI MARTINELLI, Tenor *In French* 735 10-in., 1.50
EDMOND CLEMENT, Tenor *In French* 902 10-in., 1.50
DMITRI SMIRNOV, Tenor *In French* 912 10-in., 1.50

O NATURE, PLEINE DE GRACE
(Invocation to Nature) FERNAND ANSSEAU, Tenor *In French* 6104 12-in., 2.00

FARRAR AS CHARLOTTE IN WERTHER

THE OATH (AL FRESCO PRODUCTION IN SWITZERLAND)

WILLIAM TELL

(GUILLAUME TELL)
(French)

WILLIAM TELL, outlining the story of the liberation of Switzerland, was composed in the twenties of the last century, at a time when Europe was recovering from the Napoleonic wars, and many theories of liberty were finding voice. Schiller, the German poet, had attracted considerable notice in Paris following the translation of some of his works into French, and it was but natural that Rossini should have turned to his splendid drama for an operatic subject.

Notwithstanding "Il Barbiere," "William Tell" is usually regarded as the greatest of Rossini's works, from a musical standpoint. Rossini is known to have been interested in the works of Beethoven at that time, the death of that great master in 1827 having perhaps called special attention to his works. As a result "William Tell" was a revolutionary departure from Rossini's usual style of composition. This is the more remarkable when one reflects that Rossini was then the foremost dramatic composer in Europe, having a long list of successful works to his credit. A lesser man would have thought he had nothing left to learn. Though at times careless enough in his workmanship, Rossini was unerring in his artistic judgment of others, as shown by his frank acknowledgment of the genius not only of Beethoven but of Haydn (whose string quartets he studied very closely) and Mozart. In many of his now forgotten operas he frequently pleased the public by including airs of whose banalities he was perfectly well aware; but in "William Tell" he lavished the utmost pains, showing, in addition, an amazing freshness of inspiration. Not only are the melodies exquisite and appropriate in themselves, but the harmonies are remarkably original for the period, and the orchestration a marked improvement on anything yet produced by Italian composers. The Overture of "William Tell" is noteworthy in this respect, and it was truly described by Berlioz (who usually loathed Rossini and all his works) as a "symphony in four parts." The quintet for 'cellos at

440

the opening is quite unique for the period, and the horn passages in the hunting chorus of the Second Act is also remarkable. As usual with Rossini, the vocal writing throughout is well-nigh perfect.

"William Tell" was the last of his operas. Just why a composer of genius who lived to be seventy-six should have ceased writing operas in his thirties, at the zenith of his fame, and with all the opera-houses of Europe open to his works, will ever remain a mystery. He was, to be sure, decidedly lazy, though he could display amazing energy when the fit seized him. Political and domestic disturbance may in some degree account for his long lethargy and his spasmodic working methods. The fact remains that he lived many years, his salon the chief meeting place of the most brilliant people in Paris, his influence in music of the highest importance yet produced practically nothing. After "William Tell" the only significant work was the sacred cantata, "Stabat Mater." He took some interest in the piano, describing himself (probably with accuracy) as a fourth-rate pianist, and writing trivial pieces for the instrument,—some of which he cynically dedicated to his parrot. His wittier sayings were quoted on all sides, but his criticism treated with respect, none the less, his creative genius expended itself for the most part in inventing new salads, for he was an admirable cook!

"William Tell" was a popular success, but the management of the Opera was given to presenting the work with elaborate cuts, reducing the five acts to three, and occasionally giving only one act at a time, using it as a curtain-raiser or as an accompaniment to the ballet. One day the Opera Director met Rossini on the street, and said: "I hope you won't be annoyed, but to-night we play the second act of 'William Tell'." "What, the whole of it?" asked Rossini in simulated astonishment. His wit made many enemies. His most bitter critics were perhaps Berlioz and the painter Ingres. But his admirers included Schubert, who called him "a rare genius," Schumann, who spoke of his "real, exhilarating, clever music," and Mendelssohn, who allowed none to disparage his work. With these masters, the musical world now generally agrees, —especially as regards "William Tell."

THE OPERA

OPERA in four acts; text, by Jouy, Bis and Marast taken from Schiller's drama. Music by Rossini. First presented at Paris, August 3, 1829. First London production, 1830. Produced at the New Orleans Opera, 1842. Revived at the Academy of Music by Leonard Grover's Opera Company, with Carl Formes. Produced at the Metropolitan 1888, with Fischer, and 1890, with Tamagno. Century Opera 1914, Metropolitan, 1922-23.

CHARACTERS

WILLIAM TELL, Swiss Patriot . . . . Bass

ARNOLD, suitor of Matilda ⎫ Swiss Patriots ⎧ Tenor
WALTER FURST ⎭ ⎩ Bass

MELCTHAL, Arnold's father . . . . . . Bass

GESSLER, Governor of Schwitz and Uri . . . . Bass

LEUTHOLD, a shepherd . . . . Bass

MATILDA, daughter of Gessler . . Soprano

HEDWIGA, Tell's wife . . . . Soprano

JEMMY, Tell's son . . . . Soprano

Scene and Period: Switzerland; Thirteenth Century

(The French name of the opera is Guillaume (*Gee-ohm*), G hard, and the Italian, Guglielmo (*Gool-yel-moh*) Tell).

THE Overture is a lengthy and imposing work, frequently heard in our concert rooms. It is in four parts: The Dawn, The Storm, The Calm, The Finale. It seems to be designed to furnish the "atmosphere" of the drama, the Swiss background, to suggest the beauties of nature in a land of mountainous beauty and sudden storms. The opening Andante is peaceful and serene, with a lovely, chant-like passage for 'cellos after the slowly-climbing figure at the opening:

The tranquil mood of the opening breaks up in turmoil as the rustling strings suggest the distant mutterings of a storm which finally bursts with tremendous power. After a furious crescendo, it dies away, a few liquid notes from the flute seeming to suggest the birds, restirring in the trees when the sun breaks through. Then comes a delightful pastoral melody for the English Horn, originally assigned by Rossini to an obsolete instrument of this type known as the *oboe di caccia*. As the pastoral dies away, trumpet calls introduce the vigorous *gallopade* with which the Overture closes, a splendid and stimulating quick-step usually played very swiftly, and leading to a magnificent *finale* with which the work comes to an end.

ACT I

Scene—*A Village in the Canton of Uri*

IN the year 1207, when the events are supposed to take place, Switzerland suffers beneath the German yoke, the tyrant *Gessler* ruling over the unhappy people with uncalled-for ferocity. Notwithstanding this, the people strive to carry on life with calmness, and the curtain ascends upon a peaceful scene. *William Tell* and his family are at work in the fields; nearby a group of fishermen are about to set out on the lake. *William Tell* is disturbed by their apparent indifference to the political tyranny beneath which they suffer, and he listens with grim patience when a fisherman sings a delightful barcarolle in keeping with the sunny quiet of the day. This is the "Accours dans ma nacelle" (Come, Love, in My Boat).

A horn sounds. It is the signal to open the annual Shepherds' Festival, at which three marriages are to be celebrated by *Melcthal*, the patriarch of the village. *Melcthal* rejoices in the task and he regrets that his son *Arnold*, is not among the betrothed. *Arnold*, however, though he dares not admit it, is in love with *Matilda*, the daughter of the tyrannical *Gessler*. *William Tell* has seen that the youth no longer seems to share the general hatred of the Swiss for their oppressors, and he chides him, half guessing the reason. *Arnold* then confesses to him his love for the girl, in the aria, "Ah, Matilde, io t'amo" (Matilda, I Love Thee).

Arnold is finally persuaded that his country stands first in the matter of duty, and he agrees to set aside his private wishes. He and *Tell* together join the peasants in their festivities.

While these are at their height, a sound of horns is heard across the valley, proclaiming that *Gessler* and his followers are near by, and intruding an ominous note into the general merriment. Suddenly the weddings are interrupted by *Leuthold*, a fugitive, crying "Save me, from the tyrant." He has slain one of *Gessler's* followers for attacking his daughter, and the hunters are out on his trail. He begs the fishermen to convey him across the lake into safety, but as it would mean crossing some dangerous falls, they re-

442

PASTORAL SCENE IN THE SWISS OUTDOOR PRODUCTION OF WILLIAM TELL

fuse. *William Tell*, however, comes to the rescue, and they put off just as the pursuers appear. The baffled *Gessler* then orders the village to be put to the flames, and the fields devastated. *Melcthal* is seized and slain, and the curtain descends upon a scene of desperate ruin.

ACT II

SCENE—*A deep Valley in the Alps. On the left the Lake of the Four Cantons. Twilight*

MATILDA waits for her sweetheart, *Arnold*, but, when he joins her it is only to tell her of his determination to remain with his people. She is deeply distressed, but both of them are deeplier shocked when *William Tell* brings in the news that *Arnold's* father is dead and the village burnt down in reprisal after *Leuthold's* escape. *Arnold's* desire for vengeance now overpowers even his love for *Matilda*, and it is in lament that he rejoins *William Tell*. Soon the men from the Cantons, or districts, gather and swear vengeance. *William Tell*, the best archer and strongest swimmer among

them, is naturally their leader, and he longs for action. Yet for the moment he advises caution.

ACT III

SCENE—*The Grand Square of Altdorf— Gessler's Castle in the Background. In the Foreground a Pole Surmounted by a Cap*

GESSLER, after the manner of his kind, overlooks none of the "refinements of cruelty" which are often more bitterly resented than flagrantly brutal acts. It is a holiday, and he sits, enthroned, before the conquered people. As a final insult, he has had erected a pole with a cap on it, as the symbol of his "might, majesty and dominion." It is his august will that the Swiss people shall bow before the pole; as they approach it, he watches them do so with grim pleasure. Meanwhile, there are games and entertainments, set to the "William Tell Ballet Music."

Among those who come to the fair is *William Tell*, with his little son, *Jemmy*. Disgusted at this fresh outrage, *William Tell* refuses to bow before the ridiculous symbol of power. He is promptly

443

captured, and, with *Jemmy*, brought before *Gessler*. When the tyrant learns that *Jemmy* is his only son, the fiendish idea occurs to him that he may test the prisoner's reputed ability as a bowman by having him shoot an apple from the boy's head. If he refuses, both shall suffer instant death. Having no option, *Tell* is forced to consent, his hand being none the more firm because of *Jemmy's* confidence in his powers. They stand the boy before a tree, placing an apple on his head. They offer to bind him, but *Jemmy* refuses, crying "Father, remember your skill! Fear not, I will not move."

Tell selects not one arrow but two, hiding the first in his cloak. He sends a fierce look at the tyrant, then aims with great care and looses a flying arrow. The shot is successful, despite the long range. When he realizes that the boy is safe, *Tell* faints away; as he sinks down, the second arrow falls from beneath his short cloak. "For whom was the second arrow?" asks *Gessler*, when he recovers. "For you, tyrant, if I had harmed my child!" is the answer. *Gessler* then orders them both put to death, but *Matilda*, who has entered and who has seen the whole ghastly business, boldly demands the child's life and takes him under her protection. *Tell* is borne to prison amid the curses of the Swiss.

ACT IV

SCENE I—*The Ruined Village of Act I*

ARNOLD, who knows nothing of *Tell's* capture, has come to his native village to bid farewell to the home of his boyhood. He gazes at the desolate cottage and sings his charming and pathetic air, "O muto asil," or "Asile hereditaire," (O Blessed Abode).

Swiss patriots enter hurriedly and acquaint *Arnold* with the recent events at Altdorf. He calls on them to follow him to the rescue of *Tell*, and they depart.

SCENE II—*Lake of Four Cantons. A Storm is Gathering*

TELL'S wife is resting here on her way to demand of *Gessler* her husband and son. Suddenly she hears her son's voice and is overjoyed to see him brought to her by *Matilda*. She clasps the boy in her arms, and anxiously inquires for her husband. *Matilda* says that *Tell* has been removed from Altdorf Prison, and taken across the lake. She has no sooner spoken than *Tell* appears, having escaped from the boat and sent an arrow through the tyrant's heart. *Arnold* and the patriots appear, rejoicing that *Gessler* has been slain and that the Swiss are free once more.

The storm breaks, and as if to announce liberty to Switzerland the sun bursts forth, revealing the glittering, snowy peaks of the Alps in all their dazzling beauty. An invocation to Freedom swells from every throat.

THE VICTOR RECORDS
(Sung in Italian)

ACT I

AH, MATILDE, IO T'AMO E AMORE
(Matilda, I Love Thee) GIOVANNI MARTINELLI, Tenor and MARCEL JOURNET, Bass
10009 12-in., $3.50

ACT II

SELVA OPACO
(Deep Shaded Forest) FRANCES ALDA, Soprano   537 10-in.,   1.50

TRONCAR SUOI DI
(His Life Basely Taken) GIUSEPPE DE LUCA, Baritone; JOSE MARDONES, Bass; GIOVANNI MARTINELLI, Tenor
10009 12-in.,   3.50

ACT III

RESTA IMMOBILE
(Flinch Not, Nor Stir a Limb) GIUSEPPE DE LUCA, Baritone   596 10-in.,   1.50

ACT IV

O MUTO ASIL
(Oh, Blessed Abode) GIOVANNI MARTINELLI, Tenor   6212 12-in.,   2.00

ARNOLD:

I will ne'er abandon my resolve,
My heart's thirsting for revenge!
William the tyrant has in chains imprison'd!
The hour of battle I impatiently wait!
What silence in this lone place doth reign;
I listen—my own steps alone I hear!

Oh! bless'd abode, within whose walls
Mine eyes first saw the light,
Once so belov'd, yet now thy halls,
Bring mis'ry to my aching sight.
In vain I call; no father's greeting,
Which fancy now to me's repeating,
Will ere again these ears be meeting,
Then home once lov'd, forevermore, farewell!

BLACK LABEL AND BLUE LABEL RECORDS

THE OVERTURE

Part I—At Dawn	*Victor Concert Orchestra*	17815	10-in.,	$0.75
Part II—The Storm	*Victor Concert Orchestra*			
Part III—The Calm	*Victor Concert Orchestra*	18012	10-in.,	.75
Part IV—Finale	*Victor Concert Orchestra*			
Part I—At Dawn	*Arthur Pryor's Band*	35120	12-in.,	1.25
Part II—The Storm	*Arthur Pryor's Band*			
Part III—The Calm	*Arthur Pryor's Band*	35121	12-in.,	1.25
Part IV—Finale	*Arthur Pryor's Band*			
Part I—At Dawn	*Pryor's Band*	16380	10-in.,	.75
Part II—The Storm	*Pryor's Band*			
Part III—The Calm	*Pryor's Band*	16381	10-in.,	.75
Part IV—Finale	*Pryor's Band*			

TELL REFUSES TO BOW TO THE TYRANT

ZAZA

ZAZA had to wait a long time, in America at least, for anything like recognition. Ruggiero Leoncavallo himself wrote the words, according to his custom, adapting the opera from the well-known play of Berton and Simon. It did well in Europe, and it was actually given in America as early as 1903, but only in 1920, when the Metropolitan Opera Company presented it, did the quality of the work reveal itself.

THE OPERA

OPERA in four acts; libretto and music by Ruggiero Leoncavallo. First production in Milan, 1900. First American production at the Tivoli, San Francisco, 1903. Excerpts given at Leoncavallo Festival, New York, 1906. Revived in San Francisco, 1913, under Leoncavallo himself. Notable performances during 1920 with the Metropolitan Opera Company, New York.

CHARACTERS

ZAZA (*Tsah-tsah*)..A concert hall singer
NATALIE (*Na-tah-lee'-ah*)..Zaza's maid
MILIO DUFRESNE (*Mee-lee-oh Doo-frayn'*)......A wealthy Parisian
SIGNORA DUFRESNE........His wife
CASCART (*Cas-cahr*) A concert hall singer
BUZZY.................A journalist
Actors, Singers, Dancers, Scene Shifters, Firemen, Property Men, etc.

Time and Place: Paris; the Present Time

THE first scene represents a stage divided into two sections. At one side is the dressing-room of *Zaza*, while the other represents the rear of a stage setting. *Zaza*, a concert-hall singer, has taken a fancy to *Milio Dufresne*, and she openly boasts to *Buzzy*, a "journalist," who is despised yet feared by the stagefolk, that she will have *Milio's* love. She puts forth all her feminine powers, and *Dufresne* succumbs. It is during this scene that *Zaza* and *Cascart* sing the "Il Bacio" (The Kiss), from the rear of the actual stage, in front of the imaginary audience—whence they return, flushed with triumph. The duet is a cleverly artistic parody of the music hall style; "catchy" but remarkably well-written.

In the second act, the love affair is well under way. *Zaza* is told by *Dufresne*, in her own country house, that he must go away on a business trip. The singer takes this much for granted, until *Cascart* enters, hinting that *Dufresne* may have other reasons than business for his departure. *Zaza's* suspicions rise, and she follows him to Paris.

The third act shows a room in *Dufresne's* Paris house. *Zaza* enters, accompanied by *Natalie*. Discovering there a letter addressed to *Signora Dufresne*, she thereby discovers, to her astonishment, that her lover already is married. His child enters, finally *Signora Dufresne* herself, who is equally astonished at this visitor. *Zaza* declares she has entered the wrong house. Her explanation is accepted, and she leaves.

The scene of the last act again is *Zaza's* suburban house. *Cascart*, who is really a good sort of fellow, goes there and pleads with her to give up *Dufresne*. His two numbers, "Buona Zaza, del mio buon tempo" and "Zaza, piccolo Zingara" (Zaza, Little Gypsy), have been recorded. *Zaza*, however only laughs at the idea. When *Cascart* leaves, *Dufresne* himself is announced. He greets *Zaza* in the old affectionate manner, but she informs him she knows of the marriage—though, woman-like

446

she forgives his deception. She declares, nevertheless—for *Zaza* is rather a mixture—that she has told *Signora Dufresne* of their intimacy. In a rage he curses her and throws her to the floor, and her love for him is suddenly cured. She then assures him that her first story was untrue, that *Signora Dufresne* knows nothing of the affair, and the shallow *Dufresne* leaves her.

In the original version of the play, *Zaza* returns, logically, to her stage life. As given in the United States, it had an added act, in which *Zaza*, "purified by suffering," became a great actress, and returned to philosophize with, and confute, *Dufresne*. More accurate French and Italian dramatic sense and clearer discernment of character simply returned her to the music hall.

Whatever *Zaza's* fate is, or should have been, the opera, like the original play, is a study in human character.

THE VICTOR RECORDS
(Sung in Italian)

ACT I
IL BACIO
(The Kiss) GERALDINE FARRAR, Soprano
GIUSEPPE DE LUCA, Baritone
625　10-in., $1.50

È UN RISO GENTIL
('Tis a Gentle Smile) GIOVANNI MARTINELLI　736　10-in.,　1.50

ACT II
BUONA ZAZA, DEL MIO BUON TEMPO
(Dear Zaza) TITTA RUFFO, Baritone
824　10-in.,　1.50

ACT III
O MIO PICCOLO TAVOLO INGOMBRATO
(My Desk, Like My Heart, is Encumbered with Care GIOVANNI MARTINELLI, Tenor　6194　12-in.,　2.00

MAMMA USCIVA DI CASA
(Mother Has Gone) GERALDINE FARRAR, Soprano　625　10-in.,　1.50

ACT IV
ZAZA, PICCOLA ZINGARA
(Zaza, Little Gypsy) TITTA RUFFO, Baritone　824　10-in.,　1.50
RENATO ZANELLI, Baritone
882　10-in.,　1.50

DUFRESNE DENOUNCING ZAZA—ACT IV

447

Victor Talking Machine Company, Camden, New Jersey
Printed June, 1924

CPSIA information can be obtained at www.ICGtesting.com
Printed in the USA
268059BV00003B/11/P